Charles Jackson, Abraham De la Pryme, Charles De La Pryme

The Diary of Abraham De la Pryme, the Yorkshire Antiquary

Charles Jackson, Abraham De la Pryme, Charles De La Pryme

The Diary of Abraham De la Pryme, the Yorkshire Antiquary

ISBN/EAN: 9783337018597

Printed in Europe, USA, Canada, Australia, Japan

Cover: Foto ©Raphael Reischuk / pixelio.de

More available books at **www.hansebooks.com**

THE

PUBLICATIONS

OF THE

SURTEES SOCIETY.

ESTABLISHED IN THE YEAR

M.DCCC.XXXIV.

VOL. LIV.

FOR THE YEAR MDCCCLXIX.

OF

ABRAHAM DE LA PRYME,

THE YORKSHIRE ANTIQUARY.

Abraham de la Pryme

Published for the Society
BY ANDREWS & CO., DURHAM;
WHITTAKER & CO., 13, AVE MARIA LANE; T. & W. BOONE,
29, NEW BOND STREET; BERNARD QUARITCH, 15, PICCADILLY;
BLACKWOOD & SONS, EDINBURGH.
1870.

At a Meeting of the Council of THE SURTEES SOCIETY, held in the Castle of Durham, on Tuesday, December 1st, 1868, the Rev. C. T. Whitley in the chair—it was

Resolved, that THE DIARY OF ABRAHAM DE LA PRYME should form one of the publications of this Society for 1869, to be edited by MR. CHARLES JACKSON.

JAMES RAINE,
Secretary.

INTRODUCTION.

THE Council of the Surtees Society are enabled, by the courteous permission of Francis Westby Bagshawe, esq., of the Oaks, near Sheffield, the owner of the original manuscript, to furnish its members with the volume now delivered to them. To that gentleman the cordial thanks of the Society are justly due, and, on their behalf, are hereby presented.

The manuscript consists of two volumes folio, in size about eleven inches by seven. Each volume is bound in rough calf, with folding flaps, originally secured by a single clasp of brass, with four catches. The pages of volume the first are alternately numbered. Including several original letters, printed papers, etc., occasionally inserted by the Diarist, and numbered as pages, they amounted to 573. Several pages are, however, now wanting. In volume the second, not so thick a book as the first, the pages are not numbered. Inclusive of its interleaved matter it appears at present to contain 135 pages. At the end of it many pages have been cut or torn out : but, as the latest entry is under date of the 25th Jan., 1703-4, and the writer lived only to the month of June following, and since as the later portion consists merely of entries of copies of letters to some of his antiquarian correspondents, without any notes of daily occurrences, it is probable that the missing leaves were for the most part blank, and only taken out for other purposes. The handwriting is bold and clear in character. In places where some of the church notes are given, trickings of arms, hastily executed, are made; these it has not been considered worth while to represent by engraving. Upon the whole the manuscript may fairly be regarded as being in very good condition.

Mr. Bagshawe informs me that he is unable to state for what length of time these two manuscript volumes have been in the possession of his family, or how, indeed, precisely they were at the first obtained. His belief is that they were given by one of the De la Pryme family[a] to one of his ancestors, Mrs. Darling,[b] who was connected with Thorne, the last place at which the Diarist resided, and where also he died.

The Diary has been, no doubt through the civility of its owners, lent at different times to various persons, and it is likely that transcripts of or extracts from it, printed or otherwise, may exist elsewhere. For historical purposes it was certainly, some years ago, entrusted to at least one distinguished topographical writer, than whom no one was more welcome. or more able, to extract the essence of it, and who has suitably acknowledged the benefits, which these, as well as other manuscripts of De la Pryme, afforded him in his compilation of the history of *South Yorkshire.*[c]

Upon undertaking the editorship of this work I had the pleasure of becoming acquainted with an existing member of the Diarist's family, Charles de la Pryme, esq., M.A., of Trinity

[a] On the outside of the cover of vol ii. is written "Peter Pryme, his Booke." This was the Diarist's next brother and successor, who died 25th Nov., 1724, (See *Pedigree*). The Diarist's nephew and namesake has also thus described himself within the cover of the same volume :—"Abraham Pryme, living in ye Levils of Hatfield Chace, in ye county of York, in the West Rideing thereof, near Doncaster, Anno Domini 1722."

[b] Ellen, daughter and coheiress of Richard Bagshawe, of the Oaks, married at Thorne, 8th March, 1733-4, William Chambers, of Hull, M.D., whose only daughter, Elizabeth Chambers, became the wife of Ralph Darling, of Hull. Their son, William Chambers Darling, assumed the surname of Bagshawe in lieu of Darling, and, being knighted, became Sir William Chambers Bagshawe, M.D. He was the grandfather of Francis Westby Bagshawe, esq., now of the Oaks.—See *Hunter's Hallamshire*, 1819, p. 234 ; *Gatty's Hunter's Hallamshire*, 1869, pp. 399, 400.

[c] "At the end of the 17th century Abraham de la Pryme, a clergyman. and early fellow of the Royal Society, made some not inconsiderable collections for the history, natural and civil, of the Level of Hatfield Chace, the place of his nativity. These collections, though injured by the carelessness of some former possessor, are now in the Lansdowne department of the British Museum, and

College, Cambridge, who informed me that he had been contemplating the publication of notices, collected by his family and himself, relating to his worthy ancestor. With great politeness he immediately suggested that these should be introduced as a preface to the present volume, and that such portions of the actual Diary as he had previously copied should be merged in it. This arrangement, being a great mutual advantage, has been adopted, and Mr. de la Pryme's valuable addition accordingly appears at the conclusion of these few remarks.

In this volume the original Diary is not printed *verbatim et totaliter*. A certain license, in these cases no less needful than discretionary, has been exercised in the rejection or omission of such portions as, on various accounts, seemed unnecessary in print. For the most part the original orthography has been followed, except in some instances, where the appearance of the book, and the more convenient perusal by non-antiquarian readers, seemed to demand a more modern variety of form.

Though not equal, either in the supply of information, or method, or general character, to the diaries of Pepys, Thoresby, and others, still it will probably be found that the references, as well to political as to private and personal occurrences, are of considerable interest; and the quaint, unartificial language of an old Diarist, telling us naturally what happened in his time, is always attractive.

Next to the owner of the manuscript my best thanks, as editor, are justly due to our Secretary, the Rev. Canon Raine, M.A., of York, whose long and intimate acquaintance with compilations

there I had access to them, through the kindness of Mr. Ellis, before they were generally placed in the hands of those who are admitted to the reading-room of the Museum. Besides these, De la Pryme left an Ephemeris or Diary of his life, in which he has inserted many historical and biographical matters. This last has been entrusted to me by William John Bagshawe, esq., of the Oaks, in Norton." (Mr. Hunter's preface to *South Yorkshire*, 1828.) At page 179 of vol. i. the same author again recognises "the unsolicited and kind communication" of this Diary. Mr. Hunter made copious extracts from the Diary, which are now amongst his MSS. at the British Museum.—*Additional MSS.*, 24475, pp. 33-94.

of this character has enabled him to render material help to one
who cannot lay claim to similar experience.   The Rev. Dr.
Thompson, Master of Trinity College, Cambridge ; the Rev.
J. E. B. Mayor. M.A., of St. John's College, Cambridge; the
Rev. George Ornsby. M.A., vicar of Fishlake, near Doncaster ;
Edward Peacock. esq., F.S.A., of Bottesford Manor, near Brigg;
and George William Collen, esq., Portcullis Pursuivant at Arms,
have greatly assisted me with the information supplied in the
notes.   For the testamentary notices of the De la Pryme family
and others, to be found in the Appendix,[d] and elsewhere, I am
chiefly indebted to Robert Hardisty Skaife, esq., of York, and to
Colonel Chester, of London.   Those who know what it is to be
engaged in the compilation of Pedigrees will readily appreciate
the value of being permitted a free and unrestricted access to
parochial registers and other records.   For this privilege I must
request the Rev. Canon Brooke, M.A., vicar of the Holy Trinity
Church at Hull; the Rev. Henry Hogarth, M.A., vicar of Hatfield ; and the Rev. George Jannings, B.A., vicar of Thorne, to
accept my most sincere acknowledgments.   I must not omit the
names of Rowland Heathcote, esq., of the Manor House, Hatfield,
(for the liberal facility of inspecting the court rolls under his
charge),[e] of Edward Shimells Wilson, esq., F.S.A.[f] and William
Consitt Boulter, esq., F.S.A.   And there are other gentlemen,
of whose friendly aid I bear the most grateful remembrance.

In a work of this kind, involving for its elucidation references
to so many scattered sources, so many old records, and so many
manuscript authorities, errors are inevitable.   I will only add
that I have done my best to explain, for the Surtees Society and
the Public, the obscurities which Time has thrown over the
"observable things" recorded in this Diary by one who in his
day was a remarkable man.

                                  CHARLES JACKSON.
Doncaster, 1st November, 1870.

----

[d] See *Appendix,* pp. 265-9.   [e] See *postea,* p. 257, *n.*   [f] See *Appendix,* p. 298.

PREFACE.

MEMOIR OF THE FAMILY OF DE LA PRYME, BY CHARLES DE LA PRYME.

THE antiquity of families has so long been a subject of interest to some, and of ridicule to others, that it is difficult to assign its proper limits in a biographical memoir. The De la Pryme family has claimed to be the oldest of the Huguenots that have settled in this country, whether traditionally or historically considered. Were this work intended for the votaries of what has been called the "science of fools with long memories," some pleasant pages might have been written about the descent from the last king of Troy, the crossing the Mediterranean and settling in France— first at *Troyes* and then at *Paris* (hence so called), and their consequent assumption of the prefix *De la*.

The "gentle reader" will, perhaps, be quite content to pass over in respectful silence the legendary period, and descend at once to the tamer level of the twelfth century, when we find them chief magistrates of the city of Ypres, in French Flanders.

The earliest spelling of the name was *Priem*, the next *Prijme*, the next *Prime*, and the last *Pryme;* which an herald would perhaps call respectively the Trojan, the Flemish, the French, and the English variations. The prefix *De la* has had its vicissitudes in this, as in some other families—as the De la Poles, Delafields, etc., where it has been, as it were, "on and off" for some time, and even finally dropped. In some cases it has been so with only the *De*, and in others with only the *La*. The author of "Robinson Crusoe" has been accused of taking exactly the contrary liberty with his name, by calling himself [De] Foe. During the seven years' war (1756-1763), the anti-Gallican feeling here was so strong, that Francis, who, in 1749, was elected mayor of Hull as Francis De la Pryme, was, in 1766, mayor as simply Francis Pryme. His son, Christopher, continued the mutilated form, and gave it to his son George, who revived the original name, in its trisyllabic fulness, at the baptism of his son Charles, the present representative.

There seem to have been two branches of the family, one of which possessed a chateau near Paderborn, in Westphalia, in the middle of the last century. The other, which was the original one, resided near Ypres, of which city several of them were chief magistrates. It was then one of the most important cities of northern and western Europe; its manufactures were celebrated all over the Continent; and it lent its name to the best of its fabrics, the *diaper* (which is merely a corruption of *D'Ypres*), just as our own *worsted* is so called from a place of that name in Norfolk.[g]

Among the MSS. belonging to the family, there is an old paper,[h] of which it will be sufficient to give the substance.

It appears that in 1176, Philip of Alsace carried with him to the Crusade five hundred of the citizens of Ypres. Three years

---

[g] Worstead. a parish, and formerly a market town, eastern division of Norfolk, 2¾ miles (S.S.E.) from North Walsham, and 121 (N.E. by N.) from London. This place was once celebrated for the invention and manufacture of woollen twists and stuffs, thence called *worsted* goods; but this branch of trade was, on the petition of the inhabitants of Norwich, removed to that city in the time of Richard II., where it was finally established in the reign of Henry IV. —*Lewis Top. Dict.*

[h] Stated to be compiled from old papers, and considered by the family as trustworthy. Stories of the nature here given, are, however, when unsupported by evidence, generally tinctured with so much of what is romantic, that their reception is entirely a matter to be left to the judgment of the reader.

afterwards, four hundred and thirty-six of these returned. These were amply rewarded by their leader, some with knighthood, some, it is said, with grants of arms. Among those who were honoured with the last was the ancestor of the De la Prymes, whose coat-armour is thus described :—

"Hereunder is the coat of arms of Alexander Priem, which is *Field azure, with two gilt crosses and silver poinards, with a red bar in the middle.* The motto, *Animose certavit*—He has fought as a hero. If the Turks came with so many thousand men to attack

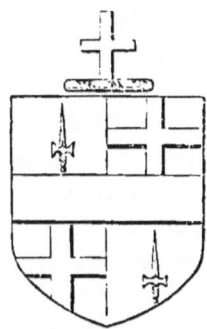 all Christian people ; and if he came with such great fury, and with numberless to cover all the fields, yet Alexander Priem has shown to many Saracens that they were not able to fight against him, for his dagger is always Priem, being a poinard, which is the name of the family, and, as before the cross, has slain upon the ground many Turks and Saracens."

The following are the names of the persons of the family of Priem that have been in the magistracy of Ypres since the year 1179, when the first Alexander received his nobility.[1]

1179.	Alexander Priem.	1567.	.... Priem.
1222.	Leo ,,	1572.	.... ,,
1276.	Arnauld ,,	1581.	.... ,,
1383.	Ignatius ,,	1612.	George ,,
1490.	William ,,	1616.	George ,,
1468.	Paul ,,	1620.	George ,,
1545.	Christian ,,	1628.	George ,,
1554.	Nicholas ,,	1680.	Robert ,,

[1] In a similar account of the early history of the family, as furnished in *Burke's History of the Commoners of Great Britain and Ireland*, 1838, vol. iv., p. 705, it is stated that Alexander Priem "received a patent of gentility and a grant of arms." The latter, however, it is believed, were unknown under Philip of Alsace ; and, upon enquiry, neither of these documents, if they ever existed, appear to be now in the possession of the present representative of this family in England.

James de la Pryme, of Naze House, near Kirkham, Lancashire, went to Ypres, at the close of the last century, to enquire after any of the family—their situation, property, etc. He found two persons of the name (which they spelt *Prijme*), and brought back their arms, and a long pedigree from the year 1100, written in the language of the country.

In August, 1851, I went with my father and mother to Ypres with the same motive. We had obtained an introduction from Lord Palmerston to the British embassy, at Brussels, from which we procured one to the burgomaster at Ypres, so as to enable us to inspect the archives of the city. We found several burgomasters of the name of Priem, not only in the archives, but on the monuments in the cathedral. A widow, Madame Rix Priem, was living there, who had the same arms as we have, and she informed us that the ancestor who was the link between us had been ignored as a heretic. We also learnt that on the death of De la Pierre, the editor of *Precis analytique des Archives de la Flandre occidentale*, De la Priem, of Bruges, had succeeded him, and was continuing the work, in the first volume of which (in 1850), mention had been made of the family at Ypres.

Alexander De la Pryme's descendants embraced the reformed religion, and have continued good Huguenots to this day; and their assumption of the original name shows that in the word good they included the word *liberal*.

The number of good families that by religious persecution was thus lost to France, and gained to England, is very surprising. Among them may be mentioned the families of Romilly, Lefevre, La Touche, Delafield, Labouchere, De la Pryme, etc.

The persecution which Richelieu had renewed against the adherents of the reformed religion, and the desperate resistance of those who were besieged in Rochelle, in 1627, rendered a residence in French-Flanders so insecure and uncomfortable, that about eighty families fled to England, and settled in the Levels of Hatfield Chase, in Yorkshire, in 1628-9. Hatfield is a village

in the middle of Hatfield Chase, seven miles eastward of Doncaster, in the west-riding, and was formerly a royal village, in
which the king had a palace,[j] of which De la Pryme says (1694)
"there is part of the palace standing, being an indifferent large
hall, with great courts and gardens about the same."[k]

Charles De la Pryme was the first of the family whose zeal
induced him to take the sad alternative of sacrificing his country
to his religion. The De la Prymes, however, retained an estate
in French-Flanders, which, after the revocation of the edict of
Nantes, one of them vainly endeavoured to recover. On settling
in England, he obtained a licence from Charles I. for a religious
service in the French and Dutch languages, which was celebrated
in my ancestor's house till the chapel at Sandtoft was erected for
that purpose; and the French and Dutch languages were preserved among these emigrants for two or three generations at
least. Charles, probably from a feeling of persecuted religion,
changed the family arms, as emigrant dissenters in America did.
He adopted the coat of a sun upon an azure ground, with the
crest of a wyvern, on, what has been probably originally intended
for a rock, or pile of stones, but which, by the mistake or carelessness of sculptors and engravers, has been represented on
monuments, and on some of our plate, as a pile of books—folio,

[j] Hatfield, for nearly five centuries after the conquest, was subject to the
feudal superiority of the Earls of Warren, lords of the castle of Conings-
borough. It was owned by a series of earls till the 20th Edward III., 1346.
It then came to the crown, and was settled on the princes of the house of
York. When they ascended the throne, it became demesne of the crown. The
earls of Warren were accustomed to resort hither for the enjoyment of field
sports; and, near the centre of the Chase, at what is now the town of Hatfield,
they had a house at which they might remain, when, fatigued with their day's
exertion, they were unwilling to return to Coningsborough. This house, when
Hatfield became royal demesne, was sometimes dignified with the appellation
of a palace. But, though occasionally the residence of our kings, it never
could have been considerable. Leland calls it the Lodge, or Manor Place. In
this house Queen Philippa was delivered of her second son, surnamed de Hatfield. Here, also, was born Henry, eldest son of Richard Duke of York, on
Friday, 10th February, 1441.—*Hunter's South Yorkshire*, i., pp. 153-155.

[k] See Diary, *postea*, p. 114.

quarto, octavo, and duodecimo, placed one upon another.[l]

Warburton, *Somerset Herald*,[m] who published a quaint map of Yorkshire, putting the arms of some of the nobility and gentry in the margin, gives among them those of the De la Prymes.[n]

These we find also on the old plate, seals, etc., belonging to the

[l] On the monument of Peter De la Pryme, 1724, in Hatfield church, the crest, formerly placed over the arms, has disappeared, but on the wreath are left two of these books, one upon the other.

[m] John Warburton, F.S.A. and F.R.S., born 28th Feb., 1681-2. *Somerset*, 6th June, 1720. Died 11th May, 1759. For the armorial illustrations on his Map of Yorkshire, it has been said that he has incurred some reproach, on account of having introduced several coats which are of doubtful authority.—*Hunter*. Note in *Thoresby's Diary*, vol. ii., p. 264.

The seals here given are copies of two now in the possession of the Rev. Edward Ryley, rector of Sarratt, Herts, who is maternally descended from the family of De la Pryme. This gentleman is also the owner of a gold and red cornelian seal, oval shaped, upon which is represented a female figure, *sejant*, in an attitude of mournful contemplation, her head reclining on her right hand, the arm of which rests upon her knee. In the back-ground is a vision of a Roman soldier's helmet, shield, and breast-plate. It is said that this was engraved for some, or one, of the family refugees, in memory of their expatriation from fatherland ; and, consequently, a proportionate value is placed upon it by those concerned in its history. Judging from its age and appearance, Mr. Ryley considers that it may have once belonged to Abraham De la Pryme, the Diarist.

[n] In this instance, either Warburton, or his engraver, by mistake, has made the field of the arms gules, or red.

family, and they are placed over the entrance of the house at Cambridge (Trinity Hostel); and are still used by the last descendant of the family who remained at Ypres.

The De la Prymes joined with Sir Cornelius Vermuyden, and others of their countrymen, in the draining of the great fens in the Levels of Hatfield Chase; and the knowledge they must have derived from the similar situation of their native country, rendered them peculiarly fitted for such an undertaking. But, either through the disadvantageous terms of the contract,[*] or from unexpected obstacles in executing it, although, as our Diarist tells us, " for a time they lived like princes, most of them were undone, and Charles de la Pryme lost many hundreds of pounds by it." Vermuyden's losses were still greater ; and losing money not only by the works, but by litigation connected with them, it is said that he died in poverty. Abraham De la Pryme has done him ample justice in his *MS. History of Hatfield*, where he says that he, " at the incredible labor and charges of 400,000*l.*, did discharge and drain Hatfield Chase, whose name deserves a thousand times more to be honorably mentioned and revered in all our histories than Scaurus' was in those of Rome, for draining a great lake in Italy, not a quarter so big as this."

Charles De la Pryme left two sons, Matthias, or Matthew, and Abraham, the father and uncle of the Diarist. The latter was, according to his nephew, " an honest, learned, pious, wise, and understanding man,"[p] and died in 1687. Matthias was born in 1645, and married Sarah, daughter of Peter Smagge (or Smaqúe) "a rich Frenchman, that, with his whole family, was forced from Paris by persecution for his faith, and was come to live on these Levels." They were married in the great hall[q] of the Dutch

---

[*] Dated 24 May, 1626. (See *Hunter's South Yorkshire*, i., p. 160). There is a copy in *Lansdowne MSS.*, Brit. Mus., 205, f. 193. See also appendix to *Peck's Isle of Axholme*, 1815.

[p] Diary, *postea*, p. 13.

[q] These words, "great hall," etc., are struck out by the Diarist in the original MS.

congregation, called Mynheer Van Valkenburg's,[r] and came to live at Hatfield. In 1680 he removed to Crowtrees Hall, a large house on Hatfield Chase, built by Valkenburg, and died in 1694. His epitaph, so quaint and characteristic, will be found in the Appendix (page 26).

Matthias had two sons, ABRAHAM, the DIARIST, and Peter, who, on his elder brother's death, succeeded to the family property, 13th June, 1704. Peter married, in 1695, Frances, daughter of Francis Wood, of Hatfield Levels, and died 25th November, 1724, leaving two sons, Abraham, born in 1697, from whom descends the Lancashire branch.

Francis, born in 1701, as a younger brother, went to reside at North Ferriby, seven miles west of Hull, where he became a very active and influential magistrate, and was twice mayor, and also sheriff in the important year, 1745, "when the town ditches had to be cleaned, and the walls repaired and newly strengthened, in fear of the Pretender and his army."

He died 7th July, 1769, leaving an only son, Christopher, born in 1739, who married Alice, daughter of George Dinsdale, of Nappa Hall, in Wensleydale. Pryme-street, Christopher-street, and Alice-street, in Hull, were called after them, as George-street has since been called after their son, and Charles-street after their grandson ; the sixth street being very appropriately called Reform-street. Pryme-street, in Manchester, received its name from the Lancashire branch. Christopher died in September, 1784, leaving an only child, George,

Born at Cottingham, 4th August, 1781.

Admitted at Trinity College, Cambridge, October, 1799.

Bachelor of Arts, January, 1803.

Elected Fellow of Trinity, October, 1805.

Master of Arts, July, 1806.

Called to the Bar at Lincoln's Inn, November, 1806.

---

[r] Not Halhenburg, as printed in *Burke*, iv., p. 706.

Married Jane Townley Thackeray, August, 1813.

Elected the first Professor of Political Economy, May, 1828.

Elected M.P. for Cambridge, December, 1832.

Re-elected in two succeeding parliaments.

Resigned his seat in parliament at the dissolution in 1841.

Died 2nd December, 1868,[*] at his house, at Wistow, Huntingdonshire, leaving that best of all inheritances, a good name, to his only son, Charles de la Pryme, its present and only representative, by whom a volume, containing *The Life and Literary Miscellanies of Professor Pryme*, is in preparation. "*Multis ille bonis flebilis occidit, nulli flebilior quam mihi.*"

ABRAHAM DE LA PRYME, the DIARIST, was born "to all the miseries of life"[*] in 1671. Before he was twelve years old he began the "*Ephemeris Vitæ; or, a Diary of my own Life; containing an account, likewise, of the most observable and remarkable things that I have taken notice of from my youth up hitherto.*" In this, he says, "My father can speak Dutch, and my mother French, but I nothing yet but English."[*] This is the only indication we have of his early education, which, under such circumstances, must have been the "pursuit of knowledge under difficulties." His great eagerness for the acquirement of it induced his father to give him the benefit of an university education. His father's inclination was in favor of Glasgow and Presbyterianism, and the son's in favor of Cambridge and the church of England, to which, after much persuasion, he was fortunately allowed to go. He was admitted a pensioner of St. John's College in April, 1690;[*] and, during his residence there, was a contemporary of Sir Isaac Newton, who was a Fellow of the neighbouring college of Trinity. Of the latter he speaks in the *Diary*, and of the circumstances connected with which a separate notice is appended to this memoir.

---

[*] See notices of him in the *Daily News*, 5th December, 1868; and the *Register*, for January, 1869, p. 48.

[*] See Diary, *postea*, p. 1.

[*] See Diary, *postea*, p. 4.

[*] See Diary, *postea*, pp. 18-20.

C

At Cambridge, he did not confine his attention to the ordinary academic studies, but applied himself diligently to natural history, chemistry, and to what was then considered by many a cognate subject, magic. Whatever smile this may now create, it was far otherwise then; and even some of the Fellows of the college, if not addicted to it, were not disbelievers in it. In the intercourse attempted to be held with the other world, by himself and some brother students, he frankly confesses his disappointment[w] that "nothing would appear, *quamvis omnia rite peracta.*" This frame of mind, however, did not last long; and, some time afterwards, he very candidly admitted this, and took pains to expose the improbability of præternatural appearances. It has been wittily said, in favor of the theory of ghosts, that *appearances* were in their favor, but not even this could be said of this form of demonology. He took his B.A. degree in January, 1693; and, soon afterwards, holy orders, and obtained the curacy of Broughton, near Brigg, in Lincolnshire. He entered upon a new course of study, suggested by the topographical antiquities of that part of the country, into which he made great researches, and of so valuable a nature, that the principal of them were published in the *Philosophical Transactions.*

Having exhausted all the materials that this neighbourhood afforded, he removed to Hatfield in 1696, with a view of writing its history; and entered into correspondence with the celebrated antiquary, Dr. Gale, dean of York. He speaks of it as a much more interesting place than we now suppose. It was a true "labor of love" to him; and (as he says), he was so "exceedingly busy in old deeds and charters, which they send me in on every side, that I cannot take time to think or write anything else." The work, with some other of his MSS., is now in the British Museum, though in a somewhat imperfect state.[x]

His antiquarian pursuits did not divert his attention from the

---

[w] See Diary, *postea,* p. 26.
[x] *Lansdowne,* 897-899. See notices in Appendix.

study of natural history, in which he corresponded with Sir Hans Sloane, and others. From his observations on marine petrifactions, he attempted to solve the problem of the connexion of these phenomena with the deluge, as recorded in Scripture, the results of which were also published in the *Philosophical Transactions*. In estimating their value as contributions to science, we must not think lightly of them because they have been superseded by modern discoveries, and more extended research, for these subjects were then, as it were, in their infancy. Let us remember, as Professor Pryme has so well said, "Justice requires us, while we admire the modern superstructure, not to forget the merits of those who laid the early foundations, or, by unsuccessful attempts, showed what parts of them were unsound. They laid the groundwork of what has been since done more accurately and completely; and by narrowing the limits of conjecture, contributed to the discoveries of those who might otherwise have been occupied, like them, in ill-directed researches, and in deducing erroneous theories."

In 1698, he was appointed curate and divinity reader of the High Church, Hull, where he applied himself with unusual diligence to methodising the records and antiquities of that town. Frost, in his notices of the early history of Hull, thus speaks of his labors in that department. "The first attempt to give a detached *History of Hull* was made by the Rev. Abraham de la Pryme, M.A., F.R.S., who filled the office of divinity reader in the Holy Trinity Church there, between the month of September, 1698, and the year 1701. He was attracted to the place by his taste for the study of antiquities, which he hoped to indulge by obtaining access to the numerous MSS. and old deeds there understood to be deposited. A three years' residence afforded him sufficient opportunity, not only to arrange and make a copious analytical index of all the ancient records of the corporation, but to compile from them a regular and connected detail, which has formed the basis and groundwork of all subsequent

XX   PREFACE.

accounts and histories of the town. His labours, though evidently intended for publication, exist yet, in MS. only; and a
copy is to be found in the Warburton Collection, among the
Lansdowne MSS., in the British Museum, in two volumes, folio,
bearing the following promising title: *The History, Antiquities,
and Description of the Town and County of Kingston-upon-Hull,
etc., collected out of all the Records, Charters, Deeds, Mayors'
letters, etc., of the said Town.* By A. de la Pryme, Reader and
Curate of the Church of the Holy Trinity of the said Town.
—*Lansdowne, MSS.*, in Bibl. Mus. Brit., No. 890-891."

Such, however, was the labor and difficulty attending these
studies, that he confesses that he "began to grow somewhat
weary thereof."[y]   Although he inherited from his father an
estate in Lincolnshire, as well as one at Hatfield, which, together
with his stipend at Hull, procured him a very good income, the
expensive nature of his studies, and the journies connected with
them, seem to have crippled his resources. He says, "my zeal
for old MSS., antiquities, coins, and monuments, almost eats me
up, so that I cannot prosecute the search of them as I would.
I am at very great charges in carrying on my studies of antiqui-
ies, in employing persons at London, Oxford, etc., to search
records, etc., even to the danger and hazard of my own ruin,
and the casting of myself into great debts and melancholy."[z]

In 1701, the Duke of Devonshire gave him the living of
Thorne,[a] near Hatfield, which enabled him to retire from his
more laborious duties at Hull. He was also elected a Fellow of
the Royal Society, which was then an honor of much greater
distinction than it has since become, and he obtained it at the
then very early age of thirty.

He did not, however, live long to enjoy these honors; and, in
June, 1704, we meet with the following sad record of his death

[y] See Diary, *postea*, p. 238.
[z] See Diary, *postea*, p. 236.
[a] See Diary, *postea*, p. 245.

in *Thoresby's Diary*, vol. i., p. 455 : "Was much concerned to hear of the death of my kind friend Mr. Abraham de la Pryme, minister of Thorne, who, visiting the sick, caught the new distemper, or fever, which seized him on Wednesday, and he died the Monday after, the 12th inst., in the prime of his age." Thoresby has preserved some of his letters in his valuable collection.

He was buried in Hatfield church, where are the monuments of most of the family,[b] under a plain gravestone, bearing an inscription, which will be found in the Appendix.[c]

His death shows him to have been a good man, as well as a great scholar. He was a man of high principle and strong religious feeling, as well as genuine warmth of friendship. His great simplicity of heart, and singular modesty, may account for his never having married ; and his first, and last, and only love, was literature, to which he seems to have been too much wedded to allow the *divisum imperium* of matrimony.

Tickell, in the preface to his *History of Hull*, says that " Pryme was born at Hull.[d] Probably it might be at the time his father, Matthew, emigrated from the city of Ypres, in Flanders, previous to his settling in the Levels of Hatfield Chase, soon after the same was drained by Vermuyden. This Abraham was some time divinity reader to the High Church, Hull, and minister of Thorne. I have been able to gather very little respecting the life of this respectable person ; but the ample list of works attached will attract the attention of the antiquarian, and awaken that respect which is due to his labours. He died in the 34th year of his age, as appears by the tablet erected to his memory in Hatfield church.

" When Pryme was divinity reader to the High Church, Hull, he was employed, by the bench of mayor and aldermen, to

---

[b] See Appendix, p. 260.
[c] *Ibid*, p. 262.
[d] This is, however, an error, as the Diarist himself tells us that he saw born in the Hatfield Levels.—*Diary*, p. 1.

inspect and arrange the ancient records of the corporation—a task he was, doubtless, well qualified to perform, and which he has executed with the greatest diligence and attention. From these original papers he has made long extracts, which are bound up in volumes, and lodged in the Guildhall, with a general index, directing us to the originals; so that any record, previous to the period bounded by the present century, may be as readily examined here, as an enrolment in one of our register offices."

Tickell compiled his history principally from the preceding papers, which he published in 4to, 1769. He adds :—

"Two folio MS. volumes of the above extracts were among Mr. Warburton's collections concerning Yorkshire, and are now in Lord Shelburn's library.—*Gough's British Topography*, vol. ii., p. 447.

"In the same library are deposited the following MSS. by Pryme.

"History of Rippon, Selby, Doncaster, and the W. Riding. 1 vol.

"History of Headon and the E. Riding. 1 vol.

"History of York and the N. Riding. 1 vol.

"History of Beverley. 1 vol.

"History and Antiquities of Winterton, 4to. 1 vol. (A copy, as corrected and enlarged by Mr. Warburton, was purchased at the sale of his books, in 1859, by Mr. Goodman, coal merchant. I have seen two copies of this MS.)

"History of the Drainage of the Level of Hatfield Chase, 4to. 1 vol. (There are many copies of this MS. in the country, but all of them very imperfect).

"After Pryme became a member of the Royal Society, there were many of his papers published in the Transactions, some of which are the following :

"Relation of two Waterspouts observed at Hatfield.

"On certain Fossil-shells found in Lincolnshire, Louth, abridged, vol. ii., p. 428.

" On Trees found underground in Hatfield Chase. Vol. iv., 212.

" Experiments on Vegetation. Vol. iv., 310.

" On Hydrophobia. Vol. v., 366.

" A Roman Pavement, near Roxby, in Lincolnshire. Vol. v., 422.

" The Roman Way, called High-street, in Lincolnshire. Vol. iii., 428.

" On the Hermitage at Lindholme, a poem. Printed by T. Outybridge."

Joseph Hunter says of him, "He died before he had the opportunity of pouring upon the world the results of a meditative life, of which it may be truly said that in a short time he had fulfilled a long one."

Edmund Henry Barker wrote, on returning the MS. Diary to my father, "Your relation was a fine specimen of primitive honesty and simplicity; learned himself, and a liberal encourager of learning; full of generous sympathies and Christian feelings, and patriotic sentiments. The whole Diary reflects so much honor on himself, that it ought to be published entire; and you may be proud of the publication. It contains many curious particulars of things and persons; and men of a right antiquarian spirit will read the book with great relish. I can furnish you with many notes by way of *garnish*, or *sauce* to the meat."

My father then (April, 1832) meditated the publication of this Diary, tho' not in its entirety; but, in December, he was elected member of parliament for Cambridge, and turned his attention to the great political questions which were then occupying the public mind, and in which he took a very active part in the House of Commons. In consequence of this, the publication was postponed *sine die;* but, shortly before his death, in 1868, he entrusted it to myself; and the Surtees Society, without any previous communication from us, offered to include the Diary in their series of antiquarian works. I cannot regret this delay, as it has led to two great advantages—the publication of the Diary almost in its entirety, and the valuable assistance of Mr. Jackson, of Doncaster, to whose very great care, attention, and ability, this work is so much indebted; and I trust he will accept this hearty and unreserved acknowledgment of his services, the value and extent of which no one has better known, or more cordially appreciated, than his ever very faithful friend,

CHARLES DE LA PRYME.

86, Gloster-place, Portman-square,
  London.

P.S.—In reference to the illness of Sir Isaac Newton, mentioned in the Diary,[f] the following extract from Sir David Brewster's *Life of Newton* will be interesting. Edinburgh edition, 1860. Vol. ii., p. 89. Chapter 17 treats of the illness of Sir Isaac in 1692, and Sir David thus speaks of it:—" In the autumn of 1692, when Newton had finished his letters on Fluxions, he did not enjoy that degree of health with which he had so long been favored. The loss of appetite and want of sleep, of which he now complained, and which continued for nearly a twelvemonth, could not fail to diminish that mental vigor, and that ' consistency of mind' (as he himself calls it), which he had hitherto displayed. How far this ailment may have arisen from the disappointment which he experienced in the application of his friends for a permanent situation for him, we have not the means of ascertaining; but it is impossible to read his letters to Locke, and other letters from his friends, without perceiving that a painful impression had been left upon *his* mind, as well as upon theirs. The state of his health, however, did not unfit him for studies that required, perhaps, more profound

---

[f] See *postea,* p. 23.

thought than his letters on Fluxions and Fluents, for it was at
the close of 1692, and during the two first months of 1693, that
he composed his four celebrated letters to Dr. Bentley."

" The illness of Newton, which increased till the autumn of
1693, was singularly misrepresented by foreign contemporary
authors, to whom an erroneous account of it had been communicated. During the century and a half which has elapsed
since that event, it has never been mentioned by any of his
biographers; and it was not till 1822 that it was brought before
the public as a remarkable event in the life of Newton.

" The celebrated Dutch philosopher, Van Swinden, made the
following communication to M. Biot, who published it with
comments, that gave great offence to the friends of Newton:
'There is among the manuscripts of the celebrated Huygens,'
says Van Swinden, 'a small journal in folio, in which he used
to note down different occurrences. It is note no. 8 in the
catalogue of the library of Leyden, p. 112. The following extract
is written by Huygens himself, with whose handwriting I am
well acquainted, having had occasion to peruse several of his
manuscripts and autograph letters :—' On the 29th of May, 1694,
M. Colin, a Scotchman, informed me, that eighteen months ago
the illustrious geometer, Isaac Newton, had become insane, either
in consequence of his too intense application to his studies, or
from excessive grief at having lost, by fire, his chemical laboratory
and several manuscripts. When he came to the Archbishop of
Cambridge,⁵ he made some observations which indicated an
alienation of mind. He was immediately taken care of by his
friends, who confined him to his house, and applied remedies, by
means of which he had now so far recovered his health that he
began to understand the Principia.' Huygens mentioned this
circumstance in a letter to Leibnitz, dated 8th June, 1694, in the
following terms :—' I do not know if you are acquainted with

⁵ Archiepiscopus Cantabrigiensis is perhaps a clerical error for *Cantuar-
ensis.*

the accident which has happened to the good Mr. Newton, namely, that he has had an attack of phrenitis, which lasted eighteen months, and of which they say that his friends have cured him by means of remedies, and keeping him shut up.' To which Leibnitz replied in a letter, dated the 22nd June :—' I am very glad that I received information of the cure of Mr. Newton at the same time that I first heard of his illness, which doubtless must have been very alarming. It is to men like you and him, Sir, that I wish a long life and much health, more than others, whose loss, comparatively speaking, would not be so great.'

" The first publication of the preceding statement produced a strong sensation among the friends and admirers of Newton. They could not easily believe in the prostration of that intellectual strength which had unbarred the strongholds of the universe. The unbroken equanimity of Newton's mind, the purity of his moral character, his temperate and abstemious life, his ardent and unaffected piety, and the weakness of his imaginative powers, all indicated a mind which was not likely to be overset by any affliction to which it could be exposed. The loss of a few experimental records could never have disturbed the equilibrium of a mind like his. If they were the records of discoveries, the discoveries, themselves indestructible, would have been afterwards given to the world. If they were merely the details of experimental results, a little time could have easily re-produced them. Had these records contained the first fruits of youthful genius, of obscure talent, on which fame had not yet shed its rays, we might have supposed that the first blight of early ambition would have unsettled the stability of a mind unannealed by the world.

" But Newton was satiated with fame. His mightiest discoveries were completed, and diffused over all Europe, and he must have felt himself placed on the loftiest pinnacle of earthly ambition. The incredulity which such views could not fail to encourage, was increased by the novelty of the information. No English biographer had ever alluded to such an event. History and tradition were equally silent, and it was not easy to believe that the Lucasian Professor of Mathematics at Cambridge, recently a member of the English Parliament, and the first philosopher and mathematician in Europe, could have lost his reason without the dreadful fact being known to his countrymen.

" But if the friends of Newton were surprised by the nature of the intelligence, they were distressed at the view which was taken of it by foreign philosophers. 'The fact,' says M. Biot, 'of the derangement of his intellect, whatever may have been the cause of it, will explain why, after the publication of the *Principia* in 1687, Newton, though only forty-five years old, never more published a new work on any branch of science, but contented himself with giving to the world those which he had composed long before that epoch, confining himself to the completion of those parts which might require development. We may also remark, that even these developments appear always to be derived from experiments and observations formerly made, such as the additions to the second edition of the *Principia*, published in 1713, the experiments on thick plates, those on diffraction, and the chemical queries placed at the end of the *Optics* in 1704; for, in giving an account of these experiments, Newton distinctly says, that they were taken from ancient manuscripts which he had formerly composed; and he adds, that though he felt the necessity of extending them, or rendering them more perfect, he was not able to resolve to do this, these matters being no longer in his way. Thus it appears that, though he had recovered his health sufficiently to understand all his researches, and even in some cases to make additions to them, and useful alterations, as appears from the second edition of the *Principia*, for which he kept up a very active mathematical correspondence with Mr. Cotes, yet he did not wish to undertake new labours in those departments of science where he had done so much, and where he so distinctly saw what remained to be done.'

" Under the influence of the same opinion, M. Biot finds ' it extremely probable that his dissertation on the scale of heat was written before the fire in his laboratory ; ' and he describes Newton's conduct about the longitude bill as exhibiting an inexplicable timidity of mind, and as ' so puerile for so solemn an occasion, that it might lead to the strangest conclusions, particularly if we refer it to the fatal accident which befell him in 1695.'

"The illness of Newton was viewed in a light still more painful to his friends. It was maintained that he never recovered the vigour of his intellect, and that his theological inquiries did not commence till after that afflicting epoch of his life. In reply to this groundless assertion, it may be sufficient to state, in the words of his friend John Craig, that his theological writings were composed ' while ' his understanding was in its greatest perfection, lest the infidels might pretend that his applying himself to the studies of religion was the effect of dotage.'

" Such having been the consequences of the disclosure of Newton's illness by the manuscript of Huygens, I felt it to be a sacred duty to the memory of that great man, and to the feeling of his countrymen, to inquire into the nature and history of that indisposition which seems to have been so much misrepresented and misapplied. From the ignorance of so extraordinary an event which has prevailed for such a long period in England, it might have been urged with some plausibility, that Huygens had mistaken the real import of the information that was conveyed to him ; or that the person from whom he received it had propagated an idle and groundless rumour. But we are fortunately not confined to this very reasonable mode of defence.

" There exists at Cambridge a manuscript journal, written by Mr. Abraham de la Pryme, who was a student in the University while Newton was a Fellow of Trinity. This manuscript is entitled ' *Ephemeris Vitæ*, or Diary of my own Life, containing an account likewise of the most observable and remarkable things that I have taken notice of from my youth up hitherto.' Mr.

A. de la Pryme was born in 1671, and begins the Diary in 1685. This manuscript is in the possession of his collateral decendant, George Pryme, Esq., Professor of Political Economy at Cambridge,⁴ to whom I have been indebted for the following extract, which is given verbatim, and occurs during the period when Mr. De la Pryme was a student in St. John's College, Cambridge :—' 1692, February 3rd. What I heard to day I must relate. There is one Mr. Newton (whom I have very oft seen), Fellow of Trinity College, that is mighty famous for his learning, being a most excellent mathematician, philosopher, divine, &c. He has been Fellow of the Royal Society these many years; and amongst other very learned books and tracts he's written one upon the mathematical principles of philosophy, which has got him a mighty name, he having received, especially from Scotland, abundance of congratulatory letters for the same ; but of all the books that he ever wrote, there was one of colours and light, established upon thousands of experiments, which he had been twenty years of making, and which had cost him many hundred of pounds. This book, which he valued so much, and which was so much talked of, had the ill luck to perish, and be utterly lost, just when the learned author was almost at putting a conclusion at the same, after his manner :—in a winter's morning leaving it amongst his other papers, on his study table, whilst he went to Chapel, the candle, which he had unfortunately left burning there too, catched hold by some means of other papers, and they fired the aforesaid book, and utterly consumed it, and several other valuable writings ; and, which is most wonderful, did no further mischief. But when Mr. Newton came from chapel, and had seen what was done, every one thought he would have run mad, he was so troubled thereat that he was not himself for a month after. A long account of this his system of light and colours you

⁴ That would be, however, under loan only, as the manuscript was then the property of W. J. Bagshawe, esq., of the Oaks, near Sheffield,—See *Introduction, antea.*

may find in the Transactions of the Royal Society, which he had
sent up to them long before this sad mischance happened unto
him."

"The story of the burning of Newton's laboratory and papers,
as stated by Mr. de la Pryme, has been greatly exaggerated and
misrepresented, and there can be no doubt that it was entirely
unconnected with Newton's illness. Mr. Edleston has placed it
beyond a doubt that the burning of the manuscripts took place
between 1677 and 1683, and I have found ample confirmation of
the fact from other sources of information.

"Dr. H. Newton, as we have seen, tells us that he had heard a
report that Newton's *Optics* had been burnt before he wrote his
Principia, and we know that no such accident took place during
the five years that Dr. Newton lived with him at Cambridge.
The following memorandum of Mr. Conduitt's, written after
conversing on the subject with Newton himself, appears to place
the event at an early period :—' When he was in the warmest
pursuit of his discoveries, he, going out, left a candle upon his
table amongst his papers : he went down into the bowling-green,
and meeting somebody who diverted him from returning, as he
intended, the candle set fire to his papers, (and he could never
recover them). Upon my asking him whether they related to
his *Optics* or his *Method of Fluxions*, he said he believed there
was some relating to both, and that he was obliged to work them
all over again.' The version of the burnt papers, in which
' Diamond ' is made the perpetrator, and in which the scene of
the story is laid in London, and in Newton's later years, we may
consign to a note, with the remark of Dr. Humphrey Newton,
that Sir Isaac never had any communion with dogs or cats.

---

 i   See Diary, *postea*, p. 23.

j   It should be observed, *en passant*, that what De la Pryme "relates" in
his Diary, 3rd February, 1692, is only what he " *heard* today ; " but he appears
to furnish us with no information as to the time when the accident befel
Newton's papers by the fire, further than that it occurred " on a winter's morning."

" By means of this extract from Mr. de la Pryme's Diary, we are enabled to fix the latest date of the accident by which Newton lost his papers. It must have been previous to the 3rd January, 1692, a month before the date of the extract; but if we fix it by the dates in Huygens' manuscript, we should place it about the 29th November, 1692, eighteen months previous to the conversation between Colin and Huygens.

" The manner in which Mr. de la Pryme refers to Newton's state of mind is that which is used every day when we speak of the loss of tranquillity which arises from the ordinary afflictions of life ; and the meaning of the passage amounts to nothing more than that Newton was very much troubled by the destruction of his papers, and did not recover his serenity, and return to his usual occupations, for a month. The very phrase, that every person thought he would have run mad, is in itself a proof that no such effect was produced ; and whatever degree of indisposition may be implied in the phrase, 'he was not himself for a month after,' we are entitled to infer that one month was the period of its duration, and that previous to the 3rd February, 1692, the date of Mr. de la Pryme's memorandum, 'Newton was himself again.' These facts and dates cannot be reconciled with those in Huygen's manuscript. It appears from that document, that so late as May, 1694, Newton had only *so far* recovered his health as *to begin to again understand the Principia.* His supposed malady, therefore, was in force from the 3rd January, 1692, till the month of May, 1694—a period of more than two years. Now, it is a most important circumstance, which M. Biot ought to have known, that in *the very middle of this period*, Newton wrote his four celebrated letters to Dr. Bentley on the Existence of a Deity,— letters which evince a power of thought, and a serenity of mind, absolutely incompatible even with the slightest obscuration of his faculties. No man can peruse these letters without the conviction that their author then possessed the full vigour of his reason, and was capable of understanding the most profound parts of his writings. The first of these letters was written on the 10th December, 1692; the second on the 17th January, 1693; the third on the 11th February, and the fourth on the 25th February, 1693. His mind was, therefore, strong and vigorous on these four occasions; and, as the letters were written at the express request of Dr. Bentley, to assist him in preparing his lectures for publication, we must consider such a request as showing his opinion of the strength and freshness of his friend's mental powers."

I am happy to be enabled to add that this opinion is entertained by Sir John Herschell, the Astronomer Royal, and the Rev. Dr. Edleston, to whose valuable work on Newton, the memory of that great philosopher is so much indebted.

DESCENDANTS OF HUGH BLAYDES AND ELIZABETH DE LA PRYME,

NIECE OF THE DIARIST.

Joseph Blaydes=Jane, dau. of Wm. Mould, mayor of Hull, 1698.

Benjamin Blaydes, mayor of Hull, 1702.

Hugh Blaydes, of Hull, born 1685; died 9 Apr., 1759, aged 74.=Elizabeth, dau. of Peter de la Pryme; mar. 28 Apr., 1728; died 21 Aug., 1772.

Joseph Blaydes=Martha Jarratt.

Rev. Isaac Thompson.=Mary Blaydes, vicar of St. Mary's, only child. Hull; ob. 1777.*

Hugh Blaydes, d. s. p.

Benjamin Blaydes, of Melton, mayor of Hull, 1771; born 5 Mar., 1735; died 29 Oct., 1805.=Kitty, dau. and co-heiress of Christopher Scott, of Aldbro', in Holderness.

Catherine, died unmarried at Melton.

Benjamin Blaydes, of Beverley, London, and Cheltenham; died at the latter place 1840.=Elizabeth, dau. of Geo. Knowsley, of Cottingham.

Hugh Blaydes, of High Paul, co. of York, and Ranby Hall, Notts.; born 9 Aug., 1777; died 15 Feb., 1829. High sheriff of Notts. 1812.=Delia Maria, dau. of Col. Richard Wood, of Hollin Hall, nr. Ripon; mar. 19 March, 1800.

Elizabeth, living at Teignmouth, co. Devon, 1869.
Katharine.
Frances, mar. Captain Beatty.
Mary Anne.
Lucy.
Emily.

Hugh Marvel, died unmarried 1836.

Charles Benjamin Blaydes, born 9 Ap., 1812.†

Caroline Martha, dau. of Captain Jackson=

Frederick Henry Marvel, in holy orders; born 29 Sept., 1818.=Fanny Maria, dau. of Sir Edward Page Turner, bt.

Delia Katherine.
Louisa Anne.

Harriet Elizabeth, died unmar., 1824.

Henrietta Christian,=Edward Parratt, esq.

Emmeline Sophia,=F. A. Blachford, esq., Captain 23rd Highlanders.

=H. T. C. Kerr, esq.; died 1845.

son, of Bronsoj, and
and next heir, about
d. 18th September,

John, son of John
·ch, 1747-8, aged 22.
p. 106 ; and Hunter,
April, 1746, guard-
ork, deceased (from
Thomas Johnson, of
ng surety in bond).
Kingston-upon-Hall,
and and houses, of

l, about half an hour
er Bosv. My mother
:her.—*Family Bible.*

l of Hatfield Chace,

etc., published in 1766, were numerous; but many of them were of an objectionable character. His journal is noticed in the *Cornhill Magazine*, May, 1868, pp. 610-640. In it he speaks of his "brother-in-law," and "half brother" (tho' it does not seem that, strictly speaking, he was either), Christopher Pryme ; to the memory of whom, an allusion, in a "rhyming" form of words, is not of the most complimentary order. He mentions, also, a married "sister Wright." He died on board the *Grampus*, of which he was commander, off the coast of Africa, on 17th January, 1786. By his will, which was proved in London in April following, he left £100 to Mary, his "ungrateful wife," in honour preferring doubly, by a bequest of £200 and other things, a certain Miss Powell, whom he styles his "faithful companion" (probably the "Emma" of the journal). His burial is directed to be at St. Giles'-in-the-Fields, near that "glorious, honest citizen, Andrew Marvell," whose seal ring he bequeaths.

p See *Burke's Commoners of Great Britain and Ireland*, 1836, vol. i., pp. 667-8 : *Dictionary of Landed Gentry*, 1868, p. 114.

q See pedigree, Gatty's *Hunter's Hallamshire*, 1869, p. 449.

r Baptized at St. Mary's, Sculcoates, Hull, 1769, Oct. 4, Ann Elizabeth, dau. of Mr. Mavson Wright, merchant. 1770, Dec. 1, Francis, son of ditto.—See *Monumental Inscription in Hatfield Church.*

s See biographical account of him in *The Register*, January, 1869, page 48. Also "*Autobiographic Recollections of George Pryme, Esq.*, etc. Edited by his daughter." Cambridge, Deighton and Bell, 1870. *The Times*, August 25th, 1870.

id next heir, about 18th September,

John, son of John b, 1747-8, aged 22. . 106 ; and Hunter, april, 1746. guard-k. deceased (from iomas Johnson, of ; surety in bond), ngston-upon-Hall, id and houses, of

about half an hour Bosv. My mother er.—*Family Bible.*

of Hatfield Chace,

etc., published in 1766, were numerous; but many of them were of an objectionable character. His journal is noticed in the *Cornhill Magazine*, May, 1868, pp. 610-640. In it he speaks of his "brother-in-law," and "half brother" (tho' it does not seem that, strictly speaking, he was either). Christopher Pryme ; to the memory of whom, an allusion, in a "rhyming" form of words, is not of the most complimentary order. He mentions, also, a married "sister Wright." He died on board the *Grampus*, of which he was commander, off the coast of Africa, on 17th January, 1786. By his will, which was proved in London in April following, he left £100 to Mary, his "ungrateful wife," in honour preferring doubly, by a bequest of £300 and other things, a certain Miss Powell, whom he styles his "faithful compa ion" (probably the "Emma" of the journal). His burial is directed to be at St. Giles'-in-the-Fields, near that "glorious, honest citizen, Andrew Marvell," whose seal ring he bequeaths.

p See *Burke's Commoners of Great Britain and Ireland*, 1836, vol. i., pp. 667-8 : *Dictionary of Landed Gentry*, 1868, p. 114.

q See pedigree, Gatty's *Hunter's Hallamshire*, 1869, p. 419.

r Baptized at St. Mary's, Sculcoates, Hull, 1769, Oct. 4, Ann Elizabeth, dau. of Mr. Mayson Wright, merchant. 1770, Dec. 1, Francis, son of ditto.—See *Monumental Inscription in Hatfield Church.*

s See biographical account of him in *The Register*, January, 1869, page 48. Also "*Autobiographic Recollections of George Pryme, Esq.*, etc. Edited by his daughter." Cambridge, Deighton and Bell, 1870. *The Times*, August 25th, 1870,

EPHEMERIS VITÆ

ABRAHAMI PRYME,

OR,

A DIARY OF MY OWN LIFE.

CONTAINING AN ACCOUNT, LIKEWISE,
OF THE MOST OBSERVABLE AND REMARKABLE THINGS THAT
I HAVE TAKEN NOTICE OF FROM MY
YOUTH UP, HITHERTO.

———————

ECCL.:

Vanity of vanitys. All is vanity and vexation of spirit.

Man's life is but a vain thing, and a series of evils. Teach us then, O Lord, so to number our days, that we may obtain everlasting bliss in thyne eternal kingdome.

A DIARY OF MY OWN LIFE, CONTAINING AN ACCOUNT OF THE MOST CONSIDERABLE THINGS THAT HAVE HAPPEN'D THEREIN.

My father, whose name was Mathias Pryme, was the son of Charles Pryme, my grandfather; he was one of those that came over in king Charles the First days from Flanders, from a citty called Eper[Ypres], upon the draining of the great fens in the Levels of Hatfield Chace;[a] but they were most of them undon by their great undertaking, as my grandfather lost many hundred of pounds by it.

My father being grown up to man's estate[b] marryd Sara the daughter of Mr. Peter Smagge, who was a rich Frenchman, that with his whole family was forced from Paris by persecusion for his faith, and was comed to live also on these Levels.

They were marryed April 3rd, in the year 1670, in the Dutch congregation in the chapple at Santoft;[c] for these forreigners had divine service there for many years together, before their chappel was built at Santoft.

I was the first born, and was born the 15 of January, in the year 1671[d] (to all the miserys of life) at a house about the middle of the Levels, about the middle way on the high road side on the left hand as you come straight from the Isle of Axholme, or Haxyhom, from Epworth to the little neat town of Hatfild in Yorkshire, in which parish and which county I was born.

[a] For an account of the general history of the Level of Hatfield Chace, its drainage, etc., see *Hunter's South Yorkshire*, vol. i. pp. 150-197.

[b] My father was born the 31 of Aug., 1645. My mother, 17 of Nov., 1649.—*Marginal note by diarist*.

[c] Sandtoft is a hamlet in the parish of Belton, which is in Lincolnshire, but close to the borders of the county of York. When Sir Cornelius Vermuy-

B

My father can speak Dutch and my mother French, but I nothing yet but Inglish.

1680.

I can remember very little observable before I was ten or eleven years old, onely my going to school and such. But in 1680 my father shifted dwelling, and went and lived at an old great larg

den took a grant of the Manor and Chace of Hatfield, he had the privilege awarded him of erecting a place for religious worship, where the Dutch and French settlers on the Levels might assemble to hear divine service performed in a foreign tongue. In 1634 a chapel was erected at this place, which was probably chosen as being centrical to the whole drainage. It was built by one Isaac Bedloe, a merchant, and, many years after, he had not received the money stipulated to be paid him. In 1650 the chapel was much defaced and injured by rioters who assembled to resist the sheriff in the execution of legal processes connected with the drainage. The noted fanatic, Col. John Lilburn, who came to reside here, is said to have employed the chapel as a stable or barn. Mr. Hunter, when he wrote in or about 1828, mentions that the register of the chapel had been carefully kept from 1641 to 1681, and was then or then lately in existence. He gives from it what he terms "a pretty complete list" of the names of the foreign settlers. Much enquiry has been from time to time since made for this register, but it is supposed to be now lost or destroyed. The following ministers occur. M. Berchett. He died 18 April, 1655, and was buried at Crowle. Phillip Castell, "Nantices, Franc. in Gallia," buried at Hatfield, 5 Sept., 1655. Johnston has a notice of the inscription over his place of interment, in the south aisle of the chancel. Jean Deckerhuel was minister in 1659. M. de la Prix. Samuel Lamber was here in 1664. Jaques de la Porte was minister in 1676. John Conrad de Werneley, or Werndley, was minister in 1681. He had no successor, it is said, and the chapel itself did not long survive the ministers. It was taken down, and cattle grazed upon its site.—*Hunter, S. Y.*, i. 165, 169, 170. Mr. W. O. Chatburn, of Sandtoft, has in his possession an oak post, which is said to have belonged to the chapel. Mr. James Dunderdale, of Tiverton Lodge, Cheetham Hill, Manchester, is the owner of a large Bible, with the Gospels, one foot three-and-a-half inches by ten inches in size, having an engraved frontispiece, and entitled *La Sainte Bible Interpretee par Iean Diodarti. Imprimee a Geneve,* M.D.C.XLIIII. It is bound in brown calf leather, and fastened with two embossed brass clasps. This book is traditionally said to be the one which was used in the services of the chapel at Sandtoft, and has been handed down through the family of Le Leu, or Le Lew, from whom, I am informed, Mr. Dunderdale is descended. In the fly leaf is written, *Appartient à Pierze le Leu;* and in several places occur the dates of births, marriages and deaths of that family. To me, however, it scarcely presents the idea of having done the hard work of a public church book. Mr. Werneley published in 1693 a book under the following title :—"*Liturgia Tigurina:* or, The Book of Common Prayers, and Administration of the Sacraments, and other Ecclesiastical Rites and Ceremonies, usually practised and solemnly performed in all the Churches and Chappels of the City and Canton of Zurick in Switzerland, and in some other adjacent countries ; as by their Canons and Ecclesiastical Laws they are appointed ; and as by the Supreme Power of the Right Honourable the Senate of Zurick they are authorised, established, and commanded, with the Order of that Church. Faithfully translated out of the Helvetian into the English tongue, by John Conrad Werndly, formerly Minister of the French and

hall in the Levels, which was built by Mijn Heer Van Valkenburg,' one of the great drainers of the country; and took two
hundred akers of land belonging thereto, for which he payd above
one hundred pound a year, and we live now of that hall yet.
It had stood empty a long while by reason of the great distur-
bancys that had been there by spirits and witches, of whome
there are many dreadfull long tales; but however we have not
this five or six years, that we have lived here, heard or seen anything more than ordinary.

1683.

In 1683 a memorable thing happend at our house relating to
the long abstinence in live creatures. The thing is this. Esquir[e]

Dutch Congregation of Sandtoff, in the Isle of Axholme, in the County of
Lincoln : and now Minister of Wraisbury-cum-Langley, in the County of
Bucks. London : printed for D. Newman, R. Baldwin, J. Dunton. 1693."
The Book has the *Imprimatur* of the bishops of London, Lichfield and Coventry,
Bangor, Norwich, Chichester, and Peterborough.
  ᵈ See Genealogical Notices in appendix.
  ᵉ When the drainage of the Level of Hatfield Chace was undertaken by
Cornelius Vermuyden, the celebrated Dutch Engineer, in 1626, his own capital
being unequal to the design, he was supported by many of his countrymen who
came over and settled in and about the neighbourhood of the works ; amongst
them were the Valkenburghs, who took a principal share and acted a prominent
part in the direction. Three brothers of the name, viz., Matthew, Mark, and
Luke, came hither as residents. They appear to have held a large stake in the
concern. It is shewn from The original MS. *Boke of Accounts of the participants of the dyckage of Haitfield chace of seueral taxes and asensments by
them laide sints 1628 vntill 1634*, in the possesion of Mr. Peacock, that the
Van Valkenburg family possessed 3204 acres on these Levels ; Luke is returned
as possessing 1247 acres, Mark 1146, and Matthew 811.
  Matthew Van Valkenburgh occurs as a commissioner of sewers at a court
held at Epworth, co. Lincoln, in 1635.
  On the 22 Jan., 1638-9, Sampson Marples was fined £10 for serving a king's
letter on Mr. Valkenburgh, one of the commissioners of sewers, during the
sessions of sewers, and was committed till he paid the money.
  In 1636 Matthew married Isabella Eyre, daughter of Anthony and sister of
Sir Gervas Eyre, of Rampton, Notts. He built a large house on the Middle
Ing, on which he resided. In the very interesting volume of " Depositions
from the Castle of York," published by this Society in 1861, we have (pp. 12
and 13) an account of a riot that occurred on the 11th Oct., 1648, in which one
Robert Kay, a Doncaster gentleman, was charged before the justices of peace
with having come to the house at "Midlins" with sixteen or eighteen men, in a
warlike manner, with muskets and swords drawn, and broken open the out gate
and four other doors, committing various outrages, terminating in Mr. Matthew
Valkenburgh being forcibly taken from his house for a quarter of a mile.
Again, on the other hand, at page 174, we have notices of indictments being
preferred, in 1657 and 1661, against Mark Van Valkenburgh, of Hatfield, Esq.,
and others, for taking horses away from their owners, probably for distresses

Ramsden' sending from Hatfield to our house to desire us to send him half a score or a dozen of hens and cocks, he being to have some strangers, it being then about the middle of Christmas. So accordingly they were gotten up, but he sending word that his strangers did not come, so that he had no need of them, they were ordered to be turned out; but through carelessness of the servant they were not, nor was any more thought of, till about ten days after, one [going] into that low vault or little [place where] they were, found them, and they . . . . . . and had not had anything to eat [all that] time, but being fat before, they were now poor; but being turned out into the fould they all lived.

1684.

In this year, in Feb[ruary],[s] dyed King Charles the Second,

for drainage "scots" or rates. So unpopular was the scheme of the drainage, that these acts of violence and disorder were neither few nor trifling. In the Court of Pleas, at Doncaster, 6 Sept., 1649, an action was brought by John Noades, gent., against Mark Van Valkenburgh, for having on the 7th May previously, at Doncaster, publicly spoken of him these "falsa, ficta, scandalosa, et opprobriosa verba," viz., "you are a thief," to his damage of £50. The jury gave a verdict for the plaintiff for £6 13s. 4d., and costs £2 12s. 8d., making £9 6s. 0d. By patent, 26 July, 1642, Matthew Van Valkenburgh was created a baronet, and in April, 1644, he died. His widow lived only to Nov. following, being then buried at Hatfield, with the addition of "Heroina" to her name in the register. Probably her courage had been not unfrequently put to the proof in defence of the great house on the Middle Ing.

f John Ramsden, Esq., son of Wm. Ramsden, a merchant of Hull, by a sister of Sir John Boynton, of Rawcliff. He built himself a handsome house at Norton, was a justice of the peace, deputy lieutenant, and member of parliament for Hull. Died 26 March, 1718, aged 61, and was bur. at Campsal. By Catherine, his wife, dau. of John, Viscount Downe, of Cowick (who d. 20 May, 1737, and was bur. in St. Martin's, Coney-street, York), he had William Ramsden, of Norton, Esq., bap. at Hatfield, 26 Jany., 1683-4, but died before his father, 8 June, 1717, æt. 34, and was bur. at Campsal. Dorothy bp. at Hatfield, 1st, and there bur. 4 Sep., 1682. Elizabeth, bap. at H. 9 Oct., 1687, m: to Richd. Roundell, Esq., of Hutton Wansdley. Ann, bap. 22 Aug., 1689, and bur. at Hatfield, 15 Feb., 1689-90. The wife of Wm. Ramsden, the son and heir, was Mary, d. and c. of Robert Robinson, Esq., of Folkerby, co. York. She d. 5 Ap., 1745. The Norton Estate was settled on Mrs. Mary Ramsden on her marriage, and she purchased the fee simple. She also succeeded to her father's estate at Folkerby. Both these estates she gave to trustees, for making additional buildings, and the support of six fellows and ten scholars at Catherine Hall Cambridge. She directed that they should be called Skern's fellows and scholars, out of regard to the memory of her kinsman Robert Skern, who had heretofore been a benefactor to the same college ; and that natives of Yorkshire and Lincolnshire should have the preference.—See *Hunter's S. Y.*, ii. 470, 473. Richard Ramsden signs the register 1604 as *minister in sacris.* He was bur. 3 March, 1628-9. Two of his children occur as baptized there, Henry, born 11 and bap. 14 Nov., 1606. Mauleverer, bp. 28 Oct., 1610. Matthew Appleyard, Esq., and Mrs. Grace Ramsden were married at Hatfield 30 May, 1682.

s Charles II. died 6 Feb., 1685.

of a disease they call an appoplexy, as they say. He is mightily
lamented by every one, as well by his enemies as friends; and
[I] heard a gentleman say that came from London, that the citty
was in tears, and most of the towns through which he came.
Yet perhaps it may be that they wept not so much for the love
they bore to him, as for fear that his brother who now reigns
should be worse than he. Good God, prevent it!

1685.

This Easter I went with some relations to see Hull. I did
not tak much notice of things as I went, because that we rid
pretty fast. The chief towns that we went thro' were Howden,
etc. Howden is a very pretty town, there being many fine
houses in it, and a pretty church. They say there [is a] mart
kept there, etc. From thence we went many a long tedious mile
over the woulds to Beverley, which is a larg delicate town
indeed. There we stayed a day or two. The minster is a fine
curius building, and there we saw several old monuments and
inscriptions which [I] could not read; and from thence we went
to Hull, where we saw most of the raritys.

[*At this point three pages are wanting in the MS., viz., 4, 5, 6.*]

1686.

This year (1686) I had leeve given me to go visite some of
our relations about York, by which means I got a sight of that
famous tho' not very fine citty. The minster, I believe, is the
biggest building in England, carrying with it in the inside a very
majestick and awfull presence. 'Tis adorn'd within, especially
in that side about the chappel, with a great many rich and costly
statues and funeral monuments of those prelates and noblemen
that have been buried there. The front of the chappel is adorn'd
with the statues of a great many of the Saxon and other kings, if
my memory faill me not. Up and down in the citty there is a
great many reliques of famous and noble houses, but especialy
there is one in the chappel yard which has been a prodigious larg
one with delicate fine gardens, fountains, etc., and statues, seven
or eight of which last (being some of the Roman emperors) are
yet standing, tho' much consumed by time.[a]

[a] The house to which De la Pryme alludes is that of the family of Ingram,
on the north side of the minster, which was one of the sights of York. The
chapel is that of St. Sepulchre, on the same side, which is now destroyed.

The camp at Hunslow Heath. This camp is ill resented all over, and everyone says that a standing army will be England's ruin.

There is great dissentions amongst them ; for the papist Irish and the protestant officers are commonly striveing for superiority.

The Dutch have picter'd the army here, and K[ing J[ames] at the head of them, shooting at butterflies in the air, which has given great offence to the king and court.

Being reading this day a book entitled "The Countess of Kent's receipts," I asked my aunt Prym, who is an ingenious woman, who this countess was, etc. Shee answer'd me that when shee, my aunt, lived in London, she lived just over against her, and knew her very well. She sayd that the countess was a widdow and never had a child in her life : that she was an exceeding good charitable woman, and that she spent twenty thousand pound a year yearly in physick, receipts, and experiments, and in charity towards the poor. Shee caused every other day a huge dinner to be got, and all the poor people might come that would, and that which spared they took home with them. My aunt says shee has seen the poor at her tables several times. Sometimes there would have been sixty, sometimes eighty, sometimes more, sometimes less. And shee sent vast quantitys of meat out to those that could not come. She would oft go to the houses of the poor, and visit them and dress their soars with her own hands ; and shee distributed a vast deal in money herself yearly to all those that stood in need. Yet for all this, as I have since heard, lived in common whoredom with the famous Selden, who she entertained as her gallant.[1]

---

[1] It is but an act of ordinary justice to the character of the noble lady whom the diarist has named in the text, to mention that the story to which he refers, whether true or false, does not, at all events, or in any way, relate to *her*. The "good Countess of Kent," so called from her deeds of charity and hospitality, was Amabel, the second wife of Henry Grey, tenth Earl of Kent (who died 1651), daughter of Sir Anthony Benn, Recorder of London, and widow of the Hon. Anthony Fane. She lived to be 92 years of age, surviving her husband forty-seven years, and dying 17 Aug., 1698. But the "Countess of Kent" who was the real subject of the evil report, was an earlier lady, viz., Elizabeth, second dau. and co-heir of Gilbert Talbot, Earl of Shrewsbury, and wife of Henry Grey, eighth Earl of Kent. The latter nobleman died in 1639, without issue, when the title passed to his cousin, Anthony Grey, ninth Earl, the father of Henry the tenth Earl, husband of the "*Good* Countess" aforesaid. Elizabeth Talbot was born in or about 1581, and died 7 Dec., 1651, aged 70. John Selden, who is here (let us hope) so unjustly brought under our notice, was the famous patriot and lawyer. He was born at Salvington, near Tarring, co. Sussex. His baptism occurs at the latter place in 1584-5—"John Selden, the sonne of John Selden the minstrell, was baptized the xxth day of January." For the life and history of this truly eminent man, the reader must be referred to

This 25, Mr. Reading[j] being new come from London, was at my father's. I heard him say that he saw Oats that discovered the popeish plot whipt according to his condemnation, most miserably; and as he was haild up the streets the multitude would much pitty him, and would cry to the hangsman or he whose office it was to whipp him, "Enough! Enough! Strike easily! Enough!" etc. To whom Mr. Oats replyd, turning his [head] cheerfully behind him, "Not enough, good people, for the truth, not enough!"

Mr. Woodcock, of this town, being lately come from the assizes at York, sayd before some gentlemen that he heard some Londoners say that judge Hayles did formerly say of my lord Jeffries[k] (when he was onely . . . .) that he never saw a man in his life have more impudence and less law. This England knows since to be very true.

This judge is reckon'd to be a very impudent, rawming, conceited fellow.

It happen'd once that he was judging a cause in the country, and having heard much, and laughed much, and abused the cause and witnesses, as he commonly dos, he sees another witness coming in, a grave old white-headed fellow, "Ho! Ho! come old gray-headed father," (says he) "What say you to this?" And, as he was declaring what he knew, "Pish! pish! (says Jeffries to him) "Old father gray-beard, you talk you know not what; you tell what you know herein, and all you know is not worth a ———, much knowledge has made you madd." "No, no, my lord, much knowledge has not made me madd, but too

---

Wood's Athenæ Oxon., etc. Educated for the profession of the law, Mr. Selden appears to have been employed as solicitor or legal steward to the Earl of Kent, the husband of Elizabeth (Talbot) above mentioned, with both of whom he was necessarily much associated, and lived for many years in the strictest degree of friendship. John Aubrey, the Wiltshire Antiquary, a great collector of the rumours of the day, has not omitted to notice that which De la Pryme had heard as to the countess and Selden. The general character furnished to us of Selden is that he possessed principles of the purest and noblest order, and that he was moreover a resolved, serious Christian. It is difficult at this day, in the absence of any positive testimony, to believe that he was likely to be a party to any shameful intrigue like that suggested. Selden died 30 Nov., 1654, at the Friary House, in Whitefriars, London, which, amongst other property, he possessed as devisee of the countess, who, by her will dated 20 June, 1649, and proved 12th Dec., 1651, appointed him her executor and residuary legatee.

[j] Nathaniel Reading, de quo vide *Hunter's S.Y.*, i. p. 167.

[k] A half-length portrait, which is said to be of this notorious judge, is in the possession of the Rev. F. W. White, vicar of Crowle, Lincolnshire; but as it bears a date which is read as 1615, there would seem to be a mistake somewhere.

little has made you a fool," sayd the fellow again.   So they were
all fit to go together by the ears; but the man got him gon, and
whether the judge ever remembered him for it I do not know,
only this 1 know, that they on whose sid the old man was lost the
cause.

The Irish soldiers that are come over are the rudest fellows
that ever was seen, and talks nothing but of killing and destroying all the hereticks, and dividing their lands and goods amongst
them.

This year was published an order against bonfires and fire-
works upon any account whatever. The vulgar and every one
soon perceived what it drove at, viz., the hindering of rejoic-
ings and sports on gunpowder treason night.   Therefore, that
nevertheless they might not loose the priviledge of haveing some
merriment, and of shewing their abhorrence of popery, they
invented illuminations; that is every house, when that night
came, set all their windows as full of candles as ever they could
hold in all the great towns in England, which caused a most
delicate spectacle.

1687.

In the year 1687 there were several memorable things happen'd which we cannot but take notice off.   Of the 28th of April
it rained wheat in great abundance at Lincoln and the towns
adjacent, several granes of which were sent as miraculous and
prodigious presents to several gentlemen about us.[l]

[l]   This was not the first time such a phenomenon is said to have been wit-
nessed in Lincolnshire, as the following extract from R[obert] B[urton's]
*Admirable Curiosities, Rarities, and Wonders, in England, Scotland, and
Ireland* (second ed., p. 139), will show :—"About April 26, 1661, in Lincolnshire, it rained wheat, some grains whereof, were very thin and hollow, but
others of a more firm substance, and would grind into fine flower (*sic.*) Several
pecks of this were taken out of church leads, and other houses that
were leaded. Several inhabitants who were eye-witnesses brought up a considerable quantity to London." Thoresby, in his Diary I., p. 85, says, that on
the 11th June, 1681, in his "cousin Fenton's best chamber, I gathered some of the
corn that was rained down the chimney upon the Lord's-day seven night, when
it likewise rained plentifully of the like upon Hedingly-Moor, as was confi-
dently reported ; but those I gathered with my own hands from the white
hearth, which was stained with drops of blue where it had fallen, for it is of a pale
red or a kind of sky colour, is pretty, and tastes like common wheat, of which
I have one hundred corns. What it may signify, and whether it doth proceed
from natural causes (of which some may be prescribed) or preternatural, such
an ignorant creature as I am cannot aver."—Mrs. Loudon, in her *British Wild
Flowers*, says :—"The seeds of ivy when deprived of the pulpy matter which
surrounds them, bear considerable resemblance to grains of wheat ; and hence
the numbers which are sometimes found lying about are supposed to have given
rise to the stories of wheat being rained from the clouds, which were once so
popular.—P. 185, as quoted in *Notes and Queries* ; 2nd s. vol. ii. p. 335."

At Thorn, a markate town about nine miles of us, was calved in May following a calf with two heads. And at Fishlake, not far of of the aforesayd town, there came up thereto in the river near fifty miles from the sea, sea dogs, a hee and a shee, and a purpose, the last of which I saw.

In August following, it being then very hot weather, I had the good fortune to behold from the beginning to the end one of those strange works of nature called spouts, or rather hurricanes. It immediately filled the air with great black clouds, as I observed day over day. And I observed that some moved from this quarter, some from that, so that they meeting in the middle created a great circumgiration or whirling, which made a noise somewhat like the motion of a milstone. Ever and anon it darted down out of itself a long spout, in which I observed a motion like that of a skrew, so that it seem'd [to] screw up whatever it met with. It went over a grove of trees, and made them bend like hazel wands ; then it came to a great barn, and catching hold of the top thereof, pluck'd all the thatch thereoff in the twinkling of an eye, filling the whole air therewith. Thence it went to a great oak tree, and falling upon one of the branches broke a huge branch thereof, and flung it a great way of of the same in a minnit. Then it came exactly over that part of Hatfield town where I then was, so that I easily beheld the circumgiration of the clouds, and the whirling noise that they made. Thence it went about half mile further, and then dissolved. The whole length of the course that it travel'd over was about a mile and a half.

Ho ! brave ! the queen's with child. Fine sport indeed ! Is it not an abuse to God to say one thing and think another, for no one scarce believes that she is realy with barn ? Is [it] not like a sin in us to thank God for a thing under the name of a blessing which will most certainly prove a curse to us ? *Kurie eleison!* They say that the Virgin Mary has appear'd to her, and declair'd to her that that holy thing that shall be born of her shall be a son. They say likewise that the pope has sent her the Virgin Mary's smok, and hallowed bairn cloaths.*"*

Aug. 11. This day I heard some gentlemen say that the king is wholly led by the nose by the jesuits, and that he dos anything that they bid him. This year, he says, there was great prayers and fastings, and pennancys amongst them, for the souls of all

* This blasphemous and ridiculous nonsense is printed merely to show what was the *vox populi* on this exciting topic.

the royal hereticks (viz., the past protestant kings of Eng[land]),
and after much to do they got King Edw[ard] the Sixth, and King
Charles the First, and King Charles the Second, out of purgatory; as
they reported in their sermons; but as for Queen Eliz[abeth] and
K[ing] Jam[es] the First, they were so fast in hell that there was
no moving of them. God forgive them! I mean these fools, and
grant that they never come there. It seems that they are so foolish as to think that they can thus impose upon us.

1687.

Towards the end of this year there happened a great inundation in the Levels by means of the much rains that fell, and the
high tides, which increased the waters so that they broke the
banks and drownded the country for a vast many miles about.
My father and every one in general that dwell there lost very
considerably in their winter corn; besides the great expences
they were put to by boating their chattel to the hills and firm lands,
with the trouble of keeping them there two or three months. I have
been several times upon these banks (which are about three yards
in hight) when the water of one side has been full to the very tops,
and nothing appeard of one side but a terrable tempestuous sea.
The water remains about half a week, and sometimes a week at its
full height, whose motions some hundreds of people are watching
night and day. But if it chance to be so strong as to drive away
before it, as it often dos, any quantity of any of the banks, then
it drownds all before it, and makes a noise by its fall which is
heard many miles afore they perceive the water. And in the
place where it precipitates it self down it makes a pond, or huge pitt,
sometimes one hundred yards about, and a vast depth, so that in
that place, it being impossible for the bank to be built again, they
all always build it half round about the same. Many of which pitts
and banks so built may be seen beyond Thorn, a markate town a
little of of my town of Hatfield, etc."

JULY THE 20. God be thankt, the bishops are deliverd out
of prison and are clear'd, and people at London shew the greatest
joy that ever was, and the soldiers at Hunsley heath are so gladd
of it they know not what or how to shew it. They tost up their

* Quoted in a note p. 116 of the Hist. Isle of Axholme, 1839, by the Rev.
(afterwards Dr.) W. B. Stonehouse, who in every instance where he alludes to
our diarist invariably writes the name Prymne.

hats into the air, and made loud huzzahs for two houers together. Now our eyes begin to be open'd, and everyone sees that we are yet in danger of our lives and religion. God defend us and take both or none!

Ju. 23. My uncle and godfather Prym[e] is dead. He was an honest, learned, pious, wise, and understanding man.

God knows what will become of poor England. All the land quakes for fear! never a day passes but one or other is asking concerning the French they ruin us all with, for the jesuits and papists here bear all down before them, and many have been heard to say that they expect to wash their hands in heretick's blood before next Christm[as]. God prevent it, for his great mercy's sake!

This day I observed at Mr. Hatfield's[p] a dunghill cock with a cock's spur growing upon his head like a little thorn. The way they do such things is this:—at the same minute they kill one cock they immediately cutt of one of his spurs, which they then clap upon another young cock's head that has just in that sayd minute also had his comb cut off. Then they tye it well on, and so it remains growing. The consideration of this made me reflect upon the story of Taliacocius's engrafting of one man's nose upon another's face, etc.[q]

[o] Abraham de la Pryme, died 23 July 1687. See Pedigree.

[p] John Hatfeild, the 3rd son of Ralph Hatfeild of Laughton-en-le-Morthing, co. York, gent. (of whom and his ancestry see *Hunters S.Y.*, i. pp. 178, 290, 291), was a captain in the Parliament Army. Soon after the civil wars he seated himself at Hatfield. Married 1 June, 1652, Frances, d. of Thomas Westby, Esq., of Ravenfield. She died 2 Sept., 1693, aged 62. Capt. H. died 28 Dec., 1694, aged 72. There is a monument for them in Hatfield Church, erected by their eldest son John Hatfeild, Esq., barrister-at-law, who died in 1720, aged 61. The great granddau. of this latter gentleman, Ann, became the wife of Wm. Gossip. Esq., of a family at Thorp-arch. This gentleman dying 26 March, 1830, left with other issue, an eldest son, William Hatfeild Gossip, Esq., who d. 15 Jan., 1856, leaving an only surviving son, who eventually became heir to his uncle by marriage, the Rev. Cornelius Heathcote Reaston-Rodes, of Barlborough, co. Derby, assuming, by his desire, the surname of De Rodes, in lieu of Gossip, and is the present William Hatfeild De Rodes, Esq., of Barlborough. He m. 7 Sep., 1854, Sophia Felicite, d. of the Hon. and Rev. Alfred Curzon, Rector of Kedleston, co. Derby. This lady (who had subsequently the precedence of a baron's daughter granted to her, on her brother becoming Lord Scarsdale), died without issue, 2d April, 1869. Of the above family of Hatfeild was the Rev. George Hatfeild, Vicar of Doncaster 1762-1785. Ralph Thoresby, the eminent antiquary of Leeds, says, 19 June, 1683, he "had the honour of a visit from Capt. Hatfield, of Hatfeild, with some pleasing discourse concerning the antiquities of that place." (Diary ii. appx. 417.) On 31 Aug., 1694, he rode to Hatfield, and was "most obligingly entertained by the good family" there. (Diary i., 262, 263.) Again 17 January. 1695. (P. 289.)

[q] Tagliacozza was a learned Italian physician. For this feat of his see

OCTOB. 2. Great talk of the prince of Orange. He is making great preparations beyond sea, and 'tis thought that they are designed for England. God's will be done !

3. They say that he has one hundred thousand men which he designs to bring over, amongst which twenty thousand are antropophagi, Laplanders clad in bear skins, that never lay in beds in their lives, but always like beasts under the open canopy of heaven.

20. My father being at Doncaster last Saturday I heard him say that there was a man there with a strong sort of a glass that openly for 10d. lets any one see therein whatt they will. My father took him to be a conjurer.

29. This day I heard that there wer lately arived out of Ireland six thousand Irish, the rudest fellows that ever were seen. Tyrconnel sent them.[r]
All the nation is in fear of being murder'd, and watch is set in all towns by the order of the magistrates to exam[ine] every passenger, etc.

1688.

NOVEMB. 5. About the end of this year happen'd here in England the greatest revolution that was ever known. I mean by that most bold and heroick adventure of the most illustrious and famous Will[iam] Hen[ry] Nassaw, Prince of Orange, who soon turned the scale of affairs, and delivered us out of all our fears of tyranny and popery, which, as farr as I can possibly see, would infallibly have faln upon us.

---

a vulgar jest in *Hudibras*, part i. canto i. line 280, et seqq. What he really did was to make artificial noses, lips, ears, &c., by transplanting portions of skin from other portions of the face. At first people did not know exactly whether to treat him as a sorcerer or liar, but, after his death, his fellow citizens set up a marble statue to his memory, at Bologna, holding a nose in his hand.

r Richard Talbot (Malahide) was created Earl of Tyrconnel, in 1685, and afterwards Duke of Tyrconnel, after James the Second's abdication. He was slain, or at all events died, at Limerick, 14th Aug., 1691. He m. Frances, widow of Sir George Hamilton, Knt., the sister of Sarah Jennings, wife of John Churchhill, Duke of Marlborough. These ladies were the daughters of Richard Jennings, of Sandridge, co. Hertford, Esq. Richard Talbot was son of Sir Wm. T., of Courtown, Bart., who d. in 1633, and brother of Sir Robt., of same place, Bart., and also of Sir Griffith Talbot, who died 26 Dec., 1723, æt. 82. The Earl of Tyrconnel was generalissimo of the Irish forces under King James II.

Qui nescit dissimilare, nescit nec vivere, nec regnare. Politick frauds is and always has been in action in all kingdomes, revolutions, and nations, which is sufficient licence for their lawfullness; and, as for their usefullness, there needs nothing to be said about that; any one that is wise must needs know that many a noble and excellent design would have perished in its birth had it not been brought into the world by such midwives as these. In this time of our revolution wee had many a strange story of long popish knives, gridirons, and instruments of torture found in at least a hundred popish houses up and down the land, with suppositious letters, speeches, and such like, to irritate the people and encourage them to obey the revolution.

But that which was the most observable of all was a general alarm, that was spread over all the land, of God knows how many thousands of Irish (who were disbanded by K[ing] James) who ravaged the country and slew and burnt all before them. This rumour begun in the south, and went northward so effectually that most people believed it, for there came expresses of it everywhere to get everyone in arms, and to meet at such a great town, on such a day, where the whole country was to go and try a brush with the enemy. Now it was that the whole nation was in such a ferment that they sweat for fear! Now all was up in arms, yet nobody knew where they were to fight! All ways was stopt up and passes, old forts, and castles mann'd, and nothing but arms sounded in everyone's mouth. Now it was that the papists was at the brink of the grave, for, wherever there was any, their houses was searched, examined; and, if they were priests, were sent to prison, etc. In all this bustle there was few that offered to run away, but all joyfully and couragiously equipp'd and armed themselves, being resolved to fight. Its almost incredible to think what a number of men there was in arms, all of them resolved to conquer or dy. Everyone when they went to exercise and meet the enemy, took their last lieves of their wives, friends, and sweethearts, with farr more sorrow than they showed for any fear they had either of an enemy or death, etc.

This newse or report ran, as I sayd, quite through the country, and for all it was some weeks a running northward, yet no one letter appear'd out of the south concerning any such thing there till it was always gone past those places where these letters were to go.

Various reports there was concerning the occation of this rumour. Yet most certain it is that it was nothing but a politick alarm raised and set on foot by the king and council to see how the nation stood effected to their new king.

Yet one thing that I exceedingly wonder at is that there was no men killed in this bustle, for I have asked and examined all over wherever I came, and I could never hear of any. But indeed tho' they kill'd nobody, yet they made most miserable of all the papist's houses that they came near; for, under pretence of seeking for arms, they did many thousands of pounds worth of hurt, cuting down rich hangings, breaking through walls, pulling in pieces of excellent ceilings, and such like. But they carried nothing away with them but what they eat or drunk, and then they secured all the papists they could get, intending to carry them all away to prison.

It is wonderful how such rumors as then was could be invented. Here came letters down from London that in a great vault hard by the parliament house they had discover'd a great many gridirons, three yards long, with strang sorts of pincers and scrus and long knives, all of which was to torment those great parliament men that would not agree with the king towards the fulfilling of his will, etc. Then again in another place there was discovered three score horses, kept underground, that had not seen light this many years, which were fed with humane bodys, and these were to tear us in pieces. Then elsewhere there was found under the earth great coppers full of oyl, and others of pitch, and tar, and lead, all which was to boyl hereticks in: and in many popeish houses round about in the country we heard what strange instruments of torment was found in their possession, etc., all which the vulgar faithfully believed; but, as for me, I gave little heed thereto, etc., for they were plainly nothing but politic frauds.

1689.

This year a strange kind of a violent and burning feaver, together with the small pox reigned so in our family that I lost two brothers and two sisters.

Towards the latter end of the aforegoing year there landed at Hull about six or seven thousand Dains, all stout fine men, the best equip'd and disciplin'd of any that was ever seen.

They brought over with them a great quantity of both money and plate, as silver tankards, tumblers, cups, spoons, pottingers, etc., which they sould up and down the country.

Their money had a great alloy of copper in it, yet, for all that, the people here took for their commoditys.

They were mighty godly and religious. You would seldome

or never heard an oath or ugly word come out of their mouths. They had a great many ministers amongst them whome they call'd pastours, and every Sunday almost, ith' afternoon, they prayed and preach'd as soon as our prayers was done.

They sung almost all their divine service, and every ministre had those that made up a quire whom the rest follow'd. Then there was a sermon of about half-an-houer's length, all *memoratim*, and then the congregation broke up. When they administred the sacrament the ministre goes into the church and caused notice to be given thereof, then all come before, and he examined them one by one whether they were worthy to receive or no. If they was he admitted them, if they were not he writ their names down in a book, and bid them prepare against the next Sunday. Instead of bread in the sacrament I observed that they used wafers,' about the bigness and thickness of a sixpence.

They held no sin to play at cards upon Sundays, and commonly did everywhere where they were suffered ; for indeed in many places the people would not abide the same, but took the cards from them.

They were mighty good-natured, and kind, and civel, and many of them where they were quarter'd would thrash or work a week for what they could get. And indeed the English were all over hereabout extream kind to them and gave them free quarter, for which they were exceeding thankful.'

Tho' they loved strong drink yet all the while I was amongst them, which was all this winter, I never saw above five or six of them drunk.

They liked England very well, "Oh! it was the finest country that ever they came in in all their lives," they would oft say, and many swore that they would be hang'd before they would leave

---

* The wafer is still used throughout the whole of Scandinavia. The name given to it in Sweden is *Oblat*, and the silver baskets in which the wafers are brought for presentation on the Holy Table are called *Oblaten schalten.*—See an article on the Swedish Church in the *Christian Remembrancer* for April 1847.

' A memorial of the Danish troops which were quartered in Yorkshire, after the revolution, is to be found (I quote *Allen's Hist. Yorks.* v. iii., p. 285, not having seen the original), in the parish register of St. Mary's, Beverley.

1689, Dec. 16.—Daniel Straker, a Danish trooper buried.

„ Dec. 23.—Johannes Frederick Bellow, beheaded for killing the other, buried.

The following doggrel is on an oval tablet on the outer side of the south wall of the nave :—

" Here two young Danish souldiers lie,
The one in quarrel chanc'd to die ;
The other's head, by their own law,
With sword was sever'd at one blow."

C

it. There was snow in their country a foot thick before they
came away, and they were so surprised, that when [they] came
hither, they found not a bit, they scarce knew what to say.

Many of them at this town, while they stayed here, acted a play
in their language, and they got a vast deal of monney thereby.
The design of it was "Herod's Tyranny;" "The Birth of Christ;"
and the "Coming of the Wise Men." They built a stage in our
large court-house, and acted the same thereon. I observed that
all the postures were shewn first of all, viz., The king on his
throne, his servants standing about him. And then, the senes
being drawn, another posture came ; the barbarous soldiers murdering of the infants, and so on : And when they had run through
all so, they then began to act both together. All which time
they had plenty of all sorts of music of themselves, for [one]
soldier played on one sort and one on another.

I heard some of them say that some of those players belonged
to the king of Denmark's play house that was set a fire, and
burnt when most of the nobles were beholding a play several
years ago, tho' how long I cannot exactly tell.

This day I heard my father say that, as he went to Doncaster
fair,[u] he overtook a company of godly Presbyterians who were
singing salms as they rid. Was not this a great peece of affected-
ness, and more out of vain glory and pride than piety ?

I have heard of a Presbyterian minister who was so precise
that he would not as much as take a pipe of tobacco before that
he had first saved grace over it.

My father alas ! inclines mightily this way, as does all the
French and Duch of these Levels, and he would needs have me go
to the University of Glasco, but I do not intend it. I hope God
will so incline my father's will as to suffer me to go to Cambridge,
which thing I beg for Jesus Christ his sake.

One thing at present which makes a great noise in the country
is an act,[v] not for liberty of conscience, as some call it, but only to

---

[u] 5th April.

[v] 1st W. & M., c. 18, "For exempting their Majesties Protestant subjects,
dissenting from the Church of England, from the penalties of certain laws,"
commonly called the Toleration Act, which enacted that neither certain acts
therein specified, nor any other penal laws made against Popish recusants
(except the test acts) should extend to any dissenters other than Papists and
such as deny the Trinity: provided, 1. That they took the oaths of allegiance
and supremacy (or made a similar affirmation, being quakers) and subscribed
the declaration against popery; 2. That they repaired to some congregation cer-
tified to and registered in the court of the bishop or archdeacon, or at the
County Sessions ; 3. That the doors of such meeting-house should be unlocked,
unbarred, and unbolted ; in default of which the persons meeting there were

exempt the dissenters from the penaltys of all the former laws that
have been made against them, upon condition that they swear to
be true to K[ing] W[illiam] and Q[ueen] M[ary] and do not
at anytime of their meeting keep the conventicle door lockd, barrd,
or bolted ; and that they do subscribe to all the 34, 35, 36, and
these words of the 20th Article, viz.,—*The Church hath power
to decree rites or ceremonies and authority in controversys of faith :
and yet :* which they could not subscribe to.

1690.

In this year about the end of April I began to set forward for
Cambridge, to be admitted there an accademian. The first day
of our journey (which was from the Levels to Sleeford beyond
Lincoln Heath) wee travelled forty-six miles, and so came through
the Fenns of Ely to Cambridge. 'Tis a strange thing that great
towns should so decay and be eaten up with time. I observed when
I came to Lincoln that several stately houses and churches are let
fall down to the ground, piece by piece ; and this which has been
such a famous citty heretofore, there is scarce anything worth
seeing in it now but the high street, it being indeed a most stately
and excellent structure, and is the chief ornament of the town.
The minster indeed looks very stately too on the outside, but
what it is within I do not know. There is an old open fortifica-
cation against it castlewise, which might (tho' there be guns nor
nothing in it) do the town some little hurt if it was well
mann'd, because it stands upon the hill of the town, etc."

We arrived at Cambridge (which I took to have been a much
finer town than I then found it to bee) on the first of May, and I
was admitted member of St. John's College the day following.
First, I was examined by my tutor, then by the senior dean,

---

still to be liable to all the penalties of former acts. Dissenting teachers were
also to subscribe the articles of religion mentioned in the Stat. 13 Eliz., c. 12
(viz., those which only concerned the confession of the true christian faith and
the doctrine of the sacraments), with an express exception of those relating to
the government and powers of the church and to infant baptism.

" Lincoln Castle must have been one of the most majestic fortresses in
England during the middle ages. It seems to have retained much of its
ancient beauty until it was taken by storm on Monday morning May 6, 1644,
by the Earl of Manchester, after which it fell into ruin. Samuel Buck's view
of the castle taken in 1727, and of the city in 1743, represents it much as it is
now ; neither of them show the interior of the fortifications. Probably in de la
Pryme's time the precincts contained many interesting remains that were
swept away when the present ugly shire-hall and prison were built.—See *A
True Relation of the Taking of the City, Minster, and Castle of Lincoln.* R.
Coates for John Bellamy. 4to. Lon. 1644.

then by the junior dean, and then by the master, who all made me
but construe a verse or two a-piece in the Greek Testament,
except the master, who ask'd me both in that and in Plautus and
Horace too.   Then I went to the registerer to be registered
member of the College, and so the whole work was done.

We go to lecturs every other day, in logics, and what we hear
one day we give an account of the next; besides we go to his
chamber every night, and hears the sophs and junior sophs dispute, and then some is called out to conster a chapt[er] in the New
Testament ; which after it is ended, then we go to prayers, and
then to our respective chambers.

Our master they say is [a] mighty high proud man, but God be
thank'd I know nothing of that as yet by my own experience.
His name is Doct[or] Gower[r] and it was him that first brought
up the haveing of terms in the college, without the keep of every
one of which we can have no degrees.

He came from Jesus College to be made master here, and he
was so sevear there that he was commonly called the divel of
Jesus ; and when he was made master here some unlucky scholars
broke this jest upon him,—that now the divel was entered into
the heard of swine ; for us Jonians are called abusively hoggs.

In this my fresh-man's year, by my own propper studdy,
labour and industry, I got the knowledge of all herbs, trees, and
simples, without any body's instruction or help, except that of
herbals : so that I could know any herb at first sight.   I studdied
a great many things more likewise, which I hope God will bless
for my good and his honour and glory, if I can ever promote
anything thereoff.[y]

---

[r] Humphrey Gower, a native of Dorchester ; the son of Stanley Gower, a
minister there during the interregnum. Chosen Fellow of St. John's Coll. Camb.
23rd March, 1658 ; M.A., 1662 ; D.D., 1676 ; Master of Jesus Coll., 11th July,
1679 ; and of St. John's, 3rd Dec. following. Died 27th March, 1711.—*Nichols'
Lit. Anecdotes*, iv., 245, 246 ; v., 125, 128, 129.   Dr. Gower was a man of great
university mark, and a large benefactor to St. John's, although not originally a
member of that college.

[y] He was admitted Scholar of St. John's, 7th Nov. 1690.   " Ego Abrahamus Prim Eboracensis juratus et admissus sum in discipulum hujus coll.
pro Dre Morton decessore Dno. Proctor."   This Cardinal Morton scholarship
was filled up 6th Nov., 1694, when Humphr. Davenport was admitted " decessore Dno. Primme."

De la Pryme was never fellow, nor did he hold an exhibition.

The college entry of De la Pryme's admission is " Abrahamus Prym,
Eboracensis, filius Matthæi Prym, generosi, natus infra Hatfield, ibidemque
litteris institutus sub Mro. Eratt, ætatis suæ 19, admissus est pensionarius tutore
et fidejussore ejus Mro. Wigley, Maii 2ndo, 1690."

1692.

JAN. : Alas ! who can refrain from tears, what learned man can but lament at the sad newse that came the other night, viz., the death of the famous and honourable Mr. Boyl,[z] a man born to learning, born to the good of his country, born to every pious act, whose death can be never enough lamented and mourned for. England has lost her wisest man, wisdom her wisest son, and all Europe the man whose writeings they most desired, who well deserved the character that the ingenious Redi gives him, who calls him, *Semper veridicus, et quavis sublimi laude dignus !* I have heard a great deal in his praise and commendation. He was not only exceeding wise and knowing, but also one of the most religiousest and piusest men of his days, never neglecting the public prayers of the church or absenting himself therefrom upon any occasion. He was exceeding charitable to the poor and needy, and thought whatever he gave to them too little ! He was a mighty promoter of all pious and good works, and spent vast summs, as I have heard, in getting the Bible and several more religious books to be translated and printed in Irish and spred about that country, that his poor countrymen might see the light of the Gospel. He was a mighty chemist, etc.

JAN. 7 : This day was in company with a gentleman scholler Mr. Bennet[a] of our coll. a very learned, ingenious, and under-

[z] The Hon. Robert Boyle, the 7th son and 14th child of Richard, 1st Earl of Cork ; Died 13th Dec. 1691, unmarried. — See portrait and biographical account of him in *Lodge's Portraits of Illustrious Personages, &c.*, vol. ix.
His life was written by Dr. Birch. It may be found in his edition of Boyle's works, 5 vols. folio, 1744 ; and was in the same year issued separately in an 8vo form.

[a] Thomas Bennett, son of Tho. Bennett, gent., born infra Cæsaris burgum, Wilts., at school there under Mr. Taylor, admitted sizar for his tutor, Mr. Browne, 31st May, 1689, æt. 15. This voluminous author was elected foundation fellow 26th Mar. (admitted 27th Mar.) 1694, in Boughton's room. He was catechis. 26 Febr. 1700-1 ; and appointed college preacher 12 June, 1701. Edm. Waller was elected 26 Mar. (admitted 27 Mar.) 1705 in Bennett's room. B.A., 1692-3 ; M.A., 1696 ; D.D., 1715 ; rector of St. James's Colchester, when he subscribed to Strype's Parker ; vicar of St. Giles's, Cripplegate, when he subscribed to Strype's Annals, vol. 3 ; of Salisbury School (*Carlile's Grammar Schools*, ii. 746), Obiit. 9 Oct., 1728 (*Historical Register* 1728, *Chronicle* p. 54) ; married to ——Hunt, of Salisbury, 8 Oct., 1717 (*Historical Register*). Made rector of St. Giles's. 4 Apr., 1717 (*Ibid.*) Lecturer of St. Olave's, Southwark, 20 Febr., 1716, (*Ibid.*, p. 118).—See *The Tanner MSS.* William Gould, Fellow of St. John's, left him £50 in 1690, (*MS. Baker*, xxvi, 278). See *Darling's Cyclopædia*, col. 2569, 2840. Subscriber to Spencer De legibus Hebr. 1727.—See *Lampe's Commentary on St John*, i. 221. *Examination of a book lately printed by the Quakers*, 8vo., Lond. 1737, *pp.* 69, 72 ; *Defence of do.*

standing young man, who comes from Salsbury, and was theer
in all the time of the late revolution, and saw most of the things
that happened there.   He says that when King Will[iam] came
first over, for three, four, or five days, he was mightily dijected
and melancholy, fearing that nobody would joyn with him : but
when the Lord Cornbury and several others were come over, he
was very well content and cheered up.   When he landed he wore
his own hair which was long and black, and looked as to his face
very pale and wan : but now he has got a wig,[b] and looks as brisk,
and has good a colour as anyone.

This gentleman was at Salsbury when the late king was there,
and he says all was in the greatest confusion imaginable.   He
saw K[ing] J[ames] ride backward and forward continnualy
with a languishing look, his hat hanging over his eyes, and a
handkerchief continnualy in one hand to dry the blood of his
nose for he continnualy bledd.   If he and his soldiers did but
chance to hear a trumpet or even a post-horn they were always
upon a surprise, and all fit to run away, and at last they did so.

All the nights there was nothing but tumult, and every question that was ask'd " Where are the enemy ? " " Where are the
enemy ? "   " How far are they off ? "   " Which way are they
going ? " and such like.

10. Yesterday I was at Mr. Hall's the bookseller, asking for a
magical book,—" Zouns," says he " Doct. you'l raise the divel,"
at which I laughed.   " But hark you," says he, " I have a
friend about 7 miles off who has lost a great many cattle by
witchcraft, and he is now in the town at the Three Tuns, prathee
go with me thither to him, and tell him what he shall do to save
the rest ? " to which I made answer that I was unwilling to go ;
and besides that I knew not how to help him.   " No matter for
that," says he, " you shall then have some discourse with him
and hear what he says, it shall cost you nought, I'll give you two or
three pints of wine."   Then I went and we had a great deal of talk.
He told me that he was once, about thirteen years ago, with several
others set to keep a witch in a room, and sayd that before them

Lond., 1737, *pp.* 35 *seq.* ; *Life of A. A. Sykes*, 88, 89, 93 ; *Newcourt's Repertorium*,
ii. 170 ; *Watts' Biblioth. Brit.*, i. 100 ; *Chalmer's Biogr. Dict.* ; *Bodl. Catal.*
vols. i. and iv. *Catal. Brit. Mus.* ; *Notes and Queries*, 2nd ser. iv. 171 ; *Catal.
Codd. MSS. Bodl.* iv. 831 ; *Ayscough's Catal. MSS. Brit. Mus.* 793 ; *Darling's
Cyclopædia* ; *Nichol's Lit. Anecd.* iii., 11., i., 412.
  [b] In an original portrait of William III., by Sir Godfrey Kneller, in the
possession of Mr. Peacock, he is represented in a long flowing wig of dark
brown hair.

all shee chang'd herself into a beetle or great clock, and flew out of the chimney, and so escaped. He told me also that a neighbour of his as he was once driving a loaded waggon out of the field, they came over against the place where a witch was shearing, and that then of a suddain (tho' there was no ill way or any thing to throwgh a waggon over) the waggon was in a minnit thrown down, and the shaves became as so many piggs of lead, so that nobody could for two hours lift them upright.

FEBR. : What I heard to-day I must relate. There is one Mr. Newton (whom I have very oft seen), fellow of Trinity College, that is mighty famous for his learning, being a most excellent mathematician, philosopher, divine,[c] etc. He has been fellow of the Royal Society this many years, and, amongst the other very learned books and tracts that he has writt, he's writt one upon the Mathematical Principles of Philosophy, which has got him a mighty name, he having received, especialy from Scotland, abundance of congratulatory letters for the same : but of all the books that he ever writt there was one of colours and light, established upon thousands of experiments, which he had been twenty years of making, and which had cost him many a hundred of pounds. This book which he valued so much, and which was so much talk'd off, had the ill luck to perish and be utterly lost just when the learned author was almost at putting a conclusion at the same, after this manner. In a winter morning, leaving it amongst his other papers on his studdy table, whilst he went to chappel, the candle which he had unfortunately left burning there too cachd hold by some means or other of some other papers, and they fired the aforesayd book, and utterly consumed it and several other valuable writings, and that which is most wonderful did no further mischief. But when Mr. Newton came from chappel and had seen what was done, every one thought he would have run mad, he was so troubled thereat that he was not himself for a month after. A large account of this his system of light and colours you may find in the transactions of the Royal Society, which he had sent up to them long before this sad mischance happened unto him.

[c] No less a personage than the great Sir Isaac Newton, *de quo vide Nichols's Literary Anecdotes,* vol. iv. pp. i. etc., etc. He was born 25 Dec., 1642. Admitted at Trin. Coll., Camb., 5 June, 1661, as a sub-sizar, a class which still exists in the college. He afterwards became Fellow of the College, and a Professor of the University, for which he was twice elected one of the representatives in Parliament, an honour which was also attained by his illustrious predecessor Lord Chancellor Bacon (a fact not generally known). He died 20 March, 1726.—See preface of this work.

29. Yesterday I began a work. God of His great mercy make me able to carry on the same! It is a book of travelling, to be entitled "The compleat Traveller, or full directions for travelling, and querys about almost everything memorable in all countrys."

30. Doct[or] Burnet Bish[op] of Sarum has given notice in all our newse letters that he will undertake to write the famous Mr. Boyl's life, which is not to be doubted but it will be done very well, tho' nevertheless it is impossible that it should be done so well as it deserves, he having been the [most] learned, wisest, and godliest man that England ever brought forth. He was a mighty strict, pious man, and seldome or never missed the publick prayers in church, and was mighty charitable to the poor. Some condemns him for being too credulous and giving too much heed to the relations of his informers in philos[ophical] matters, but this springs from nothing but ignorance and envy.

APRIL 1. The present Bish[op] of St. Asaphs,[d] Doctor [Lloyd] is a very famous man by reason of his pretending to interpret and comprehend that most hard and ambiguous book of the Revelations : for he prophesyd nothing but good therefrom, of the downfall of the French king, and the Pope, etc. It happen'd once in the present reign that there came a poor Vaudois to begg alms of him, complaining that he was forced out of his country for his religion by means of the tyranny of the French king. "Well, well" (says the honest bishop) "I cann assure you that tyrant will not live long, for God has look'd upon your afflictions, and the tyranny of that monster, and will deliver you and every one else out of every apprehensions of danger from him, and that within six months : therefore you shall go to your own country again, and I will give you money to bear your charges thither," etc., which he accordingly did ; but whether the Vaudois went home or no I cannot tell ; but the poor bishop has been sadly mistaken in many of his interpretations upon that obscure book. (*Ex relatione filii Dr. Lloyd episcop. Norwich.*)

1692

Towards the end of this year I went a course of chymistry with

[d] William Lloyd, S.T.P., consecrated Oct. 3, 1680. He was translated to Lichfield and Coventry in 1692, and from thence to Worcester, 22d January, 1699-1700. He died 30th August, 1717, and is buried at Fladbury, co. Worcester. *Le Neves Fasti.*, ed. 1854, vol. i. p. 558 ; iii. 68.

Signior Johannes Fransiscus Vigani, a very learned chemist, and a great traveller, but a drunken fellow. Yet, by reason of the abstruceness of the art, I got little or no good thereby.

In this very time of my course it was that my very great and most intimate friend Mr. Bohun* (of the year above me) hangd himself in his studdy. I missing him all that day began to inquire for him, which I observed put a great many lads then in the hall going to supper in an opinion and kind of consternation that he had hanged himself, though they knew nothing of it, nor had any reason for what they spoke or imagined. Upon which I and some more got his chamber dore key of his bedmaker, and going in we found his wigg, cap, and gown hanging over the chairs that were in his chamber : and not finding him there wee forced his studdy door open, but none of them durst go in to see if he was there. Upon which I rushed in, and found him hanging at the end of his studdy with his feet not above half or three quarters of a foot of the ground, having hung so all the day, for it appear'd afterwards that he hanged himself in chapel time in the morning. The rope that he hang'd himself in was one that he us'd to hang dogs in when he anatomized them.

Just before he dy'd he writt a very serious letter to his father, and dated it, and seal'd it up too, lying it on the table just at the door, desireing in another piece of paper that it might be sent home to his father, saying that he had given a sufficient reason to his father for the sayd act. But what this reason was I could never certainly learn. Sure I am that it was not out of any evil actions that he had committed, for he was never given to any, neither was it for want of monney, or any unkindness of his parents, for they loved him very well and gave him what he desired. He was a great student also, and a good scholar, having made great proficiency in most arts and sciences. I was one of those that was brought in to give my evidence what I knew of his nature. I depos'd that I had heard him several times talk that he was melancholly, but he knew not for what, it was his nature that led him to it, as he thought. He loved to take walks in the dark, but yet nevertheless was of as merry and jovial a nature as any one I ever see.

The night before he did this, he, I, and two or three more of us, had been walking into the town after supper, and when we were got home again he took his leave of us, and shak'd us all by

* Humfrey Bohun, son of Edmund Bohun, esq., born at Pulham, Norfolk. educated at Woodbridge school under Mr. Candler, admitted pensioner 30 May, 1689, æt. 19, under Mr. Browne. (See on him, who died 1 Dec., 1692, Bohun's Autobiography and pedigree prefixed).

the hand, clenching them (as I observed) something hard in his (just as a dying man will catch hold of anything in his reach and hold it fast), but this we did not take much notice of because he was so free and merry; but so all o' us bid him a good night, as he also did us. And he having a chum, he say'd that he went to bed and slept very well till the morning, and arising then he put on his studdying gown and cap and his stockings and shoos, and going into his studdy lock'd the dore after him, and so having written the aforesayd letter hang'd himself without making any noise or struggling.

He was the eldest son to Edm. Bohun, esq.,*f* him that has writt so many books.

Dec. 23. Tho' my friend came to this so suddain and unfortunate end, yet I desisted not from my studdys and searchings into the truth and knowledge of things : for I and my companion yester night try'd again what we could do, but nothing would appear, *quamvis omnia sacra rite peracta fuerunt; iterum iterumque adjuravimus.*

Last week I got two or three vol. of the Turkish Spy.*g* As soon as I had read a little I suspected it to be a cheat, and the further I read I discover'd it the more. There are English proverbs in it, as—*let him laugh that wins,* vol. 2, etc. And it says in several places,—such a year according to the Christian Hegira—which is nonsence, and could never proceed out of the mouth of a Mahometan, etc. However, it is a book that sells exceedingly, and my bookseller says that the ingenious Doct. Midgley that has been licencer of the press several years is the author thereoff.

1693

Jan. 1. This year begins very ill for it is exceeding cold, the Parliament are fitt to fall out together by the ears. God prevent it !

2. I dream'd yesternight that methought as I was walking I

---

f A well known person, and for some time licencer of the press.

g *Letters writ by a Turkish spy who lived five and forty years undiscovered at Paris.* First edit. 8 vols. 8vo., 1691. The work has gone through upwards of twenty-eight editions, the last of which was in 8 vols. 12mo., 1801. The work is usually attributed to Jean Paul Marana, a native of Genoa. It seems to be quite certain that the first thirty letters are his composition.—*Gent. Mag.* 1840, pt. ii. p. 409 ; 1841 ; pt. i. p. 265, 270 ; *Notes and Queries,* 1st series, vol. i. p. 834 ; 3rd. series, vol. v., p. 260.

overtook my old friend Mr. Bohun, but he seemed to be melancholy, and as we were walking, " Oh, Abraham ! " says he (calling me by my name), I could never have imagined that my father would have taken my death so ill, or else I would never have done the act." And so me-thought we parted. I observed also in my dream how he had the exact gate that he used in his lifetime, flinging out an elbow as he walked, and shaking his head when he spake.

This year, I being soph, I began to look more about me than before, and to take better notice of things, as having got more knowledge and experience than I had before.

I went lately to take a view of the new library of Trinity College in this University, and it is indeed a most magnificent piece of work within, and it is very well built without. 'Tis raised from the foundations wholy of Portland stone, and has cost finishing thus farr above three thousand pounds. 'Tis...yards long, ... broad, and......high. It is bore up by three rows of pillars each..... foot about. The starecase up into the library is excellently carved, and the steps are all of them of marble, which staircase alone cost above fifteen hundred pounds.

JAN. 8. This day I received a very kind tho' a very severe letter from the famous Mr. Edm[und] Bohun, the father to him whose unhappy death I have already related. He persuaded me exceedingly to desist from all magical studdys, and lays a company of most black sins to my charge, which (he sayd) I committed by darring to search in such forbidden things.

JUL. 9. Reading this day in Father Kircher's[A] Æd. Æg., how that the ancient Egyptians us'd commonly to have four or five or six children, it brought into my mind several relations of such great births, and, to speak the truth, it is not half so strange to have so many at a birth in England as it is beyond sea. About eight years ago the milner wife of the Leavels had four at a birth, two of which lived till they were thirty years old. Rich. More, now living at Hatfield in Yorkshire, his wife had three at a birth, about fifteen years ago,[i] and going to the parson to get

---

[A] The Ædipus Ægyptiacus of this celebrated scholar, a work in four volumes, folio, published at Rome, 1652-4.

[i] This appears to have occurred earlier than the diarist names. In the parish register of Hatfield, No. III., I find in 1659-60 there were baptized " Richard, Susanna, and Anne, children of Richard Moore, jun., and of Anne his wife, ye 6t d. of Jan." and the same three were buried on the 10th of the same month. In 1718-19, Feb. 10th, at the same place " Elihue, Guliel., Carolus, Elinna, and Ricardus filiæ[sic] Guliel. Waller," were baptized. And on the 18th Dec., 1720, " Robertus, Abrahamus, et Isaacus filii Gulielmi Fox."

them christened, he told him—that—that—that—he had got a few children to christen, at which the minister laugh'd; but they were all of them christened; but how long they lived I know not. J. Tompson's wife, about nine years ago, had three; and, about a year before I came to Cambridge, there was another woman in the sayd town that had four together. All this in but a little time and within our little parish where I was born.

I have oft enough heard of women in the country round about that has likewise had sometimes two and sometimes more at a birth, but they being out of our parish I shall not relate them.

I have likewise very oft heard of women who by superfœtation have had three, four, and some five, and some six or seven children in a year. There is now living at Bramwith, by our town of Hatfield, two sisters who were both born together, and the same year their mother was again of three more, which all dy'd.

This year there was admitted of our college one Needham,[j] a freshman of about twelve years old, a meer child, but had indeed been so well brought up that he understood very perfectly the Latin, Greek, and Hebrew tongues. But this is nothing in comparison to one of our present fellows called Mr. Wotton,[k] who

[j] Peter Needham, the well-known scholar, co. Chester, son of the Rev. Sam. Needham of Stockport, educated at a private school at Bra nam, Norfolk, under Mr. Needham, was admitted sizar for Dr. Bury, 18th Apr., 1693, æt. 12, under Mr. Orchard. On his death (I suppose at least that he is meant, and not Wm. Needham,) See *Thesaurus Epistolicus Sacrorum* i. 137 ; see also *Index to vol.* ii. He was elected foundation fellow 11th April, 1698, admitted 12th April in Wigley's room. On 19th Mar., 1715-6, Jo. Peake was elected (admitted 20th Mar.) in Needham's room. B.A., 1696-7 ; M.A., 1700 ; B.D., 1707 ; D.D., by royal mandate, 1717 ; was rect. of Stanwick, Northants, when he subscribed to Knight's Life of Colet., rect. of Conington. Subscriber to Spencer De Legibus Hebr., 1727. Vicar of Madingley in 1711 (*Madingley Register.*) *Blomefield's Norfolk*, iii., 459. J. A. Fabricius sent him a collation of Hierocles, which was lost on the road, afterwards published by Wolf (*Fabricii Vita*, 54, 55). His collections for an ed. of Æschylus (*Fabricii Vita*, p. 335; MSS. Nn., i, 16, and Nn. ii., 32, in Cambridge University Library, described in the Catalogue of Adversaria, preserved in the library of the University of Cambr., Cambr., 1864, pp. 5, 11 seq. *Monk's Life of Bentley*, 8vo., ed ii. i., 226 seq. *Bentley's Correspond. pp.*,477, 572, 534, 812.
In Baker's MS. xlii. 265, is a Latin epitaph by Sam Drake, D.D., on P. N. ridiculing his corpulence. Ob. Ash-Wednesday, 1730. Baker copied it from "a half sheet of paper, privately printed 8vo. " ; and says " These are libels upon two men of worth, both of 'em my friends ; I conceal their names." (The other was Ric. Rawlinson.)—*Watt's Biblioth. Brit.* ii. 697 ; *Catal. Brit. Mus.*; *Darling's Cyclop. p.* 2166 ; *MS. Lansd.* 989, 13 ; *Blomefield's Norf.* (8vo.) ii. 267 ; vi. 145 ; *Nichols' Lit. Anecd.*, iv. 271.
[k] Wm. Wotton, son of Rev. Henry Wotton, was admitted, pensioner, 20th June 1682, under Mr. Verdon. " We ye fellows of St Katherine's Hall in Cambridge, the master being absent, doe certefye yt William Wotton, who commenced Batchelor of Arts in January 1679-80, hath behaved himselfe soberly and studiously during his residenc amongst us, and hath free liberty to admitte himself of any other

when he came up to be admitted was but eleven years old,[1] and
understood (as I have heard from all the colledge and multitudes
of hands besides), not only the aforesaid languages, but also the
French, Spanish, Italian, Assirian, Chaldean, and Arabian
tongues. When the master admitted him, he strove to pose him
in many books but could not. He is yet alive, and I have
seen him frequently, he being a most excellent preacher, but a
drunken whoring soul. It is him that has lately translated Du
Pin's new Ecclesiastic Bibliotheke into English.

JULY 28. It is a true and excellent saying of the learned
Æneas Sylvius—*De regimine civitatum, de mutatione regnorum, de
orbis imperio, minimum est quod homines possunt (hinc vero de re-
ligionis constitutione multo minus) magna magnus disponit Deus.*
This saying pleased me mightly, and it is really owing to a good
consideration of it that I was satisfyd with the present government, etc.

The prophet Daniel likewise has a most excellent saying, which
yielded me a great deal of satisfaction, ch. ii., v. 20, 21, 22,—
" Blessed be the name of God for ever and ever ; for wisdom and
might are His : and He changeth the times and the seasons : He
removeth kings and setteth up kings : He giveth wisdom unto the
wise, and knowledge to them that know understanding : He re-
vealeth the deep and secret things : He knoweth what is in the
darkness, and the light dwelleth with Him."

Many more were the places of Scripture which I collected and
compared, and blessed be God, for He at length opened my eyes.
Blessed be His Holy Name for ever and ever.

college. In testimony whereof wee have hereunto subscribed our names, June
20, 1682.—Cath. Hall. Nicholas Gouge, Jo. Warren, W. Miller." B.A. (St. Cath.)
1679-80 ; M.A. (St. John's) 1683 ; B.D., 1691. *Darling's Cyclopædia, col.* 2622.
St. John's Coll. Library. pp. 9, 25, and 33. Subscriber to Spencer de Leg.
Feb., 1727. Evelyn and many others attest his extraordinary proficiency.
Admitted Beresford fellow, 8th Apr., 1685, in Turner's room. Rob. Grove was
elected in Wootton's (sic) place, 26th Mar., 1694 (admitted 27th Mar.) His
correspondent Dr. Thos. Dent (*Birch's Life of Boyle,* 298) ; Wotton intended to
write Boyle's Life (*Ibid.* 396-9). In the preface to the reprint of Stanley's poems
he is said to have written an eulogium on Stanley, published at the end.of
Scævolæ Sammarthani Elogia Gallorum. Letter to him from Tancred Robinson.
Bodl., Catal. iii., 291b. *Bentley's Correspondence* (ed. Wordsworth, index and
p. 719). Index to Tanner MSS. Wm. Wotton, M.A., of St. John's has verses in
Academiæ Cantabrig. Affectus, 1684-5. sign. Q 3b.—See *Nichols' Lit. Anecd.*,
iv., 253-259 ; *Dr. Gower's Testimony to his Precocity ib.*, 258.

[1] Aubrey says that Dr. Kettle, President of Trin. Coll., Oxon., came to be
scholar there at eleven years of age. Also, that Sir John Suckling went to the
University of Cambridge at eleven years of age, where he studied for three or
four years, as he had heard.

SEPT. 3. This day I was with a gentleman that was watcing man to Coll. Kirk, him that saved Londonderry from being taken by King James. He was with his master likewise all the while that he commanded at Tangiers, while the great fort there was in the English hands. Amongst a great deal of other talk that we had, he said that his master, that is Coll. Kirk, was closseted by King James, and that the king, after he had told him a great many things, spoke plain unto him, and told him he would have him change his religion. Upon which the coll. began to smile, and answered him thus—" Oh, your majesty has spoke too late, your majesty knows that I was concern'd at Tangier, and being oftentimes with the Emperor of Morocco about the late king's affairs, he oft desired the same thing of me, and I pass'd my word to him that if ever I changd my religion I would turn Mahometan," etc.

OCT. 29. This month came out a book at London, entitled the Oracles of Reason, written by Sir Charles Blount, which was sent to Cambridge and elsewhere by whole parcels, for those that sent them durst not be known ; and because they were aitheistical, the Vice-Chancellor sent the bedel to demand them all from the booksellers, and caused them to be burnt. The author a while after shot himself, because that a woman refused to have him, but the bullet did not mortally wound him, as he deserved.*

* Charles Blount was not an atheist but his opinions were very far from orthodox. He seems to have been an idealist of the school of Lord Herbert of Cherbury. He was the brother of Sir Thomas Pope Blount, son of Sir Henry Blount, a Hertfordshire gentleman, known as an author by his "Voyage into the Levant." Charles Blount was born in 1654, educated in his father's house. In 1679 he published a book called " Anima Mundi, an Historical Narration of the opinions of the Ancients concerning Man's Soul after this Life according to Unenlightened Nature." In this work he was supposed to have received the assistance of his father. The book created great excitement and was condemned by the Bishop of London. In 1680 appeared the most celebrated of his works, " The Two First Books of Philostratus, concerning the Life of Apollonius Tyaneus," written originally in Greek, and now published in English. This book was suppressed immediately on its appearance, and is now very rare. There is a copy of it in the library of the British Museum, and also one in the library of Lincoln College, Oxford, but the Bodleian does not possess one. It was supposed, at the time of its appearance, to contain notes drawn from the manuscripts of Lord Herbert of Cherbury. After this appeared "Great is Diana of the Ephesians, Religio Laici." " Janua Scientiarum." " A Just Vindication of Learning," a treatise advocating freedom of the press, and a pamphlet maintaining the claims of William and Mary to the crown of England, Scotland, and Ireland, on the ground of the right of conquest. This book was burned by order of the House of Commons. He also wrote a pamphlet defending marriage with a deceased wife's sister. His last work published after his death was "The Oracles of Reason." Charles Blount had a personal object in writing

Nov. the 3rd. This day I beheld a strange experiment, which I cannot think upon without admiration. Being in company and talking of Mr. Boyl book of the strange effects of languid motion, and some storys that he mentions therein, one amongst us, a musitioner, told us that he would shew us as strange a thing as any of those there mentioned. So the company breaking up, the before say'd fellow led us to that exceedingly strong quadrangular portico of Kaius Colledge, that looks towards the publick schools. And when we was got there he began to sing the note of a dubble *do, sol, re,* which he had no sooner sounded but that the whole portico manifestly and visibly trembled, as if there had been a kind of earthquake, and I observed that the air round about (for I stood about half a dozen yards of of the sayd portico), was put into such a tremulous motion that I could perceive several hairs of my head to tremble and shake. This is a property that has been observed to be in this portico this hundred years together.

Dec. 19, 1693. Yesternight we had good sport! There came a great singer of Israel into the college. He was a little, well-shap'd, good-like man, in handsome cloaths. He had a long beard and a sheephard crook in one hand, a Psalm-book in meeter in the other, and wherever he went he kept singing. I as[ked] him where he came from, he say'd out of the land of sin and desolation. I asked him then where he was going : to the Holy Land of Canan (says he) and the new Jerusalem that's just now descending out of Heaven. And then he began to sing again. Several such like answers about many things I had, that I urg'd to him. The lads got him into the kitchin, and there they were as joyfull of him as if he was a mountebank, and they made him sing all their supper time, and then they gave him his. And after that they carried him in tryumph, as it was, into the hall, and set him on his feet on the high round table there, and made him sing to them for an hower together, and then what became of him I do not know.

his tract on marriage with the sister of a former wife. He was anxious to form a contract of this nature with the sister of his own deceased wife. The Archbishop of Canterbury, and other theologians, having declared against it, the lady refused to marry him, and the unfortunate author died by his own hand in consequence—shooting himself with a pistol at a house in the Strand. He survived three days after this sad act of madness. His death occurred in August, 1693. See Sir Alexander Croke's *Genealogical Hist. of the House of Blount*, vol. ii., pp. 321, 331 ; *Biograph. Universelle, and Biograph. Britt.*, sub. nom.

Awhile ago another sort of an enthusiast, viz., a Quaker, ran
up and down the streets of this town, crying out, "Repent, repent, the day of judgment is att hand, and you must all be tryed
for your abominations," etc.

1694.

JANUARY. This month it was that we sat for our degree of
batchelors of arts. We sat three days in the colledge and were
examin'd by two fellows thereof in retorick, logicks, ethicks,
physicks, and astronomy; then we were sent to the publick schools,
there to be examined again three more days by any one that
would. Then when the day came of our being cap'd by the Vice-
Chancellor, wee were all call'd up in our soph's gowns and our
new square caps and lamb-skin hoods on. There we were presented, four by four, by our father to the Vice-Chancellor, saying
out a sort of formal presentation speech to him. Then we had
the oaths of the dutys we are to observe in the university read to
us, as also that relating to the Articles of the Church of England,
and another of allegiance, which we all swore to. Then we every
one register'd our own names in the university book, and after
that, one by one, we kneel'd down before the Vice-Chancellour's
knees, and he took hold of both of our hands with his, saying to
this effect, "*Admitto te,*" &c. "I admitt you to be batchellour
of arts, upon condition that you answer to your questions; rise
and give God thanks." Upon that as he has done with them one
by one they rise up, and, going to a long table hard by, kneel
down there and says some short prayer or other as they please.
About six days after this (which is the end of that day's work,
we being now almost batchellors) we go all of us to the schools,
there to answer to our questions, which our father always tells us
what we shall answer before we come there, for fear of his
puting us to a stand, so that he must be either necessitated to
stop us of our degrees, or else punish us a good round summ of
monny. But we all of us answer'd without any hesitation; we
were just thirty-three of us, and then having made us an excellent speech, he (I mean our father) walk'd home before us in
triumph, so that now wee are become compleat battchellors,
praised be God!
I observed that all these papers of statutes was thus imperfect
at the bottom, which makes me believe that they were very much
infected with Jacobiteism.
At this time Prince Lewis of Baden was highly caress'd in

our court by the king and all the nobility. He had twenty
dishes a meal allowed him, and the king, to honnour him the
more, delegated a great number of his gentlemen pentioners to
wait upon him. He was a man, they say, that could not drink
for all he was a Dutchman, yet he loved Christmas games, and
I have heard that he lost 1000l. stirling to the Earl of Mulgrave.
There was bear's baitings, bulls' sport, and cock fighting instituted for his diversion and recreation. But above all he admired
cock fighting, saying that had he not seen it he never could have
thought that there could have been so much vallor and mag-
nanimity in any bird under heaven. He liked England very
well, and once say'd, amongst some lords, that it was as happy
and glorious a country as any in Europe, but easily might be
the best of any in the world, if the inhabitants thereof would but
understand and make use of the happiness thereoff. What he
came about is as yet kept secret however. He sent an express to
the Emperor that he had succeeded in his negociation. He being
ready now for his departure, the king has presented him with
twelve of the finest horses that was ever seen, and the queen has
bestow'd upon him several household vessels of gold. Since I
writt the former, our letters tells us further that the king has
made him another gift of 1000 five pound pieces. A noble present!

FEBRUARY. Being on the 3d instant in company we began to
talk of the great strength of some men, both of ancient and
modern times. There was some gentlem[en] by that instanced
in a great many Engl[ish] of late years that we[re] prodigys of
strength. There is one Kighly now alive, a gentleman akin to the
the Earl of . . . . who would kill the best horse or ox
ith' world with a stroke of his bare fist. He is of so prodigious
a strength that he would easily with one hand break the iron
bar of a window in piece, or shatter an oak stick in pieces by
shaking of it. He would take two men from of a table upon
the palm of his hand and carry them twenty yards together. I
heard of several more that could take new horse-shoes betwixt
their hands and easily straight them, etc. Several in our company had heard of most of these things before from very good
witnesses, and they confirm'd the same.

Many believes it to be certainly true that K. Charles the 2d
dy'd a papist, and I have heard several gentlemen say that, as
soon as ever he was perceived to be sick, the papists would not
let any of the reformed come to him, but only papists. Others

D

believe charitably that he dy'd a protestant, and that this story of
his dying a papist was only an invention to delude the country,
and it is manifest that the papists beyond see even doubted whether
it was true or no, as appears from a passage in Voyages of the
Jesuites to Siam, written by father Tascard. However, let him
dy as he would, how it was is unknown to us, and only known to
God ; yet we all know how he lived, giving himself up to nothing
but debauchery, caring not what end went foremost if he but
enjoy'd his misses. But I will not say any more, these things
are better buried in oblivion than committed to memory.

FEBR. 14. This day I received twelve little retorts and three
receivers from London, to try and invent experiments, and all the
things that I shall do I intend to put them down in a proper book,
and in imitation of the most learned Democritus, to give them
the title of χειρόκμητα, as he did his, which being interpreted im-
plys *Experiments of my own Personal Trying*.

The retorts cost me 4d. a piece at London, and the receivers
6d., and I pay'd for their carriage from thence hither 1s. 6d.

MARCH. The 29th instant I began my journey from Cambridge
(having now got my degrees) into the country. From Cambridge
we went to Huntington, and then leaving the high road on our right
we went to Haverburough, commonly called Harburg, which is a
very fine, stately, magnificent market town, having a great many
good houses and tradesmen in the same. From thence wee went
[to] Leicester, which is but a large open town standing in a
valley, off no strength at all, nor indeed can it be of any, it is so
badly situated ; neither is there a castle nor anything of defence
that I could see, except a pittifull old foursquare fort, which is
turn'd into a prison. There is a good many very handsome
buildings in the town, and about five or six churches. From
thence we went (through a great many little towns of no note) to
Darby, which is a town mighty well situated, and adorned
with many good and stately buildings, and is reckoned a rich
town, tho' it is but built upon an indifferent soil. There is but some
two or three churches in it at most. The spring and well waters
tasts mighty strong of the limestone. Here are a great many
rarities to see in and near this place, but having no time I could
[not] go to see them. From thence, as I went along, I chanced
to observe a leaden pump, and as I rid through Andsley[n] by my

---

[n] Annesley.

Lord Chaworth's park, I saw sheep therein with four horns apiece. There are also therein a great many wild beasts, etc. From thence I came to Mansfield, which is a very handsome well built town ; and from thence by mistake to Redford, which is likewise well built, and of great trade. It has two churches in it, etc. From thence in a few hours I came to Bautry, and then through Hatfield, and so to the Levils, where, blessed be God! I found our whole family in indifferent good health.

In my whole journey from Cambridge hither I observed several ruins in the little towns that I went through of ancient religious houses.

Having rested myself a day or two, I went about some business to Doncaster. When Doncaster was builded is uncertain, however it sufficiently appears to be a town of considerable antiquity. Some think that it was built by the Romans, because it has a Lattine name, being derived from the word *Don* or *Dun*, which is the name of the river that runs through it, and *castrum*, a castle or fort, which they built there: others say that it was built by the Dains, and called Doncaster, *quasi* Daincaster, *a Danorum castris.*[o] About the year . . . . . it was burnt down by lightning, and in Cromwell's days there was two or three valiant acts committed there by the royalists of Pomfract, etc. However, this is and always has been a town of good note, trade, and buildings. It has had a strong castle in it, the ruins of which is visible in the walls of some houses. There has likewise been two churches, and a chappel which [has] now falln quite to ruin, except onely the great church which is dedicated to St. George. There is the reliques also of a religious house, in part of the ruins of which I have seen the entrance into a private subterranian passage, which runs under the river in full length, two or three miles to another ancient monastry.

APRIL. The 5th of this month I went to pay my respects to that ingenious gentleman Mr. Corn[elius] Lee.[p] After much kind reception he carry'd me up into the chamb[er] to see his unkle Capt.

[o] See *Hunter's South Yorkshire,* vol. i., p. 1.
[p] De la Pryme appears to be in error in calling Capt. E. Sandys *uncle* to Mr. Cornelius Lee. It was the reverse. See ped. of Lee, *Hunter's South Yorkshire,* I., 177. Cornelius Lee's sister, Elizabeth, however, married Thomas, afterwards Sir Thomas Sandys, and not Edwin Sandys, as there stated. They were married at Hatfield 12th May, 1641. Robert Lee, father of Cornelius, in his will, 5th April, 1659, names his son-in-law, Sir Thos. Sandys, to whom he bequeaths 1s. in satisfaction of his wife's portion, which portion he had had with ample addition—names Edwin, Thomas, and Henry, sons

Edwin Sandys's armoury, which indeed was very well worth

óf said Sir Thomas S. To Katherine S., dau. of Sir Thomas S., 30*l.*, when 21. Residue to Thomas Lee, his eldest son, and he exor.

The pedigree should stand thus :—

Robert Lee, of Hatfield, Esq. Will d. ⊤Frances, bur. at Hat-
5 Ap., 1659, p. at York, 8 Aug., 1663. | field, 5th Sep., 1655.

| Thomas Lee, eld. son, bap at H.,23 Sep.1624 died in June, 1699. | Cornelius Lee,of Hatfield, bap. 1 May,1629, bur. 20 June, 1701, will d. 29 Oct.,1690, pro. 6th Feb.,1701-2. A cornet of horse in the king's army in the civil wars. | Eliza-beth, mar. at Hat field, 12th May, 1641. | ⊤Sir Tho-mas San-dys, Knt. | Susan⚏John bap. 19 Septem., 1626, m. at H. 23 October, 1654. | Walker, of Mans-field, Notts, gent. |

| Thomas bap. 4th, bur. 9th Decem., 1642, at H. | Edwin Sandys Captain in the Reg., bur. at Hatfield, 19th Oct., 1702. s.p. | Thomas Sandys bap. at H. 9th Nov. 1646, of Tempsford, co. Bedford, clerk, living 1701. | Henry Sandys, of the par. of St. Mar-tin's in the Fields, London, a capt. "Chiliarchus," liv-ing 1704. | Elizabeth, bap. 7th Feb. 1648-9. bur. 7 January, 1652-3. | Kath-erine, bap. 7 Feb. 1648-9. |

Sir Thomas Sandys above named is described in the Hatfield register, at the baptism of his son Thomas, 1646, as Knight and *Baronet* (Mil. et Bar.), but that must be a mistake, for when he died, admon. of the goods etc " Dni Thomæ Sandys nuper de Hatfield *militis* defuncti" (*York Act book*) was granted to Edwin Sandys, Esq., his son, who, had his father been also a baronet, would then have succeeded to the same title.

Captain Sandys's, baptism does not occur at Hatfield, that I can discover. Nor have I succeeded in ascertaining the dates of his commissions. The Earl of Oxford's Regt. of Horse Guards, or " Oxford's Blues," is now the Royal Regt. of Horse Guards Blue. Probably Sandys entered as cadet, as men of position used in those days to do. From the *Historical Records of the British Army*, by R. Cannon, Esq., of the A. G. Office, it appears that Tangier being in 1680 threatened by the Moors, a considerable force was embarked to place that fortress in a state of defence. A troop of the Royal Regt. of H. G. under Capt. Sandys was ordered to form part of the expedition, but was afterwards counter-manded. In 1685 Capt. Sandys's troop was at the battle of Sedgemoor. In a list of officers of the Royal Regt. of Horse, 1687, Harl. MSS., No. 7018, the fol-lowing appear as his troop—Capt., Edwin Sandys ; Lieut., Charles Turner ; Cornet, Samuel Oldfield. Capt. Sandys is mentioned in the terriers of Hatfield as the donor of a clock, or "watch," to the church there.—An Edwin Sandys, a royalist captain in the regiment commanded by Thomas Colepeper, was, in 1663, a suppliant for the royal bounty.—*List of Officers Claiming to the Sixty Thousand Pounds Granted by His Majesty for the Relief of his Truly Loyal and Indigent Party*, 4to, 1663, p. 29.

Cornelius Lee was a collector of antiquities, &c., Thoresby, who was on a visit at Capt. Hatfeild's, at Hatfield, 2d Sept., 1694, says he "made also a visit to Cornet Lee's who shewed me his collection of rarities, pictures, and armoury." (*Diary* I., 263.) On the 18th Jany., 1695, he mentions that he went " to visit my cousin, Mr. Cornelius Lee, and view his collection of curiosities, when he presented me with his grand-father's pickadilly," (a ruff,) (*Diary* I., 289.) Dr. Johnston states in his MSS. that he saw in the possession of Corn-elius Lee a large wooden cup which was found in the ruins of the castle at Thorne, which had this verse carved about it in old characters :—

Weel mer hym yat wist
In whoam he mought trist.

It afterwards came into the possession of Lord Irwin. Will 29th Oct., 1699. Cornelius Lee of Hatfield, gent. All my houses and lands in Hatfield, or else-

seeing, and amongst other things I beheld a whole suit of cloathes, coat, britches, stockings, shoes, gloves, and cap, all made of badger skins withe hair on, which was outward, and told me this story of the same. The Capt., when he was in the last Irish wars, was one of those that was sent into Limerick to agree with them about articles of surrender. When he knew that he was appointed to be one of them, he put on all this apparel, and went amongst the rest into the town; but all those that saw the Capt. were so frighted that they did not know what to do; all their eyes were upon him, and none had any mind to come near him. But one ask'd him who he was. "Zounds, man "(says he) "I am a Laplander, and there be aleim [*i.e.*, eleven] thousands of us in dis country, and if yee will not agree to surrender soon, by the eternal God! we will cut you all as small as meat for pyes. Wee be all clothed in de skins of beasts, and a piece of an Irish child's flesh is as good as venison," etc. And so he hector'd them ith' town, and told several of them the same tale, which frighted the vulgar exceedingly. But, however, the town surrendered in a few days.

At this town they were put to such want of meat for their horses that they, having eaten every thing that was eatable, were forc'd at last for to send the forragers out to cut down bows of trees, and bring them to feed on, and lived of them thus for fifteen or twenty days. This I had from the cap[tain's] own mouth.

APRIL. The 9th instant I was at the house of Peter Lelew,[7] who

---

where within that manor, to John Hatfield, Esq., and Wm. Eratt, clerk, in trust (subject to a legacy of £50 to my niece Catherine Sandys,—an annuity of 24s. to sd. Cath. and dole to the poor of Hatfield and Kirk Brámwith) to the only proper use and behoof of my dear nephew, Captn. Edwin Sandys, and his heirs for ever. All my tythes, lands and ten, in Campsall, Norton and Sutton to my two nephews, Thos. and Henry Sandys, and to their heirs for ever. To my niece Lee Barker, £50. Sd. John Hatfield and Wm. Eratt, exors. They renounced 24th Jan., 1701-2, and admon. was granted, 6th Feb., 1701-2, to Capt. Edwin Sandys, nephew of sd. decd. This will is not registered.

[7] The name of Lelew does not occur in the "Lyste of the seueral owners of the Dyckage of Haitfielt Chace." Anno Domini 1635, in the before-quoted MS. in Mr. Peacock's possession. It is, however, one of those given by Hunter, in his list made from the register of the chapel of Sandtoft (see *S. Y.*, i. 169-70), and it is of frequent occurence in the parish register of Hatfield. Pieter le Leu in 1681, along with others, on behalf of themselves and the rest of the tenants of the newly drained lands, represented to the Court of Sewers their want of a minister, in consequence of which many of the lands were at that time unoccupied. (See *S. Y.*, i. p. 170). On 23 April, 1752, Susanna, dau. of Isaac and Mary le Leu, married Mr. Thomas Dunderdale, of the Levels, whose great grandson, Mr. James Dunderdale, of Manchester, now living, is the owner of a large French Bible formerly belonging to the Le Leu family, as noticed at page 4. *ante.*

because he had been exceeding sick last summer I asked him concerning his distemper, and by what methods he was cured.   He say'd he was taken almost of a sudden, as he was at an adjacent town, with an exceeding faintness, and by degrees a weakness in all his limbs, so that he could scarce go, attended with a pain in his syde, which increased day by day.   He lay thus sick, pained, and weak, several weeks, nobody thinking he would ever recover; but at last he did by this medicine (when all others were found inefficatious).   He was order'd to take the jeuice of new stoned horse dung mingled with strong beer.   No sooner had he taken a draught of this down but that it made all the blood in his veins boil, and put all his humours into such a general fermentation that he seemed to be in a boyleing kettle, etc.   And this it was that cured him.   He coveted strong beer mightily, but when he was recovered he could not love his horse for half a year after.

It is very credibly and certainly reported that the King of France sayd to King James after some few complements when they first met, "Come, come, King James, sit down here at my right hand, I'll make your enemys your footstool!" etc.   But this he sayd after that he was a little pacify'd.   But at first of all when he heard that the king was driven out of his dominions he was in an exceeding great rage, and, drawing his sword, he swore by the blood of Christ that he would never put it up till he had re-established King James on his throne; and the queen swore that she would never put off her smock till she either see or heard that that was done.

APRIL 30.   There came hither a while ago newse that the famous butcher of Leeds is going to run a great race on the 10th of the next month for five hundred pound.   This man is the miracle of the age for running.   His name is Edm. Preston,[r] and yet follows his trade, for all he has thousands of pounds by his heels.   His common race is ten or twelve miles, which he will easily run in less than an hower.

There was a great runner, a Cheshire man by birth, who was the king's footman, who, hearing of this man's fame, sent a challenge to him.   They both met about Leeds.   The Cheshire gentlemen took their countryman's side, and the Yorkshiremen took

---

[r] Thoresby alludes to this man, whom he calls " the Leeds butcher, Edward Preston, who was esteemed one, at least, of the best footmen in England.   £3000 were said to be won by him in one day, in 1683."—*Diary* I., p. 169.

their countryman's side, and 'tis thought that there were five or six thousand spectators upon the spot. Both sides were sure, as they thought, to win, so that many of them layd all they had—houses and lands, sheep and oxen, and anything that would sell. But when they ran, the butcher outran him half in half, and broke almost the poor fellow's heart, who lived not long after. But there was such work amongst the wagerers that they were almost a'l fitt to go together by the cars. Many people lost all they had. Many whole familys were ruin'd. And people that came a great many miles, that had staked their horses and lost, were forced to go home afoot. This happen'd in the last year of King James. After which he was sent up for to London, by some lord, whose name I have forgott, who kept him there under the name of a millar, and disfigured him so that no one could know him. After that he had kept him a great while, he made a match with another man, a famous runner, telling him his miller should run with him. But, in short, the miller bet and won for his master many thousands of pounds.

There are such strange storys told of this man that they are almost incredible; and I believe that Alexander's footman, that was so famous, was never comparable unto him for swiftness. I long to hear what he will win at this raise, for there is no fear but he will beat. There is gone four or five hundred people from hereabouts to see him run.

MAY 19. Yesterday I received two letters from Cambridge, giving an account of all the newse, and whatever was most memorable. In one of them I received a long account of a house that was pretended to be hanted, to this effect :—

About a month ago it began to be rumor'd abroad that Volantino Austin's house' over against our coll[ege] began to [be] haunted, and strange noises were as it were heard up and down about the house, and thus it stood for the most part of the week, but were more and more buz'd up and down the town. The second week the noises began to be greater, and pebbles and little stones began to be thrown here and there through a hole under the door. Thus the sport continued most of that week The room, which was haunted, was a low cealed room with a cellar under it, having a bed in the room in which the Mr. and Mrs. lay every night. They pretended to be mighty fearfull, and gave any one liberty to go where he would and search about the house. But the third week now coming on, on Monday night, about 2 a clock

---

' This man is by trade a painter, but a poor man. *Marginal Note by Diarist.*

at night it made a great hollow noise and gingl'd monney, and broke the windows by flinging little stones at them, and raised a stink of brimstone, and frighted several old poor women that watched, so that they run away into the street, and came there no more. But next morning all the town almost believed it, and at night there was above three score people flocking about the door to hear this spirit, among whom there was S[r.] Hall,[f] S[r.] Harrop,[*] S[r.] Millard,[v] and several other scholars of our coll[ege] of my acquaintance. "Come, sais one of them, '' fetch us a good pitcher of ale, and tobacco and pipes, and wee'l sit up and see this spirit." "With all our hearts," say'd three or four more; so they sent for the ale, and, as they went in, the people exclaimed against them sadly, crying " Oh, you wicked wretches, will you have the divel to fetch you?" etc. Then, as soon as they got in, the man and woman being in bed ith' room, they exclaimed against them again, but they cared not, but sat singing and drinking there till morning, but neither heard nor saw anything. But the night after, which was Wednesday night, Mr. Walker, minister of the Round Church, and some more with him, hearing of all that had pass'd, went to pray in the house, and, as they were praying, they heard a great bellowing voice, and in at the window out of the fold was flung a great pot of paint with such force that it broke all the glass window in pieces, and had like to have hitten Mr. Walker on the head. All which time there was at least a hundred people before the dore, but when they heard such a noise, away they all ran as if the divel was in them, and as soon as they had ended their prayers away went they, also sadly frighted, and fully satisfy'd that it was the divel ! Now the whole town was in an uproar, and nothing but the divel was in every one's mouth. Nay, Mr. Walker had no more witt but to make a long sermon the next Sunday to his people in the Round Church about it, and to tell them the whole story of the same.

Thursday night, Friday night, and Saturday night nothing was heard, tho' there was a great many earnestly expecting the

---

[f] Clifford Hall, of St. John's, son of the Rev. John Hall, born at Fordingbridge, Hants, educated at Eton, under Rodrick, admitted pensioner, 28th Aug., 1688, æt. 18, under Mr. Browne. He has verses in *Lacrymæ Cantabrig.* 1694-5. Sign. P2.; was B.A., 1692-3 ; M.A., 1696.

[*] Obadiah Harrop, of St. John's, B.A., 1693-4, M.A., 1697. Abdias (so it is in the Latin) Harrope, son of the Rev. Jas. Harrope, born at Lamesley, Durham, educated at Usworth, under Mr. Stannick, admitted pensioner 30th May, 1690, æt. 18, under Mr. Orchard.

[v] John Millerd, of St. John's, B.A., 1693-4. John Millard (so writes himself) son of Henry Millard, Esq., born at London ; educated at St. Paul's under Dr. Gale ; admitted sizar for Mr. Armstrong, 1st May, 1690, æt. 17, under Mr. Orchard.

same. But, Sunday night there being but few watchers, viz., four old women, it made a great noise and gingled money, and flung 6s. into the room, which lay there all the following day, and nobody durst take or meddle with it.

It being nois'd about that the disturber was come again, Mr. Kenyon,* fellow of our coll[ege] and Mr. Hope,* and Mr. Hedlam,* two of our fellows more, with young Sir Fran. Leicester,* made an agreement amongst themselves to go thither exactly when the disturber was playing his pranks, and to shoot off their pistols towards any place where the noise was heard. So having on Monday night by one of their spys had information that the disturber was heard, they all went, and rushing together into the room talked high and chairged their pistols before the people's faces that were there, and protested they would discharge them towards the place where any noise was heard, saying that it was a shame that a rogue and a villane should make such a noise in a town and disturb the whole neighbourhood with his knavish tricks, etc.

---

* Edward Kenyon, son of Edward Kenyon, rectoi of Prestwich, Lanc., deceased. At Stockport School, under Mr. Needham : entered pensioner 6th May, 1681, æt. 16, under Mr. Verdon. Admitted Gregson fellow, 8th Apr., 1685. His place was filled by Roger Kay, 19th Mar., 1688-9. B.A., 1684 ; M.A., 1688.

Roger Kenyon, son of Edward Kenyon, rector of Prestwich, Lanc., deceased. At Stockport School, under Mr. Needham ; admitted pensioner 10th Apr. 1682, under Mr. Verdon, æt. 15. Admitted licentiate of the Coll. of Physicians, 22d Dec., 1703. A nonjuror, died at St. Germains. Helped the publication of Chas. Leslie's Works. Admitted Ashton fellow, 15th Mar., 1686-7, in room of Ashton. on 28th Febr., 1694-5. Roger Kenyon was elected to a medical fellowship in Dr. Stillingfleet's room. Theobald was elected in Kenyon's place 10th June, 1696, but gave way again to Kenyon, 19th Apr., 1697. On 15th Mar., 1713-4. Hen. Rishton was elected (admitted 16th Mar.) into Kenyon's vacant room. B.A., 1685-6. Roger Kenyon "an able and orthodox divine," minister of Accrington, 1650 (*Whitaker's Whalley*, 123, 395) must have been of the family.

* John Hope, son of the Rev. Mark Hope, born at Keddlaston, Derby ; at Derby School, under Mr. Ogden ; admitted pensioner 24th Apr., 1682, æt. past 16, under Mr. Coke. Admitted Plat fellow, 19th Mar., 1688-9, in Churchman's room. On 7th April, 1707, Wm. Wigmore was elected (adm. 9 Apr., 1707) in Hope's room. B.A., 1685-6.

* Richard Headlam, son of the late John Headlam, Esq., born at Kexby, York. Educated at Pocklington School, under Mr. Elletson. Admitted pensioner 26th May, 1682, under Mr. Billers. Admitted fellow of St. John's, 5th Apr., 1688, in the room of Dr. Watson. On the 11th of April, 1698, Rob. Read, co. York, was elected into Headlam's room (admitted 12th Apr., 1698). On the 31st Mar., 1707, Jo. Perkins was elected (adm. 1st. Ap., 1707), into Headlam's room. B.A., 1685-6 ; M.A., 1696.

* Sir Francis Leicester, Bart., son of Sir Rob. L., Bart., born at Tabley, Chester, educated at Eton, was admitted fellow commoner, 6th Apr., 1692, æt. 17, under Mr. Orchard. He took no degree. He was M.P. for Newton, co. Lanc·; mar. Frances d. and h. of Joshua Wilson, Esq., of Colton., co. York, and widow of Bryan Thornhill, Esq., by whom he had one d. He died 5th Aug., 1742, when the baronetcy became extinct.

But the divelish disturber having att this thought it best to be packing, and never to come there more, so accordingly they frighted him so that never any more disturbance was heard there, and so ended the whole scene of imposture, for every one but old wives and other such like half-witted people never reckoned it to be anything else.

On Monday night likewise there being a great number of people at the door, there chanced to come by Mr. Newton,* fellow of Trinity College : a very learned man, and perceiving our fellows to have gone in, and seeing several scholars about the door, " Oh ! yee fools," says he, " will you never have any witt, know yee not that all such things are meer cheats and impostures ?   Fy, fy ! go home, for shame," and so he left them, scorning to go in.

It is a strange and wonderful thing to consider into what enthusiastic whimseys almost all the nation fell in Cromwel's days, but especially all those that were enemys to the king, for God surely blinded them in their own ways, and confounded them in their own paths.   Yet these men were the onely saints of the times, every one that was not of their party were accounted sinners and reprobates, and those fine times were then the days of the reforming of the church, and the rooting out of vice.   But where was there more vitious times than them ? where was there more wickedness ever done under the colour of reforming than they did ?   For they turn'd not onlly the whole land but all religion upside down, and never was a nation surely since the world begun so infatuated as they were then.   The justices of peace marryed people then, and the ceremony in many places was no more than thus—when they came before the justice, he would say thus,—" What is your name ?" to the man, then, " What is your name ?" to the woman.   When they had told him, then he sayd, " Have you a mind to be marry'd together ?"   " Yes."   " Well, then take you this man to your husband, and take you this woman to your wife,—of all which I myself am witness," said be, and so the marriage was ended. They never heeded in what place they were married, but would have mett these justices a hunting, or courseing, or at the ale house or taverns, or anywhere, and they would immediately have marry'd them.   Then, when a child was born, and was brought to be christened, it was thus :—The father himself brings his child to the church, to the reading-desk, where having a bason of water ready, the priest asks the father whether that be

* Afterwards Sir Isaac Newton.—See *ante* p. 23,

his son or no? then, " What will you have him called?" and
then nameing the name, he baptized them with the usual words,
In the name of the Father, etc. But they had such names for
their children in them days that posterity will never believe, such
as these,—*Praise God, Love Christ, Child of God, Faithful,
Increas, Chearfull, Blessed be God, Praise, Victory, Fear God,
Conquer thy Enemys,* and Cromwel had a commander call'd
Praise God Barebones if you live, and his surname was Ironsides.
And I knew two, one call'd *Love the Lord all your life Wilson,*
and the other *Deliverance Smyth,* etc.[b]

I having oft heard that King James closeted several, nay even
most, of the great men that were Protestants, and that were in
office in his times, I never understood the business so thoroughly
before as till this day that I chanced to be in company with a
great man's son whose father was done so by. And this brings
into my head that I have oft heard that ingenious young man,
Mr. Bohun (Mr. Edm[und] Bohun's son), who is now dead, tell
how that his father, who was a justice of peace, was sent for by
the king, and examined about several things very privately in
his closset, and at last he told him that if he expected his favour
he must be very kind to the Papists, and likewise be one of his
communion. To which he answered immediately that he could
not possibly be so. To which the king replyed in a great fury,
" Well, look what follows," and the very next day he was turned
out of his office, etc., etc., etc.

I have heard of a great many more that gave the king such
like answers, and they likewise were turned out of whatever office
they had. Others turn'd themselves out for fear of the worst.

Cap[tain] Edwin Sandys,[c] a very ingenious man, a good
scholar, and one that has been almost in all engagements whether
beyond sea or at home for this twenty years, being of the Earl of
Oxford's regiment, the king took occasion one day to send for
him, and having brought him into his closet he begun to talk

---

[b] In the parish register of Wadworth, co. York, occurs the marriage of
Samuel Cockaine with Jesset Banishment Deliverance Saunderson, 22 Jan, 1694-5.
The Rev. Samuel Bower, Rector of Sprotborough, 1632-1634, had a daughter
named Deliverance, wife of William Beaumont of Doncaster, Alderman,
whose widow she was in 1703.

Mr. G. Steinman Steinman communicated to *Notes and Queries* (4th S. III.,
p. 215), the fact that in the church register of St. Andrew, Holborn, it is recorded that there was buried 5th Jany., 1679-80,
" Praise God Barebone, at ye ground near ye Artillery."

[c] The diarist has first written *Esq.,* and afterwards altered it to *Kt.* without
explanation. E. S. is described in the register of his burial, 19th Oct., 1702, as
" Capt. Edwin Sands" only. Probably allusion was intended to be made to
Sir Thomas Sandys.

about this and that, and at last told him what he would do for him, and how great a commander he should be if he would but be a Catholik. To whom the Cap[tain] replied (in a bigg hoarse voyce, as he always spoke), " I understand your Majesty well enough. I fear God, and I honour the king, as I ought, but I am not a man that is given to change," which unexpected answer so stopped the king's mouth that he had not a word to say.

Within a few days after, the Cap[tain] went to the Earl of Oxford, and would needs have given his commission up and gone into Holland, etc., but the Earl would not accept of it, but whispered him in the ear, saying, " These things will not last long," meaning these actions of the king. And, just about a quarter of a year after, the revolution happened.

Yet for all this, when it was happening, yet this good Cap-[tain] got into Windsor Castle, and kept it for the king, untill he run out of the land, etc.

This relation of him I had from an intimate friend and rela-tion of his, and once I heard the Capt[ain] own it. But he is so modest a man that he never tells any of his actions but to his intimate friends in private.

Not being well pleased with the country, tho' I was mighty much made on there, and had every thing that I could desire, I however begun my journey for Cambridge again on the 1st of July, 1694. The first day I ridd by Newark (which is a very handsome town, well situated, and of great trade ; there are the reliques of a mighty large and strong old castle, built after the old manner like forts, which castle held out mightily in Crom-well's time for the king, to Grantam, which place is famous for a delicate high steeple. Having lodged there that night, the next day by noon I got to Stamford, which is a pleasant town, very large and well peopled. It has some six or seven churches in it, etc. From thence I came to Huntington, and from thence to my long wish'd for place of Cambridge.

But I had like to have forgot, as wee were coming upon the road, wee saw Belvior Castle, a castle indeed, strongly seated upon a steep mountain, and in very good repair. 'Tis the seat of the Earl of Rutland,[d] whose estate is near twenty-three thousand per annum. He keeps constantly scaven score servants in pay, and is a man mightily beloved round about in the country. At the foot of this castle on the one side is as fine gardens as can possibly bee seen, and on the other is my lord's bakehouses, brew-

---

[d] John, tenth Earl of Rutland, created 29th March, 1703, Marquess of Granby, and Duke of Rutland, died 11th January, 1711.

houses, stables, and other such like out dwellings. All their provisions the[y] got up with a mighty deal of trouble, the hill is so steep, and there is no riding up it no sort of way, unless people have a mind to break their necks, but as it were by winding stairs.

The next day I got to Cambridge, and was very well pleased to find all my friends and acquaintance in health. I blessed God for my being got out of the country, for when I was there they wearyed me almost of my life by [saying] that all learning was foolish further than that that would make the pot boyl. So little praise and thanks had I for studdying so much at Cambridge, etc.

4TH.* This morning I enquired of several about the truth of Vol. Austin's house being hanted, and I found it confirm'd on every hand, and that it was all just so as I had it written to me some months ago from Cambridge. But none that I can meet with, except old foolish women, believes that it was any thing else than a meer cheat and imposture.

5TH. Memorandum. I have heard Capt[ain] Sandys, a learned ingenious man, protest that he himself has seen Will[iam] Pen the great Quaker's name up in King James's days amongst the name of the Jesuit converts at Doway. I heard likewise from one who had been several times at Pen's house that he lives like a king, and had always plenty of all sorts of wine in his house, and good victuals, and that commonly, when he had any strangers, their meat was all served up in silver plates. I have heard likewise several times how he came to turn Quaker, from several good hands, which was this. He being brought up in Oxford was a fellow commoner there, and after that he had been there a great while desired something of them, which they would not grant. Upon which he swore he would make them all repent it. Upon which, in a great huff, he left the college, and, going down into the country, joyn'd himself to the scism of the Presbiterians; but they having cross'd him in one of his projects, he turns to the Quakers, and immediately they made him their head; and he could rule them, foolish enthusiasts, as he pleased, and so he has continued amongst them unto this day. He carried many hundreds of familys with him into Pensilvania, which he so called from himself, and gave them land there. But, alas! they were in a few years most of them either pined to dead, or else knock'd oth' head by the wild Indians.

* Month not given.

Pen bought a great many of their estates of them, and then sent them over. He changed so many hundreds of akers there with the like number of akers here, and then sent the silly deluded people over to possess it. He did abundance of such tricks in K[ing] Ch[arles] the Second's days.

On the ...... instant there passed the seals at London a grant to a gentleman to make and use post coaches, which he undertakes shall carry several persons a hundred miles in twenty hours.

[*Here several pages seem to be wanting, and the diarist next appears to be referring to Peterborough*].

My observations on the famous minster, or religious house, that was formerly thereby.

The Mi[n]ster is a most stupendous piece of work, built after a most wonderfull, majestick, manner, it being almost inconcievable what a prodigious deal of pains, cost, and labour has been spent in the raising and perfecting of the same. When I went in it, I found how much it had suffer'd in the late damnable wars, for here it was that they kept their horses, and defaced all the curious monuments therein. They pull'd some thousands of pounds of brass from the grave-stones and monuments ; and wherever there was a curious statue they pull'd it in pieces. But yet there remains several old tombstones with Saxon letters upon. They defac'd likewise [the] tomb of Queen Catharin wife to Har[ry] 8, who lys on the left side of the chappel in the minster, and likewise that of Mary the Queen of Scots, who lay on the right. There lay likewise two bishops of York, hard by the altar, who dyd above 690 years ago, but their curious monuments were likewise destroyed. The altar was one of the finest in the whole world, most of black and white marble, exalted by curious penacles, carveing, and stately figures, almost to half the hight of the chappel, but this likewise was utterly destroy'd in Cromwell's days. Harry the 8th, whose covetious fury deserves condemnation by every one, intended to pull all this stately minster to the ground, but that one desired him not to do such a think for the love of his dear queen that lay buried therein, which he heark'ned to, and so it was saved. But, alas! the most stately and magnificent monastry that in a manner encompas'd the whole minster, felt the heavy hand of covetious Harry, and was all pull'd down and defaced, onely the walls, most curiously carved, yet stands to shew what they formerly were, dwelling houses now being made out of them, and a most stately chappel or two that were in the said monastry, bigger than many churches, is converted into dwelling rooms.

'Tis not long ago that the sexton, being digging to make a grave in the minster yard, found the body of one of the old monks, not consumed by time, buried, as it was the custome in their days, in all his best habiliments, with a sort of croiser staff in one hand and a book in the other quite rotten. He had likewise boots and spurrs on, not in the least cankered.

While I was here a gentleman told me that, as he was lately coming over Lincoln heath, suddainly the[re] arises just before him, with a great cry, a buzzard, which flew straight up a great height into the sky, and then came tumbling down again. He, being surrpris'd at this, immediately rid to the dead bird, and found that it had got in its claw a great weesel, which had fixt its teeth in the breast of the buzzard and suck'd it's blood.

Here was formerly about this town or rather citty of Peterbur: four or five miter'd abotts here, another at Thorny, another at Ramsey, and others in other places. They were esteem'd as lords and sat in the house of pears in time of Parliament.

Old Rich[ard] Baxter is dead, the great and famous preacher up of reformation and puritanism. To give the divel his due, as the proverb is, this Baxter was a man (as far as my accounts can reach, as well oral as printed), of great virtue, piety, and holiness of life, but exceeding passionate, and so fond of his own oppinions and affections that he could not abide to hear them contradicted. He writt much against the Church of England, but, tho' he was sufficiently and excellently answered by several, yet he would never vouchsafe to peruse the sayd answers, but had the impudence, in several of his books, to boast that his books were never answered, that his enemys could not confute him, and such like. But the older he grew he was the more peevish, and became mighty enthusiastical, conceited, and dogmatical in his opinions.

As for his learning it was onely superficial, as is manifest from several of his books, from which it appears that he was very little versed in the writeings of the Fathers, and had little knowledge in antient Church history. About seven years ago I read one book of his, and I remember very well that he says therein, that from his birth 'till the time of his writeing that book he had but committed about five or six sins, and one of them was that he had whetted a knife on the sabl ath day, etc.

He was the great upholder of his sect of the Presbyterians, and gave that sect such roote that it is to be feared it will never be eradicated.

His arguments in almost all his books that I have seen and read (which are above half-a-score), are very weak, and has more of passion in them than sollid reason. Yet he strives to run all down before him, and calls them demonstrable, unanswerable, impregnable, and such like ; and has the impudence to affirm things for truth that are notoriously known to be false, as, amongst the rest, where he says,[f] that the dissenters were, under K[ing] James' reign, the chief that fought against popery, and asks the question likewise, who had done or suffered more to keep out popery? yet it is well enough known that there were above two hundred discourses published against popery in that reign, and there was but three of them writt by the dissenters.

He was a man that was even blinded with passion and interest, so that he condemn'd things before that he understood them, and would not hear any one that should chance to contradict him ; so that as well in his history as divinity there are a great many errors and mistakes.

All the publick affairs of state went on very well this year, and I observ'd that the common people were mighty well pleased thereat, so that there was not the least murmering either by one or other. But thre years before, the nation was sufficiently full of discontents and grumblings, so that the last year but this the king, when he landed out of Holland was so coldly received that he was scarce so much as welcom'd when he arrived at London. But, alass ! as many a fair day ends in a foul shower, so this year, tho it begun and continued well, yet it ended the most to our sorrow that any one ever did since the reign of Q[ueen] Eliz[abeth], and that by the death of our dear Queen Mary, which caused an universal sorrow in the whole nation, as well in the malecontents as others, for shee was univarsaly well beloved of every one, and the most esteem'd of any that ever was since the death of Q[ueen] Eliz[abeth] ; and by her prudent management of all sorts of affairs got the love of every one, she being generaly observ'd to be a woman of very great witt, prudence, and cunning, yet of a free, liberal, and open behaviour, but never to her own hurt and dishonour by blabing out of things that ought to be kept secret.

She brought a fashon into England that was as rare here as it was excellent, that was, that tho' shee had no need of working, yet she hated nothing more than idleness, so that wherever shee was going in her coach, or a foot, shee would either be knitting, or making of fringes. And when she had occasion to visit any one, she would always take her work with her, and work and

---

[f] In his " English Nonconformity under King Charles II. and King James II. truly stated, etc." London, 1689.

talk faster than any four or five people else. So that this sedulity and laboriousness of her's became a custome or rather fashion in London, and every lady follow'd the same, and wrought at their fringes, networks, and knittings, as they ridd in their coaches along.

They have a characteristic saying here of the K[ing], Q[ueen], and her broth[ers] and sist[ers], and that is, that—

> King William thinks all,
> Queen Mary talks all,
> Prince George drinks all,
> And Princess Ann eats all.

But this excellent Queen Mary of our's dy'd of the small-pox, a disease that has been fatal to several of the family, and her death so affected the king that he layd it most to heart that ever was seen, and fell into two swounds when he was taking his last leave of her. Her funeral obsequies is appointed to be in March ; and it is certainly thought that there will be the greatest mourning for her that ever was for a king or queen in Europe. Black cloth, that was but ten shillings a yard one day, got to be twenty the next, and well were those that could get it so. I hear that, up and down the country everywhere, all that can afford it do intend to be in mourning ; but they say that they do not mourn for the Queen of England but for the Princess of Orange.

This month came about for a sight a little Scotchman, the least man that ever was heard on, for he was but two foot and seven inches in height. He was thirty-two years old, and had a son with him that was twice as bigg as himself. He taught school in Scotland many years, and was a harsh and severe master. And having spent all he had there in good ale, he suffered himself to be carryd about for a show, so that he might but enjoy that good creature, night and day, which he constantly did in such abundance that he was very seldome sober. Telling this to a gentleman that was lately come from London, in re-quiteal for my relation—he told me another, which he would have counted well worthy of his time if he had gone thither on purpose to see him, and it was this. He saw a young, tall, slender man there, about twenty-five years of age, that did with his voyce imitate any sort of musical instruments, and play several tunes therewith so lively and so exactly that there was but few that could perceive the difference. He imitated the fiddle, the trumpet, the flute, the organs, the virginals, etc., with his voyce, and played them several tunes. Then this gentleman ask'd him if he could ring the bells, and he did it the most exactly that could be,

E

raising them by degrees, then ringing a good round peal therewith, then setting of them all one immediately after another, and
then ringing another; and then letting them settle one after
another, etc.

Feb. 9, [169]4-5 This day viz., the 29th inst. [*sic*.] being in
company with Mr. Cornelius Lee,[f] who was a great royalist and
cornet of horse in the time of the late troubles, in our discourses
about Cromwel, he gave me an account of several things that I
had not heard or red on concerning him.

He says that he himself and three more bound themselves in an
oath that they would be Cromwel's death one way or other, and
that for that end they posted *incognito* to London; and after that
they had been there a consid[erable] while, one of them inveigled
himself in with Cromwel's cook, and on a time cunningly cast a
slow but most certain poison upon some dishes of meat that was
going to his table, and convey'd himself away. And within a
fourtnight he fell sick, and of that sickness he dy'd. This he does
most constantly aver, and realy believes that he was poisn'd.

This Mr. Lee was at Lon[don] when the king return'd, and
hearing that Cromwel and Ireton and Bradshaw were going such
a day to be pul'd out of their graves and hang'd at Tyburn, he
went with a great many more to see the tragedy. Now it
happen'd that there was a plank layd over a little goit or water-
course, over which they should go. When Mr. Lee had just got
over there was an old woman that asked him where he was going.
" Going, good woman," sayd he, " I am going to see Cromwel
executed." " I, I," says shee, " many of you gos now to see
him being dead that durst not look in his face when he was alive."
" Very true," says he to her again as they walk'd along, " and
if I could get the same way back I came, I would go no further,
but the multitude of people coming will hinder me." So he
walked on, (as he told me before several gentlemen), and when
the[y] came there they found them all hung up but Cromwel,
and getting as near as he could be, just came in time to see
Crom[wel] open'd by the hangsm[an] who had no sooner cut
the sear cloaths open, but he catches hold of a great plate
whereon was written all Crom[wel's] titles, and what he was,
and when he dy'd. " This is it," say'd the hangsman, " that I
look for, I have now got it." He thought it had been gold, and
that made him so joyfull, but, to his sorrow, he found it to be
only iron dubble guilt.

[f] See *ante* p. 35.

The same gentleman told me several relations and storys of Hugh Peeters, which tho' they were very memorable, yet, because the[y] relate to such a rogue, they are not worthy of setting down.

Yet, perhaps I may spoil paper with one or two. As this Peters was one [day] walking in St. James's Park, in the times of our late destractions, there enters Cromwel likewise to take the air also ; but neither the one nor the other had walked very long before that it began to rain very hard, and Cromwel got under the shade, and bidd them carry his cloak to Ha[gh] Peters to cover him from being wet. But he refused it, and told the bearer that he begg'd his highnesses pardon, and would not be in his cloak for a thousand pounds.

A gentleman met him once in the street and whisperd him ith' ear, saying, " Peters, thou art a great knave." But he answ[ered] him again saying, " S[o] your fool, or else you would have been what I am." That gentleman had been a great sufferer in the royal cause. As he was preaching once in a church, and telling his auditors a company of delicate fine storys, as he usually did, he perceived a gentleman to be shrinking away out of the church: " Hark you, you gentleman," says he, " I have something to say to you, come hither, I'll tell you a story. There was a cock, and a frog, and an ass went once a traveling, and it came to pass that at length they came to a great river. " Well," say they one to another, " how shall we get over here ?" " As for me," says the frogg, I'll swimm it," "and I," sayd the cock, " I'll fly it over." " But the poor ass," says he, " not being willing to wet his feet wandered away be river side, and was at length taken and beat with many stripes. Verily (says he), thou art an ass or I am much mistaken, else thou woulds't not have left thy company hearing good and profitable things, and turn'd back to give heed to a simple story ; and if thou haddest thy right thou shouldest be scourged with many stripes, for, as our King Jesus says, thou deservedst it."

This Peeters was hanged amongst the regicides, and there are many that dos believe that it was realy him in disguise that cut the said king's head off. And I heard a gentleman say that he had a very great hand in those unhappy times ; that there was one that, coming by chance into this Peeter's lodgings, found in one of the windows, writ with a diamond ring this verse,

> The greatest head ith' world since Cæsar's
> Was lately crop't by Doct[or] Peters.

for so he used to stile himself. Which inscription, when he saw the gentleman take notice off, he up with his kain and broke the pain in pieces.

This fellow, I mean Peters, was the greatest buffoon in all London, and the church he commonly preached in was usually as full as ever it could hold ; for he made the people more sport than any play could do. And they would laugh as loud as if they were at some publick bull or bear bateing.

The same gentleman and me talking about Selby church steeple that fell down about six or seven years ago,[h] [by] means of the river's undermining it, he told me that in Cromwell's days there was the finest painted window there that was thought to be in all Europe. He himself saw it several times, and heard from very good hands that formerly, before the troubles began, they had twelve thousand pound offerd for it by some popish lords, to send it to Rome, but they would not take. Yet in the aforesayd holy times Crom[well's] sold[iers] broke it all in pieces.

MARCH. This 2d inst. I was in company with one Thom[as] Oldham,[i] a Quaker. That which made it observable to me was because that he was the first learned one that ever I heard on or saw. He understood Latt[in], Greek, and Hebrew, but especialy the two former languages very well. His father was carried before the judges once for some misdemeanour that the light within had promp'd him to, and because that he would not put of his hat, one that stood by pul'd it off and flung it down, at which he took such offence that he would never put on a hat after as long as he lived, but went to the markets and follow'd the plow, and did all his business ever after barehead.

---

[h] This tower fell down on Sunday March 30th, 1690.—*Morrell's Selby*, p. 204.

[i] Aldam. Amongst the freeholders of the manor of Warmsworth, near Doncaster, the principal have been of the family of Aldam, who are reputed to have been located here since before the conquest. Their names are said to be among witnesses of deeds in the thirteenth and fourteenth centuries. The Thomas Aldam, referred to by the diarist, was the grandfather of Mrs. Catherine Aldam, a maiden lady, on whose death, in 1807, the family became extinct at this place. He and his father, another Thomas, were among the first persons who were induced to adopt the peculiarities of George Fox and his associates. The father was one of the two Friends who attended the delivery of Fox's memorable declaration to the messengers of Oliver Cromwell. In Fox's journal we have an account of the interruption of one of the religious assemblies at Warmsworth ; and it appears that one or both of the Aldams were for a time imprisoned in the Castle of York. (*Hunter's S. Y.*, i., 129). The property passed, by devise, to a family called Pease, which assumed the name of Aldam, and the present representative is William Aldam, esq., of Frickley and Warmsworth, who was elected M.P. for Leeds in 1841, and is justly regarded as an active, experienced, and useful magistrate for the West Riding of Yorkshire.

The Quakers now are nothing like what they were formerly. They are the most reformed that ever was seen. They now were fine cloathes, and learns all sorts of sempstry and behavour, as others do that are not of their opinions. And within this quarter of this year they have begun all over this country to put off their hats whenever they name the name of Jesus Christ.

They do not now quake, and howl, and foam with their mouths, as they did formerly, but modestly and devoutly behave themselves in their devotions, making commonly long prayers, and then a sermon, and then a prayer after it, but this is the evil of them that [they] are full of tautology and vain repetitions, which the Apostle Paul has condemned in the service of the heathen.

When any one has a mind to marry, he did formerly take the woman that he would have into his house, and calling in six or seven of his friends and neighbours, would say thus unto them, taking the woman by the hand—" Witness, friends and brethren, that I take this woman to me to be my wife." And so there was no more to do.

When a child was born unto any of them, the father would call some neighbours together, and then would say thus—" Bear witness, neighbours, that I call this child of mine Thomas, Mary," etc., but they never christened them with any water, or any thing else.

But now, times being altered, none is wed amongst them before that they have been ask'd two years together in their meeting, etc.

Every year four or five and sometimes more of them, within the precincts of this little lordship, come over to our church, and tho' they be men and women they are baptized in full congregation.

And likewise of the Presbiterians a great many round about come over to the church. God grant, for the love of his dear Son Jesus Christ, that they may all shortly and speedily do the same. Amen.

5TH. This day I heard of a workman at Sheffield that is much cryd up for his skill and ingenuity; one exper[iment] of which was, that he could and had smooth'd two pieces of steel so exceeding smooth and plain that they stick so fast, the one upon the other, that a man could scarce sever them with all his strength. This is common in marble.

I was likewise in the church seeing the stone cutter make a

monum[ent]—which should have the names of the benefactors
thereon to the church, the school, and the poor. Amongst other
talk he told me that marble was a sort of stone the easiest to be
stain'd of any, and that it is no choice art to do the same, even
through the whole stone, if it was a yard thick ; but he could give
no reasons for the same. He says also that there is the best alabaster that ever was seen, gotten a little way beyond Nottingham.
He says the[y] frequently wett the same, or raither, to use his
term, the[y] boyl it in iron pottoks till all the humidity be
evaperated, and then it becomes a most pure white powder, which
when they have a mind to use (for molding or such like uses)
they mix water therewith, and then it makes an image or any
thing, harder by half than it would do otherwise.

1695.

11. O God, I give the humble thanks for inabling me
to make and finish now this day a book of some sixty or
seventy sheets, which I have entitled *Curiosa de se,[j]* or, *The
Curious Missellanys and Private Thoughts of one Inquisitive
into the Knowledge of Nature and Things.* O be gratious unto me,
enable me to finish the others that I am about making, for thy
dear Son's sake. Amen.

Ap. 3. Mrs. Dewey, of this town, dy'd about twelve years ago
of the small pox.[k] The thing that is observable about the same
is that, as soon as ever she went into a house where the small pox
was, she felt as it was a vehement damp, and was almost choak'd
therewith, tho' not one in the room felt or perciev'd it but herself. But this proved her death, for shee came home and dyd of
them.

My mother, being once gon to Thorn, went to see the children

---

[j] Hunter observes that "this manuscript is supposed to be lost. Antiquaries
are, of all classes of men, least prone to destroy the *litera scripta.* But perhaps
his maturer judgment might urge him to commit this to the flames." (*S. Y.,* i.,
180). Mr. Peacock, in his preface to De la Pryme's History of Winterton,
(*Archæologia* XL.), considers that Mr. Hunter's latter suggestion was made
"perhaps without sufficient authority."

[k] Will of Rebecca Dewie, of Hatfield, spinster, dated 13 December, 1678.
—to my kinsman Gregory Betney, £10 ; to Mrs. Lee (Leah?) Walker, 20s. ; to
Mr. Cleworth, 20s. ; to Mr. Simon Simpson, to preach my funeral sermon, 20s. ;
to the poor of Hatfield and Woodhouse, £5 ; residue to Cornelius Lee, gent.
He sole exor. Proved at York, 19 April, 1683, by Cornelius Lee.—*Reg. Test.*
60, fol. 18.
"Mrs. Rebeccah Dewy buryed in linnen contrary to ye Act of Parliamt" 30
March, 1682-3.—*Hatfield Register.*

of Christian Middlebrook, who were sick, tho' she did not know of what disease. Yet as soon as ever shee open'd the curtains, " Oh !" says she, '' these children are sick of the measels, I feel so by the strong smell or damp," and shee came home and fell sick of them in a day or two.

Some ascribe this dampish smell onely to fancy, because every one does not perceive it. But I believe that every body's corps are not equaly subject to these diseases, however, not at a time or together, therefore believes that those bodys that are fully ripe and apt to receive the morbific matter, inbibes the same, and that then they smell and perceive things that others may not do, by reason of their bodys not being so open as the others that are subject to infection.

20. I was with Mr. Corn[elius] Lee yesternight, and amongst other things he assured me on his own and a great many more people's words, that foxes, so many years old they are, so many livers they have, and that he himself saw one opened that had eight, and so they all judg'd him to be eight years old. I ask'd Mr. Lucas about it this day, and he says it is true. But that which I most boggl'd at is this. They sayd that, for a certain, the whelps of a shee fox never breed so long as the dam liveth, tho' they be never so old, and this is the reason, sayd they, that there are more sheep than foxes.

24. Talking with Mr. Horatio Cay,[l] he says that the ancient Romans when the[y] conquer'd this country, as they travell'd through this part of Yorkshire, they seeing a part of the country for a huge way round about boggy and full of quagmires, they gave it the name of *Balneum*, which now is called *Bawn*.

Yesterday, which was the last of this month, I preached at Bramwith,[m] about two miles hence ; it was the first sermon that

---

[l] Horace Kaye, vicar of Barnby-Don, son of William Kaye, by Elizabeth, daughter of Horace Eure, sister and coheir of George Lord Eure, married 16 May. 1673, Frances, widow of Francis Gregory, esq., of Barnby-Don.—*Hunter's S. Y.*, i., 211.

[m] Kirk-Bramwith. At a ford over the Don are two villages, one on each side, both called Bramwith, of which that on the south was included in the Warren fee and the chace of Hatfield. At the Bramwith on the north side the stream a church was erected, to which was assigned, as the parish, the vill of Bramwith. Hunter, (*S. Y.*, ii., 477) in speaking of the church of St. Mary here, does not say anything respecting the "ten or twelve Knight Templars or monks" there lying in the days of the diarist. He remarks that "no family of any consequence having ever being settled within the precincts of this parish, we have no monuments, or other memorials, except of former rectors or their curates."

ever I preach'd. I observed in that little church that ther lyese
about ten or twelve Knight Templers, or monks, who it seems
had great lands and liveings in these parts. That which is now
the parsonage was in old time some castle, and moated about.

APRIL 8.ⁿ   For this fortnight last past there has been a
fortune-teller in this town, which, as soon as I heard on, I caused
him to be apprehended and brought before the sages of the town,
where he was examined and search'd, but tho' he was a very
handsome, genteel, young man, every bit like a gentleman born,
yet he was the greatest fool that ever I cast my eyes [on]. We
got all his books and papers, but what were they, think you?

Spectatum admissi risum teneatis amici,

a company of old mouldy almanacks, and several sheets of astro-
logical scheems, all drawn false and wrong, and Wingate's
arithmetick. The fellow had scarce any sence in him, and
in his discourse frequently betray'd himself, and confest things
which the law would have taken hold on otherwise. Yett was
never a bitt under any surprise of mind, nor ever gave any one
an ill word, but as all such vagrant rogues commonly do,
prayed heartily for the good company's health, biding God to
bless them, and such like. I examined him almost an hower by
myself, but he knew nothing of any art or science, nor did not
understand that which he pretended. He behaved himself so
that every one pittyd him, and he sayd that whereever he came
the women were always his best friends. He confesses at last
that he gets thirty or forty pound per annum thus, tho' at first he
sayd this was the first time that ever he did so. He told about
fifty people in this parish that they should come to suddain death,
some be hang'd, some be drown'd, and he told several people
the divel would fetch them, others that they should be bewitched,
and named the witches, which were poor good harmless women.
In a word, he has done incredible mischief in this parish, and rob'd
the people of above five pound. It is their custom to deny every
thing that's objected against them, tho' witnesses be brought
against them. They likewise always keep a serene countinance,
sober life, and a pretended ignorance, when they come to be
examined, that they may raither be pitty'd than punished, tho'
indeed this fellow I take to have been a real fool, for he understood no Lattin, nor no art nor science, nor could scarce spell

---

ⁿ The dates are not very regularly inserted in the Diary, and cannot therefore be entirely depended on.

words right, nor write but indifferently with his pen. He should have been whipp'd, but that the women of this town begg'd his pardon, and help him to contrive his escape. We hear since of his having broke a house and stolen several things at Barmby-upon-the-More, and of several of his mad pranks, etc.

APRIL 10. Ho, brave Russell!° what honour have you brought to the English nation by your thus rideing two years together emp[eror] of not only the English, the French, the Spanish, but also of the Mediterranian sea itself. We hear that he will not let a ship of any nation pass the straits without his licence. As soon as he brought his navy hither all the kingdoms and principalitys round about trembled. The great Duke of Tuscany, and the Duke of Mantua, that before would not winter the Germans, as soon as they heard of the English being passed the straits, they agreed with them about their winter quarters. The Pope, likewise being afraid, confirm'd the Bish[op] of Leige and Collen, tho' the French did what they could to prevent it. The French in Catalonia being flushed with victory as farr as they went, being just ready to besiege Barcelona, (which if they had done they had certainly taken it) as soon as they heard of the approach of the English, they left their undertaking of, and never had any such thoughts again. The governors of Tangiers and the Algerines have sent long letters of complements to him, and promises to furnish them with what they want, and to be true friends to them. Marseils and Thoulon trembled when they heard of their approach, and many of the inhabitants sent the best of their goods farr into the country. This has rebounded more to the honour of the English than anything that has happen'd these several ages.

° Edward Russell, second son of Edward, the fourth son of Francis, fourth Earl of Bedford, the principal undertaker of that great work known as the " Bedford Level." He was gentleman of the bedchamber to the Duke of York, but on the beheading of his cousin, William Lord Russell, he retired from court ; and after the accession of James II. exerted himself to the utmost in promoting the revolution. Upon the advancement of the Prince of Orange to the throne he was made one of the privy council, and in 1690 was appointed admiral of the blue, advanced to the command of the navy, and appointed first lord of the admiralty. On the 19th May, 1692, he gave a signal defeat to the French fleet, commanded by Mons. de Tourville, at La Hogue ; in 1695, he by his diligence, prevented the intended invasion of James II., who lay with a French army ready to embark near Dieppe. For these and other gallant services, he was, 7 May, 1697, created Baron Shingey, co. Cambridge, Viscount Barfleur, in the duchy of Normandy, and Earl of Orford, co. Norfolk. In May, 1701 he was impeached by the House of Commons, but was unanimously acquitted of the articles exhibited against him. His lordship died without issue 26 Nov., 1727, having married Lady Margaret Russell, youngest daughter of his father's brother William, first Duke of Bedford.

AP. 26. This being the visitation time, I went to Doncaster to see the ceremony thereof. Amongst many other observable things that Doct[or] Chetwood,[p] the archdeacon, took notice of in his charge to us, he sayd that he did not question but that we should deliver this age down to our posterity in a better condition by half than we received it from our ancestors; he meant in matters relating to the good unity and quiet of the Church of England. " For," sayd he, "whereever I go, I hear of dissenters coming in unto the blessed Church of England," etc.

1695.

JUNE 11. About this time I was sent for into Lincolnshire, to Roxby, about a liveing. Having passed over the Trent at Althorp, or Authrop, in my going to the aforesayd town, I saw nothing observable but the barrenness of the country, and the sandy commons that I passed over; which I no sooner saw, but it brought into my mind the sandy desarts of Egypt and Arabia, which I had a most clear idea of when I beheld these sandy planes. For here the sand is driven away with every wind, and when the wind is strong it is very troublesome to pass, because that the flying sand flys in one's face, and shoos, and pockkets, and such like, and drives into great drifts, like snow-drifts. This sandy plane is some miles in length, and about a quarter of a mile in bredth. In great winds it does great damage, for sometimes in a night's space it will cover all the hedges that it is near, and cover all the corn land adjacent, etc. I have observed huge hedges quite sandyd up with it to the very top; and a cloas of thistles that was one day almost a yard tall, the wind changing, and I returning the same way the next day, I could but just discover the tops of them. This plane was formerly a much higher country than it is now, for here and there are left a few hills (now we may call them) three yards in height perpendicular, which blows away by degrees, but were formerly eaven with the rest of the blown away land, etc.

JUNE 15. I was this week at most of the towns in this corner of

[p] Knightley Chetwood became Archdeacon of York in Jan., 1688-9. In 1707 he was made Dean of Gloucester, and died in April, 1720. He was son of Valentine Chetwood, of Chetwood, esq., and was born in 1652. Educated at Eton, and King's College, Cambridge. He was a great friend of Dryden the poet, and had some literary repute. Thoresby records in his Diary (II., p. 261) 21 September. 1714. that he had been visited by "Dr. Chetwood, Archdeacon and Dean of Gloucester."

Lincolnshire. I observe that it is but a poor, barren country. Here is no land to be met with about Roxby and most of the rest of these towns that is above two, three, or four shill[ings] an aker. I was at Burton and expected to have found a fine large town there, but I was much mistaken, it being but little and ill built, and the worst market place that ever I saw.[¹] The Trent runs hard by it, and [I] heard several that was in company with me say that at low water it is fordable in several places, etc.

25. Being Monday I went to Hull from Roxby to Barton, and from thence over the water, which is about five miles, to Hull.[²] We payd a groat for our passage, and a shilling for a horse. Hull is mightily improv'd since I saw it last; but it is a mighty factious town, there being people of all sects in it.

The 29. I agreed with Mr. Hammersley,[³] minister of Roxby, to be his curate at Broughton in this shire. He ask'd me what I would have a year. I told him no more than others, viz. 30l. per an. out of which I gave 10l. a year for my table.

Broughton is as much as to say Burrow town from the vast plenty conney borrows that are round about it.[⁴] I do not find

[¹] The little town of Burton-upon-Stather has ceased to have a market for many years. The market place, which was on the brow of the hill west of the church, has long been enclosed and become private property.—*Hatfield's Terra Incognita of Lincolnshire*, p. 32.

[²] There has been a ferry over the Humber from Barton to the mouth of the river Hull from very early times, probably prior to the foundation of Kingston-upon-Hull by Edward I. A traveller, who is believed to have been none other than the author of Robinson Crusoe, crossed over this ferry a few years after Abraham de la Pryme was there. He had not a pleasant passage. " There are some good towns on the sea coast, but I include not Barton, which stands on the Humber, as one of them, being a straggling mean town, noted for nothing but an ill-favoured dangerous passage, or ferry, over the Humber to Hull, where in an open boat, in which we had about 15 horses, and 10 or 12 cows mingled with about 17 or 18 passengers, we were about 4 hours tos'd about on the Humber before we could get into the harbour at Hull."—*Tour thro' the whole Island of Great Britain by a gentleman*, 3rd ed., 1742, vol iii.. p. 11.

[³] He was ancestor and namesake, I believe, of Mr. Hugh Hammersley, of Doncaster, attorney at law, and one of the aldermen who was elected mayor 24 Sep., 1741. Alderman Hammersley married, 7 May, 1728, Elizabeth, eldest daughter and coheir of Wm. Wade, town clerk of Doncaster, and died in 1757, leaving an only son, Thomas, baptised at Doncaster 3 Nov., 1747. The latter settled in London, and originated the banking house of Hammersley and Co., in Pall Mall. He died in 1812, leaving issue.

[⁴] Borotona, Bertone, Broctone, (*Domesday*, i., 365, 376,), Berghton, (*Taxatio P. Nicholai*, 75, col. 2). The name of this place has assuredly nothing to do with rabbits, though they have for ages abounded there. Beorh, or Beorg, a hill, and Tun, an enclosure—a town in the old sense still retained by the Lincolnshire peasantry—are the words from which this name has grown up. The hill from which the name has been derived is a large circular sand hill, like a huge grave hill, but almost certainly natural, not far from the church. This mound abuts upon the old Roman way, known in books as the Ermine Street, to those who live near it in Lindsey as the " Ramper," or "old street."

anything in history about it : but, however, it seems to be ancient, there being some lady and warriours buried therein, who perhaps were the founders of the church.

12. I was with my uncle Bareel,[*] and he tould me for a most certain truth that the swine herd place at Barrow, in this country, is worth above 30*l.* a year, by reason that they keep such a vast company of swine in that town.

13, 1695. Being in company at Brigg this Friday with several clergymen and others, we had a great deal of good discourse. Some mightily talked against the late famous and excellent edition of *Cambden's Britannia*,[v] saying that it was not worth bying, and that there was a great many memorable places in England that had not been taken notice off, and such like. But, however, let them talk as they please, I am sure that it is twice as good and excellent as it was before, and I am sure that there is no book in the world of a particular country that can compare with it. Rome was not all built of a day, and it is impossible that everything memorable should of a sudden be comprehended and put in any book. Every age sees something more than another, and every year almost some monuments are digg'd up out of the earth some where or other that was not discovered before, so that it is impossible that such a book as it should be perfect *in toto et quälibet parte*.

Talking likewise of Doct[or] Busby[w], who is lately dead, one of this company told this pleasant relation of him and Fath[er] Peters.

As the doct[or] was walking out one evening in K[ing] James reign, to take the air, he met by chance with Father Peters, who had formerly been his scholar. Peters saluted him. "How," says the doct[tor] "are you that Peters that was our scholler?" "Yes," says he again. "Well, but how come you to have this garb on?" (he being a Jesuit); to whom he reply'd, "I had not had it on, honourable master, but that the Lord Jesus had need of me." "Need of thee"? (say'd the doct.) "I never heard that our Lord and Saviour had need of anything but an ass." And so he turned him about in a fury and left him.

---

[*] *Forsan* Beharell.—See *Hunter's South Yorkshire*, i., 169.
[v] The first edition of Gibson's Camden's *Britannia* was published in one volume folio, 1695. It is a learned and painstaking work, but inferior to the second edition in two volumes, published in 1722.
[w] The well known head master of Westminster school.

19. This day I went with some other company to Castor. I expected to have found it (that is so famous in both the Roman and Saxon historys) to be some great and large town, but when I got there I was deceived, it being but a little place, yet mighty famous for its great markits and fairs. It was very ill built before the great fire,* but now there are a great many good modern buildings therein. It was here that Hengist begg'd so much ground of King Vortigern as he was able to encompass with an ox-hide;▾ who, not well understanding his meaning,

---

* "The great fire" at Caistor happened in 1681, or the following year. A brief was issued for collecting money to repair the losses sustained. At Youlgrave, in the county of Derby, the sum of 9s. 7d. was collected for this purpose on the 5th of June, 1682.—*Reliquary*, vol iv., p. 193.

▾ The well known legend of the hide cut into strips is told of sundry places in every country in Europe. It was probably an old story when it became dovetailed into the legendary history of the foundation of Carthage. It need scarcely be added that there is no ground for believing, even in a substratum of fact, in the story as told above. The Diarist's authority for it, and a very poor one it is, is Geoffrey of Monmouth, who in book vi., chapter 11, gives the legend. His tale is that Hengist received as much land as he could encompass by an ox hide from Vortigern. The place so gained was called in the British tongue Kaercorrei, in Saxon Thancastre, that is Thong castle. Kemble, in his *Saxons in England*, i., p. 17, says that the same myth appertains to Ragnor Lodbrog. He quotes *Rag. Lodb. Saga*, cap. 19 and 20. As an instance how these old prehistoric legends multiply and engraft themselves on the new facts of history, he tells us that "the Hindoos declare we obtained possession of Calcutta by similar means."

A singular ceremony annually takes place at the church of Caistor, by the performance of which certain lands in the parish of Broughton, near Brigg, are held. On Palm Sunday a person from Broughton brings a large whip, called a gad whip, the stock of which is constructed of ash, or other wood, tapered towards the top : the thong is large, and made of white leather. The man comes to the north porch about the commencement of the first lesson, and cracks his whip in front of the porch door three times ; after which, with much ceremony, he wraps the thong round the stock of the whip, and binds the whole together with a whip-cord, tying up with it some twigs of mountain ash ; he then ties to the top of the whip stock a small leathern purse containing two shillings, but originally twenty-four silver pennies, and taking the whole upon his shoulder, marches into the church, where he stands in front of the reading-desk, until the commencement of the second lesson ; he then goes up nearer, waves the purse over the head of the clergyman, kneels down upon a cushion, and continues in that position, with the purse suspended over the head of the clergyman, until the second lesson is ended, when he retires into the choir, and waits the remainder of the service. After the service is concluded, he carries the whip and purse to the manor house of Hundon, a hamlet in the parish of Caistor, where they are left, and are generally given to some person as a curiosity. A new whip is made every year. In the performance of this ceremony it is said that the whip used to be cracked over the head of the clergyman in the reading-desk ; but, on one occasion, the whip coming sharply in contact with the face of the clergyman, caused that part of the ceremony to be omitted, and the purse only waved over the head. It is remarkable that this tenure is not noticed either by Camden or Blount.—*Historical Account of Lincolnshire*, anonymous, 1823, vol. i., p. 186.

granted him his request, thinking that he meant no more than he could cover with an ox-hide. But Hengist cut it all into small thongs, and by that means encompast in round about a great compass of land, and built an exceeding strong castle upon part thereof, part of whose ruins I took notice of, it being a wall five or six yards thick. But, when Christianity came in, they pull'd the castle down, and built the church in the place where it stood, of the stone that it was built off. In which church I observed one of the Knight Templars, lying with his legs a cross and his shield on his left arm, besides some few monuments besides.

Mr. Baxter, minis[ter] of that place, let me see about half a score old coins that had been digg'd up about that town, some of which were Roman and others Saxon coins, and he told us, in the pinfold hard by the church (which was in the limits of the old castle) that, about six years ago, there was digged up several huge men bones, a jaw bone of which, a very fat man, that was standing by, easily slipt upon his own jaw.

This is a good town for water, for there is springs runs out of it on every side, and one or two is so bigg that they drive a water mill about. But it is no town of strength, there being several hills that can easily command it.

About half a mile beyond the town, in the high road betwixt Horncastle and Barton, there are a great many hills cast up all along betwixt these two mentioned towns, which were undoubtedly done by the old Romans to direct their way from one place to the other.

Most of the outward stones in this wall of the castle of Castor were charg'd with lead, as Mr. Baxter told me, who had seen several of them so done.

27. It is very observable what I heard this day about Rawby church[r] in this county, nine miles of of Brigg, to witt, that for all that it stands half-way upon the side of a great hill, yet in one side of the church, and in part of the chancel, there are such great springs, that they can scarce dig any graves there for the great quantity of water that springs there upon them. The graves are always above half full when they come to put the corps in, and that the water may not be seen, they always strew chaff or straw thereon before that they put the corps in, to hinder the water being seen by the people.[s]

[r] Rawby is, I suppose, Wrawby, but that place is only about a mile from Brigg; a portion of the town of Brigg is in Wrawby parish.
[s] The practise of putting straw at the bottom of graves when there is water in them is still common in Lincolnshire.

ABRAHAM DE LA PRYME.

About the beginning of this year I went to preach at a toon called Bramwith,[b] a mile or two of of Hatfield. There was then an old clerk there that could scarce ever get a pair of spectacles that he could see with, his sight was either so vitiated or destroyed. At last an old wife tells him a way how he might see without spectacles—to get a prayer book printed upon yellow paper. At last he got such a one, and tho' it was but a small print, yet I observed that [he] saw and read with as much ease as if it had been ever so bigg.

About half a year before my father dyd he sent one of his men to Doncaster about some business; who, as he was coming whome in the night, when it was very dark, chanc'd to meet with an *Ignis fatuus*[c] in one of the lains, which went danceing and leaping before him, and frightened him sore. But, plucking up good courage within a little while (he realy takeing it to be the divel) was resolv'd to light of of his horse and beat it. And so, accordingly, he observeing that when he went it went, and when he stood still it stood still, he lights and tys his hors to the hedge, and falls at it manfully with his great stick, and beat it all to pieces, making one piece fly one way and another. And then, being all in a sweat, he got tryumphantly upon his horse and came home, attesting seriously and soberly that he had kill'd the divel, which he did realy believe for a great while after.

The like story I have heard of another man in the south; that as he was coming from his work one dark night, in a lane, there came whisking over the hedg to him an *Ignis fatuus*, which he getting a sight on ran away from it. But the faster he ran, the faster it followed him, so that he did not [know] what to do. At length, turning him about, he up with his stick to strike it, but it

---

[b] See *ante*, p. 55.

[c] Mr Ernest Baker, of Mere Down, Bath, communicated to *Notes and Queries*, 6 Feb., 1869, (4th S., iii., p. 125), that on the 18th December previous, at about 6.45 p.m., he was riding over the Downs to Mere, when there suddenly appeared on his horse's head five lights, one on each ear larger than the rest, about the size of the flame of a small taper, of a bluish colour; two on the left eyebrow, and one on the right—these were like glow-worms, or as if the parts had been rubbed with phosphorus. It was pitch dark, with a steady rain falling, yet, while the lights lasted, (which was while he rode upwards of a quarter of a mile), he could see the buckles on the bridle. There had been thunder and lightning in the afternoon. He rode steadily, trying to make out what it could be; when it disappeared as suddenly as it came. The horse had been taken from the stable, and had only travelled half-a-mile, and did not perspire in the least. At page 182 Mr. C. W. Barkley suggests that this phenomenon was a "Will-o'-the-wisp," or "Jack-a-Lantern," and he relates a similar instance, in his own family, of its appearance. In Norfolk, he says, this luminous gas is exhaled from swampy ground, and is there called "a Lanthorn-man," and the appearance is feared to this day.

flinch'd his stroke two or three times. But he being resolved to
vanquish or dy, he followed on his strokes as if it had been for
his life, but always when he lifted up his great stick above his
head to strike it, then it flew about his ears and put him in a
most miserable condition. But, however, tho' the fight was long
and fearful, yet the fellow got the victory over this divel, and beat it
all in pieces. And he told it all over that he had killed the divel
that would needs have carry'd him away ith' lane, if he could but
have gotton hold of him. But (says he) I mall'd him.

He that told me this story affirm'd that he saw the stick that
this fellow kill'd the divel with, and says that it was stained all
black within towards the end with its strokes over this *Ignis
fatuus.*

I remember likewise that I have heard a gentleman in the
country say that he once got an *Ignis fatuus,* and affirm'd that
it was nothing but a shineing froth. He sayd that it was as like
the froth of water that is made from any high dessent as can be.

AUG. 9, 1695. Guinnes has been the greatest price this year
that ever was known. At first when this warr begun they rise,
and they have kept riseing ever since, so that now this year they
go current all over for thirty shillings, and has done ever since
the king went out. The reason how they came to rise so was the
vast quantitys that the lords and gentlemen in the king's service
carry'd out of the land. But now I hear that, for all this, yet
there is more guinnys stirring at London than ever has been
known, so that they are more plenty than silver. And the reason
thereof is this; everybody seeing how much guinnes goes for,
all that had any gold, cups, spouns, etc., carry them all into the
Tower and gets them coin'd into guinnes, paying some little for
their coining, which indeed is the true reason that they are there
stirring in such vas quantitys.

These warrs went very hard the two or three first years after
that the king came in, and there were general complaints about
the heaviness of the taxes, and everybody was anctious about the
affairs of state, and full of cares, and doubts, and fears. But now
the nation haveing become used to the taxes there is none that
either now complains or that troubles them about the state affairs;
the whole country being now in as much peace as if there was
neither any taxes nor any warrs.

Silver money being exceeding scarce, and several beginning
to complain of the little money that there was in the land, perhaps it was a piece of pollicy of K[ing] Will[iam] to make

ginnes go so much above their intrinsick worth, that, by that means, the rich misers, for lucre sake, might be entis'd to coin what gold they had, (as they have done), to the end that monney might be the more plentifull : which trap has taken effect, and so everybody talks that this great price of guinnes will fall.

About seven years ago as they were digging a cellar in Lincoln, in the chief street, the[y] found a whole large boat with a great many cut and squar'd stones therein.ᵈ

MEM. They have boar'd for coals oft here in this parish of Broughton, and other parts of Lincolnshire, and found that there was coals in the soyl, but that they lay so exceeding deep that they were discourag'd from proceeding on in their work.ᵉ

AUG. 12. Yesterday I was with an ingenious old man who had been a great royalist in King Charles the First days. Amongst other very observable things that he told me, and that we talk'd about, he says that they had a dog in their troup that every night had letters put betwixt his neck and his collar, which was made

---

ᵈ Many canoes and boats have been found in the low lands in Lincolnshire, but all, except one which is preserved in the British Museum, have perished. Mr. Peacock's grandfather, Mr. Thomas Peacock, could remember one being discovered by some workmen, whilst making a drain in the parish of Scotter. He communicated the fact to Sir Joseph Banks, who came over to see it, but he considered that the workmen had mutilated it so much that it was not worth preservation. When found, it lay in the earth, bottom upwards, and the excavators cut it in two before they discovered that it was a boat. A raft, of very primitive construction, the several pieces fastened together with wooden pegs, was found about fifty-five years ago at the foot of a sand hill, called Greenhoe, in the township of Yaddlethorpe, parish of Bottesford. The wood of which it was constructed was so sound, that the late Mr. William Hall, of Hull, to whom the property belonged, used the greater part of it for spars for some farm buildings, which were being erected on the sand hill, but a stone's throw from the place. The hill has now nearly lost its old name, by being miscalled by a former tenant Yaddlethorpe grange, The late Mr. Stark, in his *History of Gainsbrough*, second ed., p. 5, mentions a canoe found, at a depth of 8 feet from the surface, near the river Witham "about two miles east of Lincoln, between that city and Horsley Deeps." It was thirty feet eight inches long, and measured three feet across in its widest part. The thickness of the bottom was between seven and eight inches, and it was hollowed out of a single oak tree. Another canoe was discovered about two years before, in cutting a drain near Horsley Deeps, but was unfortunately destroyed by the workmen. Another has been found in a meadow near Gainsbrough, not far from the bank of the river Trent ; and two others in cutting a drain through the fens below Lincoln. Stark derived the foregoing facts from a communication made by Sir Joseph Banks to *The Journal of Science and Art*, No. ii., p. 244.

ᵉ The coal beds, if coal there be in this part of Lincolnshire, are far too deep to be worked. In sinking wells, thin beds of a carboniferous shale, strongly impregnated with iron, are frequently come upon. They are not true coals, but are probably the fossil remains of sea weeds, as ammonites and other shells, once the inhabitants of salt water, are usually found imbedded in them.

F

larg a purpose, and that he would have gone to any garrison or
place they told him off within twenty miles round about.   Talking of other ways of sending letters privately, he sayd they had
but two more ways, and they were these : the one was to make
hollow the wooden heells of a pair of old shoos, and so stopping
letters therein, and then letting a flap of the inner soal fall upon
the covering, and so to put them on a beggar's feet and send
him where they pleas'd.   The other way they had was to carry
them in a hollow stick or crutch, that beggars walks with.   'Tis
an observation all over England, that all these great captains and
officers, that had any hand in fighting against King Charles the
First, are all or most of 'em become beggars, as the[y] deserve, for
committing such an abominable act as rebellion against one of
the best of men.

15. Yesterday I was at Brigg, to hear what newse there was
stirring, but there happen'd to be none observable, the Holland
males being not come.

Yet, however, it is mightily to the honour of old England to
hear what valiant sons she now brings forth, when all forreign
nations expected her past bearing coragious men.

When the king came over in 88,ƒ there was but very few
Englishmen that knew anything of the feats of warr.   In Ireland
there was but very few commanders English, all the rest being
Dutch and French.   When they besieged Lymerick, the ingeneers
were all forreigners.   But a private soldier, called Brown, taking
notice how they cast their bombs, and how slow they were in
doing of it, he desired lieve to see what he could do, and he was
so fortunate as to outdo them, and to cast two into the citty to
their one; and he was the first ingeneer that we had since this
warr begun.

But now capt. Phillips, capt. Bendbow, my lord Barclay,
and innumerable others, are so expedite and skillfull thereat, that
they cast them as well as any one ever did.   Last year, when
they burnt Deep [Dieppè], the Marq[uis] of Choiseul, the commander, sent letters to the French king, complaining that the
English mortars were so bigg that they could stand far off at sea,
out of any cannon reach from the town, and cast their bombs
therein as they pleas'd ; and we have several mortars now that
flings or casts bombs above two miles and an half, as the French
know to their sorrow.

ƒ William began his reign February 13th, 1689.

25. Mr. Selden, the famous antiquary, gatherd up all the old ballets he could meet with, and would protest that there was more truth in them than there was in many of our historians. *Ex relat. amici mei doctiss. dom. Lewis, minist.*

26. I have been at Castor again yesterday, on some business, and from thence I went to Nettle[ton],⁵ a little mile, to see something there that I thought memorable. All along the hill side there, for at least a mile, lyes a long bed of sand, which has sprung somewhere thereabouts out of the ground, and encreas'd to the aforesayd bigness, having cover'd a great quantity of good ground, and by that means undone several poor people. Within these twenty years it begun to move towards this town, and all that part of it that layd close to the hill edge (which was about twenty-five houses, with their folds and garths) has been destroy'd by it this several years, onely there is one house, which is a poor man's, that has stood it out by his great pains and labour ; but as for his folds and gardens they are all cover'd. It had destroy'd a great deal more of this town, but that, betwixt it and the aforesayd houses that were destroy'd, there runs a strong water spring, or brook, which it cannot get over, neither can it fill it, for as soon as any great rains falls, either in summer or winter, upon the hills, it dissends through this brook, and soon washes it to its old channel again, etc. So that this quicksand, not being able to get over, it goes all along by its side and the side of the hill, and last year broke a great hedge down, and has begun to enter into a piece of excellent ground, which it will most certainly destroy. And this was the memorable thing that I went to see. I have read in the Transactions of the Royal Society of a such like sand in the borders of Norfolk, which has almost destroy'd a whole town; but that moves southward, as I remember, but this northward.

[*Three pages wanting*].

1695.

8 (Sept. ?) This day I was asking several how they got wells digg'd in this country, seeing that it is so very rocky. They told me that a well will cost five, six, seven, eight, nine, ten pound digging, and sometimes more at after, as the stone proves

---

⁵ Nettleton is a small village, about one mile south of Caistor.

softer or harder. Justice Nelstrop,[h] of Scawby, our next town, had a well digg'd about a year ago, and they were forced to digg through five or six layers of stone, some three, some four, some six, some eight inches thick, betwixt which commonly was a layer of clay. The way the[y] took to get through the stone was this: they swept the surface thereof clean, and made a great fire of wood thereon, in the well, and then cast a sackfull or two of coals on, so that there was a great fire, by the heat of which the rock gave cracks as bigg as cannon, and pieces of four or six pound weight would have flown out of the very top of the well with great force. And then, when the fire was out, they fell on with their picks and chizels, and having cutt as farr as they could, then the[y] fired again, as before, untill the[y] found a spring and gott throw the rock.

16. This day I observed a Roman way to run from Lincoln, and by this town, in a direct line to Humber side. It has been paved, and in many places the pavement is very obvious at this day,[i] as, for example, a little on this side Scawby wood, where I measur'd it seven yards broad.

Septem. About the beginning of this month happen'd a most vehement storm. The wind was north, which has done an incredible deal of damage, there being reckon'd to be lost above two hundred and fifty colliars' vessels, with all their men, and of other ships, such as pinks,[j] and such, about thirty-six; and men are cast ashore in such plenty, all along these coasts of Lincolnshire, that people are forc'd to leave their harvest and carry them away in carts to bury them. Yesterday I was with one at Brigg that was in the whole tempest, and yet escap'd. He says that about an houer before it begun, they being at sea, saw a prodigious black cloud in the north, which swelled bigger and bigger, and at last it burst asunder with the dreadfulest thunder

---

[h] Justice Nelstrop is Sir Goddard Nelthorpe, the second Baronet. He married Dorothy, daughter of Hugh Henne, esq., of Rooksnest, in Surrey, and relict of Nicholas Poultney, esq. The title became extinct, 22 Nov., 1865, on the death of Sir John Nelthorpe, Bart. Arms.—Argent, on a pale sable a sword erect of the field, pommel and hilt or.

[i] The pavement of the Ermine Street yet exists in several places. It is usually visible, especially after heavy rains, in the declivity of a little hill, immediately to the south of the gate leading from the Ermine Street to Manby Hall. Probably this is the place where De la Pryme saw it. It is in the parish of Scawby, not more than two miles from Broughton.

[j] "A small vessel, masted and rigged like other ships, but built with a round stern; the bends and ribs compassing so that her sides bulge out very much."

and lightning that ever was seen, but especialy with the latter, for it came down in such flakes that all the whole sea seem'd to be of a flame, and then, immediately after, the storm arose out of that dreadfull cloud.

29. I being in Yorkshire last week, at Sir George Cook's,[k] we heard there how that Sir William Lowther,[l] a presbiterian, hearing of a great meeting of the townsmen of Pomfrit together, he goes thither, and sends them in, in the first place, a duzen of bottels of claridd, and then a duzen more, by which time, thinking they had been a little drunk, he makes bold to go amongst them, and, after haveing complemented them exceedingly, he at length begins to tell them what he drive at, to witt, of geting their votes that he might be made a parlament man, and did tell them so many fine things, and what favours and kindness he would bestow upon, so that they scarce knew what to say. But immediately one Mr. Stables,[m] sitting at the end of the table, took him up, saying, "Sir William, we thank you for your wine, but, had we understood that this was the design thereoff, we would have raither been without. And for our votes, I must tell you truly, if I had ten thousand I would not give one of them to you, nor to any such Commonwealth's man as you are." "I a Commonwealth's man!" (says Sir William) "I defy it; I scorn to be scandaliz'd so," etc. Upon which, and a great many more words, Sir William challeng'd Mr. Stables to the door. To which Mr. Stables answer'd, "To the door! I scorn to come to the door with any such presbiterian raskal." Upon which Sir William drew at him; but the company riss up against him, bid him get him gone; what had he to do to intrude into their company, and to disturb them. And so Sir William went away, curseing and swearing how he would be reveng'd of them. Thus this Mr. Stables saved the votes of all his company; for undoubtedly, if he had not stood up to him, he had got all their votes.

Octob. 2. I was yesterday with Mr. Anderson, of this town,

[k] Sir George Cooke, of Wheatley, near Doncaster, third Baronet, died 5 October, 1732.
[l] Sir William Lowther, of Swillington and Great Preston, Bart.
[m] Probably William Stables, Alderman and twice Mayor of Pontefract. Alderman [Richard] Stables was one of the volunteers in Pontefract Castle on Christmas day, 1644. Mr. Richard Stables, no doubt the same person, was an inhabitant of that borough in the following year.—*Drake's Journal; Surtees, Miscellaneous,* pp. 3, 5, 52. There is a pedigree of this family, the Stables of Tanshelf, in *Dugdale's Visit. Ebor.,* 1665-6, p. 11.

a fine gentleman, and of a great estate.   Talking of the spaw
waters of Knaresbrough, but especialy the sulphur well, and of
the great virtue it has, amongst other things he told me that he
was there this year, and had a waiting boy with him, that for
about a month before, had been subject by times to have something
to rise up in his throat, and then to vomitt blood.   He caryed
this boy to the sulfer well, and, having made him drink heartily
of the water, he vomited up a skin, somewhat like a bladder, full
of clotted blood.   It came up, he says, by pieces, at three or four
vomits.   This is very strange, and well worth taking notice of.

This gentleman's eldest son, about fifteen years old, often
times of a sudden falls down, and cannot get any breath, yet
nothing arises in his throat, and he is as lively and vigorus a
young man as can be seen.   The only thing that dos him good,
and recovers him, is the anointing his nostrills with sweet oyl,
and the pouring a little down his throat.

OCTOB. 3.   Some may be asking in future times how the
Jacobites behaved themselves under this government, which they
were so much against.   I answer, that when anything went of
their side, they were very merry and joyfull; and, on the contrary, were as much cast down when anything went against
them.   They were frequently exceeding bold, and would talk
openly against the government, which the government conniv'd a
little at, for fear of raising any bustle, knowing that they were
inconsiderable by reason of their paucity.   They set up separate
meetings all over, where there was any number of them, at which
meetings I myself have once or twice been in Cambridge, for we
had above twenty fellows in our coll[ege] that were nonjurors.   The
service they used was the Common Prayer, and always pray'd
heartily for King James, nameing him most commonly; but, in
some meetings, they onely prayed for the king, not nameing who.

About three years ago they held a great consultation at the
then nonjuring arch-bish[op] of Canterbury's house, where about
all the chief nonjurors were present in all England, in which the
arch-bish[op] gave them rules how to behave themselves, and
how they should pray for the king, and such like.

Their meetings in Cambridge were oftentimes broken up by
order of the vice-chancellor, but then they always met again in
some private house or other.

They had a custome in our college, while I was there, which
I did not like, and that was always on publick fast days, which
was every first Wednesday in every month, they always made a
great feast then and drunk and was merry; the like they did at
London.

And at that latter place made bonefires and rung the bells on King James the Second's and the Prince of Wales's birth nights. This is all I can at present remember of them, for, God knows, I was once one of them myself, untill I was at length better inform'd.

Yesterday was Castor fair; there was almost no silver to bee seen at it, nothing but gold. Every one had five, or ten, or twenty, or one hundred guinnes a piece. There was nothing almost to be seen for all sorts of things but gold.

Остов. 20. This [day] examining and talking with several of my oldest parishoners of this town about what was memorable relating thereto, they tell me that this Roman way, of which I have already made mention, is commonly call'd amongst them the High Street way.

This country has been exceeding woody to what it is now, above half of the woods being cut down and sold about forty years ago. Here was formerly very great roberys committed in them, this being the most dangerous place in the whole country, so that people durst scarce travel in companys. In this wood towards Thorholm more, is a low sunken place call'd Gipwell,ⁿ wch was formerly a mighty deep hole, so thick beset with trees, that it was impossible to see the sun. Here it was that the rogues kept their rendisvouz and carryd all those thither that they rob'd, oftentimes murdering them and casting them therein. Within these twenty years stood a mighty great hollow tree, in which, when it was cut close up by the roots, was found a pair of pothooks.

There stood a mighty great famous tree likewise by this way side, which was cut down about thirteen years ago. It was nine yards about, had twenty load of wood in it besides it's body, and spread at least twenty-five yards each way when it was standing.

There is a good law at Worlebee, a town some few miles off, which every tennant, according to the quantity of land that he takes, is bound to plant yearly so many trees thereon; but, tho' this law is yet in force amongst them, yet it is a great pitty that it is not so much regarded as formerly.°

ⁿ There is no such place as Gipwell now. There is a deep black bog on two sides of Thornholme, and it must, I think, have been some part of this that was formerly a pond or pool; and if they put their victims in, I have no doubt they would soon sink into the bog, and never be heard of again.

° There were bye-laws, in many manors, requiring the tenants to plant trees yearly. At a court of the manor of Bottesford, held April 1st, 1579, the following, among other regulations, was decreed by the lord and jury.

"Item, that everie husbandman within this lordshippe [is] to sett euery yere vj willowes, and euery cotiger iij, and to preserve them from cattel; in doing the contrary euery husbandman to forfayte xijd., and euery cotiger vjd."

Octob. 25. The other day I was at the visitation at Ganes-burrough. I met with nothing observable by the way but some places that looked like old fortifications; only at the very entrance of the town is a large green burrow, hollow at the top, under which, as I concieve, many Dains have been buried, because that they mightily infested this town in King William the Conqueror's days. The church is no splendid piece of workmanship, but low, narrow, and dark. I had not time to observe what inscriptions there were in it.[p]

Stow[q] caused a letter to be read unto us that came from the bishops, which commanded us, amongst other things, to observe to pray for the bishops and the universitys of this land in our prayer before sermons,[r] and that we should always conclude the same with that most excellent and divine of all prayers, called the Lord's Prayer. It commanded also that every one that kept a curate should allow him proportionable to the greatness of the livings in which he officiated. And ordered likewise, that every Sunday, in the afternoon, wee should catechize and make chatechetical lectures, or else preach twice on the day, etc.

Everything was exceeding dear by reason that the king intends shortly to visite some of these parts.

Nov[ber] 9th. The latter end of the last month the king made a journey to Lincoln, and so to Welbeck and Nottingham. He brought with him not above twenty nobles from London, and his guard, besides gentlemen that he had pick'd up in the country as he came along. He got into Lincoln about seven a clock at night, and next morning went to prayers in the minster, where, after prayers, all the clergy had the honour to kiss the king's hand; and then, when that ceremony was over, the king went away, and immediataly took coach for Welbeck.

He brought with him from London all his own provision, but made little use of the same at Lincoln, for he eat nothing there but a porringer of milk. As he was at prayers several throng'd mightily about him, so that he could scarce get any wind, upon

[p] An engraving of the old church at Gainsbrough may be seen in *Stark's History of Gainsbro'*, second edition, 1843, p. 364. It was evidently a building of late perpendicular date, probably erected not many years before the Reformation. With the exception of the tower, it was pulled down in 1736.

[q] The Diarist has run his pen through "Doct." before Stow, and after it ("ye Chancellour as I think"). He must mean the Archdeacon of Stow, who, at this period, was John Hutton, M.A.; he was collated to the archdeaconry 4 November, 1684, installed 21 February, 1684-5. He died 29 April, 1712, aged 63 years, and was buried at Wapenham, in Northamptonshire.—*Le Neve*, ii., p. 81.

[r] This evidently enjoins the use of the "Bidding Prayer."

which he made signs to them with his hands to stand off.

His comeing made a vast noise in the country, and prodigious number of men went from all parts to see him; even from York, and Carlisle, and Newcastle itself, as I was credibly told.

In Lincoln there was so many, that people of all sorts were forst to ly in stables and barns, and every thing was so exceeding dear that it is incredible.

The parriters [apparritors] were sent out, all ten miles round about Lincoln, to bid the clergy come in to kiss the king's hand, and all the constables had order to acquaint all towns and gentlemen with the king's comeing to Lincoln.

I am credibly told that the town of Newark presented him with a silver scepter, curiously cut and ingraved, but he would not accept thereoff. Then they presented him with a bagg of gold, but he refused that also, he telling them that the taxes were great, etc. But at Lincoln he received one of fifty broads and fifty guinneys.

1695. For all the stirr that was made at Pomfrit about Sr. Will[iam] Lowther, yet I hear to-day that, upon better consideration, when they had not got so much wine in their heads, they have chosen him for their parliament man, after that he had clear'd himself from being a Puritan.[']

21. Having heard several more things from very good hands relating to the king's being in this country, I cannot but take notice of the same. The king was mighty nobly entertained at Sr. John Brownley's,['] twelve miles or thereabouts beyond Lincoln, S^{r.} Jo. killed twelve fat oxen and sixty sheep, besides other victuals, for his entertainment, and made the most of him and his followers that can be imagin'd. The king was exceeding merry there, and drunk very freely, which was the occasion that when he came to Lincoln he could eat nothing but a mess of milk.

When he got to Lincoln, Mr. Dorell made as much of him as he possibly could, and 'tis say'd that that night's treat cost him above 500 pound.

When he came to the Earl of Kingstone's, there was provided for him the most quantity of victuals of all manner of sorts that can be imagined. There was near twenty oxen kill'd, besides

---

['] Sir William Lowther, Mr. Monckton, and Sir John Bland, stood candidates; the two first gentlemen were returned. The latter petitioned, but afterwards withdrew the petition.

['] Sir John Brownlow, of Belton, near Grantham.

great numbers of sheeps, and twenty-five messes of different meats were all served up to the king and the nobles in huge dishes of plate, and they had all sorts of wines that can be imagined. The king's guards had every one of them two bottles of different wines set at their trenchers, and liberty to go in the earl's cellars and drink what they would.

But as for the Duke of Newcastle, tho' he went to meet his Majesty at Dunham ferry, and tho' he carryed him home to his house, yet he behaved himself the sneakinglyest to him that can be imagined for a man of his quality and figure. For, as he is commonly recon'd to be one of the richest and one of the covetiousest man in all England, so he made it appear so by his entertainment of the king, who was nothing at all made off in comparison to what he was at S^r Jo[hn] Brownley's, or Lincoln, or the Earl of Kingstone's, so that 'tis sayd that the king is sayd to have sayd that Brownley entertained him like a prince, Kingstone like an emperor, and Newcastle like a clown.

The king, because that he had the first good entertainment that he mett with in the country at S^r Jo[hn] Brownley's, he has sent up for him to London, to honour him the more, and to requite him for his kindnesses.

All gentlemen and great men whenever they came were permitted to kiss the king's hand.

The king was, as they say, mighty nobly treated at Oxford by the Earl of Ormond the Chancellour, and, in a word, has got the greatest affections that ever was known by this progress into the country.

At Lincoln, before the clergy had the great honour done unto them to be admitted to kiss the king's hand, the chanter" made this following short speech to his Majesty—

MAY IT PLEASE YOUR MAJESTY !

Wee, your Majesty's most dutifull and loyal subjects, ye chapter of this your cathedral church, together with our brethren the neighbouring clergy, humbly begg lieve to bear a part in that publick joy which ye honour of your Majesty's presence has spread through their country, and presume to take this opportunity to make your Majesty ye most humble tender of duty ; and wee beseech your Majesty to believe that we are thoroughly sensible of ye wonderfull preservation and continued favours which ye people, ye laws, ye church, and religion of England owe to your sacred Majesty, and by ye blessing of God will studdy with all our might to make such a return of duty for the same as becomes our holy function ; and, as in duty and gratitude bound, we daily beseech Almighty God to preserve and bless your Majesty's person, to prosper your arms, and prolong your reign, to continue your Majesty a terror to your enemys, and glory and blessing to these your kingdoms, and a successful

" The Precentor.

defender of the church and religion you have so happily preserved and establish'd, and, in God's good time, to crown your victorys with making your Majesty
the glorious instrument of restoaring and establishing the peace of all Chris-
tendome.

This is the speech, and I had it sent to me from Lincoln
under Doct[or] Holm's own hand, having imploy'd a friend to
get it for me.

29. It having been hitherto the finest weather that can be
desired, more like summer than winter, I observed that the crows
are busy in building their nests just as if it was spring. I have read
somewhere that there has been found young crows at Christmass
time, and I remember that it was look'd upon as an ill omen, but
there's nothing ominous in it.

DEC^{BER.} 7, 1695.· I was with Mr. Castor, a learned and ingenious man, this evening, and, talking of diverse things, he tells
me that the same Collonel Lilliston[v] that was a soldier in Cromwel's days for the parliament, was a relation of his, and, that which
is observable, he says that he, the same Lilliston, was the twentyeth
child of his parents, by one man and one woman, and that they
all lived to men and woman's estate. After which Col. the same
two people had some three or four children more, all girls, which
lived.

He says that Cromwel had a great many soldiers in each
country which they calld eight-pound men, because they had
sallerys of eight pound a year whether they served in the warrs or no.

---

[v] Recent investigations into the pedigree of Lillingston can only discover
the existence of thirteen children. Colonel Lillingston married Elizabeth, dau.
of Marmaduke Dolman, of Bottesford, co. Lincoln, and is said to have died in
Holland in 1682. Some dim tradition of him is remembered by old people
sixty years ago. He was spoken of as a hard featured man, who always wore
a steel breast-plate, and held very strong puritan opinions. He had several
children, the only one whom it is needful to mention is Luke Lillingston, born
at Bottesford 22 October, 1655, when his father was the owner of the property by
parliamentary title. He entered the Dutch service, and had a subordinate command at the siege of Grave. He was afterwards appointed Colonel of an English
regiment. He served in Ireland and the West Indies, and rose to the rank of
Lieut.-General. He contributed to literature a pamphlet called "Reflections
on Mr. Barchet's Memoirs," 8vo., London, 1704. I am not aware that it has any
other interest now, except that which attaches to excessive rarity. Only some
three or four copies are known. There is one in the British Museum. He died
at North Ferriby, co. York, 6 April, 1713, and was buried in the church there
on the 9th of the same month, where there is the following inscription to his
memory. "Here lye the bodyes of Brigadier Luke Lillingston (Son of Colonel
Henry Lillingston, late of Bottesford, in the County of Lincoln) who departed
this life April the 6th., 1713, in the 60th year of his age ; and of Elizabeth his
wife (daughter of Robert Saunderson, late of Bommel, in the Province of
Guelderland), who dyed October the 18th, 1699, aged 53.

23. I heard this of my patron, that is just come from London, that the king, as he was going to Oxford, was told by one of his nobles (but upon what grounds it is uncertain) that his Majesty should be poison'd at Oxford, and desired him not to tast of any of their entertainment. Upon which, when he came to Oxford, he was exceedingly welcom'd, and carryed to the theater, which was full of gentry in all the gallerys, and there was a most splendid repast provided. But the king came in with his lords and nobles, and took a view of all, and having walked about for a while went out. As he was going out several of the mobb throng'd in, upon which the gentlemen in the gallerys hist at them; and the king, not understanding the meaning thereoff, thought they hiss'd at him, and took it very ill, until that the Chancellor and several of the heads of the university hearing thereoff went and told the king the true reason of their hissing.

A great many more things I could relate about the king's being in the country, but I am very suspitious of them, therefore shall not set any of them down.

29. Yesterday, James Middleton came over from Hatfield. He tells me a very merry thing that happen'd at Wroot, in the Isle, lately. Mr. Parrel there had a great lusty man-servant, but, as appears by the sequell of the discourse, not of very much witt. About two months ago, there comes a maggot into his head to turn padder upon the highway; so he acquaints his master with his resolution. "Master," says he, "I have been two years in your service, and what I get is inconsiderable, and will scarce suffice my expenses; and I work very hard. I fancy," says he, "that I could find out a better way to live, and by which I should have more ease and more money." "Ey," says his master, "pray what is that?" "It is," says he, "by turning padder." "Alass! John," says he, "that will not do; take my word," says he, "you'll find that a harder service than mine." "Well, but I'll try," says the man. And so, next morning, away he went, with a good clubb in his hand; and, being got in the London road, somewhere about Newark or Grantham, there overtook him on the road a genteel man on horseback. John letts him come up to him, and taking his advantage, he catches hold of his bridle, and bidds him stand and deliver. Upon which he of horseback, being a highwayman himself, he began to laugh that a thief should pretend to rob a thief. "But," says he, "harken, thou padder, I'm one of thy trade; but surely, thou'rt either a fool or one that was never at the trade before." "No sir," says John, "I never was at this

trade in my life before." "I thought so," says the highwayman; "therefore, take my advice, and mind what I say to
you. When you have a mind to robb a man, never take hold of
his bridle and bid him stand, but, the first thing you do, knock
him down, and, if he talk to you, hit him another stroke, and
say, 'Sirrah! you rogue, do you prate?' And then," says the
highwayman, "you have him at your will," etc. Thus they
walk'd on for about a mile, the highwayman teaching the other
his art; and as they were going a by way to a certain town, they
comes to a badd lane. Says the padder to the other on horsback
" Sir, I am better acquainted with this country than perhaps you
are, this lane is very badd, and you'll indanger [of] lying fast,
therefore you may go through this yate,[w] and along the field
side, and so miss all the ill way." So he took his advice, and
going that way the padder went the other way, and coming to
the place where the highwayman should ride through a gapp into
the lane again, this rogue, this padder, stands under the hedge,
and as soon as ever he sees the highwayman near him, he lends
him such a knock over the head that he brought him down
immediately. Upon which he began to say, " Sarrah, you
rogue, is this your gratitude for the good advice that I gave
you?" " Ah! you villain, do you prate?" And with that
gave him another knock. And so, having him wholy at his mercy,
he takes almost fifty pound from him and gets upon his horse,
and away he rides home to his master at Wroot, by another way,
as fast as he could go, and being got home he goes to his master
and tell's him, saying—" Tash! master, I find this a very hard
trade that I have been about, as you sayd it would prove, and I am
resolved to go no more, but be contented with what I have gott.
I have got a good horse here, and fifty pound in my pocket, from a
highwayman, and I have consider'd that I cannot be prosecuted
for it, therefore I'll live at ease," etc.

1696.

JAN. 2. The king having issued out his royal proclamation,
towards the end of the last year, that no clipped money should go
but unto such a day, it has made a vast noise in the country, and
most people grumbles exceedingly because that the time is so

---

[w] Yate. Gate, the common form of the word throughout the north of
England and Lincolnshire.

"Seest thou not yonder hall, Ellen?
Of redd gold shine the yates."

Childe Waters, l. 72, Percy's folio MS., vol. II., pt. ii., p. 271.

short, and there is no penalty layd upon those that refuses it until the appointed time. They say the rabble has been up at London about it, but they are settled again, and there was a libell flung up and down the streets, which the king and parliament have promis'd two thousand pounds to any one that will discover the author thereoff.

19. Chattel eats turnops in this country better than they'll do hay, and they make them so sportly, lively, and vigorous that they play and leap like young kidds.

Three pages wanting.

Doct[or] Pierce*z* is a very learned and ingenious man, (if he be yet alive), he preached a sermon that got him a great deal of reputation and honour, takeing for his text these words, "From the beginning it was not so." This was chiefly levell'd against the papeists, and shew'd the novelty of popery, how that it was not known in the primitive times of christianity. Not long after this, the Doct[or] (being of —— coll[ege] in Oxford), caused the bowling-green of the sayd coll[ege] to be plow'd up and sawn with turnips, because that the schollers spent a great deal of their time there in that sport. Upon which, one of them, a while after, when the turnips were grown up, made the following copy of verses, and pasted them one night upon his dore :—

> Where bools did run, now turnips grow,
> But from y*e* beginning it was not so.

Reflecting ingeniously in the latter line upon the Doct[or's] celebrated sermon.

---

z Thomas Pierce, son of John Pierce, was born at Devizes, co. Wilts., (of which town his father was several times Mayor), was Rector of Brington, co. Northampton, President of Magdalen College, Oxford, and was installed Dean of Salisbury 4th May, 1675, which dignity he kept to his dying day. In the year 1683 arose a controversy between him and Dr. Seth Ward, Bishop of Salisbury, concerning the bestowing of the dignities of the church of Salisbury, whether by the king or bishop. Dr. Pierce wrote a narrative on behalf of the king, which was answered by Dr. Ward; but neither was published. Pierce, however, wrote a pamphlet in vindication of the king's sovereign right, which was printed in London in 1683. He also wrote many other works, a list of which may be seen in *Bliss's Athenæ Oxonienses*, vol. iv., p. 299. He, dying 28 March, 1691, was buried at North Tidworth, near Ambersbury, co. Wilts., (where, several years before, he had purchased an estate), at which time a book, composed by Dr. Pierce, was given into the hands of every person invited to the funeral, instead of rings and gloves. This book was entitled " Death considered as a door to a life of glory, penn'd for the comfort of serious mourners, and occasioned by the funerals of several friends, particularly of one who died at Easter, and of the Author's own funeral in antecessum." There is a long account of him in *Catalogue of Fellows of Magdalen College, Oxon*.

Guinneys gos yet at thirty shill[ings] a piece.

All sorts of commoditys has sold very well ever since the warr begun, and bears a good price to this day. Wool is nineteen and twenty shillings a stone. Barly is twenty two sh[illings] a quarter, and in Yorkshire twenty-eight, etc.

FEBR. 5. At Upper Reasby there has been a pretty large handsome town formerly, but now 'tis all vanished but one single large farm-house. There has been a pretty larg church there, well built, as appears from part thereof now standing, and the tradition of the place says that it has had four bells, two of which were broke, and the other two given to the church of Roxby, within the memory of man.[y]

6. And this day I went to Gokewell,[z] formerly called Goy-kewell, which was a nunnery. It seems to have been a most stately place.[a] The walls has compassed in betwixt twenty and thirty akers of ground. They shew'd me a little well, which, by tradition, was once very great and famous ; this they called Nun's Well. It has run straight through the midst of this ground, being a great spring, and it fedd all the house with water, and several statues or water fountains in the courts and gardens. The part of the old building that stands is but very small, one room at most. Here was a church within this nunnery, as the constant tradition says, part of which, being fitt to fall, was pull'd down about ten years ago ; and as they digged deep, to set down a stoop for a yate, the[y] found, at about four foot deep, the pavement of the sayd church consisting of larg four square pavers all leaded. Part of the orchard walls of this nunnery is yet standing, and there has spread upon it and knitt into it an ivy that has mightily preserved it, and will keep it firm and strong many

[y] There is evidence of there once having been a village at Risby. Green mounds may still be seen, by which the forms of houses may be traced. They were probably simply cottages around the hall. This hall, once the residence of Sir John Aylmer, Kt., third son of John Aylmer, Bishop of London, has long disappeared. Its site is occupied by a farm house of the better class. The estate has been in the possession of the family of Elwes, of Great Billing, in Northamptonshire, for several generations. The church of Risby has long disappeared, the foundations alone remaining. The form of the chancel, nave, and tower, may still be distinctly made out, as also the enclosure fence of the church-yard, now but a green bank.

[z] There is but little known about this small religious house. A few sculptured stones remain of its buildings. Among the proceedings of the Lincolnshire Architectural Society for 1854, pp. 104-8, are transcripts of four grants of land which were once made to it.

[a] It was built by one Mr. Will. D'Awtrey, in lattin De altâ ripâ.—*Marginal Note by diarist.*

years, in the stones of which wall are innumerable belemnites. There was a little town, as there most commonly was wherever were religious houses; the chappel that belonged to it was pulld down and converted into a dwelling house, which stands on the north side of this nunnery, and is, to this day, called the chappel house.

7. This day I made another journey, and that was to Rantrop,[b] to enquire for antiquitys there. I find that it's true name is Ravensthorpe, and that there has been a town there, as is apparent from the foundations of many houses. I was shewed a place likewise, which the constant tradition of the inhabitants says was a chappel, and the cloas is called Chappel cloase unto this day. This place is in Appleby parish, for all that our parish of Broughton is betwixt. They talk that there has been a religious house here, or however, as I am rather apt to believe, a college of monks belonging to Thornholm in the parish of Appleby, and very probable it is that the lord of this Rantrop, tho' it was in Broughton parish, might give the same unto the monks of Thornholm, and so by that means it perhaps came to be annexed to Appleby parish, tho' it be realy and truly in this of Broughton. All the houses at this Ravensthorp is now but three or four.

When the religious houses were standing in petty towns, the towns got a great sustinence by them; but they being pull'd down, was the reason of the towns falling to ruin. Tomorrow I go see Thornton, if it be fair weather.

8. Yesterday I could not go to Thornton, as I proposed, but however went to Castrop[c] in this parish, which town was formerly

[b] Raventhorp, pronounced by the common people Ranthrup, is a detached township belonging to the parish of Appleby. There are some obscure traces of foundations yet visible. It is not probable that the place was ever much more populous than it is now. There is at present but one farm house and a few cottages. The last census return gives the population as 26.

[c] Castlethorpe, pronounced by the common people Castorp, the same exactly as the Domesday spelling. When the Domesday survey was made, it formed a part of the possessions of Durant Malet; and the following charter shews that this township, or a portion of it, was in the hands of the family of Painel, at a shortly subsequent period. The hand in which the charter is written and other circumstances, I am informed, indicate that it is not of later date than the reign of Henry II.

"Notum sit omnibus, tam præsentibus quam futuris, quod ego Willelmus Painel dono, & concedo, & hâc meâ cartâ confirmo Philippo de Alta Ripa, filio Antonii de Alta Ripa, dimidiam carucatam in Kaisthorp, quam Antonius de Alta Ripa tenuit de me; cum tofto quod idem Antonius tenuit in eadem villa in feudo & hæreditate; sibi & hæredibus suis tenendam de me & hæredibus meis, in bosco

call'd Castlethorp, from a great castle that was there in King John's days, the ruins of which are now scarce to be seen, onely the place where it stood is called Castle Hill to this day. On the east side on the town, on your right as you go down to the commons, here are a great many foundations of houses to be seen. It has been as bigg again as it is, and was once a parish of itself. They say that it had a larg chappell at it formerly, where now stands the stable on the south side of the east fold. I fancy that there has also been a religious house there where now the hall stands, because that I have observ'd, in the walls thereoff, arch'd windows, very low, near the ground, with cherubim heads on, and, in a neighbouring house over against the way, I say [saw] a piece of ceiling with these letters on in great characters, J.H.C., which signifies *Jesus hominum Salvator;* and this hall, I observe, has been moated about with a very deep ditch, as most religious houses were. This hall was built about the year 1600 (as appears from a stone over the gate), out of the ruins perhaps of the religious house.

About fifty years since there was another great hall here, that stood in the great cloase that lyes full west of this hall, the foundations of which are yet visible. There is to be seen about this hall these two coats of arms in stone.[d]

1695-6. 25. Being at Brigg yesterday with Mr. Morley, of Redburn, or Retburn, as it is in old deeds, and being talking of various things, he says that about four years ago there happened a mighty rain and a great flux of the springs, which are all about these townes here in Lincolnshire, and he says that he himself saw and beheld, in all the gutters and rivelets of water in the streets and in the flodges,[e] great quantities of little young jacks, or pickerels,

---

& plano, in pratis & pasturis, in viis & semitis, in aquis, infra villam & extra villam, & in omnibus locis, pro homagio suo, liberam & quietam ; reddendo mihi & hæredibus meis xijd. ad Pentecosten pro omnibus serviciis quæ ad me pertinent & hæredes meos. His testibus, Roberto de Gaunt, Petro de Alta Ripa, Toma Peitevin, Willelmo de Hedune, Philippo de Alta Ripa, Nigello filio Wimarc, Alexandro de Alretune, Adamo Painel, Theobaldo, Ricardo Painel, Gilberto Painel, Willelmo filio Gamelli, Willelmo de Plaiz, Hugone de Startune, Jordano filio Roberti." (Seal gone).

The township most probably takes its name from an earthwork. A castle, in the sense in which the word is now commonly used, can scarcely have existed there at so early a time.

[d] Two shields are here sketched, one of them quarterly, but the charges have not been inserted.

[e] Flodge. A small sheet of water of very slight depth, on a nearly level surface. It is no doubt a hard form of the word Flash, Flosh, or Fleesh. It bears the same relation to Flash as Splotch does to Splash, Slodge or Sludge to

G

about the length of a man's fingure, and that when the waters were gone they all dy'd. I ask'd him whence he thought they came. He sayd he could not certainly tell, but that some thought they came from the clouds with the rain, but that he for his part believed that they came out of the springs, and that they bred there in great caverns of the earth. Upon which I told him the history of the great lake in Carniola,*/ which mightily pleas'd him, and confirmed him in his opinion.

We had the newse yesterday of a great plot being discovered, and how the king had like to have been kill'd, and how that K[ing] J[ames] was ready to land, etc., which has putt the nation into an exceeding great fright; they resolving every[where], as well in citty as country, to stand by the king with their lives and fortunes.

[MARCH] 10. I was yesterday with one Mr. Nevil, of Winterton,* who I found to be a very ingenious man. He has several old MSS. by him. One is a history or chronicle of England in

Slush, or Pitch to Pick. The other form, Flash, is yet a common provincialism in Lincolnshire. Ferry Flash, near Hardwick Hill, on Scotton Common, appears in the Ordnance map.

f Carniola, a duchy in Germany, of which Lanbach is the capital.

g John Nevil, of Winterton, was a member of a family that had been settled at Faldingworth, in the county of Lincoln, from an early period. The late Mr. Williamson Cole Wells Clark, of Brumby, had a pedigree of this race, labelled "Nevil's pedigree of Faldingworth. Collected out of evidences and ancient records in the custody of Mr. John Nevile, nunc de Faldingworth, 1641, by Dr. Sanderson, bishop of Lincolne." It was not in the doctor's autograph, and contained some entries of a later period than his death, but there is no reasonable doubt of its genuineness. Many of the charters from which it was compiled are in Mr. Peacock's possession. The pedigree begins with a certain Thomas de Nová Villá, "circa tempus conquestoris Angliæ," after whom follow four generations, for whose existence there is no other evidence except in this table, then comes a Thomas de Nevil, whose wife was named Johanna ...... they are the first of the race whose existence appears to be proved by record evidence. From this Thomas, John Nevil, in whose possession the family papers were when Sanderson made the pedigree, was the twelfth in direct succession. He was born in 1605 ; his wife was Jane, daughter of Henry Nelson, of Hougham, co. Lincoln. This gentleman's second son was John Nevil, the person mentioned in the text. He married for his first wife, Ann, daughter of John Morley, of Winterton, (See *Peacock's Church Furniture*, p. 164), but had no issue by her. His second wife was Elfame Gravenor, one of the Gravenors of Messingham, but whose daughter is not quite certain, as the parish register is defective at the time her baptism would be entered. They were married 20 Nov., 1661, at that village. By this latter match he had three children, John, Edward, and Anne. Mr. Nevil filled the office of coroner for this part of Lincolnshire at the end of the seventeenth century. His papers relating to inquests are in Mr. Peacock's possession. The following is from the Winterton parish register. 1701. "Mr. Johne Neville was buried December the thirteenth." His son John, who lived at Ashby, in the parish of Bottesford, was buried at Winterton 19 April, 1736. There is no stone to either of them in church or church-yard. The Arms of the family are, Or, a chief indented vert, over all a bend gules.

many vols. folio, writ by one of his ancestors in 1577. He has also a book of heraldry in a vast large fol. as bigg as a church bible, made by the famous Bish[op] Sanderson, etc. He tells me also that Mad[am] Pelham, of Brocklesby hall, has several old MSS. belonging to mon[as]tres. This Mad[am] Pelham was daughter to Mr. Wharton, of Beverly, frequently call'd the rich Wharton, because that he was the richest man, for to be a gentleman only, that was in all England, for he was worth fifteen thousand pound a year, etc.

14. Yesterday I was sent for upon extraordinary business into the Levels, which having dispatch'd, I was told a very tragical story that happen'd at Epworth about three weeks ago; which is this. Ann, the wife of Tho[mas] White, being turned anabaptist, or dipper,[a] they went with her, to perform the cere- mony of dipping upon her, to a pond or well in one of the closes near adjoyning on the south side of the town. So the[y] put her in ; upon which shee cryd out, " Oh! something pricks me ! something pricks me !" Upon which the godly that stood by cryd out, " It's your sinns ! it's your sinns ! Lord have mercy upon you! it's your sinns !" Upon which they sayd to their elder, " Dipp her again over the head ;" she yet crys out something pricks her ! and thus they dipp'd the poor woman over the head five or six times, untill they almost drowned her, and when shee came out shee lived not over a day. It seems that there was fall'n some thorns in the well, or else some unlucky lad had put them in, and it was them that prick'd her so, and not her sins, as the godly thought. The woman was a young pretty woman, one that I had often seen formerly, and had been marry'd about half a year.

12. 'Tis a very strange thing most of the soil of this country is full of shelfish ; and such shelfish as are not described by any writers. In a quarry at Ravensthorp, or Rantrop, in this parish, was found, about half a foot within the stone, whole branches and boughs of trees, all petryfyd, and I have by me now a sort of fruit somewhat like a gord which I myself struck out of a huge stone, etc.[i]

13. I heard an old man this day, that was one [of] Crom-

---

[a] In the parish register of Crowle, co. Lincoln, is the following baptism : 1714-5. " Mary Stabler (aged about 21 years & born of Dipper parents)." Feb. 20.

[i] The fossil like a gourd was probably an Echinus, three or four species of which have been found in the Lincolnshire oolite of this neighbourhood.

well's soldiers, say that clergymen in his great master's days
were no more esteem'd of than pedlars.   He added that they
could not go any where from home but they were dispiz'd and
scoff'd at, and the little children in the streets would point at
them, and call them blackcoats, such was the abominable wickedness of them times!   He says that it was not onely the Epis-
copall clergy that were thus despis'd, but also even the Puritans
themselves, "for," say'd he, "the people grew perfectly atheis-
tical."

14. All sorts of money now goes very well again, great and
little, nobody refuses it, tho' the proclamation says that it shall
not go beyond such a time.   The nation was at a great chock at
first about it, but all is well enough now.   It was it undoubtedly
that gave breeding unto the late great plot, etc.

20. This day I was with Mr. Parker,[j] a great papist.   (He's
an esq., and an ingenious man, but hot as fire).   I ask'd him a
great many questions relating to this plott,[k] but would answer
but little.   Then I asked him if it was true what was related of
his seing an apparition two days before that we heard that the
late great plot was discoverd, and he did boldly attest it to be
true, and is as certain of it as ever he was of anything that ever
he saw.   He related it thus to me.   " Coming," says he, " home
from Gainsburrow, not being at all in drink, by moonlight,
being about ten a clock at night, I chanc'd to look on my left
hand, and I saw walking hard by me the appearancys of six men
carrying a corps, uppon which, being somewhat frighted, I
held my horse fast, and set forward, but saw it following of me
yet as oft as I look'd back.   Then, having got pretty far, I
look'd behind me once more, and instead of the corps and men
following of me I saw a bear with a great huge uggly thing
sitting thereon, which thing I saw as oft as I look'd.   Then of a
suddain it disappear'd in a flash of fire, which made my horse
leap out of the way and through [threw] me just when I had
got to . . . . . town end.   Going into the town, much
affrighted, but telling nobody, I hired a man to seek my horse,
and there I lodged."   This he will take his oath off.   But I

---

[j] Parker the papist was no doubt one of the family of Parker of Castlethorpe, some of whose monumental inscriptions are in Broughton church, (see
postea).   The family became extinct in the last century, and their property is now
in the possession of the Earl of Yarborough.
[k] The plot mentioned is the conspiracy against the life of William III.,
known as Barclay and Fenwick's plot.

not giveing much heed to such things as these—"Come," sayd I, "Mr. Parker, I'll interpret your vision unto you, that you may know what it means. The corps you saw carryd is the dead plot, which some papists have been carrying on to destroy the relm. The bear is King James that was coming, and the great uggly thing riding upon him was the King of France, for never prince would have been so ridden by the French king as he would have been had the plott taken. And the flash of fire (sayd I), in the exit of the scene, shews the suddain exit out of this life of these wicked conspirators, and their reward for the same hereafter must be fire everlasting." At which words he was so mad he did not know what to do, and went his way out of the room.

This Parker is thought most certainly to have been in the plot, and so this apparition appeared to him two days before the knowledge of the discovery of it was known in the country.

MARCH the 29th. This day I was at Mr. Edwin Anderson's,[l] and his lady and I fell into discourse about old age, and how old people lived formerly to what they do now. Shee told me that shee herself knew a woman very well that got all her teeth again, and her hair, after shee was eighty years old. Shee lived at Scotter; and I have heard since that it was most certainly true.

Shee told me also that, about twenty years ago, as her father was dressing a great pond, by or in Scotter, there was cast up out of it three or four score little pretty images about a foot long, some in one posture some in another, but delicately cutt of alabaster and other sorts of stones, and one or two there was of bras, one of which had a leg broken of.

What these has been I cannot imagine,[m] whether popish or pagan idols. Shee has promised me shee'l procure me one or two, and then I shall be better able to judge what they are. I never heard of any monastry or religious house being at Scotter, so that I cannot conceive what they have belong'd to. See Cambd[en], new ed., p. 829. Such have been frequently found in old Roman towns in Cumberl[and].

---

l Edwin Anderson.—See *postea*.

m Portions, no doubt, of tabernacle work out of some church. Some images, exactly corresponding to this description, were found at Epworth, in the Isle of Axholme, some years ago. An account of them, with engravings, was communicated by Archdeacon Stonehouse to *Willis' Current Notes*. Mr. Stonehouse's original drawings are in his interleaved copy of "The Isle of Axholme," in the library of the Dean and Chapter of Lincoln.

There are a vast number of men taken up that had a hand in the late plott. They reckon that there are above two thousand five hundred warrens out for takeing of the rogues up. But they are taken fast enough without warrens, the 1000*l.* in new mill'd monney for the greatest rogues, and 500 for the less, dos feats, and there could never [have] been invented a better way to apprehend them than by doing so. Besides, some of them have got their pardons and 1000*l.* to boot for discovering the whole conspiracy, so that in a little time we shall have a full acount of every thing that these rogues did intend to do. 'Tis sayd that there will be a great many men suffer.

APR. 1. I went this day to see Mr. Sy, minist[er] of Wintringam. I enquired and lookt about for antiquitys, but could find none scarce. The old Roman way has come streight from Lincoln thither. It leaves Winterton on the west and Wintringham on the east, and there are great foundations dug and plough'd up hard by this way near Humber, which I take to have been some old beach made by the Romans to bring and secure their shipps in, because that it encompasses a great piece of land, and is warp up. Here is a place in the town call'd chappel garth, from which we may gather that there has been a chappel. In the church there is nothing observable but a Knight Templer. Formerly, on the south side of the parsonage or minister's house, there stood a great hall, but now it is all gone. The minister of this town pays to the king two shillings with a few pence as due for the nunnery of Goquell or Goykwell. I saw also an old coin or two of the Roman emp[ire] that had been found there.

7. On the seventh instant I went to Lincoln, and took notice of the country all along as I rid, but saw nothing at all observable but the old Roman way upon which we rid to the citty. It is twenty long miles, I think, from Broughton thither, and I wonder that the Romans has left us no monuments all along this way but the way itself. Some miles of this side Spittle, as you go, here seems a bury, etc. The reason why we meet with none here is perhaps because that this part of the nation was but meanly inhabited by the old Brittons, so that when the Romans came hither they had nobody all this way to oppose them, so had no need to cast up any fortifications or intrenchments.

Spittle seems to have been an old place;" there being some old buildings there perhaps gave name to the town, that an old spittle or hospital or two, wherein were maintaind poor people infected with any contagious spreading distemper, as the plague, leprosy, or the like. Perhaps there may be some other pieces of antiquitys there also, but I had not time to alight or stay. The town seems to have been much bigger than it is now.

From thence we went to Lincoln. The old citty stood all upon a hill; and there was one inhabitant of the citty with us that let us see how farr the bounds of it had formerly gone, and that is as farr as the field now goes, which is a mile, so that now here is corn where once the citty stood. When we got near the town we observed some deep trenches, and saw the fort, and the minster, which last place is a most delicate building and mighty stately.

We overtook upon the road an English gentleman, factor in Norway, with a Norwegian gentleman in company with him, so we went to Lincoln together, and lodged together, and had a great deal of talk about Norway, it's people, religion, soil, woods, trees, beasts, birds, buildings, etc. He says that the nation is exceeding poor, and that the king gets one part of a man's yearly estate throuought the whole land: that the commonality are almost meer slaves, and mightily lorded over by their land-lords. He confirms that which Mr. Boyl says of the exceeding

" Spital-in-the-street is a hamlet in the parish of Hemswell. A hospital existed here from a remote period. Its funds were augmented by Thomas de Aston, canon of Lincoln, in the reign of Richard II. The chapel, a mean modern building, stands on the old site. On its front is the following inscription :—

FVI A⁰ D'NI 1398)
NON FVI   1594 }· DOM. DEI & PAVPERVM
SVM   1616)
        QVI HANC DEUS HVNC DESTRVET.

On the wall of a cottage, once an alms-house, is this :—
        DEO ET DIVITIBUS
        A⁰ D'NI 1620.

The sessions for the parts of Lindsey were held here in the seventeenth, and early part of the eighteenth, century. The court house remains, but it is now used as a barn. Daniel De Foe, or whoever was the author of the *Tour thro' the whole Island of Great Britain*, (ed. 1742, vol. iii., p. 10), gives an inscription which he saw upon this building.

HÆCCE DOMUS DAT, AMAT, PUNIT, CONSERVAT. HONORAT,
ÆQUITIAM, PACEM, CRIMINA, JURA, BONOS. 1620.

Which he renders into English verse a shade more rugged than the original.
        This court does right, loves peace, preserves the laws,
        Detects the wrong, rewards the righteous cause.

The stone remains still, but in a mutilated state.—See *Allen's Lincolnshire*, vol. ii., p. 38 ; *Notes and Queries*, 1st S., vol. ix., pp. 492, 552, 602 : vol. x., p. 273.

The old court-house has the arms of Sanderson upon it, with the badge of Ulster.

great heat sometimes there, so that it is not possible almost to abide it. The religion there profes'd is Lutherane, and they are mighty religious and great maintainers of the same.

They have none of our blind enthusiasticks amongst them, but has an excellent law which commands most strictly any one's head to be cutt of immediately that shall pretend to teach or inculcate any other doctrine there than that of Luther's, so that, by that means, they preserve the peace of the country and their religion mightily. There is not any one suffered to preach there unles of their faith, no not if they belong to envoys, ambassadors, or any factorys.

There are vast quantitys of bears, foxes, leopards, and wild ravinous beasts, which impoverish the country mightily by their destroying of cattel, and wolves are seen there in whole flocks like sheep.

The gentleman's name was Mr. Heddon, and the Norway man's name was James Beorgdendish; they both came from Dram,° in Norway.

When I came from Lincoln I left Spittle on the east, and so passing through Kirton, a fine larg town, (it having one of the three largest fields about it that is in all England),ᵖ came to Bottsworth,ᵠ which signifyes apple-town, and haveing some

---

° Probably the sea port of Drammen, near Christiana.

ᵖ Kirton-in-Lindsey. When De la Pryme says that this place had about it one of the three largest fields in England, he could not mean that the open fields in the parish of Kirton were very vast, as the whole parish, including the old enclosure, only contains 4,510 acres. In his time the whole of the country, with the exception of some small plots of enclosed land, was open on all sides of this place for many miles.

ᵠ Bottsworth is the present popular name for the village of Bottesford. Budlesforde, Bulesford, (Domesday); Botlesford, (Rot. Chart., 55, Hen. III., pars I); Botelford, Bottilford, (Testa de Nevil, 311b., 344); Botenesford, (Tax. p. Nicholai, iv., circa 1291, p. 75b. The manor belonged to the Knights of St. John of Jerusalem. Bottesford passed through the hands of many owners during the first fifty years that followed after the fall of the Religious Houses. In 1595 it formed a part of the large estates of the Tyrwhitt family ; on the 20th September in that year Marmaduke Tyrwhitt, of Scotter, and Robert Tyrwhitt, his son and heir, sold it to William Shawe, of Brumby, and Thomas Urry, of Messingham, from the former of whom, the present owner, Mr. Peacock, is lineally descended. The Diarist is very far wrong in his derivation of the name. It may be taken from some Saxon or Danish personal name, but it is far more probable that it is simply the village or dwelling at the ford Bòtel, Bòtl, Bùtl, Anglo-Saxon for dwelling, and Ford, a ford.

The church is a very beautiful one. The chancel being, for its size, one of the finest specimens of Early English architecture in existence, but the Diarist is wrong in saying it is "all of squared stone." The walls are rubble, with the exception of the door and window jambs and the buttresses. The clerestory windows are alternately circles and short lancets. The chancel lights are very narrow lancets, some of which are engraved in *Sharpe's Window Tracery*. The

business there, I stay'd a while, and then went to see the church, which is indeed very well and very artificialy built all of squared stone. There is no monuments in it, but it is very observable for its strange sort of windows. In the upper story of the church they are all round, but in the lower, almost all over the church, they are very long and narrow, scarce a foot wide, with a great deal of painted glass in them, representing many passages in the Bible, which renders the church somewhat dark, and, by that means, strikes some sort of a divine fear and horror in the minds of the religious that come to perform their devotions thither.

I ask'd the Norway gentl[man] about witches,[r] and he says he never saw any, nor heard but little talk of them.

1696. APRIL 10. I was with an old experienced fellow to-day, and I was shewing him several great stones, as we walked, full of petrifyd shell-fish, such as are common at Brumbe, etc. He sayd he believed that they grew ith' stone, and that they were never fish. Then I ask'd him what they call'd 'em : he answer'd

---

stained glass has all perished. Among some manuscript memoranda of the late archdeacon Stonehouse occurs the following notes on Bottesford church.

" In this church I commenced my ministerial labours as curate to Dr. Bayley, on Sunday, 16th day of October, in the year 1815. The church was then in a somewhat dilapidated condition—old benches interspersed with high square pews—there were then many remnants of fine old stained glass in the windows, especially in the great chancel and in the north transept. That in the north transept contained a representation of the crucifixion. It was purloined out of the church during some repairs. Mr. Clarke, of Ashby, told me that, when he was a boy, he used frequently to go with his playmates and break these windows to make toys of the glass ; that the church was open both by night and day, and in bad weather cattle were driven in for shelter."

One monumental stone still exists in the church, in a mutilated condition, which De la Pryme appears not to have noticed. It reads, HIC JACET JOH'A UXOR RICARDI BELLINGH'M ARMIG' . . . . . CVI A'TE P'PI'ET' DEV' AMEN. The lady commemorated was Johanna, daughter of John Harbert, and relict of William Morley, of Holme. The remains of an early English cross exist in the church-yard : it is probably coeval with the earliest part of the church. Some fragments of a Norman, or perhaps Saxon, font were found during the restoration of the chancel, about ten years ago. The present font is of Early English character. An ancient gravestone, 5 feet 3½ inches in length, was found, in 1865, over a body in the church-yard at Bottesford, in the angle formed by the north wall of the chancel and the east wall of the north transept. Bottesford was a preceptory of the Knights of St. John of Jerusalem, and it is possible that the gravestone is a memorial of one of that brotherhood. The cross on the stone is incised. A sketch of it was communicated to the Society of Antiquaries by Mr. Peacock, the local secretary for Lincolnshire, and was engraved in vol. iii. of their proceedings, 2nd S., p. 164,

[r] The word has been partly erased in the original.

milner's thumbs,' and adds that they are the excellentest things
in the whole world, being burnt and beat into powder, for a
horse's sore back : it cures them in two or three days.　He says
that there has carryers' men come out of Yorkshire to fetch the fish
thither for the sayd purpose.　So I have heard that some mid-
wifes will give anything to get these sorts of shell-fish that [are]
found here about this town of Broughton, especialy muscles,
coclites, etc., which they beat into powder, and give to their sick
women, as an exceeding great medicine *ad constringendas partes
post partum.*

10. This afternoon I went to see Kettelby, but I found that it
had never been a religious house, as I had been informed, but
only a gentleman's hall.　An old fellow told me that it was built
in K[ing] James the First's days to entertain him when he came
a hunting in these parts.　The old man sayd that he had oftentimes heard say that the king, whereever he rid, never held the
bridle fast in his hand, but always let it ly upon his horse's neck,
and so he did when he rid a hunting.　I think I have read this
also of that king, but I have forgot where.

This Kettleby hall has been a very fine structure, but they
are now pulling it down.　There are stables with almost as fine
carvings in them as ever I saw in my life.'

12. I was talking with this gentleman likewise about Greatrix,
the famous Irish stroker.　He says that he knew him very well, and
lodged over the way just against him in London.　He has talk'd
with him several times, and says that he seem'd to be a strang
conceited fellow, believing strang things of devils, spirits, and
witches, etc.　He says he fancyd him himself to be an impostor.
He had two or three young men wateing upon him, who always
pump'd the persons that were going to be stroak'd, how long
they had their distemper, whether they thought that their master
could cure 'em, etc.　He never took one farthing for any cure

' The "milner's thumb" occurs literally, I am told, by millions in the lias
beds of North Lincolnshire.　Their medicinal properties may still be known.
They are curved bivalves, the perfect ones have lids to them.　The name which
geologists give them is *Gryphæa Incurva.*　They are found wherever the lias
occurs in England, France, and Germany.　When burnt they fall into lime, and
if they are good for wounds, can have no other effect than a mineral one.

' Kettelby hall, near Brigg, was the chief residence of the family of
Tyrwhitt.　The present structure is a modern farm house.　The old hall was
moated, and the present house stands within the enclosure.　A private burial
ground was attached, over the site of which the Manchester Sheffield and Lincolnshire railway now runs.

that he did, nor would suffer his servants to do the same ; but those that were cured. out of gratitude, a good while after, presented him and his servants with anything that he or they stood in need of. While this gentleman lodged over against him, which was for about three weeks, there was brought unto him near one hundred people, of which he says that there was not over fifteen of them cured : upon which some people took notice thereoff to him. " Are they not so," says he, " I thought they had been all cured. Either they want faith, or some of my men has received money." So he called up his men, who having heard what was sayd,—" Sarrah, you rogues," says he, "some of you, I believe, has made my cures ineffectual by your roguerys. John, James, Thomas, Macko, Matko," says he, " I find you are the rogue that has received some of the poor's money, tell me ?" So he confes'd it. " Well," says he, " get you gone, I'll make an example of you." So he went down. And the next morning the stroker and all his men went out of town. Thus this gentleman told me word for word. He saw this fellow at my Lady Conway's likewise, and dos confess that he did by some way or other strange cures there. But there were several likewise that he could not cure. He might say perhaps that his servants received money, etc.

13. This day I took a walk in the woods, and the country hereabouts being full of springs, I diverted myself by weighing the waters, and casting strong spirits into them, and such like, to try whether they ran through any minerals or no, etc. ; and coming upon Thornham moor, just on the north side of Broughton wood, near the same I found a spring that turned all the grass and moss that grew about it into perfect stone (which property belonging to that spring was never known before.) I brought a great many pieces of the petrifactions thereoff home with me in curious shapes. I tryd the water, and found it to proceed from iron," etc., so that I do not question but that it is good in many distempers, for several spaws turns moss into stone, and the water itself condenses into perfect stone, as that dos at Scarburrow, etc.

Hermeston is a manour in this shire, and town is very ancient." It has it's name from a great stone erected there on the highway,

---

" Iron has been worked in this neighbourhood by the Romans. On the estate of Charles Winn. esq., of Nostel, at Scunthorpe, about four miles from Broughton, are now very extensive iron works.

" There is no place called Hermeston in Lincolnshire. Harmston is a parish in Kesteven. I am not sure that this is the place meant.

dedicated to Hermes ; for it was a custome to erect and dedicate
stones up to him, etc.

29. Mr. Howson, our apparitor, came this [day] unto me,
with the Association to sign, and I sign'd it accordingly; and over
all the whole nation there are few or none that refuses the same,
but every one signs it with the greatest alacrity imaginable.   I
was not bound with any oath or tye of allegiance to K[ing]
J[ames], therefore I might do it with more freedome and boldness.
The reason that it had not come amongst us sooner was because
that it was put off till the Visitation, but because that cannot
be in hast so it is sent about now.

There lately happened a pretty (tho' inconsiderable) thing at
London, which is mightily talk'd off all over the country.   There
are a company of rude sparks there commonly calld bullys or
baux,[w] [beaux] who, tho' most of them be but meer cowards, yet
are for picking quarrels with one, and for hectoring, cursing and
swearing, none can outdo them.   They had lately got up a
fashion of wearing great huge buttons, and these they called
bully buttons.   A maggot comeing lately in some nobleman's
head (for so he was thought to be) to affront the conceited fopps,
and so accordingly one evening he went to one of the coffy houses
where these baus commonly meet, thus cloathed ; his coat was
beset all with great turneps instead of buttons ; his hatt was
buttoned upon the side with a huge onion ; his sword had a
dishcloth hanging about it instead of a bunch of ribbons ; his
muff that he wore before him was made of a little oyster barrel,
and the wigg that he had on was all powdered with meal.   He
had six good bigg footmen wateing upon him, some of which
carryed dridging boxes by their sides, instead of powder boxes,
for his wigg.   Thus cloathed, and thus attended, he walked
through the streets of London to the baus' coffee-house, where
being entered, and having strutted about the room two or three
times, and view'd himself in the looking-glass, he went and sat
down by the fireside, because that it was winter, and because
that there was set four or five baus there.   Haveing sat there a

---

[w] Manningham, in 1602, says that "there was a company of young gallants
sometyme in Amsterdame, which called themselves the Damned Crue. They
would meete togither on nights, and vowe amongst themselves to kill the next
man they mett whatsoever ; so divers murthers committed, but not one punished. Such impunity of murder is frequent in that country." The editor in a
note adds :—"This association was not confined to Amsterdam. A club of pro-
fligates, under the same name, existed in London, much about this time, under
the captainship of Sir Edward Baynham, a well known young roysterer."—
Diary, Camden Society, pub. 1868, p. 142.

bitt, he began to cast his long meald wigg backward first over one shoulder then over another, almost in the very faces of those that sat near him, on purpose to affront them. Then says he in hectoring note—" Wee baus are peaceable men," and so he over with it two or three times. But they, tho' they whisper'd amongst themselves, and were sore vexed, yet durst not attac him. Then he called for a dish of chocolate, and, having drunk it, he gave the coffy man half-a-crown, who having asked what he would please to have again, answered, " We baus never ask any thing again." and so he went out. And hearing some that begun to talk behind his back that durst not say a word before his face, he steps in again in a great fury saying, " Who is that that has the impudence to say that I deserve to be kick'd?" (for so one sayd), but nobody sayd a word to him; upon which he sitts down again, calls for another dish of chocolate, and in his paying for it he put his hand into the wrong pocket, as he pretend[ed], and drew out a handfull of guinneys. Then, putting them up, he put his hand in the other pocket, and gave the coffee man half-a-crown, and so went his way, haveing sufficiently affronted and hector'd all the town's fopps, and out-braved them on their own dunghills.

[MAY] 8, 1696. No clipped money being to go beyond the 4th of May, it has putt all things to a stand, and makes the markates very small that was larg ones a little while since. But the people dos not half so much grumble thereat as they did at first, because that they are now used to it. This being the 8th of May, I was at Brigg, and nothing would be taken there but broad, and for all that there was not a piece of broad money to be seen before that day, everybody thinking there was none in the nation, yet now it comes out in plenty. I let with a gentleman at the inn that was just come from London, I asked him whether the king was gone or no, and he sayd " yes." Then I asked him about the conspirators and their number, and he told me that it was the deepest layd plot that was ever almost known,—" for " says he, " it appears that there was not a papist nor jacobite in the whole nation but knew of the same, etc."

15. Strang and wonderful are the actions and fancys of melancholy men ; so rideculous and surprising, that one that is not acquainted with books that treats of them, and that has not seen such people, could never believe them to be true. I have oft heard of S^r· James Brooks his thinking to shoot himself

to death, but never heard so whole and particular an account of him as this day from some gentlemen that I was with.

This Sr. James was melancholy, and had the strangest sort of actions that ever man had. In the beginning of his disease he would have stood on his head, pull'd of all his cloaths and danced naked, sung in his sleep, etc. But, in length of time, growing worse and worse, he scarce ever laugh'd, and when he walk'd he went as easily as ever he could. One day his distemper drove him to such a height that he was resolved to destroy himself, and according[ly] having got a pistol somewhere, he goes into his chamber and charges it, and then, seing himself in a looking-glass, he holds out his pistol to his own representation in the glass and shoots it off, and falls down flat on his back, crying out, " I'm kill'd, I'm kill'd !" upon which his servants running up in all hast saw the looking-glass all shot in pieces, and a great hole through the ceiling into the next room, and found their master lying there all his length, pretending he was kill'd, but, finding how it was, they were very well pleased that it was no worse, etc.

We began likewise to talk of the indirect and foolish dealings and actions of K[ing] James while he was here in the nation, and talking of several that had turned papists he told me this observable about the Earl of Salisbury, which I had heard several times before. This Earl had the ill luck to turn papist just two or three months before that the Prince of Orange came in, and became a mighty fat, unwieldy man, so that he could scarce stirr with ease about, tho' he was not over thirty-nine or forty years old. When the rumor was that the prince was coming he would almost every hower be sending his man to Whitehall to hear what newse there was. Then, when he heard that the prince was comeing and landed, and how he was received, he lamented sadly, and curst and damn'd all about him, crying, " O God ! O God ! O God ! I turn'd too soon, I turn'd too soon," etc. But, a while before this, somebody made a long copy of ingenious verses upon him, and scattered them in his chamber and about the streets. They begun thus :—

> If Cecil^x the wise
> From his grave should arise,
> And see this fat beast in his place,
> He would take him from Mass,
> And turn him to grass,
> And swear he was none of his race.   Etc.

I have forgot the rest.

^x The Earl's surname is Cecil.—*Note by Diarist.*

June 5. Being this day in Yorkshire I hear that a mint has come to York[y] to coin silver tankards, plates, cups, etc. The poor people has been up in great numbers in Ratsdale[z] by reason that their clipp'd money would not go, and was marching in great fury to one of their parliament men's houses, which they swore to pull down to the ground and ransack. But the gentlemen round about, getting immediate notice of it, soon pacifyed all by commanding that their clip'd sixpences should go if not clipped within the innermost rimm, and by promising that they would take care to change their little old money for great money, and such like, or else they would have done a great deal of mischief.

Talking this morning with Capt. Sandys of birds flying over sea in winter into hotter climates, and such like, [he] told me this very observable thing. That he himself being at Deal, in Kent, wateing to take shipping, at that time of the year when woodcocks were just a comeing over, saw a huge hurricane upon the sea, and beheld himself, the next day, some hundreds of woodcocks cast upon the sea shore all about Deal, which he conjectured had perished in the sayd storm.

7. This day I heard of one that is come from Lincoln, that the country people has been up about Stamford, and marchd in a great company, very lively, to the house of S[r.] John Brownley. They brought their officers, constables, and churchwardens amongst them, and as they went along they cryd, "God bless King William, God bless K[ing] W[illiam]," etc. When they were come to S[r.] John's, he sent his man down to see what their will was, who all answered—" God bless K[ing] W[illiam], God bless the Church of England, God bless the Parliament, and the

---

[y] Although milled money had been coined from an early time in the reign of Charles II. (1662), the old hammered money had never been withdrawn from circulation. The coinage had therefore, at this time, become so diminished in weight by wear, and by the frauds of clippers, that it was not worth intrinsically more than half its current value. A tax was laid on houses for the purpose of raising the sum of £1,200,000 to supply the deficiencies of the clipped coin. That the new money might be issued as soon as possible, mints were set up at Bristol, Chester, Exeter, Norwich, and York. The coins struck at these places are marked respectively, B, C, E, N, Y, under the king's bust.—See *Hawkins' Silver Coins*, p. 226.

Thoresby says that, 5 Nov., 1703, he went "to visit Major Wyvil (son to Sir Christopher, the author of some learned tracts against popery). The Major, being concerned in the late mint at York, when the old monies were called in, I desired an account of what monies were coined at the mint, which, by his books, he showed me was 312,520l. 0s. 6d."—*Diary*, i., p. 447.

[z] Query Rochdale.—*Sic orig.*

Lords Justices, and Sr John Brownley ! We are King William's true servants, God forbid that we should rebel against him, or that anything that we now do should be construed ill. We come only to his worship to beseech him to be mercifull to the poor; we and our familys being all fit to starve, not having one penny ith' the world that will go," etc. S^{r.} Jo[hn] hearing all this (as soon as his man) at a window where he was viewing them, sent them a bagg with fifteen pound in it of old mill'd money, which they received exceeding thankfully, but sayd the sum was so little, and their number and necessitys so great, that they feared it would not last long, therefore must be forced out of meer necessity to come see him again, to keep themselves and their familys from starving. Then they desired a drink, and S^{r.} Jo[hn] caused his doors to be set open and let them go to the cellar, where they drunk God bless King William, the Church of England, and all the loyal healths that they could think on, and so went their ways.

8. This day I was with Francis Anderson, esq., lately come from London. I ask'd him, I believe, a hundred questions about this and that. He says that Ferguson (who has a great hand in this plot) being brought before the councell, one of them sayd, " Mr. Ferguson, I'll ask you but two questions"—to whom he answered as angerly as could be, " You ask what you will, I'll answer none." No more he did, but was sent straight away to Newgate. When he came there, one of his disciples seeing him go in, " O, dear S^{r.} (says he), what, are you got hither?" " Yes, that I am, but I would not have thee to think that I was put in here for picking of pockets; " intimating that it was for something more worthy and noble (as he thought) than for such a base thing.

About a fortnight before the late great plot broke out there went several spys from London to pump the clergy almost all over England, tho' who sent them, or what their design or intent was, God knows. However, they were well arm'd, and had their pockits full of gold and silver, and were well mounted. They commonly let at an ale-house ith' town, and having learn'd what the minister's name was, and such like, they sent for him, saying they were strangers and travilers, and would be very glad to drink a pot of ale or wine with them for company sake. I myself was with a friend of mine, an ingenious clergyman of Fishlake, near Doncaster, in Yorkshire: one of them met with him at Doncaster, and being both in the house together, the gentleman desired Mr. Hall,[a] the clergyman, to sit down and drink with him. So having asked Mr. Hall what was his name, where he lived, and having pump'd all out of him that he could about King W[illiam] and the Church of England, he writt it down in a table book. The gentleman sayd he came from London, and that he was to ride all the north part of England round, and then to return to London again, and I have heard from several ministers of the towns round about, that he always drew them on to discourse about the aforesayd things, and whatever they sayd, he was never angry, but noted all down in his book, and always treated those that he sent for. Some thought this fellow was a spy to see which of the clergy stood true to K[ing] W[illiam], which not. Others thought him sent down by some presbiterians to see how many of the clergy stood affected to them; and some thought him sent for other things.

This day I was at Brigg to hear the newse. We had nothing observable but a great riseing of the mob, at and about Newcastle, about the money not going, and we do not hear that they are yet quelled.

Most people seems mightily dissatisfyed, tho' they love K[ing] W[illiam] very well. Yet they curse this parliament, not for their design of coining all new, but for their ill mannagement of it in setting so little time, in takeing no care to coin fast and send new monney out, etc.

In most places the people has got such a way of takeing money now as was never in use before: I mean not in England; and that is they take all by weight. Every one carry a pare of scales in his pocket, and if he take but a shilling in the market, he pulls out his scailes, and weighs it before that he will have it, and if it want but two or three grains they refuse it.

And for all that the act of parliament says sixpennys shall go not clip'd within the innermost rim, yet nevertheless no body will take sixpences unless they were never clip'd and be full weight.

Poor people are forced to let their clip'd shillings go for 6d., 8d., and some at 10d. a piece, and some at shops are forced to give as much more for anything they by as is ask'd for it, etc. These are very hard things, and but that the nation is so mightily in love with the king they would all be soon up in arms.

The parliament promiss'd that no man should loos anything

---

[a] John Hall does not occur amongst the vicars, and was probably curate only. In an Act of Chapter, 20 Nov., 1693, at Durham. it was ordered, "That, if Mr. Maurice Lisle resigne the vicarage of Fishlake, Mr. John Hall shall shall have the next presentation." It does not appear that Mr. Lisle did resign. See more concerning him *postea.*

II

by this thing, and layd a tax for scaven years for the makeing up
the deficiency of the clip'd silver, yet everybody must pay the
tax and loose vastly in their little money to boot.

I have seen unclip'd half crowns that has weigh'd down fifteen
shillings clipt. Some have weigh'd more. Shillings I have seen
that has outweigh'd three, four, five, six shillings clip'd.

And that which surpriz'd me to-day, one said unto [me] " Sᵣ·
I have been weighing a shilling and it wanted seven groats of
weight"; that is, he put a broad shill[ing] into one skale and a
clip'd one into the other, and seven silver groats to it before he
could bring it to the weight of the broad shilling.

'Tis sayd that the parliament was not half so wise in this
affair about money as the[y] might have been. They studdyed
and computed that all the clip'd money in the nation came not
to above . . . millions, and having guessed how much would
make up the difficiency in that summ, they lay'd this tax upon
the houses for seven years. But now it appears since that there
are above one hundred millions in the nation clip'd, so that it
will not be a tax of many scaven years that can make out so vast
a deficiency.

And people percieving this, and finding that for the future (by
reason of the narrowness of the coinage acts), that no money will
be taken of them to be new minted but by weight, they will not
receive any but by weight likewise. There are reckoned to be
now in the Exchecker . . . . millions of clip'd money, and
yet it is as plenty here in the country as ever, so that not half
nor quarter is yet put in thither.

There was a sad thing happen'd the other day at Ferriby-by-
Humber. A carefull honest pedlar woman, who had got a great
deal of clip'd money by her through her trading, was almost
madd for a week together when shee percieved that all her labour
and pains to scrape up portions for her children had been to no
purpose, and that not a penny of her money would go. Shee
took a knife and cut her own throat, and dy'd.

Several people went to see her, and amongst others there was
one there who sayd thus—" It may be questioned (says he)
whether this woman be guilty of her death or no ; I would have
all the parlament men come and touch her."[b]

I was in Yorkshire about a week ago, and there was some
that told me this sad story. A gentleman in Nottinghamshire,
near Mansfield, having a huge flock of sheep, had several shep-

---

[b] Alluding to the old belief that blood would flow at the murderer's touch.

pards to keep and take care of them. The head sheppard was a
marryd man and had a family. He came to his master saying,
"S^r," says he, "I want some money, I have had none of so
long." "John," says [he], "you shall have the best money
that I have," so he fetches him twenty shillings, and gave him
them. But John told him that he believed they would not go.
His master bid him trye, and if they would not, bring him 'em
again, for they were the best he had. So he did try, and did
bring them again because they would not go. So the poor man
was forced to go home without any money, and he and his family
lived of grass, rape, leaves, and such like, for above a week,
until they were almost starved. At last it comes in his mind,
what signifyze it, thinks he, if I take one of my master's sheep, and
kill it and eat it, to keep me from starving : my master owes me
a great deal more money than one sheep's worth. So having
taken one, killed it and eaten it, his master, hearing thereoff,
sends for him and carrys him before a justice of peace for
stealing one of his sheep. When they were come there, and that
the poor man had made his whole case known, the justice shaked
his head, and said nothing for a good while, but at last dismissed
the poor man, after a little reprimand for his boldness, but told
the master if he had no broad money he must get some, must sell
his sheep, etc.

17. I was at the Visitation at Gainsbur this day, and we were
putt to sign the Assosiation, and all did it, but onely one parson
who had been mad formerly, and was never right well since.
We signed one before, but it would not do, not being upon
parchment.

25. This day I was with one Mr. Holland, at Winterton, who
had under King James' days got a great estate by unlawfull
means, and being fear'd to be call'd to an account for the same, he
fled into America, into one of our plantations there, and is become
a great man, having many fields, and houses, and slaves. But,
finding that he was never call'd here to an account, so he ventered
to come over to see all his friends. I ask'd him a great many
things, which he gave good answers to.

JULY 10. These three or four days last past I have been at
Hatfield in Yorkshire, the place of my birth, and where many
of my relations and very good friends lives. I was in company

with S[r] Brotherdine Jackson,[e] John Ramsden, esq., Jo. Hat-field, esquire,[d] Tho[mas] Lee, esq., Corn[elius] Lee, gent., Capt[ain] Sandys, and several others, all of them learned and in-genious men, and worthy of all credit and honour. I heard them tell many observable and remarkable storys, some of which I shall here set down.

Capt[ain] Sandys sayd that as a certain man was digging in his garden at Rumford, in Essex, about fourteen years ago, he let of a small vault, which he was a long while before he could get opend. At last having opend the same he cal'd for a candle, and looking in he perceived a kind of a coffin therein, which haveing taken out, he perceived that it was made of a green sort of glass, and was in leng[th] just two foot nine inches. It was excellently well soldered or run together, so that no air could get in ; but, being broke by the country clown, he found nothing therein but ashes or dust, and the bones of an infant. The truth of this was asserted likewise by Jo. Hatfield, esq.

Capt[tain] Sandys adds that he saw part of the glass coffin, and says that it was very rudely run, and was about half an inch thick. Whether this might be the onely child of some great king or queen, or the reliques of some little martyr layed up there in the times of popery, I shall not take upon me to decide.

The same Capt[ain] told us also the following relation, to witt. That when he was quarter'd at Chelmsford, in the same county, a gardener, for the improvement of his garden, cast and cut away the skerts of a great hill or old burrow that was on one side of his garden ; and having done so several years, sometimes he found pieces of arms therein. But at last he discovered (under the bows of a huge old oak that grew on this hill) a great stone coffin between eight and nine foot long, which being open'd, there was nothing found therein but the ashes of a burnt body, and some parts of huge bones, and a bust of gold, as bigg as an egg, of the head of one of the Cæsars. This bust he sold, takeing it to be brass, for two shilling, to the minister of the town, who (out of requital for some favours) presented it to the Repository or University at Oxford. The fellow, upon discovery of all this, setts up a shed under the aforesay'd tree, and sold ale there, haveing caused it to be cryed up and down the country what he had dis-

---

[e] Sir Bradwardine Jackson, third and last baronet of Hickleton, named in the Baronetage of 1727 as then living and unmarried, but what ultimately became of him has not been ascertained.—See *Hunter's South Yorkshire*, ii., p. 136 ; *Herald and Genealogist*, part xxvii., p. 270.

[d] Of Hatfield.—*Hunter's South Yorkshire*, i., p. 177, 178 ; see *ante*, p. 13.

covered, so that he got a great trade, and the capt[ain] hearing of it sent word thereof to the Duke of Albermarle, who, being not farr of, came amongst others to see it, and [the] duke, being very inquisitive, he took some of the dust out of the coffin in his hand, and smelling thereoff percieved it to be most excellently sweet, so that he carry'd some handfulls away with him.

The ingenious Mr. Lee told us that he was present at the siege of Colchester, and that he saw the two loyal and couragious gentlemen, S[r.] Ch[arles] Lucas, and S[r.] George Lile, executed there, when the rebells took the town. He says that they were both brought bound into the castle-yard, and being loos'd, they then prayed together, and, haveing hugg'd one the other, they stood expecting the fatal bullets, which accordingly came and killed them both stark dead in a minnit, who, falling backward, lay there a good while before that they were taken up and buried. But, from that time to this, 'tis observed that no grass will grow where these two brave men fell, but that there is to this day the exact figure on the ground in hay time that they fell in ; for it is good hay and grass round about, but in these places. This was attested by Tho[mas] Lee, esq., and Capt[ain] Sandys says that he has observed it himself.

But when the king returned, the L[d.] Lucas, the brother to the dead of that name, erected a stately monument to the memory of these two brave men, with this inscription thereon,[*]

> Here lyes buried the renown'd
> S[r.] Ch[arles] Lucas, and S[r.] George Lile. basely
> Murder'd by the L[d.] Fairfax, general
> Of the Parlament army.

Several years after that the king was come in, and after that this was erected, the Lord Fairfax came to kiss the king's hand and to desire a favour from him, and as he was on his knees, kissing the the king's hand, he desired that the aforesayd monument might be demolish'd, for it was a skandal and stain to his family. Upon the hearing of which the L[d.] Lucas (that erected it), standing by, humbly entreated the king that, if he was pleased to grant Fairfax that favour, his majesty would be pleased to suffer him to erect another after the same shape. But the king answered thus, laying his hand on Fairfax's head, "No, no, my L[d.] you have been a great rebell, and I was so kind as to pardon you. And as for the monument it shall stand as long as the world endures."

This Mr. Lee, while he was cornet for the king, was with

[*] In his chapel at Colchester.—*Marginal Note by Diarist.*

his friend Robin Portington,/ at the fight at Horncastle, in this
county, but it happen'd that after a sharp fight they were beat,
so that one was forc'd to fly one way, one another. This Robin
in his flight and escape was met in an odd place by a country
parson, to whom this Robin sayd thus—" Ey, by God, we have
now beat these damn'd king's men, these roges that thought to
have destroy'd the whole nation," etc. " Ey, Sʳ· ey, (says he)
I hear of it, God be thanked for the victory, their vanquish'd,
I wish their king was but as dead as many of his adhearents are."
" Ey, you rogue," says Mr. Portington to him, " Say you so, by
God you'r a dead man," and, whipping out a pistol, he shot him ;
and, as he was falling of horseback, he cryd, " Lord have mercy
upon my soul ; " to which Robin answered, " Ey, by God, but it
is a question whether He will or no ; however, I care not whether
He have or no."

This Robin came into Marshland and lurked there, and not
very long after, as he was going over Whitgift ferry, he say
/[saw] an ape, and playing with it, it bit his hand, which bite he
slighting, it ganger'd and kill'd him. Mr. Hatfield sayd that he
had several times heard his father (who was a capt[ain] in the
parlament's army) tell this sadd story.

After which, " Come (says Mr. Corn[elius] Lee) I'll tell you a
fine comical story, after such tragical ones. When I was last at
London there was this cunning trick played. There was two
rogues sitting in the chamber of a tavern next to the street, over
against which was a merchant's house. These rogues perceives
through the window a casement open in a roome of the merchant's over against them, and observed that the merchant was
taking his morning draught with his wife before that he went out
to the exchange. They observed likewise that they drunk out of a
great silver tankard, that had part of the lidd broken off. ' See
you,' sayd one of them to the other, ' yon tankard shall be mine
before two houers end. I like it very well, it is a larg one,' etc.
' Pish,' say the other, ' how will you get it ? ' ' Let me alone
for that,' says he ; and so he go's, and in the first place went
streight into the market, and buys a great pike, and brought it to
the merchant's house, saying, ' Madam, your husband has mett
with two or three gentlemen of his relations, and intends to bring

---

/ Of a family at Barnby-Don, co. York. Hunter (*South Yorkshire*, i., p. 213)
states that he was a major in Sir William Savile's regiment, and was at the
fight at Horncastle on October 11, 1643, when Sir Ingram Hopton was slain.
Portington was taken prisoner at the battle of Willoughby and sent to Hull,
where he was confined until the Restoration. He died 23 December, 1660, and
was buried at Arksey, a few miles from Barnby-Don.

them home to dinner, therefore, fearing that you might have
nothing in the house, he has sent you this pike to prepare for
them. And, madam, (says he) your husband bid me ask you for
a silver tankard that has part of the lidd broken of, and desires
you to send it to him, and he will get the lidd mended and bring
it with him, by the same token that both of you drunk your
morning draughts in it.' ' Ey,' says shee, ' we did so,' and
so shee fetched it, and delivered it to him. And away go's he
with his tankard, and shews it to his companion, saying, ' See
you here, sarrah! (says he) I have got what I look'd for, I have
brought it with me,' etc. So they sat them down at the aforesayd place and drunk on. At noon the merchant comes home,
and as soon as his wife saw him shee fell a scowlding him, saying,
' Ey, husband, you'r always a troubleing us thus with somebody
or other, youv'e no prudence in you.' To which he sayd,
' Pray, dear, what do you mean? What do you mean, to be
thus angry with me?' ' What do I mean? (says she),
nay, what do you mean, to play us so many foolish tricks?'
' What strangers are those you'r bringing to dine with us?'
' To dine with you! I know of none—I am bringing none.'
' No! (says shee) what did you send yon pike for then?' ' I
sent none,' says he. ' Nor you did not send for the great silver
tankard to get mended neither, did you?' ' No,' says he, ' no
more I did!' At which they both stood amazed for a while, but,
recollecting themselves, they both concluded that some rogue had
imposed upon them and cheated them, upon which they both ran
out of doors, one to one goldsmith, and another to another, to lay
wait for the plate, and so they took care for the recovering of it,
and for the apprehending of the rogue."

"But, in the meantime, he sat looking out of the hole in the
glass window, and seeing them run'd one one way and the other
another way, says he to his companion, ' Jack, I'm hungry, I'll
'een go steal my pike again that I gave yon merchant, and we
will have it dress'd.' ' Pish! pish!' says the other to him,
' you'l certainly be taken and hang'd for your being so venter-
some.' ' No, no,' says he, ' I will go,' and so being somewhat disguised by pulling his sleeves of, and by tying a speckled
handkercher about his neck instead of his cravat, he goes a back
way, and comes running up the street to the merchant's, and with
great joy runs in crying, ' The rogue's taken, the rogue's taken,
God be thank'd, he's taken that stole your master's tankard, and
he has got it again, and sent the thief to Newgate.' ' God be
thank'd for it,' says the maid, ' I'm gladd of it.' ' And,' says

he, 'Your master and mistris is met at such a tavern, and they
sent me to command you to send them the great pike that the
damn'd rogue brought here ith' morning, for they intend to get
their dinners there : there are several of the neighbours met there
also, and they are very merry.'   'Well, well,' says shee ; so
shee delivers him the pike, reddy to be used, and takes down a
large silver platter and lays it thereon, and so the rogue went of
with more than what he expected.   As soon as his partner saw his
great fortune he was amaz'd, but both of them thinking it was
not safe for them to stay any longer there, they contrived a way
in a box for the carriers to get their prize off, and then shifted
for theirselves."

   " But about two houers after the maid had delivered him his
fish, in comes her master and mistris, and as soon as ever shee
saw them, ' I'm glad at heart,' says shee to them, ' that you
have got your tankard again. and discovered the rogue, God be
thank'd for it, God be thank'd,' etc.   ' What, what, what ails
the lass,' say they, ' is shee madd ?   Surely shee's madd,
she talks she knows not what.'   ' Well, well ! tho' you
make as if you had not got it, yet you have, and I am heartily
glad of it.   I sent you the rogue's pike on the great silver platter,'
etc.   ' O God ! (says he) has this rogue cheated me again,
he has not onely got my tankard but my platter also,' etc.
Upon which they were all so mightily surpriz'd that they did
not know what to do, but stood as thunderstruck, amazed at the
strangness of their losses."

   It is very observable what Mr. Ramsden sayd touching clippers, which we had been talking of.   He says that about nine
years ago, when he was at London, there was a clipper taken,
who, being a shoemaker by trade, wrought at the aforesay'd art
openly in his shop, singing aloud, " I shall ne'er go the sooner, I
shall ne'er go the sooner to the Stygian ferry."   Thus he did for
some two days together, but on the third he was taken, and in
the next assises hang'd.   He had been long at the trade, but
always did it in secret ; but being turn'd a rigid predestinarian,
he believed it in vain to work any more in secret, but took it to
be the very same to work in publick, for no one could anticedate
his own death.

   11. This day I went to see Madam Anderson, and falling a
talking from one thing to another, shee ran and fetched me down
several old coins to look at, amongst which one was a rose noble,
one of those that Ramund Lully is sayd to have made [by]

chymistry. There was another of silver, which was a medal made
upon the return of K[ing] Charles the Second; and there was
two or three old Saxon coins, such as is seen in the beginning of
Cambden, and one which was a Danish one. Concerning which
three or four last shee told me this very observable thing ; to witt,
that about four years ago, as a man was digging in the field near
unto Boston, in this county, he light upon a cave, which having
broke through the wall thereof, he discovered therein the dead
body of a man, layd in a kind of a stone coffin, which body fell
to ashes as soon as ever he touched it. And in the cave he found
great heaps of money, all black with age, which money he sold
in whole baggs full, by weight, to all the neighbouring country,
and carry'd a great quantity of it to Gainsburr, and sold it by
weight there, and there it was that this lady got those pieces
thereof that I saw. They were full as bigg as large sixpenys,
and were all of them of silver, and of a great many different coins.

Shee relates likewise that about thirty years ago there was
discovered a very strang thing at Godstow, which shee had from
many eye witnesses, and was this. As a gardiner was digging
on the side of a great hill nigh the town, he could never proceed
on his work for the great stones that he continnualy encounter'd
with, therefore one advised to digg on the top of the hill, and
having done so for half a day, he came to a causy, as he cauld it
at first, but, having pull'd up many of the stones, it appear'd to
be the roof of a great arched cave, built in manner of a church,
in which there were several old monuments and diverse images.
Some of the latter she says were taken out and putt in the church
of that place.

This brings into my mind what I heard a gentleman say, last
time I was in Yorkshire, to witt, that about the year 1659, when
he was in Somersetshire, there was discover'd in a hole on Malvern hills, a pot full of money, many of which this gentleman
had, but has lost them all. However, they were brass and
copper, and had most of them the name of Lewellin on. The
same gentleman let me se an old Athenian coin, with an owl on
it on one side, on each side of which was an omicron and a
eupsilon, on the other side a royal head with a crown on, with
two ill shaped unknown letters.

16. I was with a gentleman or two this day that came from
London, an ingenious, knowing, understanding man, and he says
that many of the commissioners and great men for the king
keep spys in the citty of London, and in the nation, who they

find with money, and gives them lieve to swear at K[ing]
Wil[liam], and to drink K[ing] James his health, and to talk
against the government, and to join themselves to all companys,
on purpose to pump them, and to find how they are inclined.
And when that they discover any thing they immediately give
notice thereof to their respective masters. He says that Monsr·
de la Rue, who is one of the chief discoverers in this plot, is a spy
of the L^d· Portland's, and that the Duke of Devonshire, the Earl
of Ormond, and others, keeps a great many more, some one, some
two, and some three, a piece.

The 18th instant, being Saturday, I went to see a place, between Sanclif and Conisby, called the Sunken Church,[f] the tradition concerning which says that there was a church there formerly,
but that it sunk in the ground with all the people in it, in the
times of popery. But I found it to be only a fable, for that
which they shew to be the walls thereof, yet standing, is most
manifestly nothing but a natural rock, which lifts itself out of
the ground about two yards high, in a continued line, like the
wall of a church, etc.

S^r· Rob[ert] Swift,[h] in 1612, had a great estate at Lancham,
Upton, Gamston, etc., in Nottinghamshire. He was son to

---

[f] Sunken Church at Sancliff yet exists, and is known by that name. The
story is that the church and the whole congregation were swallowed up by the
earth, but that on one day in the year (the anniversary, it is believed, of that
on which the church went down), if one goes early in the morning he may hear
the bells ring for Mass. The legend cannot be accounted for. A similar tale
exists, I understand, about various other places in Britain and Germany. There
has clearly been no church here. The stone is certainly natural. It is not so high
now as Pryme reports. The earth has probably washed down the hill and raised
the ground about it. There are some marks or furrows on it, which may be
very rude carvings, but this is doubtful. As large stones are a rarity thereabouts, and as this is visible at a considerable distance, it may have had heathen
rites connected with it, which have given a weird memory to the spot.

[h] See pedigree of Swyft, of Rotherham, Doncaster, and Streetthorpe, (*South
Yorkshire*, i., p. 204), where it appears that it was his cousin Frances (and not
his daughter), third and youngest daughter and coheiress of his uncle, Robert
Swyft, esq., who married Sir Francis Leake, as stated. Our Diarist, in another
of his MSS., says of Sir Robert Swift that he bought Stristerop [Streetthorpe]
where he dwelt. "He was an ingenious, witty, and merry gentleman, concerning whome this town (Hatfield) has many traditional storys. They tell how
that he having once discovered a gentleman of Cantley, a town hard by, whose
name was Mr. Slack, stealing one of the king's deer, he apprehended him, and
having heard that he was a constant transgressor, (the assizes being then at
York, and all ye other delinquents being sent from Thorn prison), Sir Robert
set out with this gentleman to ye same place; but night coming on, they took
up their lodgings by ye way, and finding there by chance a pot of good ale, this
Mr. Slack told him so many merry tails over ye same, and enticed them to drink

Will[iam] Swift, esq. Sr Rob[ert] marry'd one of his
daughters to Sr Franc[is] Leek, who had a son that was made
Ld Deincourt and Earl of Scarsdale. Another daughter he
marry'd to Sr Rob[ert] Anstrudder. Of this Sr Rob[ert]
Anstrudder, or of his father, I do not know whether, is related
this pleasant but certain story.

He was sent over ambassador to the King of Denmark, and
having been there several times before, he was highly caress'd
by the king and all the court ; and after that dinner was ended,
as the custome is, the king and him, and many others, fell hard
to drinking, and, being merry, the King of Denmark made this
pleasant proposal. "Come," says he, "my l^d ambassador, I'll
tell you what we will do. I'll send for my crown, and will set it
on the table, and you and me will drink for it. If you make me
drunk, you shall wear it till I be sober. If I make you drunk
I will wear it till you be sober." So they soon agreed to this,
and the crown was brought and set before them. So they went
to it; but, in short, Anstrudder made him so drunk he fell under
the table, and the nobles, as they were commanded, set the
crown on Anstrudder's head, who, being thus crowned, made
them call him king, and sending for the secretary of state, he
made several new laws, and commanded him to write them down,
and these laws are many of them yet kept, and call'd to this day
Anstrudder's laws. The ambassador, being thus made king, was
resolved to reign as long as he could, and took such care that he
kept the king drunk three days together, and had done it longer
had not they feared that it might have killed him, and then, with
a great many complements, he return'd him his crown again.

About a year after, Amstrudder' was sent again, and the king,
meditateing reveng, sent for him in all hast, and he comeing out
of a close shipp in a great amaze unto the king, the king after
haveing saluted him and he him, begun full bumpers, and after

so long, that he got Sir Rob. and those with him dead drunk. Upon which
takeing a piece of paper, he writt thereon these following verses :

To every creature God has given a gift,
Sometimes the Slack dos overrun the Swift.

and, having stop'd them into Sir Robert's pocket (where he found them by
chance next morning), he made his escape that night, and was not heard again
of, of a long while. But Sir Rob., seeming as if he was not at all concerned,
kept on his journey to York, and, haveing performed his business there, returned
again to his station. This Sir Rob. dyed, very much lamented by every one that
knew him, in ye year 16--, and was buried in Doncaster church." Hunter
furnishes the date of his death 14 March, 1625.

' This Amstrudder was also sent ambassador into Germany in 1630.—*Marginal Note by Diarist.*

a pretty hard tugg he fell'd Amstrudder down, so that he fell fast
asleep.   Upon which he searched his pocket, and found his
papers, and what things they were that he came about.   He
immediately dispatch'd the same, and caused them to be put in
his pocket again, and so sent him away a shippbord again, commanding them to depart immediately, and be gone.   Which being
performed, and being in their full course to England, Amstrudder,
awakening out of his sleep, begun to stare and wonder where he
was, and to be so amaz'd that he did not know what to do (after
they told him that the king commanded them to be gone in all hast
from his coasts), fearing that he should be hanged when he got
into England ; but then, searching for his papers, he found his
business done, and that pleased him very well.   Upon which
being got into England, and going to meet the king on a suddain,
the king begun to swear at [him].   " By me shaul, mon, thou
art not fitt to gang about any business, thou art so slo," etc.,
thinking that he had not yet set out on his embassage, but hearing of him that he had, he was mightily well pleased thereat,
and asked how he came to get his business so soon done, upon
which Amstrudder told him the whole, which made the king
laugh heartily.   This was told me by Mr. Corn[elius] Lee, a
relation both of Sr· Rob[ert] Swift's, and Sr· Rob[ert] Amstrudder's, and dos attest it to be a real truth, and is mentioned in
Loyd's Worthys in his life.[j]

The Marquis of Carmarthen and the Ld· Cutts has been lately
in disguise in England, sent from the king to pump the nation,
and are lately returned back.

On the 20th was taken five huge porpuses in Trent, near
Authorp, etc.

JULY 30. This day I was with one Mr. Cook, who says that
as his brother was plowing in the fields of Darfield in Yorkshire,
about sixteen years ago, his plow bared a all [sic] the earth of a
great pott like a butter pot, which, he taking notice of, he found
and discovered that it was top full of all Roman coins, amongst
which was several of gold, which he carry'd home, and sending
for a goldsmith he sold them to him for one pound, tho' they
were worth above three times as much as he gave for them.

My Ld· Portland is lately come over in disguise from Flanders, and, being unknown, was taken up in Kent for some great
person lately come from France ; but he soon discovered himself

---

[j] See quotation therefrom, etc., in *Hunter's South Yorkshire*, i., p. 55.

who he was, and so was acquitted. He came to pump the nation, and see how they were affected. He has a great many spys, and so has my Ld. Cutts, Devonshire, etc.

There are, they say, about ninety justices of peace turned out for not signing the Assosiation, and about one hundred and twenty officers in the trainbands.

AUG. 12. 'Tis sayd that the king looses above 1000*l.* per day in the excise, by reason of the ill management of the clipp'd money : for a great many ale houses all over the country, and some almost in every town, has given over brewing and selling of ale, because that they can get no good money for the ale that they shall sell.

There is great striveings now to get interest and votes to be chosen parlament men, before that they know that the parlament will be dissolved; and for all that there was an act made the very last year that they should [not] treat the country and bribe for their votes, yet, nevertheless, they carry on that course yet, and say that the act of parlament can take no hold of them, because that the old parlament is not yess [yet] dissolved, but that when it is dissolved that then they must not do so.

I have promiss'd my votes for Capt[ain] Whitchcot, and champion De Moc, commonly call'd Dimmock.* This champion holds certain lands by exhibiting on a certain day every year a milk-white bull with black ears to the people who are to run it down, and then it is cutt in pieces and given amongst the poor. His estate is almost 2000*l.* a year, and whoever has it is champion of England; but he ows more by farr than he is worth, and has no children, so that it will soon get into another family. The Dimmock has enjoyed it ever since Will[iam] the Conqueror's days, if I do not mistake.

13. This day Mr. Rawson, an old, learned, and ingenious gentleman, that was at the siege of Newark in Cromwell's days, in one sally that the besieged had made, a blackamore took a Scotch soldier prisoner; upon which the poor Scot, being almost

---

* Charles Dymoke, referred to by the Diarist, was champion at the coronation of William and Mary, and Queen Anne. He represented the county of Lincoln in parliament from 1698 to 1701. Dying s.p. 17 January, 1702-3, he was succeeded by his brother, Lewis Dymoke, M.P. for Lincoln 1702-5, and 1710-13. He died, unmarried, at the age of 91, in February, 1760, when the estate at Scrivelsby devolved, under his will, upon his cousin, Edward Dymoke, who was at that time an eminent hatter in Fenchurch Street, London. He died 12 September, 1760.—See *postea.*

frightened out of his wits, pray'd heartily, saying " O God! O God! O God! have mercy upon me sawl, have mercy upon me sawl, de deel's got my body, the deel's got my body; " and the fellow was so frightened he would not follow the black, so that he was forc'd to kill him.   He says he was in this sally, and saw this thing.

The same gentleman says he saw a young spare thin man there of about twenty years old, but of vast strength.   He would oft [have] lifted more than five men.

He says that at Nonersfield,' about twenty miles beyond York, is a vast great fortification, and that there was many silver and gold coins found there in Cromwel's days.

S[r.] Rob[ert] Amstrudder had a black, who was mighty religious, and would every morning walk out into the open field and pray to the rising sun.   At last he was converted to Christianity, and lived a very examplary and pious life.

Here is very little or no new monney comes yet down amongst us, so that we scarce know how to subsist.   Every one runs upon tick, and those that had no credit a year ago has credit enough now, the parlament has done that which God himself could scarce do, for they have made the whole land out of love [with] monney, so that, whether it be clipp'd or full weight, they know not what to do with it, etc.

SEPTEMBER 3.   I heard an old gentleman say that has lived at London all his time, that it was always the custome of Cromwel, when he had any great business in hand, or when his council asked him whether such a thing should be so or no, or whether such or such a great man should be executed for his loyalty or no, etc.,—says he always, " Stay a bitt, stay a bit, I'll go consult the L[d.] !"   and then he went up into his closset and stayed commonly about half a quarter of an hower, sometimes more, and then he always discided the thing when he came down, saying " The Lord will not have it so !"   When the king was to be executed, Cromwell's daughter who was marryed to . . . . begged upon him, as it were for her own life (all in tears and morning) that he would not suffer such a monstrous piece of murder to be performed, " which, says she, " will for ever reflect upon you,

---

' No such place occurs in the Yorkshire Directories. There is a place called Nosterfield, in the parish of West Tanfield, and liberty of Richmondshire, about three-and-a-half miles from Masham ; and we have Nunburnholme, three-and-a-half miles from Pocklington, where there was formerly a small Benedictine Nunnery, and where the villagers show a mound, a little above the village, at the bottom of a wood, as the site where the Nunnery stood.

and make you odious to the end of the world." "Well," says he, "I'll go consult the L^d and what the L^d says that will I do." So upon that he ran to his studdy, and [the] poor lady followed him, almost drownd in tears, and fell down at the studdy door, weeping and lamenting. After a while Oliver comes out, crying, " He shall dy, he shall dy, the L^d commands it, the L^d commands it."

This is somewhat like the actions of Baalam the sorcerrer, who went so oft to consult the L^d to curse the anointed of God his Israel. But now, whether Oliver, who was a great politician, did this on purpose to blind the eyes of the vulgar, and to make them believe that whatever he did was according unto the command of God, I cannot tell ; or whether he held correspondence (if there can be any such thing), with the divel, who was the l^d his god ; whom he consulted upon all occasions, I shall not determin ; but most certain it is that he was a very wicked man, one of no religion nor piety, but lived like an atheist.

OCTOB. 10. Things are very quiet yet, but the Jacobites are of undanted spirits, and continues their high, impudent, treasonable talkings and discourses, almost as much as ever.

New money beginns to grow plentyfull, there is no one almost but has some little quantity. All the mints are now in motion, and they give satisfaction to the country.

13. I have heard from Sr Edwin Sandys[m] and others, that the Lady Amstrudder had a child when shee was ten, and continued to have till she was threescore, tho' indeed most of them dyd after they were born. I knew a woman myself that was brought to bed of two children when she was eleven, and another I knew that had a child when she was thirteen, and shee bears children now, tho' shee is above fifty years old.

OCT. 18. I have been told by several learned men that some of the virtuosi both at London and beyond sea have, with their telescopes, observed that the sun has these several months been cursted over its face with some sort of tough digested matter, and some says that the same was observed above a year ago, so

---

[m] In a former page (43) the Diarist has called his friend Edwin Sandys "knight," and here again he has given him the prefix of "Sir," that is if he is alluding to the same person. His father, Sir Thomas Sandys, is styled "knight and baronet" in the parish register of Hatfield, but the latter title must be an error.—See *ante*, p. 36.

that it is notable to exert its power and heat upon those northern countrys (if not all others likewise) as much as it used to do, which is the reason that we have had no summer this year, nor very little last year, but continual rains and missts, to the great damage of harvest.

23. I was with the ingenious Doct[or] Smart, at Brigg, and having asked him several questions about antiquitys and old coins, he says that, when he was a boy about sixteen years old, as he and some more of his companions where playing and casting handfulls of sand one at another, some of them grasped three or four old coins amongst the sand, and, looking further, they found above a peckful hid in the sand hill. They were all Roman emperors, and as fresh as if they were new coined, being all of brass or mixt mettal, and about the bigness of half crowns. The town's name, where they were found, is Whitburn, a fisher town by the sea-side, and betwixt Sunderland and Schields.

About twenty miles beyond Doncaster there is a town they call Eccleston,* which has an old church at it, which for its antiquity is become the subject of a proverb amonsgt the country for a great many miles round about, who, when they would express a thing of any great antiquity, they immediatly say that it is as old as Eccleston church.

10 NOVB. I have observed it two or three times, that when I have been in trouble, that I have always met with very comfortable hopes in my reading accidentally the very appointed services of the church, so the last week I was presented for not being at the last Vissitation, and for some malitious thing layd to my charge, and the Sunday following, which was the third day of the month, in the evening prayer, I mett with those appointed Psalmns, the 41, 42, and 43, which yielded me a great deal of comfort; and being to be at Lincoln, at the court, on Monday following, when I came there, the court was exceeding kind unto me, and sayd that I might not have troubled myself in coming, but might have but sent a line or two, and I should not only have been excused and cleer'd; and so nothing was ill.

The last week I took two or three new counterfeit sixpences, but exquisitly made, and washed with silver, being copper within. Munday was a sennit, they had many new sixpences stirring at Hull, with a Y for York on them, tho' they did not begin to coin such sixpences at York till the Wednesday following, so soon is

---

* Probably Ecclesfield is intended.

our new money counterfeited, so that now they take new milled monney as well as old, onely by weight.

The k[ing] and the parl[iament] agrees mighty well.

11. Doct[or] Johnston," after thirty years labour in compiling his history of Yorkshire, gives us now some hopes to see it

° The name of Dr. Nathaniel Johnston is one which no Yorkshire antiquary can pass by unnoticed. He made very considerable collections, consisting of transcripts of records, copies from Dodsworth, trickings of monuments in the churches, and of old mansions, in Yorkshire, abstracts of evidences illustrative of the property, descent, and alliances of some of the principal families of the county of York. He put together many volumes of genealogies ; some were copied from public documents, but others were the compilation of the doctor himself, and are extremely valuable, since the facts which they contain are not perhaps elsewhere to be found. The whole is in fact the apparatus for a topographical account of Yorkshire. The value of these collections is however diminished, to a great degree, by the hasty manner in which the manual art of writing was performed by him, nor can any practice in reading after him enable a person to determine with certainty what proper name is meant in some cases where it is of importance to determine it. Canon Raine says of them that " they are, most unfortunately, written in a hand so crabbed and obnoxious that even the most practised eye must look upon them with horror and amazement."— *Yorkshire Archæolog. and Topog. Journal*, 1869, part i., p. 19.

The father of Dr. Johnston, a native of Scotland, was a member of the English Church, and, at the time of his death, held the Rectory of Sutton-upon-Derwent. He seems to have resided, at one period of his life, at Reedness, in Yorkshire, for there, it is believed, the doctor was born in 1627, and was baptised at Whitgift. Early in life he married and settled at Pontefract. His wife was a daughter and coheiress of the Cudworths, of Eastfield, in the parish of Silkstone, an ancient family of the better yeomanry or lesser gentry. His practice was extensive, lying amongst the superior gentry of the West Riding. An account of his family was furnished by him to Sir W. Dugdale at the visitation of Yorkshire in 1665. At that date he was 38 years of age. (*Surtees Society's Publications*, vol. xxxvi., p. 6). He went to reside in London, and there, it is said, he was for ever giving out that he had methodized his collections for the history of the county, and intended to publish them. The work was to be in ten volumes. It was thus when our Diarist above refers to him. The Earl of Peterborough was the antiquarian earl whom perhaps he assisted in the compilation of the history of the House of Mordaunt. From the state of obscurity into which he fell he seems not to have emerged, and Hunter says that he accidentally discovered that he died in 1705. Relative to his property, the following is a copy of an advertisement, which appeared in the *Gazette* from Monday, March 24th, to Thursday, March 27th, 1707.

" All the Estate of the late Dr. Nath. Johnston, consisting of a Great House, and several other houses and lands at Pontefract, Eastfield, Hadley House, Cravemore, and Thurgoland, in the County of York, is to be sold by vertue of a Decree of the High Court of Chancery, before Dr. Edisbury, one of the Masters of the said Court, at his Chambers in Symond's Inn, where particulars may be had."

His collections fell into good hands, for they were purchased by Richard Frank, esq., of Campsal, Yorkshire, F.S.A., recorder of Pontefract and Doncaster, himself a diligent labourer in the cause of literature, and one who carefully preserved the accumulations of others. The MSS. are now the property of the descendant of his brother, Frederick Bacon Frank, esq., the present possessor of Campsal.—See *Hunter's South Yorkshire*, ii., pp. 465, 466 ; *Ib.*, prefaces to vols. i. and ii. ; *Thoresby's Diary*, i., p. 39.

I

brought to light. He has collected, for the time, all that ever he can find in most antient authors, and has lately sent several volumes thereof down into the country to crave any one's additions or corrections. That concerning Hatfield, Thorn, Fishlake, etc., came to me, but I would not meddle to add anything in Hatfield, because that I am writing the history of that place,[p] but I have added abundance of things to Thorn, Fishlake, Bramwith, Sandal, etc.

The Doct[or] is exceeding poor, and one chief thing that has made him so was this great undertaking of his. He has been forced to skulk a great many years, and now he lives privately with the Earl of Peterburro, who maintains him. He dare not let it be openly known where he is, and the letters are directed for other people that goes to him. When I write to him he desired me

[p] The following extract, relating to Hatfield, out of De la Pryme's MSS. in the Lansdowne Collection in the British Museum, may not be unacceptable :—

"It is situated (as almost all ye towns of its name are), upon a pleasant, fruitful, and happy soil, neither too high, nor too low, too subject to durt in winter, nor too troublesome in summer by reason of its dust ; 'tis not too much exposed to winds, nor rendered unpleasant at any time by vapours or mists, but every thing conjoins in one to make it pleasant and neat. It stands in ye midst of an almost round field, not disfigured by hills and dailes, perpetually green with corn in one part or other, and ye pleasant oaks, and woody pastures and closes, which encompass this field and town round about, gives a most delectable prospect to ye eye.

"The town itself, though it be but little, yet 'tis very handsome and neat: ye manner of ye building that it formerly had were all of wood, clay, and plaster, but now that way of building is quite left of, for every one now, from ye richest to ye poorest, will not build except with bricks : so that now from about 80 years ago (at which time bricks was first seen, used, and made in this parish), they have been wholy used, and now there scarce is one house in ye town that dos not, if not wholy, yet for ye most part, consist of that lasting and genteel sort of building ; many of which also are built according to the late model with cut brick and covered over with Holland tyle, which gives a brisk and pleasant air to ye town, and tho' many of the houses be little and despicable without, yet they are neat, well furnished, and most of them ceiled with ye whitest plaster within.

"And as this town was formerly a royal village, in which ye kings had a pallace, so there is part of ye pallace standing, being an indifferent larg hall, with great courts and gardens about the same. There is likewise a hall or two of good workmanship and curiosity, with several large well built houses, an ingenious and well contrived school-house, and the most stately, magnificent, and beautifullest church that is to be seen in the whole country ; and another glory of this town is, that it is not plagu'd with any dissenters.

"Altho' this town be not dignify'd either with a market or fair, yet it stands so conveniently that it is not far off of any, haveing Doncaster five miles distant on the west, Thorn two miles of on ye east, and Bautry seaven miles on ye south, so that if it stands in need of any thing, there is but a little way to fetch ye same. But indeed ye town of itself is so well furnished with one or two of almost every trade, as butchers, mercers, chandlers, joyners, cutlers, chirurgians, etc., that other places stands in more need of them than ye latter of ye former."

superscribe his letter onely thus—For the Doctor—and then to wrap it in another paper, and sealing it, to superscribe it thus:

> This for the right reverend father in God,
> Tho[mas] Lord Bishop of St. David's, to be left with
> Mr. Monah, postmaster, over against
> Ax Yard, in King's Street, Westminster.

And then, under all, he desired me to make two strokes, thus, ———————————— which was a private mark.

24. I have lately written several letters to Doc[tor] Johnston, and informed him of a great many things of Thorn, Fishlack, Sandal, Doncaster, York, Pomfrit, Thorp, Burrowbrigs, Middleham, Darfield, Beverley, etc.

About the year 1638-9 the Levels of Ancham, where the river Ank runneth, were drained by the instigation of the Dutch, several of whome were overseers in the business. The cut or river called New Ankam (falsly for New Ank), from five miles beyond Newstead to Humber, in the cutting of which river was found oak trees lying with their tops north east, and nothing else of any note. Some of the trees were plainly broke by stress of weather; others, tho' very few, were plainly cutt, but the most were driven down root and all. The great sluce that they built at Ferriby cost above 3000*l.*, and had twenty-four doors, each of which doors were able to laid a cart and eight horses, by reason of their great thickness and weight, and the great quantity of iron that was therein. The sluce is sayd to have two or three flowers [floors], and it is added that twenty-nine waggon load of the best timber that could be found in these woods went to the pileing and the laying of the foundation of that sluce. This I had from several old men.

In Haxey Carr there are several great hills not farr from one another called Fort Hills: when the[y] were built, or what for, is not easily known.

The last time that I was in Yorkshire I was with an ingenious gentleman, a virtuoso, who had been in all the Irish warrs. He gives most lamentable accounts of every thing, too long here to mention. He says that one time he saw our carriages drive over a field in which there had been a sharp fight for the pass, and they drive over all the bodys of the men there killed, some of which was not yet dead, and their bones crack'd and broke as they drive over them. He says he saw three Irish men quarter'd alive by command of K[ing] W[illiam]. They put their knives in their breasts and so cut them up. They had impail'd two

Englishmen that they had treacherously taken. He was likewise att the time in the camp at Caricfergus, where they were almost all pined to dead, and, being but 30,000 weak sickly men, were encompass'd by 50,000 of their enemys, yet durst not attack them. He says, as I have related before, that the common soldiers when they wanted any seats to sit on, they would commonly run to the next tents and pull out a dead man or two, stiff with cold, and, drawing them to the fireside, would sit on them instead of a bench, and smook tobacco, and sing and drink, etc.

DECBR. 20. Monney goes for no more than it weys, nor for that neither. I mean no clipt monney will go now for more than 5s. 2d. an ounce, and sometimes ten, fifteen, or more shillings will but weigh that, so badly was our money cliped.

21. I was told this day a very observable thing by a very good hand, which is this. When Champion Dimock[q] let of his horse to kiss K[ing] James the Second's hand, after that he had challenged any one that durst question the king's rights to the crown, as the custome is, the champion in moving towards the king fell down all his length in the hall, when as there was nothing in the way that could visibly cause the same ; whereupon the Queen sayd, " See you, love, what a weak champion you have." To which the k[ing] sayd nothing, but laught, and the champion excused himself, pretending his armour was heavy, and that he himself was weak with sickness, which was false, for he was very well, and had had none.

In Haxey carr, in the Isle of Axholm, formerly called Haxeholm, is to be seen several great hills which have been cast up, and are called by the vulgar Fort hills.

I have writt to Doct[or] Bernard again, and have sent him a cattalogue of several more MSS., that are in the hands of some gentlemen on this side the country.

Being this day in company with one Mr. Nevil, an ingenious man, of Winterton, we fell into discourse about the great Irish hubub that happen'd soon after K[ing] Will[iam] came in. He told me of several men that was kill'd in the same, one perhaps is not unworthy of relating, and that is as follows. In the aforesayd time there was one John Smith, who, belonging to Hull, had a vessel in Grimsby Road, and, at the same time, when all the great stir was, one of his men went with the country mobb to

q See antea, p. 109,

search a papist's house not farr of. When they were come to the house, this man, because that they would not give him entrance, he puts his musket into the window and shoots a servant that belonged to the house quite through the head, upon which he dyd immediately. This being done, they got in and haild the people away to the next town. But the aforesayd Smith, hearing what his man had done, he calls him abord, and so away they steard for Hull. But, on their course, as they were sailing, this man fell by chance from off the deck of the shipp into the sea, and was drounded, etc.

The Andersons is a worthy and honourable family, great lovers of the church, and of unity and peace. Stephen Anderson was a great loyalist in K[ing] C[harles] the First's days, and was almost ruined thereby, altho' that he had a vast estate. All Appelby then was his, and he sould it to aid the king. He gave at one time 800 pounds to compound for his estate. He maintained for several years a troop of horsemen at his own charges, and had his house at Manby thrice sacked, and every thing that he had taken away from him, not onely household goods, but also all his beasts and horses. He was in the siege of Newark. He had four sons, which was then but young; which four are now alive, viz., Sr. Stephen Anderson, Edmund Anderson, Francis, and Edwin. When a party of the enemy sacked his house the last time, they enquired hard for Frances his little son, who was then at nurse in the town of Manby, to have got him, and to have made his father redeem him, which so frightened the nurse that she takes the child, dresses it and herself all in raggs, and ly's it on her back, and away she ran with it to Newark, and got safe into the town. Mr. Edmund, and a sister that he had, was carry'd about almost a whole year, from place to place, the one in one panyer, the other in another, but, God be thank'd, never got any harm. These four brothers are yet alive. This I had yesterday from one of them.

Sr. Steph[en] lives at London, in Bedford Walks; Mr. Edm[und] at Eyworth, in [Bedford]shire, in the south; Mr. Frances at Manby, and has about 800l. per annum; and Mr. Edwin at this town of Broughton.

This day I read Mr. Bohun's character of Queen Eliz[abeth]. I remember that I have heard his son, who hang'd himself, several times say that his father had had that book a long while by him to print, and had sent it several times to be licenced towards its printing, but it was not suffer'd to be printed. At last of all, when I was at Cambridge, he was made a licencer to

the press, then it was printed. But a short while after happened
the death of his son, which so disturbed him that he licenced
several books which he should not, whereupon he was brought
to the barr, and, after a confession of his fault, he received his
demitts, and was turned out of his place of licencer.

1696-7.

JAN. 2. In this church of our's, of Broughton, is an antient
monument of white marble, being the statues of one Sr. Henry
Redford and his lady, who is sayd (by tradition), to have been
the builders of this church. They are both cut of one great
stone, and are made holding one the other by the hand. They
did formerly lye in a little quire on the north of the chancel;
but, when Sr. John Anderson dy'd, his executors, that set up a
curious fine monument to him, removed the two aforesayd statues,
and now built the quire, and made his monument to be put
therein, and removed the aforesayd into the rails of the communion
table, and layd the first under an old arch which had another
monument on it formerly, and layd his lady below by him. He
lyes all in armor. Upon his leg, in modern but well cut letters,
is engraved these words, "Here lyeth Sr. Henry Retfort,
Knight."' There is his and her gravestones likewise, with their

---

' The inscription on the knight's leg is effaced. The Arms are correctly
described. There is also a rampant lion in a narrow compartment at the west
end of the tomb. The knight and lady wear each a collar of SS. Her feet rest
on two dogs collared; his on a lion with an uninscribed label coming out of
his mouth. His surcoat has the arms of Redford upon it. The two figures
are each cut out of a separate block of alabaster, which has been painted stone
colour.

Gervase Holles, in his Lincolnshire collections, noticed the following shields
in the windows. "In fenestrâ australi, 1.—Rydford : argent, fretty s., a chief
s., impaling Strange (gules, 2 lions passant arg). 2.—Rydford impaling a chief
gules. The crest defaced."

Henry Redford was sheriff of Lincolnshire in 1393 ; Sir Henry Redford,
knight, in 1406 ; and Henry Redford in 1428.

Mr. Peacock has a transcript (made by himself from the original in the
possession of a friend), of a charter of Henry Redford, of which an abstract
is annexed.

"Sciant, quod ego Henricus Redford milesdedi Willielmo Laken, Ricardo Bedford,
& Willielmo Staveley, maneria mea de Carleton Paynel, Irby, Worlyly & Kyllyng-
holm, cum advocacione ecclesiæ de Irby, ac reversionem manerii de Casthorp
[Castlethorpe, in the parish of Broughton]. Quod quidem manerium Maria,
domina de Clynton, mater mea, tenet ad terminum vitæ suæ. Testibus Hamone
Sutton, Willielmo Percy armigero, Thoma More, Thoma Chambr, & Ricardo
Gunne. Dat. apud Carleton Paynel, 19 Nov., 29 Hen. vi. (Seal circular.
Arms.—Argent, fretty sa., a chief sa. Crest.—A bull. Inscription.—SIGIL....
REDFORD MILITIS.)"

statues thereon, in brase, and has had their arms and inscriptions on formerly, but are now pull'd of. The arms of this knight and his lady is thus in the stonework :—

1.—Two lions passant. [Strange.]

2.—A fret of six, and chief, [Redford.]

3.—Redford. impaling two lions passant.

In the aforesayd little quire ly's the effigies of judge Anderson, curiously cut of alabaster, leaning his head on his arm, and holding a book in the other hand. Round about the monument are many inscriptions, which here follow.

Sr. Edmund Anderson, Kt, Ld. Chief Jus. of ye Common Pleas, had, by Magdalen his wife, ye daughter of Nich. Smith, of Anables, in ye county of Hartford, esquire, to his 3d & youngest son Will., who lived part of his time at this town of Broughton, & dying here, lys buried in ye chancel of this church. Ye sayd Will. marry'd Joan, ye daughter of Henry Essex, of Lambourn, in ye county of Barks., esq., & had by her one onely son, Edmund, born at Redburn, in ye county of Hartford, August ye 1st, 1605, who also dyed at this place, ye 19 of January, 1660, haveing been promoted to the degree of Baronett, ye 11 day of Decemb. before. In memory of whome this mon. was placed here, he haveing so order'd it to be in his last will & testament.

In another oval table thus :

Sr. Edm. Anderson, Barrt., marry'd to his 1st wife, Mary, ye daughter of Tho. Wood, of Audfield, in ye county of York, Esq., & heiress to Barnay Wood, of Killenwyck Percy, in ye county of York, Esq. He had issue by her 7 sons & 3 daughters, Will., Edm., Jo., Edm., Franc., Charl., & Steph., Mary, Franc., & Susan. After his 1st wife deceased, who dyed at Carleton, in this county, 1636, & lyeth interred there, he marryd to his 2d wife, Sibilla, ye relict of Edw. Bellot, of Morton, in ye county of Chester, Esq., & daughter of Sr. Rowl. Egerton, of Fardingoe, in ye county of Northampt., Baronet, who survived him but few months, dying at this place, 1661, & lyes interred by his side in this burying place.

In another oval thus :

Sr. John Anderson, Baronit, 3d son to Sr. Edm. (his elder brothers dying before his father) succeeded to his father's dignity & estate. He was born at this place, December ye 23, 1628, & was marryed the 5 day of Nov., 1659, to his wife Eliz., ye daugh. of Hugh Snawsell, of Bilton, in ye Annesty of ye county of York, Esq., & by her had issue one son & 4 daughters, Edm., Eliz., Kath., Frances, & Mary. He dyed at this place, ye 18 day of March, 1670, & lyes interred in this burying place, which he built according as his father had ordered it to be.

On the east end of this great monument on an oval table there thus :

Here lys also interred ye body of Mary Wood, widdow to Tho. Wood, of Audfield, who dyed at this place, November ye 16, 1665.
And likewise ye body of Frances, ye daughter of Will. Staresmoor, of Froulsworth, in the county of Leicester, who was ye 1st wife of Francis, ye 5th son of Sr. Edm. Anderson, buryed here Decemb. ye 20, 1667.

The arms of the Woods was thus :

On a bend engrailed 3 fleur-de-luces, with a wolf's head grinning, collor'd, for it's crest.[']

Over the door of this little quire is the bust of a young man, thus under-written :

In memoriam Domini Edmundi Anderson, Baronetti, qui natus est Biltoni, in agro Ebor., 15 die Augusti, 1660. Obiit autem Londini, 17 die Septemb., 1676, hocq in loco sepultus jacet (rosa immatura sic rudi carpitur manu). Mœstissimus patruus Carolus Anderson hoc monumentum poni curavit, Anno Dom. ⊕xii.[']

Upon a great gravestone of black marble, in the midst of the chancel, is this following inscription :

Here lyeth yᵉ body of Will. Anderson, youngest son of Sr. Edm. Anderson (who, by his first wife Jone, daughter to Henry Essex, of Lamburne, in yᵉ county of Birks., Esq., had issue Edmund Anderson, now liveing, and by his second wife, Eliz., daughter of Sr. Tho. Darnes, two daughters, which dy'd young). He departed this life yᵉ 2d day of August, Anno Dom. 1643, aged 62 years.

Upon a brass, in the midst of another black gravestone, is this following inscription :

Here lyeth yᵉ body of Katharin Anderson, yᵉ onely daughter of Stephan Anderson, of Broughton, in yᵉ county of Lincoln, Esq., & of Katharin his wife, daughter to Sir Edwin Sandys, of Ombersley, in yᵉ county of Worster, Knight, who dyed yᵉ 25 of September, Anno Dni 1640.[ᵘ]

Upon another stone :

Here lyeth yᵉ body of Mary, daughter of Edwin Anderson, Gent., and Mary his wife, who was buried May yᵉ 31, Anno Dom. 1681.[ᵛ]

Upon an alabaster stone thus :

Here lyeth yᵉ body of Elizabeth, the onely daughter of Josias Morley & Elizabeth his wife, who departed this life yᵉ 22 of May, Anno 1677.

['] The crest is now broken off. The following is an inscription yet remaining.—THE COATE ARMOUR OF BARNABYE WOOD, OF KILLNWICK, ESQ., WHOSE HEYRESS, MARY, WAS FIRST WIFE TO SIR EDMUND ANDERSON. And opposite to it is this. [Arms, quarterly, 1 and 4, Anderson, 3 and 4, five stars of five points]. THE COAT ARMOR OF SIR EDMUND ANDERSON, KNT., Lᴰ. CHIEFE JUSTICE OF THE COMMON PLEAS.

['] The following explanation of the ⊕xii (signifying 1678), appearing on the monument in Broughton Church, is from Mr. W. H. Black, F.S.A., of Mill Yard, London.

"⊕ is a circle divided into quarters, and therefore containing a simple cross : it so becomes a monogram of 1666, constructed thus :—

The circle with the upright or polar diameter represents ↺, the old Roman numeral mark for M (Mille) ; while the two halves, or E and W sides, signify D and C respectively. The cross represents L, X, V, and I. All these elements, if used once only, make up MDCLXVI. Add the XII, then 1666 + 12 = 1678, two years after the man's death, in 1676 (q. e. d.), the date of the monument."

[ᵘ] This is now over the chantry door.

[ᵛ] Now destroyed.

This Mr. Morley was steward to S^r ...... Anderson, and has got a mighty estate under him. He lives now at Redburn, in this county.[w]

On an old gravestone, in the quire, in letters so old that I could scarce read them, is this inscription :

Hic jacet Dom. Tho. Wats, quondam Rector hujus ecclesiæ, cujus animæ propitietur Deus.

There is another gravestone or two written on, but they being modern, are so worn out, that I could not read them.

There is a narrow black, or raither blew gravestone, with the superficies elevated, with a long cross thereon : and there I saw part of another also, which had a cross and a sword on, being a man of some millitary order.

On one of the bells is written, in old text letters, this sentence:

IN MULTIS ANNIS RESONET CAMPANA JOHANNIS.

from which it seems to appear that this bell is dedicated to St. John.[x] On the other side is this :—

CUM VOCO AD TEMPLUM VENITE, 1669.

This family of the Andersons is of no great antiquity. Judge Anderson's grandfather, from whom all those Anderson's are descended, was onely a miserly gripeing husbandman of Flix-burrow, in this part of the county, who had such good luck to scrape together as to make all his posterity great even unto this day.[y]

---

[w] There were two families of Morley in this neighbourhood. The Morleys of Holme Hall, in the parish of Bottesford, who were distinctly in the rank of the gentry, and the Morleys of Winterton, who were somewhat less clearly so. There is no evidence, that I am at present aware of, which demonstrates the connection of the two ; but I have little doubt that the Winterton Morleys were a branch of those of Holme. Fragmentary pedigrees of both are in *Peacock's Church Furniture.* It is next to certain that Josias Morley was a cadet of one of them, but he is not named in either pedigree.

[x] The bell inscribed IN MULTIS ANNIS RESONET CAMPANA JOHANNIS was broken up and recast about two years ago. A bell with a similar legend yet exists at Scotton, near Kirton-in-Lindsey.

[y] Our Diarist had been misinformed when he spoke thus contemptuously of Judge Anderson's father's family. I believe that record evidence could, if necessary, be produced to disprove it. The Andersons are believed to have come from the North of England. We first find them at Wrawby, afterwards at Flix-borough, near Burton Stather, where the moat, which once protected their mansion, is still picturesque with trees and flowering brushwood. Edmond Anderson, the judge who tried Queen Mary of Scotland, was the founder of the families now represented by the Earl of Yarborough and Sir Charles Henry John Anderson, of Lea Hall, baronet. The arms, as now borne, are : argent, a chev. between three crosses flory sable. On the Judge's seal, and others of later date, the charge is, a chev. between three crosses crosslet.

Jan. 15. New money begins now to be pretty plentiful, and the country people have now left of their curseing and daming parlament, and begins on the other side to praise and commend them.

Brigg, in this county, that I go so oft to, to see the newse, is a pretty large town: it has a good trade, there being no market-town of less than eight miles of of it. It seems not [to] be of any great antiquity. It stands in four parishes, and has no church nor chapel, so that it is plagued with dissenters. It's right name is Glenford Brigg,[z] from the consideration of which name it plainly appears either to have had its name and origin from one Glenford that built a bridge there, or else from a ford and a bridg over the river Ank (falsly called Ankam), which ford and bridg was in a shady vally, for so glen or glin signifiys in Welsh.

The ground upon which the town stands seems to have been all washed thither from the neighbouring hills, because that under it is a plain moor, as they do easily find when they digg wells; and in the sayd moor, and in the commons round about the town, is found and digged up great quantity of wood, most of it oak, which shows that there was indeed a shady vally here formerly.

Jan. 29. This day I was with one Mr. Dent,[a] of Roxby, who

---

[z] The town of Glamford, Glanford, Glandford, or Glemford Bridge, commonly called Brigg, stands in the four parishes of Broughton, Scawby, Wrawby, and Bigby. Till about twenty years ago there was no church, but a very mean room was used for the services of the Church of England. A church has now been built, sufficiently large for the accommodation of the people, but in a style of architecture, which, although we must call it Gothic, in no way reminds us of our ancient ecclesiastical edifices. As might be anticipated, the place is not in the Domesday Survey. It no doubt arose out of a collection of fishermen's huts around the ford of the Ank, or Ancholme. The first notice Mr. Peacock remembers seeing of it is a papal rescript of the time of Henry III., from which it appears that a hospital existed here, founded by the ancestors of Ralph Paynel. This hospital was subordinate to the Abbey of Selby. It seems that Ralph Paynel had complained to Pope Gregory IX. that the abbot and convent of Selby had converted to their own use this hospital. The pope therefore orders the Bishop of Lincoln (Grosseteste), and the dean and chancellor of the same church, to examine the case and do justice therein. It seems to have been decided that one of the brethren of Selby should have custody of the hospital, and reside there, but that the revenues should be expended upon the poor only. —*Monast. Anglic.*, vol. vi., p. 688. There is a notice of the chantry at Glaunford-Bridge in the *Patent Roll*, vii. Edward III., part i., no. 16; and of the *Tolls at the bridge* in that of Richard II., part i., no. 14.

[a] Probably of the family who were sometime afterwards settled at Winterton; of whom John Dent, of that place, who was born 25 June, 1703, and died in 1771, by Isabella, daughter of Thomas Aldam, of Warmsworth, was father of

tells me that he was about fifteen or sixteen years ago servant to one Mr. Van Akker, an Englishman, who haveing above 700*l.* per annum, travelled with him and his chaplain (one Mr. Broom, who has a liveing now somewhere by Dover), over all England, Wales, and Scotland, and into Holland, where this Van Akker dyd. He says that the aforenamed chaplain writt every thing down that they saw in Engl[and], etc., in two larg vol. folio, which the aforesayd chaplain yet preserves by him in MSS.

FEB. 7. I have found in an old bit of paper that there was a castle at Redburn,[b] in this county, and that when the Barron warrs was at an end, the lord of the manor pulld it down, and built the church of the town out of part of it, and a monastry out of the other part, and sold what stones spared.

FEBR. 11. Being with one Mr. Jo[hn] Worsley yesternight, a learned and ingenious clergyman, wee had a great deal of discourse about old things.[c]

He says that when that Gen[eral] Monk called a free parlament, in which was proposed the bringing in of K[ing] Ch[arles] the Second, that one Cornal King, parlament man for Grimsby,[d] started up when he heard the motion made of bringing him in, and declared that tho' he was not against it, yet he would desire them that, considering they had all been in rebellion against him, they would take care to bring him in upon such and such articles, that he might not be able to hurt them. Upon this Gen[eral] Monk answer'd, that he should be brought in like a king, and not like a slave with his hands tyd ; upon which followed many warm disputes in the house, but it at last passed that he should be brought in so as the gen[eral] had sayd.

Jonathan Dent, of Winterton. The latter individual amassed very considerable wealth, which he left to a son of his sister Catherine, wife of Robert Tricket, of Hill foot, near Sheffield, viz., Joseph Tricket, born 1 May, 1791, who, by royal license dated 11 Sep., 1834, assumed the surname of Dent in lieu of Tricket, purchased the estate of Ribston, Yorkshire, and was High Sheriff of that county in 1847.—See *Burke's Dict. of Landed Gentry*, ed. 1863, p. 363.

[b] Redburne. The statement about there having been a castle here and the church being built out of it is very doubtful. It is stated in the *Monasticon* that Richard I. confirmed to the monks of Selby the church of St. Andrew, of Redburn, which had been given by Reginald de Crevequer, with the consent of Mary his wife, and that he also gave the town with forty acres of land. It remained a part of the possessions of the abbey until the fall of the religious houses.

[c] It is believed that Mr. Worsley was an old member of the Royal Society.

[d] Edward King was one of the members for Grimsby in the Parliament that met 25th April, 1660.

This King was afterwards, when the king was restored, taken up
for these words, and sent to the Tower, where after sometimes
imprisonment, he was set at liberty, [on] paying his fee or entering penny, as they commonly call it, which always is 50*l.*   King
would not pay this so great a sum, so that there was a great stir
between him and the govern[ment], but at last they agreed to
refer the thing to the famous or raither infamous Mr. Pryn, that
was then in the Tower digesting all the records in order.   So
having gone to him he immediately answered that no prisoner
should pay above fourpence for his entrance, and brought an old
rect. and proved it.   Upon this there were many hard words, but
in fine, King got out by that means for nought, the governor
bidding him get him gone.

   This Pryn that I have here mentioned was the great rogue in
Cromwell's days, and one of the very beginners of our civil
warrs.   When the king came over, the Privy Councel did not
know what to do with this great man, nor how to keep him from
plotting against the government, so therefore, the king (to keep
him employed), made him keeper of the records in the Tower,
and commanded him to digest them all in their propper order of
time, which he did, to the great ease of any that go's to search them.
He also made him search for many particular cases, on purpose
to keep him imployd, knowing that it was almost impossible for
him, who had been a plotter and rebell so long, [to keep] from
plotting again, unless that he was so fully imployd otherwise that
he could not have time to invent and hatch mischief.   He writt
his history of K[ing] J[ames], etc., in the Tower also, to which
work he was instigated by a certain great man, for nothing
but the reason aforesayd, and afterwards became a mighty stiff
man for the king and the church, and writt a " Historical Vindication of the Supream Ecclesiastical Court," and many things besides.

   The Winns (formerly called Gwins), lords of Appleby, Thornton, etc., in this county, is but a family lately sprung up, tho'
now they are dignifyd with knighthood.*   George Win, in King
James the First's days, was but a country gentleman, but
reckon'd very rich by the gripeing methods that he used.   He
bought a great deal of land, and flourished mightily in Cromwel's days.   He bought Appleby of Stephen Anderson of Manby,

   * See pedigree of Winn (*Hunter's South Yorkshire,* ii., p. 216). George
Winn, here mentioned, purchased Nostel, in Yorkshire, of his younger brother,
Rowland Winn, an alderman of London, who had bought the estate of the
Wolstenholms, 25 May, 1654. He was created a baronet 3 December, 1660.

who, being a great loyalist, was forced to sell the same to carry
on business. The next of the name was Edmund Win, who was
knighted in K[ing] C[harles] the Second's days (or pretended
to be so). He marryd to his second wife his maid servant, who
was the daughter of one Jackson, a baker in Gainsbur, by
whome he had two sons and three daughters. His first son, S[r.]
Rowland, came to his estate about a year ago. He owns Appleby and Thornton, in Lincolnshire, and Nostell, and many more
places in Yorkshire, to the whole vallue of about 3,500l. per
annum. He is a mighty mad, proud, spark, exceeding gripeing
and penurious, and a great oppressour of the poor.[f]

1697. APRIL 1. I was asking the clark of this town of
Broughton, this day, if never anything observable of antiquity
had been ever diggd up in this town; to which he answered
nothing that ever he observed or heard of, but onely he can remember very well that, when he was a boy, he saw the then clerk
digging a grave just under the communion table, and having
opend a coffin they found a skelliton, and, about the skull, an antient
caul, which was a sort of cap or cornet that women wore formerly on their heads, which caul was of massy leaves of gold,
curiously embossd and flowered. He adds that the then minister's wife got it (who was Mrs. Waterland), having given the clark
something to hold his peace; and he says that it was constantly
reported that shee sold it at Gansburg for a great many pounds.

"Scarburg Warning" is a proverb in many places of the north,
signifying any sudden warning given upon any account. Some
think it arose from the sudden comeing of an enemy against the
castle there, and haveing dischargd a broad side, then commands
them to surrender. Others think that the proverb had it's
original from other things, but all varys. However, this is the
true origin thereof.

The town is a corporation town, and tho' it is very poor now

<hr />

[f] Sir Rowland Winn died 16th Feb., 1721, and was succeeded by three
other lineal descendants of the same name. Mrs. Cappe, of York, who has left
many notices of the Winns in the memoirs of her own life, was accustomed to
distinguish the four baronets of the name thus :—

Old Sir Rowland,
Good Sir Rowland,
Profligate Sir Rowland,
Unfortunate Sir Rowland.

Mrs. Catherine Cappe was the daughter of the Rev. Jeremiah Harrison, by
Sarah, daughter of Edmund Winn, Esq., of Ackton, second son of Sir Rowland
Winn, the second baronet.—See *Hunter's South Yorkshire*, ii., p. 216. She
died 27 July, 1821.

to what it was formerly, yet it has a . . . . who is commonly some poor man, they haveing no rich ones amongst them.
About two days before Michilmass day the sayd . . . .
being arrayed in his gown of state, he mounts upon horseback,
and has his attendants with him, and the macebear[er] carrying
the mace before him, with two fidlers and a base viol. Thus
marching in state (as bigg as the lord mare of London), all along
the shore side, they make many halts, and the cryer crys thus
with a strang sort of a singing voyce, high and low,—

> Whay ! whay ! whay !
> Pay your gavelage, ha !
> Between this and Michaelmas day,
> Or you'll be fined, I say !

Then the fiddlers begins to dance, and caper, and plays, fit to
make one burst with laughter that sees and hears them. Then
they go on again, and crys as before, with the greatest majesty
and gravity immaginable, none of this comical crew being seen
as much as to smile all the time, when as spectators are almost
bursten with laughing.

This is the true origin of the proverb, for this custome of
gavelage is a certain tribute that every house pays to the . .
. . when he is pleased to call for it, and he gives not above
one day warning, and may call for it when he pleases.

Capt[ain] Hatfield[f] was first of all in Lambert's regiment,
but when the king came in, and all the old rebellious regiments
broke, he got to be in Gen[eral] Monk's regiment, and Mr.
Corn[elius] Lee was his cornet.

S[r.] Corn[elius] Vermuden sold a great deal of the land in his
lifetime. He sold the man[or] of Hatfield to S[r.] Edw. Osburn,
who sold the same to Mr. Gibbons, and he sold it to S[r.] Art[hur]
Ingram.

Mr. Corn[elius] Lee told me this as a most certain truth ; that
Sir Phil[ip] Stapleton, who was Oliver Cromwell's great friend,
went to . . . . to desire him to advance Mr. Cromwel to
the honor of a lievetennant or captain's place, I have forgot
whether, in his regiment, which thing he readily granted, and
calling Mr. Cromwel in, the . . . . . had a great deal of
talk together, and sayd that he would grant him a commission
for the place as soon as he had time. S[r.] Phil[ip] Stap[leton]
came three times to the earl for his commission before he could

---

[f] John Hatfield was a cornet in Sir Hugh Bethel's regiment of horse, 9th
April, 1660.—*The Remonstrance and Address of the Armies of England, Scotland, and Ireland, to the Lord Monck,* 4to, 1660, p. 14 ; see *antea,* p. 13.

get it. Says the earl to him the last time, " Sr Phil[ip], I have
not withheld this favour from you nor your friend on any ill will
to either of you, but the first time I saw him, his presence made
such an impression on my spirits that [I] cannot get shut of it,
and I see by his face that if I advance him hee'll clim higher
than us all, and be our ruin. I had the commission all this
while written by me, and could not deliver the same before I
declaird this ; and now, I being somewhat at case, take it, and do
what you will with it." Sr Phil[ip], having got it, gave it to
Mr. O. Cromwell, who gladly received the same.

Wee have had a great many fast days every year since the
king came in. They were, at first, every first Wednesday in a
month as long as the king was away ; but they grew from little to
little to be so neglected that nobody heeded them, almost every
one went to their work and about their worldly concerns. The
king's council and chief magistrates considering this, thought it
not best to call the people to account for this, for fear it should
inrage them ; therefore these fast days were appointed to be kept
upon Sundays, tho' it is not handsom to fast on the day which
has always been accounted a festival. Yet the necessity of affairs
made it to be so.

19. In the chancel of [Broughton] church, in the wood work
thereof, is a coat of arms that I formerly overlooked, which is
thus. (*A rough drawing of a St. George's cross*).

21. This day I took my horse and went to see a place called
Gainstrop, which lys in a hollow on the right hand, and about the
middle way, as you come from Kirton, formerly called Chirictown, to Scawby. Tradition says that the aforesayd Gainstrop
was once a pretty large town, tho' now there is nothing of it
standing but some of the foundations. Being upon the place I
easily counted the foundations of about two hundred buildings,
and beheld three streets very fare. About half a quarter of a
mile from the sayd ruind town, on the left side of the way as you
come from the aforesayd town of Kirton, just in the road, is a
place called the Church Garth, and they say that the church
which belonged to Gainstrop stood there, with several houses
about the same, all which are now ruind and gone.

Tradition says that that town was, in times of yore, exceeding
infamous for robberys, and that nobody inhabited there but thieves ;
and that the country haveing for a long while endur'd all their
villanys, they at last, when they could suffer them no longer,

riss with one consent, and pulld the same down about their ears.

But I fancy that the town has been eaten up with time, poverty, and pasturage. 'Tis true indeed that as this roade from Lincoln to Wintringham was the onely great road in former times unto the north, and all those that travel'd thither came hereon, so by reason of the great woods, which reach'd on both sides of the way from Scawby as farr as Appleby, there were so great robberys commited that travellers durst not pass but in whole caravans together: and in this our wood of Broughton was a place called Gyp or Gip-well, which was a huge great spring and hole in the earth, near to which place a company of rogues always had their rendizvouse, and those that they robb'd they carryd them thither, and, haveing ty'd them hand and foot, cast them therein, as is certainly related here by all the whole country round about. By this well grew several huge elm and willow trees, which was cutt down and cast therein, with several loads of earth and stones to fill the same up. Near the same also the thieves had several stone cabbins, and a stable for their horses, these were likewise cast into the said well, and so choked up the same that it is scarce now to be found.

These great roberys were one of the causes that made this road, from Scawby northwards, to be neglected, so that Broughton, Apleby, Winterton, and Wintringham, that were great and populous towns formerly, and most of them had marckets, soon decay'd and came to nothing; for travelors, that they might avoyd the aforesayd dangerous woods, went over at a ford in the river Ank, then called Glenford, and now Brigg, and, so passing along, they cross'd the Humber at Barton.

While these roberys were thus frequent, no question but some thieves did live at the aforesayd place of Gainsthorp, but whether they might be the occasion of the ruin of it, or raither time, poverty, and pasturage, I shall not trouble myself to examin nor decide.

APRIL. There was a commission[h] lately at Louth; amongst other dishes of meat that was brought up, there was towards the latter end thereof a tansey.[i] After they had eaten of this tansey

---

[h] Commission. The Diarist means a meeting of the Commissioners of Sewers. Much about the Lindsey Commissioners of Sewers is to be found in *Dugdale's Embanking and Draining.*

[i] Tansey was commonly used in cookery among our forefathers. It will be remembered by readers of the *Spectator* how beautiful the widow's hand and arm appeared to Sir Roger de Coverley, when she was helping him to some tansey (*Spectator*, No. 113). It has not quite gone out yet in some parts of the country, but its use is rare. Most of the older cookery books contain recipes for making tansies.

all the commissioners fell sick. Immediately some vomited, some purged, some fainted, others were so gryp'd they did not know what to do, yet put as good face on everything as they could. After dinner their servants were call'd in, and being asked what sort of liquor they had drunk, and what sort of meat they had eaten, they told them the very same that came from their table, only they did not eat any tansey, because there was meat enough besides, and they sayd they were very well. Upon this they sent for their hostes up, and asked her where shee got so much tansey grass this cold and backward year, to make her tansey so green as it was. Shee told them shee knew what they ment, and, begging their pardons, told them that truly shee could not get any [thing] to make her tansey green, and that therefore, going into the garden, shee got a great handful of daffadilly leaves and stalks, and having brused them and squeezd the juse out, it was with them that shee had coloured it green. So they concluded that it was them alone that had wrought such effects upon them.

1697. MAY 1. This day I went to take a view of the country. Having passed through Brigg in our way towards Melton, we went by a great spring, famous in days of old, called St. Helen's Well.[j]

Being come to Melton, I could find little or nothing observable there, it being but a little poor town. The church is such a one that it dos not deserve the name of one, neither is there coats of arms, monuments, nor epitaphs therein. There is a close over against the church, on the south side, called the Hall close, from a great hall having formerly been there. Towards the north end of that close is a place which has been moated in, which perhaps has been some antient cell.

From thence I went to Kennington, where I could find nothing observable, nor any thing of antiquity. In the church, if I may give it so honourable a name, was only two or three recent coats of arms, the one being one Mr. Airy's, as we were told.

From thence I went to Crowston, betwixt Melton and which place there are certain hills (as I am told), call'd Fort Hills, but I had not time to seek the same. There is a church, but not worth seeing.

From thence I went to Ulsbee, now called Housby, which is a pretty large town. As you enter the same on the south side is

---

[j] Saint Helen's Well, so named after Helen, the mother of Constantine the Great. The water with which the town of Brigg is supplied comes from this spring.

J

a large tumulus, or bury, all hollow on the top, under which
there has been some numbers slain in some battel that has been
fought there. The church is pretty handsome and neat. In the
quire, which belongs to the Appelyards, is a great deal of painted
glass, and in the glass this coat of arms. [*Sable, five fusils in
jess between three mullets pierced or.*]

From thence I went to Thornton.[k] I was amazed to see the
vast stupendious fragments of the buildings that have been there.
There is all the gait-house yet standing, of a vast and incredible biggness, and of the greatest art, ingenuity, and workmanship, that ever I saw in my life. There is four or five images,
standing in the front thereof, of excellent simitry and workmanship, and upon every exalted or turrited stone in the battlements
of the gatehouse, and on the top of the turrits, stands images,
from the middle, of men with swords, shields, pole-axes, etc., in
their hands, looking downwards ; and I was told that upon the
battlements of the whole college, when it was standing, was in-

---

[k] Thornton College, founded by William le Gross, Earl of Albemarle,
about 1139, for canons regular of the order of St. Augustin. After the suppression of the religious orders, the site of this monastery was reserved by
Henry VIII., for the purpose of founding a college there to the honour of the
Holy Trinity. This continued only till the second year of Edward VI. (*Monast.
Angl.*, vi., 325). On 13th June, second Edward VI., the site of the college, with
the greater part of the precincts, along with divers other estates, in Thornton,
Barrow, Goxhill, Halton, and Ulceby, were granted for a term of twenty-one
years to Henry (Holbeche), bishop of Lincoln, for a rent of 44*l*. 9*s*. 8*d*. : and by
letters patent dated 3rd July, third Edward VI., the reversion of the same was
granted to Robert Wode, of the Inner Temple, London, gent., from whom the
said Henry, bishop of Lincoln, purchased the site in perpetuity. The above
Henry "Holbeache, *alias* Henry Randes, by the goodness of God, bishop of
Lincoln," by his will dated 2nd August, 1551, disposed of this property to his
wife, with remainder to his son, Thomas Randes. Thomas Randes, of the city
of Lincoln, gentleman, sold the same, 1st September, 1575, to Sir Robert Tyrwhitt, of Kettleby, knight. In 1587, dame Elizabeth Tyrwhitt was in possession
of the premises, and by feoffment dated 24th November, 1588, she conveyed the
same to her grandson, Robert Tyrwhitt, the son of her son William. On the
28th February, 1602, Robert Tyrwhitt sold the aforesaid to Sir Vincent Skinner,
of the city of Westminster, knight. In 1720 the property passed from the
Skinners, by purchase, to Sir Robert Sutton, of Kelham, in the county of Nottingham, knight, from whose family, in 1792, the estate passed by sale to
George Uppleby, esq., of Barrow, upon whose death, in 1816, it was again
sold, and conveyed to Lord Yarborough. (*Notes penes Mr. Peacock, by the
late Mr. W. S. Heselden, of Barton-upon-Humber*).
 The figures which the diarist saw on the ramparts of the gateway have
perished. There have been many views of the magnificent gateway of this
house published. By far the best is a large engraving issued by subscription,
by Mr. William Fowler, of Winterton, from a drawing by his son, Mr. Joseph
Fowler, in the year 1818. The view of it in the "*Monasticon,*" by a strange
blunder, is attributed by the engraver to Thorncham, or Thornholme, an Augustinian house, in the parish of Appleby, in Lincolnshire, not one stone of which
has remained upon another for many years.

numerable statues of the greatest ingenuity and workmanship imaginable, some in shape of soldiers, others of astronomers, others of carpenters, others of all trades and sciences,[l] so that, looking up, the battlements of all the whole building seemed to be covered with armed men. There are abundance of images yet, on various places of the gait house, of dogs, bulls, bears, foxes, lions, etc. The passage all over a vast moat is of delicate workmanship and ingenuity, so that I cannot easy describe the same.

There is ther the hugest finest court that ever I saw in my life, with two rows of trees on each side, on both sides of which trees is the ruins of vast buildings to be seen, and the like almost all over. At the north side is the fragments of the chappel, of mighty fine stone, and curious workmanship, which, by the arches that is now stand[ing], appears to be above half buried in the ground in its own ruins. The drainers that drained these levels of Ank, *vulgo* Ankham, fetch'd all the stone from this chappel that they built Ferry Sluce with,[m] and, by a just judgment of God upon [them], for applying that to profane uses that had been given to God, the drainers were all undon, and the sluce, which cost many thousands of pounds building, is now coming down.

Out of part of the old buildings is built a large but somewhat low hall, not farr of of the aforesayd chappel, which, with the whole estate, belongs to the Lady Skinner,[n] who lives at London.

There is a current story[o] that about one hundred years ago, as one was pulling down some of these old buildings, they discover'd a little hollow room, which was a monk's cell, with the exact figure of [a] monk in all his cloaths, set before a little table,

[l] This I had from tradition.—*Marginal note by Diarist.*

[m] Ferry Sluice should perhaps be Ferriby Sluice. There is no sluice at Ferry, that is Kinard Ferry, in the parish of Ouston, in the Isle of Axholme. De la Pryme gives a different account in his history of Winterton. Both statements may be true however. *See Archæologia,* XL.

[n] The Thornton College estate was purchased, in 1602, by Vincent Skynner, of the city of Westminster, esq., from Robert Tyrwhit, esq., of Kettleby. Skynner, who was secretary to Lord Burleigh, was knighted at Theobalds, 7th May, 1603, and was buried at St. Andrew's, Holborn, 29th February, 1615-16. He had represented in parliament Truro, Barnstaple, Boston, Boroughbridge, and Preston. His wife was Elizabeth, daughter of William Fowkes, of Enfield, and widow of Henry Middlemore, of that place. She died in 1633. The widow of Sir Vincent's grandson, Edward Skinner (who was Anne, daughter of Sir William Wentworth, second brother to Thomas, earl of Strafford), was probably the "Lady Skinner" referred to in the text as being the owner of the college in 1697. She died 20th September, 1707, and was buried at Goxhill. The property now forms part of the estate of the Earl of Yarborough, of Brocklesby.

[o] Stukely tells this story about some one being found walled up here with a book and a candle, and it is repeated in *Greenwood's Tour to Thornton Monastery,* 1835, p. 26, only there we are told that the discovery was made in the last century.

with an old parchment book before, and a pen and ink and paper, all which fell to ashes when they were shaked and touched.

This has been the finest place that ever I saw in my life. If the gaithouse be thus neat, undoubtedly the building of the college and the abby was one hundred times more excellent.

From thence I went to Barton. Barton has been a very great and rich town formerly, but Hull, growing up, has robb'd it of all it's trade and riches. There are two delicat fine churches, in excellent repair, the one dedicated to St. Peter (which church, and the chappel of All Saints, which formerly was in this town, but now is quite forgot, were given by Walter of Gant to Bardney Abbey in Lincolnshire), the other is dedicated to St. Mary, but, as I remember, they told me that the former is the mother church. In these two churches has formerly been a great many grave stones with brasses upon them, but they were pull'd of in Cromwell's days, when the organs also were pull'd down. There are a few brasses left. I had not the time to write all their inscriptions down, but onely this as the most observable. Upon a great black stone is the image of a monk in brass, treading on two barrels. He was not a monk, as appears from the inscription, but it was common for people that would to be buried in monks' habits, believeing there was such divine power therein the divels durst not touch them. The inscription[p] is this :—

In gratiâ et misericordiâ Dei hic jacet Simon Seaman, quondam civis et vintinarius Londoniæ, qui obiit 27 die mensis Augusti, anno Domini millessimo tricessimo tertio, cujus animæ et omnium fidelium defunctorum Deus propitietur. Amen. Amen.

In a brass about his head this :

Credo quod Redemptor meus vivit, et in novissimo die de terrâ surrecturus sum, et in carne meâ videbo Deum Salvatorem meum.

There is a great many coats of arms, which, being fresh, I did not take down. On a long kind of a cornish between two pillars is drawn the coats of arms of all the kingdoms in the world which traded with this town, as the tradition says. There is the arms of Jerusalem with this inscription in old letters,

REX HIEROSOLIMÆ, ETC.

Not farr of this town is a great old tree call'd St. Trunyon's tree, under which that St. had an altar and religious rights.[q]

---

[p] The inscriptions in the churches here were printed in a history of Barton, compiled (anonymously), from Mr. Heselden's notes, and published by Mr. Ball, bookseller, Barton-upon-Humber, about eight years ago. It is, I am informed, a carefully edited little book.

[q] St. Trunion. There was, half a century ago, at Barton, a spring, called

The field of this town is reckond the biggest in all England but Godmanchester. It is a custome here, as it is at Godmanchester also, whenever a king come by, all the husbandmen wait upon or go's to meet him with their plows.

There is smook money[r] payd at this town, which is the same with the old Peter's pence.

I will go visit all these things again some day, and take a more particular account of them.

23. This day I was at Brigg, towards night, and meeting with a very ingenious countryman he tells me that but a while ago, he himself saw a huge ash tree cut in two, in the very heart of which was a toad, which dyd as soon as it got out. There was no place for it to get in, all was as firm about it as could be. I have heard of a great many toads that have been found so likewise.[s]

1697. MAY 7. Mr. Castor, of this town of Broughton, sent me this day one of the finest and largest *Cornu Ammonis*, as it came out of a larg round blew clay stone, that ever I saw in my life. It was found in the clay pit at the east end of this town.

I was at the Visitation the other day, and there was nothing that I heard observable. There is a project come out for a lending library in every deanery. I subscribed five shillings towards the first trial of it.

I pay ten shillings a year towards the mantaineing of one Mr. Cleworth, at St. John's, at Cambridge, because he is a poor youth.[t]

St. Trannian's Spring; and in the open field a thorn, called St. Trannian's Tree.

The Very Reverend Dr. Rock suggests that St. Trannian may be St. Tron, a native of Brabant, who preached the faith in that province in the seventh century. He built a monastery there, which was called St. Tron's, or St. Truyen's. His death took place A.D. 693.—See *Butler's Lives of the Saints*, November 23.

[r] Smoke Money. Smoke silver, or reck pennies, were paid to the vicar in many parishes in Lincolnshire, as a kind of small tythe; in lieu of tythe of fire wood, it has been thought. Jacob says that in 1444 the bishop of Lincoln issued his commission "Ad levandum le Smoke-farthings."

[s] Stories of this kind have been common enough.

[t] Thomas Cleworth, son of the Rev. Thomas Cleworth, of Hatfield, Yorkshire, baptized there 15th January, 1677-8; educated at Hatfield, under Garett; admitted sizar for Wigley, 4th June, 1696, aged 18, under Mr. Nourse; B.A. 1699-1700; ordained deacon 21st September, 1701; priest 1st March, 1701-2, at York; and then admitted to the vicarage of Campsal, co. York, on the nomination of Colonel Lee. He died 22nd April, 1754, having been vicar fifty-two years. James Fretwell, a neighbour, in his diary, alluding to his death, says, that "He was universally respected, and that deservedly. He was a grave, sober, pious man, but not at all morose or cynical, but of a cheerful temper, and innocently pleasant in conversation."

I pay 13d. a quarter to the king, for my head, according to the great tax, but I was not cess'd for any money, etc.

Being this day near unto Thornholm moor, I was asking several old men what was the names of such and such great hills in that moor. When you [go] through our wood on the Roman highway, as soon as you enter through the gate on Thornholm moor, the place round about is called Bratton-grave-hill. The vulgar says that there has been by that yate several people buried that have hanged themselves ; amongst which there was one which was called Bratton, but I suspect that there is something more than this in the antiquity of the name.

About a half or rather quarter of a mile furder by the road are several hills called Gallow hills,ᵘ which sound very ancient.

A little furthur over against, and by a little house standing in Thornholm wood side, formerly called Sand Hall, are some hills called Averholms.ᵛ On the south side of Thornholme, on the moor side, is two or three great hils, called Maut Hills. I have not at present my Saxon nor my Welsh dictionary by me, or else I would strive to find out the meaning of them. There are several more parts of the same moor called by other name, but they are modern names.

Yesterday, being a day of great thunder, Madᵐ Anderson told me that about three years ago the thunder fell upon their house, or raither hall, at Broughton where they live. Part of the lightning flew in at a chamber window as a woman was shutting the casement, and scorched all the length of one side of her arm, and felld her down and almost stifled her. At the same time it came down through the chimney into the kitchin, where the family was all set, and, rebounding from the ground, part of it flew in a huge flame betwixt some of the people out of the south window, without breaking a bitt of the glass or making any hole, and the other part flew to the north side of the kitchin, and so into a little room, and through the north window thereof, makeing a larg hole. For all this nobody was hurt in the house but the aforesayd woman servant. But there was so great a smook therein, and so great a smell of gunpowder or brimston, that they were almost choked. Some that saw this lightning fall upon this hall compared it to a whole river of fire falling out of the air, and the hall seem'd to be totaly encompassed with flames.

ᵘ That is gallows hills, where the gallows stood in antient times. that be-longed to the priory. (*Marginal note by Diarist*). This seems to shew that the Prior of Thornholme had capital jurisdiction here. I am not, however, aware of any other evidence of this.

ᵛ For Moot Hills, perhaps.— *Vide* Spelman. (*Diarist.*)

14. I was at Hatfield in Yorkshire last week with the Commissioners of Sewers. Justice Simpson, of Babworth, in Notinghamshire, being one,[w] told me that either last year or this, I have forgot whether, as the workmen were digging very deep to lye the foundation of the steeple of Babworth Church, they found the skull of a monstrous giant, and some of the bones. The skull was almost two foot diamiter, in which were many teeth, but the workmen casting several great stones upon the same, as they dig'd deeper, they broke it in pieces. But the justice, hearing thereof, made the stones be removed, and tho' that the skull was found all broke in pieces, yet they gathered up about eleven teeth, all which he gave away but three of the greatest, which he keeps by him, which are about three times as great as our's.

16. This day I went to Redburn, formerly called Retburn, as the ingenious Mr. Morlay tells me. This town was very much larger than it is now. Mr. Morlay tells me that within the memory of man there were above eighty farmers therein, whereas now there is not above thirty. It is pastureing that has undon it. There has been a larg castle there, with a great moat about it, the foundations of which is yet to see. As a man was digging therein for stone, he found a silver cupp. This castle was pull'd down towards the latter end of King John's days, and out of part of it was the church built which is now standing. The church is but little, yet was given to Selby Abby, in Yorkshire, in K[ing] Edw[ard] the Third's time, by . . . . . as we find in the first vol. of the Monasticon. The church is very beautifull; there ly's an old stone in the quier under an arch on the northside, with the figure of a man engraved thereon, with a short dagger in his hand, with this inscription by him.[s] [Not inserted].

[w] 11th May, 1697, court held at Hatfield, before Samuel Mellish, Henry Cooke, William Sympson, Thomas Lee, John Hatfeild, esquires, and others. This was William Simpson, of Sheffield, and afterwards of Babworth, Notts.— See pedigree, *Hunter's South Yorkshire*, i., p. 184. Genealogical notices in *Hunter's Hallamshire*, 234.

[s] This monumental slab yet exists; it is put up sideways, near the north wall of the chancel. An engraving of it was made by the late Mr. William Fowler, of Winterton—the last work that admirable artist ever executed. The inscription, in a bold black letter character, forms two lines on the right hand of the figure. It runs thus :—HIC JACET DNS GERALDUS SOTHILL MILES QUI OBIIT ANNO D'NI MILL'IO CCCC CUIUS ANIME MISERERE DEUS. AMEN. The knight is clad in a complete suit of plate armour, girt with sword and dagger. His feet rest on a collared greyhound, which has a bell to its neck. He has a long drooping moustache, and wears a conical helmet, without visor. The head rests on a double cushion, supported by two angels. There were five Gerard Sothills. This one is probably that Sir Gerard who married a daughter of Sir Gerard Salvin.—*MS., Queen's College, Oxford*, F. 22, fol. 15.

In Cromwell's days there was a great deal of painted glass in the windows of the north alley of this church, which the soldiers broke down with such fury that they broke also the stonework of the windows, and pull'd of the sacred lead that covered that ally, and said that, seeing it was polluted and defiled by idolatrous images in the glass underneath, anybody might take it away, as they did, so that this ally fell to ruin, and was some years after totally pulled down, and the wall built under the arches of the great pillars.

Out of the ruins also of the aforesayd castle was also built a large great house or hall, on the east of the castle close (which is eighteen or nineteen acres), which, I fancy, has been a religious house, a cell to the monastry of Selby, the markes of it being a religious house are these, the cherubim heads that are to to seen in many places in stone, and the heads of men in stone in many places. The shape of the hall like such a publick hall as we dine in in the Universitys, and several windows is to be seen like chappel windows.

Of all heresys that ever were raised by the divel from Christ's days unto these, Quakerism is one of the boldest, and one that has made as great encrease, as I lately got a new book writt by De la Croose,[y] a Calvinist, an impudent man, who, to palliate their heresy, defends their monstrous tenents to the seduceing of many unstable souls, and who has writt as many lys almost as there is pages in the book, besides the impudent reflections he casts upon the glorious Church of England, the best and most pure church in the whole world.

God be thank'd I have onely one family[z] of those damn'd he[re]ticks in my parish. The woman is a great speaker, makes three or four sallys a year into the country, and has stayd out sometimes a month or two or three at a time, and never returned home with less than thirty or forty pounds in her pocket, which shee gets for the wages of her unrightiousness and heresy.

This trick of the new coining of the money at such an unreasonable time, when we were, and yet are, engaged in a doubtfull warr against France, was most certainly a French trick, as I have been lately inform'd; for, amongst the letters that were

---

[y] Gerard Croose, a protestant minister of Amsterdam, born there, 1642 : author of a History of the Quakers, 1695, octavo, in Latin, of which there exists an English translation. He also published "Homerus Hebræus, sive Historia Hebræorum ab Homero." 1704, octavo. He died in 1710, at a place near Dordrecht.

[z] The Nainbys.—*Marginal note by Diarist.*

intercepted and taken comeing from France, when about the
great plot was discovered, there was plain proofs thereof; in one
of which letters was mentioned a saying of the French King, to
this purpose. When he had heard that the design did go on in
reforming our coin—" This is well (says he), if this do not set
the English doggs together by the ears, the divel himself cannot
do't." But tho' this work has plainly done the nation more
hurt then all the warr and the taxes, yet, God be thank'd, we
are pretty well content.

19. The flowers of the lillys of the valley, which grow in
vast quantitys in these Broughton woods, are now ripe and open.
Here is come some men from Coronel Bierly's, that is above
fifty miles of, to begg lieve to gather some. Others are come,
some twenty, some thirty, some forty miles. There are at least
gather'd in these woods yearly as many as is worth 60l. or 100l.;
for when they are dry'd they are commonly sold for seventeen,
eighteen, and nineteen shillings a pound."

29. This day being Saturday I made an inroad into the
country to see and to examin what I could about the history and
antiquitys thereof.

In the first place I went to Normanby. It is but a small hamlet
belonging to the Ld Mulgrave, who was made marquis of the
same since this king came in. He has a very fine well built hall
or pallace there, but it is not great nor very stately. It is of
modern building.

From thence I went to Burton, which is a mile further. It is
but a small town, for all it is a market town, and is of itself very
poor. They have a little inconsiderable market there every
Tuesday. It stands upon the very height of the hill, and has a
mighty fine prospect all to the SW and WN. The church is
built of rough stone, and has nothing worth seeing in, there being no monuments nor no epitaphs, tho' there has been considerable men buryed there, as the late L^d and Lady Mulgraves, and
others. This church was, in times of popery, given with the
tithes to Freston Priory, in this county, by Alan de Creun. At
the east end of the quire, out of the same, ly's the body of one,
who was in times of old, vicar of the church. There has been
several brasses on the great stone, but they are now gone. With

---

^a There are great quantities of Lilies of the Valley in Broughton and
Manby woods. People still come from a great distance to gather the flowers
and take away their roots, which are medicinally valuable.

much to do I made out these words, *Orate pro anima*. In the
chancel is the Marquess of Normanby's arms, thus, [shield blank]
with two bores, supporters of the crest, which is a blew bore's
head upon a crown.

Not farr from this town is two hills like butt hills, they say,
for I did not see them, onely they are too farr one from another.
They are called Spillo hills.[b]

From thence I went all along upon the brink of the hill to
Alkburrow, commonly called Aukburrow. By the wayside I
saw a little burrow,[c] very hollow in the middle. As soon as I
came to the town I observed a four square trench encompassing
many akers of land, which tho' it be old, yet it seems to be
Roman, tho' it is but a small one.[d] That which makes me believe
that it is Roman, besides the squareness of it, is a tradition which
the people has, that there is a passage under ground from it to
Holton Bolls, which is a mile of, it being common with the
Romans, and no nations else, to make passages under ground
from their forts and camps to other places, to get aid and provisions into them the more secretly and safely in time of need.
They say likewise that there has been digg'd up about the town
several skellitons of men's bones, some of which were of a
monstrous greatness. Below this hill, hard by the waterside,
was built a strong little fort in Cromwell's days, which is since
fall'n to decay. This town is certainly of greater antiquity than
any town hereabouts ; Alkburrow signifying old town, and that
there were several old burrows there, under which men were
wont to be buried in time of warr. There is a pretty good
church there, but no epitaphs nor monuments in it at present
visible, because that the chancel, being fall'n, has buried all.
However, these words are written on a great stone in the wall of
the sayd chancel, now almost illegible :—

> Richardus Bruto, nec non Menonius Hugo,
> Willelmus Trajo templum hoc lapidibus altum
> Condebant patria, gloria digna Deo.

O ! 'tis a great shame and a skandall to see that chancel as it is.
It belongs to one . . . . Denman, esq., to repair and keep
in order, who has near 1000*l.* p[er] ann[um], and lives hard by,
and is lord of the town. Yet to his eternal shame he takes no care
thereof.

---

[b] A place in this parish is still called Spihoe or Spelhoe. There are also
two artificial mounds on the south side of Burton, on the declivity of the hill,
which seem to have been butt hills. No special name is attached to these.

[c] Called Lady, or Countess Burrow.—*Marginal note by Diarist.*

[d] Alkborough. There is a plan of the camp here in Stukely.

From thence I went to Whitten.* The town is but a little inconsiderable town, as most of these Lincolnshire towns are. It is seated mighty advantagiously, having the Humber running close by it. When I saw the town it put into my mind a song that I had heard of it, which ended at every verse thus :—

> At Whitten's town end, brave boys !
> At Whitten's town end !
> At every door
> There sits a . . .
> At Whitten's town end !

There is nothing worth seeing in the whole town. The present lord of it is one Mr. Pleadwell, who lives at London, who got it by marrying the daughter of Sᵣ John Morton, who was lord thereof before.

About twenty years ago was part of a great hall standing on the west side of the church,ᶠ in a cloase where the Mortons lived, but now onely part of the foundations appear.

It is exceeding probable, and that not without some grounds in history also, that there was a time when that the Humber broke through the woulds into the now called Ouse and Trent, and drounded and sunk many hundreds of thousands of akers of land, which now lyes all on the west of it; and, besides, Trent and Ouse falls about a mile west of this town at present (tho' I believe that formerly it fell even against this town) into Humber, and caused abundance of shipp wraks, and such like, which occasiond this common saying :—

> Between Trent-fall and Whitten-ness
> Many are made widdows and fatherless.

That which they now call the ness ly's about a mile from that place which they now call Trent-fall, which is against Foxlet-ness, in Yorkshire, which answers almost over against Alkburrow.

But, as I sayd, I do not believe that the Trent-fall was there first of all, but just over against this town, from which thing this town had it's name, for Wite, or Witen in Saxon signifys sorrow or sorrowfull, which answers to the afore going verses.

The hill which sloped the Humber, which afterwards was broke through, ran from Whitten high hill or ridge very much north east, and so butted upon the Yorkshire woulds ; but, being worn through by long success of time, it was all carry'd away and layd all along the midst, and all the north side of the

* Whitton is situate at the north-west extremity of the county of Lincoln, on a bold cliff overlooking the Humber.
ᶠ The present church is a modern structure, built about sixty years ago. Not a trace of the old one is left.

Humber, where it lys to this day, for a mile in length in a great
long bed, which is very dangerous for vessels that is not well
acquainted with the river; for commonly at low water the only
channel which lys all on this side is not above twice twelve score
yards over; so that tho' the river be very broad here, yet that
arises from the resistance to the tide that the reliques of this
hill made, which caused it to overflow, and dround so much
more on the Yorkshire side.

The church of this town is but mean, and there [is] nothing
worth seeing in it. The people has their seats full of straw to
kneel on instead of basses.

From thence I went to West Halton. This town tho' it bee but
little now is nevertheless of great antiquity. It's parish is very
large, which [is] also a good sign of its antiquity. The church
is all now faln to ruins, but appears to have been very stately,
magnificent, and larger than any one for a great many miles
round about it. There are two great bells lyes buryed amongst
the rubbish with these inscriptions upon the them . . . .
and in the quire is a great stone with this epitaph on it⁵ . . . .

As you come to this town from Whitten there is two great
burys, hollow on the top; and in the town, on the north side of
the church, is a huge hill called . . . hill, where has been
formerly a great . . . .ʰ

⁵ Spaces are left for the insertion of these, but have not been filled up.
ʰ The writer has entered in the Diary a copy of a brief that had been
issued for the rebuilding of the church, which sets forth "that the parish church
of West Halton, together with the steeple and bells, did immediately after
a violent tempest fall down, so that there has not been any public worship or
preaching therein for many years, save only in a little chancel, which is now also
become so very ruinous that the minister's dwelling-house is the only place to
which they (the inhabitants) can resort. That the charge of rebuilding the
church, chancel, and steeple is computed at £840," etc.   To this brief the
Diarist has appended the following annotations.

"Yᵉ chancel is all pretty good and firm. It will want onely a little strength-
ening and cementing together. This church at first cost, in all likelihood, some
thousands of pounds building at first, there having been a great deal of excellent good workmanship about it. Yᵉ old material is very good and fresh,
and will do good service.

"Yᵉ quakers are a mighty refractory people, and mighty backward to pay
anything of dues to yᵉ churches. Undoubtedly there will be but little money
got for this good use from them. I remember that awhile ago I was with yᵉ
pious and learned Mr. Tho. Place, Winterton, who told me, that when he began
at first to build and repair that church, that there met him suddenly in the street
a grave old long-bearded quaker, who accosted Mr. Place thus: 'Thou Place, (says
he) I have a message to thee from God, who commanded me to tell thee that
thou must desist in going out this work of the devil, yᵉ repairing of yᵉ steeple-
house of this town!' And then yᵉ quaker stamped at him, and denounced
several woes against him if he did go on. These unexpected words so frightened
and surprised Mr. Place that his hair stood almost upon an end; but having

When I was in the chancell I found that the town's chest was broke in pieces, and all the papers torn in small bitts by the birds, or else by some children. Three or four papers relating to the town's business, tho' of very small concern, I brought away with me, which I shall transcribe here, especially the most observable things in them.'

About ten years ago almost all Castor in this county was burnt down. The houses were poor mean things before, but are very neat and handsome now, and it is observed that every town is betterd exceedingly by being purified by fire.

Yesterday I was at Brigg with Doct[or] Smart, Mr. Jollence, and a gentleman call'd Mr. More,ʲ who comes out of Derbishire. He says that about twenty years ago, as his father was digging very deep in Staley parish, near Chesterfield, in the said county, that they found the perfect skeliton of a man of a monstrous bigness; the head was able to hold two pecks of corn, and this

considered thereof, he fell more hard to yᵉ work than ever, haveing really taken this fellow to have been employed by yᵉ divel to stop yᵉ same."

Among the political offenders of the seventeenth century the quakers of the day must be enumerated. They were concerned, more or less, with exceptions of course, in all the plots of the time. It was their delight to abuse the minister in the pulpit, and the judge upon the bench. They were continually violating public order and decency in the grossest manner. They prophesied. They walked about the streets in the unadorned simplicity of our first parents. They howled and bellowed as if an evil spirit was within them. They professed to use earthly weapons as the sword of the Lord and of Gideon. Madness like this was of course intolerable. In 1664-5, at Beverley, John Thompson, of Hollin, yeoman, deposed before the justices that discoursing with Peter Johnson (a quaker) concerning tithes, the said Peter took the deponent, gript and shook him, and told him that tithes should quickly be put down, and if the Lord would put the sword into their hand they would fight the Lord's battle. Further, that on Sunday after Lammas day, 1663, Peter said to Mr. Henry Salley, minister of Hollin, as he was going to Kilnsey to preach, " Harry, art thou going to tell lies as thou hast done in Hollin? repent, repent, thy calamities draw near," which he often repeated. Thomas Slinger, vicar of Helmsley, being about to inter a corpse, was openly assaulted by a party of quakers, who tore both the surplice and the book of Common Prayer. It was one of their practises to enter churches with their hats on during divine service, and to rail openly and exclaim aloud against the ministers with reproachful words, calling them liars, deluders of the people, Baal's priests, etc. One instance of this kind may be related. Mr. Fothergill, vicar of Orton, one Sunday exchanged pulpits with Mr. Dalton, of Shap, who had but one eye. A quaker, stalking in as usual into the church of Orton, whilst Mr. Dalton was preaching, said " Come down, thou false Fothergill!" " Who told thee," says Mr. Dalton, " that my name was Fothergill." " The Spirit," quoth the quaker. " That spirit of thine is a lying spirit," says the other, " for it is well known that I am not Fothergill, but peed Dalton, of Shap."—*Raine's Depositions from York Castle*, preface, etc.

ⁱ " The Cargraver's account, 1626." " Money disbursed by Antony Wright, churchwarden, 1628." " A whole Cargraver's bill of disbursements, but there is no year named."

ʲ *Forsan* Jalland and Mower.

gentleman says that he has by him now one of the teeth that was then taken out of the skull, which weighs four pound nine ounces,[k] and that which is most strange is that this skelliton was in an erect or standing posture.

25. I was at Barton yesterday with one Mijn Heer Peter Van Schelsbroot, an ingenious young Dutchman.

Hard by the church of St. . . . . . in Barton, towards the north side, stands part of an old building which has been a chantery, called chantry house to this day. There is a famous well at Barton which is called St. Catharin's well, which had the image of that S^t well cut in white marble standing by it, within the memory of several men now liveing, but it was all broke in pieces in Cromwell's time. There is a well in Barton Fields, that always rises and falls with the river Ank, now called Ankam, tho' the well is two or three yards perpendicular above the river, it being on the top of the would.

This day I was at a place called Kell Well,[l] near Aukburrow, where I got a great many pretty stones, being a kind of the astroites or starr-stones. There is many of them also at Whitton, on the cliffs, and in Coalby beck. The country people have a strang name for them, and call them *kestles* and *postles*, which somewhat sounds like Christ and his Apostles.[m]

Mr. Tho[mas] Place, of Winterton, is a very ingenious publick spirited man.[n] He spends his time in building, repairing,

---

[k] These are the figures stated in the diary, but it is difficult to imagine the writer gravely giving credit to the statement. If the story be not a joke, it is probable that they were the remains of an elephant. The bones of that animal have frequently been mistaken for human relics.

[l] Kell Well is a bubbling spring, which runs out from between the layers of Lias rock on the western face of the hill, near the Trent, between Burton-Stather and Alkborough. Keld, Keal, or Kell, is a common name for wells.

[m] The Diarist's explanation seems to be a fanciful one. The stones he speaks of are fragments of the arms of Pentacrinites.

[n] The name of such a man deserves all the perpetuity that can be given to it. In De la Pryme's History of Winterton, co. Lincoln, published by Mr. Peacock in vol. XL. of the *Archæologia*, he alludes to the miserable condition of the church of that parish after the civil wars, when so many suffered. "This particularly of this town was," he says, "through ye same, in such a state of decay that, for many years after ye Restoration, there was scarce either a bit of glass in ye windows, or of lead upon ye roof, or any good timber about it. It lay almost open to all storms, so that if either rain or snow fell ye congregation were sure to suffer thereby. Thus it continued, until that Mr. Tho. Place, a most worthy gentleman of ye said town, and general promoter of everything that is great and good, begun to commiserate its sorrowful condition and repair ye same, which he so effectually promoted and performed, that in a few years all its breaches and cranics were mended, its roof most of it cover'd with new timber and lead, its windows new glaz'd, its floors new layd, its old seats turn'd into oak pews, its walls beautifyd, its bells new cast, and its yard made level, handsome and neat, and most of this at his own proper costs and charges, so

and beautifying of churches, and most of this at his own cost.
There is a most excellent project comed in his head of building a
chappel at Brigg, because that that town being larg, farr from
their churches, and having in it all sorts of sectarys, becomes
by that means a seminary for all such like cattel the whole county
over. To stop all this, and to quell them, he is resolved to promote all he is able the erecting of a chappel* in the same ; and
that the sectarys may not, as they commonly do, call us hier-
lings, he is for having the whole neighbouring clergy to preach
there every Sunday gratis, which no one refuses, and seeing that
the Bish[op] of York has erected several weekly lectures on the
market days in many schismatic towns in Yorkshire, as at Pontefract, etc., so he is for having one to be here also, at which I have
promised to preach twice a month, besides as oft as the Sunday
preaching comes in my course.

Mr. Place being a layman is much envy'd by lay gentlemen

that it is now one of ye most beautiful churches in ye country." There are
many rich men of our own day to whom it may be said "Go and do likewise."
The Winterton Register contains several notices of this family.

1599. The 25 of December was . . . . Place buried.

1601. December the 7 daye, was Henrye Place beried.

1613. Isabell, the daughter of Will'm Place and Elizabeth his wife, May
the 24th (bap.)

1614. (?) William Place, September the 5th (bur.)

1616. Jone, ye daughter of Will'm Place and Elizabeth his wife, April 14th
bap'd (buried April 23).

1617. Thomas Place, the sonne of Will'm and Elizabeth his wife, was baptised August decimo die.

1618. Mary, daughter of Thomas Place, gent, and Elizabeth his wife, November 5 (bap.), [buried March 1st, 1620].

1622. Thomas, the son of Thomas and Elizabeth Place his wife, July 30
(bap.)

1624. Thomas Place was buried Desemb. 23.

[*There is a break in the Parish Register from 1639 to 1681*].

1683. Mrs. Mary Place, wid., was bur. August ye tenth.

1691. Mary, daughter to William Place, gent, and ffines his wife, was bapt.
April ye twenty first.

1691. Thomas Place, gent, was bur. July ye twenty third.

1693. Thomas, son to William Place, gent, and ffines his wife, was bapt.
July ye sixth.

1695. William, son to William Place, gent, and ffines his wife, was bapt.
November ye eight.

1697. John, son to William Place, gent, and ffines his wife, was bapt.
September ye fifteenth.

1703. Mrs. ffinis Place was buried April the sixth.

1720. Thomas Place, gent, was buried July the eighteenth.

[This is probably the gentleman whom the Diarist mentions].

1728. Mr. William Place bur'd November ye second.

* It is stated in *Allen's Lincolnshire*, vol. ii., p. 224, without any authority
being given, that the chapel at Brigg was founded by four gentlemen, whose
names are not told us, in 1699.

for these good deeds, therefore he has got Mr. Sye, Mr. Hargrave, and myself, who are publick spirited clergymen, to promote openly the design, and he himself will do all for it that he can underhand.

Wee was to have had a private meeting about it this day at Mr. Sy's, at Wintringham, but Mr. Place, happening to be not well, could not come, so our design was let fall. I had sent a letter to Mr. Brown, schoolmaster of Brigg (now preferred to three livings in Ireland by the Bishop of Clohar), to desire his company, but he was pre-engaged, and so writt unto me.

Mr. Baldwin, who was born at Doncaster, told me that about twenty-six years ago, in his time, there was a new window built in the church there, and that the cement to join the stone together was made of quick lime, ale, and tan water. He says that the whole in ale and tan water came to fifteen pound.

There is lately cast upon the shores of Yorkshire, in Holderness, vast quantitys of a mineral, exactly like bismuth or tin glass, many hundred cart loads. Some believes it to be silver oar. I have sent for some to try what it is. I hear that they are trying it in many places. They used to sell it at first for 1s. a bushel, but now they have raised it to three.

I was with one Mr. Kidson, of Barton, yesterday, who has been in many countrys. He says that, when he was last at Amsterdam, he chanc'd to meet with a great merchant in that citty with whom he was acquainted, and going to the coffy-house, the merchant began to tell him what he was going to do with his son. "In the first place," says he, "I will place him for a year or two with a wine-cooper in this citty, to teach him thoroughly the excellency of wine vessels and tuns, for there is non in the world have so good as them made at Amsterdam. Then," says he, "I'll send him some more years to London to learn of the English the art of makeing of wines, for," says he, "there is none in the world like unto the English for that. They'l take a small vessel of wine worth about 5*l*., and they'l make it immediately worth 50*l*.; whereas we useing the same art in Amsterdam cannot give it so lively a flavour and so natural colors. Most wines," he says, "cannot be drunk unless they be thus diluted and sophisticated." Doct[or] Merrel has writt a whole book of the mistery of Vintners.*ᴾ*

ᴾ In a previous part of the diary De la Pryme says he had heard it certainly related some years ago "that there was a man at York that made artificial wine so pure and natural like that nobody could discover it from the best wine that comes from beyond sea."

In King Charles the Second's time there came over an ambassador from Muscovy. Killegrew[q] went one morning to his lodgings to complement him, and pay him a visit. After a few ceremonys was past, the ambassador calls for his morning's draught, which was soon brought, to wit, a huge quart glass of brandy, and a great paperfull of pepper, a handfull of which he put into the glass, and haveing stir'd it well in, he drank it of to Killegrew ([who] was the king of drinkers in them days), saying "this is the King of England's good health." Killegrew look'd at him as if he would have look'd through, and was mighty loath to take such a drench next his heart, yet not knowing how to deny it, he took it off. The ambassador was for drinking several more such healths, but Killegrew (with a great deal of sorrow and shame), declined them, and takeing his leave he went to the king, swearing that he thought the divel and hell itself was in it: he had got a morning's draught that almost burnt him in pieces, and having told the whole story to the king, he laught heartily at him.

JULY 24. Wee had a Bishop's Visitation[r] on the 21st of this month at Gainsburg, and on the 24th I went to wait upon his lordship at Barton. Somebody told the bishop of the staitliness of the remaining buildings of Thornton College, upon which he went to see the same, and stood amazed with the august appearance thereof, he having never in all his life seen any building more curious and finer wrought than it. S[r]. . . . . Skinner,[s] that pull'd the college down, built a most staitly hall out of the same, on the west side of the abby plot within the moat, which hall, when it was finished, fell quite down to the bare ground without any visible cause, and broke in pieces all the rich furniture that was therein. Then S[r] Edm[und] Win, seeing no building would thrive there, he caused all the stone to [be] fetched away, and built a most delicate hall at Thornton town, but that prospered not neither, so that there is now onely a few of the lower walls to be seen thereon. After that . . . Skinner built another hall out of part of the stones that the other was built of, which hall now stands on the east side of the court

---

[q] Tom Killigrew, the famous wit, about whom so many stories are told. He died at Whitehall in 1682.

[r] He gives the following extract, "Out of y[e] church book of Broughton, anno 1540 or thereabouts. At y[e] Visitation at Spittle:—A quart and a half of claret wine, 1s. 3d. ; 3 quart of sack, 2s. ; half a quart more, 4d. ; one pound of sope, 3d. ; spent in ale upon St. Hew's day, 2d."

James Gardiner, S.T.P., was Bishop of Lincoln at this time. He was consecrated March 10th, 1694, and died March 1st, 1704.—*Le Neve*, p. 143.

[s] Sir Vincent Skinner.—See *antea*, pp. 130-131. *Note.*

K

of the abby, and is all built on arches of some of the old building. We observed the place of the huge portcullice, which was in the gait house of this abby, etc.

28. Haveing been in Yorkshire this last week, I mett with diverse learned and ingenious gentlemen, who told me a great many observable things.

It was upon Hanson's house at Hale's Hill, in Woodhouse,[*]

[*] Hatfield Woodhouse, near which place, in the centre of the great Hatfield turf-moor, were formerly about sixty acres of land, known by the name of Lind-holme. "It is a prevalent opinion," says Hunter (*S.Y.*, i., 196), "that here once dwelt some extraordinary personage who is known by no other name than that of William of Lindholme ; a species of Prospero, one who was in league with infernal spirits, and who was endued with strength far surpassing the ordinary strength of man. Two immense boulder-stones called the 'thumb-stone' and the 'little-finger-stone,' are supposed to have been brought hither by him," etc. Amongst the many traditionary stories related concerning him is one to the effect that, when he was a boy, his parents went to Wroot feast, and left him to keep the sparrows from the corn or hemp seed. The account is that he drove all the sparrows into a barn, which was then being built, and still unroofed, and con-fined them there by placing a harrow against the door. After he had done this, William followed his parents to Wroot ; and when scolded for so doing, he said he had fastened up all the sparrows in a barn, and where they found them on their return in the evening, one version says, all dead, except a few which were turned white. Since this transaction it is said that no sparrows were ever seen at Lindholme. Probably the setting of the *waggon* in the text refers to the story, as above, of placing a *harrow* against the barn door.—See more of William of Lindholme in *Hunter;* and in *Stonehouse's Isle of Axholme*, p. 393.

The following verses on the Hermit, William of Lindholme, are by the Revd. Abraham de la Pryme, F.R.S., our Diarist :—

Within an humble lonesome cell
He free from care and noise does dwell,
No pomp, no pride, no cursed strife,
Disturbs the quiet of his life.
A truss or two of straw's his bed,
His arms, the pillow for his head,
His hunger makes his bread go down,
Altho' it be both stale and brown.
A purling brook that runs hard by
Affords him drink when'eer he's dry,
In short, a garden and a spring,
Does all life's necessaries bring.
What is't the foolish world calls poor,
He has enough ; he needs no more,
No anxious thoughts corrode his breast,
No passions interrupt his rest,
No chilling fear, no hot desire,
Freezes or sets his blood on fire,
No tempest is engender'd there,
All does serene and calm appear.
And 'tis his comfort when alone,
Seeing no ill, to think of none.
And spends each moment of his breath
In preparations for his death,
He patiently expects his doom,
When fate shall order it to come.
He sees the winged lightning fly
Through the tempestuous angry sky,
And unconcerned its thunder hears.
Who knows no guilt can feel no fears.

See *Gentleman's Magazine,* vol. xvii, p. 23, 1747.

that S[t.] W[illiam] a' Lindholm set his wagon. One Hanson lived there then. Look and see when the Hansons lived, and then you may find perhaps when W[illiam] a' L[indholme] lived.

Near Gaubur Hall,[u] a mile beyond Barnsley, there is a great coal pitt which is on fire, and has burn[ed] many years.

There is a most delicate fine freestone at Brodsworth,[v] but so porose, tho' not visible, that, troughs being made of it, it will let the water run out for a year or two before that the pores are filled up with the sediment and sand carryd in the water.

The ingenious Mr. Place told me that, about ten years ago, when he was at London, he was well acquainted with one Mr. Kettlewell, a learned and ingenious barrister-at-law, who chanced to dy when he was there. When he perceived that he had but a small time to live he made his will, disposed of every thing, and sent for half a dozen fiddlers, two base viols, and other musick, and made them stand round about his bed, and play the most sweetly that ever they could, and charg'd them to play there till he was dead and an houer after, which thing they accordingly perform'd. He dyed that night, after that they had played a whole day before him; and when his will came to be look'd at,[w] it was found there that they were to continue playing before him night and day untill that the time came for him to be bury'd, and that then also they should play him even to the church porch.

AUG. 10. Mr. Place, of Winterton, being four miles from Humber, and two or three from any river, digging very lately for a well, found the ground undigged before, and at five yards deep came to the root, or stratum, or layer, or shell of stone, that

---

[u] Gawber-hall, in Bargh (Galbergh) occurs in the inquisition of Alice de Lund, in 32 Edward I. It was the estate of a family named Dodworth, afterwards of Jenkinson, Barber and Sitwell.—*Hunter's S.Y.*, ii., p. 378.

[v] Near Doncaster. (See *Hunter's S.Y.*, i., p. 314). The estate at the conquest was given to Roger de Busli. It passed through the Darels, and Wentworths, to the family of the Earl of Kinnoul, of whom was Dr. Robert Drummond, Archbishop of York, who died in 1777. By the sale of it by Robert, ninth Earl of Kinnoul, the Archbishop's eldest son, to Peter Thellusson, a London merchant, it was one of the places which, Hunter observes, became a name familiar in the courts at Westminster, under the extraordinary provisions of that gentleman's will, the particulars relating to which he supplies. The testator's eldest son, Peter Isaac Thellusson, was created Baron Rendlesham, of the Kingdom of Ireland, in 1806. From Charles, the third son, is descended C. S. A. Thellusson, Esq., born 6th Feb., 1822, who, within the last few years, has built an entirely new mansion at Brodsworth, and has greatly improved the village. This gentleman served the office of High Sheriff of Yorkshire in 1866.

[w] Colonel Chester, to whom I am greatly indebted for many other similar acts of kindness, has most obligingly made a careful search for this will in London, from 1680 to 1697, but without meeting with it.

is all over this country.   Upon it they found a great old-fashioned pot ear, and in the stone, which they were forced to cut through, the[y] found several pieces of wood somewhat heavy, but not petrifyd, which cracked and broke in pieces when it came to be dry.   He gave me a larg piece in the stone, and takeing some of it we put it in water and it swum.

Upon the top of the great ridg of the flying sand hills as you go from Santon to Burton market, in Santon parish, has been a great treasure of old copper coins hid ; they have frequently been found there by whole handfulls, but are all so eaten away that nothing can be observed upon them.   There was in the sayd sands, not long since, a fine wrought cross found, also of copper, about a foot and a half long, etc.

SEPT. The churches of Burton and Butterwic were given to Freston Priory in Lincolnshire by Alan de Creun.   Frodingham belonged to Birstal Priory, Messingham, Cletham, Scotter, Scotten, etc., to St Peter's in Peterburg.[*]

I hear that the sea formerly came up over all the marshes to Lincoln citty side, and that the parish of St Botulp's was once fined for not keeping the sea-dike banks in repair.   There is reckords of this to bee seen in the aforesayd church.

The Trent, before that the Humber broke it's way into it, all ran by Lincoln over those marshes into the sea.   There has, in the citty of Lincoln, been found great stathes and huge piles stuck down into the earth.   There was, not many years ago, an old boat found very deep, as they were digging a well, with hewn stone in it, sunk perhaps in the Roman time, when they were bringing stone to build their collony here.   There has also been found many scaled fish wholy petryfyd.

---

[*] Our Diarist has been led far astray here by the similarity of the names of places in the County of Lincoln. He thinks he is writing of Burton-upon-Stather, and East or West Butterwick in the Isle of Axholme, but the places he is really telling us of are Baston in Kesteven, and Butterwick near Boston. The Charter of Alan de Creoun and Muriel his wife to the priory of St. Guthlac of Croyland is given at length in the *Monasticon*, vol. ii., p. 120. By a typographical error Baston is printed Burton in the charter, but is given rightly in the *Minister's Account*, p. 125. Frieston was a cell to Croyland, and these properties were given " in perpetuum ad victum et ad vestimenta monachorum qui serviunt Deo in ecclesiâ sancti Jacobi Frestoniæ."

Frodingham belonged to Revesby Abbey.—*Monast. Anglic.*, v., p. 456.

The Rectory of Messingham belonged to the Augustinian Abbey of Thorn-holme.—*Monast. Anglic.*, vi. p. 357.

Cleatham, Scotter, Scotton, "et tres partes de Messingham," were in the abbot of Peterborough's fee.—*Chron. Petriburgense*, ed. Stapleton, p. 153, *et passim.*

Not far off of the Roman street that runs by Hibberstow, in Hibberstow Fields, appears to have been the foundations of many buildings. Tradition says that there has been an old citty there. I asked all ways that I could imagine to know the name thereof, but they could not tell me. Not farr from it is a place where tradition says stood a great castle belonging to this citty. I then asked if there was any old coins found there, and they answer'd some few Romans. I then asked if there was any springs hard by, and they answered that there was two ; the one called Castle Town spring, and the other called Jenny-Stanny well,[y] perhaps Julius's Stony well. This was undoubtedly some Roman town, because that it is so near the Roman street, etc.

There is a famous spring at Kerton, called Diana's head.[z] This coat of arms is in Wintringham church :—

> Or, a cross of St. George vert. Hussey, a knight family.[a]

I am told that at Lindwood, in Lincolnshire, by Marcket Rasin, ly's buried the famous civil laywer, Lindwood, under a fair monument.[b]

16. There is a great teacher amongst the quakers, who has for this last two months made it his business to go from meeting to meeting prophesying unto them that the day of judgement was to be on the six[th] day of this month, but this sixth day is over, and the quaker proves to be a lyar and decicver.

I was with Mr. Holms, min[ister] of Wrawby, yesterday. He tells as a most certain truth that about thirty-seven years ago he lived at Giggleswick (as I remember in Yorkshire, where the great school is), at which time one Mr. Lyster was min[ister] of the town. There was a quaker there, who was revelation mad, whome the spirit moved mightily to go to the church to reprehend the congregation. Accordingly, upon a fine clear Sunday,

---

[y] Jenny Scanny Well. This is at a farm in the parish of Hibuldstowe, now called Staniwells.

[z] No well called Diana's Head is now known at Kirton-in-Lindsey. There are several bubbling springs there. One is called White Well ; another Otchen Well ; and a third Esh or Ash Well. Mention has been met with of this last in a record of the early part of the sixteenth century.

[a] Hussey, Dorsetshire, Hador, Gowthorp, and Linwood, co. Lincoln ; and of Wiltshire, or a cross vert.—*Burke's Armoury.*

[b] Lyndwode, Bishop of St. David's, the canonist, was born at Linwood, in Lincolnshire, but not buried there. Of his birth-place there cannot be a doubt ; he says in his will, " Lego ecclesiæ de Lyndewode, ubi natus sum, antiphonarium meum minus de tribus." There can be no reasonable doubt but that he was buried at Westminster. He provides by his will "corpus meum sepeliendum in capella Sancti Stephani apud Westmonasterium ubi munus consecrationis accepi."

the quaker doffs him stark naked, and takeing a burning candle
in his hand he goes to the church, and as he entered into the
churchyard on the one side, a gentleman of the town hapened by
chance to enter in on the other side, who was amazed to see
him in such a state: who, calling him by his name, sayd, " N.,
where are you going ? "   " I am going (says he), to the house of
Baal."   " What house is that ? " sayd he : " That great house,"
says he, " whether thou art going."   " Why so? " sayd he :
" The spirit of God, speaking within me, commanded me to do so,
to reprehend that conjurer Lister."   " Did the spirit bid thee go
this day to reprehend the preacher Mr. Lister at this church to-
day? "   " Yea verily," sayd he, " the spirit did."   " Well, well,
fy for shame, N.," says he, " the spirit of delusion is in thee ; it is
the divel that leads and decieves ; this day Mr. Lister dos not
preach here, but one Rogers, therefore you may see how you are
deluded ; go, go home and be wiser," etc.   These words so
wrought upon the quaker that he went home much ashamed.[c]

This Mr. Homes was at London the year K[ing] W[illiam]
came in.   He says that, towards the latter end of the first parlament, the House of Commons had the impudence to pretend to
meddle with the holy things of the church, and would needs have
the cross in baptism, the surpless, and the use of the ring in marriage made indifferent things, so that people that would have them
might, and those that would not might not ; but the House of
Lords, tho' they argued long upon the bill, yet at last they cast
it out of the house.

The House of Commons are commonly a company of irreli-
gious wretches who cares not what they do, nor what becomes
of the church and religious things, if they can but get their
hawkes, hounds, and whores, and the sacred possessions of the
church.   It is plainly visible that the nation would be happier if
that there was no House of Commons, but onely a House of
Lords, who yet, nevertheless, should not have so much power as
they have, but should be onely the eyes of the country, and of the
council of the king, who should also be bound by his coronation
oath never to yield to any chang of the fixed ecclesiastic government, etc., for we commonly see that whatever mischief has been
wrought in the nation has been carryd on and back'd by the
House of Commons, etc., who vallues the weal politic above the
ecclesiastic, and their own worldly ends above their salvation.

    [c] See a similar anecdote in Canon Raine's preface to *Depositions from York
Castle, Surtees Society's Publications*, vol. xxiii.   Referred to *antea*, p. 141.

I have heard it from very many ministers and old people that the sacraments of baptism and the L^{d's} supper was so little regarded in Cromwel's time that they were in many towns and places quite left of. In many towns the L^{d's} supper was not administered for ten or fifteen years together, and people, I mean especially the presbiterians and indipendants, did not take any care to get their children baptized : so that quakerism and anabaptism spread mightily. Mr. Homes says that he has baptized since he came to Wrawby sometimes three, sometimes four, and sometimes more, altogether on one Sunday, who were at men's (or very near) estate, and that those were the sons of the aforenamed sects and not of the quakers. I have heard a great many relations of the same in other places.

23. I was this day with a gentleman that saw a larg piece of gold coin as bigg as a Jacobus, lately found at Riby in this county. He says that it was a Roman coin, and was such pure gold that [it] bended any way as easily as if it had been a thin plate of lead.

There is a pretty school-house at Brigg, but not very well situate, nor very well contrived ; it was built and endowed by one Sr. John Nelthrop after his death.^d

These Nelthorps (of which there is several in this country), [are] descended all from one Tho[mas] Nelthorp, who was taylor to Queen Elizabeth, who got a great estate under her, and purchased several houses in Hull, and several manors in this county.

I was at Authorp,^e by Trentside, yesterday. The church is

---

^d The Grammar School at Brigg was founded by Sir John Nelthorpe, the first baronet (created 10th May, 1666), son and heir of Richard Nelthorpe of Scawby, by his wife Ursula, daughter of Martin Gravenor, of Messingham. Over the school house door are the arms of the founder, Argent, on a pale sable a sword erect of the first, pommel and hilt or. Beneath them is the following inscription :—

JOHANNES NELTHORPE BART^{TUS}
SCHOLAM HANC
EX INSIGNI PIETATE
PROPRIIS SUMPTIBUS ÆDIFICAVIT
ET ANNUALI SUBSIDIO DONAVIT
IN PERPETUUM.
MDCLXXIII.

A good three-quarter length portrait of the founder is in the master's drawing-room.

The diarist has recorded "a true copy of so much of the aforesayd Sr. John Nelthorp's will, as relates to the aforesayd school," dated 11th Sept. 20 Car. 2, 1669, in which the testator is described of Grays Inn, co. Middlesex. (pp. 326-329, *MS. Diary*).

^e Althorpe.

well built of squared stone.   On the west side of the steeple are these coats of arms :—

| [1.—Neville. A saltire.] | [2.—Neville, quartering Beauchamp, and Newmarch, five fusils in fess.] | [3.—Mowbray, a lion rampant ; impaling Newmarch, five fusils in fess.] |

with a bull's head for the crest over the second.   On the south side is emboss'd on two great stones a ram with one foot touching the end of a great tun or barrel, with an old I and B over them.   This perhaps the simbol of some gentleman's name.   B perhaps stands for Bernard or Benjamin, and the ram and tun joyned together makes Ramton.   I have read of such a surname, but what their arms are I cannot tell.

The chancel seems to have been built since the church.   Over the arch of the east window is the coat of arms[f] of a lion rampant, and over that, instead of a cros at the sumit of the gable end, is a great stone crown, old fashon'd.

At the termination of the cornish, on one side of the sayd window, is the bust or germ of a king with a crown on and short curld hair, and a long broad beard.   On the other side is a bish[op] with his miter on, and a croisar staff in one hand, and the other held up in the form of blessing.

On the south side of the chancel, under the termination of the cornish of the three great windows there, there is under the 1st the bust of a venerable old man, with a cap on like a hat crown, with short curld hair and divided beard, and somewhat like a collar of SSS. about his neck.   On the other side is the bust of a beautiful lady, his wife undoubtedly, in a strang old kind of head dress.   Under the second window a bishop with his miter, etc., as before, and on the other side a man with a hat crown cap on, without a beard, with a book in his hands.

On the termination of the stone of the third window an old man's bust with a strang capp on, tyd under the chin, falling down like Danish capps, on the left side of the head, and on the other side [a] woman's bust with the aforesayd strang head dress on, onely a little more waved and gimp'd.[g]

There is nothing worth seeing in the church, there being neither monuments nor good seats therein.

Oct. 13. On the 13th of this month of Octob[er], I made a journey to Grimsby, to see that old town, and to find what I

---

[f]   "Is ye armes of ye lord Mowbray who built this chancel,"—*Marginal Note by Diarist.*

[g]   These arms and figures are given in woodcuts in Stonehouse's *Isle of Axholme*, pp. 366 and 367.

could observable about the same. In my passage thither I went throw Brigg, Bigby, Riby, and Ailsby, in which towns I found nothing memorable untill I came to Great Coats, in which there seems to have been an old religious house all built of brick. It has turrits like the old buildings, and somewhat in the walls of the gaithouse, which seems to have been nitches for images, tho' now bricked up. It is encompass'd also with a great moat. I could not get time to see the church, which look'd spatious, it being late. From thence I went over a wath,[h] which tradition says was formerly a great river, running through the haven by Grimsby, and so into Humber, which river carryd large coal vessels as far as Ailsby. From thence I went to Little Coats, about which are many foundations of buildings. From thence to Grimsby.[i] Grimsby is at present but a little poor town, not a quarter so great as heretofore. The old marqet place is lost, and that where they now keep it is in the midst of a street. There is scarce a good house in the whole town, but a larg brick one, which Mr. Moor, their parlament man, has lately built. The church, which is now standing, [is] the old great monastry church belonging to the monastry that then was in Harry the Eighth's days. It is a noble larg building of great bigness, built in form of a minster, but it all falls to decay, the whole town being not able to keep it in repair, they being so poor, and it so

---

[h] Wath is a provincial name for a ford throughout the whole of the North country.

[i] Great Grimsby, now a place of considerable note, under the wealth and activity brought to bear upon it by the improvement of its harbour and the introduction of its railways, is doubtless one of high antiquity also. It is situated near to the mouth of the Humber, about forty miles north-westward from Lincoln. Tradition ascribes its foundation or chief advancement to a fisherman named Gryme, who came originally from Souldburg, and engaged in a very lucrative traffic with Norway, Sweden, and Denmark. The numerous artificial hills in the marshes adjoining the present town proclaim the spot to have been a station of consequence amongst the ancient Britons; and to these, more probably, the origin of the name may be attributed. Works of this character are pretty generally ascribed to a power that is superhuman, and by some have been not unfrequently regarded as the works of the devil. This shews their extreme antiquity. *Grim* denotes blackness, and also the look which inspires terror. Grim's-by, the residence of the devil; Grim's-thorpe (*villa diaboli*), the village of the devil; Grim's-dyke, the devil's ditch or dyke; Grim's-shaw, the devil's wood; etc., have all their same apparent origin from this belief. The arms borne by some of the families, whose surname begins with Grim, may be said to savour of this idea, such as Grimshaw and Grimsditch, which both contain the griffin or dragon, emblematical, it may be, of the old serpent.—See Rev. Dr. Gatty's edition of *Hunter's Hallamshire*, pp. 24, 26, 396, who there refers to what Mr. Oliver has written on the origin of the name of Grimsby; and to *Notes and Queries*, first series, vols. iv. and v., for a full discussion as to the origin and meaning of the word Grim.

larg. It costs some of the house-holders 5*l.* a year yearly to-wards it. It hangs very plainly towards the north, as if it would fall that way. There are several old inscriptions and monuments in it, but so dirty'd and defac'd that I could not read them. From thence I went to a great spot of ground called the old church-yard, where tradition says that the town's church stood, which is reported to have been bigger than the monastry church, tho' now there is not as much as a stone to be seen. 'Tis said that the town made an exchang of it for the monastry church with him that had got the same in Har[ry] the Eighth's days, because that the monastry church stood more con-veniently in the heart of the town, and so that thereupon the said town's church was pull'd down and sold, and the mon[astry] church preserved. Yet, for all that, the minister of the town pays synodal, procurations, etc., for the town church, as much as if it was standing. There was in this town one great abbey bordering upon the minster, with two frierys, one of white and another of grey, and a nunnery besides, and a larg chantery, all hard by this minster, so that it seems to have been built for them all. Over the nunnery gate, which is the onely part almost now stand-ing, I observed a coat of arms of three boar heads, with a ——— bend betwixt them. A little way out of the town there was another pretty larg abbey, out of which, when it was pull'd down, the owner built a very larg stately farm-house, like a great hall, which remained untill within the memory of man; at which time there was plainly seen to come a great sheet of fire from out of Holderness, over the Humber, and to light upon which abbey-house, as they called it, which burnt it all down to the bare ground, with the men in it, and all the corn stacks and buildings about it. The shipmen in the road, and many more observed this sheet of fire to come thus, as I have related. About [a] quarter of a mile from the town eastward is to be seen the ruins of a larg hermitage, where was in the memory of man a fine orchard, with excellent fruit in it.

This town was very great and rich formerly, by its hav-ing a larg spacious haven which brought great trafic to the town; but the haven growing worse and worse for this two or three hundred years together, the town decayed more and more, and came to that poverty in which it is. Three things may be assign'd to its decay. First, the destruction of the haven, which was in former times a fine larg river, and carryd large vessels as farr as Ailsby, as I have sayd before. That which destroy'd it was the Humber's wearing away the huge cliff at

Cleythorp,[j] and bringing it and casting it all into Grimsby haven or river, and all along Grimsby coast on the north, so that the river was not onely fill'd thereby, but also a huge bay on the north side of the town, which came almost close to the town side, in which shipps did formerly ride with the greatest eas and advantage to the town imaginable. This bay being thus fill'd up, and made common for almost two miles broad, from the town's end to the Humber, the mayor and aldermen petitiond Queen Eliz[abeth] to bestow this new land for ever upon them and the town, which she did.

I was at Cleythorp to examin about this notion, and I observed how the sea washed the cliff away, which is nothing but clay and sand, and is as high as a church steeple; huge pieces is under-mined and brought down every great tide as bigg as whole churches together, and the people of the place says that they have, by tradition, that there has been several miles length of land wash'd away, and people have been forced to pull down their houses and build them again furder off.

I observed in the cliff how confusedly the layers of earth lay, sometimes sand uppermost, sometimes clay, sometimes a mixture, etc., but no stone amongst them.

The second thing which has caused the decreas of Grimsby [Grimsby] was the destruction of the religious houses there, which, whereever they were, made a town always rich and popu-lous by their promoting of all sorts of trades, arts, and sciences; and then again, they were a means for the fishing trade to be carryd greatly on, because they consumed a great deal of fish.

The third thing which occasiond it's decay was the rise of Hull, which having first of all priviledges and advantages above other towns, and a fine haven to boot, robbed them all not onely of all their traffic, but also of all their chief tradesmen, which were sent for and encourag'd to live there.

But now there is a publick spirited parlament man there, one of a noble soul, who is contriving by all means to make the town great again. He has for this two or three years last been lying a new sluce, and digging the haven (which now tho' digged not over ten yards broad at the top), to bring vessels to the townside again. But I told them their haven would never do unless that

---

[j] The village of Cleethorpe, though a separate constablewick, is a hamlet to the neighbouring parish of Clee. It is distant about two miles and a half south eastward from Grimsby. Originally a fishing hamlet, it has, from its convenience for bathing, of late years become the resort of much company during the Summer.

they make a huge stath at the aforesayd cliff to keep it from
wearing away, etc.   He is also promoting the fishery upon the
Humber mouth for the advantage of Grimsby, and there are vast
subscriptions already gotton towards the same ; some have subscribed 100*l.*, some 1200*l.*, and others even 2000*l.* a piece* ; and
five large fishing vessels are a building at Stockwith and other
places for the town.   He is also establishing the woollen manufacture there, and has already sent down out of Oxfordshire a
rugg and coverlet maker, and has given him wool, and his new
house three years, rent free.

As you go down by the haven to the Humber, there is on
your right hand three hills cast up, with moats about them,
called Blockhouse hills, made to defend the haven.

I observed in a close of Mr. King's, a butcher and ale-keeper,
who was formerly a town's 'prentice, but now one of the aldermen of the corporation, I observed there, I say, Engl[ish] beens,
with stalks three yards high, others ten foot high.

Haveing seen and learnt all at this town that I could, I returned back by Limbur, and so to Brocklesby, to the Lady
Pellham's.*   The town is but little and mean, and nothing observable in it but three things, the great quantity of fine wood that
is planted and improved about the same, which is not onely exceeding pleasant, but will also be of vast advantage to the owners.
The next thing is the church, which is little, but pretty neat.
The steeple is spired, and built upon two arches, one to the west-
wards, and the other to the eastwards, within the church, with a
wall in the middle, with a window in it, the whole thus :—

$$\left\| \frac{\text{w}}{\text{E.}} \right\|$$

The bell strings hangs within the east arch in the church.   In

---

*   "These subsc[riptions] in gen[eral] are towards y^e Royal fishery of
Engl[and] but in partic[ular] likewise for this town."—*Marginal Note by
Diarist.*

  *   Brocklesby is situate about eight miles north by east from Caistor, and
about the same distance westward from Grimsby. This place, for a great number of years, was the seat of the Pelhams, of which family the last male descendant was Charles Pelham, esq., on whose death, in 1763, the extensive and
beautiful estate came into the possession of his great nephew, Charles Anderson
esq., a descendant of a female branch of the Pelham family, whose name and
arms he then assumed.   In 1791, he was elevated to the peerage as baron
Yarborough, of Yarborough, co. Lincoln, and died in 1823.   His eldest son Charles,
D.C.L. F.R.S., &c., born 8th August, 1781, was created earl of Yarborough and
baron Worsley, in 1837, and died 5th September, 1846, leaving issue, by his
wife Henrietta Anna Maria Charlotte, second daughter of the Hon. John Bridge-
man Simpson, Charles Anderson Worsley, second earl (the late father of the present earl of Yarborough, of Brocklesby), Dudley Worsley Pelham, capt. R.N., now
deceased, and Charlotte, married to Sir Joseph William Copley, bart., of Sprotborough near Doncaster, one of the members of this Society.

the church are many curious and excellent monuments of the Pellhams, whose inscriptions Mr. Skinner, a gentleman there, has promised to send me.   There is the most painted glass in the windows that ever I say [saw], with the images of the apostles therein, one speaking one article and another another article of the Creed, it being believed formerly that every one at a councill at Jerusalem utter'd an article thereof.

The third thing here observ[able] is the seat of the Pellhams, formerly knights, tho' now the heir thereof, who is about twenty years of age, is onely an esq[uire], whose incom yearly is about 4000*l.*   The hall is a very fine stately building, built in the year 1603, when the Pelhams first came into this country out [of] Kent as I remember (where there is a knightly family of the same name).   The hall is leaded upon the top, and most excellently furnished with all manner of rich goods and pictures within, of excellent painting.

There is two carved chimney pieces of wood, of the finest workmanship that ever I saw.   One represents Diogenes in his tub, speaking to Alexander, with trees, landscips, etc. ; all the sayd work with those verses in golden letters underneath.

Here is also very fine gardens, with groves, pleasure houses, etc., and all manner of fruit.

Not farr from this town was a place called Newsom,[m] where formerly stood a famous priory with several houses about it, but now there is not as much as one stone above another to be seen, all be pulled down and squanderd, and brought to lay the foundation of the aforesayd hall.

From thence I came home, observing nothing further worthy of note.

17. Not far from Limbur is a town called Kealby, or Keelby, where there is, as they say, a double church, with a huge chancel, and several things observable about the same, but I did not hear thereof till I had got home.

---

[m]   Newhouse, Newlms, or Newsome, the first monastry of the Premonstratensian order in England, was founded by Peter de Golsa circa 1043.   It was dedicated to the honour of the Blessed Virgin Mary and St Martial, not St Michael, as has sometimes been erroneously affirmed.   St. Martial was one of the first preachers of the gospel in France.   He was the first Bishop of Limoges (see *Acta Sanctorum*, vol v., June, p. 535 573.   St. Amaber, *Vie de S. Martial de Limoges apôtre des Gaules*, Clermont 1676, 2 vols fol., Limoges 1683 and 1685). The foundation Charter and some other records of this house are printed in the *Monasticon*, vol. vii., p. 865.   A register of this house is believed to be in the possession of the Earl of Yarborough.

At Berlings,["] five miles of this side Lincoln, was in antient times a famous monastry. The church was left standing, but with all the lead of and the bells gone, which church [is] now standing, tho' in rubbish. Yet in the same is several monuments and inscriptions to be observed, as I heard this day.

When all the minsters or cathedralls and collegiate churches should have been pulled down in Cromwell's days, there were some very busy for getting a grant of Lincoln minster ; which, when one Capt[ain] Pert,[°] parlament men for Lincoln, knew, he went to Cromwell and told him that, if the minster was pulld down, Lincoln would soon be one of the worst towns in the county, and made it so plainly out that Cromwell told him it should not be touched, so it was preserved. Yet this same Pert got great part of the bishop's lands, and upon some in the citty

["] Barlings or Oxeney, a Premonstratensian House dedicated to the Blessed Virgin, founded in 1154. A register of this house, imperfect at the beginning and the end, is in the Cotton collection, Faustina B., I. *Monast. Angl.*, vii. 915.

[°] Original Peart, concerning whom Mr. Ross, of Lincoln, before mentioned, has made the following obliging communication.

"I could like myself to have possessed some particulars of the ancestry and early career of the prominent actor in the municipal drama at Lincoln during the periods preceding and following that of the Commonwealth, but, from the defect of the records of our Corporation (the interval between 1638 and 1661 being a blank), I have been able to collect nothing worth giving to you.

"He was a member of two parliaments, 1654-1656 ; at the first, along with Alderman William Marshall, and at the second, with Humphrey Walcot, the latter being then a resident of Lincoln.

"The two Marshalls, Robert and William, of great civic power at this unsettled period, were hot parliamentarians, and were both displaced at the Restoration.

"In 1640 Original Peart was sheriff along with Richard Wetherall, and, during their sherivalty, the King, on his return from Scotland after the treaty of Ripon, passed through Lincoln. He appears to have met with an unaccorded reception by the citizens : but it is said (see a small history of Lincoln published in 1817). that the sovereign was met about two miles north of the city, viz : at Burton Wall, by Mr. Sheriff Peart. The then Mayor, Robert Beck (being a well known parliamentarian, as is proved by his dismissal along with the two Marshalls), appears to have observed a silent and inactive deportment on this occasion.

"In 1650 Peart was chosen Mayor, but I can give you no particulars of his mayoralty.

"In 1686 Original Peart (perhaps the same) was appointed Town Clerk or "clericus communitatis civ. Linc.," which office he appears to have held till 1705, when Francis Harvey was chosen.

"I have some notices of Original Peart's descendants, but I am at this time unable to find them. One Robert Peart (not improbably a son of Original), was one of the chamberlains in 1655, and again in 1659, and died during his last tenure of the office. This vacancy gave rise to a dispute between the mayor John Leach, and the members of the common council, each party claiming the exclusive right of appointing the successor. The mayor submitted.

"An unmarried daughter of Original Peart died in 1751, aged 72, as may be seen on one of the pavement-slabs in the Church of St. Mary-le-Wigford."

of Lincoln built a delicate fine house, which cost him about 900*l.*, out of which he was soon turned when the bishop was restablished in K[ing] C[harles] the Second's return.

All those, all England over, that had layd hands on those lands were all turned out of the same when the king returned.

Our newse says that the presbiterians in Scotland has lately caused " The Whole Duty of Man " to be burnt by the common hangsman, and with it Whiston's " New Theory of the Earth."

I told them at Grimsby that it was no wonder that their town and trade was so decayd, and that they were so poor, seeing that they were all guilty of the horrible sin of sacrilege, as appeared by the great quantitys of religious stone that is in the walls of almost every house.

There is a family of the Tully's about Grimsby, which has 800*l.* a year, but it is spending and flying now as fast as ever it can, great part of which were religious land.

I was this day with a bookseller at Brigg, who was apprentice to one who printed that scurrilous pamplet against Sherlock intitled the " Weesels," (the author of which was Durfee).[p] He says that [he] is certain that his master got about 800*l.* by it. He says that Durfee was forced to write an answer to it which he entitled the " Weesel Trapped."

The lord or steward of this mannour of Broughton formerly had every year over and above their rents, 1s. of every one for their swine going in the woods to feed, tho' there be no acorns. He had also a capon of every husbandry, and a hen of a whole cottagry, and a chicken of a half cottagry; and in hay time every one that had a cottagry went a whole day to make hay for him in Grime cloas, and those that had half cottagrys[q] went onely one day, and the husbandry went with their draughts to fetch it home and load it; and in lieu of all this they all had a great dinner at Christmas at the lord or steward's house. This is plain villanage, and was but lately left off. Yet to this day some of the chief husbandry fetches their coals and wood.

16. Rhodes, the bookseller that bought the coppys of the " Turkish Spy," and that printed them, has got a great estate by

---

[p] Thomas Durfey, the notorious libeller and scribbler.

[q] This hen rent was a very common tax in the middle ages. Our ancient records often make mention of it. Norden and Thorpe, in their survey of the manor of Kirton-in-Lindsey in 1616, say that at Winterton there was paid to the lord of the manor of Kirton "vjd rent for six hens payable at the feaste of Christe's nativitie, and iiijd per ann. for warne of lande." M.S. *Public Lib, Cambr., Ff* 4-30, fol. 66. b.

them. He was but a poor man before, and is become now very rich.

This day I received a letter from the ingenious Mr. Skinner,[r] from Brocklesby Hall, containing the inscriptions that are in the the church there.

On the south[s] wall of the church, excellently cut out of marble and alabaster, is a glorious tomb of Sr William Pelham and his lady and children, all represented kneeling; under which monument in golden letters is written the words :—

Hic jacet Gulielmus Pelham, miles, in juventute suâ apud Scotos, Gallos, et Vngaros ob militiam celeberrimus ; in provectiore ætate apud Hibernos regni præfectus, apud Belgas exercitus mariscallus munitionis bellicæ sub augustiss : Principe Regina Elizabetha Promagister. In uxorem duxit Dominam Eleanoram Henrici Comitis Westmerlandiæ filiam, quæ hic simul sepulta jacet. De eâ tres filios totidemq. filias genuit, e quibus tres adhuc sunt superstites, quorum senior, Will : monumentum istud in perpetuam parentum memoriam consecravit. Obiit Flissingiæ mense Decemb : 1587.

Boathe liv'd at once, but not at once did dye,
Shee first, hee laste, yet boathe together lye.
Hee greate in deedes of armes, shee greate in byrthe,
Hee wise, shee chaste, boathe now resolv'd to yearth.
Needes must ye slender shrubbs expect their fall,
When statelye oakes fall down and cedars tall.
Bragge not of valloure, for this woorthye knighte,
Mightye in armes, by deathe hathe lost his mighte.
Boaste not of honour, nobler was there none
Than Ladye Ellinore, that now is gonne.
Joy not too much in youthe, these children three
Were as you are ; as they are shall yow bee.

[r] See antea, p. 131. I have made some endeavour to ascertain who this Mr. Skinner was, but without success. The Rev. J. H. Johnson, of Kirmington, obligingly inspected the registers at Brocklesby to see if he occurred as the rector or curate of that place, but nothing appeared in aid of that idea, and he further reported that there was no monumental inscription for the name of Skinner in the church. Sir Vincent Skinner's only son William Skinner, esq., of Thornton College, who died 7th Aug., 1627, æt. 32, married Bridget, 2nd daughter of the celebrated Sir Edward Coke, Chief Justice of England, by whom he had, besides five daughters, three sons, viz: Edward, who died in 1657, having married Anne, daughter of Sir William Wentworth ; William, baptised at Thornton, 30th April, 1626, regarding whom nothing that I am aware of has been ascertained further than that in his mother's will, 1648, she alludes to him as a "most undutiful son," and also that he was living in 1657, when he occurs as a legatee of 50l. in his brother Edward's will ; and Cyriack, born after his father's death in 1627, and hence so named probably as if he was peculiarly a gift from the Lord. He was entered of Trinity College, Oxford, in 1640, was an author and a man of letters, but appears to have settled down as a merchant in London, where he died in 1700. He was a friend and pupil of the immortal Milton. De la Pryme, in a previous part of his Diary (p. 160 MS.), has made an extract from the preface to the Etymologia Linguæ Anglicanæ, wherein, as he says, "the learned and ingenious Mr. Skinner, a great crittic himself, has thus excellently in short characterized a crittic." This, however, was Stephen Skinner, a physician, who died at Lincoln, 5th September, 1667. I suspect that Cyriack Skinner was the contributor to the Diarist of the inscriptions here mentioned, whilst probably on a visit at Brocklesby.

[s] Sic orig. But I am informed that this monument is on the north wall of the chancel.

There were many coats of arms about this monument which he has not sent.

On the south side of the chancel is a great altar tomb, all bannister'd about, and adorn'd with inscriptions, arms, and crests, on which lyes the images of Sr. William Pelham and his lady, with this inscription :—

Gulielmus Pelham, nuper de Brocklesby, in com : Lin : Eques auratus. In celeberrimis academiis, Strasberg, Heidelberg, Wittenberg, Leipsick, Parisiensi, et Oxoniensi magnâ cum curâ educatus, artibus liberalibus imbutus, et linguas Germanicam, Gallicam, Latinam (nec Græcarum rudis), non solum callens, sed promptè eloqui edoctus. Ab his domiciliis Mars distraxit, ubi post varias pugnas, obsidiones, etc., sed non sine vulneribus rus contulit. Annam, filiam Caroli Willoughby, Baronis de Parrham, castam virginem, connubio sibi junxit ; ex quâ liberos viginti utriusque sexûs Dei benedictione accepit, quorum septem filii et tres filiæ in vivis sunt. Vixerunt cæteri. Reliquo temporis consumpto justitiam exequendo, orando, scribendo, pauperes sublevando, sacra biblia, antiquos patres et neotericos legendo, magnam gloriam adeptus est. Et quid in his profecerit meditationes in Sancti Johannis Evangelium editæ, observationes in omnes Testamentorum tam Veteris quam Novi libros et diatribæ in sacramentum Cænæ Domini manû suâ scriptæ, et posteritati restauratæ imperpetuum testabuntur. Hisce rebus et annis circiter sexaginta transactis, fide in Christum constanti, et charitate erga proximos inviolabili, placidè in Domino obdormiens, spiritum Deo Patri Spirituum, corpus terræ matri, in die resurrectionis magno cum incremento recepturus, commendavit 13 Julii an'o D'ni : 1629.

Upon the north wall of the chancel is written the following words,' to the memory of Thomas Eton, rector and schoolmaster of this town, by Doct[or] Lake, who was the scholar of his that was so grateful to his memory.

Pietati et Solertiæ S.

Depositum Magistri Thomæ Æton, presbyteri, Bosworthi in agro Leicestrensi nati, hujus ecclesiæ Brocklesbiensis quondam Rectoris et Scholarchiæ eximii, hic subtus jacet. Qui plures per annos gregem hic sibi concreditam tam vitâ exemplari quam officiis omnimodo divinis animarum curæ incumbentibus fideliter pascendo, et pubem juventutem, non solum ò familiâ nobili Pelhamiana, tunc temporis sicut longum supra et ad præsens hic florenti, verum etiam circumquaq. vicinam et remotiorem, tantum non in ipsa studiorum incude positam sed provectiorem etiam scientiis liberalibus, tantum non universis arte perquam exquisitâ, methodo non vulgari, sed misterii instar penitus proficienti, sedulitate opera indefessâ imbuendo, perficiendo, atque exinde de patria suâ optimè meritus mortalem summû cum laude absolvit telam, suique reliquit desiderium charissimum et annorum, ... anno a partu virgineo, 1626, placidè Christianè admodum in Domino obdormivit, cujus memoriæ meritissimæ e discipulis suis olim unus minimutum hoc (meliore multo dignæ) gratitudinis ergo posuit memoriale, anno Dom : 1668.

This day I was with Mr. Jolence,^u attorney at Brigg, and steward

---

' This monument is now very high on the north wall of the chancel, and the latter part is almost illegible. It is believed that the inscription is correct.

^u *Forsan* Jalland, or Jolland. There was a George, son of George Jolland, Scalby (Scawby ?) near Brigg, Lincolnshire, gent., entered at Manchester school, 28th June, 1746 ; Fellow of St. John's, Cambridge ; A.B. 1753 ; A.M. 1756 ; died 1760.—*Chetham Soc. pub. Manch. School.*

L

to Mr. Elways (who owns most part of Brigg, Wrawby, Roxby,
etc., having an estate of about 3000*l.* per annum), he says that
about 27 years ago Mr. Elways did for ever give and grant unto
his tennants of Roxby all their land to be tithetfree, which they
have unpay'd untill this time.   It was an inpropriation unto
him.

At Scarburrow there is a wonderfull causey called Phila
causey, which runs with a great ridg into the sea.   It [is]
reckond to be above three miles long, and ten yards broad.   It
is all made of huge stones, four, five, six, and some seven yards
broad and long.   It is very dangerous to seamen, and occasions
many shipwracks.

The verses at Brocklesby Hall, under the carved work of
Diogenes in his tun speaking to Alexander, which I had like to
have forgot, are these.

> Vita quod hæc hominis tam sit brevis atque caduca
>   Non vult Diogenes ædificare domum.
> Vos domns est in quâ sapiens sua gaudia sentit
>   Contentusque suis regia nulla petit,
> Æmathioque duci quærenti qualia vellet
>   Munera responsum libera lingua dedit.
> Corde velim toto, rex augustissime, solem
>   Ne mihi surripias quem tribuisse nequis.[v]

They have a tradition at Winterton that there was formerly
one Mr. Lacy,[w] that lived there and was a very rich man, who,
being grown very aged, gave all that he had away unto his three
sons, upon condition that one should keep him one week, and
another another.   But it happened within a little while that they
were all weary of him, after that they had got what they had,
and regarded him no more than a dog.   The old man percieveing

---

[v] These lines, as well as the foregoing monumental inscriptions, have been
very obligingly collated with the originals by the Rev. J. Byron, vicar of
Killingholme ; from which it appears that the Diarist had not got them literally
correct.

[w] The Lacy's were an old Winterton family of yeoman rank.   There are
numbers of them in the register of that parish.

John Lacy, and William Lacy, occur as parishioners of that town in an award
between the prior and convent of Malton and the parishioners made by Roger
Fauconbergh, esq., 10th of August, 1456, printed in vol. xl, *Archæologia.*

A branch of the family was settled, in the 17th century at Kirton-in-Lindsey.
Henry, Robert, Brian, and John Lacy, were tenants of that manor there, in
1616.   The male line ended about the beginning of this century, when the last
of them, Thomas Lacy, died.   His little property passed to a person of the name
of Fox, who inherited some of the Lacy blood in the female line, and who was
a tenant on the Kinscliffe School farm at Northorpe.   His son, the late Mr.
Thomas Fox, of Northorpe, died without issue 31st of March, 1862.   The property is now in the hands of those who are in no way related to the old
family, as I am informed.

how he was sleighted, went to an attorny to see if his skill could
not afford him any help in his troubles. The attorny told him
that no law in the land could help him nor yield him any comfort, but there was one thing onely which would certainly do,
which, if he would perform, he would reveal to him. At which
the poor old man was exceeding glad, and desired him for God's
sake to reveal the same, for he was almost pined and starved to
dead, and he would most willingly do it rather than live as he did.
"Well," says the lawyer, "you have been a great friend of mine
in my need, and I will now be one to you in your need. I will lend
you a strong box with a strong lock on it, in which shall be contained 1000*l.* ; you shall on such a day pretend to have fetched it
out of such a close, where it shall be supposed that you hid, and
carry it into one of your son's houses, and make it your business
every week, while you are sojourning with such or such a son, to
be always counting of the money, and ratleing it about, and you
shall see that, for the love of it, they'll soon love you again, and
make very much of you, and maintain you joyfully, willingly,
and plentifully, unto your dying day. The old man having
thank'd the lawyer for this good advice and kind proffer, received
within a few days the aforesayd box full of money, and having so
managed it as above, his graceless sons soon fell in love with him
again, and made mighty much of him, and percieving that their
love to him continued stedfast and firm, he one day took it out
of the house and carry'd it to the lawyer, thanking him exceedingly for the lent thereof. But when he got to his sons he
made them believe that [he] had hidden it again, and that he
would give it him of them whome he loved best when he dyd.
This made them all so observant of him that he lived the rest of
his days in great peace, plenty, and happiness amongst them, and
dyed full of years. But a while before he dyd he ubraded them
for their former ingratitude, told them the whole history of the
box, and forgave them.

There was formerly a great hospital and a free chappel[z] at the
east end of Brigg built by S[r.] William Terwyt, *vulgo* Turrit,
vallued at 20*l.* per annum. Part of the hospital is yet standing,
and a wall of the chappel. Within the memory of man there
was a fine spacious court wall about between the hospital door

---

[z] Mention is made in the last edition of the *Monasticon*, vol. vii., p. 766,
of a hospital at Wrawby, founded by Sir William Tyrwhitt, and a reference
given to *Patent Roll*, 20th Henry VI., pars. 1. This was probably an augmen-
tation of the more ancient hospital there, of which I have before made mention.
—*Monast. Anglic.*, vii., p. 688.

and the chappel door, but it was pulld down about forty years
ago, because that part of it had fallen and killed a man; and so
they were affraid that the rest should likewise do some such like
mischief.   Part of the town of Brigg belongs to Clare Hall College in Cambridg, as dos also the impropriation of Wrawby
liveing.

Tradition says that there lived formerly at Alkburrow a famous heroic princes[s], who did many martial actions.   They say
that she had a huge hall in that piece of ground which I have
described before to be a Roman fortification, and says that the
place is call'd Countess close from her, adding that it is the most
ancient place that is in the exchequer rolls, and always first called there, etc.   The aforesayd hollow burrow before mention'd is
called Lady pitt, or Countess pitt, from the aforesayd Countess,
who perhaps was lady of the town in the Saxon (or, raither,
Dainish) days, who misserably harrasd all that and this part of the
country, and opposing some party of the enemy might be there
slayn and buryed.

They have at [this] town, as also at Appleby, two Roman
games, the one called Gillian's[y] bore, and the other Troy's walls.
They are both nothing but great labarinths[z] cut upon the ground
with a hill cast up round about them for the spectators to sitt
round about on to behold the sport.   The two labarinths are
somewhat different in their turnings one from another.

[y] Pro Julian.—*Marginal Note by Diarist.*

[z] The Appleby Labyrinth has perished, and no memory of it, as far as I
can hear remains.   The one at Alkbrough is yet perfect, but is in a decayed
condition.   There is an engraving of it in the *Reports of Lincolnshire Architectural Society,* 1852, p. 258, Hatfield's *Terra Incognita of Lincolnshire,* facing
title.   Andrews *History of Winterton,* p. 78.   There cannot be much doubt that
these curious mazes are mediæval, not Roman.   There are several examples of
labyrinths in and outside foreign churches.   There is one incised on one of the
pillars of the porch of Lucca Cathedral, *Didron Annales Archeologiques, tome
xvii,* another on the floor of the nave of Chartres Cathedral.   They may perhaps
originally have been intended as penitential pathways, but in more modern
times they were used for popular games.   They are several times referred to by
Shakespeare. e. g.

    The nine mens morris is fill'd up with mud;
    And the quaint mazes on the wanton green,
    For lack of tread, are undistinguishable.
                        Midsummer Night's Dream, Act II. Scene II.
There was formerly a maze between Farnham and Guildford called Troy
town.   A very curious German engraving of a maze is preserved in the British
Museum, press mark 1750, c 28.   In William Lawson's *New Orchard and
Garden* 2nd edition, 1648, 4to p. 84, there is an engraving of a square maze,
with a tree in the midst.   "Walls of Troy" seems to have been the name for a
labyrinthine pattern on linen as late as the beginning of the last century.   "In
the Nurserie......Two dozen and one [table cloths] of burdseye, and nine of
several knots odd, three fyn towels and five of the *Walls of Troy,"—Invent of
Furniture at Thunderton.   Dunbar, Social life in former days, p.* 210.

Nov. 20. I have now left my curacy at Broughton, in Lincolnshire, and am come to live at Hatfield,[a] the better to carry on my history of that place.

All the Dutch soldiers that are in England are going to be shipt of at Hull. All their horses are taken from [them] and it is sayd that they are to have others beyond sea, by which means the king will save a vast deal of money, who commonly pays for transporting; it is sayd that every horse will cost six or seven pound transporting.

This day I heard for a certain truth, and there are many that will give their oaths upon it, that Tho[mas] Hill, fowler for Mr. Ramsden, did shoot thirty-two pair of duck and teal at one shot in the Levels, in 1692-3.[b]

In the south west of Yorkshire, at and about Bradfield, and in Darbishire, they feed all their sheep in winter with holly leaves and bark, which they eat more greedily than any grass. To every farm there is so many holly trees; and the more there is the farm is dearer; but care is taken to plant great numbers of them in all farms thereabouts. And all these holly trees are smooth leaved and not prickly. As soon as the sheep sees the sheppard come with an ax in his hand they all follow him to the first tree he comes at, and stands all in a round about the tree, expecting impatiently the fall of a bow, which, when it is falln, all as many as can eats thereof, and the sheppard going further to another tree, all those that could not come in unto the eating of the first follow him to this, and so on. As soon as they have eaten all the leaves they begin of the bark and pairs it all of.

Snow and frost is commonly very great and very long in the peak country of Derbishire, and oftentimes the frost is not out of the ground till the middle of May and after. In 1684, when the great frost was, snow lay beyond several hills all the following

---

[a] It is said at Hatfield that the Diarist lived in the house there which is now the property of, and occupied by, Mr. W. J. Fox, solicitor, and which was surrendered 30th November, 1699, by Theseus Moore to Mrs. Sarah Pryme, the Diarist's mother. It does not appear from the title deeds (to which Mr. Fox has obligingly allowed me access), that Abraham de la Pryme was ever the owner; but, being a bachelor, he most likely resided with his mother, who, in the year 1697, was a widow of about forty-eight years of age, and outlived her son twenty-five years.

[b] A fen-man named Bury, worthy of credit, stated that he fired a large duck gun at a flock of snipes that were sitting on Bled Ground, in the vicinity of Whittlesey mere, and at one shot killed thirty-six dozen. (Memoranda furnished by J. M. Heathcote, esq., to *Lord Orford's Voyage round the Fens*, in 1774. Edited by J. W. Childers, esq., 1868, p. 107).

summer, and the frost was in the ground on the sun side till after
July came in.

1697.   In several towns on the sea side in Holderness is cast up
great quantitys of coal, all in dust, which the people makes fires
of, but it being so exceeding small that it commonly smothers all
their fires out, unless they keep perpetualy blowing the same,
they have found out this invention to keep it in.   Their houses are
set upon all points of the compass, and of each side of their
chimneys they have two holes (directly against each end of their
rangs) through the wall, these are commonly stopd with a piece
of wood or an old cloath, and when they have any need for a fire
they   . . . . . .

[*The next two pages of the Diary are pasted together*].
There is a house in Winterton, on the north side of the town, not
farr from the church, which has been a religious house.   There
was digged up a few years [ago] in the same a font very neatly
cutt.

The font that is in Hatfield church came from the monastry of
Dunscroft.[c]

Doct[or] Neal, the present Doct[or] Neal's father (that is
no[w] a dying[d]), was the first that found out the spaws at Knares-
bur, by observing the place to be very much hanted with pigions,
which came there to pick up the salt.

DECEMBER 17, 18, 19, 20.   On the 17th of this month wee
had a very great snow,'which was on the level ground about two

---

[c]   This cannot have been the case.   When John, the last earl of Warren
gave the church of Hatfield to the abbot and convent of St. Mary de la Roche,
in 1345, they required the residence of some one on the spot to look after their
temporal interests in this extensive parish.   For the management of their
revenue arising from Hatfield, they erected a grange at the place called Dunscroft, between Hatfield and Stainford; and, having certain feudal privileges
connected with their rectory estate, it came to be called the manor of Dunscroft.   Some have spoken of Dunscroft as a cell to Roche Abbey.   This is,
however, a mistake.   Dunscroft was never more than a grange; and the seal
engraved by Mr. Rowe Mores, as the seal of the cell of Dunscroft, belongs to
some other religious establishment.   The legend is imperfect, but the name of
the place is *not* Dunscroft.   (*Hunter's South Yorkshire*, i., p. 187).   In 1607,
the interest, which the monks had here, had passed to the famous countess of
Shrewsbury, and it continued in the possession of the earls and dukes of Devonshire, her descendants, for several generations.   At page 381 of the MS. Diary is
the following :—" I do hereby licence, authorise, and appoint John Hatfield,
esq,, to fish in the river Dun at his pleasure, and so farr as it runneth within
the lordship of Hatfield, in the county of York, in as ample manner as the
abbot of Roch or rector of Hatfield have used and enjoyed the same according
to a free rent yearly payd for this fishing to his Majesty's recievours.   Given
under my hand the twentieth day of June, A.D. 1672.   W. Devonshire."
[d]   But is since recovered.—*Marginal Note by Diarist.*

foot and a half thick after a pretty hard frost, which, as it thow'd, frose again for several days. The 20th it thow'd exceeding fast, upon which there came so great a flood down that the like was never known. About forty-one years ago there was then the greatest flood that was ever remembered, but that was much less than this ; for this came roreing all of a suddain, about eleven a clock at night, unto Bramwith, Fishlake, Thorn, and other towns; upon which the people rung all their bells backwards (as they commonly do in case of a great fire), but tho' that this frighted all, and called all to the banks, and bid them all look about them, yet, nevertheless, the loss is vastly great. The people of Sikehouse and Fishlake, tho' they had banks to save them, yet it topt all, drounded the people's beasts in their folds and houses, destroyd sheep, and several men lost their lives, their houses in Sikehouse, and many in Fishlake, being drownded up to the very eves, so that they reckon no less than 3000 pound damage to be done by the same in the parish of Fishlake. It came with such a force against all the banks about Thorn, which keeps the waters of the Levels, that everybody gave them over, there being no hopes to save them, and ran over them all along, and the ground being so hard they could [not] strike down stakes upon the tops of their banks, to hinder the water from running over. At last, it being impossible that such vast waters should be contained in such short and small bounds, it burst a huge gime close by Gore Steel, near Thorn, where had been a vast gime formerly, and so drounded all the whole Levels to an exceeding great depth, so that many people were kept so long in the upper part of their houses that they were almost pined, while all their beasts were drounded about them. It was, indeed, all over, a very sad thing to hear the oxen bellowing, and the sheep bleating, and the people crying out for help round about as they did, all Bramwith, Sikehouse, Stanford, and Fishlake over, as undoubtedly they also did in other places, yet no one could get to save or help them, it being about midd night, and so many poor people were forced to remain for several days together, some upon the top of their houses, others in the highest rooms, without meat or fire, untill they were almost starv'd. The slewse at Thorn had like to have gone away, which if it had, it is thought that it would never have been layd again, because that the whole country would have petitioned against it, be[cause] it keeps the waters of of the Levels, for but for it they would be drounded as much as ever, so that it would be impossible for any [to] dwell thereon, and it is sayd of all hands that, if it had gone, all the whole country would have

petitioned against its ever being built again, so that the Levels
must have thereafter remained as it was before the drainage, a
continual rendezvouz of waters; and it is my belief that one time
it will come to its ancient state again, which will be the ruin of
all those that have land therein.[e]

The waters upon the banks by Thorn that besides it overrun-
ing all over, and besides the aforesayd breach that it has broke
eight or nine breaches in the sayd bank between Thorn and
Gowl, has driven away four rooms in New Rivers great bridge,
has broke all the banks and bridges of the whole country round
about, sweeping all away before it.   In Lincolnshire, the Trent,
by the aforesayd melt of snow, has broke it's banks near the town
of Morton, hard by Gainsburrow, and has driven allmost the
whole town away, drounding several men, women, and children.
The banks of Vickar's dike and Dicken dike are also broken,
bordering upon our Levells.   In a word, the loss to the whole
country hereabouts is above a million of pounds, besides what it
dos to the whole country round about out of our limits and
circuits.

All the most oldest men that are says that it is the vastest
flood that ever they saw or heard of.

I heard this day from a very ingenious man that the Earl of
Craven's father was but a poor lad, that going up to London did
not as much as know his own name, but, coming out of Craven
in Yorkshire, they not onely gave him that for a sirname, but
also afterwards he was dignify'd with the title of that place from
which he drew his name.   He afterwards marry'd the Queen of
Bohemia, and dyd a while ago, whose son now succeeds him.[f]

[e] Stonehouse in a note *History Isle of Axholme,* (p. 116,) quotes this entry
in the Diary, and, with particular allusion to the latter portion of it (which he
has given substantially and not literally) has appended the following remark
of his own.   "N.B. From this last sentence it is evident that De la Prymne considers the works of the Participants as one cause which freely aggravated the
mischief of these floods; and, if he is correct, we cannot wonder that the
inhabitants should withhold their consent from any others being erected of a
similar nature."

[f] The ingenious man seems, as ingenious men not unfrequently are, to have
been very ignorant.   There is, I apprehend, no reason to doubt the statement in
the peerages that this family was anciently seated at Appletreewick in Craven,
from whence they spread in several branches.   The nobleman here mentioned
was William Craven, eldest son of William Craven knight, Lord Mayor of
London 1611, born 1606.   He was celebrated for his gallantry under Gustavus
Adolphus, King of Sweden, was created Baron Craven 1626, and Earl of
Craven and Viscount Uffington 1664, and died 1697, without issue.   By a
patent 11th Dec., 1665, the barony of Craven was limited, in the event of the Earl's
death, s p., to Sir William Craven, great grandson of Henry Craven, elder
brother of the Lord Mayor, pursuant to which limitation the barony devolved

Sr. Joseph Williamson^r that is now in so great state was also but one of very mean birth.

29. Sr. Clowdsly Shovel^h was a poor lad, born in Yorkshire, who was first ostler at an inn at Redford, in Notinghamshire; after that, being weary of his place, he went to Stockwith in Lincolnshire, where he turned tarpaulin, and from thence, getting acquainted with the sea, he grew up to what he now is. I heard a gentleman say, that was in the ship with him about six years ago, that, as they were sailing over against Hastings in Surry, says Sr. Clowdsley, " Pilot put neer,' I have a little business a shore here," so he put nere, and him and this gentleman went a land in the boat, and having walked about half a mile ashore, Sir Clowdsley came to a little house, " Come," says he to the gentleman, " my business is here, I came on purpose to see the good woman of this house." Upon which they knocked at the door, and out came a poor old woman; upon which Sir Cloudsley kist her, and then fell down on his knees, begged her blessing, and call'd her mother (shee being his mother that had removed out of Yorkshire thither). He was mighty kind to her, and shee to him, and after that he had payd his visit, he left her ten guines, and took his leave with tears in his eyes, and departed to his ship.

Ibid. After the aforesayd thow and inundation came several days of exceeding fine weather, but yesterday it begun again to

on William, 2nd Lord Craven, eldest son of the said Sir William. Elizabeth, Queen of Bohemia, whom the Earl of Craven is said to have married, was the only daughter of James the 6th of Scotland, and Anne, his Queen, and was born in that country 19th August, 1596. She was married to the Elector Palatine Frederic the 5th, 1613. On his decease 29th November, 1632, she remained at the Hague, living in the utmost privacy. The management of her domestic affairs she committed to Lord Craven, who was much attached to her. " The most perfect friendship and confidence, and the most open and unreserved intimacy subsisted between them, yet such was the public opinion, or rather feeling, excited by that harmony of general correctness which had always distinguished her, that not a breath of slander ever fell on their connection. It was at length believed, and probably most justly, that they had been privately married."—*Lodge's Portraits,* vols. viii and ix.

^f Sir Joseph Williamson was son of Joseph Williamson, vicar of Bridekirk, Cumberland; M.A. and fellow of Queen's College, Oxford; D.C.L.; one of the clerks of the Council; keeper of the paper office; secretary to Sir Edward Nicolas, knight, and also to Henry, Earl of Arlington. He was afterwards secretary of state himself. Knighted at Whitehall, 24th January, 1671; P.C. 11th September, 1674; president of the Royal Society. Married lady Catherine, sister and heir of Charles Stewart, Duke of Lennox, and Baroness Clifton. Left no child.

^h Sir Cloudsley Shovel is said by some to have been born in co. Norfolk, 1650. He died s.p.m., but had two daughters by his wife Elizabeth, daughter of John Hill, Esq., a commissioner in the Navy, and relict of Admiral Sir John Narborough, knight, of Knowlton, co. Kent. (*Marr. Lic. Vic. Genl. Abp.*

freez very hard, and last night and this day is falln as much
snow as was before, so that we are exceeding fearful of another
great thow and deluge.

I, having left Lincolnshire, am so exceeding busy in old deeds
and charters, which the gentlemen are pleasd to send me in on

Canterbury, 1690-1, March 6, Sir Cloudesley Shovell, of the city of London,
knight, aged 30 and upwards, bachelor, and dame Elizabeth Narborough, of
Knowlton, co. Kent, widow, to marry at Knowlton). The eldest daughter,
Elizabeth, married Sir Robert Marsham, 5th baronet, created Baron Romney
1716. Lady Shovel died 15th April, 1732. Sir Cloudsley was buried in Westminster Abbey, from his house in Soho Square, about twelve at night, according
to Le Neve's MSS. The ceremony is recorded thus in the Abbey Register, 1707,
December 22 : " Sir Cloudesley Shovell, Kt., Her Majesty's Vice Admirall, &c.,
in the south aisle, by the Lady Gething's monument." The following is the
inscription to his memory :—

Sr. Cloudesly Shovell, Knt.,
Rear Admirall of Great Britain,
And Admirall and Commander-in-Chief of the Fleet,
The just rewards
Of his long and faithfull services.
He was
Deservedly beloved of his country,
And esteemed tho' dreaded by the Enemy,
Who had often experienced his Conduct and Courage.
Being Shipwreck't
On the Rocks of Scylly,
In his Voyage from Thoulon,
The 22d of October, 1707, at night,
In the 57th year of his age,
His fate was lamented by all,
But especially the
Seafaring part of the nation,
To whom he was
A generous Patron and a worthy Example.
His body was flung on the shoar
And buried with others, in the sands,
But being soon after taken up,
Was placed under this Monument,
Which his Royal Mistress has caused to be erected
To commemorate
His steady Loyalty and extraordinary Virtues.

NOTES FROM THE WILL OF SIR CLOUDESLEY SHOVELL, OF LONDON, KNIGHT,
COMMISSIONER OF THE NAVY, DATED 20 APRIL, 1701.

Mother, Mrs. Anne Flaxman, lands at Morston, in Norfolk. Sister Mrs.
Ann Shorton's children—wife Elizabeth—children of my wife by her former
husband, Sir John Narborough—lands in Kent. Cousin John Thurston—wife's
youngest son, James Narborough—her daughter, Elizabeth Narborough—their
eldest son, Sir John Narborough, Bart.—eldest daughter, Elizabeth Shovell—
youngest daughter, Anne Shovell, when 21 or married—aunt Ringstead and her
daughter Mary Ringstead—cousin Elizabeth Thurston daughter of my aunt
Thurston deceased—William, Ann, and Abigail Jenkinson, son and daughters
of my uncle Cloudesley Jenkinson—wife executrix. Proved (C.P.C.) 13th
January, 1707-8, by Executrix.

every side, that I cannot take time to think or write of anything else. Justice Yarbur,[j] before he dyd, sent me a MS. of the lives of the Earls of Waren.

Mr. Yarbur, of Doncaster, sent me many things relating to Doncaster, etc.

Mr. Gregory, of Barmby Dunn,[k] sent me a coppy of the old

In Pulman's MSS., A. ix., p. 777 (at Her. Coll.), there is a pedigree thus commencing :—

```
.......... Shovel, of=Ann, d. of ....=..Flaxman
|.................|.............  2d husband.
```

Sir C. S. &c., born at ...., co.=	Elizabeth, daughter of John=	Sir John Nar-
Suffolk, 1651. Knighted 1May, 1689,	Hill, Esq., Commissioner of	borough,
in Bantry Bay, shipwrecked, &c. Will	the Navy. Ob. 15 Apl., 1732.	Knt.,
dat. 20 Apl., 1701.	Buried at Crayford, co. Kent.	Admiral.

In *Notes and Queries*, 1st Ser., xii., 395, is quoted a letter written by the Rev. George Crokatt, rector of Crayford, in 1708, consoling lady Shovell on the loss of her husband and two only sons. He says that Sir C. S. was *born in Norfolk* in 1650, of an ancient family, remarkable for loyalty, etc., and not inconsiderable as to estate, though lessened by their adherence to Charles I. He says the good old gentlewoman, Sir C. S's mother, is still alive, and enjoys no contemptible competency, which has been transmitted from father to son. And he adds that he writes this to correct some false stories about Sir Cloudesley's birth and education.

I regard this testimony as conclusive. It was written shortly after Sir Cloudesley's death, and by one who evidently knew the facts. His mother's second marriage, to Flaxman, may account for her being at Hastings. De la Pryme probably was misled by the "false stories" still extant in 1708.

Sir Cloudesley Shovel, knight (no other description), had a grant of arms and crest, 6th January, 1691-2, to him and his descendants. The earl marshal's warrant is dated 29th April, 1691. He is called in the grant Rear Admiral of the Blue Squadron. The arms granted were—Gu. a chev. erm. betw. two crescents in chief arg., and a fleur-de-lis in base or. Crest—out of a naval coronet, gold, a demi-lion gu., holding a sail arg., charged with an anchor sa. (*Grants*, 4, p. 103). There is no pedigree in Le Neve's Knights ; nor is Sir C. in any of the lists of knights at Heralds' College.

I am indebted to Colonel Chester for the information above furnished.

Macaulay (*Hist. England*, I., 304) says that Sir John Narborough was cabin-boy to Sir Christopher Mings, who had also entered the naval service in that capacity, and that Sir Cloudesley Shovel was cabin boy to Sir John Narborough.

The name of Cloudsley is a Yorkshire one. Thoresby, the Leeds antiquary, had a "cousin Robert Cloudsley." And Hunter states that the name became extinct at Leeds by the death, without issue, of Mr. Benjamin Cloudsley, in 1753.—*Diary*, i., p. 33.

  i "Need" in *orig.*

  j Thomas Yarborough, esq., of Campsal, co. York, justice of the peace and deputy lieutenant of the west-riding during forty-seven years. Died 30th November, 1697, aged 73.—*Hunter's South Yorkshire*, ii., 466.

  k See pedigree.—*Hunter's South Yorkshire*, i., p. 211.

charter for the fair of Stanford, and several papers relating to the chappel thereof and town.

Mr. Tor,[l] or Tur, sent me a MS. of and about the church of Hatfield, etc.

Mr. Nevil and Mr. Place, of Winterton, sent me some papers relating to Hatfield business, and a whole bundle of manumissions of villans,[m] and charters of Franciscan privileges. One or two I transcribed before in this book, and put down the rest that related to this town in my papers, as I commonly do.

I have received, God be thanked, a great many more notices about things of this town from many hands which I shall thankfully remember elsewhere.

---

[l] James Torre, a celebrated antiquary, of a family long seated at Haxey, in the Isle of Axholme, Lincolnshire. " He settled chiefly at York, and giving way most probably to the natural bent of his genius, devoted himself entirely to the study of ecclesiastical antiquities and family descents. He purchased an estate at Snydall in 1699, where he died in the same year, and was buried in his parish church of Normanton."—*Stonehouse, Isle of Axholme*, 305-308 ; See more of him, *Thoresby's Diary*, i., p. 226, *note by Hunter.*

[m] In an illuminated pedigree of the Wortley family, of the age of Elizabeth, in the possession of Lord Wharncliffe, a drawing is introduced of Sir Nicholas de Wortley (who died 1360), surrounded by his tenants, who are receiving, apparently with great satisfaction, a charter of enfranchisement from his hands. From the muniments of Sir J. W. Copley, Bart., of Sprotburgh, I am enabled to furnish a specimen of one of these deeds of manumission.

Omnibus Christi fidelibus hoc præsens scriptum visuris vel audituris Willielmus fitz William de Sproteburgh armiger salutem in Domino sempiternam, Noveritis me manumisisse et ab omni jugo servitutis liberasse Johannem Plumptre de Rotington nativum meum pro quadam summa pecuniæ quam michi dedit præ manibus, ita quod liber homo sit cum tota sequela sua bonisque mobilibus et immobilibus imperpetuum. Concedo autem eidem Johanni, cum tota sequela sua procreata et procreanda, plenam licentiam eundi, habitandi et redeundi super feodum meum ubicunque prout decet hominem liberæ conditionis et fidelis sine perturbatione mei vel hæredum meorum. In cujus rei testimonium præsentibus sigillum meum apposui. His testibus, Johanne Clarell, Willielmo Chaworth armigero, Willielmo Capron, rectore ecclesiæ de Plumptre, et multis aliis. Datum apud Sproteburgh, primo die mensis Decembris, anno ab inchoatione regni regis Henrici Sexti quadragesimo nono, et re-adeptionis regiæ potestatis suæ anno primo. [1470].

De la Pryme has copied in the *Diary* (p. 347), deeds bearing on this subject, of an earlier date than this. John de Loudham grants to William de Loudham, his brother, one Thomas Locks, of Wintrington, "nativum meum de manerio meo de Wintrington, cum omnibus liberis ejus procreatis et procreandis ac omnibus catallis ejus," etc. Dated on the Sunday next after the translation of St. Thomas the Martyr (7th July), 10th Edward II. (1316). Shortly afterwards, however, viz., on the Sunday next before the feast of St. Margaret the Virgin (20th July), in the same year, it appears, from another deed, that William de Loudham released to the said Thomas Locks all the right whatsoever in him which he had of the gift of Sir John de Loudham, knight, and made him "liberum, manumissum ab omni conditione, nexu, servitio, absolutum in perpetuum."

FEB 6. 1697-8. Mr. Raysin, of Doncaster,[n] has a mighty rare old chron[icle] in MSS., the most splendid, glorious, and beautifull that ever was seen, having the most curious antient pictures and letters in it were ever known, all in the most richest colours and best proportion, etc.

FEBR. 12. Yesterday I went into the Isle of Axholm about some business. It was a mighty rude place before the drainage, the people being little better than heathens, but since that ways has been made accessible unto them by land, their converse and familiarity with the country round about has mightily civilized them, and made them look like Christians. There is nothing observable in or about Belton Church that I could perceive. There is a pretty excellent Church at Epworth, but no monument, coats of arms, nor inscriptions are therein, that I could observe. In the north porch of the church I observed these two coats.

| 3 serpent heads with pricked up ears.[o] | A lion or lioness, which is the arms of the Mowbrays.[p] |

The chancel of the church was formerly a most stately building, almost as bigg as the whole church, and all arched and dubbled rooft, but falling to decay, they made it be taken down and a less built out of the ruins thereof, which was about twenty five years ago.

All on the east end of the Church, and over against the south thereof, stood a famous and magnificent monastry of Carthusian monks, which, upon the reformation, were all expelled, and the monastry pulled down to the bare ground, to the great shame and skandall of the christian religion; in which ground, where it stood, they tell me that there has oft been found several old pieces of English coin, and several gold rings, but they could not shew me any. The Minister thereof is the famous Mr. Wesley,[q] who set out the celebrated poem of the *Life of Christ.*

[n] Probably alderman George Rasine, who was mayor in 1683, when Sir George Cooke (the first baronet) presented the corporation with their great mace.

[o] Stonehouse, in his *Isle of Axholme*, 1839, p. 152, states this coat to be "the arms of Sheffield." That family, however, bore a chevron between three *garbs.*

The bearing most nearly resembles that of the family of Broxholme, to which, in 1580, the arms of, argent, a chevron between three brock's (or badger's) heads azure, were granted. It does not appear, from the account of Epworth, that this family had any connection with that town or it's church.

[p] "Ye same arms is also upon ye font."—*Marginal Note by Diarist.*

[q] The Rev. Samuel Wesley, M.A., born at Whitchurch in 1662, became

The Lord Cartaret' was the late lord of the Isle, but he being dead, his lady enjoys the same.

Low Melwood, in the Isle of Axholm, was (I have lately heard) in antient time a most fine and stately priory, belonging first of all to the Knight Templers, then afterwards to the Knights of Saint John of Jerusalem, and was dedicated, as I imagine, to Saint Leonard, because there is land in the Isle called Saint Leonard's land, which holds of the sayd Melwood.

I have several times been at it, but I was so young I cannot very well remember the same.

However, I can remember very well that [it] was a great and most stately building of many stores high, all of huge squared stone, all wholy built so upon vaults and arches that I have gone under the same a great way. All was huge stone starecases, huge pillars, long entrys, with the doores of both sides opening into opposite rooms. I remember the dining room also, which was at the end of one of those entrys, had huge long oak tables in it, great church windows, with a great deal of painted glass. The outside of the house was all butify'd with semi-arches jetting of the walls upon channeld pillars, and the top was all covered with lead. The doors were huge and strong, and ascended up unto by a great many steps, and places made through the opposite turrets to defend the same, and the whole was encompass'd with a huge ditch or moat.'

There was the finest gardens, orchards, and flowers there that ever I saw ; but now there is, I believe, none of these things to be seen, for, about ten years ago, all or most part being ruinous was pulled down, and a lesser house built out of the same. It is a very unfortunate place, as commonly all religious places have been to the sacrilegious and wicked devourers and raptors of the same. No family has yet possssed it one hundred years together, for it has commonly a new lord every forty or fifty years.

In a green meadow close in Stickley,' near or in Shire Oaks,

Rector of Epworth, and died in 1735. He was father of John Wesley, the celebrated founder of the people called Methodists.—See *Stonehouse, Isle of Axholme,* pp. 175-222. At page 162 that author gives him the rectory of Epworth in 1636, which must be an error.

 ' Sir George Carteret, baronet, so created 9th May, 1645, was Comptroller of the Navy *temp.* Charles I.—an officer of great courage and skill. In 1681 he was created Baron Carteret, of Hawnes, co. Bedford, and died 1695. The manor of Epworth was granted, together with some other crown lands, on a lease for 90 years, by Charles II. to Sir Geo. Carteret.

 ' *Stonehouse, Isle of Axholme,* p. 253, gives this entry from the Diary somewhat varied from the text.

 ' Stickley is probably Steetley. Steetley Church is in Derbyshire, but close to the boundaries of Nottinghamshire and Yorkshire. It is a most beautiful

in or near Worsop, in Darbyshire, stands a staitly well built chapel, all arch-roof'd, excellently enambled and gilt; the lead that cover'd the same is all stoln away, so that the weather begins to pierce through its fine roof, to its utter decaying.

One Mr. Houson, of Beaverley, has several records relating to Doncaster and Hatfield.

FEBR 29. I have written Doct[or] Johnston, the great anti-quary, seven or eight sheets of pedigrees, memorable things, etc.

The pedegs [pedigrees] of the Anns of Frickley, the Went-worths of Elmsal, the Stapletons, the Snasels, the Latimers, the Cholmundleys, the Ardingtons, the Husseys, the Salvens, the Bruces, the Bulmers, the Boyntons, the Musgraves, the Maliverers, the Fairfaxes of Waltham [Walton], the Elands, Vavasors, Spekes, Copleys; the whole pedigrees, for many hundred years together, of the Hothams, Salvins, Bulmers, Whartons, Eastofts, etc.

I have sent him an account also [of] Phila Causey, of many towns on the sea side, of the feeding of their sheep with holly leaves about Bradfield and elsewhere. Epitaphs (out of an old MS. formerly belonging to Dunscroft coll), in Doncaster church and chapels, Snayth church, etc., with a whole description of Doncaster at larg, and of all the memorable things and places belonging thereto.

The MS. aforesayd, which I mightily prize, contains, tho' in short, very many observable epitaphs in the aforesayd churches and chapels, and many in Fishlake church, Hatfield church, Thorn church, Holden [Howden] church, Crull [Crowle] church, and Haxey, Epworth, and Belton churches; but the paper is so farr consumed and gone, that they are scarce legible, and some not. It belongs to Mr. Canby," of Thorn, and is bound up with ma[n]y records relating to his estate, so that he will not part with the same out of his presence. I have sent the Doct[or] as many of them as I transcribed at one time, and if I can pick out the meaning of any more for him, I intend to do it. Those rela-

Norman building, now roofless and deserted. Around it is a church yard, but no burials have taken place there in modern times. It consists of a nave and apsidal chancel; the door on the south has a slightly projecting porch; the arch is composed of zig zag and beaked mouldings; on its shafts are foliage and signs of the zodiac, and the arches of the chancel and apse are even more highly ornamented.

" Hunter, in his preface to *South Yorkshire*, vol. I., states that he had endeavoured in vain to trace this MS., and was fain to content himself with the few extracts from it incorporated with other topographical collections made by De la Pryme. He added, in a MS. note, that " Mr. Elmhirst, who represents Mr. Canby, has it not."

ting to Crull, Haxey, Belton, and Epworth, I will set down, when I have time, in this book.

MARCH 16. This day I had the following papers sent me to interpret from almost twenty miles beyond York, there not being any one, lawyer or whatever, that could do the same, tho' it had been sent and shewd to many. It is a transcript out of Doomesday book, and, as near as I can imitate the letter and brevity thereof, I will set it down here.

[Here follows a long extract which it is unnecessary to repeat.]

APRIL 23. This two or three days has been exceeding bad weather, we have had a great deal of snow and a hard frost ; and indeed this winter has been so sevear that scarce anybody living ever saw the like. We have had six winters in this winter, mighty sevear and cold, between every one of which was great floods (one of which was the greatest that ever was known, topping almost all the Partisipants' banks on every side), between every one of which was a week or above of as fine weather as could be, and then another storm came, etc.

Mr. Geree,[v] of London, has a larg MS. in many vols. folio of of the antiquitys and history of Lincolnshire, written by Doct[or] Sanderson, Bish[op] of Linc[oln.]

I hear much of the religious assemblys and societys that are fixing in every city and great town of England, against al manner of prophaness and immorality, but as yet cannot give a full account thereof.

I was the other day with Mr. Wesley, min[ister] of Epworth, the famous author of the poem of the Life of Christ. He says, that while he was at London, he knew a parrot that by its long hanging in a cage in Billingsgate street (where all the worst language in the city is most commonly spoke), had learned to curse and swear, and to use all the most bawdy expressions imaginable. But, to reform it, they sent it to a coffy-house in another street, where, before half-a-year was at an end, it had forgot all it's wicked expressions, and was so full of coffy-house language that it could say nothing but "Bring a dish of coffy;" "Where's the

[v] See *postea.* There was a John Geree, a Yorkshireman, either a butler or servitor of Magd. Hall. Oxon., in the beginning of the year 1615, who became minister of Tewkesbury, etc. Died in Ivy Lane, London, 1648.
    Stephen Geree, elder brother to the above, also of Magd. Hall, Oxon., 1611, became minister of Wonnersh, near Guildford, and afterwards of Abinger, Surrey.—*Wood's Athen. Oxon.*

news," and such like. When it was thus throughly converted, they sent it home again, but within a week's time it got all its cursings and swearings and its old expressions as pat as ever.

Contrary to all expectation corn of all sorts is exceeding dear,*w* and the weather very cold.

This day I had a large old book in folio sent me, entitled thus— " *Y^e right devout, much laudable, and recomendable boke of the liffs of the olde auncyent faders hermyts, traunslatyd first out of Greke into Latyn by ye Blessed and Holy Saunt St Jerom, right devout and approved Doctoure of ye Chirche, and translated out of Latyn into Frenche, & dylygently corrected in the Cyty of Lyon, anno 1486, and, after, to witt in the year of our L^d 1491, reduced into English, following the coppe alway under the correction of the Doctours of the Chirch.*"

The book itself, after such a fine title-page, is full of lyes, storys, legends, foppery, and popery. It ends thus :—" *Thus endyth the moost Vertuouse Hystorye of the Devoute and right renouned Lyves of the houly faders lyvyng in deserts, worthy of remembraunce to all well dysposed persons, which hath been translated out of French into Englishe, by William Carton, of Westmynster, late deceased, and fynyshd it at ye last day of his lyfe. Enprinted in the sayd town of Westmynstre by Mynhevr Wynkin de Worde, ye yer of our Lord, 1495, and ye 10 year of our Soveragn Lord, K. Henry ye 7th*"

Mr. Hall, min[ister] of Fishlake, has several old MSS., both history and heraldry, written by Mr. Perkins, in Queen Elizabeth's days, a worthy and ingenious man, some of which I have borrow'd.*x*

Mr. Prat, parson of Boswel*y* beyond York, has gathered up a fine collection of medals.

My Lady Wentworth, of Banks, near Barnsley, has also a delicate collection.

Mr. Adwick, of Arksey, has several old papers, deeds, and MSS., as has also Mr. Washington, of Adwick hall, of which he has promiss'd me a sight.

There is a town called Kimberworth,*z* two miles of of Rother-

---

w The average price of wheat for the year 1698 in given as £3, 0s. 9d., in a table reprinted from the *Mark Lane Express* in *Notes and Queries*, 2nd S., vol. v., p. 144.

x See *postea*.

y Bossall.

z Hunter had observed this passage in the Diary. He remarks that " an early antiquary would connect the name of this township with the Cimbri ; but De la Pryme lived before much attention had been paid to the principles on which we

M

ham, so called from y⁰ old Cimbri : Kimberworth, signifying in
English the town of the Cimbri.

Mr. Midleton, of Sutton, can give larg account of the family
of the Lees of Hatfield.

Mr. Kitchingman, Min[ister] of .... by York, has
written a larg Chronology, mighty ingenious and accurate, in fol.
MSS. at Mr. Hall's of Fishlake.

MAY 4. Ever since that May came in there has been a great deal
of snow and frost, the like never seen in memory of man.   In the
west the frost was a great deal bigger than here, for it frose there
above an inch thick in one night, whereas it was not over half as
thick the same night here ; the snow that fell here was also less than
that which fell there, but however, if that it had layd, [I] believe
that it would have been very near a foot thick.   It has done great
damage to all sorts of corn and fruit, and there is so little grass that
the greatest number of cattle have dyd that ever was known.
About Hallifax side the necessity of the winter has caused them to
find out a strang new meat for their goods in winter, and that is
this, when all their fother was done, they took green whinz, chopt
them a little, put them in a trough and stampt them a little to
bruise all their pricles, and then gave them to their beasts, which
eat on them, and fedd them better than if it had been the best hay.

6. On the sixth of this month was the Visitation of the Arch-
Bishop of York,* who was personal there with us at Doncaster.
He is an exceeding strict, religious, and pious man, exceeding
humble, affable, and kind.   He gave us a great deal of most excellent advice, and talked severaly against drunkenness, loos
living, keeping of company, and such like ; desired us all to be-
ware of the same, and beg'd on us to enter into religious associa-
tions one with another, and with the chief of the town to suppress
all vice, profaness, and immorality, in our respective parishes,
etc.

Having finished the beautifying of the church of Hatfield,
the chief of the parish, to the number of thirty, when[t] to Doncaster to the Bishop with the ingenious and worthy min[ister] hereof,

may hope to analyse the terms found in our local nomenclature. The probability
rather is that we have the name of some early settler prefixed to one of the usual
terminals.   In *Domesday* it is Chibereworde, an orthography which is also found
in the *Recapitulatio ;* but as the letter m is found in very early charters as a
part of the name of this place, and is, moreover, an efficient portion of the
name, it is probable that it ought to have made a part of the name as written
by the Norman scribes." See more.—*Hunter's South Yorkshire*, ii., p. 26.
  * John Sharp, D.D., consecrated 5th July, 1691, died 2nd Feb., 1714.

Mr. Eratt,[b] to thank him for haveing given them liberty and power to regulate the pews, and to present him with two maps of the platform of the church, as every one was seated, to get them signed by him, and to desire a confirmation thereof under the seal of the office. As soon as ever we were got to the house where he was, Mr. Eratt when[t] in to acquaint [him] that we were come. The Bishop would not let us come any furder to wait upon him, but came streight down into our room to wait upon us, exprest a great deal

[b] William Eratt, son of Wm. Eratt, of Wartre, in the East Riding of Yorkshire, educated at Pocklington School, was admitted Sizar of St. John's College, Cambridge, 4th May, 1672, when 16 years old. A.B., 1675 ; A.M., 1696 ; came to be minister of Hatfield in September 1689. Married 4th January, 1680, Mary, d. of Thomas Fitzwilliam, of Doncaster, the town clerk of that borough, and widow of John Gilby gent., and mercer of London. *(Jackson's History S*. *George's Church Doncaster*, appx., xlvi.) By her Mr. Eratt had issue, with others, William Eratt, of Doncaster, M.D., who died 13th March, 1727, leaving a daughter and heir, Jane, afterwards married to Edward Forster, Esq., of Thorne, but died s.p. In 1701 there was published, " A Necessary Apology for the Baptized Believers : wherein they are vindicated from the Unjust and Pernicious Accusations of Mr. William Eratt, the Parish Minister of Hatfield, near Doncaster, in Yorkshire, in his Epistle to John Woodward. By Joseph Hooke, a Servant of Christ, and a hearty lover of all men." Our Diarist was a pupil of Mr. Eratt's, and he has recorded in the Diary the following specimen of versification by him :—

" A MANIFESTO OF KING JAMES' RUIN."

Hark, most unhappy and deluded king,
Unto the cause that did thy ruin bring ;
For thee the sockless child and parent mourn'd,
When th' trees 'ith west were unto gallows turned ;
For thee time-serving favourites appear'd
When neither truth nor justice cou'd be heard ;
For thee the Popish judges gave the cause
Against all right, and liberty, and laws ;
For thee some faulty doctors did betray
Their church : mandamus's they had for pay.
The freeman in his land was quite undone,
And the miser scarce could call his gold his own ;
For thee poor Teague was forced to run away,
To save his bones he fled without his pay ;
For thee the merchant had lost all his trade,
And hence the seaman was in harbor stay'd ;
In spite of law thou didst our law suspend,
And fain would new ones had to serve thy end.
Thy patriot's aim in all their loyal votes
Was to invent and contenance sham plots ;
By thee no credit in the land was left,
And little coin not counterfeit nor clip'd ;
Yet still thy loyal slaves desire to be
Under their former yoke of tyranny,
To their own country's good they're strangers grown,
Peace they would have abroad but war at home.
What wonderous fools they are all will conclude
To call thee just who never kept thy word.
Bewitch'd they're sure to sign the Popish rolls,
That priests may suck their blood and d—n their souls.

Will. Eratt, M.A., Minist. de Hatfield, f.

The Rev. Wm. Eratt was buried at Hatfield 30th March, 1702. The arms borne by his family, as they appeared on Dr. Eratt's gravestone in Doncaster church, were :—A fess between three estoiles.—See *Mon. Ins. Jackson's St. George's Church, Doncaster*, p. 112.

of respect unto us, and when we let him see the mapps he was
exceedingly pleasd therewith, and sayd they were exceeding fine
and neat, well contrived, and mighty decent, etc., and asked several times before he signed them, whether every one was content
and willing, and well pleased at the regulations made, which they
all affirmd they were.　Then he signed them, thanked us all,
talked a while, and as he was going out, he turned again and
told us he would next year come to Hatfield, would give us a
month's notice, and would confirm there, etc.

7th.　This very day Mr. Theseus Moor,[c] our next neighbour,
caused a hen to be killd for his Sunday dinner, but, when they had
killd her, they were all amazd when they begun to o, en, all
between her body and her skin was contained a huge quantity
of a transparent matter, just like starr shot jelly (about an inch
thick in most places, and spread round about almost all over her).
It was a water contained in tough bladers, very adherent one to
another, but not glutinous, nor had it any smell or tast.　The whole
quantity of this stuff is almost as heavy as the whole hen.　I have
a good quantity of it, which I do intend to try experiments on.
The hen thrive[d] very well, and ate heartily, seemd to be very
fatt, and nobody suspected that she aild any thing.

Her distemper was perhaps a kind of a dropsy, or a gathering together of a subcutanious water, occasioned by the obstruc-
tion of the pores of the skin, which were perhaps filld up by
some blasting or some excess or storm of this could winter, for it
has been observed that some ones, that have been great starr
gazers in winter nights, have by the could contracted a distemper,
which has obstructed the pores of the skin, and caused the vapours, that were to exhale, to gather between the skin and the body
etc., an instance of which in a man is in the Transactions of the
R.S. for the year 1665 p. 138.

I borrowed not long ago two MS. in folio of Mr. Hall,[d]

[c] On the 30th Nov., 1699, Theseus Moore surrendered in the court of the
manor of Dunscroft, by the hands of Peter Prim, one of the tenants, a house in
Hatfield to Sarah Prim, the Diarist's mother, who was then admitted. 10th March,
1718, Sarah Pryme, by Peter Pryme, surrendered the premises, described as a messuage or cottage at the east end of Hatfield, near the church, in which William
Marryott lately dwelt, to Margaret Greenhalgh, w⁰·　She, by will, 16th Oct., 1740,
devised it to her daughter, Emelia De la Pryme, w⁰· ; by whose devisees, James
De la Pryme, of Sheffield, and James Greatrex, of Manchester, it passed, 28th
Feb., 1772, to the Rev. Francis Proctor, Incumbent of Hatfield.　Of his descendants, the Rev. Thomas Fox, a subsequent incumbent, purchased, from whom
it has come to his son, Mr. W. J. Fox, solicitor, who has obligingly communicated this information.

[d] 1695-6.　Johannes Hall, cler., et Sarah Perkins, Vid., 17th Feb.　(Marriage at Fishlake, ex inform. Rev. G. Ornsby, Vic.)

min[ister] of Fishlake, who had mar[ried] the relict of Mr. Perkins.'

The first I have entitled:

Of the antiquity of Ensigns and Armes, to which is joined a catal[ogue], of the Creation of the Nobility of every King since the Conquest to Queen Elizabeth's days. By Thomas Perkins, of Fishlake, Esq.

The other I have entit ed:

A book of the arms and pedegrees of many of the Yorkshire nobility and gentry : Collected by Thomas Perkins, of Fishlake, Esq.

In which last book is contained the pedegrees of the Anns, of Ask, of Bigod, Bruce, Bohun, Babthorp, Boynton, Birdhead,ʄ Barmby, Beiston, Clarrel, Copley, Constable, Clare, Castelion, Denman, Eastoft, Frobisher, Furnival, Ferrers, Fitzwilliam, Fairfax, Gascoign, Harrington, Hilliard, Hilton, Holm, Hotham, Hastings, Lov . ., Lovetoft, Lacy, March, Montney, Melton, Marshal, Nigil, Nevil, Oldwarck, Peck, Portington, Perkins, Quinzy, Rotherfield, Rockley, Rearsby, Stappleton, Sothell, Swift, Strangbow, Skearn, Salvin, Stanfield, Talboys, Talbot, Triggot, Urslet, Vernon, Westby, Wortley, Wallis, Wentworth, Worral, Woodrofe and Wombel.

"14th June, 1694, Johannes Hall, clericus, admissus fuit ad inserviendum curæ animarum in ecclesia de Gisbrough, in eccl. de Upletham, et in eccl. de Fishlake, diæc. Ebor."

He had a son, John Hall, who was Fellow of Sᵗ· John's College, Cambridge. 24th May, 1719, in the church of Sᵗ· Mary, in Nottingham, "Johannes Hall, A.B., e coll. Jesu Cantab." was ordained deacon, and priest in York Minster on March 5th, 1720-1. On April 4th, 1722, Johannes Hall, clericus, A.M., admissus fuit ad inserviendum curæ animarum in ecclesiâ de Gisborough, ac etiam in eccl. de Upleatham, in com. et diæc. Ebor. His successor, Richd. Cuthbert, A.M., was admitted to the same cures 20th Nov., 1722. The son died in 1722, aged only 26, and was buried in the church at Hatfield, where there is a monument to his memory, with the following inscription :—(Arms, arg., a chev. engr. between 3 talbots heads erased sable).

Juxta situs est
Vir verè Eximius et Marmore Dignus
Johannes Hall, A.M.:
Colleg. Jesu Cantab. nuperus e socijs,
Ecclesiæ apud Guisbrough Pastor
Fidus et Amabilis.
Primævæ puritatis Indagator Sagax,
Pietatis Æmulator Sanctissimus,
Vixit Filius, Frater, Amicus, Optimus :
Obijt, ah Juvenis !
Æternitati tamen (si quis alius), maturus
A.C. 1722, Ætat. 26.
Imitemur.

ᶜ On the 4th Feb. 1721, Thoresby was engaged in the afternoon "making an index to Mr. Perkins's manuscripts till near evening."—*Diary*, ii., 34.
ʄ *i.e.* Burdett.

In the first there is . . pages, in the second there is 232.

He has lent me also the fragment of an old MS. Chron[icle] in which are several things very observable, especially that about St. Augustine the monk killing many hundreds of the Brittans, because they would not submit to him, and acknowledge the Pope for universal Bishop.

At Trumfleet[f] water mills there [are] commonly every May such vast numbers of young eels comes over the wheels with the waters and runs into the mill, that they are forced to give over working, and to send into the town for the swine to devour them, for they are innumerable as the sand on the sea shore.

I was a fishing in Went the other day. It is a narrow river, not over six yards over, but the crookedest and the deepest that ever I saw in my life, therefore it is rightly called Went, which signifys deep in Welsh. Every turn of the river makes a great bogg on the other side, on which the water is thrown by the current; and there is delicate fish therein; but such quantitys of eels that the like was never seen. Sometimes there will break out, or fall out of the hollow bank sides, when people are a fishing, such vast knots of eels, almost as bigg as a horse, that they break all their netts in pieces.

Wroot church is of pretty great antiquity (but not so old as it is pretended, to witt, antienter than Lincoln minster). It is dedicated unto St. Peter, as may appear by its feast, which always has been, and is, kept upon St. Peter's day unto this time; tho' I have seen an old will in which was this sayd, that he gave five shillings to the altar of St. Pancratius, in Wroot.[h]

There is a famous k[ing] of the gipsys, that's call'd Mr. Bosvill,[i] a mad spark, that, haveing an estate of about two

---

[f] A hamlet in the township and parish of Kirk-Sandal, six miles west from Thorne, west-riding of Yorkshire.

[h] The village of Wroot is situate on the west side of the Isle of Axholme, Lincolnshire, about five miles westward from Epworth. Stonehouse (*Isle of Axholme*, p. 385), states that this church "was rebuilt in the year 1794, on the old site, and about the same dimensions. The antient fabric, like the present, consisted only of a nave and a chancel," etc. He does not say to whom it is dedicated. At the present day the inhabitants appear to consider that they enjoy the patronage of St. Peter.' In the *Doncaster Chronicle*, of 16th July, 1869, it was stated that, at that place, "the feast, or anniversary of the dedication of the parish church, commenced on Sunday last," 11th July, which was old St. Peter's day.

[i] Hunter notices him (Charles Bosvill) in *South Yorkshire*, i., p. 68. Miller, in his *History of Doncaster*, p. 237, erroneously calls him *James* Bosvill. The following is the entry of his burial in the Register at Rossington, near Doncaster : "Charles Bosvill was buried on Sunday, January 30th, 1708-9, without affidavit." "This person," observes Hunter, "is still remembered in the traditions of the village as having established a species of sovereignty

hundred per annum, yet runs about. He is mighty fine and brisk, and keeps comp[any] with a great many gentlemen, knights and esq[uires].

Hoppkinson's MS.[*j*] collections are now in the hands of Mr. Thornton, of Leeds; there is another coppy more correct, with additions, in the hands of Mr. Parker, formerly of Marlow, now near unto Skypton in Craven.

On the 26 of May last, about five in the morning, in a dry time, I went into the garden and gathered a pint or two of dew, and having filtered it through a clean cloth I put it in three glasses, one of which I cork'd fast, the other little at all, just to keep dust out, and the other not at all, the first and the last I set in the north window of my chamber, and the second in the south window against the sun, the second soon grew greenish, and so continues; that which was stopt fast continues its first colour almost as pellucid as water; but that which was not stopp'd is of a golden colour like urine.

About the 10th of June I took the aforesayd bottle that was unstopp'd and set it in my south window, and put both into it, and into the other that had stood in the south window from the first, a wheat corn apiece; the wheat corn in that which had stood in the south window all along germinated and shot forth roots, a stalk, and two blades many inches long, but the other is not yet germinated.

among that singular people called the gypsies, who, before the inclosures, used to frequent the moors about Rossington. His word amongst them was law; and his authority so great that he perfectly restrained the pilfering propensities for which the tribe is censured, and gained the entire good will for himself and his people of the farmers and the people around. He was a similar character to Bampfield Moore Carew, who, a little later, lived the same kind of wandering life. No member of this wandering race for many years passed near Rossington without going to pay respect to the grave of him whom they called their king: and I am informed that even now, if the question were asked of any of the people who still haunt the lanes in this neighbourhood, especially about the time of Doncaster races, they would answer that they were "Bosvile's people." Miller says that one of the accustomed rites of the gypsies from the south, when they visited Bosvill's grave, was to pour a flagon of ale thereon. In the burial register of Tickhill, a few miles from Rossington. occurs. "1693. July the 25th. Susanna, daughter of Charles Boswell, gent., a stranger." In the church of Winslow, co. Bucks, it is said that under a flat stone "lieth the body of Edward Boswell, gent., who died Aug. 30th, 1689," of whom it is a tradition in the parish that he was king of the beggars. *Topographer*, vol. i., p. 53.

In the churchyard of Beighton. co. Derby, is a stone in memory of Matilda Bosswell. who died Janry. 15, 1844, aged 40; also of Lucretia Smith, "Queen of the Gypsies." who died Nov. 20th. 1844, aged 72. Again. at Calne. is one for Inverto Boswell, with the figure of a horse rampant, of which a coloured drawing was exhibited at the meeting of the Wiltshire Archæological Society at Chippenham in Sept., 1855. by Mr. Alfred Keene. of Bath.

[*j*] These MSS. are now divided between the British Museum and Matthew Wilson, Esq., of Eshton Hall.

Mr. Robert Geree,[a] that has the MSS. of Bish[op] Sanderson, cont[aining] the his[tory] of Lincolnshire, lives at Islington, and and is minister there.

In the digging of the well at Mr. Place's, at Winterton afore-sayd, they found the earth and stone thus, three yard sand, one foot fine warp, in which was found the ear of a pot, two foot deeper a blew clay, under that, a foot deeper, a blew stone, in the surface of which was found wood, half wood, half stone.

The Marquess of Normanby's hall, or pallace raither, at Nor-manby, by Burton in Lincolnshire, was built, most part of the hewn stone of it, out of Butterwick chappel[i] which was pulled down to build it.

Several projectors have been exceeding busy this last sessions of parliament to have had the rivers Ayre and Chalder navigable, and there has been the greatest lugging and pulling on both sides, the one to effect, the other to hinder the same, that ever was known, and thousands of pet[it]ions have been sent up *pro* and *con* about the same ; but the parlament has broke up before that the bill was three times read.

There is huge papers in print of reasons both for and against it, but those on the latter side are farr the strongest, tho some of them are weak enough, as for example this. In the bill they say that the sea hath water enough to supply all rivers, and that the making or cutting of never so many rivers out of or into any antient river will not abate the tide of such antient river, which (this answer says) is falls [false] and then proceeds thus. The sea onely continues flowing six hours, and such flowing is received into the rivers as their proportion affords room for the time to receive the same. The river Humber, being larg, first takes in the tide plentifully where it flows about twenty-four foot at Hull, and from thence continues about twenty five miles to Owse mouth, where it flows sixteen foot, thence continues about ten miles to the mouth of Ayre (the river growing narrower), where it flows twelve foot, and at York flows onely two foot and a half, and that which is very observable is that the water ebbs at the mouth of the river Humber an houer before that it begins to flow at the mouth of the river Ayre. That no more water can come out of the

---

[a] See *antea*, p. 176.

[i] It is said that one of the family, George Sheffield, great uncle to the Marquess of Normanby, "broke his neck in a new riding house, said to have been made out of an old consecrated chapel."—*Stonehouse*, p. 270.

Compare this with what the Diarist says in the *Hist. of Winterton (Archæo-logia)*, about Ferriby Sluce being built out of Butterwick Chapel. The present hall at Normanby is a new structure, built on the site of the old one by the late Sir Robert Sheffield.

sea but what came in before the ebb, so that the making any new
cutts out of the river Ouse will take out and lessen or divert part
of the tide of the said river, as is proved by experience, there
having been a new river at Gowle (about four miles nearer the
sea'than the mouth of the river Ayre), for the draining of Hatfield Chase into the river Ouse. A sluce was erected to hinder
the tide of Ouse from flowing into the sayd Gool river, and
while the sayd sluce was kept in repair, the tide at York flowed
two foot more than it does now, but the sluce falling into decay,
about forty years since (which the country is not able to make
up), Gowl river takes so much of the tyde that York hath lost
two foot of their tyde.

'Tis true that Gool does take some of their tyde back, not
half so much as is here pretended, because that it is fenced out
with huge stathes, for, if all the water might be sufferd to come
in that would, it would weare the entrance or mouth of the river
a vast bredth and dround and destroy the whole Levels. When
the tides dos come, and the water rises, the Ouse water is a great
deal higher than the water in this river, tho' it pouers therein all
it can, because the narrownes of the mouth hinders its flowing in
so fast as to keep it with a level with Ouse.

July 26. We have all of us been this week voteing for parlament men at York. The three competi[t]ors were the Lord
Downs, Lord Farefax, and Sir John Kay ; with much to do after
a soor pull, we got the two Lords chosen. The common-free inhabitants that made above 40s. a year of their common did, according as formerly, swear themselves worth above 40s a year freehold, and were acordingly polld. Our common is freehold unto
us, and the lord has nothing to do with it. We have charter for
the same."^m

^m The following letter is interleaved :—

"Mellwood, 1st Aug., 1698.
" Kinde Sꞃ.,
        " I am pritty well assured that both your selfe and brother are
freeholders in our county. If you please both of you to be so kinde as honor me
with your good companys and interest on Wednesday next at Lincolne, it
would be a very obliging favour. And as I aske for myself, so I likewise begg
yᵉ same favour for my friend the Champion, wherein you shall ever oblige,
                " Yoʳ· faithfull humble
                        " Servt.,
                                " Geo. Whichcot.
    " All the clergy and neighbourhood in the Isle goe along with me, will meet
altogether at the watering place two miles on this side Lincoln, on Wednesday
morning by nine of the clock, and so goe into Lincolne together.
    " All the clergy goe into Lincolne to-morrow and will be glad of your good
companys.

I found in the newse at York that one Mr. Ardsley, a Quaker, is chosen parlament man for Wicham, which is such as was never known before; but it came to be voted whether he should sit or no, so he was cast out.

I have this day bought several old Roman coins of the bas empier for shillings a piece that were digged up at Alburrow, not far of of Burrowbrigs, at which place not long ago was found, as a man was plowing, a great plate of gold, which the country clown sold for five shillings to a Scotchman, who, coming over the field, chanced to see it, who sold it again for fifty pounds.

I was very well acquainted in Cambridge* with an ingenious young man, one Tim[othy] Wallice, whose father, as I have lately heard, is minist[er] of a town in or near Holderness; which man, about fourteen years ago, had so violent a fitt of the cold palsy, that, when he was recoverd out of it, he had forgot every thing, and was become a perfect ignorant man again. For when he was recovered, he could remember nothing of his former life or of his actions, nor nothing, so that he could neither write nor read, nor know his own children, so that he was forced to learn both to read and write after, and the other things that people learns when they are young. After which time he has had at least half a score fitts more (which is as strange as the aforegoing), but always stoppd them before that they came to the height by a most excellent palsy water which he has gotten.

"[Addressed] To the Reverend Mr. Abraham Prim, or to his brother Mr. Peter Prim. Present."

* The Diarist has here interleaved the following letter from his college friend Bennet, to which no year is given, and for the month it seems to be placed not where it should be.

"Dear S

"I received yr. letter and humbly thank you, and do by this answer assure you how willing I am to renew yr. former acquaintance. You desire to know, Sr., wt. proficiency I have made in Heb. or Arab., but alas Sr. I am sensible I am master of nothing, and though I were as learned as I could wish myself, yet it does not become me to talk of my own abilities. As for news of books I am pretty much a stranger to them, not going as I used to ye booksellers, for I keep myself pretty retired, and mind such studies as yt my reading will not be able to furnish you with any memories; though otherwise I should be extreamly ready. I heartily wish you all ye success imaginable in yr. studies. That MS. of Butcher's is called *Antiquity Reviewed* and his design is to treat of the counties, but if ever I observe anything in it, of yt nature you speak, I shall take notice of it. Yr. chamber fellow Sibbald (now Harvy Soph in order to his degree in physick) has signelized his behaviour. Rob. Read is troubled with an asthma.

"I am, Sr.,
"Yr. humble servant,
"T. B.[ENNET].

"Feb. 18.
"(Addressed).—These To Mr. Abraham Prym at Broughton, near Glenford Brigg, in Lincolshire."

SEPT 1. On the first of September, being then at Hatfield carrying on my history of that town, I was met with by the ingenious and reverend Mr. Banks,° rector of the High Church of Hull, who, declaring that he wanted a Reader there, enticed me to go and accept of the place, which, after a while consideration, I did.

The town is a very fine town, exceeding well governed, and kept in very great aw. There is two sermons every Sunday, and a sermon every Wednesday. There is seven or eight hospitals in the town, and yet, for all that, the maintaining of the poor cost them about 1700l. a year, etc. I shall give a greater account of this town hereafter, if God please, for I have some thoughts of writing the history of it.

Towards the middle of this month, Mr. Banks going to York to preach his course sermon, I gave with him an *Elenchus Librorum et Capitum Historiæ meæ Hatfieldiensis*, to shew the Bishop, who took it very kindly, and shewd it to the famous editor of so many old chronicles, the learned Doct[or] Gale,ᵖ who was likewise very glad thereof; who sent word to me that he would be very glad to be acquainted with me, and would feign see me.

As soon as the time of the Ordination came on I went to York, and from thence to Bishopthorpe, to get into priests orders. Having been examined by the Bishop's two chaplains, who made me conster in the Greek Testament and in Cicero's Epistles, and having asked me a great many questions, how I proved the being of the Trinity against the Socinians, and such like, I then went to the Bishop, who likewise asked me a great many questions relating to divinity, and then fell of talking of antiquitys, asked me whether I had any old coins, whether I had any in my pocket, to which I answered "yes," and, upon his desire, shewd him several, which he was well pleased at, and bid me pursue my studdys, and I should not want encouragement. He sayd he liked my design of Hatfield very well, but sayd that I could not

---

° Robert Banks, A.M., of Christ's Coll., Cambridge—Vicar of Trinity Church, Hull, 1689—1715; Prebendary of Stillington at York, and Rampton at Southwell; a correspondent of Thoresby and Sir Philip Sydenham. Married Millicent, dau. of Sir Edward Rodes, and widow of Charles Hutton, esq., of Poppleton. On 14th Feb., 1714-15, admonⁿ. was granted to Millicent, his widow.

ᵖ Thomas Gale, S.T.P., of the family of Gale, of Scruton, the well-known scholar and antiquary. He was Fellow of Trinity College, Cambridge; master of St. Paul's School, 1672-1697; and Dean of York from 1697 to 1702. He is better known for his historical collections than for his classical works, although he was an excellent scholar. His collection of MSS. is in the Library of Trinity College, Cambridge. Roger and Samuel Gale, both of them antiquaries of repute, were his sons.

prove what I proposed in the three or four first chapters of my Elenchus, but only by conjecture and probability, to which I replied that that was enough where nothing else was to be had, etc.

Then I went to Mr. Dean, that is the aforesayd famous Doct-[or] Gale, who was very glad to see me; with whom I had a great deal of discourse. He enquired of me about old MSS. and historys, for he is yet collecting all he can towards another vollume of authors, two vollumes being allready published by him, to his great honour and the good of the whole nation. He tells me [he] has searched all England, Scotland, and Ireland, and can find no author older than Bede, and says that all that has written some hundreds of years after him took all what they had of former times out of him.

He says that Venerable Bede in his lifetime published two editions of his history; the first was small and is yet extant in MS., which small one K[ing] Alfrid, lighting on, translated into Saxon, which was printed in the same by Wheelock. He says that Wheeloc was a very superficial fellow, and that he scarce understood what he pretended to publish, as plainly appears, says he, by the Saxon MSS. he made use of in his edition, for he publish'd the very wost of them, full of barbaritys and errors, and left the best in MSS.

The larger edition that Bede set out in his lifetime is that which is so common, printed also with the Saxon of the small one by Wheeloc. He says that he found the same in MSS. above six hundred years old, written in the Saxon character, which he compaird with the present Bede, as he did a great many more, but found no material difference betwixt them.

He says, that he fully believes that whatever is related of Hatfield, in Bede, must be Hatfield by Doncaster.

He says that the Romans, in their marches, always pitch their camp on the south side of rivers in England, with the river between them and their enemy's. Says that the antient citty of York was undoubtedly all of it on the south side of Owse, and says that he believes that the first church that Edwin built in York was not where the minster now stands, but that it was in the old citty upon or near Bishops hill, near Skeldergate postern, etc.

He says that the great battel, mentioned in Bede to be fought in Winwid field, or Winwid stream, was not near Ayre, as Mr. Thorsby in the new edition of Cambeden has affirmed, but that it was near the river Went, formerly called Wennet, and before that time Winnid.[9]

He told me of a battel fought by the river Dun by King Arthur, &c., and, having encouraged me in my studdys, I took my leave of him.

The Sunday following I was ordain'd. The chair ges wa ust eleven shillings, besides my jorney charges, etc.,

Mr. Dean is a mighty ingenious man; keeps correspondance with all the learned men in England, and has searched all the kingdome over for old MSS., which he is for publishing, but can find none no where older than, [or] better than, those he has published.

He says Sir. Sim[on] Dews was a very braggodocio and superficially learnd fellow, that he pretending [pretended] to things he neither knew nor were able to perform.

Octor. 25. There is at present great noise in the country, and many virulent books written about one Dugdale[r] of Sury, in Lancashire, who pretended formerly to be possessd, and the presbiterians pretend that they, after a great many prayers and fastings, cast the divel out, tho' it is a plain cheat and an abominable imposture, and whether Mr. Joly, the great presbiterian, knew of it or no is uncertain. However, he makes it his by his foolish defending of it.

Nov. 2. K[ing] W[illiam] is not comed over yet from beyond sea that we hear of. 'Tis observable of him that he cannot stay or abide long under deck, it makes him so exceeding sick, so

---

[9] In a letter from the Diarist to Ralph Thoresby,. dated May 17th, 1703 (*Thoresby Correspondence*, vol. ii., p. 3), he alludes to "the pretended battle of King Edwin at our Hatfield, which," he says, "since, I have found belongs to Edwinstone, in Nottinghamshire, *i.e.*, the plain above the river Vinvid, or Win-wid-stream, was. Dr. Gale would needs persuade me always that it was our river Went that divides this manor from Pollington, but I always told him again that I thought that was rather Winnet by Stapleton, called Innet, in Cheshire or Lancashire, from a charter in the *Mon. Angl.*, vol. i., and, I think, p. 862, where Rob. de Lacy grants to the monks of Kirkstal communitatem totius moræ quæ vocatur Winnemoor, et unam acram terræ in Winnet et occidentali parte pontis super ripam aquæ."

[r] Hunter alludes to him as "a wretched imposter named Dugdale, living in the wildest parts of Lancashire, whose artifice falling in with the opinions of too many of the Puritans respecting possession, many were deceived, and especially some of the most influential amongst their ministers. A catalogue of the tracts relating to this affair may be seen in *Gough's British Topography*, vol. i., 506. Mr. Carrington, who published the first account of this person, was a young minister, then lately settled at Lancaster."—*Thoresby's Diary*, vol. i., p. 296, *note*.

that he is oftentimes forced to have a great chair tyd above deck to the mast, and there to sit sometimes many hours together with his nobles about him.

Doct[or] Fall,' præcentor of York, did lately acquaint Mr. Wesley that father Simon, the author of many books, did employ him to speak to.

Having lately recieved a kind letter from Mr. Taylor, I have this day returned him this following answer to the same.

Reverend Sir,

Haveing been most of this month seeking antiquitys in ye country, I recieved your kind and oblieging letter as soon as I got home, and am exceeding glad to understand your good resolution of not laying down ye prosecution of ye Sury cause, tho' your great and worthy studys otherwise might move you to ye same.

I cannot but wonder sometimes at ye fate of writers, just as this very business has called you from other weighty studies, which ye vanity (as you are pleased to term it) of your fancy led you to think might have been of some service to ye publick, even so has it happend to me, none of all ye skandalous lying pamphlets that ye godly have published these many years awaked me so much as this pretended divel they'd conjurd up, it being in my eys like to do more mischief, not only amongst ye mobb, but also amongst others that are superficialy learnd, and that cannot penetrate into ye depth of ye design, so that I flung by my Hist[ory] and Antiq[uities] of Hatfield, near Doncaster, my Hist[ory] and Antiq[uities] of ye famous citty of Jerusalem from its first building unto this day, my Introduction to ye excellent knowledge and studdy of Antiquitys, my Origins of Nations and Languages, some almost finished, and took pen in hand to draw up something to quell this monster of ye godly with, in such a form, and on such heads, as I have in my former letter mention'd unto you. But, as for my performance, I have neither had time nor opportunity nor those plenty of books that are requisite to make such an undertaking either perfect or indifferent, yet, upon ye reception of your kind letter, I have begun to review and new modell the same, but what I shall do therewith I know not yet.

I am very glad of that challeng that you give ye papist priests, and their brethren in iniquity, about ye existence of corporial possessions in these latter days, not doubting at all but that it may easily be proved that they are all seasd long ago, as I have briefly indeavourd to shew from ye fathers, councells, and divines, of ye Church of England.

But that I am so farr of off your country, and has so much business on my hands, I would willingly make a jorney on purpose to examin Dugdale, for to try to make him confess his knavery, and shew how he did his tricks, and who set him on work. I humbly move this unto you to enquire furder into him, by spys and underhand, and secret dealings and examinations, and to see to catch him in drink, and such like ways, as also after ye same manner to pump his father and relations, who must necessarily be confederate with him.

You promise, towards ye latter end of your letter, that if I desire to see the heads of ye chapters of your MS. you will communicate them. If you please you may, and I shall communicate anything I have. You add furder that I may do you a great kindness in somethings which relate to things you could not so handsomly take notice of in your sheets. To this I answer as freely as

---

' James Fall was at one time Principal of the University of Glasgow, and in 1692 he became precentor at York, and subsequently Archdeacon of Cleveland. He was buried in York Minster June 13th, 1711. He edited the works of Archbishop Leighton.

to ye former, that, if you please to name what it is that may be acceptable unto your design, I shall very willingly communicate it unto you.

Above all things I desire a furder correspondence with you, and, if you please, ye knowledge of those other works that you are working upon. In honouring me as above, and acquainting me with which, you will exceedingly obliege

Your most affectionate and humble broth. and serv.,

Hull, Novemb. 25, 1698.　　　　　　　　　　　　　　　　　ABR. PRYME.

This day I was with one Mr. Fiddis,[1] a minister in Holderness, who told me that, about six years ago, going to bed at a friend's house, some had out of roguery fixed a long band to the bedclose where he lay. About half an houer after he was got to bed they begun to pull, which, drawing the bedclose of by degrees put him into a suddain fright, and, looking up, he did really think and believe that he saw two or three spirits stirring and moveing about the bed, and says but that he discovered the string, and the partys confessing the fraud, he durst almost have sworn that he realy saw strang things, which shews the effects of suddain frights.

　　　　　　　　　　　　　　　　　　　　　　　　　"Wigan, Dec. 27, '98.
" Revd. Sr.,

The throng of business upon my hands, when your letter came, occasioned my deferring to answer it till I had more leisure, for I was desirous to have my first book transcribed, that in these holidays my friends might peruse it. The heads of the chapters that it consists of are these.

1. *Quid per dæmonium a quo dæmoniaci sunt dicti in sacrâ paginâ intelligendum est.*

2. *An sint dæmoniaci (viz.) homines malo spiritu corporaliter accepti.*

3. *Qui sint dæmoniaci quoad corpus affecti ?*

4. *Qui sint dæmoniaci quoad animam affecti ?*

5. *Unde fit quod spiritus malus, et animam & corpus dæmoniacorum suo arbitrio ullatenus vindicat.*

6. *Exturbatio dæmonum Evangelica inter opera, quæ Miraculum postulant ponenda est.*

7. *Pseudexorcistas esse plurimos, quorum opere Satanas collusivè Satanam ejicit.*

8. *Exorcizandi Charisma, quamdiu in ecclesia florebat.*

9. *Dæmoniaci verè et proprie dicti quomodo sint dignoscendi ?*

10. *Dæmonii potestate Divinâ ejecti Criteria.*

11. *Pseudexorcistæ, ut dignoscantur.*

12. *Miraculosa Dei potestas in dæmoniis expugnandis ut dignoscatur.*

"The second book will wholly be a Thesis on the question I sent you showing from the aforesaid principles that there is no such thing as dœmoniacks among Christians. The fanatical villany at the Surey led me to inquire into these matters, and diverted my thoughts from prosecuting an attempt at accommodating (as far as possible) the LXX. version, and the Hebrew text, wch. in a short time now I hope to return to. It bears this title, *Massora duplex ; sive Puritas Textus Hebraici ex hac parte ex illâ Versionis LXX. viralis, mutuis inter se collationibus et adminiculis, Quâ potuit Industria, sibi ipsis restituta.* I have

---

[1] For an account of Richard Fiddis and his works, see *Davies' Memoirs of the York Press*, pp. 123-5.

some years since finished an essay towards it on yͤ New Testament, wᶜʰ. I intend for a preface, wᶜʰ. (when the poet's date is out, and it wants not much of it, *nonumque prematur in annum*), if God preserves my life and health, shall see the light. This sort of learning leads me to dip a little in the Orientall languages (I say dip, for I cannot pretend to be a master of them), and if any observations I have made may be assisting to you in your treatise of the origin of nations and languages (which, as the others you are ingaged in, will be of excellent use) on the least intimation you may command them : and I think you do very judiciously in joining these two together, for I think the dialects, etc., of languages to be the best rationall guide we have to judge of the origin of nations, after what we have from revelation and history.

" The Surey impostor is so arch a knave that he stands on his guard, and all the means we have used to bring him to a confession are fruitless, wᶜʰ. confirms me in my opinion that yͤ Popish preists were at the bottom of it, for he dares not own a correspondence with them : besides the distance I live from him is so great that I cannot attend his motions, and some who are near, that should have undertaken the cause themselves, were not so serviceable to me as they might have been.

" The pleasure I intimated you might do me, when you publish your papers, was some reflections wᶜʰ. the dissenters are pleased to make on me, on account of my father, as if I should, against his conscience, have pressed him to conformity, of wᶜʰ., when your papers are ready for the press, I shall give you a full account.

" The stationer at London, Jones, yᵗ is to print my answers, I fear is a knave, and communicates yᵐ. to the adverse party, for he has had them in his hands since the beginning of September, and I can yet hear nothing of them.

" I know not but that I may be cal'd to London the next month about our Election here for Parliament men : I find myself yͤ inconvenience of not having a corrector of the press at London, and if any treatise of your's will be finish'd by that time (if I be there), I shall be ready to serve you in that office, as being,

" Sʳ.,

" yr. humble servᵗ. and bro.,

" ZACH. TAYLOR."

" Our town being a post town, your readyest direction of your letters will be to me at Wigan, without taking notice of Manchester, for that may occasion a miscarriage.

" [Addressed.] For the Rvd. Mr. Abraham Pryme, at his house over against the Great Church in Kingston-upon-Hull, in Yorkshire, these."

Having received a large pacquet of papers from Doct. Johnston, with a letter, I returned him this answer.

The pacquet was eight or ten sheets of collections of pedegrees, monuments, and raritys that I had sent him last spring, which I desired again as soon as he had done with them.

" The writer of this letter, Zachary Taylor, was the son of another Zachary Taylor, master of Kirkham School. He was rector of Croston. This letter adds not a little to the information of him that we possess. He seems to have been a learned Hœbraist, but the subject uppermost in his mind when he was writing this letter was the case of James Dugdale, the pretended demoniac of Surey, near Whalley. Into this controversy Taylor threw himself with no little enthusiasm, and two or three pamphlets attest his skill. A man was certain to arouse a number of hornets in those days who said a word against the popular belief in witchcraft.

Honoured Sr.

It being my fate to stay commonly no longer in one place than till I have got the antiquitys thereof, and the view of what MSS. and old deeds that I can meet with, having heard that there was several old things at Hull, which would be very acceptible unto me, 'tis about sixteen weeks ago that I removed thither, and, going over yᵉ last week unto Hatfield, I found the packet of papers that you had directed for me at Mr. Hatfield's. They were but just come to his hands, and where they had lay'd ever since yᵉ 22d of July, (for that is yᵉ date of them), I know not. I received your letter with yᵉ same, and shall here answer to those things that you desire, as far as I at present can, being both now absent from my books and my other helps. I am glad that yᵉ papers about Doncaster and yᵉ description of yᵉ church found acceptance at your hands. As to yᵉ coats of arms that you enquire about, they are all excellently and gloriously cut in great scutchions in stone, a foot and a half or thereabouts in length, in yᵉ ringing loft of yᵉ steeple,ᵛ standing half a foot out of yᵉ stone work of yᵉ steeple, and all of them hangs as it were in their natural position but one (tho' which I have forgotten), which lys sideways ; which intimates, I suppose, that yᵉ owner was dead before yᵉ steeple was finish'd. As for yᵉ order of succession of yᵉ arms I have forgot that, but I remember furder that in other great shields over yᵉ sayd arms, on yᵉ four inner sides of yᵉ steeple, is fower old characters of great bigness : yᵉ first is yᵉ common old abreviation of Jesus, IHC., the second *Maria* thus, ... and what yᵉ two others are I have forgot, and as to that shield with a name on I shall take notice of it next time I go, and inform you furder, and of other things. I have just now heard that there is one Mr. Thwaits,ʷ a mercer of Doncaster, lately dead, who has most certainly left 20*l*. per an. towards an afternoon sermon every Sunday in yᵉ sayd church of Doncaster.

As to yᵉ charter of Conan, Duke of Richmond, I shall compare it as soon as I have time. The letter about Trygot's daughter, that you desire to know what authority I have for yᵉ same, is in a large MS. in folio of pedigrees of several Yorkshire familys, (of which I have formerly given you an account), in yᵉ hands of Mr. Hall, min[ister] of Fishlake.

As to yᵉ MSS. of Hampolᶻ and Mr Nevel's, I long exceedingly myself to see them. I am fully satisfyd that there is an abundance of observable things in them.

As to yᵉ family of yᵉ Westbys, Mr. Westbyʸ has a larg schrool, eight yards long, of all his discent, an account of which Mr. Hatfield (who is a relation of his) has promised to send you.

As I went into Yorkshire last week I went through a town two miles of this side Houdon call'd Easterton,ᶻ in which is a fine church, on yᵉ outside of which

---

ᵛ See *Miller's Hist. Doncaster*, 91. *Hunter's South Yorkshire*, i., 38-9. *Jackson's St. George's Church*, 33-34.

ʷ Robert Thwaites, by his will, d. 6th Oct., 1698, and proved at York 22nd March, 1698-9, left the yearly sum of £20 for the use, benefit, and sole advantage of some discreet and learned minister who should preach every Sunday, in the afternoon, in the Parish Church of Doncaster. He further directed that such minister should " preach a sermon every year on the day of his death, in order and to the encouragement of charity and good works of this nature, without having any reference to this bequest." The benefactor died 3 Nov., 1698, æt. 32.

ᶻ Richard of Hampole, whose writings are well known.

ʸ Thomas Westby, of Ravenfield, near Rotherham, esq., returned M.P. for East Retford, 1710, (see ped. *Hunter's S. Y.*, i., 397). From one of this family, Henry Westby, of Car-house, in par. Rotherham, whose dau. and heir married Edward Gill, Esq., M.P., a commander in the Parliament Army, etc., is descended Francis Westby Bagshawe, esq., of the Oaks, near Sheffield, the owner of this Diary.—See Rev. Dr. Gatty's edition of *Hunter's Hallamshire*, 399.

ᶻ *i.e.* Eastrington.

N

I saw five or six great coats of arms cut very artificially in ye stone work, which, if you have not taken down, I shall send them ye next time I go that way.

When I got to Houdon I stayd there all night on purpose to view the poor church, which has been a most noble building, and of very excellent work. There is many images yet standing, on ye outside, of ye S^{ts.}, as St. Catharin with her wheel, St. Lawrence with his gridiron, etc., and the stone work of the spoot ends is the prettyest fancys, and ye best proportion, that ever I saw. One spoot end is Sampson astride upon a lyon, and very naturaly twineing his arm about his neck, and with his hands pulling his jaws wide open, out of which water flows. In another place is a shipp of stone jetting out, out of which looks out a water nymph, with a pitcher in her arms, with the mouth bended downwards, out of which pitcher ye water flows, etc. In other places other pretty fancys and many coats of arms.

This chancel, which was of most curious workmanship and great bigness, was most sacrilegiously sufferd to fall into decay about fifty or sixty years ago, so that ye lead was taken of and sold, and ye fine monuments therein defaced ; and on Michaelmas day two years the whole roof fell down, and pulld down with it most part of the walls and pillars, so that it lys now in rubbish.

Adjoining upon this curious chancel on the south side, stands ye chapterhouse, yet very well carvd and adornd. Over ye door as you go in out of ye ruined chancel is these two coats of arms :—^a

[1. Six willow wands inter-   [2. Six willow wands interlaced in saltire.]   laced crosswise.]

And on the outside of ye sayd house is several more coats of arms in great shields, one of which is ye Howards', another is a chev[ron] with three ermins thereon between three starrs ; another is a plane saltier, etc. Amongst others, in ye windows of ye church, is gules, a great cinq[ue] foil arg. persd [pierced] or, and in ye church on a great altar tomb of plain workmanship is 8 or 9 old coats of arms, and under an old fashond black marble gravestone, born up by four short pillars, lys ye body of one Walter, a monk of Durham, without date. This church had formerly 350*l.* a year belonging to it, which is now sacrilegiously usurpd by ye family of ye Allisons, of Houden, and other gentlemen thereabouts.

Hard by ye church, on ye south side, stands ye ruins of some great old religious house, which the constant tradition of ye town says was a great Bishop of Durham's pallace.^b On ye front of ye great porch is this coat of arms :—

[Bishop Skirlaw, six willow wands interlaced crosswise.]

And over ye great gate, that went to ye backside, this coat, with a mullet in ye midst of ye first barr :—

[Cardinal Langley, Bishop of Durham, paly of six.]

In ye court of this formerly great pallace the Londoners keep their mart every year. The *Notitia Monastica* tells us that there was in former times at this town a colledge of ten prebendarys, perhaps this might be it.

Not far of this town is Hemyngburrogh, of which you will find something observable in Roger Hoveden's chron. ad. an. 1072, about ye gift of ye sayd place by Will[iam] the Conqueror to St. Cuthbert's in Durham.

In an old MS. in my hands, formerly belonging to Mr. Perkins, of Fishlake, I find an old inquisition of ye customes of the manour of ye same town, which,

^a These are the arms of Skirlaw, Bishop of Durham. He sometimes used the cross in saltire.

^b A minute survey of this palace in the reign of Elizabeth, before it was dismantled, has been recently published by Mr. Raine in the *Transactions of the Yorkshire Architectural Society.*

because that perhaps you have not met with it. I will here transcribe. It is without date :—

Dicunt Juratores supra sacramentum quod man. de Hemyngbrough est de antiquo dominio coronæ, etc.

Et dicunt quod Prior Dunelmiæ est dominus ejusd. man. et quod habet visum franci plegii bis in anno, scilicet, ad fest. Paschæ, et Sti. Michaelis, et omnia ei tangentia, et curiam de tribus septimanis in tres, et quod quilibet tenens dicti manerii (excepto presbytero tantum) sectam debet ad curiam prædictam de tribus in tres, etc.

Et dicunt quod quinque tenentes ad quamlibet curiam sedebunt et jurabunt quod omnia judicia in eadem curia reddend. inter dominum et tenentem, et tenentem et tenentem, et tenentem et forinsecum, recte judicabunt, quæ per eosdem juratores per liberum judicium in eadem curia reddend. pertinent judicari.

Item dicunt quod consuetudo est ibi quod quilibet hæres masculus post decessum antecessoris ejus hæreditare debet tenementum antecessoris sui secundum legem communem, et si aliquis decesserit et habet hæredem femellam . . .

. . et exitus ejus hæreditabit secundum consuetudinem, et dicti hæredes post decessum antecessoris dicti releviare debent.

Item dicunt quod si aliquis deforcivit aliquem de hæreditate sua, seu de libero tenemento, et voluit idem tenementum alienare etc., quod tunc breve de recto claus. ballivo dicti Prioris, etc., et in eadem curia facta est protestatio, etc., secundum quod materia sua requirit, et quod processus in eadem curia talis est quod prius somoniatur ; et si non venit resamoniatur ; et si non venit attachiatur ; et si non venit distringetur ; et si adhuc non venit, amittet tenementum suum petitum per defalt. ; et si aliquo tempore compertum fuit, ut postea defalt. fecerit, exeat magna distric. 16 cap.

Et dicunt quod ibidem est consuetudo quod si alicui placuerit tenementum suum alienare, quod veniat in plenâ curia coram seneschallo, si præsens sit, et ibidem sursum reddet in manum domini tenementum ad opus ejus et hæredis sui, qui dictum tenementum habet, et in eadem curia irrotulabitur prædicta sursumrenditio ; et per pactum surrendri et irrotulamenti ipse qui dictum tenem. habebit faciat finem cum domino prout concordare poterit. Et si cum domino concordare non poterit, tunc prædicti quinque juratores dictum finem adjudicabunt, et licet dominus seu seneschallus absens fuerit, vel quod cum domino concordare non potest, tunc quod ipse qui dictum tenement. etc., per eorum absentiam non impediatur dictam terram et tenementum occupare et manu tenere, ita quod ipse seu aliquis pro eo paratus fuerit ad finem illum faciendum.

Et si seneschallus absens fuerit, ut prædicta sursum-renditio coram se fieri non poterit, quod tunc partes prædicti venient coram ballivo villæ prædictæ et coram quatuor tenentibus, vel coram quatuor tenentibus, si ballivus absens fuerit, et coram eis si ipse dimittere voluerit sursum reddere potest, et tunc prædictus ballivus vel quatuor tenentes, si ballivus absens fuerit, prædictam surrenditionem in plenâ curia coram seneschallo, cum venit, presentabunt, et ibidem jurabunt modo et forma, prout supra declaratum est.

Et si alicui placuerit dimittere tenementum suum ad terminum annorum extra curiam, quod bene licebit facere fine aliquo inde reddendo, vel si in curiâ, quod tunc solvet pro irrotulamento prout cum seneschallo concordare potest.

Item dicunt quod si uxor cum viro coopt. se dimittere voluerit de tenementis suis tam viro quam cum alio, quod eadem mulier coopt. veniat coram seneschallo, vel coram ballivo et quatuor tenentibus, vel coram quatuor tenentibus, si seneschallus et ballivus ambo absentes fuerint, et coram eis sursum reddere potest ; et ibidem examinetur ; et secundum sursum-renditionem ; et examinatio in plenâ curiâ irrotulabitur pro fine inde habendo, modo et formâ prout supra declaratur.

Item dicunt quod quælibet vidua post decessum viri sui dotem debet habere, et quilibet sponsus omnes terras et tenementa uxoris suæ post exitum ejus per consuetudinem durante vitâ suâ possidebit.

Item dicunt quod si aliquis concedere voluerit renditionem tenementi sui in dotem per legem Angliæ vel aliter ad terminum vitæ quod bene licebit ei hoc facere secundum consuetudinem, et si tenens taliter ad terminum vitæ attorniari voluerit, compellatur per quandam querelam in eadem curiâ quæ dicitur QUID JURIS CLAMAT, *et hæc concessio coram seneschallo vel balliro et quatuor tenentibus, vel coram quatuor tenent. pro fine inde faciendo, modo et forma prout superius declaratur.*

Here endeth yᵉ inquisition. It was so very badly writt that it seems to be some hundreds of years old, and savors enough of yᵉ barbarity of yᵉ age.

I have mett with yᵉ Escheat rolls that you formerly sent me word of that an attorney in Holderness had, as also some old charters of Haltenprise Priory, etc., and many things relating to this town which I am coppying over, which I shall not be backward to communicate to you, or any ingenious man.

Pray let me know whether this has found acceptance, and whether it be come safe to your hands, by yᵉ next post, and so wishing you all the success imaginable in your great and noble design,

I rest your humble friend and serv.,

ABR. PRYME.[c]

I have this day also written a long letter to Mr. Tompkinson, Fellow of St. John's Coll[ege], in Cambridge,[d] adjureing, begging, and praying of him to search all his old papers and deeds that he has, and to send me an account if he have anything about Hatfield, and to send me what relation he can of his father, who was one of the famousest and best men that the town ever had.[e]

[c] There is an interleaved reply from Dr. Johnston, dated 6th December, 1698, acknowledging the receipt of the above "most acceptable letter." He says, " I return you a thousand thanks ; for I never had from any correspondent so full and so apposite disertations as from yourself, and I most earnestly desire the continuation of your judicious observations ; and am glad you are now fixed in a place where you will have opportunity to make many remarks both concerning Hull and Beverley," etc.

[d] Thomas Thomkinson, son of the Rev. Thomas Thomkinson, of Hatfield, in Yorkshire, was baptized there 30th Aug., 1652. Was at school for two years at Belton, under Balden ; admitted pensioner of St. John's Coll., Cambridge, 1st May, 1668, æt. 15, under Watson (afterwards Bishop Watson of St. David's). He was B.A., 1671-2 ; M.A., 1675 ; B.D., 1682. Subscriber to *Collier's Church History*, vol. ii. A nonjuror. ob. 9, Maii. 1724, sep. in sacello Coll. (MS. *Baker*, xxxiii., 255). Minister of Trinity Church, Cambridge, 1683 (MS. *Cole*, xix, 100a). Buried in St. John's Chapel, 11th May, 1724—Register of All Saints, Cambridge, in MS. *Cole* III., 141a. Admitted Rookby Fellow of St. John's, 14th Mar., 1675-6, (co. Yorks.) Leonard Chappelow was elected 21st Jan. (adm. 22d Jan. 1715-6) in Thomkinson's room. This was an irregular election, only five seniors being present ; several other nonjuring fellows, among them Thomas Baker, were expelled at the same time.

[e] Thomas Thomkinson, the father of the above, was vicar or Minister of Hatfield from 1639 to 1669. The marriage of one "Gulielmus Thomkinson et Isabella Willson," occurs 29th June, 1639 ; and there is the burial of Mary, daughter of Wm. T., 12th Oct., 1644. Thomas Thomkinson, senr., was bur. 11th March, 1644-5, and Isabella Thomkinson, widow, 19th Feb., 1649-50. Probably the parents of the vicar. Besides Thomas, I find the vicar had other children, viz., Mary bap. 22 Sept., 1644. Jane, 21st July, 1646. Helen, 18th June, 1650, under the entry of her burial, 10th March, 1653, her father has recorded of her :—

Ἄγυος ἐμοὶ βίας ἦν, ἰκμὰς δὲ τάχισταί παρῆλθε,
Ἀμνου παρθενίκου νῦν ἀκόλουθος ἐγώ.

[1699.]

JAN. 1. This day I went to preach at Ferriby and Kirkeller. The first is a little town curiously seated by the Humber side, and very pleasant, there being three or four very good and larg halls therein. The first is a very fine and stately square building where the old priory stood (of which priory I observed nothing standing but a small part of the gate). It was built, as I am told, by Mr. Lockwood, an alderman of Hull, who retired thither in summer, but never thrive after, so he dyd, and lys buryed in the church there, about 1670 ; and now the hall belongs to one Mrs. Ransom, who is fast selling it. The second is a very staitly hall, at the farr end and upper part of the town, built by Mr. Anderson, rector of the high church of this town of Hull about fifteen years ago, which his widdow lives on. The third is a very pretty hall built about two or three years ago by Alderman Carlin of Hull, prettily situate and handsome. The fourth is a fine pretty house on which the onely gentleman resident in the town lives, and that is Mr. Dawson, who has about 300*l.* a year. The church is but a mean building, and has a row of pillars in the middle, and nothing in it observable. In one of the windows, on the north side of the chancel, I saw this imperfect inscription*f* and these coats of armes. By a woman kneeling with four children behind her :—

Under her this coat :—

[Wentworth, a chevron between three leopard's faces, a crescent for difference.]

Furder on this :—

[Paly of four arg. and sable, on a bend of the first three mullets or.]*g*

Robert, 28th Jan., 1654-5, bur. 12th Feb., after. Isabel, bur. 22nd July, 1656. The burial of Jane his wife is thus entered :—

" Jana fidelissima Thomæ Thomkinson, cler. A.M. σύζυγης superas evasit ad auras (beatorum repositorium) quarto die Junij anno Domini, 1661."

The vicar himself died 17th June, 1669. Hunter (*S. Y.*, i., 191), states that the inscription on his grave-stone no longer existed, and he has printed one taken from the MSS. of De la Pryme. Most of the upper portion is still, however, to be seen at the west end of Hatfield church. Together with a version of it in Johnston's MSS., it may be read with greater probability of correctness, thus :—

Thomas Thompkinson, beatæ memoriæ, diaconus anno, 1636 : in artibus magister ac presbyter canonice ordinatus anno 1639. Huic ecclesiæ per annos 30 fidelis evangelii minister. Junii 17 anno dom. 1669. ætatis suæ 58, hic sepultus.

Pacificus, charus, doctissimus, ordine mystis,

Præbebunt villæ sæcula nulla parem.

f The inscription is so incorrectly given by the Diarist that it is not worth repeating. It appears to have been for Elizabeth Halldard, dau. of John Wentworth, 1562.

g This is as the Diarist has tricked them, but such would be, of course, false heraldry. The coat is probably intended for that of Dransfield, viz., paly of six sa. and arg. on a bend gu. three mullets or.

Not farr of was this coat of armes:—

[Gules, a chevron between three boars' heads couped arg. arm'd or.]

Yᵉ arms of the knightly family of yᶜ Whites of Hackney, Middlesex.

Jan. 12. This day I writt the following letter to the Dean of York, the famous and learned Doct[or] Gale.

Very Rev. Sr.,

    Haveing been so happy as to have been admitted into your presence when I was at York, and to have your commands layd upon me for yᵉ procuring of what old Roman coins I could meet with for your use, I have accordingly gotten eleven from a friend of mine at Doncaster, who tells me that they were found not many years ago at Alburrow by . . . (some of which I formerly shewd to his lordship our right revⁿᵈ· diocesan), which my very good friend yᵉ rev. bearer hereof would needs take ye trouble to bear them unto you. If all or any of them be any way acceptible unto you they are heartily at your service, and if any prove less acceptible unto you by your having specimens of yᵉ same, I begg them again towards yᵉ laying of a foundation for a collection for myself. I do not question but that you have met with my name in yᵉ Cat[alogue] of yᵉ MSS. printed at Oxford. If they were to do again, I could send them yᵉ knowledge of many more besides those which I already have, and am daily collecting for myself. I hear that Sr· Willoughby Hickman, of Gainsburgh, has an old MSS. chron[icle] in his possession. I writt lately to Mr. Wesley, min[ister] of Epworth, to send me a whole account thereof that I might transmit yᵉ knowledg thereof unto you.

    I have lately found a monument in this town which was brought either from Beverley or Patrington, which I take to be Roman, because of it's being cutt out of hard milston greet, as all ye Roman monuments that I have seen in England are, and because that yᵉ letters thereon are great Roman ones, a fuller account of which I shall send you hereafter, if that I might understand that it would be acceptible unto you.

    I have made bold to present you with a bottle of brandy which I sent up with one of Mr. Bankes's by yᵉ carrier last.

    I heartily begg pardon for giving you yᵉ trouble of these lines, and makes bold with all hearty affection to subscribe myself,

Your most humble servant,

AB. PRYM.

The coins that I sent him were these:—

> *Imp. Caius. Pub. Licin. Val. Postumus Aug.*
> *Dom. nost. Constantius Pius Felix Aug.*
> *Dom. nost. Valentinianus Pius Felix Aug.*
> *Imp. Trajanus Germanicus, etc.*
> *Imp. Caius Marcus Aurel. Victorinus Aug.,*
> *Gallienus Pius Felix Aug.*
> *Salonina Augusta.*
> *Imp. Caius Postumus Pius Felix Aug.*
> *Romulus Remus et Roma.*
> *Julia Maesa Augusta.*

Having lately received a letter from the Revd. Mr. Taylor, I returned him this answer:—

Hull, Jan. y⁰ 20, 1698-9.

Rev. Sr.,

I received your kind letter but this very week, tho' it might by y⁰ date it bears[a] have been here long before, and thank you for giving me an idea of your papers, which are undoubtedly writ with an abundance more of accuracy than mine can pretend to, I liveing in a great and troublesome town, and wanting both leasure, opertunity, and books, to carry on anything to perfection ; but as you have given me an idea of your papers, so I shall here give you one of mine, as I promised.

Mine is a loos discourse in form of a letter, where, in y⁰ first place, after an introduction, I speak of y⁰ certainty of y⁰ being and power of evil spirits, and of their actions in y⁰ times of y⁰ Old Testament, but especially of their extraordinary and miraculous power and actions, and y⁰ reason and necessity for y⁰ same in y⁰ times of y⁰ New Testament, and as long as y⁰ wonder working age lasted. Then haveing mention'd their wonderfull actions, that is possessions, in our Saviour's days, I continue y⁰ same out of Just. Martyr, Tertullian, Origen, Cyprian, Minutius Felix, Lactantius, Firmicus, etc., untill that they ceased in y⁰ church with y⁰ power of y⁰ gift of miracles. That they then ceased I have not only proved from y⁰ reasonableness thereof, but also from y⁰ down right assertions of both Papists and Protestants, of Aretius, Firemee (?), Becanus, Chemnitius, Doc[tor] Scot, Pool, etc. Then that miracles are ceased (which cannot be if true possessions exist), I have proved not onely from reason but also y⁰ testimonys of St. Chrysost., St. Cyp., St. Austin, Greg. Mag., Stella, Acosta, Alsledius, Rivetus, Doct. Barrow, Bishop Jewel, B. White. B. Morton. B. Laud, B. Taylor, B. Hacket, B. Tillotson, etc., and from forreigners, Abutensis, Trithemius, Musso, Espensæus, etc. Then Limborg, Stella, etc., haveing yielded that there are dæmoniacs amongst y⁰ Indians, Americans, etc., I prove by Salmeron, Acosta, etc., that it is a vulgar error. Then I reduce y⁰ origin of this oppinion of y⁰ present existence of dæmoniacs to those four heads—1. A misunderstanding of that verse in St. Mat., ch. 17, v. 21, and that of St. Mark, ch. 16, v. 17 ; 2ndly, to a vain ambitions emulation that was in y⁰ beginning times of Popery of counterfeating this gift, and continnuing y⁰ order of exorcists in y⁰ church ; 3rdly, to y⁰ great ignorance of most men in y⁰ wonderfull power of many distempers, as of y⁰ epilepsy, nightmare, strong convulsions, consumptive long fastings and raptures, madness, histerical fitts, melancholy, and the power of speaking strang languages, in which I have quoted Simocata, Lamzweend, Lentulus, Willis, a Lapide, Salmon, Thuanus, Borellus, Citois, Sennertus, Paracelsus, Sanquerdus, Kircher, Moravius, Galen, Lavater, Gordonius, Cardanus, Fulgosus, Platerus, Cattier, Aristotle, Aritæus, Apporor, l'omponatius, Guianerius, Fernelius, Guyo, Raguseius, Bennivenius, Cassaubon, Sirenius, Lemnius, Huartel, Helmont, etc. Then I prove y⁰ sillyness and insufficiency of a balneum diaboli in melancholy distempers. Then I come to y⁰ four causes which I ascribe to be to y⁰ multitudes of impostures put upon the world in this kind, both of possessions and dispossessions, instanceing in Mahomet, St. Frances, Joan of Ark, Jetzer, y⁰ nuns of London, y⁰ body of Campen in 1685, etc. Then comeing to domestic ones, I instance in all y⁰ famous presbiterian and papist imposters and dæmoniacs, as Hacket, Somwers, y⁰ boy of Burton, Sarah Williams, Jo. Ash, y⁰ boy of Bilson, John Fox, Michael Smith, y⁰ chief presbiterian ministers in Cromwel's days, y⁰ Ld. Grandison's pretended steward, Tho. Sawdy, Greatrix, Spatchet, and others, from Q. Eliz. days to our's, which then brings me to Dugdale's, y⁰ whole history of whom and his fitts I shall give, first of his artificial fitts, then of those epileptic ones, which he fell into after his drunken boot at Whalley, showing that there is nothing very strang or uncommon therein unto any but country bumpkins, which I prove by many instances out of many books. Then I continnue y⁰ history of what has happened about y⁰ impostor unto this day, concluding with a few reflections.

[a] See *antea*, 27th Dec., 1698.

All which I have just now finished as briefly as ever I could in about thirty sheets of paper, but, I am so fearfull and diffident of anything I do, I doubt I shall scarce be so bold as to suffer it to be printed, tho' I have received this week a kind letter from Mr. Coggan, bookseller, in the Inner Temple Lane, begging the coppy thereof ; but, he being a virulent presbyterian, I shall keep it out of his hands, and if you be at London next month I shall be very glad to venture it with you, and heartily thank you for your proffer of kindness unto it.

I have writt many letters into your country and the west of Yorkshire about this business, tho' I have got but few answers and none very material.

I should be very glad to have notice of any old MSS. chronicles which you may have seen or heard of anywhere in yͤ country round about.

I am your most humble

Servant and brother,

AB. PRYME.

I have this day been in company with Alderman Gray, and Alderm[an] Carlin of this town. They do both attest that there was an old woman of Cave, who dyd about twelve years ago, that was universaly believed to have been born in Edw[ard] the Sixth's days. Many people went and has gone for this forty years, from time to time, to see her.

Having received the aforegoing most kind and obliging letter[i] from Doct[or] Gale, the Dean of York, I returned him this answer.

Very Revͩ. Sͬ.,

I am so overjoyd at yͤ sight of your letter that I want words to express my thankfulness with ; for as all sorts of antiquitys, MSS., curiositys, raritys, and coins, are my chief delight (next to that sacred one of my calling) so I am resolved to dedicate all my days to yͤ same ; and as I never met with any that gave me yͤ least encouragement besides yourself, so I am not onely eternaley obliged unto you for yͤ same, but shall always be ready to serve you to yͤ utmost of my power.

I will take particular care to send you yͤ account of yͤ Roman trough stone that I hinted at in my former letter, as soon as I can make out yͤ legends on yͤ same, which is very difficult by reason of yͤ loss of many letters.

I saw in my jorney to York many hundreds of tumuli, which I take to be Roman, at a place called Arras,[j] on this side Wighton, not mentioned in any author, which I intend next summer to digg into and take a whole account and description thereof, and of all other Roman stations, monuments, streets, places of battle, coins, or whatever is observable whereever I come.

Most heartily begging pardon for giveing you yͤ trouble of these lines I make bold to subscribe myself your

Most humble servant,

AB. PRYME.

[The following letter is inserted :—]

" Sͬ.,

I doe remember I promised to give you something that's ancient in Campsall church, and haveing this opertunity by my kinswoman, doe give it as

---

[i] The letter referred to has been taken out of the journal.

[j] A hamlet in the towship and parish of Market Weighton, E. R. Yorkshire. Many of these tumuli were investigated some years ago by the Rev. E. W. Stillingfleet, with very remarkable results.

it is cutt in wood between the church and chancell. The carracter is such as every one canott read :—

> 'Let fal downe thyn ne and lift up thy hart,
> Behold thy maker on yond. cros al so torn,
> Remembir his wondis that for the did smart,
> Gotyn withownt syn, and on a virgin born,
> Al his hed percid with a crown of thorne.
> Alas man thy hart oght to brast in too ;
> Bewar of the divyl when he blawis his horne,
> And prai thy gode Aungel convey the.[k] .... '

" There is on the balke at the west end of the church the figures 161. wch. many very much wonder at ; most conjecture ye church was built in 1161, and soe then one figure ommitted. I pray for yor. health and happines, and rest,

" Yor. most humble servant,
"THO. MIDDLETON.

" Sutton, 25th Feb., 98-9.
" (Addressed).—These for my worthy ffreind Mr. Primm, at his house in Hull. Present."

Haveing heard that the liveing of Finningley[l] is about falling, my friends will needs have me put in for it. I have written several letters, and they many, to John Harvey, of Ikwelbury, near Norrel, in Bedfordshire, Esq., the patron thereof.

There is no form for certificates, but are made accordingly as the person merits, and they are exceeding strict and sevear therein at this time in signing anything but what is truth.

My very good friend Mr. Bankes procured me this before I was aware thereof.

These are to certify whome it may concern that Mr. Abr. Pryme, curat of St. Trenity's, in Kingston super Hull, is a person of a sober life and exemplary conversation, very studious, of loyal principles, a lover of his sacred Majesty and the present government, conformable to y doctrin and discipline of ye Church of England as by law established, and deserves encouragement in ye same.

Witness our hands ye 8 day of Febr., 1698.

RICH. KIDSON, B.D., and Lectr. of Hull.
ROB. BANKS, Vic. of St. Trinity's in Hull.
NATH. LAMB, Min. of St. Mary's in Hull.
THO. GALE, Dean of York.
[JOHN] BURTON, D.D.
[WILLIAM] PEARSON.
[JONATHAN] DRYDEN.

6. Our newse this day acquaints us that the Duke of Bolton is dead.[m] He was a man much talk'd of in K[ing] James the

---

[k] See the inscription printed in *Hunter's S.Y.*, ii., p. 468. "It seems," he says. " as if a word was wanting to complete the last line." He attributes the date of it to perhaps the latter part of the reign of Edward VI., but they seem to have a ring of Richard of Hampole.

[l] In co. Notts, near Bawtry.

[m] Charles, sixth Marquess of Winchester, created 9th April, 1689, Duke of Bolton, in whose descendants that title continued through a succession of six

Second's days. He pretended to be distracted, and would make
all his men rise up at midnight, and would go a hunting with
torch light, and such like tricks he would of[ten] play ; but when
King William was comed in he was then a man of a quite other
nature. His estate, which falls to his son, the Marquis of Winchester, is wourth 20,000*l.* a year.

Haveing heard for a certainty that Mr. Sheppard," min[ister]
of Finningly is dead, I writt this letter to Squire Harvy, patron
of the liveing :—

Honourd Sʳ.
  Begging pardon for giveing you yᵉ trouble of a few lines, I humbly
crave a favour at your hands, which I hope your goodness will not deny me of,
that is, that you would be pleased to honour me so much as to admitt me to
yᵉ rectory of Finningly, in your gift, now falln vacant by yᵉ death of Mr.
Sheppard. None shall be more thankfull, more carefull to serve yᵉ church,
none more mindfull of you in my prayers, none more observant of your commands, which I perhaps may be serviceable to you in in my being one of yᵉ Participants of Hatfield Chace,* etc, none shall be more vigilant to promote peace,
love, virtue, and friendship amongst your tennants, and to make them, to your

dukes, till 25th Dec., 1794. Burnet says of him that " he was a man of a strange
mixture. He had the spleen to a high degree, and affected an extravagant
behaviour ; for many weeks he would not open his mouth till such an hour of
the day when he thought the air was pure. He changed the day into night,
and often hunted by torchlight, and took all sorts of liberties to himself, many
of which were very disagreeable to those about him. He was a man of profuse
expense, and of a most ravenous avarice to support that ; and though he was
much hated, yet he carried matters before him with such authority and success,
that he was in all respects the great riddle of the age." His eldest son,
Charles, who succeeded him as second duke, was Lord Lieutenant of Ireland in
1717. The tradition of the Marquess's wild hunting still lingers in Swaledale.
  " Peck (*Hist. Bawtry and Thorne*, etc., 1813, p. 73) has given an imperfect
copy of his monumental inscription, in which it is stated, " obiit quinto die
Aprilii 1699," and that he was " eruditus," and " probitate valde ornatus."
  * The Participants of Hatfield Chace were and still are, the representatives
in estate of those lands which were, on the drainage of the Level, temp. Car.
I., assigned to the celebrated Sir Cornelius Vermuyden, the drainer, and his
partners or participants in the undertaking, who were to be rewarded with
one third of the recovered lands.—See an interesting account of this drainage
in *Hunter's South Yorkshire*, i., 159.
  De la Pryme appears to have given some attention to the affairs of the
Levels, for I find that when a new Commission of Sewers was opened at Hatfield, 12th Oct., 1702, before the Vicount Downe and others, he (Abraham Prim,
clerk), was sworn as a commissioner. His attendance is recorded at the
following courts afterwards :—Hatfield, 5th Nov., 1702 ; Epworth, 20th Nov.,
1702 ; Hatfield, 2d March, 1702-3 ; Epworth, 24th March, 1702-3 ; Turnbridge,
15th April, 1703 ; Bawtry, 27th May, 1703 : Turnbridge, 29th June, 1703 ;
Kennell-Ferry, 16th Aug., 1703 ; Turnbridge, 4th Oct., 1703 ; Hatfield, 20th Dec.,
1703 ; do. 12th Jan. 1703-4 ; do. 29th March, 1704 ; do. 2d May, 1704 ; Turnbridge, 8th May, 1704 ; Epworth, 11th May, 1704. He died in the June following.

great honour and their everlasting good, both happy in this world and that which is to come, than I, who am, and always will be,

Honourd S^r.

Your most humble serv.,

A. P.

Hull, Aprill 19, 1699.

Haveing the oppertunity of sending a letter to the dean of York, by Mr. Banks's going thither, I writt him this following :

Very Revnd. Sr.,

Being overjoy'd at this oppertunity of conveying a letter unto your hands, I could not but lay hold of ye same. I most humbly and heartily thank you for the great honour you did me, in subscribing ye certificate Mr. Banks sent you, but to my sorrow I had not ye happiness to succeed. My zeal for old MSS., antiquitys, coins and monuments, almost eats me up, so that I am sometimes almost melancholy that I cannot prosecute ye search of them so much as I would, which, if I had obtained the place I sought for, I should have been able to do. Y^e inscription upon ye great trough I had sent you long ago, but that ye winter weather hath so fortifyd it with dirt that there is no comeing nigh it. As soon as ever ye weather permitts I shall send you it.

I received, a while ago, ye following inscription (which I take to be very observable), from of a great stone in ye ruins of ye chancel of ye church of Alkburrow, just on ye other side of Humber, in Lincolnshire.

Richardus Bryto necnon Menorius Hugo
Willelmus Trajo templum hoc lapidibus altum
Condebant patria, gloria, digna Deo.

That which makes it observable, is, that these men were ye murderers of S^r. Tho. Becket.

I rest, most worthy S^r.,

Your most oblieged humble Servant,

March 16, 1698-9. A. P.

A coppy of a letter from Mr. Taylor. [No date].

" Revnd. Sr.,

Not doubting but that you have received my last letter long ago, that I writ unto you in Febr. last, in which I gave you an idea of ye papers I had drawn up about ye Sury business, this is to congratulate unto you ye pleasure that I have had in reading your answers to your (pretended) friend's 2nd letter, and Jolly's vindication, in both of which, and in all that you have writ, you have most excellently managed the business, according to ye truth ; and I am exceeding glad to find that they cannot take hold (with reason) of anything that you have writ. Truth being such a noble thing that it stopps ye mouths of all gainsayers, tho' not ye hearts, from inventing ways to turn things off.

"As in ye papers of mine, that I sent you an idea of, there is contained in about 8 sheets a short history of ye whole Sury business, so I perceive that you have in ye press a book wholy of ye same nature, I should be very glad to understand that your notions and mine, and ye thread of ye management of ye same villany jumps alike, so that there may be no discrepancy between them when published.

" Therefore I make bold to set before you ye history as thus.

" That Dugdale was put into Jolly's hands before ye Revolution by ye papists.

" That Jolly understanding nothing of ye cheat," etc. (*The letter ends here*).

APRIL THE 9. This day I writ the following letter to Doct. Johns[t]on, of London :

Honour'd S^{r.},

Haveing not heard or received any letter from you of a long while, I write now unto you to begg ye favour of knowing how you are in health, and how ye great work gos on that is under your hands—I mean ye history of our country, which, as I have been, so always shall be very ready to promote and furder, by adding to your valluable treasury ye small mites that are in my custody.

I have just now finish'd a short account of ye antiquitys of Kingston-upon-Hull, ye succession of ye Mayors, all the observable things relating unto the town that happened in their times, in about 20 sheets of paper;^p as also another vol., of ye antiquitys, coats of armes, monuments, etc., of ye two churches, in about 50 sheets ; but, being at a loss of what is related of this town in Doomsday Book, which was then called Wyke, and of Myton, Scul-coats, Drypool, and ye saltpitts that were here, I begg of you that you would be pleased to send me, out of your collections, what Doomsday Book says of ye sayd towns, by ye next post, and I shall be exceeding thankfull.

I have just now got two epitaphs from ye monument maker of this town, which, because they are for your purpose, I here send them.

" Here lyeth ye body of Sr. Henry Thomson, late of Middlethorp, K^{t.}, some-time Ld. Mayor of this Citty,^q who departed this life ye 25 of Aug., in ye year of our L^{d.} 1692, aged about 60 years ; and Lady An, his wife, daught. of Alderm. Will. Dobson, late of Kingston-upon-Hull, merchant, who departed this life ye 20 of April, in the year 1696, aged 66 years ; and two of their sons ; Will., aged about 5 weeks, who dyed ye 21 of Decem., 1665, and John, aged 19 years, who dyed ye 16 of May, in ye year 1690."

The[y] left no heirs males, and what became of their estate I cannot tell, except 20l. a year apeece, which they charitably gave to ye poor of ye citty of York, for ever.

The other epitaph is on a new monument, lately erected in Campsal Church, in these words :

Tho. Yarburg[h] de Campsall,
In com. Ebor., Armiger,
Ortus
Ex antiquâ stirpe Yarburgorum
(De Yarburg[h] in agro Lincoln.),

^p Writing to Thoresby four years afterwards, viz., 17th May, 1703, the Diarist remarks to him, " As for my history of Hull, which I drew out of all the records of that town, by particular order of the mayor and aldermen, I have not altogether finished it ; neither must I dare to publish it, till some be dead that are now living."—*Thoresby's Correspondence*, ii., p. 3.

The Rev. R. Banks, of Hull, to whom De la Pryme was sometime curate, also writing to Thoresby, 29th December, 1707, says, " Mr. Pryme, a little before he left me, took some pains to collect what he thought remarkable out of those records, and records in this town (Hull) which the mayor and aldermen pur-chased of his brother, who was at Hatfield, after his death. As to the rest of his MSS., they were, about two years since, in his brother's custody ; and it may be easily known whether he has disposed of them or no, and to whom."—*Ibid.*, p. 85.

Many of the Diarist's MSS. and topographical collections passed into the hands of John Warburton, the Somerset Herald, and form the most valuable part of Warburton's Yorkshire collections, which are now in the Lansdown department of the British Museum.—*Thoresby's Diary*, ii., p. 264.

^q York. This monument is at St. Mary's, Castlegate.

primariis annis
Conservator pacis constitutus,
per quadraginta et septem annos
Magistratum exercuit.
Vir prudens, temperans, et æquus ;
Bonis adjutor, malis obstes ;
tam diu et tam bene
Se gerebat,
Posteris exemplar
Vixit,
In septuaginta et quatuor annos,
et obiit ultimo die Novembris,
1697.[r]

I am, S[r]., your most humble servant,

A. P.

Hull, Aprill ye 9, 1699.

This year we have had a fast day, to pray God to turn the hearts of the enemys of our holy religion from persecuting the poor Vaudois and French protestants.

It is certain that they are very grievously persecuted in all the inland towns of France, and the farr provinces thereof, but not very much so in the cittys and places we trafic to.

To ballance this persecution, the papists have raised a report beyond sea that we do most grievously persecute, rost, boyl, and torment those of their religion here, and they have had great fasts and processions in all the papist countrys for this imaginary persecution.

[Letter to the dean of York].

Very Rever[nd]. S[r].,

Haveing formerly had the honour to acquaint you with a mon[ument] in this town, which I looked upon as somewhat observable, to wit, an old trough, in which some famous Roman had formerly been buryd ; I lately (upon this good weather and happy season) went to y[e] place where it was, to witt, y[e] sign of y[e] Coach and Horses, a publick house in this town, where I found it applyd to y[e] use of watering horses in. I asked how they came by it ; they sayd they bought it of Ald[erman] Grey, and then went to him and asked how he came to it. He answer'd, his father had it before him. The trough is of a very hard milstone greet, eight foot long, three foot broad, and three foot deep, and y[e] bottom and sides are half-a-foot thick ; y[e] cavity is of an equal bredth both at y[e] head and feet, and hath been so as long as can be remembred, and hath no inscription but on y[e] fore side, which is exactly and lineally thus.[s] The rest of y[e] letters in y[e] upper line are so worn out that I cannot send you as much as y[e] vestigia thereof. However, you may boldly and safely depend upon those that I have sent you ; and y[e] figure of y[e] trough, as described and delineated, which any body will find to be exact that dos but view and understand y[e] same. I shall say nothing of y[e] meaning thereof, or of y[e] word *Cubus* here

<hr>

[r] Printed in *South Yorkshire*, ii., p. 469.
[s] A sketch of the stone and inscription is subjoined. As both appear in Mr. Wellbeloved's *Eburacum*, it is unnecessary to reproduce them.

met with, because that I doubt not that you have met with ye like in Gruter, and others.

I have several accounts of great inscriptions on stones, from my correspondents (particularly of a great one at Upper Catton, in ye Wolds, etc.), but they send me such lame accounts of them that I darr not trust to them, and I cannot get ye time to go see them at present, which perhaps I may hereafter, some time or other, have y^o oppertunity to do, which I shall most gladly send you.

I have, for about this half year, been collecting all that I can find memorable relating to this town, which I have just finnished, in one hundred and odd sheets of paper, in folio; and am daily collecting other things.

Begging hearty pardon for giveing you this trouble,
I am, Very Rev. S^r.,
Your most obed. humble serv.,
A. P.

P.S.—Chanceing just now to look into Camb[den], ye last edit[ion], p. 718, I find either ye same, or an inscription very very like that which I have here sent you in ye former page, and, to ye best of my memory, there are several great I's or numeral letters, tho' scarce in ye least perceptible; but there is not a letter of Diogenes. This may be some other soldier, that belonged to Petuaria or Pretoriu (?) and not ye same whose epitaph Mr. Cambden gives, both because that *Cubus* is not mentioned in his, and that nobody would give themselves ye trouble to convey such a great mon[ument] as this is from York hither, seeing that it is so little good to. Pardon, good S^r., my suddain thoughts hereof. If I have erred, it is but like a man.

Hull, May ye 15, 1699.

Mr. Watson, min[ister] of South Ferriby, after haveing been madd a whole year, and nothing could do him good, was cured by a salivation in a little time.

For the Rever[end] Mr. Z. Taylor:
Hull, July 7.
Revnd. S^r.,

Haveing long ago before Christmass drawn up a few papers about ye Snry business, and flung them by again as a too tedious work, yet, a coppy getting from me was, unknown to me, put into ye press ye 4th of this month, with many imperfections therein; however, not knowing how to help myself, I must, whether I will or no, be father thereof.

I therefore, as I could not but make very honourable mention of your name in them, as one I must respect, so I begg that you would not be angry with me at ye mention thereof. In one page there is ye following expression about you, which, if true, I begg you would let it pass; if not, it shall be blotted out:

"Mr. Z. T., a man as eternaly to be commended for turning from ye scism and abominations of ye presbiterians, in which he was brought up, as any of ye multitude of ye others, their teachers, deserve to be, that have done ye same within these few years."

I bless God that I myself was once also one of them however brought up in that way.

Before Christmas, while I was busy in composing ye aforegoing papers, there was a stranger oft came to see me, who pretended that he came from London, and that he was going to Holland, to take possession of an estate that was faln unto him by ye death of his brother. He was one of ye learnedest and ingeniousest men that ever I talked with in all my life, and gave me several accounts about ye Sury impost[or], who is since accordingly gone. Since which time, I hear for a certain truth, that he had been preaching twelve months together amongst ye presbiterians at Manchester, in ye chief meeting-house of that town, under ye chief priest, etc., ye particulars of which being too long here to relate, I think I shall draw them up, and take the oppertunity of adding them to yᵉ end of yᵉ aforegoing papers. He went by yᵉ name of Midgley here, but had another name in Manchester, which I cannot recover. If you please to do me the favour to write thither, any of your friends will tell you what his surname was that he there went by, which will be a great kindness to me if you please to send me it. Yᵉ fellow was assistant to yᵉ chief presbiterian min[ister] of yᵉ town, and was perhaps a jesuit.

I begg your pardon that I did not write to you before this ; I all along, from day to day, stayd expecting your pamphlet of Yᵉ *Divel turned Casuist*, but never got it.

If you would add anything to yᵉ end of my papers you shall be heartily welcome, if I can prevail.

I am, your most humble and affectionate brother and serv.,

A. P.

1699, JULY. I heard last week that Tho[mas] Lee, esq., of Hatfield, was dead,ᶦ and then buryd. I took pen in hand and writ the following letter thereon unto Mr. Corn[elius] Lee, his brother.

Hull, July 10.

Dear Sir,
I cannot but trouble you with condoling yᵉ great breach that God has been pleased lately to make in your family, by yᵉ death of your dear brother. Mortality is a thing that we are all subject to, and yᵉ dark and silent grave is yᵉ long home that we must all arrive at. That is yᵉ house appointed for yᵉ liveing ; that is yᵉ place where, after all yᵉ fateagues, after all yᵉ miserys, after all yᵉ afflictions and troubles of this life, yᵉ weary shall find rest and quiet, and sleep with ease. without disturbance, with yᵉ greatest kings and emperors of yᵉ earth, in yᵉ soft lap of our mother out of which we came, and unto which we must all return in yᵉ good appointed time of God, which we ought, with all patience, humbly and meekly to wait for.

Tho' that long life is troublesome, yet it is a blessing and favour of God, a way by which he fitts and ripens us for his kingdom, and after, in our old age, receives us like a shock of corn comeing in in its propper and full season :ᵘ gives us joy for all our sorrow, eternal life for yᵉ vain transitory one that we here possessed, and pleasures so great that ey hath not seen yᵉ like, nor ear heard thereof, nor could they possiby enter into yᵉ heart of man to be conceived. So that tho' our change is great, yet it is fortunate, it is a happiness that we are to dy and not live here for ever, and one of yᵉ greatest benefits that can befall us in this world, for indeed, as Solomon says, yᵉ day of death is (if we do but rightly consider it) better than yᵉ day of one's birth. We are born unto a miserable world, but we dy unto a happy one ; we are here clothed with corruption, but shall there put on yᵉ white garments of incorruption, immortality, and light ; so that St. Paul, when he thought thereon, could not but desire to be dissolved and to be with Christ, that he might be quit of this miserable world, and possessor of that glorious one. So that as an old poet says,

> Why are undecent howlings mixt
> By liveing men in such a case?
> Why are desires so sweetly fixt
> Reprov'd with discontented face ?

ᶦ See *South Yorkshire*, i., p. 177. His burial is not recorded at Hatfield. "The Regester of the Burials from the date hereof, viz., the 27th of Aprill, 1690, to the year 1700, were not set down by Mr. Eratt, minister."—*Memorandum in Parish Register.*
ᵘ Job, v., 26.

> For all created things at length
>   By slow corruption growing old,
> Must needs forsake comported strength,
>   And disagreeing webbs unfold.
>
> But our dear Lord has means prepared
>   That death in us may never reign;
> And has undoubted ways declared
>   How members dead may rise again.
>
> Dull carcasses to dust now worn,
>   Which long in graves corrupting lay,
> Shall to yᵉ nimble air be borne,
>   Where souls before have led yᵉ way.
>
> Earth take this man with kind embrace,
>   In thy soft bosom him receive,
> For humane members here I place,
>   And generous parts in trust I leave.
>
> When yᵉ course of time is past,
>   And all our hopes fulfill'd shall be,
> Then opening must restore at last
>   The limbs in shape which now wee see.

For as our bodys have been partakers also of the troubles of this world, as well as our souls, so they shall likewise be raised up to enjoy yᵉ pleasures of yᵉ world to come.

And as it is a favour and a honour unto us for God to be so kind unto us, poor contemptible dust and ashes, as to take us unto himself, out of the miserys of this life, unto yᵉ glorious liberty and joys of yᵉ sons of God, so happy is our deceased brother that has performed his pilgrimage and persevered unto yᵉ end ; happy is he that is received into Abraham's bosom ; happy is he that has now all tears wiped away from his eys, freed from all sorrows and troubles, and that now sitts in yᵉ glorious presence of God, singing halleluiahs unto his most holy name ; unto whose blessed company, and unto which blessed place, that God may of his great and infinite mercy bring us all to is the hearty prayer of,

Sʳ, your most humble and oblieged Servant,

A. P.

[Letter from the Dean of York].

"York, July 12, '99.

" Sir,

Yours of May yᵉ 15 I had, and in it yᵉ inscription which Mr. Camden saw here. It is certainly yᵉ very same, tho' now somewhat hurt and maimed in some letters. As for yᵉ CVBVS in yᵉ beginning of yᵉ 3d line I know not what to make of it, except we could discover yᵉ want of another line after yᵉ word BITVRIX, of which line yᵉ letters CVBVS might seeme to be a part . . . . . . CVM PORTICVBVS HIC S.V.F, that is BALNEUM CUM POR . . . ., etc. I fancy out of Gruter, or Rheine, Sims's Inscriptions, yᵉ like might be produced. Sir, seeing yᵉ owners of yᵉ trough make soe little esteeme of it, I would buy it of them, if a small matter would redeeme it, but you know tis now of very little value. I wish you yʳ satisfaction from yʳ correspond. about Catton, and elsewhere, and, good Sir, desist not from yᵉ pursuit of these studyes ; I hope time will help my Lᵈ Archb. (to whom lately I recomended you), to give you something for incouragement. My service to Mr. Bancks. I rest

" Your assured friend,

" This for Mʳ. A. Pryme, at Hull, etc."   " T. GALE.

[Letter from Rev. Z. Taylor].

" Wigan, July 20, '99

" Sir,

The Bp. being here I have not time to enlarge so much as I would, and therefore am constrained to enclose the account I received from yᵉ Warden of Manchester, Dr. Wroe, my ever honoured tutor, to whom I sent yours, entreating his answer. If anything be uneasy to you in his expressions, you must pardon it, for, had I had time, I would have transcribed what had been proper to you, but I had not. Your mistake in my character, I suppose, ariseth from my father, whose Christian name was Zachary, as well as myself, and was some time in the Presbyterian interest, but I thank God he left it, and died a School-master regularly licensd, which ye Presbyterians say I was the cause of, and will not forgive me for it. I think the paragraph you transcribed should either be struck out, or alterd, and do whether is pleasing to you, for either will be satis-factory to

"Sr.,

"Your humble servt. and bro.,

"ZACH. TAYLOR.

"You will, I know, pardon my haste, ye bishop being to be attended.

"(Addressed).—For the Rnd. Mr. Pryme, at his house, over against the great church, in Kingston-upon-Hull, in Yorkshire. These. By London."

I have lately received the aforegoing letter, which is fixed here,[f] from the learned dean of York, a man never enough to be prased, for the great service that he hath done in rescuing the antiquitys of his country from oblivion, and this day I writt the following answer thereto.

Very Rev. Sir,

Your kind letter came to my hands towards the end of ye last week. As for ye trough, I went immediatly to examine ye owner about its price ; he says that it cost him 36s., and that it is so very usefull unto him that he would not willingly part with it for almost as much more. Ye inscription is very much defaced and worn, and but just legible, but no letters are more fair than CVBVS, and there is no casm or abreviation, or want either of line or letter near them, there being nothing wanting but ye word or two that is in Cambden, which are worn out since his days in ye upper line. I have neither Reinesius nor Gru-ter, but I take ye whole inscription to be read thus :—

Marcus Verecius
Vir Coloniæ Eboracensis idemq.
Mortuus, Cives Biturix Clarissimus Vir bene
vivens hæc sibi vivus fecit.

For so are these letters, CVBVS, commonly interpreted upon medals and old monuments.

The reason why Cambden left this part of ye inscription out, was, in all probability, because that he knew not what to make thereof.

I most humbly and heartily thank you for your recomendation of me to our good diocesan, and for your encouraging of me to prosecute these studdys, than which nothing is more sweet, nothing more pleasant unto me, and I am resolved ardently to follow ye same. I do already find that there are a great many old antiquitys, monuments, inscriptions, and records, in many parts of this country, but there [are] very few that observes such things ; they lye buryed in oblivion, and becomes lost and forgotton. I heard, ye last week, of two old fonts applyd to profane uses, with old images and inscriptions on them, but I am so confined to ye reading of prayers twice every day, that I cannot get time to go see them. There is also in Rudston church-yard a great pillar, with strang ingraveings[u] on it. But that which is more observable, and perhaps more worthy of your note, is, that, about ten days ago, was discovered in Lincolnshire, a curious Roman

[f] See antea, p. 208.
[u] The great stone at Rudstone has now quite a plain surface.

O

pavement of mosaic work, of little stones of all sorts of colours, about half ye bigness of dice, set in most curious order and figures. It was but just bared, and then cover'd up again, until that ye lord of ye soil comes down, which will be about a month hence, and then I will be there, if it be possible, to take ye whole figure and description thereof, and will either begg it or buy it, and contrive some way to take it up whole, and so set it in a table frame at my house at Hatfield, whither I send all ye antiquitys and raritys that I can procure. Upon account of this, I have sent for Ciampini's famous book of ye Rom[an] mosaic pavements, that came out at Rome, in folio, in 1690, and shall take care to send you everything observable relating to ye aforegoing one that is so lately discover'd. Mr. Banks presents his most humble service to you.

I am, most worthy Sr.,

Your most obliedged humble serv.,

A. PRYME.

Haveing been taking a view of the said Roman pavements towards the end of the last week, I writ the learned dean this following letter concerning the same.

Hull, July 22.

Very Revnd. Sr.,

Haveing made bold, in my last letter unto you, dated ye ...... of this month, to acquaint you with ye recent discovery of a Rom[an] pav[ement] in Lincolnsh[ire], so I could not for my life (through ye vehement love and affection that I have to antiquitys), any longer forbear going to take a view thereof than yesterday, which haveing perform'd, I shall here, as I promissd, give you a larger account thereof. But because that it is by a famous old Roman highway, or street, as it is commonly call'd, I will make bold to describe its course unto you as briefly as I can. In ye first place, because that nobody has done it before me, and because that I am very well acquainted with all that part of ye country.

I have observed many Roman ways in that county of Lincoln, but none more observable than this, which runs almost directly in a straight line from London to Humber side.

This is it that is slightly mentioned by Mr. Cambden (nov. ed., p. 470), as running, says he, from Lincoln northwards, unto ye little village call'd Spittle in ye street, and somewhat furder. From this Spittle, in this street, and his somewhat furder, I shall continue it's course, and what I have observed worthy of note about ye same, unto Humber aforesayd.

It is not, perhaps, unworthy to note, that this way is call'd all along by ye very country people, ye high street, and is so visible that it is a great direction and guide to strangers and passengers to keep the road. It is cast up on both sides, with incredible labour, to a great height, and discontinued in many places, and then begun again, and so on to Humber side. I have observed, that where it runs over nothing but bare woulds and plain heath, that there it consists of nothing but earth, cast up, but, where it comes to run through woods, there it is not only raised with earth, but also paved with great stones set edge-wise, very close to one another, in a strong cement or morter, that ye roots of ye trees which had been cut down, to make way for ye causey, might not spring up again and blind ye road. Which paved causey is yet very strong, firm, and visible in many places of this street, where woods are yet standing on both sides, as undoubtedly they were in ye Roman times, else it had not been paved, and in other places it is paved, where nothing of any wood is to be seen, tho' undoubtedly there was when it was made. In one place I measured ye bredth of ye sayd paved street, and I found it just seven yards broad.

This street, or causey, in its course full north from Spittle aforesayd, runs by yᵉ fields of Hibberston, in which fields, not farr of this street, is ye foundations of many Roman buildings to be seen, as is manifest from their tile there found, and tradition says that there hath been a citty and castle there; and there are two springs, yᵉ one called Julian's Stony Well, and yᵉ other Castleton Well, and there are several old Roman coins found there. Perhaps this might be some little old Roman town, by their highway side, and was perhaps called Castleton, or Casterton, from its being built in or by some of their camps that were then in these fields.

About a mile furdur to yᵉ northward, on yᵉ west side of yᵉ sayd street, upon a great plain or sheep-walk, there is very visible the foundations of another old town, tho' now there is neither house, stone, rubish, tree, hedge, fence, nor close to be seen, belonging thereto. I have counted yᵉ *vestigia* of yᵉ buildings, and found them to amount to about one hundred or more, and yᵉ number of yᵉ streets and lanes, which are five or six. Tradition calls this place Gainstrop, and I do very well remember that I have re'd, in yᵉ 2nd volume of yᵉ *Mon. Angl.* of lands or tenements herein given unto Newstead priory, not far of this place, in an island of yᵉ river Ank, falsly called Ankam.

About a mile or two hence, yᵉ street runs through Scawby wood, where it is all paved, and from thence close by Broughton town end, by a hill which I should take to be a very great barrow, and that yᵉ town had its name from it *quasi* Barrow, or Burrow town, but that it seems to be too excessively great for one. However, I have found fragments of Roman tiles there.

From thence yᵉ causy, all along paved, is continued about a mile furder, to yᵉ entrance upon Thornholm moor, where there is a place by yᵉ street called Bratton Graves, and a little east, by Broughton wood side, there is a spring, that I discovered some years ago, that turns moss into stone, and not farr furder stands yᵉ ruins of yᵉ stately priory of Thornholm, built by k[ing] Stephen.

Opposite to this priory, about a quarter of a mile on ye west side of yᵉ street is a place called Santon, from yᵉ flying sands there, which have overrun and ruin'd some hundreds of acres of land, amongst which sands was, in antient times, a great Roman pottery, as yᵉ learned doct[or] Lister shews, in yᵉ Trans-[actions] of R.S., v. ..., p. ..., from yᵉ reliques of yᵉ ruinous furnaces, and yᵉ many fragments of Roman urns and potts yet to be met with. I have also found a great piece of brass, in yᵉ bottom of yᵉ ruins of one of yᵉ furnaces, like a cross, which perhaps was part of a grate to set some potts on.

Returning back again to yᵉ street, there are several hills, like barrows, thereby, on yᵉ top of one of which is erected a great flat stone, now so far sunk into yᵉ earth that there is not over half a foot of it to be seen; but I could not observe any inscription thereon, tho' undoubtedly it has not been set there for nothing.

Entering, then, into Appelby lane, yᵉ street leads through yᵉ end of yᵉ town, at which town is two old Roman games yet practiz'd, yᵉ one call'd Julian's Bower, and yᵉ other Troy's Walls.

From hence yᵉ street runs straight on, leaving Roxby, a little town, half a mile on yᵉ west, where yᵉ Roman pavement is discover'd that I shall describe unto you." And Winterton,ʷ a pretty neat town, where yᵉ worthy familys of yᵉ Places and Nevils inhabit, promoters and encouragers of everything that is good, and great lovers of antiquitys.

ᵛ An engraving of the Roman Pavement at Roxby was published by the late Mr. William Fowler, of Winterton.

ʷ Winterton. In 1866 Mr. Peacock exhibited to the Society of Antiquaries the original manuscript of our Diarist's history of this place, which he stated was given to him by his friend, the late Ven. W. B. Stonehouse, vicar of Owston, Lincolnshire, and Archdeacon of Stow, the historian of the Isle of Axholme. The latter had found it, about thirty years before, in a cottage in one of the

Then, about three or four miles furder, leaving Wintringham about half a mile to yᵉ west, yᵉ said street falls into Humber, and there ends.

All this end of yᵉ country, on yᵉ west side of this street, hath been full of Romans in old time, as may be gathered from their coins and many tyles, which are found all hereabouts, especially at a cliff called Winterton Cliff, where has been some old Rom[an] building ; and furder, about two miles more westward, is Alkburrow, which seems to have been a Rom[an] town, not only from its name, but also a small four-squair camp there, on yᵉ west side of which is a barrow, call'd Countess barrow, or pitt, to this day.

Haveing thus given you an idea of this part of yᵉ country, and how and whereabouts this town of Roxby stands, where this Roman pavement is discovered, I shall now proceed to give you an account thereof, as I took it upon yᵉ place, yᵉ latter end of yᵉ last week.

Being got thither with Mr. Place and Mr. Nevil, two Winterton gent[lemen], we found that yᵉ close or garth lyes in yᶜ town aforesayd, on yᵉ south-west side of yᵉ church. Yᵉ lord of yᵉ soil is Mr. Elways, a south country gent[leman]. Yᵉ tenant's name is Tho[mas] Smith. Yᵉ occasion of its discovery was his digging to repair a fence between this close and another, which, as soon as he had discovered, he bared a little thereof (it lying about a foot and a half in yᵉ ground), and digged in many places, and found it to be, as he guesses, about six or seven yards broad, and as many long, if not more ; but, he being not at all curious thereof, yᵉ school-boys went and pull'd several curious figures in pieces, that he had bared, which were set in circles.

Haveing got a spade, a shovel, and a besom, we fell to work, and with a great deal of labour, bared about a yard and a half squair ; in bareing of which we cast up many pieces of Roman tyle, yᵉ bone of yᵉ hinder legg of an ox or cow, broken in two, and many pieces of lime and sand, or plaster, painted red and yellow, which had been yᵉ cornish either of some altar, or some part of yᵉ building that was there, whatever it was ; and we observed, likewise, that several great stones, in their falling, had broke through yᵉ pavement, and there layd, untill that we removed them.

Then, haveing swept yᵉ space aforesayd, that we had bared, very clean, yᵉ pavement look'd exceeding beautifull and pretty, and one would not imagine that such mean stones could make such pretty work, for they are nothing but four squair bitts of brick, slate, and cauk, set in curious figueres and order, and are only of colours red, blew, and white, specimens of all which I have sent by yᵉ bearer ; amongst which there is one as larg again as any of yᵉ rest, of which many whole rows and rectangular figures of yᵉ same bigness, consisting of blew, red, and white, were composed all on yᵉ outside of yᵉ smaller work. Yᵉ material that these little pavers are set in, is a floor of lime and sand, and not plaster, as many are, which floor is so rotten with time, that one may easily take up yᵉ little pavers, some whole flowers of which I intend to take up whole, and send to Hatfield, if it be possible. I stay only yᵉ coming down of yᵉ lord of yᵉ soil, to see it, who, I am sure, will not regard it· Of these pavements you may see many accounts in Camb[den's] nov. edit., p. 451, 603, 604, 607, etc. Ciampini's book upon this subject, which I thought to have got, is not to be had in all London.

villages near Owston. From the signature on its cover, and the autograph at the end, it evidently once belonged to George Stovin, esq., a celebrated antiquary in his day, and a member of a gentilitial family that had been long settled at Tetley, in the Isle of Axholme. He died in 1780. The MS. is styled *A short view of ye History and Antiquities of Winterton. At ye request of Thomas Place, Gent, of ye said Town, collected by A. P., Min. of Thorn, 1703.* This MS., accompanied by prefatory observations on the family and the life and writings of Abraham de la Pryme, the Diarist, was printed by the Society in *Archæologia,* vol. xl.

I have inclosed herein an exact draught of as much of this Rom[an] pav-[ement] as we bared and discover'd, with ye colours of ye little stones as they stand in ye work, which I took upon ye place; and when that I discover and take ye rest, I shall make bold to present ye same unto you, with some of ye very figures, if I might be so happy as to know that this and they would be acceptible unto you. Humbly begging pardon for thus troubling you with so long and teadious a letter, .

I am, your most humble serv.,
A. P.

Our newse from London this day, the 27th of August, 1699, says, that upon the lord major's proclaiming Bartholomew fair, last week, there gather'd a vast crowd about him, who cry'd out " God bless the king and the lord major, that stands up for the church of England! God bless the king," etc., as before, thousands of times.

[Letter inserted].

"For the Rev. Mr. Primme, at Kingston-super-Hull.

"Gainsburgh, Aug. 29 (99).

" Sr.,

" I was lately inform'd that there had bin at Hull a person who came from Manchester, where he had bin, for some time, a teacher to a presbyterian assembly, and had a mighty reputation amongst them, who shipt from Hull for Holland; a man, as I am told, of Socinian principles, and some think a Jesuit. If you can give me any account of this business, I beg the favour of you to do it. I would hope it might be serviceable to let some misguided persons see, that they are, at this day, as much imposed on as their ancestors were by one Faithfull Comin, and Heath. Be pleased to give me an answer to this as soon as possible, and it will be a great kindness, to

" Sir.

" Your very humble servant,

"A. SMYTHE.

Hull, Aug. ye 31, '99.^x

Revnd. Sr.,

Your letter came to my hands yesternight, and, in obedience to your desire, I answer, that all that I told Mr. Wesley, and others, about ye person that you enquire of, is a real truth.

He came to this town about ye middle of Septem[ber] or Octob[er], last year, from London, as he sayd, to go into Holland, to take possession of an estate that was faln to him there by ye death of an unkle. He was of middle stature, in black cloths, had a sword by his side, was very neat and fine, and one of ye most pleasant mercurial fellows, and one of ye most universal scholars that ever I mett with, haveing all notions, new and old, and all ye most noble arts and sciences at his finger ends. He spoke very good Lattin, and had a tongue ye best hung that ever I met with; had gold and silver plenty, and kept company with most of ye great men of this town, especial the Jacobites. Sayd that his name was John Midgley, and writ it so, and that his brother, doct[or] Midgley, and him, were ye composers of ye *Turkish Spy*, and

---

^x This letter is not addressed, but it is evidently an answer to the preceding one.

that he was about thirty-five years of age, etc. I became aequainted with him, by chance, at ye bookseller's shop. After that he came almost every day to prayers in the church, and from thence to my chamber, where we sat and had a great deal of talk about all sorts of learning. I soon found that he was a ridged deist and Socinian. He turn'd of with a great deal of seeming inge-nuity all ye arguments and quotations that are commonly brought out of the antient fathers for ye divinity of ye Son and Holy Ghost, and quoted very readily other expressions, both in Greek and Lat[in], out of ye same fathers, against it. He rediculed infant baptism exceedingly, and made all religion nothing but state pollicy; which pernitious whimseys he made it his business to propogate in all company he came in, bringing them in one way or other, etc. I remember that I asked him what he thought of ye Sury business, to which he readily answer'd that he had seen all ye papers thereon, and did believe that it was a damn'd cheat. I have heard him at other times plead mightily for king James, and ye celebacy of ye clergy, and say that, as he was not marry'd, so he never had, nor never would defile himself with woman kind, etc. Haveing stay'd here about a month or six weeks, ye wind strikeing fair, over he went to Holland; was landed at Rotterdam, kept company with several there; stay'd some days, and then what became of him is not certain. Some think that he went to St. Omer's, to give an account of his negotiations amongst ye dissenters in Manchester.

Thus all noise of him ceased at this town, and we never thought more of him, 'til about half a year after, Mr. Colling, of this town, rideing to Manchester, on a py'd horse that he had bought of this spark, no sooner got he into ye town, but almost every body knew ye horse; and ye old owner living there challeng'd him, sayd he lent him such a day and time to such a one, one of their assistant preachers, ye best man in ye whole world, tho' he had ridden away with him. So that by this means ye whole villany came to be discover'd and found out: how that the horse was Mr. Greves's, of ye said town, that ye above sayd Midg-ley was certainly ye man that had been preacher amongst them about a year, that he went there by ye name of Gacheld, had been curate to ye chief presbi-terian man of that town about twelve months, that he passed there for one of ye most pious and religiousest men that ever lived, that he administer'd ye sac-raments, etc., was cry'd up for ye most heavenly gifted man that ever came to town, and preached and pray'd wonderfully, etc.; so that, when he went away, pretending that ye L^d. had given him a call to West Chester, he dissolv'd them all into tears at his farewell sermon, and told them that, tho' he should be absent, yet he would pray as much for them, that they might stand stedfast in ye faith, as if he was yet present with them, that he doubted God would let them see his face no more, etc., and that they would be pleas'd to administer somewhat of their abundance unto his necessity, for, being to take a jorney, he had not wherewithall to carry him on, etc. Upon this, great offerings were made him; some gave him five pounds, some six, some seven, some eight, some more, some less; and amongst others, besides a larg sum that the above-sayd Mr. Greves presented him with, he proffer'd to lend him his horse to West Chester, upon condition that he would take care to return him speedily again, etc., but mounting, insted of going to West Chester, he came streight to this town, and lived as before related. Yet, for all this, tho' ye wise godly were thus basely imposed upon, and tho' they acknowledge and confess that they were cheated, yet they have a very great love, veneration, and respect for him unto this day. Doct[or] Wroe, mast[er] of Manchester coll[ege], in a letter of his to me, says, that he preached them out of above 100*l.* that year. Other letters I have out of Lancash[ire], since, which say that it is reported that he has been seen at London, and that he is at present chapl[ain] to ye duchess of Somerset. But I look upon this as a presbiterian invention and trick, to bring him off from being supposed to be a papist or Roman emisary, that they them-selves might come of ye better.

I leave it to your ingenuity and judgment to judge what he was, whether he was a papist, which 'tis exceeding probable that he was not. The presbiterians were exceedingly to blame. However, yᵉ substance of all of it, with a better account of yᵉ Sury delu[sion] than that which Mr. Taylor has given us, with a presbit[erian] impost[er] at Dublin, in '94 or '95, will speedily be publish'd, they being almost printed off.

I begg pardon for my tediousness; and, as I shall always be most ready to serve you in any thing in my power, so

I am, Sʳ.,

Your most humbl. ser.,

A. P.

[Not addressed].

Dear Sʳ.,

I am exceeding glad to hear by Mr. West that you are design'd for yᵉ East Indys. Oh! how I wish that I had yᵉ happiness of waiting upon you thither, of seeing all yᵉ raritys that you'l see, yᵉ strang birds, beasts, fishes, and wonderful works of God. Well, I am so ty'd and confined to my country, that I cannot attend you, or have yᵉ liberty and good fortune that you have. Above all things, I earnestly beseech you to take great care of your health, to forbear all manner of excess of strong drinks and strang meats, and to begin to leave of feeding much of flesh before you go abord, for I look upon nothing more prejudicial to us when we come into hot countrys than our eating so much flesh. There are other rules for health that I would give, if I thought that you was not already provided of such. Amongst other things observable about Bombaim, whither I suppose you are bound, I earnestly besieech you to make yᵉ most diligent inquisition that can be into yᵉ antiquitys of yᵉ country, yᵉ originals of yᵉ people, and their languages, what traditions they have, and for yᵉ better understanding of several things in the Minor Prophets, to compare their superstitions and religious rites therewith, for as they are yᵉ more obscure, so I am of oppinion that yᵉ right understanding of yᵉ supersititions of yᵉ heathen cannot be better illustrated and clear'd than by yᵉ old traditions and practises that yᵉ most barbarous people of yᵉ east yet uses. I also earnestly intreat you to get what old books you can in yᵉ language of those babarous countrys you come in, and to get them translated, and take down every inscription, epitaph, and hierogliphick that you shall see or hear of, if possible, and inquire of yᵉ country people into its meaning. There is a great island call'd Canovein, near unto Bombaim, in which wonderfull reliques of antiquity are to be seen. There is yᵉ top of a vast rock, inaccessible to above two or 3 abreast, cut out into a citty call'd after the name of the island, or was perhaps antiently a great heathen temple. In one place there is, as it were, Vulcan's forge, all cut out of yᵉ hard rock, supported by two mighty collosses. Next, a temple, with a beautiful frontispiece, not unlike yᵉ portico of St. Paul's west gate at London, within yᵉ gate on each side stands two monstrous giants, where two lesser and one greater gate give a noble entrance into a temple, or vast room, which receives no light but by yᵉ doors and windows of yᵉ porch. Yᵉ roof is, as it were, arched, or perhaps is really so, and seems to be born up with vast pillars of yᵉ same rock, some round, some squair, thirty-four in number, and yᵉ cornish work is of elephants, horses, lions, tygres, etc. At the upper end it rounds like a bow, where stands a great offertory, somewhat oval: the body of it without pillars, they onely making a narrow piatzo about, leaving yᵉ nave open, it may bee one hundred foot in length, and in height sixty or more.

Beyond this, by the same mole like industry, is worked out of yᵉ hard rock a vast court of judicature or place of audience, as those that shew it name it, fifty foot square, all bestuck with imagrey, well engraved, according to old sculpture. On yᵉ side over against yᵉ door sitts a great image, to whome yᵉ Bramins that shew strangers all these things pay always great respect and reverence, tho' for what they say they do not know. Him they call Jongee, or yᵉ holy man. Under this vast building are innumerable little cells, or rooms, like stalls in stables for horses, at ye head of every one of which, is nitches or corbells with images in them, which seems to shew that this vast work was a seminary of heathen devotees, and that these were their cells and dormitorys, and ye open place their common hall or school. Multitudes of other buildings there also are in ye rock, with stately porticos and entrances, which will require a great deal of time to view. Pray view them all, take an exact account of them, and ye draughts of all the most observable images and characters, and hieroglyphicks, which I take to be nothing but Chinese letters; and enquire if there be any medals or coins ever found thereabouts, which may inform us who was ye wonderfull contriver and former of this extraordinary and miraculous work.

Not far of this same island of Canova, in ye same bay of Bombaim, is an island call'd Elephanto, from a monstrous elephant, cut out of a main rock, bearing a young one on its back. Not farr from it is ye effigies of an horse stuck up to ye belly in ye earth in the vally. From thence, climbing up unto ye sumit of ye highest mountain on ye island, there is another rock cutt into ye shape of a temple or fane. It is supported with forty-two pillars, (pray examine of what order they are), being a square open on all sides, but towards ye east where stands a statue with three heads crowned, with strang hieroglyphics, which be sure to coppy out, I being pretty sure that they are Chinese and may be interpreted. On the north side, in an high portico, stands an altar guarded by gyants, and immured by a square wall all along. Ye walls are loaded with huge giants, some with eight hands, making their vanquish'd knights stoop for mercy. Before this temple there is a great tank, or cistern, full of water, and a little beyond it another place full of images. 'Tis sayd that this seems to be of a latter date than that at Canoven, because perhaps that it has not suffered so much by ye Portigals as ye first hath; they striveing to demolish and break all these old reliques of Paganish.

If you have any conveniency of going into Persia, or of sending thither, I should be very glad to have a full acconnt of ye staitly ruins of Persepolis, now called Chulminoor, or ye forty pillars, tho' now there are but, as they say, eighteen standing. I am fully satisfyd with ye oppinion of ye learned Doct[or] Frier, that this was never any king's pallace, but onely a vast heathen temple; ye images of ye captives that are cutt there are exactly in ye old Persian garb or habit, and much ye same which ye Gaurs, or Gabers, which are descended from them, wear to this day. These ruins are so exactly described by many that I will not trouble you with ye being more exact in them, onely I besieech you transcribe all ye inscriptions that you can see; and if you find anything new, be pleas'd to take notice of it. In ye mountains about these ruins, are an abundance of vast reliques, images, tombs, inscriptions, etc., which I most earnestly besieech you to take an exact account of. I will lay no furder burthen upon you, dear Sr., [v] pray, for God's sake, bear and answer but this, and I will never trouble you again. In ye meanwhile my prayers shall never be wanting to ye true God, ye God of sea and land, ye author and preserver of health, in whome wee live, and move, and have our being, that he would be please'd to grant you a good voyage, perfect health, full oppertunity, and good success, in all those things, and that he would bring you safe home again; which is, and always shall be, ye most humble prayers, untill I hear from you again, of your most humble friend and servant,

A. P.

Not many years ago, as a gentleman was digging to lay the foundation of his house in Boston, in Lincolnshire, the workmen

---

[v] It is to be regretted that the name of the correspondent, upon whom this gentle burthen was laid, is not supplied.

found in a great hollow'd stone, in a great many boxes and foldings, the following record, in parchment, in very old English.

Memorandum. Anno 1309, in yᵉ 3d year of Edw. yᵉ 2d, yᵉ Munday after Palm Sunday in yᵉ same year, yᵉ miners began to break ground for yᵉ foundation of Boston steeple, and so continued till Midd summer following, at which time they were deeper than the haven by five foot ; at which depth they found a bed of stone upon a firm sand, and under that a bed of clay, yᵉ thickness of which could not be known. Then, upon yᵉ Munday next after yᵉ feast of St. John Baptist, in yᵉ same year, was layd yᵉ first stone by Dame Margery Tilney, upon which shee layd five pounds sterling. Sʳ· John Tusedail, then parson of Boston, gave also five pounds, and Richard Stevenson, a merchant in Boston, gave 5l. more, which was all yᵉ gifts given at that time.

I am sorry I cannot hear whether there were not any more records found with it, and I have written thither to know furder.

'Tis sayd for a certain truth that the altitude of the steeple and length of the church are equal, viz., each ninety-four yards.

The number of the stepps are 365, equal to the days. The windows fifty-two, equal to the weeks; and the pillars twelve, equal to the number of the months in a year.

In the 21, 22, 23, 24, and 25 years of Edw[ard] the 1st, the majorality of York was in the king's hands, and Sʳ· John de Melsa, or Meaux, was governour of the citty, who was a great man of stature, and a warriour, as appeareth by some of his armes, namely, his helmit, still to be seen in Holderness, at Albrough church, where he lyeth bury'd under a fair monument, no ways defaced; upon which is ingraven, in stone, the arms of Roos, Oatrced, Fulco de Oyry, Hastings, Lassels, Hiltons, and others, this present year, 1693, still to be seen.[a]

Upon several reparations makeing in our church of the Holy Trinity of Kingston-upon-Hull, considering that no way is better to preserve anything to posterity than to hide the same, it came suddainly into my head, seeing a convenient place, to lay some books up there to future ages. Upon which, haveing a great veneration for that most excellent of kings, k[ing] C[harles] the 1st, who is so much reviled and despised now-a-days, I wrapped carefully up his Είκων Βασιλική, of the first edit[ion] in '48, doct[or] Wagstaff's Vindication of the same against Tooland ; Gilbert and Young's Defence of him ; and Boscobel, or the wonderfull account of k[ing] Ch[arles] the 2nd's preservation after

---

[z] This is noticed in *Thompson's History of Boston*, ed. 1820, p. 91. See a communication in *Notes and Queries*, 4th S. v., pp. 27, 133, upon Foundation and Dedication Stones.

[a] *Poulson*, ii., 13. Warburton specifies fourteen coats of arms, but does not name the eleventh, which is Richmond.

P

Worster fight; and, takeing a piece of parchment, I writt the following verses thereon.

In perpetuam rei memoriam, in
Perpetuam optimi Principis
Caroli Primi, Martyris, Piissimi,
Doctissimi, Mitissimi, Patris
Patriæ Regisq. Regum, memoriam,
Posuit
In hoc loco hos tres libros,
Servus Christi indignissimus
Abr. de la Pryme, de Hatfield,
Juxta Danum, hujus S. S. Eccl.,
Lector quotidianus.
Qui hujus Bibliothecæ catal.
Primo fecit.
Hujus ecclesiæ, oppidi, et
Comitatus, historiam primo
Composuit, etc.
Anno ab Incarnatione
Filii Dei 1699.

Then, haveing roll'd it up, and wrapt them together, I committed them to fate.[b]

Nov. THE 10. This day I received the following letter, and an old coin, from the worshipfull Mr. Mason, alderman of this town, who lives at Welton.

                           "Welton, 24 Octr., 1699.
" Mr. Prime,
      " This peece of coyne, which I reckon beareth a Roman face, was found by a neighbour of mine, a waller, in digging a well at Brough, a ferry towne,

---

[b] See *South Yorkshire*, i., p. 180, note.
[c] He had no son, it is believed, of the name of Robert, but a son in law.

Rev. Valentine Mason, bp. at Cherrington, co. Oxon., Nov., 1583.—Grace Rhodes, married at St. Vicar of Driffield 1 Dec., 1615, to 3 Aug., 1635. Vicar of Ellough- | John's, Beverley, 11 October, ton 21 Aug., 1623, till his death, in 1639. | 1626.

Other   Robert Mason, third son, born 1632 or 33. Sheriff of Hull—Elizabeth .... stated
issue.   1675, mayor 1681 and 1696. Died 26 Feb., 1718-19, aged | by Beckwith to have lived
          86. Will d. 5 Dec., 1712, then of Welton, gent. By sur- | 60 years as his wife.
          render, 16 Nov., 1694, gave £1 14s. 8d. to the poor of
          Welton.

Hugh Mason,—..   Rev. Thomas Mason, rector   Elizabeth, wife   Mercy,=Robert   Mason,
living 1680.   of Thornton, bp. at St.   of Erasmus   bur. at St. | bur. at St. Mary's,
1734.   Mary s, Hull, Feb., 1661.   Darwin.   Mary's, Hull, | Hull, 19th April,
                                                  26 Nov., 1728. | 1717.

Rev. William Mason,=   Robert,   Elizabeth, bap. 25
vicar of Holy Trinity,   bp. 2 Sep.,   September,
Hull.   1696.   1696.

Rev. William Mason,
the POET.

eight miles from Hull, one antient ferry towne formerly belonging the crowne ; the towne is on this syde Humber, nigh Trent, and is in the parish of Ellaughton, a lordpp. bought from the crowne. The finder would gladly believe it to be gold, but I deeme it bras or copper. I reckon you curious in such enquiries, so send it for your veue, and, after yowr remarkes taken of it, pray returne it to my sonn Ro[bert],[c] who brings it, and give him your thoughts thereupon, who will communicate the same to Sr.,

"Your friend,
"ROBERT MASON."

Unto which I returned, this day, the following answer.

Worshipfull Sir,
I most heartily thank you for ye honour you did me in sending me ye old coin that was found at Brough. Your kind letter and it came to my hands yesterday. It is not gold, as ye finder imagined, but onely a mixture of copper and brass, as most of ye old Roman coins are. Ye effigies on it is that of ye famous emperor Hadrian, who, hearing that ye Brittons that his ancestors had conquer'd were upon ye point of rebellion, came with a mighty power into this land, about ye year of Christ 124, and, haveing settled all in peace, returned triumphantly home. Ye inscription about that his coin which you was pleased to send me is this :—

Imperator Cæsar Nerva Trajanus
Hadrianus Augustus Pontifex maximus Pater Patriæ ....

On ye reverse is ye image of Liberty, sitting at peace and ease in a chair, with a spear in her left hand, and a sacryfiseing dish in her right, as offering thanks to ye gods for ye happiness ye empire enjoy'd under his reign, circumscribed, Libertas Publica, and, under all, C. S., that is Senatus Consultu, as being coined to ye honour of his memory by the advice of ye senate.

As to ye town where it was found, it was an old Roman town, ye landing place of their forces out of Lincolnshire, and at it, as soon as they had got over, they cast up three huge banks, one of which ran towards York, another towards ye north, by Ripplingham—yet to be seen—and another towards Beverley, and thence to Pattrington, scarce now visible.

And, last of all, when ye Roman forces were all sent for home, in great hast, about ye year 400, to defend their own country from the barbarous natives that invaded, ye soldiers and Roman inhabitants that were very rich here hid their money and treasure in thousands of places in this land, in hopes to have return'd again and possess'd it, but they never returning is ye reason that there are such great number of their coins found in this nation.

I am your most humble and oblieged servant,
ADR. PRYME.

Constant tradition says that there lived in former times, in Soffham,[d] *alias* Sopham, in Norfolk, a certain pedlar, who dreamed that if he went to London bridge, and stood there, he should hear very joyfull newse, which he at first sleighted, but afterwards, his dream being dubled and trebled upon him, he resolv'd to try the issue of it, and accordingly went to London, and stood on the bridge there two or three days, looking about

[d] Swaffham.

him, but heard nothing that might yield him any comfort. At
last it happen'd that a shopkeeper there, hard by, haveing noted
his fruitless standing, seeing that he neither sold any wares, nor
asked any almes, went to him, and most earnestly begged to
know what he wanted there, or what his business was; to which
the pedlar honestly answer'd, that he had dream'd that if he
came to London, and stood there upon the bridg, he should hear
good newse; at which the shopkeeper laught heartily, asking
him if he was such a fool to take a jorney on such a silly errand,
adding, "I'll tell thee, country fellow, last night I dream'd that
I was at Sopham, in Norfolk, a place utterly unknown to me,
where, methought behind a pedlar's house, in a certain orchard,
and under a great oak tree, if I digged, I should find a vast
treasure! Now think you," says he, "that I am such a fool to
take such a long jorney upon me upon the instigation of a silly
dream? No, no, I'm wiser. Therefore, good fellow, learn witt
of me, and get you home, and mind your business." The
pedlar observeing his words, what he sayd he had dream'd, and
knowing that they concenterd in him, glad of such joyfull newse,
went speedily home, and digged, and found a prodigious great
treasure, with which he grew exceeding rich; and Soffham
church, being for the most part fal'n down, he set on workmen,
and re-edifyd it most sumptuously, at his own charges; and to
this day there is his statue therein, cut in stone, with his pack at
his back, and his dogg at his heels; and his memory is also preserved by the same form or picture in most of the old glass
windows, taverns, and alehouses of that town, unto this day.

Haveing received, the last week, a kind and obliedging letter
from the famous dean of York, which is the letter here before
inserted,ᵉ I returned him this answer.

Very Revnd. Sr.,
          Being gone yᵉ last week about some very earnest business, out of this
town unto Bautry, I had not yᵉ happiness to meet with your most kind and
acceptable letter (for which I most heartily thank you), unto Saturday last that
I got back.
          It being my vanity, or curiosity, to take a strict view of all places that I
come at, I think that I have discover'd something that may be acceptable unto
you, or which, perhaps, may be a hint to some other of your noble discoverys.
That yᵉ Romans cut down and destroyed yᵉ vast forrest, that grew upon
yᵉ Levels of Hatfield Chace, which contains about ninety thousand acres, is
pretty certain. Upon yᵉ borders of yᵉ sayd Levels, I found yᵉ last week an
antient town called Osterfield, on this side Bautry, and, hard by it, a great four-
squair Roman fortification. When I saw this, I began to consider and conjec-

ᵉ Not now in the Diary.

ture that this town might take its name from Ostorius Scapula,*/ that he fought
a field or battel there, and that ye Roman encampment there found might be
raised by him, that ye enemy he fought against might be ye old Brittains of
ye great levels, morasses, boggs, and woods adjoining, and that when he had
vanquish'd them, he might be ye man that caused to be burnt, cut down, and
destroy'd, ye vast forrest that spread itself over ye sayd low grounds.

I shall say no more, but submit this conjecture to your most pierceing and
happy judgment, onely adding, that to ye best of my memory, ye Roman way
from Agelorum to Danum runs not farr of from ye aforesayd place.

As to ye Nantz brandy, I have got you a quart of ye best that I could, and
sent it by ye bearer, which I most humbly beseech you to accept of, as a present
from

Your most humble, most obleged,
And obedient Servant,

Hull, Nov. 20, '99.   A. P.

---

*/ Hunter (*South Yorkshire*, i., 79), when writing about Austerfield, says,
"We may dismiss, as scarcely worth a moment's attention, De la Pryme's conjecture that the name is derived from that of the Roman general Ostorius.
The instances are so rare, if indeed there are any instances, of a Roman patro-
nymic entering into our local nomenclature, that it cannot in any case be
admitted without the most indisputable evidence. And when we observe how
many of our villages derive their names from the cardinal points, we shall
probably not err in assigning its origin to the old form of the word *east*. The
earth-work near the village is however evidently a camp of Roman construction."

VOLUME THE SECOND

LIFE

OF

ABRAH. DE LA PRYME,

CONTAINING AN ACCOUNT OF
ALL THE MOST OBSERVABLE AND REMARKABLE THINGS
THAT HE HATH TAKEN NOTICE OF,
FROM THE YEAR 1700,
BEGINNING AT JANUARY, UNTO THIS TIME,
TO WITT, THE YEAR 17....

THIS day, Jan. the 7th, I happened to be in company with an ingenious old lady of my acquaintance, who, having tabled several years in the family of one of the king's physicians, in King Charles the Second's and King James the Second's times, she tells me that there is no better medicine in the world for an asthma and shortness of breathing than this, etc. [Here follow recipes].

Our late newse out of the north tells us that the great fire under ground, near Newcastle, which some years ago[f] burnt and layd wast seven miles of ground round about it, destroying several villages, has lately begun to smook exceedingly again, which very much frights the neighbours, and makes them fear that it is going to spread furder and break out again.

JAN. 28. This day I went to Swine,[h] in Holderness, to give them a sermon, haveing long'd to see that church and town a great while. The town has formerly been very larg and handsom, as the people report, before the times of the Reformation, tho' now 'tis very mean and inconsiderable, nobody inhabiting the same but a few country clowns. There is but three things that renders it now remarkable, to wit, the greatness of its parish, which hath nineteen towns and villages in it;[i] secondly, the ruins of a famous old nunnery there built by Erenburch de Burtona, wife to Ulbert Constable,[j] which are scarce now

---

[f] In *Sykes's Local Records*, i., 128, there is a brief notice of this fire. It was at Benwell, near Newcastle. But *Major e longinquo reverentia!* Distance has lent enchantment to the Diarist's description.

[h] A parish and township 7 miles N.E. from Hull, in the east-riding of Yorkshire. See *History of the Church and Priory of Swine, in Holderness*, by Thomas Thompson, F.A.S., Hull, 1824. And *Poulson's Holderness*, Hull, 1841, vol. ii., pp. 197-273.

[i] "Containing the hamlets of Arnold and Rowton, Benningholme and Fairholm, Burton-Constable, Bilton, Coniston, and Ellerby; comprising Dowthorpe, part of Langthorpe, Owborough, and Woodhall, Ganstead and Turner Hall, Marton, North and South Skirlaugh, Thirtleby, and Wyton."—*Poulson.*

[j] According to Tanner, in the *Notitia Monastica*, the Priory of Swine was founded by Robert de Verli, before the end of the reign of king Stephen. Of his history little is known. The house, which was dedicated to the Virgin Mary, consisted of a prioress and fifteen nuns, at the least, of the Cistercian order. Erenburgh de Burton, wife of Ulbert de Constable, was only one of the benefactors to it. She gave a carucate of land in Freistingthorpe (Fraisthorpe), in Dickering.—*Dugdale's Monast. Anglic.*, vol. i., p. 834.

visible; and thirdly, a larg, capacious, and indifferently magnificent church, which by the broken pillars and old arches,
now walled up, seems to have been much larger and neater in
former times;[a] but, considering the havock that was made of all
sacred things in the days of the Reformation, it is a mercy and a
particular and great providence of God that we have what we
have. In the body of the said church there is the old organ
loft, and a small case of organs yet standing and perfect, tho' all
the pipes are gone. And under an arch in the south wall lyes a
knight in armer, with his lady by him, cut out of most white
marble, with great exactness and curiosity. Her head-dress is a
cap encompass'd with a roll of coronets or chaplets, by which she
seems to have been a Tilleyol, but who he was cannot now be
known, all the coats of armes being totally worn of : his crest,
upon which his head lyes, is a boar's neck and head muzzled.

In the chancel are sixteen cannons' seats, yet perfect, eight
on the one side and eight on the other, with the canopy over
them.[l] And in a little quire, on the north side of the sayd
chancel, was the burying places and the chantery, in which, upon
great altar tombs, cut out in white marble, lye the effigieses of
some of the Hiltons, Tillyols, and others, with their ladys by
them, made with great neatness and exactness. Round whose

---

[a] There is not the least doubt, says Thompson, that the church of Swine
was, about three hundred years ago, or at the time of the dissolution of monasteries, more than double the size it is at present.

[l] Thompson says, "on the south side of the chancel are still left eight folding seats of oak;" and Poulson, "there are sixteen ancient seats placed in
front and on each side of the pulpit, with seats to turn up, having grotesque
carvings under them ; they have backs, with a place for the head."
The canopy has disappeared. The Rev. C. B. Norcliffe, in 1858, noticed the
following carvings on the Misereres.

North Side.

1, 2, 3, 4, 5. All modern, and the carving renewed.
6. Woman's face.
7. A pitcher.
8. A man's head, wreathed.

South Side.

1. A Saracen's head, wreathed, blowing a horn.
2. Two imps, or monkeys, dos á dos, between them a man's face.
3. A preacher's head and cap, or a judge.
4. A man's head put between his own legs.
5. A wivern.
6. A winged griffin.
7. A man's face, with a beard.
8. The face of a devil.

monuments hath formerly been many coats of armes, but now
all eaten of with time, but the four following ones.

1. [Melton]. A cross moline."[m]
2. [Hilton]. Two bars.
3. [Sutton]. A lion rampant, oppressed or debruised by a bendlet.
4. Luce's. Three lucies or pikes haurient.

These four monuments are yet encompass'd about with great iron
bars and rails, tho' very much worn and eaten away with time.

Upon both of the breasts of the said two knights is three
chaplets apiece, which, if my memory fail me not, are the arms
of the old family of the Tilleyoles."[n]

On the north side of the said quire or chantery lys another
knight, by himself, upon a great altar tomb, most exactly and
neatly cut out of white marble, all in armer.   But who it was is
unknown, only it appears to have been one of the Tilleyols by
his crest, which is an eagle's head.[o]

In the sayd quire, upon a bras plate, on a great stone, is a
larg writeing in old munkish verse, not now legible, furder than
that it says that a son of S[r.] John Melton, K[t.], lys there.[p]

All the aforesayd curious monuments are most miserably
broken and crack'd, for the fury of blind zealous men, and for
want of repairing are now fitt to fall to the ground, the great
stones under them all giving way.

In the entrance into this chantery is two great lines of writeing, most curiously cut out in wood, the first containing these
words :—[q]

---

[m] The arms of Melton are said to be—azure a cross patonce arg.   It is
possible that, from their imperfect condition, the Diarist may not have sketched
them correctly.

[n] The Diarist has first written "Darcy's," and altered it to "Tilleyole's."
The arms of Darcy were, in some instances, three roses, and three cinquefoils.
Those of Tiliol were a lion rampant oppressed by a bendlet.   The arms of three
chaplets of roses, are those of Hilton, of Swine, and were by them adopted as
being derived from their maternal ancestors, Lascelles, of Kirkby-under-Knoll.
In several instances the Hiltons, of Swine, used as their arms two bars, and
over all a fleur-de-lis.

[o] This was Sir Robert Hilton, knight, lord of Swine, 1321. (See engraving
in *Thompson's History of Swine*, p. 92). Arms on surcoat—two bars, over all
a fleur-de-lis, quarterly, with three chaplets.   Glover, *Somerset Herald*, describes this crest as a griffin's head. (*Visitation of Yorkshire*, 1584).   And
Edmondson states that in a ducal coronet to have been the crest of Lascelles.

[p] John Melton, Esq., son and heir of Sir John Melton, married Margery,
daughter of William, Lord Fitz-Hugh, of Ravensworth castle, Richmondshire.
Warburton, the herald, who was here in 1652, describes this monument as
"a fair gravestone, and on it two pictures of brass." He also gives the "munkish verse," which Thompson has printed, p. 93.

[q] Warburton, *Lansdown MSS.*, 894, gives the original inscriptions at full
length.—See *Thompson*, p. 88.

.... Thomæ domini de Darcy et heredum suorum, et finitum est hoc opus tempore Domini Theo [r].......... Darcy, militis [filii] et heredis domini Thomæ Darcy.

And the other these, with the following five coats of armes inserted between several words in it.

Orate pro animabus Thomæ Biwater, Capellani hujus cantariæ [Beatæ Mariæ] et [omnium] aliorum capellanorum tam præteritorum quam futurorum.[s]

[Arms].

1. .... *A cross flory, or patonce.*
2. .... *A cinquefoil.*
3. .... *A fleur-de-lis.*
4. .... *A branch of acorn, of three leaves.*
5. .... *A trefoil.*

There appears to have been a great many more coats of armes upon the little shields over the sayd door, but time hath eaten them of.

These are all the coats of armes that are any where visible in the said Church, either on the outside or inside.

This day, to wit, February the 11th, I went to preach at Cottingham. This town was very famous in former days, not onely for its largness, its great castle, call'd Baynard's castle, and its great market, but also for its church, which is at present, after all the storms of fate, very larg, beautifull, and handsom, and escaped any sort of demolishing in the Reformation, save of the many chanterys in the inside, which were totaly ruin'd, in which were many monuments of the Estotevils, De la Wakes, and others, of which not the least fragment is now to be seen.

In the body of the church is nothing now observable but the old organ loft, where now the clock stands, and these two following inscriptions, the first of which, which is that which immediately follows, is writ upon a little table in capital letters, and nail'd a great height upon a pillar, which I could not read untill I had got a ladder to clim up to it, in these words, which seems to have been set up in the time of the civel war, and to relate to something then done.

DEO ADJUTORE

BERNARDUS AWMOND[t] ET ROBERTUS

---

[r] A mistake, for Geo[rgii].

[s] *Thompson*, p. 88. *Poulson*, ii., 212.

[t] St. Mary's, Castlegate, York, 1745, Oct. 20, Mary, wife of Mr. Bernard Awmond, buried; 1656, April 5, Mr. Bernard Awmond, buried.

BELTHAM CUM ALIIS
COTTINGHAMENSIS PAROCHIÆ PRIVILEGIORUM
ADVERSUS OPPRESSIONES
PONDEROSI PESTILENTISSIMIQUE
CONSERVATORES.
LAUS TIBI DOMINE!

The other is this epitaph, upon a great black marble altar grave-stone, on the south side of the church:

Here lyeth the body of Sr. William Wise. late of Beverley, in the county of York, who dyed the 2d day of April, 1677.[u]

The chancel is a larg, capacious, and neat building, tho' now carelessly and negligently kept. In the roof of it, in four great pains, are the following four coats of armes, old painted, with the proper supporters.

France and England, quarterly.

Under-written thus:

Henricus. Rex Angliæ.

The second is thus:

Or, a lion rampant gules.

And under-written thus:

Jacobus, Rex Scotorum illustrissimus, anno 18.

The third is thus:

Or, a lion rampant gules, impaling France and England, quarterly.

Under-written thus:

Margareta primo genita Henrici. Regina Scotorum præclarissima.

And the fourth is the armes of the causer of all these, with a miter thereon.

Quarterly 1 and 4, argent a nagg's head sable, 2 and 3, azure a chevron between three fishes erect argent. (Forman).

Thus under-written:

Andreas Episcopus Moravien, anno consecrationis.

[u] 1654, September 26, Right Worshipful William Wise, Esq., the recorder, and Mrs. Frances Hartforth, of York, married. St. Mary's, Beverley.
It appears by an indenture of 25th Feb., 1655-6, that she was widow of Richard Hartforth, and had a house in Jubbergate, York (which Sir W. Wise sold for 50*l.*, 15th Nov., 1670), and near one hundred acres of land in Barleby, from her former husband.
1663-4, Feb. 19th, Frances, wife of William Wyse, esq., recorder of the town of Beverley, buried. St. Mary's, Beverley. 1677, April 12, Sir William Wyse, buried at Cottingham.

With the following little coat of armes on the both sides of the greater :

> Argent, a saltire engrailed sable.

And on the side of a whole balk is this furder inscription concerning the sayd bishop :

> Andreas Forman, Episcopus Moravien[v] et commendatorius de Pettenven[w] in Scotia, et Cottingham, hanc trabem cum novâ tecturâ fieri fecit, per Magistrum Gilbertum Hauden nostrum procuratorem. Anno salutis humanæ mvᶜiv.

Hard by, in the same roof, in less and more contemptible scutchions, is to be seen the following coats of armes, with inscriptions also, which I could not read.

> Gules, on a bend arg. [sic] three eagles with double heads displayed (qu. proper), or.
> Fitz Hugh. Three chevrons braced in base or, a chief of the last.
> Tilleyole. Arg., three chaplets gules.

Under all these, on both sides of the chancel, is yet standing, and yet to be seen, thirty-two prebendarys' or channons' seats, sixteen on the one side and sixteen on the other, with seven other such like seats, but smaller, and lower than the rest, on the south wall. In the turning up of the seats in most of which canons' stalls is discover'd great coats of armes, curiously cut on the lower sides. On the right side, or south side, beginning at the chancel door, and so proceeding, they follow thus :

1. Three bars.
2. An eagle, double-headed, and displayed.
3. Six lozenges pierced. 3, 2, 1.
4. A fess nebulee between six crosses crosslet fitchée. [Lovel].
5. Pool. A fess between three lions' faces.
6. Scroop. A bend.
7. A cross moline. [Monceaux].
8. Boynton. A fess between three crescents.
9. Peche. A fess between two chevrons. [Lisle? who married De la Pole].
10. A fess dancette between six crosses, four in chief, two in base. [Engaine].
11. A chevron between three covered cups.
12. A lion rampant, within a bordure charged with fourteen cinquefoils.

In the other side of the chancel, beginning at the aforesayd dore, and so proceeding, they follow thus :

1. On a bend, three pairs of wings. [Wingfield, who married Pole, earl of Suffolk].
2. A cross flory. L[d.] Lassels, of Sutton.
3. A fess between six crosses flory.

---

[v] Vulgo Murray.—*Marginal note by Diarist.*
[w] Vulgo Pettenween, a great monastery.—*Ibid.*

4. A lion rampant, crowned. [MORLEY, who married de la Pole].
5. A chevron between three escallops.
6. A cross engrailed. in the dexter quarter a rose. [UFFORD].
7. Chequy, on a bend six (uncertain what)? a bend fretty.
[CHENEY].
8. Six escallops, 3, 2, 1. EASTOFT's armes.

Many are spoiled, and so consumed with age, on both sides, that I could not possibly make anything of them.

Upon the fore-fronts of the great seats, that they lay their books on, is the miter, and the aforesayd bishop's coat of armes in many places.

In the south window of the sayd chancel is yet to be seen the two following coats of armes in great shields:

1. Arg., three fusils in fess gules. [MONTACUTE].

This is under-written thus:

Hen. Earl of Salsbury.
2. Quarterly, 1 and 4 gules. In the first quarter of this was some sort of a cross [query NEVIL.] 2 and 3 chequy, az. and or. [NEWBURGH].

In the east window is a great deal of painted glass, containing the representations of Moses, David, Solomon, and Christ and his apostles, very well done, but somewhat defaced. And, amongst other armes in the sayd window, there are onely these three most visible and plain.

1. S. within a bordure arg., three lions passant guardant or.

This is undoubtedly the armes of Edmund Plantagenet, Earl of Kent, who married Margaret, the daughter and heir of Thomas, Lord Wake; or else is the armes of his son; or perhaps of Thomas Holland, who was Lord Wake in 1397; or of his son, who dyed 1400.[x]

3, 4. Quarterly, first and fourth or a fret azure semee-de-lis. second and third, or three bars sable.
5. Quarterly, first and fourth grand quarterly, first and fourth sable, a tower or, second and third arg., a lion rampant sable, second and third a fret, semee-de-lis (as above). The armes of the family of TOWARS.[y]

[x] Query. of Elizabeth, sister to king Edward IV., wife of John de la Pole, duke of Suffolk. It is a very common thing for *Gules* to become *Sable* through age.
[y] The said coats in the east window follows thus: 1, the three lions; then a fret, with the former three lions, which belonged to a woman and heiress, empareld or quartered with it. 3 and 4, fret as marked 3, 4. The 5 as marked Towars. 6 and 7, two more frets, as 3 and 4.—*Marginal note by Diarist.*
Bartholomew Towers, of Leeds, was living 26th Nov.. 1690, when his father-in-law, Christopher Richardson, alderman of Hull, and apothecary, made his

The next and last thing observable in this church, I mean the chancel thereof, is the monument of a monk, in a shaven crown, upon a great black gravestone, with his effigies thereon, all en-layed at length, in brass, with the following inscription on, in brass, round about him :

Hujus* erat rector domus Nicholaus humatus, factor et erector nida quæso beatis pono vices Christi gestans dedit prebendas isti Beverlaci sex famelicos pallit rixantes pacificavit, nudos armavit fæneratum nam gemmavit sed quia labe carens sub cælo nullus habetur. Natum virgo parens animæ pete propiti-etur. Obiit in die mensis Junii, anno Dom. m.ccc.lxxxiii.ª

Bordering upon this church-yard did Mr. Wardel,⁵ of Hul-bank, whose lady is now living, erect and build an alm-house for six poor folk, and intended nobly to endow the same, but that he dy'd before that it was finished. But tho' that he did not endow it, yet the aforesayd number of poor people doe live therein. He built also a small school-house near adjoyning,ᶜ and did actualy

will. Hannah, his wife, died 3rd December, 1678, aged 33, M I at St. Peter's, Leeds. Her sister, Sarah Richardson, was wife of Charles Mann, of Eltofts, buried 23rd October, 1723, at St. Maurice, York, but had no children. Her sister, Dinah Richardson, married Mark Kirkby, of Hull, merchant (will 16th September, 1712), a native of Cottingham, to the parish school of which he gave "a close called Paradise, with three stray of meadow in the Inglemire, a turf pit, or graft, in the common, and two gates in the Firth," now represented by sixteen acres of land. From his two daughters and co-heirs descend Torre of Snydall, and Sykes, of Sledmere, baronet.
ˢ This epitaph, as the scholar will at once see, is in hexameters, and has been given by the Diarist in a very incorrect way. Since the time of De la Pryme the inscription has been mutilated, and it has fared even worse in an attempted restoration, which took place some years ago. Anything more ill-advised could scarcely be imagined. This fanciful restoration has rendered it impossible to present the inscription to the reader as it once stood. The fol-lowing is a conjectural restoration of it.

Hujus erat rector domus hic Nicholaus humatus
Factor et erector, de Luda, quæso beatus.
Porro vices Christi gestans dedit ecclesiarum
Præbendas isti Beverliaci, quoque Sarum.
Famelicos pavit, rixantes pacificavit,
Nudos armavit fænoratam rem geminavit,
Sed quia labe carens sub cælo nullus habetur
Natum, Virgo parens, animæ pete propitietur.
Etc.

On May 16, 1361, Dan Nicholas de Luda (Louth), chaplain, was instituted to the rectory of Cottingham on the presentation of Edward the Black Prince. On July 23rd, 1355, he was collated to the stall at the altar of St. Catharine, at Beverley.
ª This I do not understand, but I writ it down as it is there to be read.— *Marginal note by Diarist.*
ᵇ 1668, May 21st, John Wardell, of Hull Bank, gent., buried, St. John's, Beverley. 1676, July 22nd, Mrs. Ann Wardell, widow, gent.
ᶜ Of this school-house Mark Kirkby makes mention in his will, as situate in Cottingham church-yard.

endow it with five pounds per ann[um], which is constantly payd; whose arms is over the door, and is as follows:

[Sketch. Gu., three scymetars, or swords, laid fesswise, the handles towards the sinister.]

Yesterday I went upon some business to Hatfield, by Doncaster, where my relations lives, and where I set up a noble monument, in the church, for my father.[d] Amongst others, I went to see old Mr. Cornelius Lee, a man of the finest and exactest symetry of parts that is in the whole world. He told me, in a great deal of other discourse that I had with him, that he had a relation named Mr. Rooth, that was so dull that he could learn nothing at school, nor could scarce read English, being onely one degree from a natural fool, who fell into a violent sickness and feaver when he was about twenty-one years of age, and, in the extremity of his sickness, spoke Latin, and discours'd readily in that language; but, as soon as he was cured, he returned to his aforesayd simplicity and weakness. This he does attest to be a real truth.

He says also that the occasion of the murder of Henry the Fourth, king of France, was his haveing discover'd to James the First, king of England, the design and plot of the gunpowder treason; which discovery the Jesuits took so hainously that they hired Raviliac to stabb him, who accordingly did.

This relation, he says, he had from the mouth of a great popeish lord, in king Charles the First's time, who had it discover'd to him by his confessour. That which makes this very probable is the words of Raviliac, which he utter'd in relation to king Henry, when he was examined, which were, that the king was false-hearted to the catholic cause, that he did not look upon him as one faithfull to their interests, and such like, as is related in many historys.

Yesterday I went to Sutton, in Holderness, to bury a corps for Mr. Oxnard, the minister of that town,[e] who is not well. Sutton is about two miles from Hull, and stands upon a hill of about a thousand acres, encompass'd, formerly, with morasses, but now, for the most part, with low commons and meadows. There was, in antient time, a famous colledge[f] there, for several

[d] This is still in the church.
[e] A Mr. Oxnard occurs as minister of Marfleet in 1687; and Simon Oxnard as instituted incumbent of Waghen, or Wawne, 6th November, 1691.
[f] The chapel or college of St. James. In the 31st year of the pontificate of Walter Gray, 1247, he released to Saer de Sutton all his right to the advowson of the chapel of Sutton. In 1347 Sir John de Sutton, knight, having first

Q

fellows, endow'd with thirty pounds a year, in Harry the Eighths' time, tho' it was then given in to him but at thirteen. All the old building has been pull'd down, time out of mind, and in the place where it stood is built a great house, wherein Mr.......[s] the son of ......, of the south, and parlament man for ...... lives, in whose family it has been three or four generations, which is a very great wonder. Which gentleman has about 500*l.* per year, with the colledg lands, and tythes of the fields of Sutton, etc. The church is built of brick, but for such a little town is pretty larg, great, and handsome. In the quire has been seats for the collegians, turning up like the prebendary's seats in collegiate churches, with the armes of the builders thereon, onely one of which is now remaining, which is a cross flure, which I take to have been the armes of the Lassels.

But, in the very midst of the quire, upon a great antient tomb,[h] lys a knight, all in his armor, with his shield on his left arm, and his armes thereon, which is a lion rampant beyond a dexter bendlet; and on the lower part of the monument, round about, was twelve more coats of armes, some of which are now so very much consumed with time that they are not visible. Those that I could make out are as follows :

1. A plain cross.
2. LUCY. Three pikes haurient.
3. A saltire.
4. Five lozenges conjoined crosswise.
5. [DARCY or SALTMARSH.] Semee de crosses crosslet, and 3 cinquefoils.
6. A fess nebulee between three fleur-de-lis.
7. Barry, three chaplets.
8. A fess dancette between six lozenges.
9. LORD ROSS. Three water bougets.

obtained the king's license, etc., gave the advowson of St. James, of Sutton, which was held of the king *in capite*, for the sustentation of six chaplains, to celebrate every day in the said chapel *pro salute animarum.*

[s] 21st June, 1709, Richard Broadreffe, esq., of Hull, and Elizabeth, his wife, sells the rectory of Sutton, tithes, and site of the college, to Hugh Mason, and trustees, Charles Parr, of York, and Francis Langley, of York.

1740-1, Jan. 12th, Indenture between William Mason, of Hull, clerk, and Andrew Perrott, alderman, touching the rectory of Sutton, the site of the college of the said rectory, 23 acres of arable glebe, 32 acres of meadow, 23 beast gates, Oxlands Close of 30 acres, and Rowbanks, late the estate of Hugh Mason, gent., deceased, father of the said William.

Out of these premises 10*l.* was payable to the curate of Sutton, and 1*l.* 17*s.* 4*d.* fee farm rent to dame Mary Barnardiston.

[h] Poulson (*History of Holderness*, vol. ii., 338), gives a representation of this monument, which, from the arms on the shield, would appear to be that of a Sutton—a lion rampant, oppressed by a bend gobony. That writer adds that the date of the monument, from the style of the armour, is decided by Sir Samuel Meyrick to be that of Sir John de Sutton, who died in the 12th of Edward III., 1338-9, rather than that of his son, who died in the 30th Edward III., 1356-7.

Tradition says that this is the monument of one Sir John Saar,[i] lord of this town, and other lordships adjoyning, who built for himself a great castle in the midst of the carr, about a quarter of a mile to the north of this town, where he liv'd, which is called Castle hill to this day.

But I rather take him to have been Sr. John Meux, lord of this town, Bewick-by-Alburrow, upon the sea side, in Holderness, and other great possessions, who dy'd about the year 1377, and was the last of his name; some of whose ancestors lys interr'd at Alkburrow aforesayd, under a such like monument, with many of the same coats of armes on it, as I have heard. Of this family of the Meux's, see the *Mon. Aug.*, vol. i., p. 704; etc.

In the east window of the chancel of Sutton is this coat of armes—Gules, a lion rampant or in an orl of billets of the second; which seems not to be over one or two hundred years old, tho' perhaps it may be more.

In a window on the north side of the church is the armes of the Percys, viz.—Or a lion rampant azure. And another— Argent bendways three lozenges sable. To whome it belongs I cannot tell. This is all that I found observable in the sayd church.

For this last half year, and above, I have been so exceeding busy in viewing, methodizeing, etc., the old records and antiquitys of this town, that I have not had time to consider of anything that is done elsewhere.

Yesterday, being August 2, 1700, I writ the following letter, word for word, unto the very reverend, and my very good friend, the dean of York.

Very Revnd. Sir,

I have not had the happiness to hear of anything very observable in antiquity since I had the honour to be your company the last time that I was at York. There hath, indeed, since then, been a small canal, or Roman aqueduct, or pipe, discover'd about a mile on this side Lincoln, about a foot underground, and about a foot square in cavity, of Roman brick and tile, and plaister'd within, conveying, in former times, water from a certain spring there, unto the citty; but I am sorry that I can give you no better an account of it. When I had the honour to be at your chamber, I think, to the best of my memory, that you was for fixing of Prætorium at Preston. Yesterday I saw a fine copper medal, lately found in the fields of that town, with an empresse's head on the one side, circumscribed Agrippina August.; and on the other a goddess, with this inscription—Diana Elucinia, and S. C.; which, if I could have purchas'd, I would have sent it to you.

[i] Tradition is true. His name was John (perhaps Meux), Lord Lassels and Baron Sayer; when he liv'd I do not find, but I find one of the same name and titles that dy'd about the year 1200.—*Marginal note by Diarist.*

I most earnestly beseech your worship that, whereas I am at very great charges in keeping correspondence, and in buying of books, and in carrying on my studdy of antiquitys, even to the danger and hazzard of my own ruin, and the casting of myself into great debts and melancholy, I most earnestly beseech you not to let me fall under the burthen, but, as you have encouraged me, so be pleased to begg of his grace (to whome I present my most humble duty), any the first poor living that falls, that I may be at rest to prosecute my great (and I may realy say to my sorrow), unfortunate studdys.

I most humbly beseech you to aid me herein, as soon as can be, and heartily beggs pardon, for this my great but necessitous boldness.

               I am, very revnd. Sir,

                     Your most humble servt.,

Hull, Aug. 3rd, 1700.   A. P.

To the aforegoing letter*j* that I received from the dean of York, I returned the following answer.

Very Revnd. Sr.,

     I most heartily thank you for the very great honour that you did me in this town, and for presenting my duty to my lord archbishop ; and shall always reckon myself happy in your favour and commands. I thought it would not be very propper for myself to be seen in the matter of the stone coffin, because that I had, half a year before, oftentimes ask'd the price of it, and endeavour'd to have bought it for you ; therefore I got a countryman, one that I could trust, to go and understand the lowest price of it. And when he came there, shee and her friends sayd that it was a valuable rarity, and that the dean of York had been to see it, and that it was so usefull they could not part with it under three or four pounds. and would take no less for it. A day or two after I went and found her in the same tune, so that I left her. The best way to get it would perhaps be to send her some such like old trough for it, and to give her a little money in exchange. I am very much troubled that I should be so much more unfortunate than others, in not being able to get any little liveing, that I might be the more able to serve you and his grace. My most humble duty to his lordship, if you please.

               I am,

              Your most ready and most affectionate servant,

                                 A. P.

[? To Dr. Sloane].

Honoured Sir,

     I most heartily thank you for the new Transaction that you have sent me, tho' I have not yet received it, and especialy for the honour that you have done me in reading my letter before your society, whom I have, and always have had, the greatest respect for of any men in the world. You make me in love with the studdy of shells ; and tho' I cannot be so vain as to flatter myself that I can gather anything new therein, after the ingenious Lister, Llhwyd, Hook, or Woodward, yet, however, I shall augment my own collections thereby, and oblicge my friends. And, as you desire, I will consider Dr. Hook, and

---

j The Diarist has probably inserted the letter referred to in his MS. as was occasionally his practice, but it is not there now. The Dean appears to have been desirous of purchasing the old stone coffin before mentioned at pages 205 and 208.

others, upon this subject, if that the ingenious Woodward do not soon come out, as I hope it will, in whome I doubt not but to have full satisfaction in all the abstruse parts of this curious matter. I would not have desired you to print my letter *verbatim*, but onely for the sake of them monuments therein, because they relate to a gentleman from whome I expect some favour, there being nothing to be had in this town. However, I will not hereafter trouble you with anything but what relates to natural history. I could have added some things to my former letter relating to plants and shells, but, being at work night and day upon the history and antiquitys of this town, I shall, when I see my letter again, give you another thereon, and shall send you the letter that I promiss'd you out of the East Indies.

I am
Your most humble oblieged friend and servant,
A. P.

To the honour'd Doctor Slone.

Honour'd Sir,
I most heartily thank you for the Transaction that you sent me. There are several people in this town and country great admirers of them, and that constantly buys them.

I have sent you a small rose of petryfy'd shel-fish, and some things that I know not what names to give to them. I would have sent more, if that I thought they were worthy of your acceptance and charge, and with them a letter containing a larg account of the quarrys out of which I got them, and a new solution of their phenomenon, and of the Noachian deluge, which, if you think worthy to be inserted in your Transactions, I begg that it may have that honour, *verbatim et totaliter*. I put the letter in the post, and both of them into the carrier's hands this morning, but I doubt that they will not come to you till the end of the next week. I will send you the next month the coppy of a very curious letter, out of the East Indies.

I am
Your most humble and oblieged friend and servant,
Hull, Sept. 18, 1700.   A. DE LA PRYME.

To Dr. Johnston.

Honour'd Sir,
Tho' that the long silence that has been betwixt us might justly make it a doubt to one another of us whether we are yet or no in the land of the liveing, yet I hope that these lines will find you as I am. I have been labouring night and day since I writ last unto you, upon the history and antiquitys of this town, and of the six or seven towns in the county thereof, and have carefully seen, perused, and transcribed every record out of the town's hall (where are huge quantitys), that was anything observable, and have searched all printed chronicks and MSS. that I could possibly hear of relating anything concerning the same. After all, I confess myself at a great loss for the book of Meaux, which is in Cotton's library, for Hutton's Analecta, and some few records in the Towar and other places (tho' perhaps, tho' I know it not, I have most things allready that is in them), and knowing that your collections are mighty exact, and contains in them all that can possibly be found in the south, in any place whatsoever, on these subjects, I humbly propose unto you, that if you will be pleas'd to communicate the few things out of your papers that I want concerning this town and county unto me, that I will faithfully and honestly send you everything that I have relating to any town or towns in Yorkshire, or elsewhere, and

shall celebrate and acknowledge everywhere in my book your extraordinary
civility and kindness, as the greatest benefactor, promoter, and encourager of
the work; by, and through whome, and which means, I shall be able to have it
in the press in less than half a year, in folio.

I not knowing how to write or direct this my letter unto you, I was forced
to wrap it in another, and send it to Mr. Coggan, bookseller, in the Inner
Temple Lane, to present it into you.

I am,

Your most humble and affectionate friend and servant

A. P.

Having now gather'd and gotten almost all the antiquitys
that I can relateing to this town and the country round about,
I begin to grow somewhat weary thereof, and am at present
striveing to obtain some liveing or other, where I may live out
of the noise and hurry of the great business that I am now by
my office in this great parish involv'd in; therefore I writ the
following letter to my good friends the Mayor and Aldermen of
this town.

Honoured Gentlemen,

Haveing had the happyness by you to be promoted to the sacred office
and place that I now possess in this church, which, out of respect to my duty
and to your worships, I have (tho' I say it) hitherto faithfully discharged, tho'
it hath been both exceeding troublesome and of but very mean profit unto me,
and having with great labour and pains put the records of the Corporation in
good order, and in many other respects made it my business to serve you and
honour your town in every thing that I could, so by your good connivance and
leave I have almost finish'd and prepared for the press the whole history,
antiquitys, and description thereof in long folio, containing a successive
historical account of its original building, increas, and fortune in warrs, battels,
sieges, revolutions of state and government, &c., from its first building unto this
time, which, when published, will be exceedingly to the honour and glory of
the town, and the future peace, good and welfare thereof.[A] And tho' I have been

---

[A] I had hoped to have been able to have given here some better account
than I can of the De la Pryme MSS. relative to Kingston-upon-Hull, etc.
Through the friendly and obliging assistance of Mr. Alderman Atkinson, of
that place, the town council, at a meeting held on the 5th of August, 1869,
very courteously passed a resolution in my favour, on the motion of the mayor,
(J. Bryson, esq.), seconded by Mr. Richardson, that the town clerk be authorized
to allow me such an inspection as he might think proper of our Diarist's
collections of historical and other local incidents, which he had intended to
publish, in order that I might for myself see if there was anything contained
in them which might be introduced into the notes, or the appendix, to the
Diary now published. The privilege thus intended to be allowed to me, was
not, however, facilitated in the manner which, under the foregoing circumstances, I expected, and, consequently, it was rendered practically inoperative.
It is due, however, to the town-clerk, to observe that he informed me of my in-
correctness in assuming that the corporation was in possession of any original
collection of historical MSS. relative to Hull, by De la Pryme, for that the
document in his possession was only a fair copy of the compilation for the
intended history of Hull. To the civility of Mr. Leng, the bookseller, of Hull,
I am, however, indebted for a sight of what is, no doubt, another copy of the

at great charges in employing my friends at York, London. Oxford. Cambridge, and other places, in searching records there relating to the same, and in running through almost an infinite fateague, night and day, of continual writeing, reading, searching, comparcing, reviewing, and composing of books, records, papers, and deeds, concerning the same, and inserting them into the same : yet I desire nothing at your hands for all these services nor for to enable me to finnish and print them, but onely that as you have interest with your parliament men, and with the Duke of Newcastle, and other nobles, so that you would be pleased to send up letters by Alderman Carlil to them in my commendation, and to begg of them to procure for me either from the King, or the Lord Chancellor, the very first moderate living that falls in his Majesty's gift, which is a thing that they will readily grant. And at the same time, I will second the same in my letters to the Bishop of York, and to the Duke himself, to whome I shall present some books that I have lately been concern'd in. I humbly conceive that this request is not unreasonable, else I would not have moved it unto your worships. Mr. Prat,[1] of Boswell, by York, upon his peruseing and puting in order the records of that famous and old citty, about eighteen years ago, desired the same favour at their hands, and got the sayd living that he now possesseth. And I earnestly beseech your worships not to deny me herein, that I may be speedily the better to serve you, and to finnish those books and papers, to your honour and glory, that I have under my hands, and thereupon shall ever remain,

Your worships' most obliged humble servant

April the 5th, 1701.   A. P.

Which letter their worships took very kindly, and thereupon writt up to London in the following words.

[*Their letter is not given.*]

same MS. It is intituled *The History, Antiquities, and Description of the Town and County of Kingston-upon-Hull, or the Annals of the said Town, containing a Successive and Historical account of its originall Building, increase, and fortune, and all the most observable things that have happened therein or related thereto, from its first building unto this time : Collected out of all the Records, Charters, Deeds, and Evidences of the said Town. By Abraham de la Prime, Reader and Curate of the High Church of the Holy Trinity of the said Town.*"

Mr. Frost (in his *Hist. Hull*, 1827, p. 3), alludes to the foregoing compilation as being "the first attempt to give a detailed history of Hull," and says it formed the basis and ground-work of all subsequent accounts and histories of the town. Afterwards, however, he states that it had been suggested to him that archbishop Bramhall probably occupied himself on the history of Hull prior to the time when De la Pryme wrote, viz., *circa*. 1643. Gent, Hadley, Tickell, Symons, and others, have all drawn largely upon De la Pryme's industry. Mr. Frost also observes that Wm. Chambers, esq., M.D., a gentleman of considerable talents and eminence in his profession, compiled, with great apparent fidelity, from the records of the corporation, a collection of annals of the town of Hull, from the earliest times to the year 1766, about which period it appears to have been written, and that the MS. had been entrusted to him since his (Mr. Frost's) own *Notices* were printed, by Henry R. Bagshawe, esq., of Lincoln's Inn, barrister-at-law.

A longer notice of De la Pryme's collections for the history of Hull will be found in the Appendix.

[1] Thoresby mentions having at York, August 1st, 1695, "found Parson Pratt, an antiquary, and had much of his company."—*Diary*, i., p. 307.

He had a small collection of antiquities.

See him mentioned *antea*, p. 177. Boswell is Bossall.

At the same time I writ the following letter to the Duke of Newcastle.

May it please your Grace,

I having been some few years an inhabitant of the famous town of Kingston-upon-Hull (that is blessed in your Excellencies' government of it) and the honourable Royal Society having printed several of my communications unto them, I have here, as I take myself in duty bound, made bold, with all humility, to lay some of them as a present at your grace's feet, knowing your grace's happy genius and great ingenuity in such things. I have also written and almost finnished the history, antiquitys, and description of the famous town of Kingston-upon-Hull, in larg folio, from its first building unto this day, and humbly beggs that I may have the honour and happiness (when I am in a capacity to get it printed) to dedicate it unto your honourable name and memory, that you not only be famous, as you are, to this age for all noble and princely vertues, but may be so, also, to all future ages and prosterity for ever; which is the humble request and endeavour of your grace's

Most humble, most obedient,

and most devoted servant,

[A. P.]

At the same time also I writ the following letter to the Bishop of York.

May it please your Grace,

I have made bold upon the coming of this worthy gentleman to London, to prevail upon him, if that he have the happiness to see you, to present my most humble duty unto you, with some Transactions of the Royal Society, in which they have been pleased to print several letters of mine, and which whole society have honour'd me with their public thanks for my communications unto them, to whome I shall continnue every month to send some very observable or curious things or other. I have also written and almost finnish'd the whole history, antiquitys, and description of this town, in larg folio, which I shall print as soon as ever I am able. I have acquainted his highness the duke of Newcastle, our governour, with the above mention'd particulars, and also writ of the same to the parliament men of this town, Sr. William St. Quintin and Mr. Masters. In short, having lived here almost three years in a state of great fatcngue and little profit, but, (tho' I say it,) with an universal love and good conscience, I humbly begg of your grace and his highness that you would be pleased speedily to procure for me from his majesty (which I humbly concieve you may very easily do,) the infallible gift of the very first moderate liveing that falls in the king's presentation, and it will not only put me into a capacity of doing more good, (which I glory in,) and of carrying on of my most laborious studdys of antiquitys, but also of rendering myself more fully, in every thing to the utmost of my power,

Your grace's most dutifull son and servant,

A. P.

To the honble. Sir. Wm. St. Quintin, and William Masters esq,, humbly present.

Honourable gentlemen,

I reckon it not one of the least of the favours of my life that I have the happiness to be known unto you, to have lived now almost three years in your town, and to have, by your good connivance and leave, perused all the old records of this famous corporation, put them into order and drawn out therefrom the whole history, antiquitys, and description thereof, in larg folio, to the great honour of the town, and the future peace, glory, and welfare thereof. And, that I may be in a capacity to finnish and print it, I have writ to the bishop of York to procure for me the first moderate liveing that falls in the king's gift, which I humbly concieve may be easily obtained. I have also writ to the duke of Newcastle concerning the same ; the coppys of my letters to them I here send you, and do earnestly beseech you to furder the same that I may be in a capacity the better to serve you and this famous corporation. .... *[here a blank occurs.]* therefrom and from multitudes of others at York, London, Oxford, Cambridge, and elsewhere, the whole history, antiquitys, and description of this famous town, to the great honour, glory, and future peace and welfare thereof. which, as soon as I am able, I will print in larg folio. for all which I most humbly begg but this favour at your hands, that, knowing you have interest with the duke of Newcastle, that therefore you would be pleased to procure him to beg of the king, or the lord chancellor. the very first living that is of any moderate vallue, that falls in his majesty's gift, for me (which, as I concieve, will easily be granted,) that I may be the better enabled to carry on my studdys, to the honour of this town, and the more perfectly to finnish and publish the history thereof. I have written to the b[ishop] of Y[ork] to be pleased to move also in this cause for me, and in my letter to the d[uke] of N[ewcastle,] (coppys of all which I have here sent you,) I have somewhat tho' obscurely hinted at the same. I most humbly beseech you, by all that is dear unto you, to obtain the above sayd favour as speedily as you can,

For your most humble &c.

Kingston-upon- Hull,

Wee, whose names are subscribed, do very well know Mr. Abraham Pryme, clerk, and have such an esteem of him for his learning and vertue, and prudent behaviour and loyalty to the present government, that we do not doubt, whereever he shall be placed, he will do God and his church good service, and give great satisfaction to all good men, as he has done whilest curate here. Witness our hands the 24th of April, 1701.

ROBERT BANKS, Vicar of St. Trinity & Prebendary of York.
RICHARD KITSON, B.D. and Lecturer of the sayd town.
NATHANIEL LAMB, Minister of St. Mary's.

DANIEL HOAR, MAYOR.
PHILIP WILKINSON,
SIMON SISSON,
ROBERT TRIPPET,
WILLIAM HYDES,
RICHARD GRAY,
} ALDERMEN.

JOHN CHAPPELLOW,
BENJAMIN WADE,
RICHARD BEAMONT,
ETC.

[After inserting two printed papers, one, " A word to the wise," dated 29 Jan., 1701, and the other "Considerations on the present posture of affairs," dated Feb. 1, 1701, the diarist proceeds.]

The aforegoing papers gives a sufficient idea of the state of Europe upon the meeting of the parliament, and the king layd most passionately before them the security of the protestant religion, the settlement of the crown, and the safety of the nation upon the French king succeeding to the crown of Spain. Never was there more need of a good parliament than now, and scarce ever had we a worse. Instead of falling to business they begun to

quarrel with one another about the silly business of elections. Sir
Edward Seymor, a man that has been famous in the house of
commons many years, one of the old East Indy company, and exceeding gilty of bribery himself, crys out first against the new East
Indy company, how they had bribed in the elections of this session ;
thereupon impeaches Sheppard and his sons, with many others of
the same, and blew the house of commons into such a heat
that they sent them to the Towar. But, being heated, they then
condemn'd the treaty of partition as mere nonsence and stuff,
basely reflected upon the king for the same, and Jack How,[m] in
particular, sayd that his majesty had made a fellonious treaty to
rob the king of Spain of it's dues and rights. And furder had the
impudence to say that the king of Spain had not made the sayd
will, if that the king had not made that base and scandalous treaty.
Thereupon they impeach'd the earl of Portland that sign'd it, tho',
to behold their great impartiality, they sayd nothing to the earl of
Jersey, secritary Vernon, or others that were equaly concerned
in it. Then they impeached Russel, earl of Orford, the lord
Sommers, and Montague, earl of Halifax, for many frivolous and
vexatious things not worth mentioning, which clearly shew'd
their spight, malice, and vilany. And for two months together
they did nothing but scold, quarrel, and contend one with another,
about the aforesay'd things, neglecting all manner of the necessary
business of the nation. The Dutch writ memorials and letters to
the king and them of what great danger not onely they but
this nation and the protestant religion was in, yet, for all they
heeded none of them, but went on in their villanys, till the whole
nation was enraged against them. As for the king's friends that
were in the house, they could not [stay] the current of the inundation, do what they could, so that they were forced to be quiet.
At last the Kentish men petitioned them to consider the good of

[m] John Grubham Howe, esq., M.P. for the county of Gloucester, obtained
the manor of Langar, county of Notts (where he fixed his abode), by marrying
Annabella, illegitimate daughter, but coheir, of Emanuel Scrope, lord Scrope
of Bolton, and earl of Sunderland. (The said earl having no issue by his wife,
lady Elizabeth Manners, settled his estates upon his natural children, by Martha
Jones, and the only son of this connection dying unmarried, in 1646, the three
daughters of the same became coheirs). In 1663, Charles II., granting to Mrs.
Howe the precedency of an earl's legitimate daughter, she became, thencefor-
ward, lady Annabella Howe. Of this marriage there were four sons and five
daughters ; the eldest son, sir Scrope Howe, born November, 1648, was elevated
to the peerage of Ireland, 16th May, 1701, as baron Clenawly, county Fermanagh, and viscount Howe. The second son, to whom reference is made by the
Diarist in the text, was the right hon. John Grubham Howe, M.P. for Gloucestershire. He made a distinguished figure in parliament in the reigns of king
William and queen Anne, and was remarkable for his strenuous opposition to a
standing army.

the nation &c., which they took so hainously that they committed [them] to the gaithouse, calling them factious, seditious, mutinous and rebellious fellows. But, hearing that the citty of London and many other countys were also about petitioning to the same purpose, they not [only] grew a little calmer, but also the king's party took heart. Whereupon the lord Hartington told Seymour that he was as guilty as anybody in briberys, and that he had sent Sheppard to the Tower for nothing but to save himself from going thither. Upon that the house took it very ill, and cry'd out "to the barr, to the barr," but he, clapping his hand on his sword swore G——d——them all, he'd be the death of the first man that offer'd to bring him to the barr, which made them all mute. Soon after this, that impudent fellow Jack How (who is brother to Sr. Scroop How who usualy, when he sees him begin to stirr, crys out "now, what is that impudent son of a w—— going to say, if he begin there's nobody must put a word in but himself," &c.,) got a copy of verses upon the parliament which was cleav'd upon the door. He call'd this a libell, and brought it, in a great passion, into the house, and made..................... [imperfect—inserted—" the Kentish petition," at the quarter ses-[sions held at Maidstone 29 April, 13 Wm. III.] The worthy gentlemen of Kent, who, as they had always in former times the honour to lead the van of our armies for the good of the nation, so now, in this seditious and mutinous parliament, con-sidering the strang doings therein, and the danger of the nation, how that it would be ruin'd if they went on in their unwarantable proceedings, assumed their antient honour, composed the afore-say'd petition, signed it, as aforesayd, and sent the same to their representatives in parliament by five of their countrymen, gentlemen of great estates, whose names were William Cole-peper, esq., Thomas Colepeper, esq., David Polhill, esq., Wil-liam Hamilton, esq., Justinian Champneys, esq., which, being by them deliver'd to one of their representatives, he presented it to the house, who were exceedingly enraged thereat, and, calling the five gentlemen in, ask'd them if that were their hands, to which they all unanimously answer'd in the affirmative; whereupon they were severely abused, and reprimanded, and committed to the custody of a sergeant-at-armes, and soone after to the gait house, without any warant or commitment in writing, as the law requires, and there they remain'd until the prorogation of the parliament. But, in the meantime, several of the house of com-mons, dealt privatly with 'em to have them begg pardon, or sub-mit themselves to the house, but they totaly refused, answering that they would make them guilty of some crime against the laws of the land, which they were sure they were not guilty of in what they had done. And their healths were daily drunk with that of the fouer lords, under the name *Cater* and *Cinque*, by the whole nation, and even in taverns and coffee-houses, in the very presence of the members of parliament, while it was sitting. But, after the parliament was risen, then they were all acquitted and set at liberty, but would not pay a farding to the sorjeants. Then their healths were drunk openly by every one, and [they] was hugg'd and carres'd from one end of the citty to the other; were treated one day by five hundred gentlemen of the citty at a treat which cost so many guinneys, at which treat was present nine earls. Then they were treated by the company of Fishmongers, or Ironmongers, I have forgot whether, and made free, and, haveing stay'd in the citty about a fortnight or three weeks, went out of the citty in the night, to avoyd tumult, and, proceeding forward to their own country, were met by four hundred coaches, and a great number of gentlemen on horseback. Since which some of them have sou'd the serjeant-at-armes, upon a clause of the *habeas corpus* act, for not producing the warrant of their commitments, when demanded, and they will certainly cast the serjeants therein.

At the same time that this petition was makeing in Kent, there were the like on foot all over the nation. There was one from Staffordshire in town, ready to be presented, signed with twenty thousand hands. The citty of London also made one, and when it was sign'd, and came to be voted in the common councell whether it should be presented or no, it was carry'd in the negative by the single vote of sir — Bedingfield, one of the councel, and also parliament man for Heddon, to the great grief of the royalists and true patriots.

[Not addressed].

Rev. Sir,

Amongst the multitude of the papers, records, and deeds, that I have been forced to turn over towards my history and antiquities of this town of Kingston-upon-Hull, I have discover'd, under original hands and seals, some of the original indentures and deeds, yet in full vertue and force, of the foundation of a considerable hospital, and the larg endowment of the same in your town, about the year 1622, by one Mr. Edward Latimer, of which yourself, the churchwardens, and others, are perpetual trustees. And tho' all this is nothing to me, yet, being curious of such things, and not being able to know otherwise, I begg of you that you would be pleased to honour me so much as to let me understand whether the sayd hospital has escaped the rapacious hands of sacrilegious times, and whether it yet flourishes, or no; and if the records which I mention may be anything serviceable unto you, they shall be sent by your

Most humble, tho' unknown servant and brother,

A. P.

May it please your Grace.

As the multitude of favours that you have been pleased to honour me with shall never be forgotten, so the last of your's, in condescending to write on my behalf to his grace the duke of Devon[shire], shall always possess my soul with the greatest thankfulness that can be, for, by the blessing of God, and your kindness, it was that the duke readily granted my request. The liveing of Thornⁿ is a donative, and so dos require either institution or induction, and, my presence being necessary amongst them, I am forced to be in a great hurry, otherwise I would have immediatly wated upon your grace, to render your grace my most humble thanks by word of mouth, and to begg your blessing upon all my ministerial indeavours.

I am your grace's most obliged, most affectionate,

And most obedient son and servant,

ABR. PRYM.

[The original paper, of which the following is a copy, has been inserted in the Diary].

Oct. 16, 1701.

I, Abraham de la Pryme,ᵉ clerk, now to be admitted to serve the cure of the church of Thorn, in the diocese of York, do declare that I will conform to the Liturgy of the Church of England as it is now by law established.

ABRAHAM PRYME.

Seal of Archbishop Sharp.	These are to certify that this Declaration was subscribed before us by the sᵈ. Abraham de la Prime, when he was admitted to serve yᵉ cure above mentioned. Given at oʳ. manʳ. of Bishopthorpe, under oʳ. hand and seal manuall, the day and year above written.ᵖ

JO. EBOR.

Which sayd Abraham de la Pryme did, within yᵉ time limited by yᵉ Act in that case made and provided, on a Lord's day, during Divine Service, to wit, on yᵉ 13th of November, 1701, publickly read yᵉ aforegoing certificate and declaration in yᵉ church where he dos officiate, before yᵉ congregation there assembled. In witness whereof, wee, his auditors, have hereunto set our hands, yᵉ day and year above written.

JOHN SMYTH.   JNO. WILBURN.

Dear Friend,

I have your two letters before me concerning the prince of Wales, and must needs thank you for the surprizeing newse in the latter of them—that the French king should have the impudence, contrary to the treaty of Reswick, and other secret allyances, to trump him up at this time of day, and imperiously proclame him the soveraign of these dominions. I am very sorry that your sentiments of that prince is not the same as mine, for I think that I have more reason to believe him suppositious than ever can be brought to prove him real; and because that you so earnestly demand of me what I have to say thereupon, I

ⁿ In the parish register of that place is the following entry, in the Diarist's own writing.—"1701, 1 Sept., Abr. de la Pryme obtin. Donationem Hujus Eccles. de Thorn."

ᵉ Prime has been turned into Pryme here.

ᵖ "Oct. 16, 1701.—Abrahamus de la Pryme, Art. Bac., admissus fuit ad inserviendum curæ animarum in ecclesia de Thorn."—York Registry.

will here freely give you my opinion of him, but must conjure you, as you love your friend, not to shew anybody these lines but your two good brothers, whome I very much respect, for their prudence and faithfull services unto me. I desire you to do me this kindness, not out of any fear of any man, but out of ease and quiet to myself, who dos not love to have my name publick in such state matters. It is well known that supposititious princes is no new thing. Many historys mentions such being trump't upon the world, and even ours, of this nation, hath two or three well-known relations thereof. And did not a former queen, Mary (who is as infamous in history as the latter will be), offer to put a like trick upon the nation ; pretended to be with child, and of a son too, made prayers be made and thanks given for the same all England over, ... that the nation might not want a prince, and the catholick cause a supporter? And this had been effected and brought about, but that God was pleased to strike her husband's (king Philip's), heart with so much amaze and astonishment thereat, that he refused to let such an impudent cheat be put upon the kingdom, which was honestly and nobly done by him. The whole story of which you may read more at larg in Fox's Martyrology, and other credible historians. Why should you think it strang, then, that another queen, of the same name, should offer such a thing again? Was there not the same need? Was there not the same occasion? Was not the mighty Babel of popery to be establish'd now as well as formerly? And this the only way left to bring their mighty designs about? And is not the circumstances of the breeding of the former pretended prince as like those of the latter as anything can be? And perhaps, if king James had been as honest as king Philip, we had been no more troubled with the latter than with the former. .... The duke succeeding to the crown, after his brother's decease, and being resolved to establish popery, knew that all his indeavours towards the same would signify nothing unless that he had a son to support it after he was gone. Thereupon, as soon as ever he was well setled in the kingdome, the monks and freers, and the rest of the bald-pated tribe, begun to fling out many prophesys, revelations, and visions of a prince that should be born to the king in his old age. Upon the pillars of the kingdom should for ever remain how that miracles were not ceas'd, and that God would now, as well as he had done of old, quicken dead flesh, and grant a child to their majestys about the time that the sun should enter into the tropic of Cancer. Upon this, wagers ensued amongst the popeish priests of ten, nay, ten guinneys to one, that it should be a son. Masses were publickly commanded and sayd for the young bantling, and prayers commanded in all churches, to thank God for the same. The pope sent over consecrated clouts for the brat, part of the Virgin Mary's smock to wrap it in, and part of her milk to suckle it with ; and the lady of Loretto, like the oracle of Delphos, prophesy'd that for certain it should be a son. ....

The Prince of Orange, in one of his declarations, soon after his landing, promised to make out the birth of the prince spurious, and it came to all, he either could not do it, or, however, did not do it, which is much the same, for, as it is in law, *Quod non patet non est*. But pray, seing that none of the lords or commons doubted of it, or required it at his hands, which, if they had, he was ready to do, what need was there of such a thing? Besides, upon his pretended father's abdication of the crown, and the settling of the succession upon another head, and the makeing all papists incapable of ever succeeding, there was no manner of need to go about so useless and ridiculous a subject ; and since that they have lately, the last year, excluded the house of Savoy, the duchess dowager of Orleans and her children, Edward prince palatine of the Rhine and his numerous offspring, whose births were never question'd, and that for nothing but their being papists, and consequently sworn enemys both to the church and state of this land, why should any one pretend to insist more upon the prince of Wales than them? As to the depositions you tell me of, I saw them twelve years ago ; they signify little or nothing, being *coram non judice*, and so not valid in law. But, suppose they were, they are not direct to the business and point in hand. But, suppose furder, if they were that they are not to be trusted, they proceeding most of them from known papists, whome their priests had beforehand prepared for the business, and the other few, that came from protestants. were known to come from such who were meer court weathercocks, and vallued oaths no more than their honestys.[q]

To the Honoured Dr. Sloan.

Thorn, Febr. 2d, 1701-2

Honr^d. Sir.

According to my promiss, I have sent you by the last carrier a box with a score or two of those sort of cones in it that are so frequently digged up in these Levels, concerning which I gave you my furder thoughts in my last.

In the same box I have sent you also the following things: a bottle of Nostock, or that hitherto unknown substance that is called Star Slough, or Star Shot Gelly, and Nostock, by Paracelsus, from Nore, *nasus*, and the Teutonic stecken, *pungere*, *quia fœtido odore nares ferit*. Robertus de Fluctibus says that it is, what is commonly called, a substance that falls from the starrs, and thereupon adds that, as he was one evening walking in the field, he had the happiness to see a starr shoot or fall not far from him, and that, after some seeking, he found a great lump of the usual gelly, which had many black spots in it ; and, looking by chance yesterday in the learned Chauvin, I was sorry to find him give the same origin thereof. Indeed I could wish, with all my heart, that it was the product of a star, or the *flos Cœli*, as some call it, for then I might, I think, with some reason, expect it to be impregnated with some of those wonderfull vertues that Paracelsus and others have ascribed unto it. The ingenious Borellus tells us how mightily the chemists prize it, pretending that they can draw an insipid menstruum therefrom that shall raddicaly dissolve gold ; and I remember that, when I learned that noble science with Seignior Vigani,[q] he preachd us a whole lecture of the virtues of this wonderfull substance, but was so ingenuous as to confess that he never made tryal of the same. My lord Verulam was a most acute man, and one of the most ingenious that this nation ever bred ; yet, in Mr. Bushel's extract of the Abridgment of his Philosophy, there is such an odd account of a certain strang stone that his lordship made out of this and other substances, that I cannot but set it down, which he presented unto prince Henry, son of k[ing] J[ames] the 1st, in the following words.

" Most Royal S^r.,

Since you are by birth the prince of your country, and your vertues the happy pledge to our posterity, and that the seignory of greatness is ever attended more with flatterers than faithfull friends and loyal subjects, and therefore needeth more helps to discern and pry into the hearts of the people than private persons, give me leave, noble S^r. (as small rivulets run to the vast ocean to pay their tribute), so let me have the honour to shew your highness the operative quality of these two triangular stones (as the first fruits of my philosophy), to immitate the pathetic motion of the loadstone and iron, altho' made up by the compound of meteors (as star-shot gelly, and other such like magical ingredients, with the reflected beams of the sun), on the purpose that the warmth distilled into them, through the moist heat of the hand, might discover the affection of the heart by a visible sign of their attraction and appetite

---

[p] There is a publication styled—*A Chain of Facts in the Reign of King James II., being an exact Narrative of every transaction preparatory to, and at that laboured event, the birth of a pretended Prince of Wales in the year* 1688, 8vo., wrapper, 70 pages, 1747.

[q] See *antea*, p. 25.

to each other, within ten minnits after they are layd upon a marble table or the theater of a looking glass."

Which pretious stones the said Mr. Bushel says that he was never quiet in mind untill that he had procured them, after the prince's decease, of Mr. Archy Prymrose, his page, but adds nothing furder about them.   However, I hope I may have the boldness to say that, if there ever were any such such real jewels, that they had something of more extraordinary vertue in them than any that could proceed from this gelly, or else were but of little worth.

I think that I have formerly read in a book of the learned Dr. Merril's, a once famous member of your honourable society, what this wonderfull substance is. in the following words :—" Stella cadens est substantia quædam alba et glutinosa plurimis in locis conspicua quam nostrates Star Faln nuncupant, creduntque multi originem suam debere stellæ cadenti hujusque materiam esse ; sed Regiæ Societati palam ostendi solum modo oriri ex intestinis ranarum a corvis in unum locum congestis, quod alii etiam ejusdem Societatis viri præstantissimi postea confirmarunt."

The substance he means is undoubtedly that which is all over England called star-shot gelly, but to his and others their origin thereof I cannot yield, unless that for the same thing there may be different causes, and that the froggs spawns in the warm south in October or November, which they do not do here in the cold north untill March and April following.   And as for their spawn I am sure our country crows will not touch it.

Sir, this strang substance is never found in this country but in the very beginning and end of winter, when the days are very warm and the nights pretty sharp, when there is no such thing as frogg spawn to be seen or heard of ; and I have always observed that it is most common upon bank and dike sides against the sun, especialy where it has shone pretty hot the day before ; and, at last, after having gather'd many hundred lumps of it, to try experiments upon with alcalis and acids, I found oftentimes small parts, as if they were of worms, amongst them, very pellucid or transparent, and united to the verry gelly itself.   This made me search more narrowly into the origin thereof, and then I discover'd that, in the beginning of winter, when there was a fine hot sunshine day, that many of the great sorts of earth-worms would creep out of their holes to warm and comfort themselves, but, being benum'd by the suddain setting of the sun, and the approach of cold, and not able to get into their holes again, they are, by the sharp frost of the following night, frozen to death, and their bodys all bursts, swells, expands, and becomes a perfect gelly, which soon turns into water, and disappears.   I have, in gathering of the sayd gelly, oftentimes found some worms half got into their holes, half out, the uppermost part of them all gellify'd and expanded ; then, opening the grass with my knife, I have found another part, that was a little within the ground, white, as if it was boil'd, and a third part, a little deeper, natural, and all strongly adhering one to another. Some that have been all gellify'd I have oftentimes (when they are taken fresh the next morning), opened out to the length of four or five inches.   Others, when the frost was not strong enough perfectly to gellify them, have been whiteish, as if boil'd, not very transparent, and exactly half gelly half worm, one part pretty thoroughly dissolved and another part not.   I have also oftentimes found others lying at the very roots of the grass, and there being frozen and gellify'd, it has all bursten upwards, because that there was not room enough beneath for it to expand in.   Some of these greater lumps of gelly that are now and then to be found, may perhaps have been freggs, that uither have been surprized as before, or else as they lay at the roots of the grass, or in bank sides, where they commonly hide themselves all winter; for the learned Helmont says, that froggs digged up out of the earth in winter, and expos'd to the frost, will turn into lumps of transparent gelly.   But I must needs confess that I never found any the least member of that creature in the many hundreds of lumps that I have gather'd with my own hands.

Haveing put the sayd gelly into bottles, and letten it stand a week or two, it all turns into a water of a soure tast, and a faint, nasty smell, well answering the derivation of the aforegoing word that Paracelsus gave it ; but. being let stand a year or more, it becomes purely insipid and inoffensive, as this is that I have sent you in the bottle.

I have here, withall, furder sent you a specimen of Aparine Plinii, well pictur'd and described by Johnston upon Gerrard, but not found by the industrious Mr. Ray, or any of our learned botanists, that I have heard of, growing in England. I got it plentifully in a garth of Richard Rogison's, of Broughton, in Lincolnshire, amongst the corn.   In another paper I have sent a sort of sissil stone, easily divisible into thin plates, frequently found in the plaster of Paris pitts that are here in our neighbourhood, which, whether it be the old fossil vitrum of the ancients, or Muscovian glass, or what it's name is, I should be very glad to know.

There are so many sorts of fungi and tubera that I do not know how to name them, some of which, not hitherto taken notice of by any author, are very observable, of which I will instance, at present, in no more than fragments of two that I have sent you.   The first of which, a four-square piece of exceeding lightness, and a curious fine texture, belonged to a fungus or tuber which may be called the biggest of all others.   It grows from a small thready root to the roundness and biggness of a great bomb.   This to which the specimen did belong I plucked up with my own hands, and, with a sharp [knife]. and a plank to compress it, I cut it into a square of about a foot every way, which was of a most lovely russit colour.   Which great rarity being accidentally pull'd in pieces. I have sent you part thereof, which has lost much of its colour that it had some years ago.

The other round substance is the bottom part of a great cup mushroom, or fuz, which, when fresh and in full perfection, with the sides riseing up round about from the bottom, like a cupp, will hold a quart of water, after a shower, many of which I have formerly got upon the woulds, in Lincolnshire, in the hedges.

Lastly, to help to fill up, I have put into the box a piece of the black oak that is digged up in this country, observable for its colour and hardness.   All which things I hope will come safe to your hands, and I wish may be acceptible to you.

                                               I am your, &c.

To Dr. Slone.

                                               Febr. 26, 1701-2.
Honrd. Sr.
    I not onely heartily thank you for the Transactions you sent me, but also haveing been pleas'd to convince me that those trees, that I called pitch trees, found in the Levels of Hatfield, are one of the sorts of the true fir trees. That which led me into an error was not onely the expressions of some famous authors, who had not accurately enough distinguish'd the trees, but also the defference that I would fain have had to the honour of the most famous Cæsar, who so positively says that no firs grow in Brittain, tho' indeed, I might, with reason, have given as little heed to him in that as to the next trees that he mentions.   I mean the beech, which he totaly excludes also.   But, in short, it appears that he was no more infallible than I am, and, as certainty is that which we all seek for, and is valuable with all good men, so pray be pleased to insert a line or two into some of your next Transactions, or these very lines that I now write, that I am thoroughly convinced that the trees found in the abovesayd Chace are the true fir, and not the pitch tree, and that the rest of all the particulars of them, upon a fresh and narrow examination of them, are all, to the best of my knowledge, true and certain.

    I thank you also, very heartily, for informing me what the christaline
R

substance was that I sent you, and am also glad to hear that the Aparine Plinii etc., were described in the late volume of the ingenious and accurate Mr. Ray, whose memory deserves, what I hope it will have, eternal knowledge, and whose book I had not as then seen.

As for the Nostock of Paracelsus, as I would not for the whole world impose upon any one unless I was first imposed upon myself, so I do really believe that it is nothing but that contemptible substance or thing that I named unto you. 'Tis strange that it should have been so cry'd up, and have such wonderfull powers ascribed unto it; but indeed ignorance is sometimes the mother of devotion.

I am infinitely obliged to the Royal Society for their pleasing to countenance my studdys, and accept of my weak endeavours. I cannot tell how to shew my thankfulness to the same, furder than my most humble thanks, and the dedicating of the most part of that time that my vacancy from my divine calling will allow me, wholy unto their service, which I shall always most willingly do.

You was pleas'd, I very well remember, about two months ago, in a letter of your's to me, to desire lieve to nominate me one of your honourable fellowship. I writ back that I could never have expected so great an honour, but, since that you was pleased to name it to me, I would not be so rude as to refuse it, but, on the contrary, most gladly receive it. But, having heard nothing from you of that matter since, I am apt to believe that my letter miscarry'd.

The press, indeed, has committed several errors in my letter, which I ascribe to his negligence and my short writeing, the chief of which are these following. [Left blank].

To Dr. Sloan.

Thorn, March 27, 1702.

Honrd. Sr.,

Your's came to my hands some days ago, but, being performing my last duty to a dying friend, I could not have the happiness of answering it untill now.

I most heartily thank you for the last Transaction, and the prodrom of the learned Count Marsigli, tho' I have not, as yet, received them. But, above all, I am most infinitely obliged to the Royal Society for the great honour that they have been pleased to do me, in chuseing me one of their members. Pray be pleased to give my most hearty thanks unto them, and assure them that I will always make it my business to answer the ends of their most noble foundation, and to serve them in everything to the utmost of my power and knowledge.[r]

It is certain that nothing advances knowledge more than a ready and free communication of what passes curious in every part; so, tho' many have writ *de venenis, et de his a canibus rabidis momorsi fuerunt*, as the learned Paræus, Donatus, Codronchus, and others, and have communicated relations of such to

---

[r] March 18, 1701-2. Mr. Cheyne and Mr. De la Pryme were proposed as members, ballotted for, and chosen.

April 1, 1702. A letter was read from Mr. de la Pryme, dated March 27, 1702, wherein he thanked the Society for the honor they had done him in choosing him a member; and gave a particular account of the accidents which happen'd on the biting of a mad dog, etc. He was thanked for this communication.

(From the Journal Book, Royal Society, vol. x., as obligingly communicated to me by Mr. Walter White, assistant secretary, who adds that, finding a blank against the diarist's name, under the head "Admission," he concludes that he never came up to be formally admitted).

The following is a list of papers by Abraham de la Pryme, printed in the Philosophical Transactions and Abridgement.

the learned world, yet give me leave to ad another, that happened in the family
of one of the nearest relations of mine, in these parts, some few years ago,
upon the bite of a madd dog, which may perhaps yield you some speculations
not unacceptable, and help to discover the subtilty of the poison of these
creatures, and how it affects man.

In 1695,[*] my brother had a pretty greyhound bitch, that had whelps. Soon
after came a madd dog, and bit the bitch, unknown to the family. Upon which,
about three weeks after, shee ran mad, and they were forced to kill her, but
saving her whelps, because that no sign of madness appeared in them. About
three weeks more they all pull'd out one another's throats, except one, which,
escapeing, my brother's men vallued and nourish'd, made much of it, and
stroak'd it. At length, perceiving that it could not lap, nor swallow any liquid
thing, they put their fingers in its mouth, and felt its tongue and throat, but
finding nothing wrong therein, as far as they could discover, they let it alone
a day or two longer, and then it ran madd and dyed.

They being thus dead and gone were soon forgot, untill that, about three
weeks after, my brother's head servant, a most strong laborious man, that had
frequently put his fingers into the whelp's mouth, began to be troubled now and
then with an exceeding acute pain in the head, sometimes once, sometimes
twice a day, so very vehement, that he was forced to hold his head with both
his hands, to hinder it from riveing in two, which fitts commonly held him
about an houer at a time, in which his throat would contract, as he sayd, his
pulse tremble, and his eys behold everything of a fiery redd colour. Thus was
he tormented for a whole week together. But, being of a strong constitution,
and returning to his labour, in every interval he sweat and wrought it of without any physic.

But it went far worse with one of his fellow servants, a young apprentice of
about fourteen years of age, who had made as much of the whelp as he, but
was not of so strong a constitution. He was seiz'd also with a pain in his head,
was somewhat feverish, sometimes better, sometimes worse, cough'd much, yet
had a good stomach, eat heartily, but could drink nothing. "I know not what
I ail," says he, "I cannot swallow any beer," etc., and so laugh'd at it. When
he went out of door, tho' there was but a small north wind, yet he always ran
as if it had been for his life; when they asked him why he did so, he told them
he could not tell, but that the wind would needs stop his breath. A day or
two after this he was worse, and vomited a strang nasty sort of matter, like
black blood, which stunk like sallet-oyl, but much stronger, which he did
several times, after which he would be pretty well, and walk about, but most
commonly ran as hard as ever he could; first out of one corner, then into
another, then up stairs, then down again, as if it was for his life. But, upon
the third day of his confinement within doors, he grew perfectly madd; would
start, and leap, and twist his hands and arms together, point at people, and laugh,
and talk anything that came into his mind. In some of his fitts, he was so strong
that he was too hard for four young men to hold him down in the chair where

	Phil. Trans.	Abridg.
Account of some Roman antiquities found in Lincolnshire	xxii. 561	iii. 428
Letter concerning Broughton, in Lincolnshire, with observations on the shell-fish observed in the quarries about that place	xxii. 677	ii. 428
Account of trees found underground in Hatfield Chase	xxii. 980	iv2 272
On the biting of mad dogs	xxiii. 1073	iv2 218
Account of subterraneous trees	xxiii. 1073	iv2 218
Observations concerning vegetation	xxiii. 1214	iv2 310
Observations on water-spouts seen in Yorkshire	xxiii. 1248	iv2 106
Observations on a water-spout seen at Hatfield	xxiii. 1331	iv2 107

[*] The Diarist has recorded this at p. 131 of vol. i. of the MS. Diary, 2 Jan.,
1696, as having occurred "about three months ago."

he sat. But, as soon as they were over, he was lightsom, and laugh'd and talk'd very boldly, but all his discourse was of fighting, and how, if that they would but let him alone, he would leap upon them, and bite, and tear them to pieces. And, when any one sayd unto him that he was sure that he would not hurt him, hee'd been always his friend, he answer'd sharply, that friends and foes were all alike to him, hee'd tear them all in pieces, etc. About an houer after this his fit came again, which soon made him speechless, seiz'd wholy upon his brain, and then he dy'd, just before that the physician came in.

Sr., I will not here presume to search into the particles of this poison, what figure they are of, how they move, how they multiply, how they are able to infect a many of other particles millions of times bigger than themselves, and destroy and dissolve those most curious bodys that are so fearfully and so wonderfully made. Neither will I conjecture why they should ly so long. commonly three weeks or a month, and oftentimes much longer, before that they begin to stir ; why water or beer, or any cold liquid, is against them, etc. ; because that such things cannot certainly be known but by great niceness, and repeated labour and inspection. 'Tis pity that the most noble of creatures lys at the mercy of the most ignoble of particles, and most wonderfull that a few attoms should be able to destroy a whole world, millions of times bigger than themselves.

Sr., I am, etc.

Roger Mowbray, mentioned in my last letter, did not live in 1390, as I writ by mistake, but in 1100, so that what I sayd about some reliques of old forrests of fir, then standing in these levels, is more observable than I thought of.

To Mr. Banks, in answer to his of February 15, 1702-3.

Rev. Sir,

    I most heartily thank you for your kind letter, and, in answer thereto, do confess that, while I lived in your town,' I made great collections of valuable

---

' The following notice relative to the diarist's appointment to the readership of Holy Trinity Church, Hull, occurs in his M.S. *penes* Mr. Wilson, page, 238.

"In 1698 Mr. Abr. de la Pryme, upon the removal of Mr. Wykes, succeeded to the office of Reader and Curate in the church. Mr. Banks, assuming the whole right of chusing and inducting of one to that office himself, brought him in without leave of the Bench, who, through much business, forgot to take notice of the same ; but he afterwards, understanding the badness of his tenure, went into the Town's Hall unto the Mayor and Aldermen assembled in councel, and acquainted them therewith, who readily thereupon confirm'd him in the said office, without Mr. Banks's knowledge, and appointed him to be their Reader of the High Church."

19 Sept., 1700.—" Upon reading of the Petition of Mr. Abraham D' La Prime, clerk, the present Curate of St. Trinitie's Church, it is ordered that hee continue in the said place for the year ensuing att the usuall salary."—(*Hull Town Records.*)

"In March, 1700," he continues, "they put so much trust in him that, at his request, they gave him public leave to search into, peruse, and view all their old charters, records, and memorials of the Town, upon his request to them, in the following words."—

The order here alluded to is not copied by him into the MS., but, at my request, it has been extracted from the records, as follows :—

B.B. 8, p. 432.

Tempore Wmi. St. Quintin Bart. Major : Ao. 1699.

21st March, 1699-[1700.]

"Mr. Abraham de la Prime the Reader in St. Trinitie's Church, came and desired of the Bench that they would permit him to look over and view the Antient Charters and other Records and Antiquities belonging to this Corporation and Town, in order to compose a catalogue thereof, and revive the antient rights and privileges of this town. It is ordered that his request be granted, and that the Town Clark do attend and assist him."

papers and MSS., but am infinitely sorry that I have little or nothing amongst them that might be serviceable to the great and noble design of the learned and ingenious Sir P. Sydenham, unto whome pray be pleased to present my most humble service, and let him know that, if he have not obtained the inscriptions upon the monuments of the archbishops of York, that I will purposely go to transcribe them for him sometime this summer.

As concerning bishop Skirlaw,[u] I have nothing furder of him than what is in the *Angl. Sac.*, Goodwin, Cambden, and other printed books, excepting onely that Speed, in *Cal. D. Relig. in Chron. suo*, says that he built a great college of Prebendarys in Hull, the certainty of which may be found amongst the returns of Edward VI., in the Court of Augmentations, at London.

But, as for bishop Alcock, the most learned and pious man of his time, I have somewhat furder observable of him. Bishop Goodwin, and from him others say that he was born at Beverley, which seems not at all probable to me. First, because that his ancestors, William Alcock, Thomas Alcock, sheriff in 1468, and mayor in 1478, and Robert Alcock, the bishop's father, who was sherif in 1471.[v] and mayor in 1480, were all of them famous merchants of this town, and lived here. Secondly, because that old records of the town positively say that he was the son of the aforesayd Robert Alcock, mayor. Thirdly, because that, when he founded the great free school in the town of Hull, he founded it upon his own lands, that had descended to him from his grandfather, William Alcock, merchant, of the same place, being a great garden, fifty-five royal ells in length, which he had bought in 1432, of John Grimsby, merchant. And fourthly, because that it was most commonly the custom of them days to build their chanterys, and chappels, and schools, and such like, in the towns where they were born, as the aforesayd bishop Skirlaw did his at Skirlaw, and others. This Dr. Alcock was first bishop of Rochester, and then of Worster in 1476. While he sat there, in 1484, he founded and built a little chappel, upon the south side of S. Trinity Church, in Hull, joining upon the great porch, and dedicated it to the Holy Trinity, erecting two altars therein, the one to Christ, and the other to S. John the Evangelist, and therein and thereat fixed a perpetual chantery and chantor, to chant psalms and prayers every day for the souls of King Edward 4th, his own, his parents', and for all Christian souls, which he endow'd with £14 6s. 4d. a-year, issuing out of houses and lands in Hull, Keilby, and Bigby. About fourteen years after this, awhile before his death, at the earnest request of Alderman Dalton, who had marry'd one of his sisters, he founded a great free school in the sayd town, and endow'd it with £20 a-year (tho' in the survey taken of it in Edward 5th's time 'tis but return'd in £10), out of which the master was bound to pay 40s. a-year to the clark of Trinity Church to teach boys to sing, and to give yearly to ten of the best scholars in the school 6s. 8d. a-piece, if the revennues and other exigencies would allow of the same; and all children coming to the sayd school were to be taught *gratis*. About the same time did he also, by another grant, give twenty marks a-year to the assistant minister of S. Trinity church. All which charitys were ruin'd and lost in Edward 6th days, and the school and schoolhouse pull'd down and sold.

As for Roger de Askham, I have nothing at all of his, but a book entitled, *The Schoolmaster; or a plain and perfect way of teaching children to understand, speak, and write the Lattin tongue, but especially purposed for the bringing up of youth in Noblemen's houses, and commodious for such as have forgot the Lattin tongue, and would by themselves, without a Schoolmaster, in short time and with small pains recover it.* Printed at London in 1571. Which indeed is a very learned and ingenious book, and has many things in it

---

[u] The name of Skirlaw, or Skirlew, is of frequent occurrence in the parish register of Thorne. The college of prebendaries is Howden, not Hull.

[v] There is more exact information about the Alcocks in the *Testamenta Eboracensia*.

relateing to his life and conversation in St. John's College, Cambridge, and elsewhere, which, if desired, shall be readily sent, tho' no question but he that is composing his life has seen it.

As to Dr. Honiwood's epitaph, tho' that I have it somewhere amongst my papers, yet I cannot find it at present. Yet in searching I found some others such like. There is one in St. Martin's church, in Leicester, in the following words :—"Here lys the body of John Heyrick, of this parish, who dyed in 1589, aged 76 years, who lived with his wife Mary, in one house, full 62 years, and had issue by her 5 sons and 7 daughters, and all that time never buryed man, woman, nor child, tho' they were some times 20 in household. The sayd Mary lived to 97 years, and dyed in 1611. Shee did see, before her departure, of her children and children's children, and their children, to the number of 142."

In 1656 dyed the Lady Hester Temple, wife to Sir Thomas Temple, of Latimer, in the county of Bucks, Knight, who had 4 sons and 9 daughters who lived to be marry'd, and so exceedingly multiplied that this lady saw 700 extracted from her own body before shee dyed.

Other nations as well as this have been as fruitful. Ludovicus Vives tells of a village in Spain of one hundred houses, whereof all the inhabitants issued out of one certain old man, who then lived, and observes that the Spanish language did not afford a name whereby the youngest should call the eldest, since they could not go above the great-grandfather's father. etc.

I am Sir, your most, etc.

To Mr. Parrol, in London.

Thorn, March 9, 1702-3.

Honrd. Sir,

It is now above six years ago that I begun to write an exact and faithful history of the drainage of the great Levels of Hatfield Chace, on purpose to preserve the worthy memory of the first noble undertakers of the same, and the great troubles and sorrows that they suffer'd therein, which, by the great blessing of God, I have almost finish'd in some hundreds of sheets of paper, onely some things I want relating to the Vermuydens, Vernats, the Curteens, the Cattzs, and others, which makes me most humbly begg that if there be any papers in your hands relating to their births, country, and pedegrees, estates, lawsuits, callings, or when or where they died, or in what condition, or where I might get their coats of armes, or pictures, or what became of Sir Cornelius Vermuden's son and two daughters, or where they live, that I might write or go to them. These, if you will be pleased to communicate the knowledge of to me, it shall be most graitfully and thankfully received. Or, if that you have anything relateing to your family (which I suppose was one of those concerned in the drainage)[w] that you have a mind to make publick, I shall

[w] This name does not occur amongst the list of foreign settlers given by Hunter in *South Yorkshire*, i., pp. 169-170. The Diarist's correspondent was probably connected with Mr. David Peroll (sometimes spelled Parrol and Prole), who is mentioned as surveyor for the Level of Hatfield Chase, on the 19th May, xi. Car. I. (1635), in the records of the Court of Sewers. In an order of the court, dated 23rd October, 1648, he is said to have " beene very carefull and vigilant in his office, and endeavoured, with all his abilities and skill, both by night and day, to preserve the works thereof." (Vol. i., p. 386). In 1649 he was absent, being "ymployed in ye greate fennes;" and on 17th September, in that year, two other persons were jointly appointed to execute the office of surveyor. Mr. Peroll, however, was present again at a court held 29th September, and afterwards, but appears to have died in 1655. Cornelius Peroll, or Perole, was appointed a sub-surveyor of the court under John Hatfield, esq., surveyor general of the level, by a law of sewers dated 12th July, 1677.—See page 76, *antea*.

be very faithfull therein. Myself am descended of the first drainers, am a participant commissioner of suers, fellow of the Royal Society, etc., and therefore you may be sure shall be very carefull to represent every thing to the best that I can, yet strictly according to truth. I will add no more, but, begging pardon for this trouble,

I am, etc.

To Mr. Thoresby, in Leeds.

May 17, 1703.

Honrd. Sr.,

I received your's yesterday from Mr. Hall, of Fishlake, and have returned this, by post, in answer thereto, hopeing that it will come safe to your hands. I am very much obliged to you for the great favour that you express towards me, and my poor studdys and endeavours ; yet none could be more desirous of seeing you than myself th' last year when I was at your town, to have got (what I so earnestly desire) a personal acquaintance with you, and been satisfy'd in some antient affairs that then stuck a little hard upon me, such as the pretended battel of King Edwin's at our Hatfield, and such like, which, since, I have found belongs to Edwinstow, in Nottinghamshire, *i.e.*, the place where Edwin fell. Another was where the antient river Vinvid, or Winwid stream was mentioned in Bede. Dr. Gale would needs perswade me always that it was our river Went that divides this manour of Hatfield from Pollington, but I always told him again that I thought it was raither Winnet, by Stappleton, called Innet in Cheshire, or Lancashire, from a charter in the *Mon. Angl.* vol. i., and I think p. 862, where Robert de Lacy grants to the monks of Kirstal *communitatem totius morœ vocatur Winnemore et unam acram terrœ in Winnet, e.e occidentali parte pontis super ripam aquœ ;* but I doubt not but to be rightly informed of this and other things by you when I have the happiness of seeing you at your town, which I hope will be about a month or six weeks hence. As for my history of Hull, which I drew out of all the records of that town by particular order of the Mayor and Aldermen, I have not altogether finish'd it, neither must I dare to publish it till some be dead that are yet living, remembering Camden's fate. The MSS. that I have got together have cost me both trouble and charge, tho' indeed not much, and I am daily augmenting the number of them, haveing got several since I writ that catalogue[v] of them that you saw, one of which I will here give you the title of :—*Compendium Compertorum per Doct. Leigh et Doct. Layton, etc.* This rare book, that had escaped the eyes of the famous Dodsworth, Dugdale, Burnet, and others, was found by me the last year, in his grace the Duke of Devonshire's library, at Hardwick, written in H[enry] 8 or Ed[ward] 6 days, which, upon my request, was immediately lent me home, of which I have taken a coppy in ten sheets of paper. I will not mention any other things at this time unto you, for fear of being tedious ; I will onely add that I have here sent you what you desired about farthings, and shall be always very glad to serve you in any thing that lays in my power.

I am, Sr., your, etc.

To Dr. Sloan.

Thorn, June 26, 1703.

H. Sr.,

'Tis some time ago that I sent you an account of a spout that myself and many others saw in Hatfield parish in 1685, with some few conjectures

---

[*] *Vide antea*, pp. 188-189.

[v] 17 December, 1702.—" Ordered that 8 guinnyes be given as a gratuity to Mr. Pryme for inspecting the Town's Records and Papers, and making an Index thereof."—*Record Book.*

upon the cause of it. Since that time I have been so happy as to see another in the same place, which very much confirms me in my notion of the nature and origin of them. The weather here in this part of the country hath been exceeding] wett and could, insomuch that it seem'd raither to have been spring than midsummer. Yet, for all that, Monday, the 21st ditto, was pretty warm, on the afternoon of which day, about two of the clock, no wind stirring below, tho' it seem'd somewhat great in the air, the clouds begun to be mightily agitated and driven together, whereupon they became very black, and were most visibly hurry'd round, as in a circle, whence proceeded a most audible whirling noise like that commonly heard in a mill. After a while, a long tube or pipe came down from the center of the congregated clouds, in which was most plainly beheld a swift spiral motion, like that of a skrew, or the Cochlea Archimedis when it is in motion, by which spiral nature and swift turning water assends up into the one as well as into the other. It travell'd slowly from west to north east, broke down a great oak tree or two, frighted the weeders out of the field, and made others ly down flat upon their bellys to save being whirl'd about and kill'd by it, as they saw many jackdaws to be, that were suddenly cattch'd up, carry'd out of sight, and then cast a great way off amongst the corn. At last it passed over the town of Hatfield, to the great terror of the inhabitants, filling the whole air with the thatch that it pluck'd of from some of the houses; then, touching upon a corner of the church, it tore up several sheets of lead, and roll'd them straingly together. Soon after which it dissolved and vanish'd, without doing any furder mischief.

There was nothing more extraordinary in this than in the other that I gave you a former account of, and, by all the observation that I could make of both of them, I found that, had they been at sea, and joyn'd to the surface thereof, they would have carry'd a vast quantity of water into the clouds, and the tubes would then have become more dense, and opake, and strong, than they were, and have continued much longer.

It is commonly sayd that at sea the water collects and bubles up a foot or two high under those spouts before that they be joyned; but the mistake lys in the pellucidity and fineness of those pipes, which do most certainly touch the surface of the sea before that any considerable motion be made in it, and that then when the pipe begins to fill with water it then becomes opak and visible.

As for the reason of their small continuance and dissolving of themselves, after that they have drunk up a great quantity of water, I take it to be by and thorow the great quantity of water, that they have carry'd up, which must needs thicken the clouds and impede their motion, and by that means dissolve the pipes.

I am, Sr., etc.

[To Mr. Thoresby.]

Thorn, January 25, 1703-4.

Hon. Sr.

I received your's sometime ago, but had not the opportunity of answering it untill now, being busied in transcribing the whole court rolls of the manour of Hatfield, from Edward the 1st's days untill now, (which will take me eight or ten volumes in folio) in which are an infinite number of things very observable.[z] I am very glad that the comp[osition] was acceptable unto

---

[z] At page 53 of the 1st vol. of the MS., the diarist has entered the substance, taken from an old paper he says he had by him, "of a strange cause that was brought to a hearing in Hatfield court," in the 11th year of Edward III. (1337), between Robert de Rotherham, plaintiff, and John de Ithon, defendant, relative to the breach of an agreement, made at Thorne, for the sale and

you, (I am sure it would not have been so to the papists in King James the 2nd's time, if it had been then printed, to whome it would have given a mortall blow.) You may direct it to Mr. Hardwick, at Rawcliffe, for me, by which means I hope it will come safe to my hands. As to your other querys, I answer them as follows.

Rob[ert P[ortington] whose heroic deeds I have mentioned in my MSS., was second brother to Roger P. of Tudworth: which Roger had originally but a small estate, untill that there dy'd one Sr. Roger P. of or near Leeds, who left his whole estate, about £1,600 a-year, to the disposal of his wife, they haveing no issue. And shee being old and full of piety, caus'd her coffin to be made and set in her chamber by her, and designed, when shee dy'd, to leave all shee had to a young nephew of her's called Mr. Nevil, of Chete,[a] and had accordingly given it so in her will. He, knowing this, was impatient of her death; and, being once in a merry humour, went to see her, as he did frequently, and observing her coffin stand by her, he fell a playing thereon with his fingers, and sayd, " O Aunt ! when shall I hear that you'r layd up in these virginalls?" Shee, hearing these unfortunate words,[b] sayd little, but immediately alter'd her will, and gave all she had to this same Roger Portington, of Tudworth, because he was her husband's double name-sake, tho' not at all related.

This Roger haveing got such a fine addition to his estate, came to the manour hall of H[atfield], and lived there untill the time of the breaking out of the civil war, in which he took the King's part, was a captain, rais'd and maintain'd a troup at his own cost, untill at last, haveing spent above £9,000, he was taken prisoner, and sent to London, where they made him pay £1,890 more for composition money for his estate that was left, and kept him in prison eleven years, until the King's return, after which he came and lived at Barmby-upon-Dun, and there dy'd and was bury'd.[c] As for his estate that was left, he bequeathed it to his wife for her life, and, after her decease, to the Portingtons, of Portington, to whome I think it went long ago, and is now almost, if not wholly, spent.

The aforesayd Robert P., this Roger P.'s second brother, was major in Sr. W. Savil's regiment, was a valiant soldier and brave man, plunder'd the Isle of Axholm, was in the fight at Willoughby, there taken prisoner and sent to Hull, where he lay untill the king was restored, and then comeing over Bouth-ferry, or, as others say, Whitgift, he there received the sleight bite of an ape, that was then by chance in the boat, in his hand, which gangreen'd, and shortly after carry'd him to prison again in the dark and silent grave.[d]

delivery by the latter to the former of no less an article, whether corporeal or incorporeal, than a devil, bound in a certain ligament—" Diabolum ligatum in quodam ligamine "—in consideration of the sum of 3½d. The subject has been often transcribed and reprinted, and the purport of it may be read in *Hunter's S. Y.*, i., p. 197. From an occasional inspection of these court-rolls, with which, through the courtesy of Rowland W. Heathcote, esq., of the Manor-house, Hatfield, I have been favoured, I am in a position to endorse the statement in the text, that they certainly do contain "an infinite number of things very observable " by the antiquary and genealogist. Most of the early ones, however, have suffered from a want of care on the part of their custodians, with which they are, at all events, not now chargeable.

[a] Chevet, near Wakefield. See ped., *Hunter's S. Y.*, ii., 393.

[b] This "unseemly jest" is referred to by Hunter as taken from De la Pryme's Diary, in *S.Y.*, i., p. 213, where, and at p. 214, see pedigree, and further information as to the Portington family.

[c] Died in 1683. See mon. insc. in *Miller's Hist. Doncaster*, p. 233. *Hunter's S.Y.*, i., p. 214. "1683, Roger Portington, of Barnby, Esq., was buried, contrary to act of parliament, ye 11th of December." [*i.e.* concerning the burying in woollen.]—*Barnby Dun par. register.*

[d] Died 23 December, 1660, buried at Arksey. See mon. insc. *Miller's Hist. Doncaster*, 229. *Hunter's S. Y.*, i., 214.

Hen[ry P[ortington] the great royalist, of whome I sent you the book, was the son of Robert P., esq., of Staynford, but descended from Barmby-upon-Dun, and was nephew to the aforesayd Roger and Robert, of Tudworth ; and, dying without issue, left what he had to a brother named William, who had a son named Henry, who spent all.

All this I took in writing, some years ago, from Mr. L[ayton ?] before he dy'd.*

* This is the last entry in the Diary. The MS. volume, at this point, presents the appearance of having had many leaves cut or torn out; but Mr. Hunter, who, previously to 1828, had had the book for the service of his *History of South Yorkshire*, there states that the above communication to Thoresby was at that time the latest entry in it.—See *Hunter's South Yorkshire*, i., p. 181.

APPENDIX.

GENEALOGICAL NOTICES.

[Inside the cover, at the commencement of the Diary, in the Diarist's own writing.]

Mat. Prym, my father, was born ye 31 of August, 1645.
Sarah Smagg, my mother, was born in November, 1649.
They were marryd 3d of April, 1670.
Abraham Prym, ye first born, and ye author of this Book, was born ye 15th of Jan., 1671.

1. Peter Prym was born ye 29th of April, 1672.
2. Sarah Prym was born ye 14 of Sept., 1677.
Mary Prym was born ye 17 of Octob., 1685.
Frances Prym was born ye 15 of Febr., 1687.

1. Peter Prym marryd Frances, ye daughter of Franc. Wood, of ye Levels, July ye 25, 1695.
1. His first born, dyed soon.
2. His 2d son was born Munday ye 6t. of 7ber. at 10 a clock at night, 1697.
2. Sarah Prym was marryd unto William Oughtibridg, of Woodhouse, in 1696, and by him had a son named Thomas, born...........ye ....1699.

[In a different hand.]

Thar was 5 childer more ho dyed before me father.
Daved, 3yr. ould, Jacob, 8yr. ould, Elez., 13yr. ould, Mary, half a yr. ould, Elez., 1yr. ould, Frances, 2yr. ould.

[*The following entry occurs at page* 69 *of the Diary.*]

EXTRACTED OUT OF Yᴇ REGISTER OF Yᴿ CHAPPPEL OF SANTOFT.[a]

"Le 4 d' Avril, 1670, sont maries Abram Barcel et Francoise Sterpin, et Mathew Pryme, et Sara Smaque. Le 15 Janvier, 1671, naquit Abrah. fils de Math. Pryme, et de Sarah Smaque, et a ete baptize le 22 du dit mois a Santoft, son parein est Abrah. de Prim et sa marcine Fransois Sterpin, femme de' Abr. Beharcel. Le 9 de' Avril, naquit Pierre fils de Mat. Prieme, et de Sara Smaque, et ete baptize a Santoft, le 14 de Juillet, son parein est Pierre Smacque, et sa marcine Sara Jacob, femme de Isanbaer Chavatte."

———

A College friend of the diarist's named Read (who had been on a tour into Derbyshire with Sir Thomas Bendish), in a letter dated Cambridge, March 3ᵈ 1695-6, sends him a note of one " Phillip Pryme, Gent, of Normanton in Derbyshire. I lookt in yᵉ map and found on town of yᵗ· name abt· 3 miles south of Derby itself."

———

MONUMENTAL INSCRIPTIONS IN HATFIELD CHURCH.

Sacred to yᵒ Honour of God & yᵉ Dead. At yᵉ foot of This Pilʳ· lyes Bury'd in certain hope of riseing in Christ yᵉ Body of Matthew Pryme, of yᵒ Levels, Gent· son of Charles De la Pryme,[b] of yᵉ citty Ipres, in Flanders, who marryed Sarah, yᵉ daugh. of Peter Smagge, Gnᵗ· cit. of Paris, & haveing lived 49 yearˢ in this vain world (a patern of vertue, honesty, and industry), departeᵈ to a better yᵉ 29 of Iuly, A.D. 1694, leaueing behind him a good name, a mournfull wife, & of jj children whome God had given him onely five liveing, Abraham, Peter, Sarah, Mary, and Francis, who out of gratitude to God & duty to yᵉ excellent memory of the dead did most freely, willingly, thankfully, and deservedly, erect this mon. to his

———

[a]   It is much to be regretted that the Registers of this chapel are not now to be met with. Stonehouse (*Isle of Axholme*, p. 355), says, "part of them have been preserved by Mr. Stovin." Hunter, writing in 1828, and giving the names of many of the Dutch and French settlers on the Hatfield Levels, says, "of these it is possible to collect a pretty complete list from the register of the chapel of Sandtoft, which was carefully kept from 1641 to 1681, and is still in existence, or lately was so. It was in the French language." (*South Yorkshire*, i., p. 169). Many enquiries have been made about these records but hitherto without success.
[b]   Both Peck and Hunter have omitted to give these words of paternity.

ABRAHAM DE LA PRYME.

memory.* Here allso lyes yᵉ body of Mrˢ· Sarah Pryme, wife
to yᵉ aforesᵈ Mʳ· Matthew Pryme, she dyed 1729, aged 82.

Near
this place lyes
PETER DE LA PRYME,
Gent., of yᵉ Levels,
Who dy'd Nov. 25ᵗʰ 1724, aged 52 years.
Also
FRANCES, his wife, who dyᵈ IIʸ 12, 1707.
Also 4 children
MATTHIAS, MATTHEW, SARAH, & DAVID.
Here allso lies ABRAHAM DE
LA PRYME, Gent. eldest son to
yᵉ aforesᵈ PETER & FRANCES, he
died Octoᵇ· 6, 1740, aged 40
years.
Also Emily, Relict of Abraham De La Pryme.
who died July, 1769, aged 76.
Also
2 children of his son,
Abraham De La Pryme, Gent.,
Peter & Margret.

Sacred to the Memory of FRANCIS & GEORGE WRIGHT,
Great Grandsons of Peter De La Prime, the former of whom
fell a Victim to the climate of Tobago, the 2ᵈ of Septʳ· 1801,
aged 29 years. And the latter to the bursting of a Gun when
on Duty, at the same Place, the 27ᵗʰ Octʳ· 1805, aged 26 years.
This Monument was erected by their Sister, SALLY WRIGHT, to
fulfil the Intention of their afflicted Mother, SALLY WRIGHT,
who died 7ᵗʰ Janʸ· 1809, aged 64 years, and whose Remains
lie at the foot of this Pillar.

* "This," says Hunter, "is a beautiful specimen of what I would call the
English epitaph ; full of that information for which people resort to the monuments of the dead ; not extravagantly encomiastic, but doing justice to the memory of a man whom we cannot doubt to have deserved all that is said of him ;
at the same time, simple, tender, affecting."—*South Yorkshire*, i., p. 190.
The arms represented on the De la Pryme monuments, at Hatfield, when Peck
wrote his *History of Bawtry and Thorne*, 1813, were said to be *azure a sun
argent ;* and Hunter, 1828 (*South Yorkshire*, i., p. 190), also describes them as
a silver sun upon an azure field. When I saw them, in 1869, the sun had been
painted by some one *sable.*

Here Lies all
that was mortal
of ABRAHAM DE LA
PRYME, F.R.S.,
Minister of Thorn, in the
County of York,
Son of Matthew de la Pryme
& Sarah his mournful Relict.
he died June y^{er} 13th, 1704,
in ye 34th year of his age.

Tho' Snatch'd away
in youth's fresh bloom,
Say not that he
untimely fell;
he nothing owd
Y^e years to come,
and all that pass'd
was fair & well.

A painful priest,
A faithfull fre^{n}d,
A vertuous soul,
A candid breast,
usefull his life
& calm his end,
he now enjoys
eternal Rest.

[The above is on a plain stone at the foot of the north-east pillar of the tower. *Viro monumentum haudquaquam dignum.*[d]]

---

[d] Hatfield Burial, 1704, June 14, Mr. Abraham Prym.
"Mr. Pryme, min., dyed upon June ye 12th, 1704, and was buried at Hatf., June 14th."—*Memorandum in the Register of Thorne.*

In memory of Emelia, wife to William Greene, esq., of
Chesterfield, in yᵉ county of Derby, who died April yᵉ 1st, 1760,
in yᵉ 28th year of her age.   Daughter of Abraham and Emily
De la Pryme, above mentioned.

Near This? Place lyes yᵉ Body of Sarᵃʰ yᵉ wife of Wᵐ·
Outibridge, of Hatfᵈ· Woodʰˢ· & Daugᵗʳ· of Matᵂ· Pryme,
Gentᵗ· Diᵉᵈ Marᵍʰ 27, 1708.   Also 2 daugᵗʳˢ· viz. Sarʰ· burᵈ·
Augˢᵗ· 12,ᵉ 1708, & Elizᵇ· burᵈ Augˢᵗ· 25, 1714.

T. Oughtibridge, Engraver.

D.M.S.

Near yˢ Place Lye yᵉ Bodyes of Wᵐ· Oughtibridge & Sarah
his wife, he was buryᵈ Iuly 30,ᶠ 1728, agᵈ 56.   She dyᵈ 1708.
Allso 4 children, Suˢⁿ·, Matᵂ·, Sarʰ·, & Elizᵇ·   Also Thoˢ·
Oughtibridge, Son to Willᵐ· and Sarah, he died December 26ᵗʰ,
1756,ᵉ Aged 54 years.

Arms: Or on a fess sable 3 lozenges gules, impaling, azure
a sun sable.ʰ

(On a Brass plate.)

Here Lieth the Body of W. Oughtibridge, of this Parish,
Gent., Buried July 1728, aged 56 years.

Nigh unto this place lies the Body of FRANCES, the wife of
JOHN COCK,ⁱ daughter of MATHEW and SARAH PRYME, who
departed this Life the 3ᵈ of June, J745, Aged 53.   Also two
Children HANNAH & MATTHEW, who died Infants.   And IOHN,
who died the J3ᵗʰ of March, J747, Aged 22.   Also SARAH, who
died the 8ᵗʰ of March, J763, Aged 48.

ᵉ 10th in Register.
ᶠ Buried 29th, in the Register.
ᵍ So on the monument, but an error for 1753.   His will was dated 8 Dec.,
1753, and proved at York 19 June, 1754. The burial register is 28 Dec.,
1753.   Peck, in his *History of Bawtry and Thorne*, 1813, p. 105, has it 1753.
ʰ I give the heraldry as I find it, though there is obviously some irregu-
larity in the colours. Peck has Oughtibridge thus, in his *History of Bawtry
and Thorne*, 1813, p. 105.
ⁱ Peck (*Hist. Bawtry and Thorne*, 1813) has misprinted this name *Cooke.*
Hunter the same, *S.Y.,* i., 190.   Pedigree in *Archæologia*, vol. xl., has it
so also.   It is clearly Cock, both on the monument and in the register.

Near this place lye ye remains of Thos. Johnson, of Brumby. in ye County of Lincoln, Gent., buried June 29, 175J, aged 63 years. Also Mary, his Wife, who was Buried Iune the J4, J767, aged 82 years.

T. Oughtibridge, Sculp.

Arms: Arg. a lion (or leopard) passant guardant, on a chief...3 fishes palewise, heads downwards...impaling Pryme.

From a Gravestone near the font, in St. Paul's Church, Sheffield.

In Memory of Elizabeth, the wife of James De la Pryme, who died October the ..., 1766, aged 36 years.

Also of Charles, son of James De la Pryme, Born April the 7th, 1759, died Novr. the 11th, 1760. Also of the second Charles, his son, Born April the 9th, and died May the 24th, 1763. Also of Peter, who was Born April 22d, 1765, and died August the 15th, 1768.

On a Tablet in North Ferriby Church.

Mr. Francis Pryme, of Hull, died the 7th July, 1769, aged 67.

Rebecca, his wife, the 28th May, 1750, aged 39.

Frances their daughter, the 31st Oct., 1746, aged 8 years.

Christopher Pryme, Son of Francis Pryme, by Mary his first wife, the 20th Oct., 1784, aged 46.

Alice, his Widow, died at Hull, on the 16th of October, 1834, aged 86.

———

Beneath is a shield, intended, it is presumed, to exemplify the arms of Mr. Pryme and those of his two wives, as follows:—Per pale, the dexter half parted per fess, the upper portion being paly of eight or and azure, on a chief of the first a lion passant guardant gules: and the lower portion, azure the sun or: sinister half, vert a greyhound salient argent. Here, again, is a variance in the De la Pryme arms, the sun being given as *gold*.

ABSTRACTS FROM THE WILLS AND ADMINISTRATIONS OF THE NAME OF PRYME, IN THE REGISTRY AT YORK.[j]

27 Dec., 1669.—CHARLES PRIME, of the Levell, in the parrish of Hatfeild, yeoman.—Item, I give unto the poore of the French and Dutch congregation of Santoft the summe of three pounds.—Item, I give unto my three sonns, that is, Abraham Prime, and Matthias Prime, and David Prime, all my lands which is in Flanders, equally divided amongst them three.— Item, I give unto my sonne Abraham Prime the summe of 18l. 6s., as above 20l. which I am ingaged for my sonne Abraham att Gainsbrough, to be paid by my executors hereafter nominated, which, with one hundred and sixtie-one pound 17s. alreadie paide to him, makes the summe of 200l.—All the rest of my houses, leases, tenements, and goods whatsoever, I give unto my wife Prudence, and to my sonns Matthias and David, to be equally divided amongst them three, and make them jointe and sole executors.—Witnesses, Isaac Germe, Abraham Beharrel. [Proved 10 Janry., 1669-70, admon. to Matthias & David Prime, the exrs.]—*Reg. Test.* 50, fo. 451b.

2 Janry., 1669-70.—PRUDENCE PRIME, of the Levell, widow. —To my son Jacob Coakley, 20s.—All my part of houses, leases, tenements, and goods whatsoever, to my sons Matthias Prime, and David Prime, they paying the third part of what they shall be valued at to my son Abraham Prime.—Said Matthias & David Prime exrs. [Proved 10th Janry., 1669-70, admon. to Matthias & David Prime, sons & exrs. of sd. decd.]—*Reg. Test.* 50, fo. 452.

30 Janry., 1671-2.—DAVID PRYM, of the Levells, yeoman.— My wife Mary sole exx—The 3d part of my personal estate to my son David P., when 21 or married,—the other 2 parts to my sd exr.—Should my wife die in her widowhood, and also my son, then the moiety of what she dies seized of to my brethren Abraham and Matthias Prim, or to their heirs or assigns, and the other moiety to be at her own disposal.—Benjamin Guey,

j For the contribution of these testamentary notices the Editor is indebted to R. H. Skaife, Esq., of York, a gentleman who has been upon all occasions most ready to assist him, and whose qualifications for the labours of the antiquarian scholar have been well displayed in the publication of "his first literary essay," *Kirkby's Inquest*, which forms the 49th volume of the works of this Society.

S

and the said Abraham & Matthias Prim, to be supervisors of my son David.—[Proved 26 Aug., 1672; admon. to Abraham Prymme brother of s^{d.} decd.. to whom tuition of David P., son of s^{d.} decd., was also granted.]—A second grant was issued (& the above cancelled), 26 Oct., 1672, to Susanna Guoy, the mother, & Abraham Prym, the brother of s^{d.} deceased.—*Reg. Test.* 53, fo. 324*b*.

Nuncupative will of MARY PRYM, widow and relict of David Prym, of Haines, in the parish or chapelry of Thorne, made on or about 21 Aug., 1672.—All my land to my son David Prym, if he live to accomplish his full age; if he die before, then to Suzans Guoy, my mother, for her life.—rem. to Suzans Flahant, wife of John Flahant, and to her heirs.—All my goods and personal estate whatsoever to my son David Prym (except my rings and silver thimbles, which I give to Suzans Gouy, my mother).—To Sarah Moore, my god-daughter, 10s.—Tuition of said David to my mother Suzans Gouy. [On 26 Oct., 1672, probate of the will of Mary Prym, late of Levell, par. Hatfield, & admon. granted to Susanna Guoy, mother of s^{d.} decd., & Abraham Prym, gent., brother of s^{d.} decd. Same day tuition of David Prym, son of s^{d.} decd., was granted to the said Susanna Guoy, his grandmother.]—*Reg. Test.* 53, fol. 192.

6 Oct., 1684. Admon. of the goods, etc., of DAVID PRYMM, late of Levells, but dying (intestate) at Pursland, par. Crowland, co. Linc., granted to Susanna Gouy, his grandmother.—*Act Book, Pontefract Deanery.*

26 July, 1694.—MATTHIAS PRIM, of the the parish of Hatfield, yeoman.—£18 per ann. to my wife Sarah P., to be paid quarterly, during her life, out of all my houses and lands at Hatfield & Hatfield-Woodhouse, & my old farm in the Levell, late Mr. Dawlings.—Also to my s^{d.} wife £50 within 12 months after my decease.—To my son Abraham P., and to his heirs, all that my farm at Goodcock, in the occupation of Isaac Amory, as also 49 acres in Wroot Ca..., with the buildings, and all my right, title, and interest in Vanheck land.—To my s^{d.} son, Abraham, £100 out of my personal estate, to be paid within 12 months after my decease.—My houses and lands at Hatfield & Hatfield-Woodhouse, and my old farm in the Levell, to my son Peter P., and his heirs, paying £18 yearly to his mother, as above bequeathed.—To my three daurs. Sarah, Mary, & Frances, each £200, when 21 or married.—Tuition of s^{d.} 3 daurs. to my

wife, and to my trusty & welbeloved friend Wm. Erratt, clerk,
& Edward Forster, gent.—£5 to Wm., son of Wm. Erratt, clerk,
—To Charles Prym, my nephew, £5.—To ye poore that come to
my funerall, five pound, to be dealt in dole in Hatfield church,
after I am buryed.—Residue to Peter P., my son ; he sole exr
[Probate of the will of Matthias Prim, gent., of the Levell,
granted to Peter Prim. gent., son of said deceased, and sole
executor, 25 March. 1695].—N.B. This will is not registered.

Inventory, taken 17 Janry., 1694-5, amounted to £1316 19s. 0d.
His funeral expenses were £20.
Paid to ye Dr. & Apothecary, £17.
Francis Oxley & Charles Prim, of [Ledle?], yeoman, enter
bond.

2 April, 1711, 10 Anne.—JAMES GREENHALGH, of Hooton-
Roberts, clerk.—To my son, Thomas Greenhalgh, £300 when
21.—To my son James Greenhalgh, 300, when 21.—To my daur.,
Emelia Greenhalgh, £300, when 21 or married.—Tuition of sd.
children to my wife Margaret. She sole exx [Pro. 8th Janry.,
1718-9, admon. to Margaret Greenhalgh, widow, the sole exx]
—Reg. Archiep. Dawes, fo. 106.
Mem.—21 Feb., 1692-3. James Grenehalgh, clerk, inst. to
Hooton-Roberts.
26 Janry., 1718-9. Charles Willats, clerk, inst. to Plumtree,
vice James Greenhalgh, deceased.

20 Nov., 1724.—PETER PRYM, of the Levels, par. Hatfield,
gent.—I give unto my son Francis Prym all my share of lands
in the Levells, late Mr. Vanheek's, and the house and land at
Goodcop, in the mannor of Epworth, to him and his heirs for
ever, also £300 in money, to be paid him within 12 months after
my decease by my executor.—Item, I give unto my son, Abram
Prym, all my copyhold land and messuages, buildings, and
appurtenances whatsoever, in the lordship and mannor of Hatfield, to him and his heirs for ever, and the 151 acres in Bryerhills.—To my daur. Elizabeth Prym, £600, to be paid within 6
months after my decease. To Susan Oughtibridge, £5, & to
Thomas & William Oughtibridge, each £1 1s.—Residue to my
son Abram Prym. He sole exr. Witnesses, Wm. Errat, Wm.
Rodwell, & Timothy Moore. [Proved 29 May, 1725, admon. to
Abraham Prym, son and sole exr.]—Reg. Test. 78, fo. 117.

16 Oct., 1740.—MARGARET GRENEHALGH, of Hatfield, widow.

—To my granddaur. Emilia de la Pryme £200, when 21 or married.—To my granddaur. Elizabeth de la Pryme £200, when 21 or married.—My late son, James Grenehalgh, dec^d.—Residue of my personal estate, and also my copyhold house in Hatfield, to my daur. Emelia de la Pryme, widow, her heirs, executors, & administrators, subject to an annuity of £10 to Mrs. Frances Elice, for payment of which my brother, Mr. Hugh Bosvile, became bound with me unto Mrs. Dorothy Briscoe, dec^{d.}, mother of the said Mrs. Alice (*sic*), about May 26th, 1721. Said daur. Emilia sole ex^x [Proved 14 July, 1754, admon. to Emelia de la Pryme, widow, daur. & sole ex^x of s^{d.} dec^{d.}]—*Reg. Test.* 98, 221b.

18 Aug. 1768.—FRANCIS PRYME, of Kingston-upon-Hull, esquire.—To my daur. Elizabeth Pryme £500, to be paid within 6 months after my decease,—also £500 more, to be paid within 12 months after my decease.—also a sum of about £93, left to her by her uncle and aunt, William & Rebecca Thompson, & now in my hands, to be included in the above legacy.—To my s^{d.} daur. Elizabeth £20, to be p^{d.} wthin one month after my decease.—To my daur. Nancy Pryme, £500, within 6 months, and £500 within 12 months, and £20 within one month after my decease.—To my daur. Sally, the wife of Mayson Wright, £20. —To my son-in-law Mayson Wright, £20.—My real & personal estate, charged with the above legacies, to my son Christopher Pryme. He sole ex^{x.} [Proved 18 Dec., 1769, admon. to Christopher Pryme, son and sole ex^r]—*Reg. Test.* 113, fo. 273.

2 June, 1769.—EMELIA DE LA PRYME, heretofore of Hatfield, but now of Sheffield, widow.—To my son, James De la Pryme and to his brother-in-law, James Greatrex, of Manchester, gent., my copyhold house in Hatfield, and my copyhold land at Hatfield-Woodhouse, in trust to sell the same, etc.—My granddaur. Mary De la Pryme (under 21).—To my grandson, James De la Pryme, my silver tankard.—To my grandson, Abraham De la Pryme, and to my grandson, Francis De la Pryme, my five table spoons, marked with the Grenehalghs' crest.—To my granddaur. Emelia De la Pryme, my three silver castors, and two little waiters, marked with the Grenehalghs' crest.—Residue to my son, James De la Pryme. He sole ex^{r.} [Proved 5 Nov., 1770, admon. to James De la Pryme, son & sole ex^{r.}]

10 May, 1782.—CHRISTOPHER PRYME, of Kingston-upon-Hull, merchant.—Mentions his wife Alice, his son George

Pryme (a minor), and his (testrs.) sisters, Nancy Pryme, Sally, wife of Mayson Wright, and Elizabeth Robinson.—In a codicil, dated 2 Oct., 1784, he mentions his brother-in-law, the Rev. Owen Dinsdale. [Proved 11 Nov., 1784, admon. to the Rev. Owen Dinsdale, clerk, one of the exrs.]—*Reg. Test.* 128, fo. 430.

22 April, 1771.—ELIZABETH BLAYDES, of Kingston-upon-Hull, gentlewoman.—To my daur. Frances Blaydes, £1500.—To my nephew, James De la Pryme, of Sheffield, gent., £100.—and to his two sons, Abraham and Francis, £50 each,—and to James, Mary, and Amelia, the three other children of my said nephew, James De la Pryme, £10 each. To my nephew, Mr. Christopher Pryme, my two nieces, Elizabeth and Nancy Pryme, and to my nephew-in-law, Mr. Mason Wright, and Sarah, his wife, £10 each. [Proved 12 Nov., 1772, admon. to Benjn. Blaydes, esq., & Frances Blaydes, son and daur. of sd. decd.]

RECORD OF THE DEATH OF THE DIARIST, AND ADMISSION OF HIS HEIR, AT THE MANOR COURT AT EPWORTH, CO. LINCOLN.[a]

MANERIUM DE EPWORTH.—Visus Franc. Pleg. cum magna Cur. Leta, Cur. Baron. et Cur. placitorum honorabilis Domini Johis Carterett, Baronis de Hawnes, domini manerii prædicti, infantis, per honorabilem dominam Graciam Carteret, gardianum suum ibidem tent. 18 Octob., 3 Anne, A.D. 1704, coram Augustino Sampson, seneschallo curiæ ibidem existente.

OBITUS ABRAHAMI PRYM.—Ad hanc curiam compertum est per homagium quod Abrahamus Prym gens. unus customarius domini tenens hujus manerii tenuit sibi et hæredibus suis per copiam rotulorum curiæ, secundum consuetudinem ejusdem manerii, unum cotagium sive tenementum, cum horreis et aliis ædificiis eidem spectantibus, jacens et existens infra parochiam de Belton, et vocatum per nomen de Goodcopp, nunc vel nuper in tenurâ sive occupatione Samuelis Amory, et unum clausum terræ arrabilis prope eidem adjungentem, continentem per æstimacionem sex acras (plus vel minus), abbuttantem super farnam terræ vocatum Sands Toft farm ex oriente, et altam viam ducentem inter Hatfield et Sand Toft ex boreali, et etiam unum parcellum terræ vocatum a tack, unam piscariam in rivo vocato le Old Idle, ac etiam seperalem aliam piscariam in quodam

---

[a] Copied from the original, under the obliging permission of the present lord of the manor, Alfred Parkin, Esq.

loco vocato Thorn Bush Carr.........cum pertinenciis in Belton, obiit inde seisitus, et quod Petrus Prym est frater ejus, proximus hæredum, et plene ætatis; cui dominus manerii prædicti per senescallum suum concessit inde seisinam per stramen, secundum consuetudinem ejusdem manerii, habendum et tenendum præmissa prædicta eidem Petro hæredibus et assignatis suis secundum eandem consuetudinem perredditus et servicia per consuetudinem inde prius debita et de jure consueta. Et dat domino de fine pro hujusmodi statu et ingressu ut in margine, et fecit domino fidelitatem, et sic admissus est inde tenens.[l] (Fin. xxxs. & viiid.)

DE LA PRYME OF THE ISLE OF MAN.

The following Petition, addressed to the Commissioners of Inquiry for the Isle of Man, and published in their report printed in 1805, alludes to the first establishment of Cotton Manufacture in the Isle of Man, which had to be abandoned in consequence of the customs of Liverpool insisting upon the goods paying a Foreign Duty, after being admitted duty free for ten years. The works, situated at Ballasalla had, in consequence, to be abandoned, and the manufacture of cotton was never resumed in the island.[m]

To the Honourable His Majesty's Commissioners of Enquiry in the Isle of Man. The humble Petition of Abraham de la Pryme, Sheweth,

That your petitioner, in the year 1779, removed with his family from England to the Isle of Man, for the conveniency of water, and the low price of labour, to carry on the manufacture of spinning and weaving cotton; and, at a very great expence,

---

[l] This appears to be the same property which had been held by Matthias Pryme, the father of the Diarist. 28 January, 1684-5, Richard Kingman, gent., and Ann his wife surrendered a cottage or tenement, with barns, &c., in the parish of Belton, called Goodcopp, then or late in the occupation of Isaac Amory, with a close of arable land adjoining, containing six acres, abutting upon a farm called Sandtoft farm east, the highway leading between Sandtoft to Hatfield north, a parcel of land called "una Tacka" [a Tack], a fishery in the river of old Idle, and a several fishery in Tornebush Carr Paunsh, in Belton, to the use of Mathias Prim, of the Levill, in parish of Hatfield, gent., his heirs and assigns.—*Epworth Manor Court Rolls.*

[m] The Rev. Wm. Gill, of the Vicarage, Malew, Ballasalla, writes in 1869, —"The old people here still speak of the Prymes as having been noticeable in their generation. Abraham lived at Ballatrick, Francis in Ballasalla house. The factory which Francis built still remains, but in a ruined condition. It is now used as a threshing-mill."

erected there a mill and other buildings; has ever since employed
a great number of the inhabitants in the said manufacture,
which employment is their whole support; has always imported
cotton from Liverpool, of the growth of the British Plantations,
and regularly for ten years exported the manufacture of the said
cotton, either in cloth or yarn, from the said Isle, by proper
certificate to Liverpool, free from duty, as being the manufacture
of the said Isle.

That, last month, your petitioner imported into Liverpool, by
proper certificate, three packs containing six hundred and thirty
pounds yarn, and six pieces cloth in the grey, manufactured in
the said Island, from the said cotton, which said packs are
detained in the Custom House for the payment of the duty,
which is next to a prohibition ; and, if not speedily redressed,
the erection of the mill and other buildings will be nearly a total
loss to your petitioner, and he will be under the disagreeable
necessity of removing with his family out of this Isle. How far
his removal will be a general loss thereto, your petitioner must
submit to your judicious consideration.

Your petitioner begs leave to observe, that he did not apprehend that cotton wool of the growth of His Majesty's Plantations,
and spun by your petitioner, should be deemed foreign growth.

Your petitioner also begs leave to observe that, by a late act
of Parliament, cotton yarn spun in Ireland from cotton of
foreign growth may be imported into Great Britain, duty free,
and that a like indulgence might have been obtained for the Isle
of Man, if it had been mentioned at the time.

Your petitioner prayeth that the honourable Commissioners
of Enquiry may be pleased to take his case into consideration,
and, reporting the same to Government, obtain for him such relief
as he trusts it will be found to merit, and your petitioner will
ever pray.

ABRAHAM DE LA PRYME.

Isle of Man,
  21 Octr., 1791.

    vide Commissioner's Report, 1805.   Appendix B, No. 92.

ADDITIONAL LETTERS.

[No address].

" Hornsey, Decembr. 21st, 1693.
" Sir,

I received your's of the 5th instant. I wish I could furnish
you with any observations fit to promote the laudable design you
are employed in, but fear I cannot; however, I shall tell you
what I think of the particulars named in your letter. Our
steeple is indeed a noted sea-mark, but how long it will be so
I know not, for it is very ruinous, and, I fear, this parish not
able or not willing to repair it. The marr is a mile and an half
in length, and in one place near a mile in breadth; it is fed by
the waters that run into it off the adjoyning higher grounds from
the north, south, and west; eastward it runs into the sea, in a
ditch called the stream dike, when the clow is opened; there are
many springs in it also; the soyl is, in some places, gravelly, in
others a perfect weedy morass. The water is always fresh. It
is well replenished with the best pykes, peirches, eles, and other
fish; the three named the best and largest that ever I saw or
tasted. I have taken pykes a yard long, and peirches sixteen
inches. Nuts hav bin often found in the cliffs and wood at the
down-gate, at the beck, and other places; but at the down-gate
there is, or was very lately, a vein of wood which looks as black
as if it had been burnt. The beck water, whence the houses are
so called, comes from a ditch betwin the east feild and a pasture
call'd the leys, and emptys itself into the stream dike, about
twenty yards off the clow, which is not abov a stone cast, or
little more, from the houses called the Hornsey Beck. I had
almost forgot to add that there are three hills (islands we call
them) in the marr, two of them, at the season of the year, are
so full of tern-eggs and birds as can be imagined. A man must
be very careful if he tread not on them. I can say nothing of
Albrough. Bridlington, I think, is taken notice of by Cambden, for
the priory; part of its church is now the parish church. The
best and largest collection of old coyns that ever I saw was that of
my good friend's Mr. Alderman Elcock," late of York. I suppose

---

" When Thoresby was at York 26 April, 1683, he dined at Alderman
Elcock's, and spent the rest of the day in perusing his collection of Roman
coins and modern medals.—*Diary*, vol. i, p. 165. And, on the 5th Sept. following, he " had Alderman Elcock's (of York) company viewing Roman coins and
antiquities."—*Diary*, ii, *Appendix*, 420.

his son, Mr. Alexius Elcock, hath them yet, and I dare say he
will be ready to communicate them, but it is probable he may
hav bin consulted in this busines. I hav bin told that wood (and
I think nuts too), hav bin digged out of Arnell or Ryston carr,
not abov a foot deep from the swarth; but that is so ordinary
that I suppose it must be taken notice of elsewhere, particularly
about the Levels in Yorkshire and Lincolnshire. This, sir, is all
I can think on in answer to your's. I expect to be at Hull about
three weeks hence, and, if you hav not made your return before,
shall explain to you, if you liv there, anything I have writt, if
there be need, and it may be useful, which you may better judg
of than I can do. One thing more: I hav bin told long ago, by
one that could know it, that Mr. Smales, of Preston, had a
catalogue of many towns in Holderness now swallowed by the
sea; his daughter, Mrs. Saunders, lives there now. It may be
she, or Mr. Joseph Stor. of Hilston (who was, I think, his clark),
may help you to it. If any, or all of this be impertinent, I beg
your pardon. I would, if I could, willingly serv you, or any
industrious person, in such an affair.

" Your very humble servant,

" W. LAMBERT."

Francis Elcock, mercer and grocer, was chamberlain in 1654; on Dec. 31st,
1673, he was elected alderman *vice* Thomas Bawtry, deceased, and in 1677 filled
the office of Lord Mayor. In August, 1685, he (with four others) was displaced
by the king, and died October 26th in the following year, aged 65, being buried
in the little chapel, on the north side of Christ Church, Oct. 28th. His will
(which has not occurred to me) bears date Dec. 24, 1684.—Alderman Francis
Elcock married, 1st. Sarah, daughter of Nicholas Arlush, gent., of Knedlington,
co. York. She was buried at the above church, 21 Oct., 1653; 2ndly, Aug.
14th, 1655, at St. John's, Beverley, Sarah. daughter of Christopher Ridley, esq.,
of Beverley. She was buried " in the clositt " at Christ Church, 24 Feb., 1699-
1700. At this church, Alexius, [only surviving] son of Mr. Francis Elcock,
grocer, was baptized Aug. 15, 1659. He married Margaret, eldest daughter of
Wm. Weddell, esq., of Earswick, near York. (by Margaret, 2nd daughter of Sir
Wm. Robinson, Knight, Alderman of York), by whom he had (with other
issue) Richard, baptized at Christ Church, April 10, 1692. This Richard Elcock
married (settlements dated 14 January, 1714) his cousin, Barbara Tomlinson,
daughter of Joseph Tomlinson, apothecary, York, (by Dorothy, 4th daughter of
the above-mentioned Wm. Weddell, esq.). and assumed the surname of Weddell,
pursuant to the will (dated 7 May, 1747) of his uncle. Thos. Weddell, esq., who
bequeathed to him the greater part of his estates. Thomas Elcock, eldest son
of the above Richard and Barbara, died s. p. in 1756. William, the younger
son, assumed the name of Weddell, and married in 1771, Elizabeth, daughter
of Sir John Ramsden, Bart., of Byram, but died s. p. in 1792, and was buried
at Newby. I omitted to say that the above Alexius Elcock was buried at Christ
Church, 22nd April, 1700. *His* descendants inherited Knedlington, and their
property descended to their relative, the late Earl de Grey. Alderman Elcock
gave the clock to Christ Church. In (the so-called) Torre's Antiquities of
York, his arms are thus blazoned :—" Gu. a saltire varrie O. & B. inter 4
Cocks O."

Alexius Elcock, whose will bears date 19 Apl, 1700, does not allude to his coins.

" Camb[ridge], March the 3d, 1695-6.

" Honest Ab^m.,

I rec[eived] yours, and return you many thanks for your
kindness in writeing.   I am hearty glad to hear you are so well.
I thank God I am pretty well now.   My distemper, I believe,
was neither pleurisy nor asthma, but a great and inveterate cold,
which nothing would work upon till I was fomented.   I have
writ you here what you desired out of Pettus and Blowe.   I wish
you a good journey, and wish myself with you there, and should
be mighty glad if you would give me a short acc[ount] of your
travells.   You need not to have been so fearfull of troubling (as
you call it) me.   Farther, I should be glad to be so employ'd in
serving you, it would be *utile dulci*, so never spare for that reason
again.   Mr. Bennet and sir Tennant are at London this week,
for orders.   Sir Tennant is to be conduct. of K's.   Our election
is not till the 30th of this month ; we look upon sir Lovell,
Foulkes, and Ayzerly, of our year, to come in ....
......

" From thence we went to Eldon Hole (being on the top of the
highest hill in the peak fforest), which we computed to be above
an .... long, and more than one hundred broad.   The
bottom (as 'twas told us), not to be fathomed ; and, by pry-
ing, I had certainly fall'n into it (for the ground is slippery), if I
had not been caught hold of.

" But sir Tho[mas] Bendish, with whom I travail'd, espying
some workmen makeing of walls, for there, and in other stony
countryes, they make their inclosures of loose stones or slates,
instead of which, in Suffolk, Norfolk, etc., they make ditches,
and plant them with quicksetts on the sides of the banks ; but
in Devonshire they use high mounds of earth and flag, and plant
them upon the very top of the mounds, and both are beneficial
fences by their products, whereas those walls afford none ; but
he, resolving to try some experiment, did ride to them, and, by
our generous promises, perswaded three of them, with their
pickaxes and tools, to mount behind us to the holes, where first
they digged a pretty large stone, which we tumbled in, and the
noise of its motion pleased us.   Then they digged a second stone,
as much as six of us could well roul in, (for the mouth of the hole
was declineing), and presently laid our ears to the ground, and
we could tell eight score distinctly before the noyse of its motion
ceased, and then, to our apprehension, it seemed to plunge itself
into water ; and so we tryed a third stone, of more than the for-

mer magnitude, with the like observations, which pleased the
labourers, with the addition of our gratuity."

" From whence we went to Buxton's well, bathed ourselves
that night, and the next morning (of which I shall speak more
in the word water), we went to the Devil's .... of Bake,
where we saw a large .... in the bottom of a steep hill, on
the top of which stood an ancient decayed castle (of which you
may read in *Cambden's Britannia*). We had candles, and saw
as much as we could till we were hindered by running streams.
Now, of these two holes there are many famous storyes, but,
some years after, upon viewing other mines, and their shafts and
andils to them, I apprehended that this Eldon Hole was an
ancient shaft (made in the Romans' time), to a mine, and that
the Devill's A...... was the mouth of an andil to it . . and
I am the rather of that opinion because I conceive that the levell
of the water, which stopt our further passage into that andil or
fundament of the mine, is level with the water at the .... of
Eldon Hole, and the word .... may be applyed on two
accounts, first, that upon a mistake of the word .... for the
Latin word *ars*, or art, where the Romans, when they brought
out their oars of lead, and probably made silver of it, and did
thereby shew their *ars metallica*, which the British, not being
latinized, called Ars, and as an art which they did not understand, they (as the vulgar do yet) attribute it to the devill, and
so called the Devil's ...., or *ars diabolica*. Or, it might come
from *arce*, the ablative of *arx*, a castle, and probably this
castle was originally built to defend the treasure which came out
of the hole under it, or to keep the miners in awe (there being
the like castles at the Roman mines, on the Darren hills, in
Wales), and possibly the governour of it being severe in his
duty, the vulgar (as they are apt) might call him and it *Diaboli
arx*, and since, opprobriously, the Devill's ....

" Here my friend interrupted me, and asked how Eldon Hole
(from the usuall proportion of a shaft) came to be so large. I
answer'd that *Gutta cavat lapidem*, and if one drop by often
cadency will make an hole in a stone, it is easy to be credited
that the fall of clouds of waters (from the time that this was a
shaft, being about two thousand years), might well widen it from

---

* Thoresby had been at this place a few years earlier. 22 July, 1681, he
says, " Came by Eldon hole, which is indeed of a huge wideness, exceeding
steep, and of a marvellous depth, into which I throwing a large stone it fell
from one rock or partition as it were to another, with a great thundering noise
for a pretty considerable time. Speed saith that waters trickling down from
the roof of it congeal into stones."—*Diary*, i., 92.

Virgill's dimension, of three ulnas, yards, or ells square (for I conceive he meant the shaft of a mine), to this great dimension; at which he smiled.

"Blome, Derbyshire.

"The Bake abounds with lead, and not without veins of antimony, quarries of millstones and whetstones, wherein are divers strange things, or rather wonders to be seen, as the Devill's . . . Eldon Hole, and Pool's Hole; the chief wonder is the vastness of the height, length and depth of those caves, and the strange irregularityes of the rocks within the water that comes from the Devill's ...., which is said to ebb and flow as doth the ebbing and flowing well not far distant. In Pool's Hole the water falling down is congealed to a kind of white, brittle, shining stone.

"I consulted the word waters, which sir John Pettus refers to above, but found nothing under about the Peake, or like it.

"Philip Pryme, gent, of Normanton, in Derbyshire. I look't in the map and found one town of that name about three miles south of Derby itself.

" . . . . and it may be you may go before you receive this (which I would not . . . first, tho' I doubt does not answer your expectations).

"Honest Ab..............
"Your ....
" ....

"(Addressed). For the Revd. Mr. Abra. Pryme, minister of Broughton-by-Brigg, in Lincolnshire, by way of Lincoln. Post paid 2d. at Cambridge."

"Cambridge, July the 18th, 1696.
"Honest Abraham,

I rec[eived] both your's, and humbly beg your pardon for my fault, but 'tis no wonder all your charms and powers could not...... me, for it was impossible to find me out. I am now got here again. I came but on Thursday, and this is the first opportunity since of writeing. I know not how long I shall continue here, for I think of going into orders this next time, and then will exercise myself where I could light on, till further opportunity; and I wish heartily it might be my fortune to come near you. You tempt me very much in telling me what great liveings you have, and I am mighty glad to hear your fortune is so good; and I will assure you, if I go to York (which I know not

when 't will be), I will certainly call upon you. And now to
tell you of my travells. It were enough to say I have been in
most places about London, for it would cost a man some years to
know all. I took a turn over to Green[wich?] where I saw the
fine park, the k[ing] and q[ueen's] houses, Mr. Flamstead's
house,[v] where he makes all his astronomicall observations, which
was all very fine. From thence by Blackwall, and famous ship,
where we saw severall great merchants and men of war, as also
all the way from London bridge to Deptford, to the number of
severall thousands, I believe ; we went by Woolwich, and severall
other little places on the Thames. We passed by many great
ships, men of war, and were call'd aboard one (for they searched
our barge for seamen) ; at last we came to Gravesend, a good
close little town, and over against that Tilbury fort ; its strength
lyes most in ditches and palisades, so that it makes no great
shew at a distance, except on pretty large round tower, where
there is, on great days, the royal standard display'd, which wo
saw. All ships are to touch there, on account of the custome,
before they pass, which one refuseing lately was shot at, and
presently disabled, and so taken. I saw severall men of war,
Dutch and English, and other great ships, as East Indiamen,
etc. ; and it was very pretty, when one came in, to see her fire
her guns, and the others answer her, and, after all, the fort. It
looks mighty pretty to see them spit fire and smoake on both
sides ; and 'tis no wonder they are blinded in sea fights, where
there are so many, and the sport so hot, since, after the fireing
of but half a dozen guns in on ship, she is so clouded with
smoak as I could not see her scarce in $\frac{1}{2}$ quarter of an hour ;
and I saw the guns spit their fire, I believe, a full minute from
the crack. I saw there, one evening, when the sun shone very
bright, from an hill, two or three hundred large ships and colliers,
under saile all together. 'Twas a fine sight, for they came just
against the sun, and the full white sayles look't very fine. 'Tis
a pleasant place, and fine walking in the vast cherry orchards,
which are all in strait rows, look which way you will, that 'tis
very pleasant liveing there, only those great guns sometimes, by
neglect of the gunners, are fired with ball when they should not,
and sometimes from the ships, that not long ago (but this was
upon occasion too), they killed ten h[orses?] in the low grounds
with endeavouring to sink a ship that was on fire by accident,

---

v Thoresby, 14 July, 1714, says he walked into the park, which was most
pleasant, to the Astronomical House upon the height of all, but missed of Dr.
Flamstead, the famous Astronomer, who was gone to London.—*Diary*, ii., 236.

and might have done great damage to the rest, if not . . . . .
We staid there some time, but not without visiting severall
neighbouring towns for a dose of good nappy ale or wine, when
the place could afford such.   We visited some parsons now and
then, where we might have good bottled ale, for that is theire
treat, and pipes and tobacco, for I met with none that did not
smoak, and none met with me when I did not.   'Tis a place
where there is abundance of chalk and limestones, and many
huge pits, where there are excellent and curious plants, which we
sometimes gathered, for we all pretended a little to that, tho' I
have forgot since you taught me, I am so ill a scholar.   We went
one day over a fine hill and delicate prospect to Rochester, about
eight or ten miles, where I saw nothing but an old ruinous castle,
or rather nothing but ruine itself; a poor sorry cathedral (but
very clean kept, and a good organ); and a poor inconsiderable
city, hardly so good as Grantham.   I believe, too, I have given
it more than its due.   From thence we walk't into Chattam, a
small tarpaulin town, joyning to Rochester.   We saw the king's
stores and the docks, which are incredible things almost; three or
four large men of war mending, and the sad scheleton of the Royall
Soveraigne.   Here we refreshed ourselves with a quart or two
of indifferent claret, and so took boat over the station of the
grand fleet of the world, when at home, a place rather commodious than large, for 'tis but a sudden widening of the river Medway for a little space, like a lake, 'tho the river itself I take to
be near a quarter of a mile broad.   From thence we came to
Upner castle, but durst not attempt it, for fear of being soundly
duck't in punch, which would not have been agreeable in so hot
weather, and after drinking before too.   So we slip't by, and
came home sober.   That was the castle the Dutch passed, when
they burn't our fleet there, in the late wars.   I saw the broken
chain and bomb that was laid across the river to hinder them,
but they broke it, and some demon or other had charged all the
guns in the castle with sand, so the Dutch had litle to do but
mind their business they came for.   I have given you an account
on that side, now for the other side.   Monday morning, 5 o'clock,
etc., we sayle from Blackfryars staires, so passed by all the city
of London and Westminster to Lambeth and Chelsey, Cheswick
and Putney, and other places, which you have either heard of or
which are not worth your hearing.   We came then to Mortlack,
and there landed ; a small town situate on the Thames.   From
thence we walked two miles, as if we had been in Paradise, to
Richmond, where we saw an old house, built by John of Gaunt,

now called the king's house; there we went over Richmond green, saw the wells and park, which are very fine, and a brave prospect from the park over to London, on side, and so all about, the town is but indifferent. We saw my lord Rochester's house, who is ranger of the park, and a great many fine seats of noblemen, gentlemen, and merchants of London, and the old lady Lauderdale's house, at Ham. Thence we went by Kingstone to Hampton Court, where the king's house, queen's dayry, and gardens, are the finest things I ever saw, and which would fill another sheet to relate, so let it all pass. From thence we went to Windsor, where we saw the castle, where we saw things inexpressibly fine, as St. George's Hall and Chappell, the armory, king and queen's bed, closets, withdrawing rooms, dressing rooms, canopys of state for audience to ambassadours, with the chappell or the cathedrall, where hang up all the acheivements of the knights of the garter, the vast high terras walks, etc., 'tis the finest prospect . . . . of you in the world. We saw Eaton college and school, not anything fine there; and so home, *per varios casus quos nunc proscribere longum est.* Well, honest Abraham, I have writt now 'till I am weary. You must take it as it comes in my head, for I took no notes. As to my way of living at London, I had good company, German and Dutch doctors, travellers, residents, chymists, etc., all countrymen, and so acquainted, and one brings one in to all three or four nights a week at a tavern, but, mind me, not all night. There is all languages spoke, Dutch, German, French, Italian, Latin, Greek, and I know not what. Pray excuse me any further, at this time, and excuse me to the . . Maxwell and Lovell are gone to Ireland.

"Honest Abraham, let me hear from you.

"I am your most affectionate friend and servant,

"R. READ."[1]

"(Addressed). For the Revd. Mr. Abraham Pryme, Minister of Broughton-by-Brigg, in Lincolnshire, by way of Lincolne. Post paid 3d. at Cambridg."

[1] Robt. Read, son of Clement Read, of York, grocer, by his first wife, and grandson of Clement Read, of Buttercrambe, Yorkshire, gentleman, born at York, educated at the school there under Mr. Tomlinson, admitted sizar for Mr. Hotham, 2 May, 1690, æt. 18, under Mr. Wigley. (See under Headlam). B.A. 1693-4; M.A. 1697; B.D. 1705. On 31 March, 1707, Jo. Perkins was elected (adm. 1 April) to Read's vacant fellowship. Died at York, 2 Dec., 1706.—Note in *St. John's College Register*, vol. 2, at the beginning; See *Hardy's Le Neve,* iii., 641,

Clement Read, of York, married, 2ndly, at St. Saviour's, York, 17 Aug., 1686, Elizabeth, d. and c. of Roger Wilberfoss, of that city, haberdasher, (Sheriff 1678) by whom he had Roger, baptized 1687, and Wilberfoss Read, who was living at Grimthorpe, co. York, in 1754.

"From Ipsden,' Oxfordsh[ire],
          "Near Wallingford, in Berksh[ire].

"Honest Abraham,

For so I will still call you.   I am still the same, and
I hope you will be as free with me, if I may deserve that appellation.   I received your's, with great joy to hear from my old
friend; and who, notwithstanding the longest absence of any of
my familiars, is the dearest to my memory and highest in my
thoughts.   Honest Abraham, I thought you had quite forgot me,
for the ceasing of our correspondence was not my fault, as I
may conclude from your own wherein you say you received
my last to you, since which I never had any again; this made
me believe you were angry with me, and the reason I thought
was that I did not answer your request concerning two folios
writ by one Butcher, if my memory don't fail me, MS. you
desired me to epitomise them for you, which I would not have
refused you, tho' a great task, if I had had the books myself, or
could have had conveniently those in the library, but at the time,
if am not mistaken, I had not the use of the library.   Besides,
these are lockt up in the inner study, and not to be lent out.   I
writ you what I cou'd, and I hope you have pardoned what I
cou'd not, by writeing to me again.   Sir Walter Raleigh thought
himself pardoned by a new commission;   tho' he was mistaken, I hope I am not, tho', as he, I cannot at present open
those mines you desire of me.   Honest Abraham, I shou'd have
been very ready to have served you, if I had been in College,
but where I am I can not, tho' here is a study of books of the
old parson's, who was a very learned man, but nothing in that
way in his study.   I believe you know how I come to be here
from sir Wilkinson, at York, and I suppose he told you I shou'd
be at College as last Michaelmas, which indeed I did think I
shou'd, but Mr. Headlam, our present incumbent, is still at York,
and desires me to stay till he comes.   I shou'd have answered
you sooner, but by the date I perceive your letter had laid a
great while at College, so 'tis not my fault.   I can send you
nothing from hence but what is in Dr. Plot.   I shall be in
College before Easter, however, so you may command any thing
I can do this present, if it be not too late, so pray let me know
and hear from you whilst here.

          "I am your ever most affectionate friend and servant,
                                        "R. READ.

     ʳ There is no date to this, but being directed to him at Hull, it would be
after September 1698.

" Write to me, by London, at the vicarage at Ipsden, to be left at the George, in Wallenford, Barksh[ire].

" (Addressed). For the Rev. Mr. Abraham Pryme, near the High Church, in Hull, in Yorkshire, by London."

PART OF THE DRAFT OF A LETTER FROM THE DIARIST TO ONE OF HIS ACQUAINTANCE, WHOSE NAME IS NOT GIVEN.

[*Sans* date. Bound up in *Lansdowne MSS.*, 891.]

Right Worshipful Sir,

Thankfulness is such an indispensible duty that I commonly begin all my letters with it, and by this I give you my thanks for the favours that I received at your hands the last time that I was in your town. I had returned the same to you sooner but that this Corporation layd their commands upon me to spend all my time in the searching of their records in relation to some suits they are going to be involved in. I hear that Mr. Gilby was last Sunday at your town, and that he told my brother that he'll never go more, and likewise that the liveings are not disposed of, so that I have yet hopes that God will incline your hearts to bestow the same upon me. I am sure that none shall more mind his duty, none live more peaceably amongst you, none more faithfully serve you than myself. If you desire any furder certificates of my life and conversation I could send you several from Mr. Raikes, Min[ister], of Hazil, Mr. Westby, of Ranfield, and other of my friends, but I am feard of being too troublesome unto you. I am infinitely obliged to the honoured Mr. White and his son for their great civilitys unto me, and had written unto them if I had had any thing worthy of their cognizance, to both whome pray present my most humble service when you have the happiness to see them. I should be very glad to know when you dispose of your liveing, or whether it would be well taken if I should come over again. We have here the articles of impeachment against the Lord Summers, in Dutch, which one of our ships this week brought from Holland, a short coppy of which I have here sent you in English, because that perhaps you have not seen the same.

PROPOSALS BY WAY OF CONTRIBUTION, FOR WRITING A NATURAL HISTORY OF YORKSHIRE,' By Jo. Browne, Dr. of Laws and Physick.

First of all, The author proposes to take into consideration

' The above printed Prospectus is inserted by De la Pryme in the Diary in

T

the disposition of the heavens and temperature of the air in respect to the various changes and alterations therein, and first the longitude and latitude of the country shall be reckoned in respect of London; likewise the usual salubrity or insalubrity of the air, and with what constitutions it agrees better or worse than others.

2ndly, The water will be considered, as first rivers, with their bigness, course, and inundations, with all the different species of plants, insects, and fishes, that are to be found in them; likewise lakes, ponds, springs, and especially mineral-waters, as of what medicinal use they are of, what sorts of earth they run through, their kinds, qualities, and virtues, and how examined.

3rdly, The earth shall be observed, and first in its self, as to its dimentions, situation, figure, or the like, its plain, hills, or valleys, with the several kind of soyls that are there, as of clay, sand, gravel, &c., what are its products as to minerals, vegetables, or animals; moreover, how all or any of these are or may be further improved for the benefit of man. Then 2ndly, the inhabitants themselves will be considered, that have been long settled there, particularly as to their ingenuity, diet, inclinations, &c., with what improvements of arts have been made in those parts of late years; and further, the products of the earth will be more nicely examined, with all the peculiarities observable therein, as plants, trees, fruits, animals, and insects of all sorts; with clays, marles, boles, earths, axungiæ, coals, salts, atoms, vitriols, sulphers, and all other minerals of what kind soever that the earth yields, and to what use they are, or may be apply'd either to meat, physick, or any other kind.

4thly, All gentlemen of the same county, that contribute to this work, shall have the summ contributed specified, with their names, armes, and titles inserted, and more particular descriptions given of their several houses and families, and exact

---

1697, but I have not been able to discover anything relating to the Dr. Browne, by whom it was issued. He is not now recognised by antiquarian authorities at York. The Mr. [Robert] Clark, Bookseller, occurs at the Angel and Bible, in Low Ousegate, 1686, and at the Crown at the Minster Gate, in 1695. He was also Sheriff of the city in 1690-1.

There was an author, of the same name, of the following work, of which the Rev. Canon Raine has a copy. Was he identical?

Adenochoir adelogia; or, an Anatomick-Chirurgical Treatise of Glandules and Strumaes, or King's-Evil, Swellings; together with the Royal Gift of Healing, etc. By John Browne, one of His Majestie's Chirurgeons in Ordinary, and Chirurgeon of His Majestie's Hospital. London, 1684, thick 8vo.

This book contains some curious information as to the touching for the evil, and records the numbers touched by Charles II., amounting to 92,107.

prospects taken of every gentleman's seat that are contributors.

5thly, All burough towns, towns corporate, and other market towns, shall have prospects and particular observations taken, with their several towns and respective constitutions faithfully described, if they be contributors hereto, for the design is not intended a geographical, but Natural History.

6thly, The Author proposes to make exact maps of every wapontake or hundred, which, with the several other cuts necessary to be inserted, will take above 150 copper plates; for that he has, and further designs to take an impartial survey of all towns and places, so that he may impose nothing credulously upon the world from the unexamined traditions of the ancients, but true and just observations taken from the natural state of things faithfully represented, so that by this means he cannot perfect such a vast work without great time and expences.

7thly, Contributions will be received by Mr. Smith and Mr. Walford, at the Princes Arms, in Paul's Church-yard; Mr. Bentley, in Covent Garden; Mr. Bosvile, at the Dial over against St. Dunstan's Church in Fleet-street, London; by Mr. Clark, Bookseller; and the Author in York, who will give receipts to all contributors that their money shall be returned to them again, if the undertaking be not finished within 3 years.

☞ *Note.*—The design has already received very good encouragement from several persons of quality.

FINIS.

Page 5. Note. VAN VALKENBURGH FAMILY. Since this was printed, I have met with the will of Sir Matthew Van Valkenburgh (or Vaulconburgh, as he writes it), baronet, dated 1st May, 1643, and proved in London, 23rd August, 1648. From this, we learn that Robert Kay, the Doncaster gentleman, who was charged with the riotous conduct alluded to in the note, had married Isabella, the widow of Sir M. Van Valkenburgh. It seems that Lady Van Valkenburgh was named the sole executrix of her husband's said will, but that she had never proved it. Indeed, it would appear either that a will had not been known of, or that it had been, for some reason or other, purposely suppressed; for, an administration, as in the ordinary case of intestacy, had been granted by the court at York to Sir Matthew's nephew, Mark Van Valkenburgh, on the 22nd January, 1645. Lady Van Valkenburgh's marriage with Kay must have taken place not long after the death of her first husband, Sir Matthew

Van Valkenburgh (who died in April, 1644), and not long, too, before her own decease, which took place so soon after as the month of November following. Still, it was not, apparently, until the fourth year after her death, that the will of Sir Matthew Van Valkenburgh came in for probate, and then the administration was committed to Robert Kay, as the husband of the executrix, who, as before observed, had omitted to apply for it. Possibly it was under some claim of right arising out of this, his then legal position of executor, or administrator with the will annexed, that Kay attacked, *vi et armis*, the house at Middle Ings, and forcibly ejected Mark Van Valkenburgh, in the manner stated.

Mark Van Valkenburgh, esq., one of the Commissioners of Sewers for the Level of Hatfield Chase, appears to have acted as their collector and expenditor, he being mentioned, 28th August, 10 Car., 1635, as having received divers sums of money of the Participants, and made several disbursements, and being ordered to account " in Englishe " on the 1st of September, at Turnbridge.

In a MS. note by Mr. Hunter, the author of *South Yorkshire*, etc., he states that in the 21 Car. I., Sir Matthew Valkenburgh, bart., was outlawed, together with Sir Cornelius Vermuyden, and Sir Philibert Vernatti, knt. and bart., at the suit of Sir Arthur Ingram. (The 21st Car. I. was 27th March, 1645— 26th March, 1646, and Sir Matthew was buried on 4th April, 1644).

18 Nov., 1656. Filibert Vandervert surrendered three fishings in Wrangdon, Wrangdon Hill, one Lodge Hill, whereon a lodge lately stood, called Patrick's Lodge, in Midlings, etc., the lands late of Mark Vaulkenburgh's, esq., deceased, in Thorne, to the use of Roger Tockets, of Tockets, esq., who was admitted thereto.

20 Nov., 1660. Marc Van Valkenburgh, gent., and Anne his wife, surrender lands called Low Middlemarsh, lying upon Middlemarsh Hill, in the graveship of Thorne, to John Langwith, of Doncaster, gent.

1675. At the archdeacon's visitation, Hatfield, Mark Van Valkenburgh, gent., was presented for not paying his church assessment.

1684. Do. Thorne. Marcus Van Valkenburgh, of Crowle, co. Lincoln, for detaining a legacy of 3*l.* due to the minister of the parish of Thorne.

At a Court of Sewers, held at Bawtry, 14th September, 1675,

VAN VAULCONBURGH, OR VALKENBURGH.*

Matthew Van Vaulconburgh, of Middle Ings, near Hatfield, co. York. Created a baronet 26th July, 1642. Buried at Hatfield, 4 April, 1644. Admon. granted at York to Mark Van Valkenburgh, his nephew, 22nd January, 1645. *Postea* Will dated 1 May, 1643; proved in London, 23 August, 1648, by Robert Kaye, esq. = Isabella, dau. of Anthony Eyre, and sister of Sir Gervas Eyre, of Laughton and Rampton, knt. Married 1636. Buried at Hatfield, 21 November, 1644, as "Heroina." (*Par. Reg.*) = Robert Kaye, esq., second husband.

Mark Van Vaulconburgh. Buried at Hatfield, co. York, as "senior," 17 October, 1653.

Luke Van Vaulconburgh. Is said to have died on the Hatfield Levels, leaving two sons, who returned to Holland. = Cornelia. died Dec. 1665. of Tocketts, in par. Guisborough, co. York. Died intestate. Admon. granted to his son, George, 21 Dec., 1683. = Roger Tocketts, esq. of Tocketts, in par. Guisborough, co. York. Bur. at Guisborough, co. York.

Sir John Anthony Van Vaulconburgh, baronet. Bap. at Hatfield, 16 June, 1640. Admitted of Gray's Inn, London, 31 May, 1660. Buried at St. Margaret's, Lincoln, 1 Sept., 1679. No will or admon. found at Lincoln or London.

Matthew Van Vaulconburgh. [Query.] Buried at Doncaster, 18 November, 1660].

Mark Van Vaulconburgh. Died at Crowle, co. Lincoln, and there buried, 26 April, 1694. Will d. 21st April, and proved at Lincoln, 4 May, 1694. = Ann, daughter of John Starkey, of Thorne, co. York. Bap. 20 January, 1632. Married at Thorne, 16 October, 1639; buried there 31 August, 1672.

Edmund Thompson,† second husband, m. at Crowle, to Febry., 1659-60. Buried at Crowle, 28th June, 1736, aged about 70. (M.I.) = Kather-ine, bap. at Hat-field, 23 July, 1680; bur. there 14 Jany., 1691-2. Named in her father's will, 1694. = John Margrave, of Crowle, co. Lincoln. M. at Crowle, 29 July, 1680; bur. there 14 June, 1693. Will d. 17th April, 1691, and proved at Lincoln, 22 April, 1692.

Anne, bap. at Hat-field, 11 Feb. 1661 -2.

Eliza beth, bap. at Hat-field, 11 Feb., 1661- 2.

Eliza beth, bap. at Hat-field, 7th May, 1663.

Abigail bap. at Hat-field, 25th July, 1664. Bur. at Thorne 20th July, 1682.

John, bap. at Hat-field, 20 Sep, 1665. Bur. at Thorne, 21st Feb., 1665-6

Mary, bap. at Hat-field, 20 Sep, 1665. Bur. at Thorne, 6 Oct, 1665.

Mary, bap. at Hat-field, 13th Feb., 1667-8 Named in her father's will, 1694. = Edward Fox. Mar. at Crowle, 28th April, 1692.

Pene-lope. Named in her father's will, 1694. = ... Knipe.

Mark, bur. at Hat-field, 14th Octo-ber, 1666.

John, bap. at Hat-field, 24th Feb., 1668-9 bur. there 29th Nov., 1669.

---

* The orthography of this surname, as might be expected, has not been without its varieties in a non-indigenous land. The signature to the will of Sir Matthew, the first baronet, represents it as Van Vaulconburgh. In the hands of the old parish clerks, and others, it has been subjected to numerous distortions. † From this marriage is descended the Rev. William Hepworth Thompson, D.D., F.S.A., some time Regius Professor of Greek, and now Master of Trinity College, Cambridge.

it was ordered that the 90 acres in Durtness of Sir John Anthony Van Valkenburgh's, late in the possession of James Cressey, be let to Jane Anker, widow, at £24 per annum, she paying £9 in part of the arrears of scotts, and the remainder as it became due, (£5 5s. fee-farm rent being deducted.) On the 16th December, 1675, Robert Wright petitioned the Court that he might be tenant of 64 acres in Beningtack, near Tunnel-pit, the lands of Sir J. A. Van Valkenburgh, who is willing the scott thereon should be paid out of the rents thereof, and he prayed the Court would admit him tenant, he paying the taxes out of his rent.

Mr. Hunter, speaking of various single houses dispersed through the newly recovered country, on the drainage of Hat-field Chase, says (*South Yorkshire,* i., p. 165), "Another good house was built, by Matthew Valkenburgh, on the Middle Ing, near the Don, which afterwards became the property of the Boynton family." Sir John Boynton, in a codicil to his will, dated 11th October, 1688, gives to his nephew, William Apple-yard, "all the lands I purchased of Mr. Van Valkenburgh."

RAMSDEN, page 6. Note. In 1621 Mr. John Ramsden is spoken of as "being then the chief merchant" of Hull.

"1637. In this year, the 7th December, died Mr. John Ramsden, merchant, and mayor of this town, of the plague, who was a pious, learned, and ingenious man, and was carried by visited people into St. Trinity's church, and there buried in the chancel, under a great marble stone, with a long inscription thereon. And Mr. Andrew Marvel ventured to give his corpse a Christian burial ; and there was preached a most excellent funeral sermon to the mournful auditors, which was afterwards printed."—*De la Pryme's MS. History of Hull.*

1660. William Ramsden was mayor of Hull. At York, the name occurs in mercantile circles. William Ramsden, late apprentice with Mr. William Ramsden, was admitted to the freedom of the Fellowship of Eastland Merchants residing in the city of York, 25th December, 1650. George Ramsden, son of William Ramsden, late alderman, deceased, the like, 16th August, 1661. Charles Fishwiske, 31st March, 1664, John Pearson, 21st September, 1669, and John Crofts, 6th May, 1675, were severally apprenticed to Mr. George Ramsden, merchant adventurer, and a free brother of the Eastland Company, within the city. John Pemberton, 19th June, 1667, John Drake, 26th July, 1678, and Joseph Thompson, 31st July, 1683, the like, to

Mr. William Ramsden, of the same fraternity.—*Mr. Skaife's MS. Collections.*

In 1631 Anthony Worrall, and Alice his wife, took proceedings in the Consistory Court of York, against one Henry Ramsden, of Hatfield, for attacking the fair fame and good character of the said Alice.

Elizabeth, bap. 17 May, 1635; Henry, bap. 1 April, 1638; Grace, bap. 30 August, 1640; and Francis, bap. 16 February, 1644-5, occur as children of Henry Ramsden.—*Hatfield Parish Register.*

Anthony Ramsden, of Woodhouse, buried 6th June, 1669. Joseph Ramsden, of the Levels, bur. 23rd July, 1669. Peter Ramsden, bur. 14th September, 1634. Richard, son of Henry Ramsden, bur. 28th October, 1639. Isabel, wife of Andrew Ramsden, bur. 10th May, 1660.—*Ibid.*

The name of Ramsden continued at Norton into the present century, there being a monumental inscription in Campsall church yard for Edmund Ramsden, late of Norton Priory, interred January 1st, 1809, aged 87 years. It is recorded of him that he was "a truly pious man, an affectionate friend, a father to the fatherless, a helper of the friendless;" and that "His deeds were done in love to Him who died to cleanse his soul from sin," etc.

EXTRACTS FROM THE PARISH REGISTER OF THORNE, RELATING TO FLOODS. [p. 12].

1681-2. Mem. A great flood, with highe winds, did break our banks in severall places, and drowned our towne round, upon Sunday at night, being January the 15th.

1682. Mem. Our bankes did break in ye same places, and drowned our towne round, upon Thursday, April the 27th.

1696. Mem. That a great flood came onn very suddenly, and the highest that has been known, on Munday, the 13th of December, in the night, and on Wednesday the 15th broke our bank by Gore stile, and run over the banks in many places besides.

1700-1. Jan. 18. Mem. That a great flood then came down, being Saturday, and broke the banks in the Ashfields, and run over in many places besides.

1706. A memorandum. That on Thursday and Friday, being 18th and 19th daies of this inst. July, there was a great flood, insomuch that the banke was in great danger.

P. 27. The Rev. John Symon, M.A., Magd. Hall, Oxford,
1679; rector of Langton, E.R.Y., 29th March, 1670 till 1689,
when he refused to take the oath to William and Mary, had three
sons at a birth, who were baptized and buried the same day, 30th
November, 1678.

Thoresby (13th October, 1720), mentions being "at church,
where were baptized Abraham, Sarah, and Rebekah, the trimelli
of Abraham Scholefield, of the Shambles."—*Diary*, ii., p. 301.

Mem. Nov. 3, 1772. On this day, being Tuesday, between
seven and nine of the clock in the morning, Ann, the wife of
William Appleyard, of Snaith, was brought to bed of four female
children, born alive, but died soon after the birth. William
Williams, vicar.—*Snaith Parish Register.*

Descending to our own times, it was announced in the
Doncaster and Pontefract News, 14th July, 1870, that on the 4th
of that month, the wife of Joseph Drew, of Egborough, a plate-
layer on the Lancashire and Yorkshire railway, was delivered
of three full-grown healthy children, one boy and two girls:
and that Her Majesty's usual gift, on such occasions, of three
sovereigns, arrived on the Monday following. These were christened together shortly afterwards at Kellington church, and
were reported to be doing well.

Page 43, and Note. CURIOUS NAMES.
1602-3. Thorne. Feb. 19. Barjona Griffin and Elizabeth
Mirfield, married.

1659. Thorne. May 25. Mehitophell Gillam, buried.

1692. ,, Phineas Todd and Filia Clara Redman,
married.

1698-9. York, All Saints, Pavement, March 9, Moddoracion,
wife of John Lupton, buried.

1703-4. Fishlake. Feb. 16, Misericordia Todd, buried.

1799. Rawcliffe. July 20, Laus Deo Langdale Gent, buried.

1680. Pontefract. Nebuchadnezzar Tod, living,

Page 56. WITCHCRAFT AND SORCERY.

Doncaster. Depositions against Joan Jurdie, wife of Leonard
Jurdie, of Rossington, were taken before Hugh Childers, Mayor,
Sir John Ferne, knt. Recorder, etc., on the 6th February, second
James I., 1604-5, the 18th April, and the 16th and 18th October,
third James I., 1605; and at the Borough Sessions she was
indicted for having on the 10th April, sixth James I., 1608,
feloniously practised witchcraft and sorcery upon Hester Dolphin,

and on the 5th June, same year, upon Jane Dolphin, the daughter of Wm. Dolphin : also, the like upon George Murfin, son of Peter Murfin, on the 27th September following. These persons are severally alleged by the Grand Jury, upon their oaths, to have died from the effects of her wicked arts.

1623. At the Sessions, Jane Blomeley, widow, was indicted for having on the 25th June, twenty-first Jac. I., and on divers other days, feloniously practised and exercised certain detestable arts, called witchcraft and sorcery, upon Frances the wife of Marmaduke Craven, of Doncaster, yeoman ; by which arts the said Frances, from the said 20th June to the 30th of the same month, dangerously and mortally sickened and languished, and on the 30th died ; and the jurors presented that the said Jane Blomeley *ex malicia sua precogitata, voluntariter, diabolice, nequiter, et felonice, per artes predictas, occidit ac interfecit* the said Frances Craven. She was buried on the 1st July, 1623.

1640. Roos. John Curteis, for going to a witch in time of his sickness, to seek a remedy. Confessed his wife did go to one suspected to be a wizard, to enquire of the recovery of a child.

1682. At the archdeacon of York's visitation, Spofforth, co. York, Henry Wheelhouse, of Linton, presented, for going to a sorcerer to enquire after some stolen goods.

Archdeacon's Vis. E. R., 1688. Kirkby Grindalyth. Thomas Robinson, for resorting to a sorcerer, to consult him in order to his health.

Page 60. BEHARREL. An Abraham Beharell occurs as a witness to the will of Charles Prime, the first of the family at Hatfield, 27th December, 1669. (See *Abstracts of Wills*). To those interested in the name, the following may be useful.

Margaret Beharrel, widow, bur. 6th Feb., 1731-2. Holy Trinity, Hull.

John Beharrel, bur. 24th Jan., 1653-4. Thorne.

Isaac, son of Isaac Beharrel, bap. 5th Dec., 1669. Hatfield.

Isaac Beharrel, and Jane Dearman, married, 28th Nov., 1666. Hatfield.

Elizabeth, wife of Abraham Beharrel, bur. 11th, May, 1668. Hatfield.

1691. Nov. 30. Joseph, son of Mr. Abraham Beharrell, bap. Waghen.

1702. July 12. Abraham, son of Samuel Beharrell, bap.

1708. Dec. 22. Jacob, son of Jacob Beharrel, bap. Bur. 8th April, 1733.

1686-7. Jan. 20. Mrs. Jane Beharrell, widow, bur.
1691. Oct. 6. Mr. Abraham Beharrel, bur.
1696. April 14. Isaac Beharrell, bur.
1714. April 6. Mr. David Beharrell, bur.

St. Martin's, Micklegate, York. John Beharrell, of Snaith, and Rachel Gooben, married, 26th May, 1729.

In St. John's church, Peterborough, are memorials of Abraham Beharrel, gent., who died 20th March, 1765, aged 49. Elizabeth, his wife, 19th June, 1807, aged 83. Rebecca B., spinster, 2nd Nov., 1830, aged 79. Ann B., spinster, her sister, 5th August, 1837, aged 83.

RATSDALE, page 95. This is Rochdale. In the *History of Roche Abbey*, by Dr. Aveling, 1870, p. 134, is a notice of a royal grant, of the 35th Henry VIII., to Arthur Assheton, of estates of the late monastery of Roche Abbey. Amongst these is a tenement in Saddleworth, in the parish of Ryche Dale, otherwise Rattesdale.

Page 102. PORTINGTON. (*From De la Pryme's MS. History of Hatfield. Lansdowne MS.*, 897, *p.* 205-206). Be it remembred that the pious and good Charles the First, with many of his nobles, in a jorney that they were in out of the south, came from Rossington briggs unto Armethorp, drunk there at a landlady's that kept an alehouse, by the gravel-pit side; from thence they went to Hatfield and Thorn; and so by the guide and conduct of one old Mr. Canby (unkle to Mr. Edw. Canby, of this town), an old officer in the late Chace, was led over John-a-more Long to Whitgift ferry, and from thence went to Beverley.

The same most excellent king, also, in a jorney from Beverley to Nottingham, where he set up his standard, came over at the aforesayd ferry of Whitgift to Gool, and so along the great banks into this town; call'd and drunk at an alehouse at the north end thereof; pass'd quite through the same, and so through the Levels, with design to go through the Isle into Gainsbrow, but being got to Santoft, where a guard was kept by the Islemen against the king's party then at Hatfield under Robin Portington, who, as soon as they saw a great number comeing against them, all fledd; the king, learning there that the Isle were all in armes against them, turn'd his course, and went down the great bank on the right hand, and so to a place called Bull Hassoks; and leaveing Haxey, and all the Isle on the left hand, passed onwards to Stockwith, and so to Gainsburrow, whence to Lincoln, and thence to Nottingham.

When the commission of array came out, Sir Ralf Hansby and .... were appointed to sit thereupon, upon Scausby Leys, beyond Doncaster, and to summon and list all men that could be spared in all the country round, upon which, above half of the inhabitants of this manor appear'd and offer'd themselves, with their lives and fortunes, to serve the king.

When the king's party took Leeds, in which siege Robin, Roger, and Henry Portington did great service, all this lordship was summon'd into work at the fortifying of the town, where one Pool, of Thorn, got a rich booty upon the defeat of a party of the enemy.

Oliver Cromwell, that great rebel and villane, marched through Hatfield and Thorn, with several companys of horse, into the north, and came the same way back.

Page 104. "I shall ne'er go the sooner to the Stygian Ferry." The words occur in the well-known duet, by Travers, 1725-1758, (author of "I, my dear, was born to-day;" and "Haste, my Nanette.") Query. The words are older than Travers—are they by *Prior*?

Old Chiron thus said to his pupil, Achilles:

"I'll tell you, young gentleman, what the gods' will is:
You, my boy, must go—
The gods will have it so—to the siege of Troy,
Upon those fields to be slain,
Thence never to return to Greece again.
But drink and be merry,
You'll ne'er go the sooner (*bis*) to the Stygian Ferry."

Page 114. *De la Pryme's MS. History of Hatfield* is comprized within *Lansdowne MSS.*, 897, Brit. Mus., and contains about 315 folio pages, all written very legibly in the author's own hand. Bound up with it is a copy of notes relating to Hatfield, Fishlake, and Barnby Don churches, by Torre, taken from his MSS. in the Dean and Chapter's Register at York, in August, 1724, by J. Warburton, *Somerset Herald*. There are also included within it an old map of Hatfield Chase, "surnayed in the year 1633, by mee Josias Aerlebout," (since engraved and published in *Stonehouse's History of the Isle of Axholme*); a "South-east Prospect of Hatfield Manor;" a "Bill of all the Names of Freeholders within the liberty of Howdenshire that hath 40s. per annum and above;" "the South-east Prospect of Hatfield Church;" "the South Prospect of Thorn;" "the South-west Prospect of Fish-

lake Village" (shewing the houses of Mr. Simpson and Mr.
Perkins) "Barnby Dunn, the seat of Roger Gregory, esq., to
the south;" and a north-east prospect of the same, as " the seat of
Roger Portington, esq."

ADDITIONAL NOTES CONCERNING THE QUAKERS.[1]   [pp. 141-143.]

   1695. *Archdeacon of York's Visitation.*   Presentments.
Hatfield. Christian Middlebrooke, and Thomas Lee, esquire, for
not paying their assessment.
   1664. Thorne. Christian Middlebrooke and his wife for not
being marryed according to law.
   1667. Arksey. Samuel Barlow, and Mary his wife, quakers,
for keeping two of his children unbaptized.
   1667. Snaith. Magdalen Dawney, John Dawney, and Susanna
Dawney, for not coming to church, being quakers.
   [Paul Dawney, son of Robert Dawney, of Pollington, was
bap. at Snaith, 28th January, 1613-4; his sister, Susan, 29th
September, 1618; his son, Richard, 16th July, 1640. Magdalen
Dawney was bur. 5th November, 1679].
   1669. Batley. William Watson, for despiseing the booke of
common prayer, and the homylyes, together with those that read
them, protesting that he would rather hear a song of Robin
Hood.
                  Archbishop of York's Visitation.

   1674. Thorne. Thomas Middlebrooke, senior, for with-
holding a close called Swanland, in Thorne, from the church.
   Hatfield. Jacob, John, and Isaac, sons of Isaac De Cow,
for being unbaptized. Isaac De Cow, for keeping his children
unbaptized.
   Drax. Abraham Decowe, and Sarah his wife, and Jane
Decowe, for not coming to church.

                  Archdeacon's Visitation.

   1680. Addingham. Edward Dodgson, for refusing to bring
his dead to the church to be buried, but burying it in a place
called a sepulchre.
   Pontefract. Nebuchadnezzar Tod, for not coming to church.
   1683. York, St. Mary's, Bishophill senior. Thomas Fox,
who boasted that he had been att a hundred conventicles.

   [1] From the collections of the Revd. C. B. Norcliffe, who has obligingly
communicated several other pieces of information.

Archdeacon of East Riding's Visitation.

1675. Owthorne. Stephen Eiles, for suffering his winde-mill to grinde upon Easter Sunday.

1677. Owthorne. Joanna Mare, widow, for dispraceing the common prayer, and calling itt witchcraft, and not paying her church taxes.

1665. Flambrough. Thomas Rickaby, senior, master and mariner, of Bridlington Key, and Timothy Preston, woollen draper, for keeping their hatts on in sermon tyme, upon the 29th of January.

Rillington. William Trambe, brewster, for not standing upp att the Creed and the *Gloria Patri*, and for not kneelinge at the Lord's Prayer.

1670. Hollym. Peter Johnson, for keeping his two sons, John and Isaac, unbaptized, and his daughter Rebecca also unbaptized.

Sherburn. George Owston, for a frequent goer to Quaker meetings, and for shuttinge the church doore upon the parishioners, taking away the key, and tying upp the bell-rope.

1675. Hedon. Timothy Rhodes, for drinking in time of divine service, and playing at cards on Christmas Day.

Page 193. De la Pryme's account of Doncaster consists of about ten folio pages in *Lansdowne MSS.*, 898, British Museum. Sundry matters are bound up with it, such as a letter from from Ralph Thoresby, of Leeds, dated 8th November, 1703, accompanying a transcript from *Leland's Itinerary* of what relates to Doncaster and the neighbourhood. There are also a map of the west-riding of Yorkshire, performed by Johan Speede, 1610; a map of twenty miles round Leeds, dedicated by Mr. John Boulter to the inhabitants and others of that place; a pen and ink sketch of the east prospect of Selby; an unfinished one of the south-east of Escrick Hall, the seat of Beilby Thompson, esq.; several old engraved views of seats of gentry, such as Sprotburgh, Sir Godfrey Copley's; Tong, Sir Geo. Tempest's; Whixley, Chr. Tancred's, esq.; Swillington, William Lowther's, seq.; Great Ribston, Sir Henry Goodrick's; Newby, Sir Edwd. Blackett's, bart.; Temple Newsam, Viscount Irwin's; with "prospects" of the towns of Leeds and Wakefield, by Buck, etc. The account of Doncaster has been evidently submitted to Dr. Johnston, as it bears upon it remarks in his handwriting. All or most of the information it contains has become embodied in the several printed works relating to the town, which renders it scarcely necessary to reproduce it. After giving an account of the former church of St. George (unhappily destroyed by fire on the 28th February, 1853[u]), he appears to have taken a stroll through the town, upon which the following may, perhaps, serve as a specimen of the remarks he has recorded.

Near this church, in some of the old buildings, is yet to be seen the ruins of the old castle, which the Romans built when they remained here; from which castle this town derives its name.

On the east side of this church, bourdering upon the church yard, is a larg old sacred building, of the bigness of a larg chappel, now used by the tanners. I take it to have been a great chantery.

Furder southwards, in the town, stands the nave and chancel of a great church called St. Mary Magdalen's, (which was formerly a chappel, but was made a parochial church afterwards.) The two isles, both on the north and south sides, were pull'd down, and now the arches are wall'd up, and this great sacred building is now most wickedly and sacrilegious[ly] apply'd to secular uses.[v] In the church or chappel yard about it is commonly digg'd up men's bones, and sculls, and gravestones with old Saxon letters on, etc.

Going furder on, we come to the south-east end of the town. The first thing observable there is a great cross, commonly call'd the Hall Cress,[w] standing a great height. Before the pillar for the crosses begins to arise, the pillar is made thus [sketch], with four round pillars running up the sides of it. I find that it is cemented together with oyster shells, for between every stone there is planely visible oister shells, some of them whole. Upon the top of this pillar, before Cromwell's days, there stood five curious gilt crosses, a great height, which the rogues in his time did most wickedly shoot down, and were resolv'd to pull the whole building down to the ground, but could not. About ... years ago, when Mr. William Pattison was mayor,[x] he caused this cross to be repair'd, and a ball and fane set upon the top thereof; and as they were viewing the pillar very narrowly, and rubbing the moss of that was grown thereon, he discover'd several old Roman letters, containing an inscription round the pillar, in great letters, which he caused to be clensed and gilt with gold, which inscription is this:—[+], ICEST · EST LA · CRVICE · OTE·D·TILLI · A · KI · ALME DEV EN FACE MERCI. AMEN. XI. XII.,[y] which I take to mean thus: Here is the cross of Otto de Tilly, unto whome God shew mercy. Amen.

[u] See *The History and Description of St. George's Church at Doncaster*, destroyed by fire Feb. 28th, 1853, by John Edward Jackson, M.A., of Brazenose College, Oxford, rector of Leigh Delamere, and vicar of Norton, co. Wilts. London, 1855.

[v] It had been converted into a Town Hall, and a portion of the lower part of it was used as the Grammar School. In 1846-7 it was taken down for the purpose of making some new arrangements for market purposes, when a very interesting discovery of the ruins of the old church of St. Mary Magdalen took place, a history of which, with several illustrations, was compiled by the Rev. J. E. Jackson, M.A., in 1853.

[w] See *Miller*, pp. 31-33; *Wainwright*, p. 60; *Hunter's South Yorkshire*, i., p. 10; *Jackson's St. George's Church*, appendix, lxxxix. Entirely removed in 1792, and a very indifferent substitute erected on Hob Cross, or Hall Cross Hill.

[x] Wm. Patterson, elected 26th September, 1678.

[y] The numeral figures are believed not to have been on the cross itself, but merely on the margin of an old painting of it, belonging to R. Thoresby, of Leeds, from which an engraving was made by G. Vertue in 1753, where they were set as a memorandum of the hours at which the sun traversed the dial which was set thereon.

OTHO DE TILLI'S, OR THE HALL CROSS, DONCASTER,
IN 1678.

Or, perhaps thus, if *étré* may be understood, which is most probable :—Here lyes under this cross Otto de Tilly, on whose soul good God have mercy.

What the following figures should mean I cannot tell, unless it be eleven hundred, 12 and 1, that is 1113.

On the right hand, over against this cross, is an old house with old cherubims' heads, angels, etc., where Mr. Pattison lives,[z] which was a great religious house in days of old, call'd a gild or hall, purposely design'd for the lodgment and entertainment of all pilgryms in their travels. There was another of these halls down the street, allmost at the far end of the town, by the brigg, for the same purpose.[a]

About the middle way down the street from the aforesaid great cross, on the left hand, is to be seen in the walls the ruins of the White Friars, a great Priory.[b] There is yet good gardens within, and the walls encompass the same all on the backside, as they did before its destruction. Over the gate that comes in on the back side is engraven, in very old characters, these words, with an odd sort of a coat of arms between the words, thus :—

E Th :	Prior
Anno Do:	1515.

Going on thus from this door, all along on the backside, wee come to a gate called St. Fulcher's gate, which is now not onely a gate, but a prison also: but in former times this gate and prison was a stately chappel, built by the monks of the White Friery aforesayd, upon which it almost joyns; for it was a common thing in time of popery, not onely to build a chappel by every gate of every great town, and make the passage through the chappel, and to adorn all the inside of the chappel gate with images of the saints, etc., for to invite and begg of the enterers in unto the town, or the goers out, to bestow some thing upon the poor monks of such or such an order, for if they were never so rich yet they always pleaded poverty. And then, another piece of cunning they had herein to save and preserve the town from enemys, for as when a town is besieged the chief efforts are made against the gates thereof, so the enemy seeing that these were hallowed gates, sanctifyed entrances into the town, through and belonging to a holy chappel, which whoever violated was curs'd, therefore nobody would, in them dark times, assault a town here, so that they were a great safety to those places that had such chappel gates. This sayd

[z] Hall Cross House, purchased and much altered, in 1811, by John Branson, esq., who had the honour of entertaining here her present majesty, when Princess Victoria, on her visit to Doncaster races, from Wentworth house, 15th September, 1835. Thomas Walker, esq., afterwards purchased it, and resided here. It is now occupied by the Rev. Wm. Gurney, M.A., head master of the grammar school.

[a] "Such," says the Rev. J. E. Jackson (*History of St. George's Church*, lxxxviii.), "appears to have been the standard history of almost every old house in De la Pryme's days. But whatever Hall Cross House may have been, this was certainly not the case with the other." The latter stands at the northern end of St. Mary's bridge, in the parish of Arksey, and was for some time the residence of a family of Wildbore. Edmund Wildbore, gent., "ad pedem pontis," died 26th April, 1694. His arms, carved in stone (a fess charged with a trefoil betw. two wild boars passant, crest, a boar's head erased), and dated 1690, were, until within a few years ago, to be seen fixed over the door of a building in the garden at the rear of the premises. The shield is now in my possession. Mrs. Mary Cooke, widow, first of John Battie, esq., of Warmsworth, and secondly of George Cooke, esq., was living here when she made her will, 1st June, 1764, being there described of Bridge house, in the parish of Arksey. She died 22nd May, 1775, and was buried at Warmsworth.

[b] The house of the Carmelites, or White Friars, stood in that part of Hall gate which is now called High-street, or rather, it occupied the site of land now

ch[apel] was dedicated to St. Pulcheria.[c]

From the aforesayd gate south-westward, in the street going towards Balby, is to be seen the ruins of a larg and once stately chappel dedicated to St. James, all now in rubish.

Returning therefore again, and going through St. Pulcher's chappel gate, and so into the High-street, and turning down unto the river, there has, before you come thereat, been some religious places, but what they were cannot now be known.

Comeing to the river there is an excellent stone brigg over the same, of a great height from the water, but for all that it is so high the water was this winter higher than it, and drive many of the battlement stones off, (and has quite broke down the famous great stone bridge at Tadcaster.)

As soon as you are pass'd over this Doncaster first bridge, in a great green close on the right hand, stood in former times the famous monastry of Black Friars,[d] (at which, as I remember, Cardinal Wolsey lodg'd in his jorney from Cawood to Leicester, where he dy'd,) but now there [is] nothing to see. Furder on yet you come to another bridge, which has formerly had a large chappel, over and besides the same, dedicated to St. James, most of which chappel is yet standing, and is now becom a dwelling-house. In the gate is nitches where the 12 apostles stood, which were but pull'd down in Cromwell's days ; and into the chappel was a door and several open places, like windows, for the monk that was appointed to watch to gather alms, to see when people came through.

Upon this river stands a water mill belonging to Doncaster, as built at their joint charge, which [is] one of the fines[t] in England, and is about one hundred pound a year.

On the left side of the way, just having got over the bridge, stands a famous old cross, of curious excellent workmanship, with nitches for three images to stand in.[e]

Furder on, beyond this, stands on the righ[t] hand a gentleman's house, which was formerly a great hall for the entertainment of pilgrims, as the[re] was another at the other end of the town, as I observed before.

Furder on, beyond this, on the left hand, stands the ruin of a hermitage,[f]

covered by the Mansion House, the Ram Inn, and other house property, intersected by Priory-place, and extending to Printing-office street. The great gate house stood over against the south-west end of Scot-lane. After the dissolution, there was here a capital messuage or mansion called the New Building. Mary, Viscountess Carlingford, wife of Barnham Swift, Viscount Carlingford, and daughter of the Earl of Dumfries, resided here. King Charles I. dined with her, in one of his journies through Doncaster, and planted a pear tree in the garden. Part of this royal memorial was blown down by a violent storm, 18th September, 1809, but the rest of it (quam sæpe vidi), stood till the latter end of 1841.

[c] See Hunter, (South Yorkshire, i., p. 17,) who observes that "it is too much to invent a chapel to explain a name. There is a total absence of proof of any chapel of St. Pulcheria, and the name of [St.] Sepulchre-gate existed before the house of Carmelites."

[d] Probably the grey friars. Though Burton says that a house of Dominicans, or black friars, was founded at Doncaster, in the reign of Edward II., etc. Hunter considers that "it is nevertheless doubtful whether such a house ever existed."—South Yorkshire, i., p. 19.

[e] See representation of it in Jackson's St. George's Church, appendix, xci.

[f] Among the ecclesiastical foundations in the parish of Sprotburgh, was a chantry or free chapel called the Hermitage. The endowment was a house for the cantarist, with a garden, meadow, and wood, a rent of 5s. from Conings-borough, and of 60s. from a farm at Creighton [Criglestone], within the lord-ship of Wakefield.—Hunter's South Yorkshire, i., p. 348.

THE MILL BRIDGE CROSS, DONCASTER, 1764.

with the house ho.d by that found him with meat to keep body and soul together.

I was in the hermitage, and the people shew'd us where the altar stood, where he every day digged a little and little of his own grave, and told us how that every day he gave the blessed Sacrament to those that came to receive the same.

Thus much for Doncaster.

In the midst almost of Poteric Carr,[f] beyond Doncaster, upon a small hill almost inaccessible by reason of the morass round about, is the ruins of a stately chappel dedicated to St. John. It is probable that here was either some great hermitage or little monastry, nunery, or priory, here.

I hear that one Mr. Houson, of Beverley, has several old records of Doncaster.

In the 1 vol. of Dug[dale's] Monast[icon] is the char[ter] of Nigel de Fossard, the grant of his tithes in Doncaster to St. Mary's mon[astery] in York. In the same vol. is several charters relateing to Osterfield, (which in former times belonged wholy unto the knight templars, and then to the knights of St. John, of Jerusalem, and there the court was held for all the lands in all the country round about, as I have heard; and there every house is bound, by their tenure, to have crosses upon them,) to Bautry, Barnsley, Pomfret, Selby, Hampol, &c.

Mr. Williamson, of Leeds, is a most ingenious workman at clock work; he made a clock a while ago for Sir John Lowther, which he sold for 35l., which, besides the many curious works therein, goes a whole year together.

Under the north quire of this church is a large spacious charnell house almost full of bones, yet curiously arched over. [Addit. by Torre.]

Page 197. Note f. The same imperfect inscription is given in some church notes, taken at North Ferriby, bound up with some of De la Pryme's MSS. at British Museum, *Lansdowne*, 890, only there the lady's name is given as Elizabeth Haldenbi, who died in 1562. In the south window of the quire were, it is said, the arms of Wentworth (a chevron between 3 leopards heads, a crescent for difference,) borne quarterly with (as tricked) paly of four, on a bend 3 mullets. This guides us at once to the marriage of Elizabeth, daughter of Sir John Wentworth, of

---

[f] Pottery, or Pawtry Carr, an extensive piece of level and low lying land lying to the south of Doncaster, extending towards Loversal and Rossington, containing about four thousand acres. It was formerly a morass. In 1616, Roger Gifford, of Doncaster, gent., conveyed a close called the Greater Gauble close, in Balby, which abutted *super paludem vocatam communiter Pawtrie Carre*. In 1764 an Act was obtained for draining and allotting the whole carr.—See more in *Hunter's South Yorkshire*, i., p. 64.

U

North-Elmsal, co. York, (descended from John Wentworth, of that place, by Agnes, sister and coheir of Sir Wm. Dronsfield, of West Bretton,) with Francis Haldenby, as may be found in *Hunter's South Yorkshire*, vol. ii., pp. 243 and 453.

Page 239. The *History of Hull*, which forms No. 890 of the *Lansdowne MSS.*, British Museum, is not in De la Pryme's own handwriting, but is a copy only of the compilation made by him. The title-page is signed by "J. Warburton, Somerset Herald, owner, March 24th, 1729." In the account of the churches are bound up notes in another writing, probably that of James Torre.

Lansdowne MS., 891, contains a collection of sundry manuscripts, notes, and documents relating to Hull and the neighbourhood, very little of which appears to be in the writing of De la Pryme. Much of this is evidently a transcript of another, and, being an original, a more valuable compilation, which is now in the possession of Edward Shimells Wilson, Esq., F.S.A.,[k] of Melton, near Hull. This latter, without any doubt, is in the handwriting of De la Pryme. It is bound in rough calf, lettered, and has a printed pagination. Its size is 13 by 9 inches, and $2\frac{1}{2}$ inches in thickness. Mr. Wilson states that he obtained it from the late Mr. Charles Frost, F.S.A., of Hull. Included in it are several trickings of coats of arms, noted by the author, from the windows and monuments of the churches at Hull, and other places mentioned therein.

This MS. consists of 703 foolscap pages. The first 242 contain "A short description and account of ye two churches of the Holy Trinity and St. Mary, in Kingston-upon-Hull, with many other things relateing thereto."

Then follows "The description of ye town of Kingston-upon-Hull, with ye history and antiquities of all ye famous places that either formerly have been, or at present are, therein."

At page 309 is "A short account of all the religious houses, viz., the monastrys, frierys, colleges, hospitals, gilds, and lands, given to pious uses, that either have been or are within ye town and county of Kingston-upon-Hull."

At page 409, "Of the colledge at Sutton, near this town."

At page 427, "Halton price."

---

[k] The privilege obligingly afforded me of inspecting, at leisure, this interesting manuscript, was much enhanced by the very kind and hospitable manner in which I was received and entertained by Mr. and Mrs. Wilson, who left nothing undone that could promote my comfort and convenience during my visit at their pleasant residence at Melton.

At page 439, " Mr. Bury's gift of an exhibition to Cambr."

At page 443, " The orders and rules of ye gild or fraternity of St. John ye Baptist, in Kingston-upon-Hull."

At page 455, " A short history of all ye towns that are in the county of Kingston-upon-Hull ; to which is added also a brief account of Dripool, Sutton, and Cottingham."

This includes :—

	Page.
North Ferriby	457.
Hessell	471.
Kirk-eller	477.
Tranby	481.
Anlaby, pedigrees of Anlaby and Legard, of	487.
Willarby	491.
Haut Emprice	494.
Scowscots	495.
Myton cum Tupcots	507.
Drypool	513.
Sutton and Stone Ferry	521.
Cottingham	526.

At page 537 is " An exact catalogue of all ye wardens, bailifs, mayors, sherifs, and chamberlains of Kingston-upon-Hull, that can anywhere be found upon record." [1298-1570.]

At page 553, " The reasons and causes of ye general decay of trade, and scarcity of money, in ye town of Kingston-upon-Hull, layd before ye Privy Councel, by John Ramsden, merch."

At page 565, " Catalogus Universalis librorum Bibliothecæ Sacro-sanctæ Trinitatis Ecclesiæ Regioduni super Hull."

At page 615, " An exact account of all ye lands, tenements, incomes, and reciets belonging, in ye year 1695, to ye Right Worshipfull ye mayor and burgesses of Kingston-upon-Hull, with ye disbursements and charges then going and payd out of ye same."

At page 643, " The most antient laws, ordinances, and constitutions of ye town, which were according to custom proclaimed every year in ye market-place."

At page 645, " An abridgment of all ye old laws, customs, orders, and constitutions, K.S.H. of 18 regni regis H. 6ti., etc.

At page 673, " Of ye admiralty of this town."

At page 683, " The customes of ye major and aldermen upon election day and other days."

At page 685, "The dutys and salerys of ye major's officers."

At page 687, "The incorporation of merchant adventurers."

At page 691, "A catalogue of ye benefactors and benefactions to ye town and corporation of Kingston-upon-Hull."

At page 694, "Trippet."

At page 695, Mention of a "licence for ye renewing of that antient and laudable custom, (as they themselves call it,) of reading Divine Service daily in ye said church, morning and evening," etc., 27th Nov., 1638, by Richard, Archbishop of York.

At page 697, "The case of ye reader of Trin[ity] upon Hull," etc., etc.

At page 699, "An account of ye fee farm rents payd by ye major and burgesses of Kingston-upon-Hull."

At page 701, "Of ye rents of ye town of Kingston-upon-Hull, and ye fees paid by ye corporation in K. Henry ye VIII.'s time."

At page 703, "Of the benefactors and benefactions that have been made to ye parochial church or chappel of St. Mary's in Kingston-upon-Hull."

CYRIACK SKINNER. Page 160. The statement as to his appearing to have settled down as a merchant, in London, is believed to be incorrect. The supposition arose from the information, given by Aubrey, relative to one of Milton's unpublished compositions, styled *Idea Theologiæ*, in manuscript, which the former says was "in the hands of Mr. Skinner, a merchant's sonne, in Mark Lane." Anthony a' Wood repeats this, with mentioning Cyriack Skinner as the depository of this relic, and what the one calls *Idea Theologiæ*, the other adopts, but also terms it *The Body of Divinity*, at that time, "or, at least, lately," he adds, "in the hands of Milton's acquaintance, called Cyr. Skinner, living in Mark Lane, London." But Archdeacon Todd, in his Life, etc., of Milton, 1842, shews, certainly, that it was into the hands of quite a different person that this MS. had passed : viz., a Mr. Daniel Skinner, supposed by Mr. Pulman, of the Herald's College, to be the eldest son of Daniel Skinner, merchant, of the parish of St. Olave's, Hart-street, which parish comprises a considerable part of Mark Lane. This Daniel Skinner had been educated at Westminster School, which he left for Cambridge, in 1670, where the dates of his admission, as a minor and a major fellow of Trinity College, are in October, 1674, and in May, 1679. Together also with the *Idea Theologiæ* were some MS. *State Letters*, both of which Daniel Skinner had designed to have printed by Elzevir, at Amsterdam. The latter, however, from political reasons, declining to do so, Skinner took away the manuscripts, which afterwards found their way into the Old State Paper Office, at Whitehall, where they were discovered, in 1823, enclosed in a cover directed to Mr. Skinner, merchant. (See more in Dr. Sumner's Preface to *Treatise on Christian Doctrine, by J. Milton*, 1825. *Todd's Poetical Works of Milton*, 1842, pp. 184-190.) Cyriack Skinner was entered of Lincoln's Inn, 31 July, 23 Car. I., 1647. but there is no record of his call to the Bar at that Inn. He is named, in 1657, as of the parish of St. Martin-in-the-Fields, where he was buried on the 8th August, 1700.

JULIAN BOWER. Page 164. See also an engraving of the one at Alkborough in *An Historical and Descriptive account of Lincolnshire*, 1828, Vol. 1. p. 176 :—An account of another at Horncastle, *ib.* page 236. Likewise *Notitie Ludæ*, or *Notices of Louth*, 1834. page 238.

DUNSCROFT. Pages 166-75. In the *History of Roche Abbey*, by Dr. Aveling, 1870, p. 110 (note), the author states that the opinion of the venerable historian of *South Yorkshire*, respecting Dunscroft, remained unaltered. In answer to his enquiries, Mr. Hunter, on the 13th April, 1860, wrote to him, he says, as follows :—" I had been long suspicious that there was some mistake about Dunscroft, when I met with Rowe Mores' engraving of the seal. The legend is imperfect, but there is enough to shew that the name of the place is not Dunscroft, to which he erroneously, as I believe, ascribed it. If there had been really any cell there, I must have met with something more decisive than the report of the antiquarian of the time of Torre,—some deed or document of the time when it was in existence, or, at least, some mention of it in such surveys as the ' *Valor* ' of King Henry VIII. I have seen nothing to distrust the opinion expressed in the *S. Y.* that it was the grange at which resided the person who attended to the interest of the monastery at Armthorpe, and in the level, a superior one, as the officer was probably a person of a superior class to the ordinary *grangiarii*. I should not have expressed myself so strongly had I had the least doubt about the mis-reading of the legend on the seal."

SAUNDERSON, MSS, pages 176 and 184. Robert Saunderson, D.D., born at Gilthwaite, in the parish of Rotherham, Yorkshire,

19th Sept., 1587, of Lincoln Coll., Oxford; rector of Wibberton,
co. Lincoln, 1618, and shortly afterwards of Boothby-Pagnell.
Consecrated Bishop of Lincoln, 28th Oct., 1660. Died 29th
Jany., 1662.

Saunderson was greatly attached to genealogical and heraldic
studies, which he appears to have pursued more by way of
recreation than with any definite object. Of the extensive collections which he left behind him in manuscript the larger portion
were for a time, after having been dispersed, reunited in the
library of the late Sir Joseph Banks. At his death they were
excepted out of the number bequeathed to the British Museum,
and were very probably designed to be heir looms at Revesby:
they, however, became the property of his widow, and from her
descended to the Knatchbulls. One MS. volume, which contained
the Saunderson pedigree, remained from the first with the
bishop's descendants, who, in process of time, falling in the
social scale to the rank of farmers, and caring little about
matters of ancestry, used the book for agricultural purposes, so
that the prices of the sale of corn, and the registers of breeding
of cattle, were scribbled in an ill-spelt and vulgar hand over the
pages of the good bishop's elaborate entries. This MS. is, or was,
in the possession of a Mr. Clarke, now or late Cole, living near
Normanby, in the county of Lincoln.

See Raine's *History of the Parish of Blyth*, 1860, pp. 73-78.

PRATT, OF BOSSALL. Pages 177 and 239. The following
note, stated to occur on the fly-leaf of a book, was communicated
to the *Miscellanea Genealogica et Heraldica*, 1866, page 77.

" This was the booke of my dear father, Mr. William Pratt,
A.M., of Emmanuel Colledge, in Cambridge, who was Vicar of
Bossall 28 years; he was a man of great learning, and a great
antiquary, excellently skilled in all sorts of medals. Obiit Anno
Domini 1701, Jan. the 2 day.

" This alsoe was the book of my dear and pious brother, Mr.
John Pratt, A.M., of Sidney Sussex Colledge, in Cambridge; a
man of great learning and piety, who was Vicar of Bossall 16
years. Obiit August the 25 day, Anno Domini 1718.

" MARGARET PRATT."

Page 178. The following petition, which occurs in Lansdowne
MSS., B.M. 897, is curious, as shewing that the turning of open
seats into pews was formerly considered, by the inhabitants of
Hatfield, to act as the possible means of healing certain disorders
in their parish church :—

To the Most Reverend Father in God, John, Lord Archbishop of York, His Grace.

The Petition of the Minister, Churchwardens, and Inhabitants of the Parish of Hatfield, within your Grace's Diocess, humbly sheweth,

That whereas we have a great parish, and an antient and large parish church, but that our seats therein are very old and irregular, and that there are at least forty householders of good quality amongst us, who pay considerably to the repairs of our sayd church, yet have no seats at all therein that they can claim any right to; and, likewise, that there are differencys and disputes about the sayd seats amongst several others. For the regulating of which disorders, and the incouragement of all persons to come to Divine Service, and to hear the Word of God preached, and to preserve peace, unity, and concord amongst us,[1]

---

[1] These pews, of the old high and square order, still exist in the church of Hatfield. Galleries, too, fill up the upper portion of the arches in the nave, and on the front of them, in the wood-work, is a little ornamental moulding. At one end of the south gallery the whole of an arch is fitted up for a "squire's pew" appurtenant to the former residence of the Hatfeild and Gossip families, and carefully boxed off from the rest in the line, *more theatrali.* On the opposite side a second is similarly arranged, probably for their servants. Another of these capital enclosures, on the floor, underneath the chancel screen, within the nave, is set apart for the use of the manor house. A large gallery fills the space at the western end, erected probably during the time when Wm. Drake, M.A., was minister (1739-57), and when Joseph Youden, Wm. Hobson, Robert Atkinson, and John Benson, were churchwardens, their names being placed thereon. Chained to a desk is a black-letter book of Homilies, dated "from Sarisbury 11th Dec., 1569, whereat, if so minded, the passer by may stand and refresh himself with a perusal of "The defence of the Apologie of the Church of England," or with "Sermons preached by Bishop Jewel," etc. The church of Hatfield is a spacious and handsome edifice, built in the form of the cross, the tower rising at the intersection of the limbs. It is not now rich in monuments, and many, no doubt very interesting memorials of the past, perished in the great repairs and the new pewing, which took place upon "the beautifying of the church" in 1697 (p. 178). For another, and perhaps more judicious, restoration (which such an edifice as this certainly deserves) the good vicar of the present day is, I believe, very desirous, and plans have been procured with that view. The spirit is willing, but the *quiddam necessarium* is not so ready. We want a greater number of Thomas Places than we have.—See p. 142.

Whilst upon this subject it may not be out of place to note that, a century earlier, the new ordering of pews appears to have had a somewhat contrary effect at the good town of Hull to that produced by it at Hatfield. Our Diarist, in his M.S. History of the churches there, mentions that at the Holy Trinity Church, in 1599, "all the old pews in the body of the church, which were very irregular and unhandsome, were pulled up, and those made in the room thereof that are now standing ; and, as in such alterations, many contentions commonly arise, about priority, and the right and title to seats, so the ladies, in particular, were so offended, that the mayor, aldermen, and churchwardens, were forced to get an order from her majesty's high commissioners for causes ecclesiastical, to quiet and settle them in peace, in such and such seats." On the 31st

Wee, therefore, humbly pray your Grace to issue out your Grace's commission, out of your Grace's Ecclesiastical Court, directed to [blank for names of Commissioners] empowering them to regulate the sayd seats, which we conceive may best be done by turning them into pews, and that an assessment may be layd by hous row for that purpose, through our sayd parish, to be assessed according to equity and justice, answerable to ye number of every family.

And your Petitioners shall ever pray for your Grace's long life and pious government over us.

DEAN GALE, pp. 208, 209.—The Rev. Dr. Thomas Smith writing to Pepys, 16th April, 1702, mentions that on Sunday morning last, he heard of the death of his learned friend the Rev. Dr. Gale: he doubts not but that his sons will take all possible care of his papers, and especially of those which relate to the illustrating *Camden's Britannia*, and publish, in convenient time, to the honor of their father's memory, which, with those learned books he himself published in his lifetime, would render him more illustrious to posterity than any monument they could erect in York Minster.—*Pepys' Diary*, ed. 1849. v. 404.

PERKINS' MSS. Extracts from the wills of Rev. John Hall, and his son. (See page 181.)

7 Sept., 1721. John Hall, of Gisbrough, clerk.—To be buried in the church yard of the parish where I shall dye.—I give to my son, John Hall, fellow of Jesus College, in Cambridge, but now resident at Stockton, in the county of Durham, clerk, all my books, boxes, papers, and parchments, in my study, or elsewhere, belonging to me, except such as my wife shall chuse for her own reading, desiring that no person, learned or unlearned, shall either rifle, ransack, search, or examine the same, till my son John, if living, or some person appointed by him, come to

October, 1598, an order appears to have issued from Matthew Hutton, archbishop of York, and others, authorizing the mayor, etc., "to place every of the said gentlewomen in places already made, or to be made, according to their callings or dignities, so as Mrs. Mayoress, for the time being, may keep her pew or place, and the other gentlewomen, the aldermen's wives, their pews or places, by themselves, as had been accustomed, and not thereafter to be troubled or molested by others, so that all gentlewomen resorting thither, to hear divine service and sermons, might have fit place assigned them for that purpose." It further appears to have been a part of the sword-bearer's duty "to place all new Mrs. Mayoresses, Mrs. Sheriffs, Mrs. Chamberlains, and any new Alderwomen, in the church."—*De la Pryme's MS. History, penes Mr. Wilson,* pp. 11-685.

examine, view, or dispose of the same. But if he be dead before me, I leave all my books to my wife, her administrators, and assigns, and my papers I will and desire to be all burnt. Item, I give unto my son, John Hall, aforesaid, and his heirs for ever, all my reall estate, whether freehold or copyhold, lying and being in the manor of Hatfield, provided and upon condition that he pay to his affectionate mother, my affectionately tender wife, Mrs. Sarah Hall, one-half of the clear yearly rent of and for the said land, for and during the term of her life.—Provided also, that if my son, John Hall, shall dye without issue, lawfully begotten, then my will is that one halfe of my real estate shall be equally divided amongst such of the surviving children of my affectionate wife as shall then be living, by her first husband, or among such of them as she shall appoint by writing under her own hand.—S^d wife and son ex^rs.—[Pro. 4th Apr., 1722, admon. to John Hall, clerk, son of s^d dec^d.]

18 Sept., 1722. John Hall, of Guisbrough, clerk, being sick in body.—I give and bequeath unto my loveing brother, Thomas Perkins, of Hatfield, co. York, gent., Matthew Mazline, of Cawood, clerk, and Samuel Gibson, of Lombard Str., London, druggist—all my estate, whether freehold or copyhold, lying in Fishlake, within the mannor of Hatfeild, co. York,—in trust to be by them sold for the best advantage, for the payment of my debts, legacies, and funeral expenses.—To my uncle, Ralph Hall, in Ireland, £5.—To each of my aunt Sanderson's sons, of Kirkby Huer, each £10.—To my dear and affectionate freind, Mrs. Anne (Nills?), of Scoley, the bed and furniture of my own room, the glass, and ten guineas. Residue to be equally devided amongst all my brothers and sisters; my sister Barrett's children to come in for a sister's share.—My said loveing brother Thomas Perkins, Matthew Mazline, and Samuel Gibson, ex^rs.—[Pro. 15th Oct., 1722, admon. to Thos. Perkins, gent., one of the ex^rs.]

Page 187. *Lansdowne MSS.,* 899.

HISTORIA UNIVERSALIS OPPIDI ET PAROCHIÆ HATFIELDIENSIS, OR, Y^E HISTORY AND ANTIQUITYS OF Y^E TOWN AND PARISH OF HATFIELD, BY DONCASTER. In small Books, with many Copper Cutts.

Elenchus Librorum et Capitum Historiæ Prædictæ.
Book ye 1st, intitled
HISTORICUS.

The Dedication.
The Preface.

Ch. 1.   The difficulty of finding yͤ originals of towns : that this part of yͤ country over which this town and parish extends itself was some thousands of years ago a wilderness full of pitch trees, fir trees, all wild beasts, etc., uninhabited with mankind.

Ch. 2.   The discovery of yͤ island by yͤ Cimbri, their planting all yͤ east and south parts of yͤ same ; their original strang customes, manners, etc.

Ch. 3.   The next discoverers of this island was yͤ Phœnicians, their seating of themselves in yͤ south parts thereof ; manner of fighting, customes, etc. ; wars with yͤ Cimbri.

Ch. 4.   Yͤ discovery of this island by Grecians, under Phileus Taurominitos, 150 years before Cæsar's days ; their seating themselves in yͤ south parts thereof, their wars with the Phœnicians, etc.

Ch. 5.   Of yͤ invasion of all yͤ south east parts of this island by yͤ Gauls and Belgians, about 60 years before Cæsar's days ; of their seating themselves all along yͤ seaside, and yͤ inland adjacent countrys on yͤ south east of this island ; of their wars with yͤ Cimbri, and their driveing them northwards to dwell in yͤ before uninhabited forests and wildernesses, by which means this formerly woody country, yͤ subject of my history, came to be peopled, etc.

Ch. 6.   These Cimbri, that being thus forced to live in this part of yͤ country, and to inhabit yͤ morasses and boggy woods of this parish, were called Brigantes by the Romans ; their assaults made upon them in the woods of this parish ; their consultations, wars, etc., under Cartismandua Ven . . . . etc., with yͤ conquest . . . . . by yͤ Romans . . . . return and bickering . . with yͤ Romans . . . . parish, which occasioned yͤ Romans to burn and cut down yͤ great forest of fir trees that grew in yͤ morasses of this parish that harboured them, etc.

Ch. 8. [sic] The country hereabouts being by this means render'd quiet, yͤ Romans cause yͤ conquer'd Britons to build themselves houses and inhabit here, by reason of yᵉ richness and pleasantness of yᵉ soil, etc., which gave origin to this town, its antient increase, settlement, name, revolutions, etc., untill yᵉ year of Christ 600 and odd.

Ch. 9. How that it was a king's seat in yᵉ Saxon's time; of yᵉ dwelling of Edwin, first Christian king of yᵉ Northumbers here; history of his life, and a full account of yᵉ great battal that was fought against him in yᵉ fields of Hatfield, by Penda, king of Mercia, and Caadwaller, king of yᵉ Brittans, in which Edwin and his son was slayn, and yᵉ whole town burnt down, etc.

Ch. 10. The building of yᵉ town again, its increase and flourishing condition under yᵉ succeeding kings of yᵉ Northumbers, and of several things that happened therein. Of a great synod that was held there under Egfrid, king of yᵉ Northumbers.

Of yᵉ ravages that yᵉ Dains made in these parts; of their sacking of yᵉ town of Hatfield, and burning it down again unto yᵉ bare ground.

Of its destruction again by yᵉ Dains, and yᵉ revolutions, famines, inundations, etc., relateing thereto, unto yᵉ year 13. . .

Of a great earthquake that exceeding shoke this town, and yᵉ whole country round about.

Ch. 11. Of yᵉ destruction of this town by Thomas, Earl of Lancaster, in . . . . yᵉ whole history of yᵉ invasion thereof.

Of yᵉ reversion of yᵉ town and parish unto yᵉ king; of Phillipa, queen to Edw. yᵉ 3ᵈ· that was brought to bed of a Prince, at this Hatfield, in 1335.

Of a blazeing starr and a great mortality of men in Hatfield, anno 1391.

Ch. 12. Of Hen. yᵉ 8th jorney into Yorkshire, and his intended comeing into this town of Hatfield, to hunt in yᵉ chase thereof.

Ch. 13. Of yᵉ progress that Henry, Prince of Wales, (son to King John yᵉ 1ˢᵗ·) took into Yorkshire, and his comeing to this town of Hatfield, etc.

Ch. 14. A full description of yᵉ town, both as it has formerly been, and at present is; its state, condition, delicate situation, neatness, conveniences, etc.

Of yᵉ nature of its air, of a hurricane that happened there in 1687. Of yᵉ great storm of wind in 1695, with somewhat observable concerning yᵉ same, and mists.

Of yᵉ nature of yᵉ water that yᵉ town is supplyd with; with somewhat observable relating to springs and wells.

Of yᵉ nature, humours, and dispositions of yᵉ people of this town and parish. Of their sports, recreations, etc.

Of their sicknesses, diseases, distempers, etc.

Of yᵉ king's pallace that was at this town, part of which is yet standing, etc.

Ch. 17 [*sic*]. Of yᵉ chace of Hatfield, its antiquity, bounds, and greatness, and its destruction by yᵉ Dutch.

Of yᵉ vast numbers and plenty of deer that was therein, etc.

Of yᵉ old laws and customes of yᵉ chase, etc.

Of yᵉ officers thereof, yᵉ king's bow bearer, yᵉ park keeper, yᵉ surveyor, yᵉ regarders, and their stations, etc.

Of yᵉ park of Hatfield, its antiquity, bigness, and destruction by yᵉ Dutch in 1631.

Book yᵉ 2nd, intitled VILLARIS.

Ch. 1. Of yᵉ origin of parishes, of yᵉ largeness and extent of this at Hatfield.

Ch. 2. Of yᵉ towns and hamlets that both formerly were, and at present are, in yᵉ parish of Hatfield; and first of Thorn, its antient state, etc.

Ch. 3. Of yᵉ antiquity of Stainford, its greatness in former times; of a famous chappel that was there formerly, pull'd down by K. Edw. yᵉ 6; of yᵉ present state of yᵉ town now, etc. Of Tudworth, its antient and present state; of yᵉ great fisherys that were there formerly, etc.

Of yᵉ antiquitys of Dunscroft; of yᵉ cell belonging to Roch monastery that was there, etc.

Ch. 6. [*sic*] Of Woodhouse, its original greatness; and antient and present state, etc.

Ch. 7. Of Bereswood, its antiquity and present state, largeness, etc.

Ch. 8. Of ye old and famous place of Lindholm, and what it has been.

Book ye 3rd, intitled ECCLESIASTICUS.

Ch. 1. Of ye 1st establishing of ye Christian religion in this land; of ye first that preached Christ in this parish, and of ye first church built there.

Ch. 2. Of ye building of ye present stately church that now is, with ye history, ye armes, and genealogies of those worthy men, ye Hastings, ye Ricards, ye Nevils, ye Dawneys, and others that contributed thereto, etc.

Ch. 3. Of ye solemnity of ye dedication and consideration thereof, with all ye ceremony belonging thereto, and ye great feasting that ensued thereon, etc.

Ch. 4. The history of ye advowson of ye church of Hatfield. Of ye tithes, their impropriation, first unto ye monastery of St. Pancrace, then to St. Mary's in York, and then to Roch Abby; with an ordinance for ye maintenance of ye vicar of Hatfield.

Ch. 5. The church of Hatfield, and mother church of ye chappels subordinate thereto in former days. How Thorn came to be parochial. Y^e charter of ye chappel of Thorn, with observations thereon.

Ch. 6. A full and perfect description of ye church of Hatfield; of all ye pictures, images, inscriptions, epitaphs, and reliques, that was therein a few years before ye Reformation.

Ch. 7. Of ye great need of ye Reformation when it happened, to clense and purify religion from all ye fopperys of popery, and restore it to ye pureness and undefiledness of ye primative ways, such as was first preachd and tought in this nation before that Austin ye monk landed, etc., and of ye performance thereof.

Ch. 8. Of ye sad havok that was made of religious things in ye time of ye Reformation; how much churches and ye poor suffered thereby, and especially this of ours, etc.

Ch. 9. Of ye reparations that have been made of and to this of ours, especially within these late years; with a whole account thereof, and a full description of ye church as it now is, etc.

Ch. 10. Of yᵉ exsellency of epitaphs and funeral monuments, with an account of all those that have escaped the rage of men and time, and that are yet in yᵉ sayd church.

Ch. 11. Of yᵉ Encænia, or aniversary feast of yᵉ dedication of yᵉ church, and yᵉ antient and present man[ner] of solemnizing of yᵉ same.

Ch. 12. Of yᵉ old customes that are observed in this church in christnings, maryages, burials, etc.

Ch. 13. Containing yᵉ names, lives, and memorable deeds of all yᵉ ministers of this town of Hatfield, from yᵉ most antient accounts unto this day.

Part 2.

Ch. 1. Of yᵉ origin of yᵉ monastic life, and yᵉ excellency thereof, if not abused. Of yᵉ religious places that have been in this parish, and first of Lindholm, as yᵉ most antient, with yᵉ whole life of St. Will. a Lindholm.

Ch. 2. Of yᵉ origin and building of yᵉ little monastry or cell of Dunscroft; of yᵉ number of monks therein, etc.

Ch. 3. Of their order, rule, maner of life, devotions, houers of prayer, admittance of novices, etc.

Ch. 4. Of yᵉ dissolution of yᵉ sayd little monastry, and yᵉ abominable means and ways they took to perform yᵉ same; and of yᵉ allienation of all yᵉ lands by King Henry yᵉ VIII., etc.

Ch. 5. Of yᵉ cursed ways and means that Henry yᵉ VIII. took to dissolve and suppress all yᵉ rest of yᵉ monastrys and religious houses in yᵉ land, and that it was plain sacriledge, and that every one commits yᵉ same sin in keeping yᵉ sayd lands, etc.

Part 3.

Ch. 1. Of yᵉ preceptory of knight Templars; afterwards of yᵉ knights of St. John of Jerusalem that was at Crooksbroom, in this parish; of yᵉ lands belonging thereto, etc.

Ch. 2. Of yᵉ maner of life of those two orders; of their customes, ceremonys, devotions.

Ch. 3. Of ye miserable end of ye first order, and ye abrogation of ye latter in Harry ye VIII.'s time, and ye allienation of their lands, etc.

Ch. 4. Of St. Catharin's cross that stood in ye west end of Hatfield, with the life of that pure saint.

Ch. 5. Of St. Langton's cross in ye fields; why so call'd, etc., with an account of ye patron to whome it was dedicated, and of all ye troubles that ensued through him, in which may be seen a specimen of popeish tyranny, etc.

Ch. 6. Of ye free school that is in this town, its foundation, dedication, endowments, etc.

Ch. 7. Of ye benefactors since ye Reformation to ye church, ye poor, and ye sayd school, etc.

Ch. 8. Of ye charitable donation unto this town that, having been lost this 70 years, was lately, with great charges and trouble, recovered by ye sayd town, etc.

Book ye 4th, intitled CURIOSUS.

Seu de rebus curiosis Hatfieldiæ. Containing an account of all ye curiositys and raritys that are either in ye musæum of ye author at ye sayd town, or dispersed elsewhere in ye privat hands of those that dwell in ye parish. As of almost 100 old Roman, Saxon, Dainish, and Grecian coins, and late medalls of great rarity, etc. As also petrifyd fish and shell-fish of various sorts, with other petrifactions of grass, moss, water, wood, bones of fish, etc. Strang experiments made by ye author with microscopes concerning the pores of glass, the particles of water, ye vegetation and seeding of worts, etc. With copper cutts, discriptions, and solutions of them all, etc.

Book ye 5th, intitled CURIALIS.

Seu de rebus curiæ.

Ch. 1. What manours, lordships, and townships are, ye original of them, and their various customes.

Ch. 2. Of ye original of copyhold and freehold, etc.

Ch. 3. Of ye strang customes of this manour of Hatfield, etc.

Ch. 4. Of yᵉ old custome of rideing upon yᵉ wooden horse, in yᵉ court-house.

Ch. 5. Of yᵉ fellow that sold yᵉ divel.ʲ

Book yᵉ 6th, intitled VITALIS.

Containing yᵉ history of yᵉ lives and memorable acts of yᵉ known lords of yᵉ manour and town of Hatfield, etc.

Ch. 1.   Yᵉ life of King Edwin.

Ch. 2.   Yᵉ life of Earl Godwin.

Ch. 3.   Yᵉ life of Earl Harold.

Ch. 4.   Yᵉ life of William yᵉ Conqueror.

Ch. 5.   Yᵉ life of William, yᵉ 1st Earl Warren.

Ch. 6.   Yᵉ life of William, yᵉ 2nd Earl Warren.

Ch. 7.   Yᵉ life of William, yᵉ 3rd Earl Warren.

Ch. 8.   Yᵉ life of William, yᵉ 4th Earl Warren.

Ch. 9.   Yᵉ life of Hamlin, Earl Warren.

Ch. 10. Yᵉ life of William, yᵉ 6th Earl Warren.

Ch. 11. Yᵉ life of John, yᵉ 7th Earl Warren.

Ch. 12. Yᵉ life of John, yᵉ 8th and last Earl Warren.

Ch. 13. Yᵉ life of Edm. de Longley.

Ch. 14. Yᵉ life of Edw. Plantagenet.

Ch. 15. Yᵉ life of Rich. Plantagenet.

Ch. 16. Yᵉ life of Edward Earl of March, made king of England by yᵉ name of Edward 4th.

Ch. 17. A short account of King Edward 5th.

Ch. 18. A short account of King Richard 3rd.

Ch. 19. A short account of Henry 7th.

Ch. 20. A short account of Henry 8th.

Ch. 21. A short account of King Edward 6th.

Ch. 22. A short account of Queen Mary.

ʲ See *antea*, p. 256, note.

Ch. 23. A short account of Queen Elizabeth.

Ch. 24. A short account of King James 1st.

Ch. 25. A short account of King Charles ye 1st.

Ch. 26. Y^e life of Sir Cornelius Vermuden.

Ch. 27. Y^e life of John Gibbons, esq.

Ch. 28. Y^e life of Sir Edward Osburn, knt.

Ch. 29. Y^e life of Sir Arthur Ingram.

Ch. 30. Y^e life of William Wickham, esq.

Ch. 31. Y^e life of Sir Henry Ingram.

Ch. 32. Henry, Lord Viscount Irwing, ye present lord.
Part ye 2d.
The life of Thomas, Bishop of Durham.
The life of Sir Martin Frobisher.

Ch. 2. Y^e life, history, and genealogy of ye Portingtons.

Ch. 3. Y^e life of ye Wests.

Ch. 4. Y^e history and genealogy of ye Lees.

Ch. 5. Y^e history and genealogy of ye Woodcocks.

Ch. 6. Y^e history and genealogy of ye Whites.

Ch. 7. Y^e history and genealogy of ye Greens.

Ch. 8. Y^e history and genealogy of y^o Wormels. [Worm-leys].

Ch. 9. Y^e history and genealogy of ye Hatfields.

Ch. 10. Y^e history and genealogy of ye Prymes.

Ch. 11. Y^e history and genealogy of ye Beamonts.

Ch. 12. Y^e history and genealogy of ye Ricards.

Ch. 13. Y^e history and genealogy of ye Atkinsons.

Ch. 14. Y^e history and genealogy of ye Oughtibriggs.

V

Ch. 15.   Yᵉ history and genealogy of yᵉ Broughtons.

Ch. 16.   Yᵉ history and genealogy of yᵉ [blank].

Book yᵉ 7th, intitled BELGICUS.

Ch. 1.   A short recapitulation of what was sayd in yᵉ beginning of yᵉ first book of yᵉ peat forrest that ran over part of yᵉ morasses or levels in Hatfield parish and the country adjoyning; of yᵉ burning and chopping of yᵉ same down by the Romans ; that the trees falling crossways over yᵉ rivers stopped their currents, and occasioned not only the reliques of this forrest, but yᵉ whole country round about, to be drounded and subject to perpetual overflowing.

Ch. 2.   Of yᵉ great height that yᵉ rivers Ayre, Trent, and Humber ran, in respect of what they do now, which was also an occasion of rendering this sayd low country a perpetual randezvouz of waters.

Ch. 3.   Of yᵉ many rivers that ran formerly through these levels, with the names of them, etc.

Ch. 4.   Of yᵉ many great floods that happen'd in this drownded country from yᵉ most ancient accounts untill yᵉ drainage in 1630.

Ch. 5.   How that, in success of time, yᵉ muddy waters of ye Don and Idle, that ran through those levels, deposited so much silt and warp that they made a great deal of high land on both sides of their streams.

Ch. 6.   Of yᵉ great trade that people carry'd on in those levels before yᵉ drainage, both betwixt town and town, and also in fishing, fowling &c.

Ch. 7.   Of yᵉ great benefit that yᵉ grassmen of this town and manour made by yᵉ priviledge of joysting goods upon yᵉ common, granted them by King Edward yᵉ 4th.

Ch. 8.   Of a design that one Mr. Lavrock and his partners had of draining these levels, in Queen Elizabeth's days, and ye miscariage thereof, &c.

Ch. 9.   Cornelius Vermuden gets a sight of those levels when

he came down into this country with Prince Henry ; his negotiations with King Charles 1st. about the draining of them ; with
ye articles agreed of betwixt them.

Ch. 10.   Vermuden communicats his design to several of his
countrymen, who gladly joyn with him in ye draining of ye same;
begins ye same ; meets with great difficultys, &c.

Ch. 11.   Yet, for all that, overcoms them, finishes the drainage,
which was looked upon as a vast and wonderfull work, for which
he was knighted ; gets the same divided, and his part set out ;
divides it amongst his partners ; buys also ye whole manor of
Hatfield and several more, with ye King's part also, and divides
it amongst his partners.

Ch. 12.   The [y] send for their relations and tennants from
beyond sea, build houses in ye levels ; lives like kings ; they build
also a town at Santoft, a chappel and parson's house, &c.   The
names of all those that came over from beyond sea, &c.

Ch. 13.   Of ye troubles that ensued this drainage, and the
causes thereof; how all the old drainers sold their portions in the
sayd levels, and were for the most part ruind and undone, and
went and lived elsewhere, &c.

Ch. 14.   Of ye suit that Crowl had with the Participants, and
the decree thereupon.

Ch. 15.   Of ye suit that Hatfield, Thorn, &c., had with ye
Participants, &c.

Ch. 16.   Of y^o suit that Fishlake, Pollington, &c., had with
them, and of a suit now depending in ye Exchequer between
them, &c.

Ch. 17.   Of ye great disturbances in ye Isle ; of their rising
against ye Participants, ye then possessours and enjoyers of ye
drained lands in their parishes ; of their destroying of ye cropp
of 7400 acres there ; their pulling down of all y^o houses thereon,
ruining of Santoft, &c.

Ch. 18.   Of ye great suit that commenced thereupon between
the Participants and them, with ye whole account thereof unto

this time, it not being yet ended ; and the abominable mischiefs the Isle men have lately done.

Ch. 19. Of yᵉ present state of yᵉ levels ; of yᵉ care that is taken to preserve them dry, &c.

Ch. 20, 21, 22, 23, [blank].

Book yᵉ 8th, intitled GEORGICUS.

Ch. 1. Containing an account of yᵉ high ground, yᵉ nature thereof, its cultivation, proper grain, encreas, &c.

Ch. 2. The nature of yᵉ level ground, and the town's closes, their cultivation, proper grain, encreas, &c.

Ch. 3. Of yᵉ origin of yᵉ moor grounds in this parish, their nature, property, &c.

Ch. 4. Of their digging of them into turves ;[a] of the memorable things that they find under the same, &c.

Ch. 5, 6, 7, [blank].

Book yᵉ 9th, intitled BOTANICUS.

Containing an alphabetical enumeration, with short discriptions, of all yᵉ trees, shrubs, hearbs, grasses, and flowers, as well hortal as wild,) that grows within yᵉ bounds of this parish, with yᵉ particular places where every one of them grows, &c.

Here will follow a larg map of yᵉ whole parish, having every field, ingg, close, mested, croft, cavel, intack, &c., in the whole parish in it, with yᵉ bigness and number of akers in them ; and who are the present owners thereof ; with yᵉ reasons why they are called by such and such names.

———

Abraham de la Pryme contributed to the compilers of the *Catalogi Librorum Manuscriptorum Angliæ et Hiberniæ*, Oxon., 1697, the following information :—

[a] In the MS. Diary, p. 207, De la Pryme says, 8 Aug., 1696, " I was told that the sodds that they digg up within this country, for fiering, will, if they be got in thoue [? thaw,] and wett, ferment and take fire, as hay and corn will when they are in stacks ; which is very true"

Libri Manuscripti R. V. Abrahami Pryme, Lincolniensis.

1. A true and faithful account of the amours of Henry the IVth, king of France, to the princess of Conde, and the wars that had like to have ensu'd thereon, but were prevented by the death of the king. Written by Mr. Mary, an eye-witness of most things. In 25 large sheets, folio.

2. The propositions made by the Lord de la Thuille, ambassadour extraordinary of France, to the states of the united provinces, in 164., with severe reflections and observations thereon. In 8 sheets, folio.

3. Several speeches of Sir Edw. Philips, to queen Elizabeth, king James, and queen Ann,[b] at her coming to the coronation, in both houses of parliament, etc., with their answers, by queen Eliz., king James, etc. In 16 sheets, folio.

4. A true copy of the information that Mr. Titus Oates gave in unto Sir Edmundbury Godfrey, about the popish plot, in 81 articles; to which is added his examination before the house of commons, and the discovery that Mr. Bedloe made to both houses of parliament. In 15 sheets. fol.

5. Five speeches made in parliament, in Cromwell's days, about the frequent calling of parliaments; the reforming of episcopacy, etc.; with one in defence of the earl of Strafford. In 6 sheets, large 4to.

6. A letter out of the East Indies, by one Mr. John Marshal, giving an account of the religion, notions, traditions, and knowledge of the Bramins. In 3 sheets, fol.[c]

---

[b] These speeches can scarcely have been delivered by the same person. From the death of queen Elizabeth, 24th March, 1603, to the accession of queen Anne, on 8th March, 1702, are 101 years. A Mr. Phillips appears to have acted as recorder of Doncaster, probably as deputy to Mr. Serjeant (afterwards Sir Richard) Hutton ; for, in April, 1617, the chamberlains "paid to Mr. Phillips, for his halfe yeare's fee, due at our Lady-day, xls." And, on the occasion of king James I. passing through the town, on the 8th of the same month, there was a payment "to Mr. Phillips, when he came to make the speech to the kinge, xliiiis."

[c] This is noticed and copied in the MS. Diary, pp. 135-148. He says, under 13th January, 1696, "Haveing had by me, in a loose paper, this three or four years, an epistle that was writt out of the East Indys, some time ago, to a great man now alive, it will not be amiss if I, for the better preservation of the same, transcribe it here in my Diary. It was written from Foettipore, or else

7. The life of Cardinal Woolsey, written by Mr. Cavendish. Fol.

8. A book made in queen Elizabeth's time, in answer to a popish book. Dedicated to her majesty. In 8 sheets, 4to.

9. Large excerptions out of diverse histories, in 15 sheets, 4to, with part of a French sermon at the end, of one that was converted to the protestant faith.

10. The true doctrine of Christianity, layd down in questions and answers. In 14 sheets, 8vo. This is a Socinian piece, and proves against the Trinity, original sin, etc.

11. Curiosa de se ; or, the curious miscellanies and private thoughts of one inquisitive into the knowledge of Nature and things. Enrich'd with great variety of matter, both curious, profitable, and pleasant, with a few cursory notes. —Vol. ii., part 1, page 254.

Auctarium Librorum vii. Manuscriptorum Quos transmisit D. Abrahamus Pryme, Lincolniensis.

1. The depositions of the islemen in 1642-8, about the ancient state of the Levels, etc., before that they were drained by the Dutch. In 12 sheets. *Penes* D. Abrahamum Pryme.

2. A large chronicle, writt by Mr. George Nevil, about the year 1577, in six vols., folio, from Brute's days unto the aforesaid year.[d]

3. Dr. Saunderson's Heraldry, writt with his own hand ; containing the coats of arms, pedigrees, etc., of all the families of the north of Trent, with a great many others of gentlemen elsewhere. In folio. *Penes* D. Joannem Nevil, de Winterton, in com. Lincoln.[e]

M............, by one Mr. Marshall, about the year 1680. I got the copy of it from Doct[or] Coga, while I was in the university. Yet, this is not the whole coppy of the epistle, but onely an extract of the most considerable things thereoff ; for the doct[or] himself had it [not] whole, so it was impossible that I should. However, as I had it, so I shall set it down."

[d] See the note on John Nevil, p. 82 of Diary.

[e] Bishop Saunderson's book of Heraldry was in the possession of the late Williamson Cole Wells Clarke, of Brumby, who died about eighteen years ago. From him it passed to Mr. Francis Wells, of Dunstall, in the parish of Corring-

4. A large register of all the lands, farms, tenements, etc., that were given to the priory of Newstead, in the said county. Folio: Latin. *Penes* Dom. Pelham, de Brocklesby, in com. Linc.

The same also translated into English, for the use of her ladyship.

5. A large MS. in folio, containing the lives, actions, and deaths of the earls of Warren, with several things relating to their affairs. *Penes* D. Yarburrow, de Campsel [Campsall], in com. Ebor.

6. All the works of old Chaucer, in long folio. This vol. belonged to the monastery of Canterbury. *Penes* D. Edmund Canby, de Thorne, in com. Ebor.

7. Great part of a large book of heraldry, curiously blazon'd, containing the coats of arms of all the gentry, etc., in the west-riding of Yorkshire. Writ by Thomas Perkins, esq., in the beginning of queen Elizabeth's reign. *Penes* virum reverendum D. Hall, de Fishlake, in com. Ebor.—Vol. ii., part 1, page 160.

NON-CONFORMITY. The following entry in the Diary, illustrative of the strong views entertained on this subject by the writer, and which was omitted in its proper place, may be here introduced.

1696. Oct. 10. " Having been a little melancholy this day, I was very pensive and sedate, and, while I remained so, there came several strange thoughts in my heart, which I could not get shutt of. Methought I foresaw a Religious Warr in the nation, in which our most apostolick and blessed church should fall a prey to the wicked, sacrilegous, non-conformists, who

ham, and from him to his nephew, William Cole, of Newstead, in Ancholme, in the possession of whose widow it now is. Mr. Peacock has examined it carefully; the first part, he says, is a copy of *Tonge's Visitation of the Northern Counties.* The remainder of the volume is a collection of coats of arms, not confined to any special locality. The greater portion of the volume is in a hand earlier than the time of Saunderson, but some, he thinks (but he speaks very doubtfully), is in his autograph. None of the other manuscripts can be traced.

should almost utterly extinguish the same, and set up in the place thereof their own enthusiastick follys, which God prevent! however, I foresee the downfall of those famous patriots the Bishops, and that those that shall be the authors thereof shall have farr less religion and goodness in them than them, and that, whatever their pretence is, the chief thing that they shall pluck down this holy order for will be to get their lands and estates. Then will England be fill'd with all manner of confusion and horror, and shall stand like a drunken man, many years, untill that God have pour'd out all the wraith of His cup upon it.

INDEX OF NAMES.

(The letter *n*. after the number of the page refers to the note.)

A

ABUTENSIS, 199.
Achilles, 291.
Acosta, 199.
Adwick, 177.
Acrlobout, 291.
Agrippina, August., 235.
Airy, 129.
Albemarle, Duke of, 101.
Albemarle, Earl of, 130 *n*.
Alcock, 253.
Aldam, 52 *n*., 122 *n*.
Aldwark, 181.
Alexander, 39, 157, 162.
Alfred, King, 188.
Algerines, the, 57.
Allen's Lincolnshire, 87 *n*.
Allen, 143 *n*.
Allison, 194.
Alretune, A. de, 81 *n*.
Alsace, Philip of, x., xi. *n*.
Alsledius, 199.
Amaber, St., 157 *n*.
Americans, the 199.
Amory, 266, 269, 270 *n*.
Anlaby, 299.
Ann, 175, 181.
Ann, Princess, 49.
Anne, Queen of Scotland, 169 *n*.
Anne, Queen, 109 *n*., 242 *n*., 317.
Anstruther, Sir R., 107, 108, 110.
Anstruther, Lady, 111.
Anderson, 69, 85, 96 ; family of, 117, 119 ; Judge (Sir E.), 119, 120, 121 ; S., 117, 120, 124 ; Edmund, 117, 119, 120 ; F., 117 ; Edwin, 117, 120 ; Madam, 104, 124 ; Sir J., 117 ; Magdalen, 119 ; Sir E., bt., 119, 120 ;

William, 119 ; Sir J., bt., 119, and family, 121 ; C., 120 ; W., *ib*. ; Katharine, *ib*. ; Mary, *ib*. ; Sir C. H. J., 121 *n*. ; C., 156 *n*., 197.
Andrew, bishop of Murray, 229, 230.
Andrews, 164 *n*.
Anker, 286.
Aparine Plinii, 249, 250.
Appleyard, Matthew, 6 *n*., W., 286, 288 ; (arms of,) 130.
Apporor, 199.
Archimedis Cochlea, 256.
Ardsley, 186.
Arctius, 199.
Aristotle, 199.
Aritœus, 199.
Ark, Joan of, 199.
Arlington, Earl of, H., 169 *n*.
Arlush, 273 *n*.
Armstrong, 40 *n*.
Arthington, 175.
Arthur, King, 189.
Asaph, St., Bishop of, Lloyd, 24 *n*.
Ash, 199.
Ashton, 41 *n*.
Assheton, 290.
Ask, 181
Askham, de R., 253.
Aston, de Thomas, 87 *n*.
Atkinson, Alderman, 238 *n*. ; Robert, 303 *n*., fam. of, 313.
Aubrey, John, 9 *n*., 29 *n*., 300.
Augustin, St., 130 *n*.
Austin, 39, 45.
Austin, St., 199, 309.
Aveling, 290, 301.
Awmond, 228.
Aylmer, 79 *n*.
Ayzerly, 274.

B

BAAL, house of, 150.
Baalam, 111.
Babthorp, 181.
Bacon, Lord Chancellor, 23 *n.*
Baden, Prince Lewis of, 32.
Bagshawe, H. R., 239 *n.* ; R., vi. *n.* ;
  Sir W. C., vi. *n.* ; W. J., vi., vii. *n.*,
  xxix. *n.* ; F. W., 193 *n.*, v., vi.
Baker, 196 *n.* ; E., 63 *n.*
Balden, 196 *n.*
Baldwin, 5 *n.*, 144.
Ball, 132 *n.*
Bangor, Bishop of, 5 *n.*
Banks, Rev, R., 187, 198, 201, 203,
  204, 208, 210, 241, 252 ; Sir J., 65
  n., 302.
Barber, 147 *n.*
Barchet, 75 *n.*
Barclay, 84 *n.* ; Lord, 66.
Barebones, 43.
Bareel, 60, 260.
Barfleur, Viscount, 57 *n.*
Barker, L., 37 *n.* ; E. H., xxiii.
Barkley, C. W., 63 *n.*
Barlow, 292.
Barmby, 181.
Barnardiston, 234
Barrett, 305.
Barrow, 199.
Battie, 295 *n.*
Bawtry, 273 *n.*
Baxter, 47, 62.
Bayley, 89 *n.*
Baynham, Sir E., 92 *n.*
Beauchamp, 152.
Beaumont, 43 *n.*
Beamont, 241, 313.
Becanus, 199.
Beck, R., 158 *n.*
Becket, St. Thomas, 203.
Beckwith, 218 *n.*
Bede, 188, 255.
Bedford, Earl of, Francis, 57 *n.* ; Wil-
  liam, Duke of, 57 *n.* ; W., 118 *n.*
Bedingfield, 244.
Bedloe, 4, 317.
Beharell, 60 *n.*
Behareel, or Beharrel, 260, 265, 289,
  290.
Beiston, 181.
Belgians, the, 306.
Bellow, J. F., 17 *n.*
Bellingham, 89 *n.*
Bellot, Edward, 119 ; S., *ib.*
Beltham, 229.
Bendish, 260, 274.
Bendlow, Capt., 66.

Benedictine Nunnery, 110 *n.*
Benjamin, 152.
Benn, Sir A., 8 *n.*
Bennet, 274 ; T., 186 *n.*
Bennett, Thomas, 21, *ib. n.*
Bennivenius, 199.
Benson, 303.
Bentley, xxv., xxxi., xxxii.
Beorgdeudish, 88.
Berchett, M., 4 *n.*
Bernard, Dr., 116 ; 152.
Bethel, Sir H., 126 *n*,
Betney, G., 54 *n.*
Bierly, Col., 137,
Bigod, 181.
Billers, 41 *n.*
Bilson, boy of, 199.
Biot, M., xxv., xxvii., xxxi.
Birch, Dr., 21 *n.*
Bishops, the, 320.
Biwater, 228.
Black, W. H., 120 *n.*
Blackett, 293.
Bland, Sir J., 73 *n.*
Blaydes, 269 ; pedigree of, xxxiii.
Bliss, 78 *n.*
Blomeley, 289.
Blount, Sir C., 30 *n.* ; Sir T. P., 30 *n.*
Blowe, 274.
Bohemia, Queen of, 168 *n.*, 169 *n.*
Bohun, 117, 181 ; Edmund, 25 *n.*, 26,
  27, 43 ; Humphrey, 25, 27, 43.
Bolton, Duke of, 201.
Borellus, 199, 247.
Bosswell, M., 183 *n.*
Bosvill, C., 182.
Bosvile, 268, 283.
Boswell, C.S.I.E., 183 *n.*
Boughton, 21 *n.*
Boulter, J., 293 ; W. C., viii.
Bower, 43 *n.*
Boy of Bilson, 199.
Boynton, 175, 181, 230 ; Sir J., 6 *n.*,
  286.
Boyle, 21, 24, 87.
Bradshaw, 50.
Bramhall, Archbishop, 239 *n.*
Bramins, the, 215, 317.
Branson, 295 *n.*
Brewster, xxiv.
Brigantes, the, 306.
Briscoe, 268.
Britains, the, 86, 153 *n.*, 182, 219, 221,
  306, 307.
British, the, 275.
Broadreffe, 234 *n.*
Brooke, Canon, viii.
Brooks, Sir J., 93.
Broom, 123.

Broughton, 314.
Brown, 66, 114.
Browne, 21 n., 25 n., 40 n., 281, 282 n.
Brownlow, Sir J. 73, 74, 95, 96.
Broxholme, 173 n.
Bruce, 175, 181.
Brute, 318.
Bruto, R., 138.
Bryson, J., 238 n.
Bryto, Richard, 203.
Buck, 19 n., 293.
Bulmer, 175.
Burdett, 181.
Burke, xi. n., xvi. n., 123 n., 149 n.
Burleigh, Lord, 131 n.
Burnet, 202 n., 255 ; Dr., 24.
Burton, 201, 296 ; boy of, 199.
Burtona, de, E., 225.
Bury, 165 n., 299 ; Dr., 28 n.
Busby, Dr., 60.
Bushel, 247, 248.
Busli, R. de, 147 n.
Butcher, 186 n., 280.
Butler, 133 n.
Byron, Rev. J., 162 n.

C

CAADWALLER, 307.
Cæsar, 100, 249, 306.
Camden, 105, 188, 206, 208, 209, 210, 212, 253, 255, 272, 275.
Camden's Britannia, 60, 85, 304.
Camden Society, 92 n.
Campen, 199
Canby, 175, 290, 319.
Candler, 25 n.
Cannon, R., 36 n.
Canterbury, Archbishop of, 31 n., 70.
Cappe, Mrs. C., 125 n.
Capron, W., 172 n.
Cardanus, 199.
Carew, B. M., 133 n.
Carlil, 239.
Carlin, 197.
Carlingford, Viscount and Viscountess, 296.
Carmarthen, Marquis of, 108.
Carrington, 189 n.
Carteret, Lord, 174 ; Sir G., 174 n.
Carterett, 269.
Carthusian Monks, 173.
Cartismandua, Ven., 306.
Cassaubon, 199.
Castell, P., 4 n.
Castelion, 181.
Castor, 75, 133.
Catharine, Queen, 46.

Catherine, St., 142, 194.
Cattier, 199.
Cattz, 254.
Cavendish, 318.
Caxton, W., 177.
Cay, H., 55.
Cecil, 93.
Chamber, T., 118 n.
Chambers, 239 n., vi. n.
Champneys, 243.
Chappelow, L., 196 n.
Chappellow, J., 241.
Charles I., 3, 12, 65, 66, 117, 171 n., 174 n., 217, 233, 290, 296 n., 313, 315, xiii.
Charles II., 6, 12, 33, 46, 95 n., 105, 123, 125, 145, 159, 174 n., 225, 242 n., 282 n.
Chatburn, W. O., 4 n.
Chaucer, 319.
Chauvin, 247.
Chavatte, 260.
Chaworth, Lord, 35 ; W., 172 n.
Chemnitius, 199.
Cheney, 231.
Cherbury, Lord Herbert of, 30 n.
Chester, Col., viii., 147 n., 171 n.
Chetham Society, 161 n.
Chetwood, Dr., 58 ; Val., 58 n.
Cheyne, 250.
Childers, J. W., 165 n. ; H., 288.
Chinese, 216.
Chiron, 291.
Choiseul, Marquis of, 66.
Cholmondeley, 175.
Chrysostom, St., 199.
Churchman, 41 n.
Ciampini, 210, 212.
Cimbri, 177 n., 178, 306.
Citois, 199.
Clare, 181.
Clarrel, 181.
Clarell, J., 172 n.
Clark, 282 n., 283.
Clarke, 89 n., 302.
Clark, W. C. W., 82 n., 318 n.
Clenawly, Baron, 242 n.
Cleveland, Archdeacon of, 190 n.
Cleworth, 54 n., 133, ib. n.
Clifton, Catherine, Baroness, 169 n.
Clogher, or Clohar, Bishop of, 144.
Cloudsley, 171 n.
Clynton, Maria de, 118 n.
Coakley, 265.
Cochlea Archimedis, 256.
Cock, 263.
Cockaine, 43 n.
Codronchus, 250.
Coga, Dr. 318 n.

Coggan, 200, 238.
Coke, 41 *n.* ; Sir E., 160 *n.* ; Bridget, *ib.*
Cole, 302, 319 *n.*
Colepepper, T., 36 *n.*, 243.
Colin, M., xxv., xxxi.
Collen, G. W., viii.
Collier, 196 *n.*
Colling, 214.
Comin, 213.
Conan, Duke of Richmond, 193.
Conde, Princess of, 317.
Conduitt, xxx.
Constable, 181 ; U., 225.
Constantine the Great, 129 *n.*
Conway, Lady, 91.
Cook, 108.
Cooke, Sir G., 69, 173 *n.* ; 263 *n.*, 295
　　H., 135 *n.*
Copley, 175, 181 ; Sir J. W., 156 *n.*,
　　172 *n.* ; Sir G., 293 ; Lady C.,
　　156 *n.*
Cork, Boyle, Earl of, 21 *n.*
Cornbury, Lord, 22.
Cotes, xxvii.
Cotton, 158 *n.* 237.
Coverley, Sir R., 128 *n.*
Craig, J., xxviii.
Craven, Earl of, 168 ; family of, 168
　　n., 169 *n.* ; F. and M., 289.
Cressey, 286.
Creun, A. de, 148, *ib. n.*, 187 ; Muriel
　　de, 148 *n.*
Crevequer, R. de, 123 *n* ; Mary, 123 *n.*
Croese, de la, G., 136.
Crofts, 286.
Crokatt, G., 171 *n.*
Cromwell, 35, 42, 43, 44, 46, 50, 51, 52,
　　75, 83, 109, 110, 124, 126, 127, 132,
　　136, 138, 142, 151, 158, 199, 291,
　　294, 296. 317.
Crusoe, Robinson, 59 *n.*
Curzon, A., Hon. and Rev., 13 *n.* ; S.
　　F., 13 *n.*
Cudworth, 113 *n.*
Curteis, 289.
Curteen, 254.
Cuthbert, R., 181 *n.*
Cutts, Lord, 108, 109.
Cyprian, 199 ; St., 199.

D

Dalton, 141 *n.*, 253.
Danes, the, 16, 17 *n.*, 35, 72, 152, 164,
　　307.
Daniel (prophet), 29.
Darcy, 227 *n.*, 228, 234.
Darel, 147 *n.*

Darling, vi.
Darnes, Sir T., 120 ; Elizabeth, 120.
Darwin, 218 *n.*
Davenport, H., 20 *n.*
David's, St., Bishop of T., 115 ; Wat-
　　son, Bishop of, 196 *n.* ; Lyndwode,
　　Bishop of, 149 *n.*
Davies, 191 *n.*
Dawes, 267.
Dawling, 266.
Dawney, 292, 309.
Dawson, 197.
Dawtry, 79 *n.*
De-alta-ripâ, 79 *n.*, 80 *n.*, 81 *n.*
Deckerhuel, J., 4 *n.*
De Cow, 292.
De Foe, Daniel, x., 87 *n.*
De Grey, Earl, 273 *n.*
Deincourt, Lord, 107.
Delafield, ix., xii.
De la Pierre, xii.
De la Pole, ix., 230. 231, 231 *n.*
De la Pryme, see Pryme.
De Moc, 109.
Democritus, 34.
Denman, 138, 181.
Denmark, King of, 18, 107.
Dent, 122 ; John, 122 *n.* ; Jonathan,
　　123 *n.* ; Dr. Thomas, 29 *n.*
Devonshire, Dukes of, xx., 106, 166 *n.*,
　　245, 255 ; Lord, 109.
Dewes, Sir S., 189.
Dewey, Mrs., 54.
Diana Elucinia, 235.
Dieppe, 57 *n.*, 66.
Diodorti, 4 *n.*
Diogenes, 157, 162, 206.
Dimmock, 109.
Dinsdale, xvi., 269
Dobson, 204.
Dodgson, 292.
Dodsworth, 113 *n.*, 147 *n.*, 255.
Dolman, E., 75 *n.* ; M., *ib.*
Dolphin, 288, 289.
Donatus, 250.
Dorell, 73.
Downe, Viscount, 6 *n.*, 185, 202 *n.*
Drake, S., 28 *n.* ; J., 286 ; William,
　　303 *n.*
Dransfield, 197 *n.*
Drew, 288.
Dronsfield, Sir W., 298 ; Agnes, *ib.*
Drummond, Dr. R., 147 *n.*
Dryden, 58 *n.* ; 201.
Dugdale, Sir W., 113 *n.*, 128 *n.*, 225,
　　255, 297 ; J., 189, 190, *n.* 192 *n.* ;
　　199, 203.
Dumfries, Swift, Earl of, 296.
Dunbar, 164 *n.*

Dunderdale, J., 4 *n.*, 37 *n.*
Dunton, J., 5 *n.*
Durfey, T., 159.
Durham, Langley, Bishop of, 194 ;
 Walter of, 194 ; Skirlaw, Bishop of,
 194 ; Thomas, Bishop of, 313, 318.
Dutch, the. 66, 115, 165, 242, 308.
Dymoke, C., 109 *n.*; E., *ib.*; L., *ib.* ;
 Champion, 116, 185 *n.*

E

EASTLAND MERCHANTS, 286.
Eastoft, 175, 181, 231.
Edisbury, Dr., 113 *n.*
Edleston, xxx, xxxii.
Edmondson, 227 *n.*
Edward I., 59 *n.*, 147 *n.*, 217, 256.
—— II., 172 *n.*, 217, 296 *n.*
—— III., 135, 234 *n.*, 256 *n.*, 307.
—— IV., 231 *n.*, 253, 312, 314.
—— V., 253, 312.
—— VI., 12, 130 *n.*, 200, 201 *n.*, 253,
 255, 308, 312.
Edward the Black Prince, 232 *n.*
Edwin, King, 188, 189 *n.*, 255, 307, 312.
Egerton, Sir R., 119.
Egfrid, King, 307.
Egyptians, 27.
Eiles, 293.
Eland, 175.
Elcock, 272, 273, and *n.*
Elice, 268.
Elizabeth, Queen, 12, 48, 117, 151,
 155, 160, 177, 181, 199, 313, 314,
 317, 318, 319.
Elletson, 41 *n.*
Ellis, vii. *n.*
Elmhirst, 175 *n.*
Elways, 162, 212.
Elzevir, 301.
Elwes, 79 *n.*
Engaine, 230.
England, king of, 145.
English, the, 144.
Eratt, 20 *n.*, 37 *n.*, 179, and *n.*, 207 *n.*,
 267.
Espensœus, 199.
Essex, H., 119, 120 ; Joan, *ib.*
Estotevil, 228.
Eton, Thos., 161.
Eure, 55 *n.*
Evelyn, 29 *n.*
Eyre, Anthony, 5 *n.*, 285 ; Isabella, 5
 n., 285 ; Sir G., 5 *n.*, 285.

F

FABRICIUS, J. A., 28 *n.*
Fairfax, 101, 175, 181, 185.
Fall, Dr. J., 190.
Fane, Hon. A., 8 *n.*
Fauconberg, R., 162 *n.*
Felix, Min., 199.
Fenton, 10 *n.*
Ferguson, 96.
Ferne, Sir J., 288.
Fernelius, 199.
Ferrers, 181.
Fiddis, R., 191.
Firemee, 199.
Firmicus, 199.
Fishmongers' Company, 244.
Fishwiske, 286.
Fitz Hugh, 237 *n.*, 230.
Fitzwilliam, W., 172 *n.*
Fitzwilliam, 179 *n.*, 181.
Flahant, 266.
Flamstead, 277.
Flaxman, A., 170 *n.*, 171 *n.*
Fluctibus, de Robert, 247.
Forman, 229, 230.
Forster, 179 *n.*, 267.
Fossard, N. de, 297.
Fothergill, 141 *n.*
Foulkes, 274.
Fowkes, W., 131 *n.* ; Elizabeth, *ib.*
Fowler, W., 130 *n.*, 135 *n.*, 211 *n.* ;
 Joseph, 130 *n.*
Fox, 27 *n.* ; G., 52 *n.* ; 162 *n.* ; W. J.,
 165 *n.*, 180 *n.* ; Rev. T., 180 *n.* ; 199. ;
 246, 285, 292.
Frances, St., 199.
Frank, F. B., 113 *n.* ; R., 113 *n.*
Frederic, the 5th Elector Palatine,
 169 *n.*
French, 57, 66, 85 ; the King of, 241,
 245.
Fretwell, J., 133 *n.*
Frier, Dr., 216.
Frobisher, 181, 313.
Frost, xix., 239 *n.*, 298.
Fulgosus, 199.
Furnival, 181.

G

GABERS, 216.
Gacheld, 214.
Gale, Dr. Thos. (Dean of York), 40 *n.*,
 187, 188, 189, 198, 200, 201, 203,
 208, 209, 220, 255, 304, xviii. ; Roger
 and Samuel, 187.
Galen, 199.

Gamel, 81 *n.*
Gant, Walter of, 132.
Gardiner, T., Bishop of Lincoln, 145 *n.*
Garrett, 133 *n.*
Gascoigne, 181.
Gatty, Rev. Dr., vi, *n.*, 153 *n.*, 193 *n.*
Gauls, the, 306.
Gaunt, R. de, 81 *n.*
Gaurs, or Gabers, 216.
George, St., 35 ; arms of, 127 ; cross, 149 ; church of, 294 ; Prince, 49.
Gent, 239 *n.*
Geree, 176, 184.
Germans, the, 57.
Germe, 265.
Gerrard, 249.
Gething, Lady, 170 *n.*
Gibbons, 126, 313.
Gibson, 305.
Gifford, R., 297 *n.*
Gilbert, 217.
Gilby, 179 *n.*, 281.
Gill, E., 193 *n.* ; W., 270 *n.*
Gillam, 288.
Glenford, 122, 128.
Gloucester, Dean of, 58 *n.*
Glover, 227 *n.*
Godfrey, Sir E., 317.
Godwin, Earl, 312.
Golsa P. de, 157 *n.*
Goodman, xxii.
Gooben, 290.
Goodrick, 293.
Goodwin, 253.
Gordonius, 199.
Gossip, A., 13 *n.*; W., *ib.*; W. H., *ib.*
Gossip family, 303 *n.*
Gouge, N.. 29 *n.*
Gough, xxii., 189, *n.*
Gould, W., 21 *n.*
Gouy, 266.
Gower, Dr., 20 ; S., 20 *n.*
Granby, Marquis of, 44 *n.*
Grandison, 199.
Gravenor, 82 *n.*; M., 151 *n.*; U., *ib.*
Gray, 200, 205, 241 ; Walter, 233 *n.*
Greatrix, 90, 199.
Greatrex, J., 180 *n.* ; 268.
Grecians, the, 306.
Greene, 263, 313.
Greenhalgh, 180 *n.*, 267.
Greenwood, 131 *n.*
Gregory, 55 *n.*, 171, 292 ; IX., Pope, 122 *n.*
Grenchalgh, 267, 268.
Greves. 214.
Grey, Henry, Earl of Kent, 8 *n.* ; Anthony, Earl of Kent, 8 *n.*
Griffin, B., 288.

Grimshaw. 153 *n.*
Grimsditch, 153 *n.*
Gross, le W., 130 *n.*
Grosseteste, Lincoln Bishop of, 122 *n.*
Grove, R., 29 *n.*
Gruter, 206, 208, 209.
Gryme, 153 *n.*
Gucy, 265.
Guiannerius, 199.
Gunne, R., 118 *n.*
Guoy, 266.
Gurney, 295 *n.*
Guthlac, St., 148 *n.*
Guyo, 199.
Gwins, 124.

H

HACKET, 199.
Hadley, 239 *n.*
Hadrian, 219.
Haldenbi, 297, 298.
Halifax, Earl of. 242.
Halldard, 197 *n.*
Hall, 22, 40 ; William, 65 *n.* ; J., 97, 304, 305 ; 177, 178, 180, 181, 193, 255, 305, 319.
Hamilton, Sir G., 14 *n.* ; Frances, 14 *n.*; W., 243.
Hammersley, 59 ; II., 59 *n.*; & Co., 59 *n.*; Thomas, 59 *n.*
Hampole, Richard of, 201 *n.*
Hansby, Sir R., 291.
Hanson, 147.
Harbert, 89 *n.*
Hardwick, 257.
Hardy, 279 *n.*
Hargrave, 144.
Harold, Earl, 312.
Harrington, 181.
Harrison, Rev. J., 125 *n.*
Harrop, 40.
Hartforth, 229 *n.*
Hartington, Lord, 243.
Harvey, F., 158 *n.* ; J., 201, 202.
Hastings. 181, 217, 309.
Hatfield and Hatfeild, 13, *ib. n.*, 36 *n.*, 37 *n.*, 59 *n.*, 100, 102, 126, 135 *n.*, 164 *n.*, 166 *n.*, 193, 254 *n.*, 303 *n.*, 313.
Hauden, G.. 230.
Hawkins, 95 *n.*
Hawnes de Baron, 269.
Hayles, Judge. 9.
Headlam, 41, 279 *n.*, 280.
Heath, 213.
Heathcote, J. M., 165 *n.* ; R., viii., 257 *n.*

Heddon, 88.
Hedune. W. de. 81 n.
Helen, St., 129.
Helmont, 199, 248.
Hengist. 61, 62.
Henne, H., 68 n.; Dorothy, ib.
Henry. Prince. 247, 307, 315.
—— 2nd, 80 n.
—— 3rd, 122 n.
—— 4th, x. n.
—— 6th, 172 n.
—— 7th, 177, 312.
—— 8th, 46, 130 n., 153, 154, 234, 255, 290, 300, 301, 307, 310, 312.
—— 4th, King of France, 233, 317.
Herald and Genealogist, 100 n.
Hermes, 92.
Herschell, xxxii.
Heselden, W. S., 130 n., 132 n.
Heyrick, 254.
Hickman, 198.
Hill, T.. 165.; Elizabeth, 169 n, 171 n.; J., ib.
Hilliard, 181.
Hilton, 181, 217, 226, 227.
Hoare, 241.
Hobson, 303 n.
Hogarth, H.. viii.
Holbeche, H., 130 n.
Holland, 99.
Holles, G., 118 n.
Holm, Dr., 75.; 181.
Holmes, 149, 150, 151.
Holy Trinity, the, 130 n.
Honiwood, 254.
Hooke, 179 n.
Hook, 236.
Hope, 41.
Hopkinson, 183.
Hopton, Sir I., 102 n.
Hotham, 175, 181, 279 n.
Houson, 175, 297.
Hoveden, R., 194.
Howard, 194.
Howe, 242, 243.
Howson, 92.
Huartel, 199.
Hugh, St., 145 n.
Hugo, M., 203.
Huguenots, the, ix., xii.
Hunt, 21 n.
Hunter, J., vi. n., vii. n., xiii. n., xiv. n., xv., xxiii., 4 n., 37 n., 54 n., 55 n., 100 n., 102 n., 107 n., 108 n., 113 n., 124 n., 125 n., 135 n., 146 n., 147 n., 153 n., 166 n., 171 n, 172 n., 175 n., 177 n., 178 n., 182 n., 189 n., 193 n., 197 n., 201 n., 202 n., 221 n., 254 n., 257 n., 258 n., 260 n., 261 n., 263 n.,

284 n., 286, 294 n., 296 n., 297 n., 298, 301,
Hussey, 149, 175.
Hutton, J., 72 n.; 237, 317 n.; Dr. M., Archbishop of York, 304 n.; C., 187 n.
Huygens, xxv., xxviii., xxxi.
Hydes, 241.

I

INDIANS, the, 199.
Ingram, 7 n., 284; Sir A., 126, 313; Sir H., ib.
Ireton, 50.
Ironmongers' Company, 244.
Irwin, Lord, 36 n., 293, 313.
Israel, 111.
Ithon, de J., 256 n.

J

JACKSON, Sir B., 100.
Jackson, iv, viii, xxiv. 125, 179 n., 193 n., 294 n. 295 n., 296 n.,
Jacob, 133 n., 260.
Jacobites, 70, 111.
Jalland, 141 n., 161 n.
James, I. & II. (kings), 8, 12, 14 n., 15, 22, 30, 38, 39, 43, 45, 48, 57 n., 60, 70, 71, 85, 90, 92, 94, 99, 106, 116, 124, 179 n., 201, 214, 225, 233, 246, 247, 247 n., 257, 288, 289, 313, 317.
James, king of Scotland, 169 n., 229.
James, St., 233 n., 234 n.
Jannings, G., viii.
Jeffries, Lord, 9.
Jenkinson, 147 n.; W. A. A. C., 170 n.
Jennings, Rd., 14 n.; S., ib.
Jersey, Earl of, 242.
Jerusalem, knights of St. John, 88 n., 89 n., 174, 310.
Jesuits, the, 233.
Jesus, 51, 53, 60, 81, 82.
Jetzer, 199.
Jewel, 199, 303 n.
Joan of Ark, 199.
John, King, 81, 135, 307.
John, St., 121, 297, 299.
Johnson, 264.
Johnson, Rev. J. H., 160 n.; P., 141 n., 293.
Johnston, Dr., 4 n., 36 n., 113, 114, 175, 192, 196 n., 197 n., 204, 237, 249, 293.
Jolence, 161.
Jolland, G., 161 n.
Jollence, 141.

Jolly, 203.
Joly, 189.
Jones, 192, 242 n.
Jongee, 215.
Jurdie, 288.

K

KAY, Robert, 5 n., 283, 284, 285 ; Sir J., 185.
Kaye, H., 55 n. ; W., ib.
Keene, A., 183 n.
Kent, Countess of, 8 ; Amabel, 8 n. ; Earl of, Anthony Grey, 8 n. ; Henry Grey, 8 n., 9 n. ; Edmund Plantagenet, 231.
Kentish Men, 242, 243.
Kenyon, 41.
Kettle, Dr., 29 n.
Kettlewell, 147.
Kidson, 144, 201.
Kighly, 33.
Killigrew, 145.
King, Col. E., 123, 124 ; 156.
Kingman, 270 n.
Kingston, Earl of, 73, 74.
Kinnoul, Earl of, 147 n.
Kircher, Father, 27, 199.
Kirk, Col., 30.
Kirkby, 232 n.
Kirkby's Inquest, 265 n.
Kitchingman, 178.
Kitson, 241.
Knatchbull, 302.
Kneller, Sir G., 22 n.
Knipe, 285.

L

LABOUCHERE, xii.
Lactantius, 199.
Lacy, Robert de, 189 n., 255 ; family, 162, 181.
Lake, Dr., 161.
Laken, W., 118 n.
Lamb, 201, 241.
Lamber, S., 4 n.
Lambert, 126, 273.
Lamzweend, 199.
Lancaster, T., Earl of, 307.
Langdale, 288.
Langley, 234 n.
Langwith, 284.
Lansdowne Collections, 114 n., 281, 290, 291, 293, 297, 298, 302, 305, xv. n., xviii, xx.
Lapide, a, 199.

Laplanders, 14, 37.
Lassels, 217, 227 n., 230, 234, 235 n.
Latimer, 175, 244.
La Touche, xii.
Laud, 199.
Lauderdale, Lady, 279.
Lavater, 199.
Lavrock, 314.
Lawrence, St., 194.
Lawson, W., 164 n.
Layton, 255, 258.
Leach, J., 158 n.
Leake, Sir F., 106 n., 107.
Lee, Elizabeth, 35 n., 36 n. ; Frances, 36 n. ; Thomas, 36 n., 100, 101, 135 n., 207, 292 ; Cornelius, 35, 36 n., 50, 54 n., 55, 100, 101, 102, 108, 126, 233 ; Colonel, 133 n. ; family, 178, 313 ; Robert, 35 n., 36 n. ; Susan, 36 n.
Lefevre, xii.
Legard, 299.
Leibnitz, xxv., xxvi.
Leicester, Sir F., 41.
Leigh, 255.
Leighton, Archbishop, 190 n.
Leland, xiii. n., 293.
Le Lew, 4 n., 37.
Lemnius, 199.
Leng, 238 n.
Lentulus, 199.
Le Neve, 145 n., 170 n., 171 n , 279 n.
Lennox, Duke of C., 169 n.
Leslie, C., 41 n.
Lewellin, 105.
Lewis, x. n., 67.
Lichfield and Coventry, Bishop of, 5 n.
Lilburn, Colonel, 4 n.
Lile, Sir G., 101.
Lillingston, 75.
Limborg, 199.
Lincoln, Bishop of, 82 n. ; Grosseteste, 122 n. ; Holbeche, *alias* Randes, 130 n., 133 n., 145 n., 176, 302.
Lincoln, Dean and Chapter of, 85 n.
Lindholme, William of, 146 n., 147, 310.
Lindwood, 149.
Lisle, M., 97 n. ; 230.
Lister, 149, 150 ; Dr., 211 ; 236.
Locke, T., 172 n. ; xxiv.
Lockwood, 197.
Lodge, 169 n.
London, Bishop of, 5 n., 30 n. ; Aylmer, 79 n.
—— Lord Mayor of, 126.
Longley, Edmund de, 312.
Loretto, Lady of, 246.
Loudham, J. de, 172 n. ; W., ib.

Loudon, 10 *n.*
Lovel, 230.
Lovell, 274, 279.
Lovetoft, 181.
Lowther, Sir W., 69, 73 ; W., 293 ; Sir J., 297.
Loyd, 108.
Lucas, 55 ; Lord, 101 ; Sir C., 101.
Lucy, 227, 234.
Ludā, (Louth), Nicholas de, 232 *n.*
Ludovicus, Vives, 254.
Lully, R., 104.
Lund, Alice de, 147 *n.*
Lupton, 288.
Luther, 88.
Llhwyd, 236.
Lloyd, Dr., 24.

M

MACAULAY, 171 *n.*
Mahomet, 199.
Malet, D., 80 *n.*
Manchester, Earl of, 19 *n.*
Mann, 232 *n.*
Manners, Lady Elizabeth, 242 *n.*
Manningham, 92 *n.*
Mantua, Duke of, 57.
Marana, J. P., 26 *n.*
March, 181 ; Edward, Earl of, 312.
Mare, 293.
Margaret, Queen of Scotland, 229.
Margrave, 285.
Marlborough (J. C.), Duke of, 14 *n.*
Marples, S., 5 *n.*
Marshal, 181.
Marshall, Ald. W., 158 *n.* ; R., *ib.; J.,* 317, 318 *n.*
Marsham, Sir R., 170 *n.*
Marsigli, 250.
Martial, St., 157 *n.*
Martyr, Just., 199.
Marryott, 180 *n.*
Marvel, A., 286.
Mary, 317 ; Queen, 19, 46, 48, 49, 121 *n.*, 246, 312; St., 132; Magdalen, 294; Virgin, 11, 157 *n.*, 158 *n.*, 225 *n.*, 246, 297.
Mason, Robert, 218 *n.*, 219 ; Ald. and family, 218 ; Ped. of, 218 ; H. & W., 234 *n.*
Masters, 240.
Mauliverer, 175.
Maxwell, 279.
Mayor, viii.
Mazline, 305.
Meaux, 217
Mellish, S., 135 *n.*

W

Melton, 181, 227.
Melsa, or Meaux, Sir J., 217.
Menonius, H., 138.
Merrel, Dr., 144, 248.
Meux, 235.
Meyrick, 234 *n.*
Michael, St., 157 *n.*
Middlebrook, 55, 292.
Midgley, Dr., 26, 207, 213, 214.
Middlemore. H., 131 *n.*
Middleton, J., 75 ; 178 ; 201.
Millard, 40.
Miller, W., 29 *n.*; 182 *n.*, 183 *n.*, 193 *n.*, 257 *n.*, 294 *n.*
Milner's Thumbs, 90.
Milton, J., 160 *n.*, 300, 301.
Mings, Sir C., 171 *n.*
Mirfield, 288.
Monah, 115.
Monceaux, 230.
Monck, Lord, 126 *n.*
Monckton, 73 *n.*
Monk, Gen., 123, 126.
Montacute, 231.
Montague, 242.
Monteney, 181.
Moor, 153 ; 180.
Moore, R., 27 ; S. and A., 27 *n.*
Moore, S., 266 ; T., 267 ; T., 165 *n.*
Moors, the 36 *n.*
Moravius, 199.
Mordaunt, 113 *n.*
More, T., 118 ; 141.
Mores, R., 166 *n.*, 301.
Morley, 81, 82 *n.*; 89 *n.*; Fam., 121 *n.*; Eliz., 120 ; Jos., 120, 121, 135 ; 231.
Morocco, Emperor of, 30.
Morrell, 52.
Morton, 20 *n.* ; Sir J., 139 ; 199.
Mowbray, 152, 173, 252.
Mower, 141 *n.*
Murfin, 289.
Mulgrave, Earl of, 33 : Lord, 137.
Musgrave, 175.
Musso, 199.

N

NAINBY, 136 *n.*
Nanette, 291.
Narborough, Sir J., 169 *n.*, 170 *n.*, 171 *n.*; Elizabeth, 170 *n.*; Sir J., Bart., 170 *n.* ; Elizabeth, dame, 170 *n.* ; James, 170 *n.*
Neale, Dr., 166.
Needham, 28 *n.*, 41 *n.* ; P., 28 *n.* ; Rev. S., 28 *n.* ; W., 28 *n.*
Nelson, 82 *n.*

Nelstrop, 68.
Nelthorpe, Sir G., 68 *n.* ; Sir J., 68 *n.*, 151 ; Richard, 151 *n.* ; T., 151.
Nevil, 82, 116, 172, 281, 192, 211, 212, 231, 257, 309, 318.
Neville, 152.
Newburgh, 231.
Newcastle, Duke of, 74, 239, 240, 241.
Newman, D., 5 *n.*
Newmarch, 152.
Newton, Dr., xxx. ; Sir I., xvii., xxiv., xxxii., 23, 42.
Nicolas, Sir E., 169 *n.*
Nigil, 181.
Nills, 305.
Noades, J., 6 *n.*
Norcliffe, 226 *n.*, 292 *n.*
Norden, 159 *n.*
Normanby, Marquis of, 138, 184.
Northumbers, the, 307.
Norwich, Bishop of, 5 *n.*
Nostock, 250.
Notes and Queries, 87 *n.*
Nourse, 133 *n.*
Novâ Villâ, T. de, 82 *n.*

O

Oatreed, [Ughtred] 217.
Oates, 9, 317.
Ogden, 41 *n.*
Oldfield, S., 36 *n.*
Oldham, T., 52.
Oliver, 153 *n.*
Orange, Prince of, 14, 57 *n.*, 94, 246 ; Princess of, 49.
Orchard, 28 *n.*, 40 *n.*, 41 *n.*
Orford, Earl of, 57 *n.*, 242 ; Lord 165 *n.*
Origen, 199.
Orleans, Duchess Dowager of, 246.
Ormond, Earl of, 74, 106.
Ornsby, Rev. G., viii., 180 *n.*
Osborne, Sir E., 126, 313.
Oughtibridge, xxiii. ; pedigree of, xxxiv., 259, 263, 264, 267, 313,
Owston, 293.
Oxford, Earl of, 36 *n.*, 43, 44.
Oxley, 267.
Oxnard, 233 and *n.*
Oyry, F. de, 217.

P

Painel, 80 *n.*, 81 *n.*
Parœus, 250.
Palmerston, Lord, xii.

Paracelsus, 199, 247, 249, 250.
Parham, Lord, 161.
Parker, 84, 85 ; 183.
Parkin, 269 *n.*
Parr, 234 *n.*
Parrel, 76.
Parrol, 254.
Participants, the, 168 *n.*, 176, 202, 315.
Pattison, or Patterson, 294, 295.
Paul, Apostle, 53.
Paynel, R., 122, *n.*
Peacock, viii., 5 *n.*, 22 *n.*, 37 *n.*, 54 *n.*, 65 *n.*, 82 *n.*, 88 *n.*, 89 *n.*, 118 *n.*, 121 *n.*, 122 *n.*, 130 *n.*, 142 *n.*, 211 *n.*, 319 *n.*
Peake, J., 28 *n.*
Pearson, 201, 286.
Peart, Cap. O., 158 ; R., *ib. n.*
Peche, 230.
Peck, xv. *n.*, 181, 202 *n.*, 260 *n.*, 261 *n.*, 263 *n.*,
Peitevin, T., 81 *n.*
Pelham, 83, 319 ; Sir W., 160, 161 ; Lady, 156 ; C., 156 *n.* ; family of, *ib.*, 157, 161 ; H. A. M. C., 156 *n.* ; D. W., *ib.*
Pemberton, 286.
Penda, 307.
Penn, W., 45, 46.
Pentacrinites, 142 *n.*
Pepys, vii., 304.
Percy, W., 118 *n.* ; 235.
Perkins, 41 *n.*, 177, 180 *n.*, 181, 194, 279 *n.*, 292, 304, 305, 319.
Peroll, 254 *n.*
Perrott, 234 *n.*
Peterborough, Earl of, 113 *n.*, 114.
Peters, H., 51, 52, 60.
—— pence, 133.
Peter, St., 132.
Pettus, 274, 276.
Phileus, Taurominitos, 306.
Philip, King, 246.
Phillipa, Queen, xiii. *n.*, 307.
Phillips, Captain, 66 ; Sir Edward, 317 ; Mr., *ib. n.*
Phœnicians, the, 306.
Pierce, Dr., 78.
Pierre, De la, xii.
Place, 140 *n.*, 142, 143 and *n.*, 144, 147, 172, 184, 211, 212, 303 *n.* ; family registers of, 143 *n.*
Plaiz, de, W., 81 *n.*
Plantagenet, Edward and Richard, 312.
Platerus, 199.
Pleadwell, 139.
Plot, Dr., 280.
Plumptre, J., 172 *n.*

Pole, de la, ix., 230, 231, *ib. n.*
Polhill, 243.
Pomponatius, 199.
Pool, 199, 230, 291.
Porte, de la, J., 4 *n.*
Portington, 102, 181 ; 257, 258, 290, 291, 292, 313.
Portland, Earl of, 242; Lord, 106, 108.
Portuguese, 216.
Poulson, 217 *n.*, 225 *n.*, 226 *n.*, 228 *n.*, 234 *n.*
Poultney, N., 68 *n.*
Prat, or Pratt, 177, 239, 302.
Preston, E., 38 ; T. 293.
Pretender, the, xvi.
Prior, 291.
Prix, de la M., 4 *n.*
Proctor, 20 *n.*, 180 *n.*
Prole, 254 *n.*
Prospero, 146 *n.*
Pryme, de la Pryme, Prime, iv., vi., vii., viii., 3, 8, 13, 20 *n.*, 106 *n.*, 114 *n.*, 131 *n.*, 142 *n.*, 144 *n.*, 146 *n.*, 161 *n.*, 165 *n.*, 168 *n.*, 171 *n.*, 172 *n.*, 175 *n.*, 177 *n.*, 180 *n.*, 186 *n.*, 192, 201, 202 *n.*, 204 *n.*, 208, 209, 212 *n.*, 213, 218, 219, 221 *n.*, 223, 232 *n.*, 237, 238 *n.*, 239 *n.*, 241, 245, 250 *n.*, 252 *n.*, 255 *n.*, 259, 260, 261, 262, 263, 264, 265, 266, 267, 268, 269, 270, 271, 276, 279, 280, 281, 286, 289, 290, 291, 293, 295 *n.*, 297, 298, 304 *n.*, 313, 316, 317, 318 ; Family Memoir of, &c., iv., xxxii ; and Pedigree of, xxxv.
Prymrose, A., 248.
Pryn, 124.
Pulman, 171 *n.*, 300.
Puritanical Names, 43.
Puritans, 84.

Q

Quincy, or Quinzy, 181.

R

RAGUSEIUS, 199.
Raikes, 281.
Raine, iv., vii., 113 *n.*, 150 *n.*, 141 *n.*, 194 *n.*, 282 *n.*, 302,
Raleigh, 280.
Ramsden, 6 *n.*, 100, 104, 165, 273 *n.*, 286, 287, 299.
Ramton, 152.
Raudes, Thomas, 130 *n.*

Ransom, 197.
Raviliac, 233.
Rawlinson, R., 28 *n.*
Rawson, 109.
Ray, 249, 250.
Raysin, 173.
Read, R., 41 *n.*, 186 *n.*, 260, 279, 280.
Reading, 9.
Redford, Sir H., 117, 119.
Redman, 288.
Reinesius, 209.
Rendlesham, Baron, 147 *n.*
Reresby, 181.
Rhodes, 293.
Rhine, Prince Palatine of, E., 246.
Rheine, 208.
Rhodes, 159, 218 *n.*
Ricard, 309, 313.
Richard I., 123 *n.*
——— II., x. *n.*, 87 *n.*
——— III., 312.
Richardson, 231 *n.*, 232 *n.*, 238 *n.*
Richelieu, xii.
Richmond, C. Duke of, 193 ; 217 *n.*
Rickaby, 293.
Ridley, 273 *n.*
Ringstead, 170 *n.*
Rishton, 41 *n.*
Rivetus, 199.
Robert Jordan, son of, 81 *n.*
Robin Hood, 292.
Robinson, M., 6 *n.* ; Robert, 6 *n.* ; T., 29 *n.* ; E., 269 ; M., Sir W., 273 *n.* ; T., 289.
Rochester, Lord, 279.
Rock, Dr., 133 *n.*
Rockley, 181.
Rodes, C. H. R., Rev., 13 *n.* ; de, W. H., 13 *n.* ; Sir E., 187 *n.* ; Millicent, *ib.*
Rodrick, 40 *n.*
Rodwell, 267.
Rogers, 150.
Rogison, 249.
Romans, the, 35, 55, 62, 86, 91 *n.*; 138, 148, 149, 151, 186, 188, 275, 294, 306, 314.
Romilly, xii.
Romney, Baron, 170 *n.*
Rookby, 196 *n.*
Roos, 217.
Ross, Lord, 234 ; 158 *n.*
Rooth, 233.
Rotherfield, 181.
Rotherham de, Robert, 256 *n.*
Roundel, R., 6 *n.*
Rue, de la, 106.
Russell, Admiral E., 57 ; Lady M., *ib.* ; William, Lord, *ib. n.* ; E., *ib.*

Russel, Earl of Orford, 242.
Rutland, Duke and Earl of, 44.
Ryley, Rev. E., xiv. *n.*

S

SAAR, 235.
St. Andrew, 123 *n.*
St. Augustine, 182.
St. Catharine, 194.
St. Jerome, 177.
St. John, 253, 297.
St. Lawrence, 194.
St. Leonard, 174.
St. Margaret, Virgin, 172 *n.*
St. Mary, 297.
St. Pancratius, 182 ; Pancrace, 309.
St. Peter, 182.
St. Pulcheria, 296.
St. Pulcher, *vel* St. Sepulchre, 296.
St. Quintin, 240, 252 *n.*
St. Thomas, martyr, 172 *n.*
Salley, H., 141 *n.*
Salmeron, 199.
Salmon, 199.
Salisbury, Dean of 78 *n.* ; Bishop of,
    ib. ; Earl of, 94, 231.
Saltmarsh, 234.
Salvin, 135 *n.*, 175, 181.
Sampson, 194, 269.
Sandys (family, etc.), 35 *n.*, 36, 36 *n.*,
    37 *n.*, 43, 43 *n.*, 45, 95, 100, 101, 111,
    111 *n.*, 120.
Sanderson, 305 ; Dr., Bishop of Lin-
    coln, 82 *n.*, 83, 87 *n.* ; Dr., 176, 184.
Sanquerdns, 199.
Santon, 148.
Saracens, the, xi.
Saunders, 273.
Saunderson, 43 *n.*
Saunderson, R., 75 *n.* ; Bishop, 301,
    302, 318, 319 *n.*
Savile, Sir W., 102 *n.*, 257.
Sawdy, 199.
Saxon Coins, 62, 311.
Saxon MSS., 188.
Saxons, 164, 307.
Sayer, 235 *n.*
Scapula, O., 221.
Scarsdale, Earl of, 107 ; Lord, 13 *n.*
Scaurus, xv.
Scawby, 68.
Schelsbroot, Van, 142.
Scholefield, 288.
Scot, Dr., 199.
Scotland, James 6th of, 169 *n.* ; Anne,
    Queen of, *ib.*

Scrope, of Bolton, Em. Lord, 242
    Annabella, 242 *n.*
Scroop, 230.
Seaman, S., 132.
Selden, J., 8, *ib. n.*, 9 *n.*, 67.
Sennertus, 199.
Seymour, 242, 243.
Shakespeare, 164 *n.*
Sharp, Archbishop of York, 178 *n.*,
    245.
Shawe, 88 *n.*
Sherlock, 159.
Sheffield, 173 *n.* ; G., 184 *n.* ; R., *ib.*
Shelburn, Lord, xxii.
Sheppard, 202, 242, 243.
Shingey, Baron, 57 *n.*
Shorton, A., 170 *n.*
Shovel, Sir C., 169, 170 *n.*, 171 *n.* ;
    Lady, 170 *n.* ; E., 170 *n.* ; A., *ib.*
Shrewsbury, Earl of (G. Talbot), 8 *n.* ;
    Countess of, 166 *n.*
Sibbald, 186 *n.*
Sim, 208.
Simocata, 199.
Simon, Father, 199.
Simpson, 54 *n.* ; W., 135 ; Hon. J. B.,
    156 *n.*, 292.
Sirenius, 199.
Sisson, 241.
Sitwell, 147 *n.*
Skaife, R. H., viii, 265 *n.*, 287.
Skearn, 181.
Skern, 6 *n.*
Skinner, Sir V., 130 *n.*, 131 *n.*, 145,
    160 *n.*; Lady, 131 ; Edward, *ib. n.*;
    Anne, *ib.* ; 157, 160 ; W., 160 *n.*;
    B., *ib.* ; Edward, *ib.* ; Cyriack, *ib.*,
    300, 301 ; Stephen, *ib.* ; Daniel,
    300, 301.
Skirlaw, 194, 253.
Slack, 106 *n.*
Slinger, T., 141 *n.*
Sloane, xix., 236, 237, 247, 249, 250,
    255.
Smagge, S., 3 ; P., xv., 3, 259, 260.
Smales, 273.
Smart, Dr., 112, 141.
Smaqúe, xv., 260.
Smith, J., 116, 117 ; Nicholas, 119 ;
    L., 183 *n.*; M., 199 ; T., 212 ; Rev.
    Dr. T., 304 ; 283.
Smyth, D., 43 ; J., 245.
Smythe, A., 213.
Snasel, 175.
Snawswell, Elizabeth, 119 ; H., *ib.*
Society Royal, 67.
Somers, Lord, 242.
Somwers, 199.
Somerset, Duchess of, 214.

Sothill, 135 n., 181.
Spanish, the, 57.
Spatchet, 199.
Spectator, 128 n.
Speed, 253, 275, n., 293.
Speke, 175.
Spelman, 134 n.
Stabler, 83 n.
Stables, 69.
Stanfield, 181.
Stanley, 29 n.
Stannick, 40 n.
Stapleton, 148 n.; Sir P., 126, 127; 175, 181.
Staresmoor, F., 119; William, ib.
Stark, 65 n., 72 n.
Starkey, 285.
Startune, H. de, 81 n.
Staveley, W., 118 n.
Steinman, 43 n.
Stella, 199.
Stephen, King, 211, 225 n.
Sterpin, 260
Stevenson, 217.
Stillingfleet, 41 n.; 200 n.
Stonehouse, W. B., 12 n., 85 n., 89 n., 146 n., 152 n., 168 n., 172 n., 173 n., 174 n., 182 n., 184 n., 211 n., 260 n., 291.
Stor, 273.
Stovin, 212 n.; 260 n.
Stow, Archdeacon of, 72.
Stafford, Earl of, T., 131 n., 317.
Straker, D., 17 n.
Strange, 118 n., 119.
Strongbow, 181.
Stukeley, 131 n.; 138 n.
Suckling, Sir J., 29 n.
Suffolk, Pole, Earl of, 230; Duke of, 231.
Summers, Lord, 281.
Sumner, Dr., 301.
Sunderland, Earl of, 242 n.
Surtees Society, iv., v., viii,, xxiii., 113 n., 150 n.
Sutton, H., 118 n.; Sir R., 130 n.; arms, 227; S. de, 233 n.; J. de., ib., 234 n.
Sweden, King of, Gustavus Adolphus, 168 n.
Swift, Sir R., 106, 107, 108; W., 107; 181; B., 296.
Swyft, 106 n.
Sye, 144.
Sydenham, Sir P., 187 n.
Sykes, 225 n., 232 n.
Sylvius, Æn., 29.
Symon, 288.
Symons, 239 n.

T

TAGLIACOZZA, 13 n.
Talbot, G., Earl of Shrewsbury, 8 n.; Elizabeth, 8 n., 9 n.; Sir G., 14 n.; Richard, Earl of Tyrconnel, ib.; Sir Robert, ib.; Sir William, ib.; 181.
Talboys, 181.
Taliacocius, 13.
Tancred, 293.
Tanner, 225 n.
Tascard, Father, 34.
Taylor, 21 n.; Rev. Z., 190, 192, 198, 199, 203, 206, 208, 209, 215.
Teague, 179 n.
Tempest, 293.
Templars, Knights, 55 n., 56, 62, 86, 88, 89 n., 174, 310.
Temple, 254.
Tennant, 274.
Tertullian, 199.
Thackeray, xvii.
Thellusson, C., 147 n.; C. S. A., ib.; P. J., ib.; P., ib.
Theobald, 41 n.
Thomkinson, 196 n., 197 n.
Thompson, J., 28, 141 n., 217 n.; T., 225 n., 226 n., 228 n.; W. and R., 268; E., 285; Rev. Dr., viii. 228; J., 286; B., 293.
Thomson, Sir H., 204; Lady Ann, ib.
Thoresby, vii., xiv., xxi., 10 n., 13 n., 36 n., 38 n., 58 n., 95 n., 113 n., 171 n., 172 n., 181 n., 187 n., 188, 189 n., 204 n., 239 n., 255, 256, 258 n., 272 n., 275 n., 277 n., 293, 294 n.
Thornhill, 41 n.
Thornton, 183.
Thorpe, 159 n.
Thuanus, 199.
Thuille, de la, Lord, 317.
Thurston, J., 170 n.; E., ib.
Thwaites, 193.
Tickell, xxi., xxii., 239 n.
Tilli, Otto, or Otho de, 294, 295.
Tillotson, 199.
Tillyoll, 226, 227, 230.
Tilney, 217.
Tockets, 284, 285.
Todd, Tod, 288, 292, 300, 301.
Tomlinson, 273 n., 279 n.
Tompkinson, 196.
Tonge, 319 n.
Tooland, 217.
Torre, J., 172; 232 n.; 273 n., 291, 297, 298, 301.
Tourville, Mons. de, 57 n.
Towars, 231.
Trajo, W., 138, 203.

Trambe, 293.
Trannian. St., 133.
Travers, 291.
Tricket, Catherine, 123 n. ; Joseph, 123 n. ; Robert, 123 n.
Triggot, 181.
Trippet, 241, 300.
Trithemius, 199.
Tron, St., 133 n.
Troy. King of, ix.
Trunyon, St., 132.
Truyen, St., 133 n.
Trygot, 193.
Tully, family of, 159.
Turks, the, xi.
Turner, 29 n. ; C., 36 n.
Tuscany, Duke of, 57.
Tusedail, 217.
Tyrconnel, Earl of, 14.
Tyrwhitt, 88 n. ; 90 n. ; Elizabeth, 130 n. ; R.. ib. ; Wm., ib. ; R., 131 n. ; Sir R., 130 n.
Terwyt (Turrit), 163.

U

Ufford, 231.
Ughtred, or Oatreed, 217.
Uppleby. G., 130 n.
Urry. 88 n.
Urslet, 181.

V

Valkenburgh, Van, or Vaulcon-burgh, xvi.. 5, and n., 6 n., 283, 284, 285 ; pedigree of, 285, 286.
Van Akker, 123.
Vandervert, 284.
Vanheck, 266, 267.
Van Swinden, xxv.
Vaudois, 24 ; the, 205.
Van Vaulconburgh, or Valkenburgh, 283, 284, 285 ; pedigree of, ib,, 286.
Vavasour. 175.
Verdon, 28 n. ; 41 n.
Verecius, M., 209.
Verli, R. de, 225 n.
Vermuyden, Sir C., xv., xxi., 3 n., 5 n., 126, 202 n., 254, 284, 313, 314, 315.
Vernatti, 254, 284.
Vernon, 181, 242.
Verulam, Lord, 247.
Victoria, Princess, 295 n.
Vigani, J. F., 25, 217.

Vintners, the, 144.
Virgil, 276.
Vives, L., 254.
Vortigern, 61.

W

Wade, Elizabeth, 59 n. ; William, ib.; B., 241.
Wagstaff, Dr., 217.
Wainwright, 294 n.
Wake, de la, 228 ; Lord Thomas, 231.
Walcot, H., 158 n.
Wales, Prince of, 71, 245, 246, 247 n., 307.
Walford, 283.
Walker, 36 n., 40 ; L., 54 n. ; T., 295 n.
Waller family, 27 n. ; E., 21 n.
Wallice, T., 186.
Wallis, 181.
Walter of Durham, 194.
Warburton, xiv., xx., xxii., 204 n., 217 n., 227 n., 290, 298.
Ward, Dr. S., 78 n.
Wardel, 232.
Warren, Jo., 29 n. ; Earls of, xiii. n., 166 n., 171, 312, 319.
Washington, 177.
Waterland, Mrs., 125.
Wats, Thomas, 121.
Watson, Dr., 41 n. ; Bishop, 196 n. ; 206, 292.
Weddell, 273 n.
Wellbeloved, 205 n.
Wells, 318 n.
Wentworth, Sir W., 131 n., 160 n. ; Anne, ib.; Elizabeth, 297 ; Sir J., ib. ; J., 298 : 147 n. ; 175, 177, 181 ; arms, 197, 297.
Wernelcy, or Werndley, J. C., 4 n.
Wesley, Samuel, 173, 176, 190 ; John, 174 n. ; 198, 213.
West, 215, 313.
Westby, F., 13 n. ; T., ib. ; 181, 193, 281.
Westmerland, H., Earl of, 160 ; Elea-nor, dau. of do., ib.
Wetherall, R., 158 n.
Wharncliffe, Lord, 172 n.
Wharton, 83, 175.
Wheelhouse, 289.
Wheelock, 188.
Whichcot. G., 185 n.
Whiston, 159.
White, 9 n., 83, 198, 199. 250 n., 281, 313.
Whitley, C. T., iv.

Wichcote, 109.
Wickham, 313.
Wigley, 133 n.; 279 n.
Wigmore, 41 n.
Wilburn, 245.
Wildbore, 295 n.
Wilkinson. 241, 280.
Willats, 267.
William the Conqueror, 72, 109, 194, 312.
——— King, 19, 22, 49, 64, 66, 84 n., 95, 96, 97, 106, 115, 116, 150, 189, 202, 242 n., 243.
——— and Mary. 109 n., 288.
Williams, 199.
Williamson, 297; J., 169 n.; Sir. J., 169.
Willis, 199.
Willoughby, 257; C., Lord Parham, 161; Anne, ib.
Wilson, F., 41 n.; J., ib.; 43; M., 183 n.; E. S., viii, 252 n., 298, 304 n.
Willson. Isabella, 196 n.
Winchester, Marquis of, 201 n., 202.
Wingfield, 230.
Winn, C., 91 n.; family of, 124; G., ib.; Rowland, ib. n., 125; Edmund, 125; S., ib. n.; Sir E., 145.
Wilberfoss, 279 n.
Wise, 229.
Wode, Robert, 130 n.
Wolf, 28 n.
Wolsey, Cardinal, 296, 318.
Wolstenholm, 124 n.

Wombwell, 181.
Wood, Mary, 119, 120; Thomas, 119; R., 119, 120; arms of, 120; a'Anthony, 300; Athen. Ox., 176 n.; F., xvi., 259.
Woodcock, 9, 313.
Woodrofe, 181.
Woodward, 179 n., 236, 237.
Worde, W. de, 177.
Wormley, 313.
Worral, 181, 287.
Worsley, Baron, 156 n.; J., 123.
Wortley, 172 n., 181.
Wotton, W., 28 n., 29 n.; Rev. H., 28 n.
Wright, A., 141 n.; 261, 268, 269, 286.
Wroe, Dr., 208, 214.
Wyvil, 95 n.

Y

YARBOROUGH, 156 n., 171, 319; Earl of, 84 n., 121 n., 130 n., 131 n., 156 n., 157 n.
Yarburgh, 204.
York, Archbishop of, 46, 143, 147 n., 178, 208, 239, 240, 241, 292, 300, 303, 304 n.; Dean of, Gale, 187 n., 188, 198, 200, 203, 205, 208, 209, 220, 235, 236; Archdeacon of, 58 n., 289, 292; Duke of, 57 n., xiii. n.; Princes of, xiii. n.
Youden, 303 n.
Young, 217.

INDEX OF PLACES.

A

ABINGER, 176 *n.*
Ackton, 125 *n.*
Accrington, 41 *n.*
Addingham, 292.
Adwick Hall, 177.
Agelorum, 221.
Ailsby, 153, 154.
Aire, River, 184, 188, 314.
Albrough, Holderness, 217, 235, 272.
Alburrow, near Boro'bridge, 186, 198.
Alkborough, 138, 139, 142, 164, 203, 212, 235, 301.
All-Saints, Barton, 132 ; York, 288.
Althorp, 58, 108, 151.
Ambersbury, 78 *n.*
America, xiii., 99.
Amsterdam, 92 *n.*, 136 *n.*, 144, 301.
Anables, 119.
Ancholme, or Ankholme, 115, 122, 131, 142, 211, 319 *n.*
Andrew's, St., Holborn, 43 *n.*
Ank, River, 115, 122, 128, 211.
Anlaby, 299.
Annesley, 34.
Appleby, 80, 117, 124, 125, 128, 130 *n.*, 164, 211.
Appletreewick, 168 *n.*
Arabia, 58.
Arksey, 102 *n.*, 177, 257 *n.*, 292, 295 *n.*
Armeu, 273.
Armthorpe, 290, 301.
Arnold, 225 *n.*
Arras, 200.
Ash (or Esh) Well, 149 *n.*
Ashby, 82 *n.*, 89 *n.*
Ashfields, 287.
Audfield, 119.
Austerfield, 220, 221 *n.*, 297.
Averholme, 134.
Ax Yard, 115.
Axholme, Isle of, 3, 5 *n*, 12 *n.*, 83, 85

n., 116, 131 *n.*, 148 *n.*, 168 *n.*, 172 *n.*, 173, *ib. n.*, 174, *ib. n.*, 182 *n.*, 185 *n.*, 211 *n.*, 212 *n.*, 257, 260 *n.*, 290, 291, 315.

B

BARWORTH, 135.
Bake, 275, 276.
Balby, 296, 297 *n.*
Ballasalla, 270.
Ballatrick, 270 *n.*
Balneum, 55.
Banks, 177.
Bantry Bay, 171 *n.*
Barcelona, 57.
Bardney Abbey, 132.
Bargh, 147 *n.*
Barlborough, 13 *n.*
Barleby, 229 *n.*
Barlings, 158 *n.*
Barnby-Don, 55 *n.*, 102 *n.*, 171, 257, 258, 291, 292.
Barnby Moor, 57.
Barnsley, 147, 177, 297.
Barnstaple, 131 *n.*
Barrow, 60, 130 *n.*, 211.
Barton, 59, 62, 128, 130 *n.*, 132, 142, 144, 145.
Baston, 148 *n.*
Bath, 63 *n.*, 183 *n.*
Batley, 292.
Bawtry, 35, 114 *n.*, 201 *n.*, 202 *n.*, 220, 261 *n.*, 263 *n.*, 284, 297.
Bawn, 55.
Baynard's Castle, 228.
Bedford, County of, 36 *n.*, 117, 174 *n.*, 201 ; Level, 57 *n.* ; Walks, 117.
Beighton, 183 *n.*
Belton, 3 *n.*, 73 *n.*, 173, 175, 176, 196 *n.*, 269, 270.
Belvoir Castle, 44.
Beningtack, 286.

Benningholme, 225 n.
Benwell, 225 n.
Bereswood, 308.
Berkshire, 119, 120, 280, 281.
Berlings, or Barlings, 158.
Beverley, xxii., 7, 17, 83, 115, 141 n., 175, 196 n., 198, 218 n., 219, 229, 232, 253, 273 n., 290, 297.
Bewick-by-Albnrrow, 235.
Bigby, 122 n., 153, 253.
Billing, Great, 79 n.
Billingsgate Street, London, 176.
Bilson, 199.
Bilton, 119, 120, 225 n.
Birstal Priory, 148.
Bishop's-Hill, York, 188, 292.
Bishopthorpe, 187, 245.
Blackfryars Stairs, 278.
Blackwall, 277.
Bled-ground, 165 n.
Blockhouse Hills, 156.
Blonne, 276.
Blyth, 302.
Bombaim, 215.
Bommell, 75 n.
Boothby-Pagnell, 302.
Booth Ferry, 257.
Boroughbridge, 115, 131 n.
Boscobel, 217.
Boston, 105, 131 n., 148 n., 216, 217, ib. n.
Bosworth, 161.
Bossall (or Boswell), 177, 239, 302.
Bottesford, viii., 65 n., 71 n., 75 n., 82 n., 88 n., 89, 121 n.
Botulph's, St. (Lincoln), 148.
Brabant, 133 n.
Bradfield, 165, 175.
Bramwith, 28, 37, 55, 55 n., 63, 114, 167.
Branam, 28 n.
Bratton, 134.
Bratton Graves, 211.
Bretton West, 298.
Bridekirk, 169 n.
Bridge-house, Arksey, 295 n.
Bridlington, 272, 293.
Brigg, viii., xviii., 60, 61 n., 62, 66, 68, 81, 90 n., 93, 97, 112, 122, 128, 129, 133, 141, 143, 144, 151, 153, 159, 161, 162, 163, 164.
Brington, 78 n.
Bristol, 95 n.
Britain, 106 n., 249.
British Embassy, xii.
British Museum, vi. n., vii. n., xviii., xx., 114 n., 183 n., 204 n., 291, 293, 297, 298, 302.
Brocklesby, 83, 131 n., 156, 160, 161, 162, 319.

Brodsworth, 147.
Brough, 219.
Broughton, xviii., 59, 61 n., 65, 68 n., 80, 84 n., 86, 90, 91, 117, 118, 119, 120, 122 n., 125, 127, 128, 133, 134, 137, 145 n., 159, 165, 186 n., 211, 249, 251 n., 276, 279.
Bruges, xii.
Brumby, 82 n., 88 n., 89, 264, 318 n.
Brussels, xii.
Bryerhills, 267.
Bucks, County of, 5 n., 183 n., 254.
Bull Hassocks, 290.
Burton, 59, 59 n., 137, 138 n., 148, 184.
Burton Constable, 225 n.
Burton Stather, 121 n., 142 n., 148 n.
Burton Wall, 158 n.
Burrow, Lady or Countess, 133 n.
Buttercrambe, 279 n.
Butterwick, 148 n., 184.
Buxton Well, 274.
Byram, 273 n.

C

Caistor, or Castor, 61, 62, 67, 71, 141, 156 n.
Calder, River, 184.
Calne, 183 n.
Cambridge, vii., viii., xv., xvi., xvii., xviii., xxiii., xxv., xxvii., xxviii., xxix., xxx., 6 n., 18, 19, 28, 30, 34, 35, 39, 44, 45, 57 n., 58 n., 65, 70, 117, 133, 186, 187 n., 239, 241, 260, 274, 276, 279, 299, 300, 302, 304 ; All Saints, 196 n. ; Catherine College, 6 n., 28 n. ; Christ's College, 187 n. ; Clare Hall, 164 ; Emmanuel College, 302 ; Jesus College, 181 n., 304 ; Round Church, 40 ; St. John's Chapel, 196 n. ; St. John's College, viii., xvii., xxix., 161 n., 179 n., 181 n., 196, 254, 279 n. ; Sidney Sussex College, 302 ; Trinity Church, 196 n. ; Trinity College, vi., viii., 285 n. 300 ; Hostel, xv., xvi., xvii., xxviii., xxix.
Campsal, 6 n., 37 n., 113 n., 133 n., 171 n., 200, 204, 287, 319.
Canovein, or Canova, 215, 216.
Canterbury, 170 n., 319.
Cantley, 106 n.
Car-house, 193 n.
Carleton, 109 n.
Carleton-Paynel, 118 n.
Carlisle, 73.
Carniola, 82,

Carrickfergus, 116.
Casterton, 211.
Casthorp, 118 *n.* (*vel.* Castlethorpe.)
Castlegate (St. Mary's), York, 204 *n.*
Castle-hill, 81, 235.
Castlethorpe, 80 *n.*, 81, 84 *n.*
Castleton, 211.
Castleton Well, *ib.*
Castletown, 149.
Castrop, 80.
Catalonia, 57.
Catherine College, Cambridge, 6 *n.*, 28 *n.*
Catton, Upper, 206, 208.
Cave, 200.
Cawood, 296, 305.
Chatres, 164 *n.*
Chatham, 278.
Cherrington, 218 *n.*
Cheshire, co., 28 *n.*, 38, 41, 189 *n.*, 255.
Chester, 95 *n.*
Chesterfield, 141, 263.
Chelmsford, 100.
Chelsea, 278.
Chevet, 257 *n.*
Cheetham Hill, 4 *n.*
Chete (Chevet), 257.
Chibereworde, 178 *n.*
Chichester, 5 *n.*
Chippenham, 183 *n.*
Chirictown, 127.
Chiswick, 278.
Christ's College, Cambridge, 187 *n.*
Chulminoor, 216.
Church-Garth (Kirton), 127.
Clee, 155 *n.*
Cleethorpe, 155.
Clermont, 157 *n.*
Cletham, 148.
Clogher, or Clohar, 144.
Coalby, 142.
Coates, Great, 153 ; Little, *ib.*
Colchester, 21 *n.*, 101.
Collen, 57.
Colton, 41 *n.*
Commons, House of, 150.
Coney Street, 6 *n.*
Coningsborough, xiii. *n.*, 296 *n.*
Conington, 28 *n.*
Conisby, 106.
Coniston, 225 *n.*
Corringham, 318 *n.*
Cottingham, xvi., 228, 229, 230, 232 *n.*, 299.
Courtown, 14 *n.*
Covent Garden, 283.
Countess Barrow, 212.
—— Close and Pit (Allkburrow), 164.

Cowick, 6 *n.*
Cravemore, 113 *n.*
Craven, 168, 183.
Orayford, 171 *n.*
Creighton, *vel.* Crigglestone, 296 *n.*
Cripplegate (St. Giles), 21 *n.*
Crooksbroom, 310.
Croston, 192 *n.*
Crowland, 266.
Crowle, 4 *n.*, 9 *n.*, 83 *n.*, 175, 176, 284, 285, 315.
Crowston, 129.
Croyland, 148 *n.*
Cumberland, 85, 169 *n.*

D

Danish Coins, 311.
Danum, 218, 221.
Darfield, 108, 115.
Darren Hills, 275.
David's, St., 149 *n,*
Deal (Kent), 95.
Denmark, 153 *n.*
Delphos, 246.
Deptford, 277.
Derbyshire, 13 *n.*, 41 *n.*, 141, 165, 174 *n.*, 175, 183 *n*, 260, 263, 276.
Derby, 34 ; School, 41 *n.*, 260, 276.
Devil's A...... (Derbyshire), 275, 276.
Devizes, 78 *n.*
Devonshire, 274.
Diana's Head Spring (Kirton), 149.
Dicken Dike, 168.
Dickering, 225 *n.*
Don, or Dun, River, 35, 55 *n.*, 166 *n.*, 189, 286, 314.
Doncaster, vi. *n.*, viii., xxii., xxiv., 5 *n.*, 6 *n.*, 13 *n.*, 14, 18, 35, 43 *n.*, 52 *n.*, 58, 59 *n.*, 63, 69 *n.*, 96, 106 *n.*, 107 *n.*, 112, 113 *n.*, 114 *n.*, 115, 144, 147 *n.*, 156 *n.*, 171, 173, 175, 178, 179 *n.*, 182 *n.*, 183 *n.*, 188, 190 *n.*, 193, 198, 233, 283, 284, 285, 288, 291, 293, 295 *n.*, 296, 297, 305, 317 *n.*
Dorchester, 20 *n.*
Dordrecht, 136 *n.*
Dorsetshire, 149 *n.*
Dover, 123.
Doway, 45.
Dowthorpe, 225 *n.*
Downs, the, 63 *n.*
Drax, 292.
Driffield, 218 *n.*
Drypool, 204, 299.
Dublin, 215.
Dunham Ferry, 74.

Dunscroft, 166, 175, 180 n., 301, 308, 310.
Dunstall, 318 n.
Durham, co. of, 40 n., 304.
—— 97 n. ; St. Cuthbert's in, 194 ; Prior of, 195 ; Castle of, iv.
Durtness, 286.

E

EARSWICK, 273 n.
Easterton, 193.
Eastfield, 113 n.
East Indies, 215, 237.
Eastland, 286.
Estrington, 193 n.
Eburacum, 205 n.
Ecclesfield, 112 n.
Eccleston, 112.
Edwinstowe, 189 n.
Edwinstow, 255.
Egypt, 58.
Egborough, 283.
Elephanto, 216.
Eldon Hole, 274, 275, 276.
Ellerby, 225 n.
Elloughton, 218 n., 219.
Elmsall, 175.
Eltofts, 232 n.
Ely, 19.
Elmsal, North, 298.
Enfield, 131 n.
England, xi. n., xii., xiii., xxviii., 7. 8, 9, 10, 12, 14, 17, 19 n., 24, 27, 33, 38 n., 48, 60, 66, 70, 77, 82, 83, 88, 90 n., 96, 97, 108, 109, 123, 126 n., 133, 145, 156, 157 n., 159, 165, 176, 188, 189, 229, 245, 246, 248, 249, 270, 320.
—— Church of, 58, 95, 96, 97, 113 n., 122 n., 136, 190 n., 201, 213, 303 n.
Eper, 3.
Epworth, 3, 5 n., 83, 85 n., 173, 174 n., 175, 176, 198, 202 n., 267, 269, 270 n.
Ermine Street, the Roman, 59 n., 68 n.
Escrick, 293.
Esh (or Ash) Well, 149 n.
Eshton Hall, 183 n.
Essex, 100.
Eton, 40 n., 41 n., 58 n., 279.
Europe, x., xxvi., xxvii., 241.
Exchequer Court, 315.
Exeter, 95 n.
Eyworth, 117.

F

FAIRHOLM, 225 n.
Faldingworth, 82 n.
Fardingoe, 119.
Farnham, 164 n.
Fermanagh, 212 n.
Fens, 165 n.
Fenwick, 84 n.
Ferriby, 98, 115, 184 n., 197.
—— North, xvi., 75 n., 264, 297, 299.
—— South, 206.
—— Sluice, 131 n.
Ferry Flash, 82 n.
—— Sluice, 131.
Finningley, 201, 202.
Firth, the, 232 n.
Fishlake, viii., 11, 96, 97 n., 114, 115, 167, 175, 177, 178, 180 n., 181, 193, 194, 255, 288, 291, 305, 315, 319.
Fladbury, co. Worcester, 24 n.
Flamborough, 293.
Flanders, ix., xii., xiii., 3, 108, 260, 265.
Fleet Street, 283.
Flixborough, 121.
Foettipore, 317 n.
Folkerby, 6 n.
Fordingbridge, 40 n.
Fort Hills, 115, 116, 129.
Foxletness, 139.
France, xii., 38, 90 n., 108, 136, 137, 157 n., 205, 229, 317.
Fraisthorpe, 225 n.
Freistingthorpe, ib.
Freston Priory, 137, 148.
Frickley, 52 n., 175.
Frodingham, 148.
Froulsworth, 119.

G

GAINSBOROUGH, 65 n., 72, 84, 98, 105, 125, 145, 168, 198, 213, 265, 290.
Gainstrop, 127, 128, 211.
Galbergh, 147 n.
Gallow-hills, 134.
Gamston, 106.
Ganstead, 225 n.
Gauble Close, Balby, 297 n.
Gauber Hall, 147.
Gaunt, O', J. house, 278.
Geneve, 4 n.
Genoa, 26 n.
Germains, St., 41 n.
Germany, 82 n., 90 n., 106 n., 107 n.
Giggleswick, 149.

Gillian's (or Julian's) Bower, 164, 301.
Gilthwaite, 301.
Gipwell, 71.
Gisborough, 181 *n.*, 285.
Glasgow, xvii., 18 ; University of, 190 *n.*
Glenford Brigg, 122, and *n.*, 186 *n.*
Gloucestershire, 242.
Godmanchester, 133.
Godstow, 105.
Gokewell (or Goykewell), 79, 86.
Goodcock, 266.
Goodcop, 267, 269, 270 *n.*
Goole, 168, 185, 290.
Gore Steel, Thorne, 167, 287.
Gowthorp, 149 *n.*
Goxhill, 130 *n.*, 131 *n.*
Grantham, 44, 73 *n.*, 76, 278.
Grave, 75 *n.*
Gravesend, 277.
Gray's Inn, 151 *n.*, 285.
Great Britain, 271.
Greece, 291.
Grecian Coins, 311.
Greenhoe, 65 *n.*
Greenwich, 277.
Grime Close, 159.
Grimsby, 123, 152, 153, 155, 156, 159, 253 ; Road, 116.
Grim's-dyke,, 153 *n.*
Grim's-shaw, *ib.*
Grim's-thorpe, *ib.*
Grimthorpe, 279 *n.*
Guelderland, 75 *n.*, 164 *n.*, 176 *n.*
Guisborough, 285, 304, 305.
Gyp, or Gipwell, 128.

H

HACKNEY, 198.
Hadley House, 113 *n.*
Hador, 149 *n.*
Hague, the, 169 *n.*
Haines, 266.
Hale's Hill, 146.
Halhenburg, xvi. *n.*
Halifax, 178.
Hall Cross, Doncaster, 294.
—— House, *ib. n.*
Haltenprise, 196, 298, 299.
Halton, 130 *n.*
—— Price, 298, 299.
—— West, 140.
Ham, 279.
Hampole, 193, 297.
Hampton Court, 279.
Hanson's House, 146.
Hants., co. of, 40 *n.*

Harburg, 34.
Hardwick, 255.
—— Hill, 82 *n.*
Harmston, 91 *n.*
Hastings, 169, 171 *n.*
Hatfield, viii., xii., xiii *n.*, xir. *n.*, xviii., xx., xxi., xxii., 4 *n.*, 5 *n.*, 6, 11, 12, 13 *n.*, 20 *n.*, 27 and *n.*. 28. 35, and *n*, 36 *n.*, 37 *n.*, 54 *n.*, 55 *n.*, 63. 76,.99, 106 *n.*, 111 *n.*. 114, 126, 133 *n.*. 135, 146 *n.*, 165, 166, 172, 175, 178, 179 *n.*, 180, 181 *n.*, 187, 188, 189 *n.*, 190 *n.*, 193, 196, 197 *n.*, 202 *n.*, 204 *n.*, 207, 210, 212, 218, 233, 255, 256, 257, 260, 261 *n.*, 262, 265, 266. 267, 268, 269, 270 *n.*, 284, 285, 287. 289, 290, 291, 292, 302, 303, 305, 307, 308, 309, 310, 311, 312, 314, 315.
—— Court Rolls, 256 *n.*, 257 *n.*
—— Chace, vi. *n.*, xii., xiii., xv., xvi., xxi., xxii., xxiii., 3. 4 *n.*. 5 *n.*, 37 *n.*, 55 *n.*, 185, 202, 220, 284, 286, 291, 308.
—— Levels, xvi., xxi. *n.*, 249, 251 *n.*, 254, 260 *n.*. 285, 287, 290.
—— Woodhouse, 146 *n.*, 287, 308.
Haut Emprice. 299.
Haverborough, 34.
Hawnes, 174 *n.*
Haxey, 115, 116, 172 *n.*, 175, 176, 290.
Hedingly Moor, 10 *n*,
Hedon, xxii., 244, 293.
Heidelberg, 161.
Helmsley, 141 *n.*
Hemingborough, 194, 195.
Hemswell, 87 *n.*
Herald's College, London, 171 *n.*, 300.
Hermeston, 91.
Hertford, co. of, xiv. *n.*, 14 *n.* 119.
Hessle, 281, 299.
Hibberston, 211.
Hibberstow, 149.
Hibbuldstow, 149 *n.*
Hickleton, 100 *n.*
High-Street-Way, 71.
Hill Foot, 123 *n.*
Hilston, 273.
Hogue, La, 57 *n.*
Holderness, 144, 154, 166, 186, 191, 196, 217, 225, 233, 235, 273.
Holland, 44, 48, 66, 75 *n.*, 114 *n.*, 123, 206, 213, 214, 281, 285.
Hollym, 293.
Hollin, 141 *n.*
Holme, 89 *n.*
—— Hall, 121 *n.*
Holton Bolls, 138.
Housby, 129.
Hooton Roberts, 267.

Horncastle, 62, 101, 102 n., 301.
Hornsey, 272.
Horsley Deeps, 65 n.
Hougham, 82 n.
Howden, 7, 175, 193, 191, 253 n.
Hull, vi. n., viii., x., xvi., xix., xx., xxi.,
  6 n., 7, 16, 59 and n., 65 n., (river,
  59 n.), 102 n., 112, 116, 117, 132,
  151, 155, 165, 184, 187, 191, 192, 193,
  196 n., 197, 199, 201, 203, 204, 205,
  206, 207, 208, 209, 210, 213, 217,
  218, 219, 221, 225 n., 231 n., 232 n.,
  233, 234 n., 236, 237, 238 n., 239 n.,
  240, 241, 244, 252 n., 253, 255, 257
  264, 268, 269, 273, 280 n., 281, 286,
  289, 298, 299, 300, 303 n.
—— Bank, 232.
Humber, River, 59 n., 86, 115, 128,
  139, 140, 147, 148, 153, 154, 155,
  156, 184, 197, 203, 210, 212, 219, 314.
Hundon, 61 n.
Hunslow Heath, 8, 12.
Huntingdonshire, xvii.
Huntingdon, 34, 44.
Hutton Wensley, 6 n.

I

Ickwelbury, 201.
Idle, Old, River, 269, 270 n., 314.
Indies, East, 215, 237, 242, 317.
—— West, 75 n.
Inglemire, 232 n.
Inner Temple Lane, 233.
Innet, 189 n., 255.
Ipres, 260.
Ipsden, 280, 281.
Ireland, 8, 10 n., 14, 15, 66, 75 n.
Irish Wars, 115, 126 n., 144, 147 n.,
  188, 202 n., 242 n., 271, 279, 305.
Irby, 118 n.
Islington, 184.

J

James's, St., Freston, 148 n.
—— Park, 51.
Jenny Stanny (or Scanny) Well, 149.
Jerusalem, 132, 157, 190 n., 297.
Jesus College, Cambridge, 20, 181 n.
John-a-more-long, 290.
John's, St., College, Cambrige, 133.
Julian's Bower, 211, 301.
—— Stony Well, 211.
Julius' Stony Well, 149.

K

Kaisthorpe, 80 n.
Katherine's Hall, Cambridge, 28 n.
Kealby, or Keelby, 157.
Kedleston, 13 n., 41 n.
Keilby, 253.
Kelham, 130 n.
Kellington, 288.
Kell Well, 142.
Kennell Ferry, 202 n.
Kennington, 129.
Kent, 108, 157, 169 n., 170 n., 171 n.,
  244.
Kerton, 149.
Kesteven, 91 n., 148 n.
Kettelby, 90, 130 n., 131 n.
Kexby, 41 n.
Killingholme, 162 n.
Kimberworth, 177, 178.
Kinard Ferry, 131 n.
Kinscliffe, 162 n.
King's College, Cambridge, 58 n.
Kingstone, 279.
King's Street, 115,
Kirk Ella, 197, 299.
Kirkby Gryndalyth, 289.
—— Huer, 305.
—— under Knoll, 227 n.
Kirkham School, 192 n.
—— xii.
Kirk Sandal, 182 n.
Kirkstall, 255.
—— Abbey, 189 n.
Kirton-in-Lindsey, 88, 121 n., 127,
  149 n., 159 n., 162 n.
Kilnsey, 141 n.
Kilnwick Percy, 119, 120.
Kirmington, 160 n.
Knaresborough, 70, 166.
Knedlington, 273 n.
Knowlton, 169 n., 170 n,
Kyllingholm, 118 n.

L

Laibach, 82 n.
Lambeth, 278.
Lambourn, 119, 120.
Lamesley, 40 n.
Lancashire, xii., xvi., 41 n., 189 n.,
  214, 255.
—— and Yorkshire Railway, 288.
Lancaster, 189 n.
Lancham, 106.
Langar, 242.
Langthorpe, 225 n.
Langton, 288.

Lapland, 37.
Latimer, 254.
Laughton-en-le-Morthing, 13 *n.*
Laughton, 285.
Lea Hall, 121 *n.*
Leicester, 34. 254, 296.
Leicestershire, 119.
Leeds, 13 *n.*, 38, 52 *n.*, 171 *n.*, 183, 231
    n., 232 *n.*, 255, 257, 291, 293, 294 *n.*,
    297.
Leipsick, 161.
Levels, vi. *n.*, 3, 12. 18, 19, 27, 35, 37
    n., 165, 167, 168, 185, 220, 247, 259,
    260, 261, 265, 266, 267, 270 *n.*, 273,
    285, 287, 290, 318.
Leyden, xxv.
Lichfield and Coventry, Bishoprick of,
    24 *n.*
Liege, 57.
Limbur, 156, 157.
Limerick, 14 *n.*, 37, 66.
Limoges, 157 *n.*
Lincolnshire. xviii., xx., xxii., xxiii.,
    3*n.*, 5 *n.*, 6 *n.*, 10, 58, 59, 62 *n.*, 65,
    68, 77 *n.*, 79 *n.*, 81, 82 *n.*, 83 *n.*, 89 *n.*,
    90 *n.*, 91 *n.*, 109 *n.*, 118 *n.*, 120, 125,
    132, 133 *n.*, 139, 142 *n.*, 143 *n.*, 148
    n., 149, 156 *n.*, 164 *n.*, 165, 168, 169,
    170, 172 *n.*, 176, 184, 186 *n.*, 203,
    204, 209, 211, 216, 219, 249, 251 *n.*,
    264, 266, 269, 273, 276, 279, 284,
    285, 301, 302, 317, 318, 319.
Lincoln, 65, 68, 72, 73, 74, 75, 86, 87,
    88, 95. 109 *n.*, 128, 130 *n.*, 148, 153
    n., 158, 159, 160 *n.*, 185 *n.*, 210, 235,
    276, 279, 285, 290.
—— Castle, 19 *n.*
—— Heath, 19, 17.
—— Minster, 182.
Lincoln's Inn, xvi., 239 *n.*, 301.
Lindholme, xxiii., 146 *n.*, 309, 310.
Lindwood, or Linwood, 149.
Lindsey, 87 *n.*, 128 *n.*
Linton, 289.
Liverpool, 270, 271.
Lodge Hill, 284.
London, viii., x. *n.*, xx., xxx., 7, 8, 9
    and *n.*, 12, 16, 30, 34. 36 *n.*, 39, 40
    n., 46, 48, 49, 50, 52, 59 *n.*, 64, 70,
    72, 74, 76, 78, 79 *n.*, 90, 92, 93, 96,
    97, 102, 104, 105, 109 *n.*, 110, 111,
    113 *n.*, 117, 120 and *n.*, 124 *n.*, 130
    n., 131, 132, 139, 144, 147 and *n.*,
    150, 160, 170 *n.*, 176, 179 *n.*, 192,
    200, 204, 206, 209, 210, 212, 213,
    214, 215, 219, 220, 239, 240, 241, 243,
    244, 253, 254, 257, 274, 277, 278, 279,
    281, 282, 283, 300, 305.
—— Nuns of, 199.

Londonderry, 30.
Lords, House of, 150.
Louth, xxiii., 128, 232 *n.*, 301.
Loversal, 297 *n.*
Lucca, 164 *n.*
Luda (Louth), 301.
Lyons, 1

M

MADINGLEY, 28 *n.*
Magdalen College, Oxford, 78 *n.*
—— Hall, Oxford, 176 *n.*
Maidstone, 243.
Malew, 270 *n.*
Malton, 162 *n.*
Malvern Hills, 105.
Man, Isle of, 270, 271.
Manby, 68 *n.*, 117, 124, 137 *n.*
Manchester, xvi., 4 *n.*, 37 *n.*, 161 *n.*,
    180 *n.*, 192, 206, 207, 208, 213, 214,
    268.
—— Sheffield and Lincolnshire Rail-
    way, 90 *n.*
Mansfield, 35, 36 *n.*, 98.
Marfleet, 233 *n.*
Mark Lane, 177 *n.*
Market Rasin, 149.
Marlow, 183.
Marseils, 57.
Marshland, 102.
Martin's, St., in Fields, 36 *n.*, 301.
Marton, 225 *n.*
Mary, St., le Wigford, 158 *n.*
Masham, 110 *n.*
Maut, or Moot, Hills, 134.
Meaux, 237.
Mediterranean Sea, 57.
Medway, River, 278.
Mere Down, 63 *n.*
Melton, 129.
—— (near Hull) 298.
Melwood, Low, 174, 185.
Mercia, 307.
Messingham, 82 *n.*, 88 *n.*, 148 and *n.*,
    151 *n.*
Middleham, 115.
Middle Ings and Midlins, 5 *n.*, 6 *n.*,
    284, 285, 286.
Middlemarsh, Low, 284.
—— Hill, *ib.*
Middlesex, 151 *n.*, 198.
Middlethorp, 204.
Mill Yard, 120 *n.*
Morston, 170 *n.*
Mortlake, 278.
Morton, 168.
—— co. Chester, 119.

Muscovy, 145.
Myton, 204, 299.

N

NANTZ, 221.
Nantes, xiii.
Nappa Hall, xvi.
Naze House, xii.
Nettleton, 67.
Newark, 44, 73, 76, 109, 117.
Newby, 273 n., 293.
Newcastle, 73, 97, 225.
Newgate, 96, 103.
Newhouse, or Newhus, 157 n.
New Rivers Bridge, 168.
Newsom, 157.
Newstead, 115, 319.
———— Priory, 211.
Newton, 41 n.
Nonersfield, 110.
Norfolk, co., x., 28 n., 57 n., 63 n., 67, 169 n., 170 n., 171 n., 219, 220, 274.
Normanby, 137, 184, 302.
Normandy, Duchy of, 57 n.
Normanton, 172 n., 260, 276.
Northamptonshire, 72 n., 78 n., 79 n., 119.
North Elmsal, 298.
Northope, 162 n.
Norton, vii. n., 6 n., 37 n., 287.
Norway, 87, 88, 89, 153 n.
Norwich, x. n., 95 n.
Nostel, 124 n., 125.
Nosterfield, 110 n.
Nottingham, 54, 72, 181 n., 290.
Nottinghamshire, 5 n., 36 n., 98, 106, 130 n., 135, 169, 174 n., 189 n., 242, 255.
Nunburnholme, 110 n.
Nun's Well, 79.

O

OAKS, THE, v., vi., vii. n., xxix n., 193 n.
Ombersley, 120.
Orton, 141 n.
Osterfield, 220, 221 n., 297.
Otchen Well, 149 n.
Owborough, 225 n.
Owston, or Ouston, 131 n., 211 n., 212 n.
Owthorne, 293.
Oxeney, 158 n.
Oxford, xx., 45, 74, 76, 78, 100, 135 n., 161, 198, 239, 241, 302; Lincoln College, 30 n., 302; Magdalen College, 78 n.; Magdalen Hall, 176 n., 288; Queen's College, 169 n.; Trinity College, 29 n., 160.
Oxfordshire, 156.
Oxlands Close, 234 n.
Ouse, 139, 184, 185, 188.

P

PADERBORN, x.
Paradise (a close), 232 n.; 278.
Paris, ix., 3, 26 n., 161, 260.
Patrick's Ledge, 284.
Patrington, 198, 219.
Paul's, St., London, 40 n.
Peak, the, 276.
Pensilvania, 45.
Persepolis, 216.
Persia, ib.
Peterborough, 5 n., 46, 47, 148, 290.
Peter's, St. (Petersburg), 148.
Pettenween, or Pettenven, 230.
Phila Causey, 162, 175.
Physicians, College of, 41 n.
Plumptre, 172 n.
Plumtree, 267.
Pocklington (School), 41 n.
———— 110 n., 179 n.
Pollington, 189 n., 255, 292, 315.
Pontefract, or Pomfret, 35, 69, 73, 113 n., 115, 143, 228, 292, 297.
Pool's Hole, 276.
Poppleton, 187 n.
Portington, 257.
Poteric, Pottery, or Pawtry Carr (Doncaster), 297.
Preston, (Great, 69 n.
———— 131 n., 273.
———— Prætorium at, 235.
Prestwich, 41 n.
Pulham, co. Norfolk, 25 n.
Pursland, 266.
Putney, 278.

R

RAMPER, the, 59 n.
Rampton, 5 n., 187 n., 285.
Ranfield (Ravenfield), 281.
Rantrop, 80, 83.
Ratsdale, 95, 290.
Ravenfield (Ranfield), 13 n., 193 n., 281.
Ravensthorpe, 80, 83.
Ravensworth, 227 n.
Rawby, 62.
Rawcliffe, 6 n., 257, 288.
Reasby (Upper), 79.

Redburn (or Retburn), 81, 119, 121, 123, 135.
Reedness, 113 *n.*
Reswick, 245.
Retford, 35, 169; E., 193 *n.*
Revesby Abbey, 148 *n.*, 302.
Ribston, 123 *n.*, 293.
Riby, 151, 153.
Richmond, 278, 279.
Richmondshire, 110 *n.*, 227 *n.*
Rillington, 293.
Riplingham, 219.
Ripon, xxii., 158 *n.*
Risby, 79 *n.*
Roche Abbey, 166 *n.*, 290, 301, 308, 309.
Rochelle, xii.
Rochester, 253, 278.
Rochdale, 95 *n.*, 290.
Roman Way 59 *n.*, 68, 71, 86, 149; High-street, xxiii.
Roman Coins, Games, Monuments, Pavement, etc., 62, 85, 86, 164, 198, 200, 205, 208, 210, 211, 212, 219, 220, 251 *n.*, 272, 311; Emperors, 112.
Rome, 52, 60, 210.
Romford, 100.
Rooksnest (Surrey), 68 *n.*
Roos, 289.
Rossington, 182 *n.*, 183 *n.*, 288, 290, 297 *n.*
Rotington, 172 *n.*
Rotherham, 106 *n.*, 177, 193 *n.*, 301.
Rotterdam, 214.
Rowbanks, 234 *n.*
Rowton, 225 *n.*
Roxby, xxiii., 58, 59, 79, 122, 162, 211, 212.
Royal Society, vi. *n.*, xx., xxii., xxix., xxx., 123 *n.*, 249, 250, 253.
Rudstone, 209 *n.*
Ryche Dale, *alias* Rattesdale, 290.
Ryston Carr, 273.

S

SADDLEWORTH, 290.
St. Andrew's (Holborn), 131 *n.*
St. Catharine's Cross, Hatfield, 311.
St. Dunstan's Church, 283.
St. John's College, Cambridge, 161 *n.*, 179 *n.*, 181 *n.*
St. John (Evangelist), Altar of, 253.
St. Langton's Cross, Hatfield, 311.
St. Margaret's, Lincoln, 285.
St. Martin's-in-the-Fields, London, 36 *n.*, 301.
St. Mary's Abbey, York, 309.

St. Mary's, Bishophill, York. 292.
St. Mary Magdalen, Church of, Doncaster, 294.
St. Omer's, 214.
St. Pancras, Monastery of, 309.
St. Paul's School, London, 187 *n.*
——— Churchyard, 283.
Salisbury School, 21 *n.*
——— 22, 78 *n.*
Salvington, 8 *n.*
Sanclif, 106.
Sandal, 114, 115.
——— Kirk, 182 *n.*
Sandhall, 134.
Sandridge, 14 *n.*
Sandtoft, xiii., 3, 4 *n.*, 5 *n.*, 37 *n.*, 260, 265, 269, 270 *n.*, 290, 315.
Santon, 211.
Sarisbury, 303 *n.*
Sarratt, xiv. *n.*
Sarum, 232 *n.*
Scandinavia, 17 *n.*
Scarburgh, 125, 162.
Scausby-Leys, 291.
Scawby, 122 *n.*, 127, 128, 151 *n.*, 161 *n.*, 211.
Scilly, 170 *n.*
Scrivelsby, 109 *n.*
Scoley, 305.
Scotland, xxix., 10 *n.*, 23, 49, 113 *n.*, 123, 126 *n.*, 158 *n.*, 159, 188, 230.
Scotten, 148.
Scotter, 65 *n.*, 85, 88 *n.*, 148.
Scotton, 121 *n.*
——— Common, 82 *n.*
Scowscots, 299.
Scruton, 187 *n.*
Sculcoates, 204, 299.
Scunthorpe, 91 *n.*
Sedgemoor, 36 *n.*
Selby, xxii., 51, 293, 297.
——— Abbey, 122 *n.*, 123 *n.*, 135, 136.
Sepulchre, St. (York), 7 *n.*
Shap, 141 *n.*
Sheffield, v., xxix. *n.*, 53, 123 *n.*, 180 *n.*, 193 *n.*, 264, 268, 269.
Sherburn, 293.
Shireoaks, 174.
Shields, 112.
Siam, 34.
Silkstone, 113 *n.*
Skeldergate, York, 188.
Skipton, 183.
Skirlaugh, North and South, 225 *n.*, 253.
Sleaford, 19.
Sledmere, 232 *n.*
Snaith, 175, 288, 290, 292.
Snydall, 172 *n.*, 232 *n.*

Soho Square, London, 170 n.
Somersetshire, 105.
Southwark (St. Olave's), 21 n.
Southwell, 187 n.
Souldburg, 153 n.
Spain, 241, 242, 254.
Spelhoe, 138 n.
Spihoe, 138 n.
Spillo Hills, 138.
Spittle, 86, 87, 88, 145 n., 210, 211.
Spofforth, 289.
Sprotborough, 156 n., 172 n., 293, 296 n.
Staffordshire, 244.
Stainford, 166 n., 167, 172, 258, 308.
Staley, 141.
Stamford, 44, 95.
Staniwells, 149 n.
Stanwick, 28 n.
Stapleton, 189 n., 255.
State Paper Office, Old, 301.
Stather, Burton on, 59 n.
Steetley, 174 n.
Stephen's, St. (Westminster), 149 n.
Stickley, 174.
Stillington, 187 n.
Stockport, 28 n., 41 n.
Stockton, 304.
Stockwith, 156, 290, 169.
Stone Ferry, 299.
Stow, 211 n.
Strasburg, 161.
Streetthorpe, 106 n.
Stygian Ferry, 104, 291.
Sutton, 298, 299.
Swaffam, 219, 220.
Swaledale, 202.
Swanland (close in Thorne), 292.
Sweden, 17 n., 153 n.
Swillington, 69 n., 293.
Swine, 225, 226 n., 227 n.
Switzerland, 4 n.
Suffolk, 171 n., 274.
Sunderland, 112.
Sunken Church, 106.
Surrey, 169, 176 n.
Sury, co. Lancaster, 189, 191 n., 192, 203, 206, 214, 215.
Sussex, county of, 8 n.
Sutton, 37 n., 178, 201, 230, 233, 234, 235.
Sutton-upon-Derwent, 113 n.
Sydenham, 253.
Sykehouse, 167.
Symond's Inn, 113 n.

T

TABLEY, 41 n.
Tadcaster, 296.
Tanfield (West), 110 n.
Tangiers, 30, 36 n., 57.
Tanshelf, 69 n.
Tarring, 8 n.
Temple, Inner, 130 n.
Temple-lane, Inner, 200, 238.
Temple Newsam, 293.
Tempsford, 36 n.
Tetley, 212 n.
Thames, the, 277, 278.
Theobalds, 131 n.
Thirtleby, 225 n.
Thorparch, 13 n.
Thorp, 115.
Thorne, vi., viii., xx., xxi., 11, 12, 36 n., 54, 106 n., 114, 115, 167, 168, 175, 179 n., 182 n., 202 n., 212 n., 245, 247, 250, 253 n., 254, 255, 256, 261 n., 262, 263 n., 266, 284, 287, 289, 290, 291, 292, 308, 309, 315, 319.
Thorn Bush Carr, 270.
Thorney, 47.
Thornholm, 71, 80, 91, 130 n., 134, 148 n., 211.
Thornton College, 130 n., 131 n.; Monastery, ib., 145, 160 n.
Thornton, 80, 124, 125, 130, 145, 218 n.
Thoulon, 57, 170 n.
Thunderton, 164 n.
Thurgoland, 113 n.
Tickhill, 183 n.
Tidworth, North, 78 n.
Tilbury Fort, 277.
Tiverton Lodge, 4 n.
Tobago, 261.
Tocketts, 384, 285.
Tong, 293.
Tower, the (London), 64, 124, 237, 242, 243.
Tranby, 299.
Trent (River), 58, 59, 65 n., 108, 139, 142 n., 148, 151, 168, 219, 314, 318.
Trent-fall, 139.
Trinity College, Cambridge, 23, 27, 42, 187 n.
Troy, 211, 291.
Troy's Walls, 164.
Troyes, ix.
Trumfleet, 182.
Truro, 131 n.
Tudworth, 257, 258, 303.
Tunnel-pit, 286.
Tupcots, 299.

Y

Turnbridge, 202 n., 280.
Turner Hall, 225 n.
Tyburn, 50.

U

ULLSBEE, or Ulceby, 129, 130 n.
Upleatham, 181 n.
Upner Castle, 278.
Upper Catton, 206.
Upton, 106.
Usworth, 40 n.

V

VICKAR'S-DYKE, 168.
Vinvid. River, 255.

W

WADWORTH, 43.
Waghen, or Wawne, 233 n., 289.
Wakefield, 257 n., 293, 296 n.
Wales, 123, 275.
Wallingford, 280, 281.
Walsham, North, x.
Warmsworth, 52 n., 122 n., 295 n.
Wartre, 179 n.
Wapenham, 72 n.
Wath, 153.
Walton, 175.
Wawne, or Waghen, 233 n., 289.
Weighton, Market, 200.
Welbeck, 72.
Welton, 218.
Wensleydale, xvi.
Went, River, 182, 189, 255.
Wentworth House, 295 n.
West Bretton, 298.
———— Chester, 214.
———— Halton, 140.
Westminster Abbey, 170 n.
———— School, 60 n., 300.
———— 115, 130 n., 131 n., 147 n., 149 n., 177, 278.
Westphalia, x.
Whalley, 192 n., 199.
Wheatley, 69 n.
Whitburn, 112.
Whitechurch, 173 n.
Whitefriars, 9 n.
Whitehall, 94, 145 n., 169 n., 301.
White-well, 149 n.
Whitgift, 102, 113 n., 257, 290.
Whittenness, 139.
Whittlesey-mere, 165 n.

Whitton, 139, 140, 142.
Whixley, 293.
Wibberton, 302.
Wickham, 186.
Wigan, 191, 192, 208.
Willarby, 299.
Willoughby, 102 n.
Wiltshire, co., 78 n., 149 n., 183 n.
Windsor, 279.
———— Castle, 44.
Winnemoor, 189 n., 255.
Winnet, 189 n., 255.
Winslow, 183 n.
Winterton, xxii., 54 n., 82, 86, 99. 116, 121 n., 122 n., 123 n., 128, 130 n., 131 n., 135 n., 140 n., 142, 143 n., 147, 159 n., 162, 164 r., 166, 172, 184, 211, 212, 318.
Wintringham, 86, 128, 144, 149, 212.
Wintrington, 172 n.
Winwid field and stream, 188, 189, 255.
Wistow, xvii.
Witham, River, 65 n.
Wittenberg, 161.
Woodbridge, 25 n.
Woodhall, 225 n.
Woodhouse, Hatfield, 146, 259, 263, 266, 268, 287.
Woolwich, 277.
Wolds, the, 206.
Wonnersh, 176 n.
Worcester, Bishoprick of, 24 n.
———— co. of, 120.
———— 218, 253.
Worksop, 175.
Worlebee, 71.
Worstead, x. n.
Wraisbury-cum-Langley, 5 n.
Wrangdon and Wrangdon Hill, 284.
Wrawby, 62 n., 121 n., 122 n., 149, 151, 162, 163 n., 164.
Wroot, 76, 77, 146 n., 182.
———— Carr, 266.
Wyke, 204.
Wykes, 252 n.
Wyton, 225 n.

Y

YADDLETHORPE, 65 n.
York, vii., viii., xxii., 6 n,, 7, 9, 36 n., 54 n., 73, 95, 106 n., 107 n., 110, 112, 115, 125 n., 133 n., 172 n., 176, 177, 178, 184, 185, 186, 187, 188, 190, 200, 204, 206, 208, 217, 219, 228 n., 229 n., 232 n., 234 n., 235, 239, 241, 245, 265, 272, 273 n., 276, 279 n.,

230, 282 n., 283, 286, 287, 288, 290, 292, 297, 309.
York, St. Mary's Abbey, 309.
——— Castle, 5 n., 150 n.
——— Dean and Chapter's Register, 291.
——— Ecclesiastical Court of, 304.
——— East Riding Visitation, 283, 293.
——— Minster, 190 n., 304.
Yorkshire, vi., xiv., xxi., xxii., 3, 6 n., 17 n., 27, 38, 41 n., 43 n., 52 n., 55, 69, 75 n., 79, 90, 98, 99, 105, 108, 110 n., 113, 115, 119, 123 n., 124 n.,

125, 133 n., 135, 139, 140, 143, 144, 146, 147 n., 165, 168, 169, 174 n., 179 n., 181, 182 n., 192, 193, 200, 209, 227 n., 229, 237, 251 n., 273, 279 n., 281, 289, 293, 298, 301, 305, 307, 319.
Yorkshire Archæological Society, 194 n.
Ypres, ix., x., xi., xii., xv., 3.

Z

ZURICH, 4 n.

FINIS.

RIPON: PRINTED BY A. JOHNSON AND CO., MARKET-PLACE.

ADDENDA ET CORRIGENDA.

Page viii., line 22, for *William* read *Walter Consitt Boulter.*

,, xvi., line 5, the page referring to Appendix should be 260, not 26.

,, xxxiv., Oughtibridge pedigree, note *c*, the marriage of " *William Outybridge and Margret Parnel*" is registered at Fishlake, 18th August, 1710.

,, 4, note, line 16, M. Berchett's name was *Peter.*

,, *ib.* To the list of French Ministers at Sandtoft may be added M. Caruill, or Carvill. His name occurs in the following entry in the register of Fishlake :—"1658. Peter Mazingarb and Hester Pinchan were maryed in our parish church of Fishlake upon the xiith day of August, by Master Caruill, Minister of the French Church att Santoft, he then preaching, and takinge the text out of the third chapter of Genesis and partt of the xixth verse—*for dust thou art, and unto dust thou shall returne.*" Whether this comforting assurance was specially addressed to the newly-married pair, or formed the topic of the general discourse, does not sufficiently appear.

,, 6, note, line 4, John Nodes, gent., was buried at Hatfield, 3rd April, 1669.

,, 9, note. Reading. Jasper, son of Nathaniel Reading, esq., was buried at Hatfield, 26 April, 1669.

,, 17, note, line 9, after *Bellow* read *a Danish trooper,* In the parish register of Carleton, near Snaith, it is recorded.—"1690. Deans and Polanders were quartered here six weeks, and yⁿ went for Ireland under King William yea 3rd."—*Ex inform. Rev. C. B. Norcliffe.*

,, 23, line 9, after *Febr.* insert 3.

,, 82, line 4, for *Lanbach* read *Laibach.*

,, 83, note *h.* In the parish register of Snaith, under date 13th April, 1762, occurs the baptism of Elizabeth, daughter of William Ackars, of Rawcliffe, aged 79.

,, 97, note. The Rev. C. B. Norcliffe states it does not appear that Mr. Maurice Lisle resigned before the Visitation of 1695. John Hall occurs, he says, as vicar, 1699—1706. Within the cover of the register is written " John Hall, minister de Fishlake, in com. Ebor., 1702." The living was vacant at the visitation 1707. John L'Isle was instituted 27 Aug., 1707.

,, 133, note, line 13. *Garett* is a mistake, most likely, for *Eratt.*

,, 141, note, for *Hollin* read *Hollim* ; for *Salley* read *Lathley,* minister there 6 Oct., 1641 to 1687.

,, 161, note *u.* A George Jalland was assistant curate of Holy Trinity Church, Hull, 20 Sept., 1756 to 1759.

,, 171, note. Cloudsley—a Peter Cloudsley, of Leeds, clothier, married, 27 April, 1630, Katherine, daughter of Edward Norton, of Gowdall.—*Snaith Par. Regr.*

,, 177, note *w*, line 1, for *in* read *is.*

,, *ib.*, note *y.* William Pratt, A.M., was curate of Bossall, 10th May, 1673 ; vicar 1700. John Pratt, A.M., vicar 1701, buried August, 1718. See also Appendix, page 302.

,, 179, note, line 9, for *Forster* read *Foster.*

,, 180, note *c.* One Theseus Moor was a witness, 11 April, 1709, to the will of Richard Mainsman, of Dikemarsh, proved at Snaith. A Theseus Moore, son of Henry M., was baptized 14 Feb., 1666-7, at Hatfield.

,, 181, note, line 4, for *St. John's* read *Jesus.*

,, 186, line 12. Wallice. Timothy Wallis, M.A., 18 July, 1673, R. Leven, resigned. Timothy Wallis, A.B., his son, 23 Dec., 1704. Do., T. W., the father, reinstituted.

,, 187, note *o*, line 2, read 1714. Rev. R. Banks being buried 14 Nov. in that year.

,, 196. The Greek lines at the bottom of the note should be read :—

Ἄγνος 'εμο'ι β'ιος ἦν, ἱκμὰς δὲ τάχιστα παρῆλθε,
Ἄμνου παρθενίκου νῦν ἀκόλουθυς ἐγώ.

,, 201, for *Kidson* read *Kitson.*

,, 202, note *o*, line 9, for *Vicount* read *Viscount.*

,, 257, note, line 6, for *Rowland W. Heathcote* read *Rowland Heathcote.*

,, 289, line 1, for *daughter* read *daughters.*

,, 293, line 36, for *seq.* read *esq.*

,, 294, line 34, the numeral figures should be xi., xii., i.

,, 303, note, line 25. Hatfield Church. Since these remarks were written I have seen a paragraph in the *Doncaster Gazette,* of the 14th Oct., 1870, relative to this church, the substance of which is stated to be taken from Hunter and De la Pryme, wherein we are told "that the fine parish church of Hatfield is to be added to the list of churches in this neighbourhood which have been restored to the purer style that prevailed in ecclesiastical architecture when the most ancient of our churches were built. . . . We are unable," the writer adds, " to give any details of the intended alteration, but one obvious object will be the removal of the deformities which characterized the designs of the so-called church improvers during the greater part of the Georgian era."

,, 335, first column, third line, should read *Wigley,* 20 *n.*, 28 *n.*; 133 *n.*; 279 *n.*

,, *ib.*, first column, after line 24 insert *Wimare, Nigello filio,* 81 *n.*

THE SURTEES SOCIETY.

REPORT FOR THE YEAR MD.CCC.LXVIII.

THE Council have but little to report this year to the members of the Society. The prosperity of the Society seems now to rest upon a firm footing, and the number of changes each year in its list of associates may be calculated with an almost mathematical precision. To fill up the vacancies which regularly occur there is always a more than sufficient number of candidates for admission.

The Council refer with satisfaction to the recently completed volume of the works of Symeon of Durham. In that work every exertion has been made to present a correct text of the great northern chronicler, and to free it as far as is possible from corrupt readings, and the additions of extraneous writers, which have in many places completely overlaid Symeon's own composition. The Council propose to give in a second volume the History of the Church of Durham. To this will be appended several unpublished or little known historical tractates connected with the North, together with a Spicilegium of miscellaneous letters and papers which will exhaust, as far as is possible, the annals of the palatinate of Durham to the reign of Richard I.

The Council regret the delay that has taken place in the completion of the second volume of the Memorials of Fountains Abbey. This has been caused by the very serious and prolonged illness of its editor, Mr. Walbran. The greater part of the work is ready for the press, with the exception of the notes, and five sheets have been already printed off. This volume will present what may be considered an almost perfect Bullarium of the Cistercian order in this country, and the utmost pains have been taken by its learned editor to render it complete and accurate.

For the other works that are in progress or prospect the members are referred to the list of proposed publications.

THE SURTEES SOCIETY,

ESTABLISHED IN THE YEAR 1834,

In honour of the late Robert Surtees, of Mainsforth, Esquire, the Author of the History of the County Palatine of Durham, and in accordance with his pursuits and plans; having for its object the publication of inedited Manuscripts, illustrative of the intellectual, the moral, the religious, and the social condition of those parts of England and Scotland, included on the east between the Humber and the Frith of Forth, and on the west between the Mersey and the Clyde, a region which constituted the ancient Kingdom of Northumbria.

NEW RULES AGREED UPON IN 1849; REVISED 1863.

I.—The Society shall consist of not more than three hundred and fifty members.

II.—There shall be a Patron of the Society, who shall be President.

III.—There shall be twenty-four Vice-Presidents, a Secretary, and two Treasurers.

IV.—The Patron, the Vice-Presidents, the Secretary, and the Treasurers, shall form the Council, any five of whom, including the Secretary and a Treasurer, shall be a quorum competent to transact the business of the Society.

V.—The twenty-four Vice-Presidents, the Secretary, and the Treasurers, shall be elected at a general meeting, to continue in office for three years, and be capable of re-election.

VI.—Any vacancies in the office of Secretary or Treasurers shall be provisionally filled up by the Council, subject to the approbation of the next general meeting.

VII.—Three meetings of the Council shall be held in every year, on the first Tuesday in the months of March, June, and December; and the place and hour of meeting shall be fixed by the Council, and communicated by the Secretary to the members of the Council.

VIII.—The meeting in June shall be the anniversary, to which all the members of the Society shall be convened by the Secretary.

IX.—The Secretary shall convene extraordinary meetings of

the Council, on a requisition to that effect, signed by not less than five members of the Council, being presented to him.

X.—Members may be elected by ballot at any of the ordinary meetings, according to priority of application, upon being proposed in writing by three existing members. One black ball in ten shall exclude.

XI.—Each member shall pay in advance to the Treasurer the annual sum of one guinea. If any member's subscription shall be in arrear for two years, and he shall neglect to pay his subscription after having been reminded by the Treasurer, he shall be regarded as having ceased to be a member of the Society.

XII.—The money raised by the Society shall be expended in publishing such compositions, in their original language, or in a translated form, as come within the scope of this Society, without limitation of time with reference to the period of their respective authors. All editorial and other expenses to be defrayed by the Society.

XIII.—One volume, at least, in a closely printed octavo form, shall be supplied to each member of the Society every year, free of expense.

XIV.—If the funds of the Society in any year will permit, the Council shall be at liberty to print and furnish to the members, free of expense, any other volume or volumes of the same character, in the same or a different form.

XV.—The number of copies of each publication, and the selection of a printer and publisher, shall be left to the Council, who shall also fix the price at which the copies, not furnished to members, shall be sold to the public.

XVI.—The armorial bearings of Mr. Surtees, and some other characteristic decoration connecting the Society with his name, shall be used in each publication.

XVII.—A list of the officers and members, together with an account of the receipts and expenses of the Society, shall be made up every year to the time of the annual meeting, and shall be submitted to the Society to be printed and published with the next succeeding volume.

XVIII.—No alteration shall be made in these rules except at an annual meeting. Notice of any such alteration shall be given, at least as early as the ordinary meeting of the Council immediately preceding, to be communicated to each member of the Society.

PUBLICATIONS OF THE SURTEES SOCIETY,

WITH THEIR RESPECTIVE SALE PRICES.

N.B.—Of several of these volumes the number of copies on hand is very small; some will not be sold except to members of the Society under certain conditions, and all applications for them must be made to the Secretary.

1. Reginaldi Monachi Dunelmensis Libellus de Admirandis Beati Cuthberti Virtutibus. 15s. Edited by Dr. Raine.

2. Wills and Inventories, illustrative of the History, Manners, Language, Statistics, &c., of the Northern Counties of England, from the Eleventh Century downwards. (Chiefly from the Registry at Durham). Vol. I. 15s. Edited by Dr. Raine. *(Only sold in a set).*

3. The Towneley Mysteries, or Miracle Plays. 15s. Edited by James Gordon, Esq. The Preface by Joseph Hunter, F.S.A.

4. Testamenta Eboracensia; Wills illustrative of the History, Manners, Language, Statistics, &c., of the Province of York, from 1300 downwards. Vol. I. 30s. Edited by Dr. Raine.

5. Sanctuarium Dunelmense et Sanctuarium Beverlacense; or, Registers of the Sanctuaries of Durham and Beverley. 15s. Edited by Dr. Raine. The Preface by the Rev. T. Chevallier.

6. The Charters of Endowment, Inventories, and Account Rolls of the Priory of Finchale in the County of Durham. 15s. Edited by Dr. Raine.

7. Catalogi Veteres Librorum Ecclesiæ Cathedralis Dunelm. Catalogues of the Library of Durham Cathedral at various periods, from the Conquest to the Dissolution; including Catalogues of the Library of the Abbey of Hulne, and of the MSS. preserved in the Library of Bishop Cosin at Durham. 10s. Edited by Dr. Raine. The Preface by Beriah Botfield, Esq.

8. Miscellanea Biographica; a Life of Oswin, King of Northumberland; Two Lives of Cuthbert, Bishop of Lindisfarne; and a Life of Eata, Bishop of Hexham. 10s. Edited by Dr. Raine.

9. Historiæ Dunelmensis Scriptores Tres. Gaufridus de Coldingham, Robertus de Greystanes, et Willelmus de Chambre, with the omissions and mistakes in Wharton's Edition supplied and corrected, and an Appendix of 665 original Documents, in illustration of the Text. 15s. Edited by Dr. Raine.

10. Rituale Ecclesiæ Dunelmensis; a Latin Ritual of the Ninth Century, with an interlinear Northumbro-Saxon Translation. 15s. Edited by the Rev. J. Stevenson.

11. Jordan Fantosme's Anglo-Norman Chronicle of the War between the English and the Scots, in 1173 and 1174. Edited, with a Translation, Notes, &c., by Francisque Michel, F.S.A. 15s.

12. The Correspondence, Inventories, Account Rolls and Law Proceedings of the Priory of Coldingham. 15s. Edited by Dr. Raine.

13. Liber Vitæ Ecclesiæ Dunelmensis; necnon Obituaria duo ejusdem Ecclesiæ. 10s. Edited by Rev. J. Stevenson.

14. The Correspondence of Robert Bowes, of Aske, Esq., Ambassador of Queen Elizabeth to the Court of Scotland. 15s. Edited by Rev. J. Stevenson.

15. A Description or Briefe Declaration of all the Ancient Monuments, Rites, and Customs belonging to, or being within, the Monastical Church of Durham, before the Suppression. Written in 1593. 10s. Edited by Dr. Raine.

16. Anglo-Saxon and Early-English Psalter, now first published from MSS. in the British Museum. Vol. I. 15s. Edited by Rev. J. Stevenson.

17. The Correspondence of Dr. Matthew Hutton, Archbishop of York. With a selection from the Letters of Sir Timothy Hutton, Knt., his Son, and Matthew Hutton, Esq., his Grandson. 15s. Edited by Dr. Raine.

18. The Durham Household Book; or, the Accounts of the Bursar of the Monastery of Durham from 1530 to 1534. 15s. Edited by Dr. Raine.

19. Anglo-Saxon and Early English Psalter, Vol. II. 15s. Edited by Rev. J. Stevenson.

20. Libellus de Vita et Miraculis S. Godrici, Heremitæ de Finchale, auctore Reginaldo, Monacho Dunelmensi. 15s. Edited by Rev. J. Stevenson.

21. Depositions respecting the Rebellion of 1569, Witchcraft, and other Ecclesiastical Proceedings, from the Court of Durham, extending from 1311 to the reign of Elizabeth. 15s. Edited by Dr. Raine. *

* Members have the privilege of purchasing the first twenty-one volumes, or any of them, except No. 2, at half-price.

22. The Injunctions and other Ecclesiastical Proceedings of Richard Barnes, Bishop of Durham (1577-87). 15s. Edited by Dr. Raine.

23. The Anglo-Saxon Hymnarium, from MSS. of the Eleventh Century, in Durham, the British Museum, &c. 16s. Edited by Rev. J. Stevenson.

24. The Memoir of Mr. Surtees, by the late George Taylor, Esq. Reprinted from the Fourth Vol. of the History of Durham, with additional Notes and Illustrations, together with an Appendix, comprising some of Mr. Surtees' Correspondence, Poetry, &c. Edited by Dr. Raine. (Only sold in a set and to a Member).

25. The Boldon Book, or Survey of Durham in 1183. 10s. 6d. Edited by Rev. W. Greenwell.

26. Wills and Inventories, illustrative of the History, Manners, Language, Statistics, &c., of the Counties of York, Westmorland, and Lancaster, from the Fourteenth Century downwards. From the Registry at Richmond. 14s. Edited by Rev. J. Raine.

27. The Pontifical of Egbert, Archbishop of York (731-67), from a MS. of the Ninth or Tenth Century in the Imperial Library in Paris. 11s. Edited by Rev. William Greenwell.

28. The Gospel of St. Matthew, from the Northumbrian Interlinear Gloss to the Gospels, contained in the MS. Nero D. IV., among the Cottonian MSS. in the British Museum, commonly known as the Lindisfarne Gospels, collated with the Rushworth MS. 14s. Edited by Rev. J. Stevenson.

29. The Inventories and Account Rolls of the Monasteries of Jarrow and Monkwearmouth, from their commencement in 1303 till the Dissolution. 12s. Edited by Dr. Raine.

30. Testamenta Eboracensia, or Wills illustrative of the History, Manners, Language, Statistics, &c., of the Province of York, from 1429 to 1467. Vol. II. 25s. Edited by Rev. J. Raine.

31. The Bede Roll of John Burnaby, Prior of Durham (1456-64). With illustrative documents. 12s. Edited by Dr. Raine.

32. The Survey of the Palatinate of Durham, compiled during the Episcopate of Thomas Hatfield (1345-1382). 15s. Edited by Rev. W. Greenwell.

33. The Farming Book of Henry Best, of Elmswell, E.R.Y. 12s. Edited by Rev. C. B. Robinson.

34. The Proceedings of the High Court of Commission for Durham and Northumberland. 14s. Edited by W. H. D. Longstaffe, Esq.

35. The Fabric Rolls of York Minster. 25s. Edited by Rev. J. Raine.

36. The Heraldic Visitation of Yorkshire, by Sir William Dugdale, in 1665. Edited by Robert Davies, Esq. (Only sold in a set and to a Member).

37. A Volume of Miscellanea, comprising the Letters of Dean Granville, the Account of the Siege of Pontefract by Nathan Drake, and Extracts from the Rokeby Correspondence. Edited by Rev. George Ornsby, Mr. W. H. D. Longstaffe and Rev. J. Raine. (Only sold in a set and to a Member).

38. A Volume of Wills from the Registry at Durham; a continuation of No. 2. Edited by Rev. W. Greenwell. (Only sold in a set and to a Member).

39. The Gospel of St. Mark, from the Northumbrian Interlinear Gloss to the Gospels contained in the MS. Nero D. IV., among the Cottonian MSS. in the British Museum, commonly known as the Lindisfarne Gospels, collated with the Rushworth MS. ; a continuation of No. 28. 10s. Edited by Mr. George Waring.

40. A Selection from the Depositions in Criminal Cases taken before the Northern Magistrates, from the originals preserved in York Castle. Saec. XVII. Edited by Rev. J. Raine. (Only sold in a set and to a Member).

41. The Heraldic Visitation of the North of England, made in 1530, by Thomas Tonge, with an Appendix of Genealogical MSS. Edited by Mr. W. H. D. Longstaffe. (Only sold in a set and to a Member).

42. Memorials of Fountains Abbey. Vol. I. Comprising the Chronicle relating to the Foundation of the House, written by Hugh de Kirkstall ; the Chronicle of Abbats, &c., and an historical description of the Abbey, with illustrations. Edited by Mr. J. R. Walbran. (Only sold in a set and to a Member.)

43. The Gospel of St. Luke, from the Northumbrian Interlinear Gloss to the Gospels contained in the MS. Nero D. IV., among the Cottonian MSS. in the British Museum, commonly known as the Lindisfarne Gospels, collated with the Rushworth MS. ; a continuation of No. 28 and 29. 14s. Edited by Mr. George Waring.

44. The Priory of Hexham, its Chronicles, Endowments, and Annals. Vol. I. Containing the Chronicles, &c., of John and Richard, Priors of Hexham, and Aelred Abbat of Rievaux, with an Appendix of documents, and a Preface illustrated with engravings, pp. 604. £2 2s. Edited by Rev. J. Raine.

45. Testamenta Eboracensia, or Wills illustrative of the History, Manners, Language, Statistics, &c., of the Province of York, from 1467 to 1485. Vol. III. 25s. Edited by Rev. J. Raine.

46 The Priory of Hexham. Vol. II. Containing the Liber Niger, with Charters and other Documents, and a Preface illustrated with engravings. 16s. Edited by Rev. J. Raine.

47 The Letters, &c., of Dennis Granville, D.D., Dean of Durham, from the originals recently discovered in the Bodleian Library. Part II. 16s. Edited by Rev. George Ornsby.

48 The Gospel of St. John, from the Northumbrian Interlinear Gloss to the Gospels in the MS. Nero D. IV. (A continuation of Nos. 28, 39, and 43). 14s. With Preface and Prolegomena. Edited by Mr. George Waring.

49. The Survey of the County of York, taken by John de Kirkby, commonly called Kirkby's Inquest. Also Inquisitions of Knights' Fees, The Nomina Villarum for Yorkshire, and an Appendix of illustrative documents, pp. 570. 25s. Edited by Mr. R. H. Skaife.

50. Memoirs of the Life of Ambrose Barnes, Merchant and sometime Alderman of Newcastle-upon-Tyne. 21s. Edited by Mr. W. H. D. Longstaffe.

51. Symeon of Durham. The whole of the works ascribed to him except the History of the Church of Durham. To which are added the History of the Translation of St. Cuthbert, the Life of S. Margaret Queen of Scotland, by Turgot Prior of Durham, &c. Edited by by Mr. John Hodgson Hinde. 25s.

52. The Correspondence of John Cosin, Bishop of Durham. Vol. I. 16s. Edited by Rev. George Ornsby.

53. Testamenta Eboracensia. Vol. IV. From 1485 to 1509. A continuation of Nos. 4, 30, and 45. 21s. Edited by Rev. J. Raine.

The Council propose to select their future volumes out of the following manuscripts or materials, or from others of a similar description.

1. The Ephemeris or Diary of the Rev. Abraham De la Pryme, the Yorkshire Antiquary, in the latter part of the 17th century. Now being prepared by Mr. Charles Jackson.

2. The Memorials of Fountains Abbey. Vol. II. To contain the Papal Bulls, the Royal Charters of Privilege, etc. With engravings of seals, &c. Five sheets have already been printed under the editorial care of Mr J. R. Walbran.

3. The Articles and Injunctions issued by the Bishops and Archdeacons within the Province of York, from the earliest period to 1662. Now being prepared by the Hon. and Rev. Stephen Lawley.

4. Symeon of Durham. Vol. II. To contain the History of the Church of Durham, with an Appendix consisting of several historical tractates, illustrative of Symeon's work. To be edited by Mr. Hodgson Hinde and the Secretary. *Dead*

5. The Account Rolls, Charters, &c., of Durham (Trinity) College, Oxford, with lists of its early members, and other authentic and original information relating to it. To be edited by Rev. Wm. Stubbs.

6. The Correspondence of John Cosin, Bishop of Durham. Gathered together for the first time from the original MSS. Vol. II. To be edited by the Rev. George Ornsby.

7. The Lords of the Soil of the County of Durham from the earliest period to the Reformation, comprising the descent of the estates and various other particulars, genealogical and heraldic, relating to their owners, illustrated with engravings of seals, etc. To be prepared by Mr. W. H. D. Longstaffe and the Rev. William Greenwell.

8. The Letters, Despatches, Extracts from the Household Books, and other works and papers of Lord William Howard of Naworth, from the originals at Castle-Howard, Naworth Castle, and London. To be prepared by Mr. Robert Davies.

9. The Lives of S. Wilfrid by Eddi, Eadmer, and Fridegodus, with other Biographical and Historical Documents relating to the Church of York and its rulers. To be prepared by Rev. William Stubbs, M.A.

10. A Volume of Early Rituals, supplementary to those already published by the Society, to contain as many of the unpublished Pontificals as the Society can obtain access to, including that of St. Dunstan in the Imperial Library at Paris. To be prepared by Rev. Dr. Henderson.

11. A Volume of Documents relating to the Ancient Guilds in the City of York; to contain, especially, the Register of the Guild of the Corpus Christi, which is preserved in the British Museum. To be prepared by Mr. Robert Skaife.

12. The Inquisitions Post Mortem for the North of England, from the originals at London and Durham.

13. A Volume of Extracts from the Depositions preserved in the Ecclesiastical Court at York, from the fourteenth century downwards.

14. The Visitation of the County of York in 1584, by William Flower.
15. A Volume of Wills relating to the Counties of Cumberland and Westmerland, principally from the Registry at Carlisle.
16. A Collection of Letters and Papers relating to the Dissolution of the Northern Monasteries, the proceedings of the Visitors, and the opposition of the Monks.
17. The Annals of the Pilgrimage of Grace, derived from unpublished documents of the greatest interest and curiosity in the State Paper Office and the British Museum.
18. A Concluding Volume of Extracts from the Proceedings of the Ecclesiastical Court of Durham.
19. A Continuation of the Testamenta Eboracensia.
20. Memorials of Kirkstall Abbey; The History of its Foundation; the Chronicle of Kirkstall; and Extracts from the Charter Books of that ancient house.
21. Selections from the yearly Rolls of the Bursar of the Monastery of Durham, beginning in 1270.
22. The Charters and Account Rolls of the Cells of Lytham and Stamford.
23. The Chartularies of Holm Cultram, and other documents relating to that Monastery.
24. The Chartulary of Whitby Abbey, and the Chronicle of that house.
25. St. Mary's Abbey, York, its Annals, by Abbot Simon de Warwick; with Extracts from the Chartularies.
26. The Charter Book of St. Leonard's Hospital at York, with several of the early Account Rolls, Wills of Benefactors, etc.
27. The Evidences of the ancient Family of Calverley, from the originals in the British Museum.
28. Letters, hitherto inedited, relating to the Outrages, Feuds, etc., on the borders of England and Scotland.
29. The Autobiography of Anne Countess of Pembroke, Dorset and Montgomery, with other Documents relating to the house of Clifford.
30. The Correspondence of Thomas Baker (the "Coll. Jo. socius ejectus"), with the Literary Men of his day.
31. The Correspondence of Dr. George Hickes and Hilkiah Belford, the celebrated Non-jurors and Antiquaries.
32. The Correspondence of Adam Baines, the first M.P. for Leeds.
33. A Glossary of Ancient North Country Words to illustrate and explain, especially, the Works already published by this Society.

List of Officers and Members, June, 1868.

PATRON AND PRESIDENT.

His Grace the Duke of Buccleuch and Queensberry, K.G., etc.

VICE PRESIDENTS.

Edward Akroyd, M.P., Bank Field, Halifax.
Robert Henry Allan, F.S.A., Blackwell Grange, Darlington.
John Booth, jun., Durham.
Rev. Canon Chevallier, B.D., Durham.
Rev. John Dixon Clarke, M.A., Belford Hall.
James Crossley, F.S.A., President of the Chetham Society, Manchester.
Rev. John Cundill, B.D., Durham.
Robert Davies, F.S.A., York.
John F. Elliot, Elvet Hill, Durham.
John Fawcett, Durham.
Rev. William Greenwell, M.A., Durham.
Edwin Guest, L.L.D., Master of Caius College, Cambridge.
Thomas Duffus Hardy, Her Majesty's Deputy-keeper of Records, London.
William Henderson, Durham.
~~John Hodgson Hinde, Sterling-Hall, Gateshead.~~ *Dead*
W. H. D. Longstaffe, F.S.A., Gateshead.
Richard Lawrence Pemberton, The Barnes, Sunderland.
Rev. Daniel Rock, D.D., F.S.A., 17, Essex Villas, Kensington, London.
Sir Walter Calverley Trevelyan, Bart., F.S.A., Wallington, Newcastle-on-Tyne.
The Very Rev. George Waddington, D.D., Dean of Durham.
John Richard Walbran, F.S.A., Fall Croft, Ripon.
Albert Way, F.S.A., Wonham Manor, Reigate.
Rev. C. T. Whitley, M.A., Bedlington, Newcastle-on-Tyne.
Sir C. G. Young, F.S.A., Garter King at Arms.

SECRETARY.

Rev. James Raine, M.A., York.

TREASURERS.

John Gough Nichols, F.S.A., 25, Parliament Street. Westminster.
Samuel Rowlandson, Durham.

MEMBERS, WITH THE DATES OF THEIR ADMISSION.*

Richard Abbay, Great Ouseburn, Boroughbridge. 13th December, 1861.
Sir John Dalberg Acton, Bart., Aldenham Park, Bridgenorth. 17th June, 1861.
George E. Adams, Rouge Dragon Pursuivant of Arms, Heralds' College, London. 13th December, 1862.
Rev. E. H. Adamson, M.A., St. Alban's Parsonage, Gateshead. 14th December, 1860.
The Advocates' Library, Edinburgh. 13th March, 1851.
Edward Akroyd, M.P., F.S.A., Bank Field, Halifax. 15th December, 1859, (*Vice-President*, 1866-8).
William Aldam, Frickley Hall, Doncaster. 13th December, 1862.
Robert Henry Allan, F.S.A., Blackwell Grange, Darlington. (*Treasurer*, 1834-1844. *Vice-President*, 1844-1868.)†

---

* The number of three hundred and fifty members, to which the Society is limited, is now full. Judging from past experience, there will be ten or twelve vacancies every year, and these will be regularly filled up. New members will be elected by the Council according to priority of application, unless the son or the representative of a deceased member wishes to be chosen in his place.

William Anderson, Stonegate, York. 13th December, 1861.
The Society of Antiquaries, London. 1st March, 1864.
The Society of Antiquaries, Newcastle-on-Tyne. 24th September, 1853.
John Reed Appleton, F.S.A., Western Hills, Durham. 15th December, 1859.
George John Armytage, Kirklees Park, Brighouse, 2nd June, 1868.*
The Library of the Athenæum Club, Waterloo Place, London. 13th December, 1861.
J. H. Aveling, M.D., Sheffield. 14th December 1860.
J. H. Backhouse, Darlington. 5th June, 1866.
Rev. William Baird, Vicar of Dymoke, Gloucestershire. Dec. 6th, 1864.
Charles Baker, F.S.A., 11, Sackville Street, London. 13th December, 1861.
E. B. Wheatley Balme, Cote Walls, Mirfield, Normanton. 8th December, 1863.
J. W. Barnes, Durham. 7th March, 1865.
Thomas H. Bates, Wolsingham. 7th June, 1864.
Rev. Thomas Bayly, B.A., Sub-chantor of York Minster, and Treasurer of the Yorkshire Architectural Society. 14th December, 1860.
William Beamont, Warrington. 28th September, 1843.
Wentworth B. Beaumont, M.P., Bretton Hall, Wakefield. 14th March, 1862.
George S. Beccroft, M.P., Abbey Lodge, Kirkstall, Leeds. 8th December, 1863.
Alfred Bell, 49, Lincoln's Inn Fields, London. 31st March, 1849.
George Bell, York-street, Covent Garden, London. 31st March, 1864.
The Royal Library at Berlin. 14th March, 1863.
Sir Edward Blackett, Bart., Matfen, Newcastle-on-Tyne. 15th December, 1859.
Robert Willis Blencowe, Secretary of the Sussex Archæological Society, The Hooke, Lewes. 13th March, 1851.
John Booth, jun., Durham. 18th June, 1862. (*Vice-President* and *Local Secretary*, 1864-8).
Rev. Joseph Bosworth, LL.D., F.R.S., Professor of Anglo-Saxon in the University of Oxford, Water-Stratford, Bucks. 14th December, 1861.
E. C. Boville, Willington, Burton-on Trent. 15th March, 1860.
John Bowes, Streatlam Castle, Durham.†
Richard Bowser, Bishop Auckland. 14th March, 1863.
Rev. Canon Boyd, M.A., Rector of Arncliffe, Skipton-in-Craven. 7th March, 1865.
The Viscount Boyne, Brancepeth Castle, Durham. 15th December, 1852.
Rev. J. S. Brewer, M.A., Reader at the Rolls, and Professor of English Literature, King's College, London. 13th December, 1862.
Thomas Brooke, Armitage Bridge, Huddersfield. 14th December, 1860.
Douglas Brown, 15, Hertford Street, Mayfair, London. 11th March, 1858.
James Brown, M.P., Rossington Hall, Bawtry. 13th December, 1862.
Alfred Hall Browne, 5, West Hills, Highgate, London. 13th December, 1861.
Rev. John Collingwood Bruce, LL.D., F.S.A., &c., Secretary of the Society of Antiquaries, Newcastle-on-Tyne. 6th June, 1856.
The Duke of Buccleuch and Queensberry, K.G., &c., Dalkeith. (*The first President of the Society*, 1834-1837. *President*, 1865-8.)†
Rev. W. E. Buckley, M.A., Middleton Cheney, Banbury. 13th March, 1851.
Robert Anthony Burrell, Durham. 17th June, 1861.
Thomas Burton, Turnham Hall, Selby. December, 1857.
Rev. William Bury, Chapel-house, Kilnsey, Skipton-in-Craven. 14th December, 1860.

† Those gentlemen to whose names a cross is appended have been members of the Society since its foundation in 1834.
* Those gentlemen to whose names an asterisk is attached have become members during the past year.

C. H. Cadogan, Brinkburn Priory, Morpeth. June 4th, 1867.
Rev. Thomas Calvert, B.A., Dinnington, Newcastle-on-Tyne. 13th December, 1862.
Ralph Carr, Hedgeley, Alnwick. 26th September, 1844.
Rev. T. W. Carr, Barming Rectory, Maidstone, 13th December, 1861.
William Carr, Little Gomersal, Leeds. 5th December, 1865.
Edward Cayley, Wydale, Scarborough. 13th December, 1861.
Rev. Reginald Arthur Cayley, Rector of Scampton, Lincoln. 13th December, 1861.
William Chadwick, Arksey, Doncaster. 5th December, 1865.
John Barff Charlesworth, Hatfeild Hall, Wakefield. 14th March, 1862.
Edward Charlton, M.D., Secretary of the Society of Antiquaries, Newcastle-on-Tyne. 6th June, 1856.
Rev. James Allen Charlton, Gosforth, Newcastle-on-Tyne. 8th December, 1853.
William Henry Charlton, Hesleyside, Hexham. 31st May, 1849.
Joseph Chester, 14, St. George's Terrace, Blue Anchor Road, Bermondsey, London. 5th December, 1865.
The Chetham Library, Manchester. December, 1857.
Rev. Temple Chevallier, B.D., Canon of Durham, Professor of Mathematics and Astronomy in the University of Durham. 12th July, 1836. (*Vice-President*, 1836-1868).
The Library of Christ's College, Cambridge. 13th December, 1862.
The Ven. Archdeacon Churton, Crayke, Easingwold. 3rd March, 1868.*
Rev. John Dixon Clarke, Belford Hall. 1st June, 1853. (*Vice-President*, 1855-1868.)
Rev. John Haldenby Clarke, M.A., Hilgay, Downham, Norfolk. 5th December, 1865.
J. W. Clarke, M.A., Trinity College, Cambridge. December, 1857. (*Local Secretary*, 1858-1868).
Thomas K. Clarke, jun., John William Street, Huddersfield. 8th December, 1863. (*Local Secretary*, 1864-1868).
J. W. Clay, Rastrick, Brighouse. 2nd June, 1868.*
Edward Clayton, New Walk Terrace, York. 7th June, 1864.
John Clayton, Newcastle-on-Tyne. 8th December, 1853.
The Duke of Cleveland, Raby Castle, Staindrop. September, 1841.
Alexander Cockburn, 12, Walker Street, Edinburgh. 6th June, 1854.
Rev. William Collins, M.A., St. Mary's, Ramsey, Huntingdon. 15th December, 1859.
W. H. Cooke, M.A., Q.C., F.S.A., 42, Wimpole Street, London. 6th June, 1855.
John Cookson, Meldon Park, Morpeth. 15th December, 1852.
The Royal Library at Copenhagen. 14th March, 1863.
Sir Joseph William Copley, Bart., Sprotborough, Doncaster. 13th December, 1862.
Rev. G. E. Corrie, D.D., Master of Jesus College, Cambridge. 28th December, 1837.
Rev. Thomas Corser, M.A., F.S.A., Rector of Stand, Manchester. 28th September, 1837.
Joseph Crawhall, Morpeth. 3rd March, 1868.*
Christopher Croft, Richmond, Yorkshire. 8th December, 1853.
R. Cross, Bottoms Lodge, Tintwistle, Manchester. 6th December, 1864.
James Crossley, F.S.A., President of the Chetham Society, Booth Street, Manchester. 11th March, 1858. (*Vice-President*, 1861-1868).
Matthew T. Culley, Copeland Castle, Wooller. 13th December, 1861.
Rev. John Cundill, B.D., Perpetual Curate of St. Margaret's, Durham. 31st May, 1849. (*Vice-President*, 1849-1868).
Rev. J. W. Darnbrough, M.A., Rector of South Otterington, Thirsk. 6th Dec., 1864.
Robert Darnell, jun., Mount Villas, York. 16th March, 1861.

Rev. William Darnell, Bambro', Belford. 5th December, 1865.
The Lord Bishop of St. David's, Abergwili Palace, Caermarthen. 13th March, 1851.
Robert Davies, F.S.A., The Mount, York. 13th March, 1851. (*Vice-President*, 1861-1868).
Rev. Thomas Dean, M.A., Warton, Lancaster. 16th March, 1861.
Robert Richardson Dees, Wallsend, Newcastle-on-Tyne. 15th December, 1859.
Rev. William Denton, M.A., 48, Finsbury Circus, London. 17th June, 1861. (*Local Secretary*, 1862-1868).
William Dickson, F.S.A., Alnwick. 12th July, 1836.
Rev. James F. Dimock, Barnburgh Rectory, Doncaster. 8th December, 1863.
George Dodsworth, Clifton, York. 13th December, 1862.
Rev. W. W. Douglas, M.A., Rector of Salwarpe, Worcester. 7th Nov., 1865.
The Hon. and Very Rev. Augustus Duncombe, D.D., Dean of York. 15th December, 1859.
The Right Hon. Sir David Dundas, Inner Temple, London. 30th December, 1858.
The Lord Bishop of Durham, Auckland Castle. 13th December, 1861.
The Library of the University of Durham. 16th June, 1858.
Rev. John Edleston, D.C.L., Vicar of Gainford, Darlington. 8th Dec., 1863.
Rev. J. H. Eld, B.D., Fellow of St. John's College, Oxford, Fyfield, Berks. 14th March, 1863.
John F. Elliot, Elvet Hill, Durham. 12th July, 1836. (*Vice-President*, 1849-1868).
Edmund Viner Ellis, Gloucester. 17th June, 1861.
William Viner Ellis, Gloucester. 30th December, 1858.
Charles Elsley, Mill Mount, York. 5th December, 1865.
Rev. Richard Elwyn, M.A., Head Master of St. Peter's School, York. 5th December, 1865.
Rev. Dr. English, Warley House, Brentwood. 14th March, 1862.
John Errington, High Warden, Hexham. 14th March, 1862.
The Lord Bishop of Exeter. 5th December, 1853.
The Very Rev. Monsignore Eyre, Newcastle-on-Tyne. 11th December, 1856.
Rev. W. K. Farmery, 18, Bank Street, Leeds. 7th March, 1865.
James Farrer, Ingleboro', Lancaster. 31st May, 1849.
Miss ffarrington, Worden Hall, Preston. 14th December, 1860.
G. W. J. Farsyde, Fylingdales, Whitby. 8th December, 1863.
John Fawcett, Durham. 29th September, 1842. (*Vice-President*, 1843-1868).
The Lord Feversham, Duncombe Park, Helmsley. 24th June, 1867.
John Fisher, Masham. 14th March, 1862.
Matthew Ford, 8, Lincoln's Inn Fields, London. 5th December, 1865.
Charles Forrest, Lofthouse, Wakefield. 1st March, 1864.
The Vicount Galway, M.P., Serlby Hall, Bawtry. 15th December, 1859.
Henry H. Gibbs, St. Dunstan's, Regent's Park, London. 15th December, 1859.
William Sidney Gibson, F.S.A., Tynemouth. 26th September, 1844.
The University of Göttingen. 8th December, 1863.
Nicholas Charles Gold, Whitefriars-street, Fleet-street, London. 8th December, 1863.
The Very Rev. William Goode, D.D., F.S.A., Dean of Ripon. 8th Dec., 1863.
John Edward Thorley Graham, Scarbro'. 5th December, 1865.
William Grainge, Harrogate. 25th February, 1859.
William Gray, York. 15th March, 1860.
Rev. William Greenwell, M.A., Librarian of the Dean and Chapter of Durham. 28th September, 1843. (*Treasurer*, 1843-1849. *Vice-President*, 1849-1868).
John Beswicke Greenwood, Dewsbury Moor House, Dewsbury. 14th December, 1860.
The Earl de Grey and Ripon, Studley Royal, Ripon. 15th December, 1859.

Edwin Guest, LL.D., F.S.A., &c., Master of Caius College, Cambridge. (*Vice-President*, 1856-1868).†

Edward Hailstone, F.S.A., Horton Hall, Bradford. May, 1846.

The Ven. W. Hale Hale, M.A., Archdeacon of London, Canon Residentiary of St. Paul's, and Master of the Charter House. 26th September, 1839.

The University of Halle. 8th December, 1863.

John Hammond, East Burton, Bedale. 8th June, 1864.

Rev. William Vernon Harcourt, M.A., Canon of York, Nuneham Park, Abingdon. 14th March, 1862.

Philip Charles Hardwick, F.S.A., 21, Cavendish Square, London. 14th March, 1850.

Thomas Duffus Hardy, H.M. Deputy Keeper of Records, The Rolls, London. 13th December, 1862. (*Vice-President*, 1865-1868).

William Harrison, Ripon. June 2nd, 1868.*

William Harrison, F.S.A., &c., Samlesbury Hall, Preston. 17th June, 1861.

Rev. W. Estcourt Harrison, M.A., Clifton, York. 13th December, 1861.

The Right Hon. T. E. Headlam, M.P., Chancellor of the Dioceses of Durham and Ripon, 20, Ashley Place, Victoria Street, London. 13th December, 1855.

Alfred Heales, F.S.A., Doctors' Commons, London. 3rd December, 1867.*

Henry Healey, Smallbridge, Rochdale. 14th December, 1860.

William Henderson, Durham. 27th May, 1847. (*Treasurer*, 1847-1858. *Vice-President*, 1858-1868).

Rev. W. G. Henderson, D.C.L., Head Master of Leeds Grammar School. 31st May, 1849. (*Secretary*, 1849-1852).

The Lord Herries, Everingham Park, Hayton, Yorkshire. 15th December, 1859.

Rev. William Hey, M.A., Canon Residentiary of York. 14th March, 1862.

Rev. William Hildyard, M.A., Market Deeping, Lincolnshire. 14th March, 1862.

John Hodgson Hinde, F.S.A., &c., Stelling Hall, Stocksfield-on-Tyne.† (*Vice-President*, 1843-1868).

Rev. James F. Hodgson, Staindrop, Darlington. 6th December, 1864.

Richard Wellington Hodgson, North Dene, Gateshead. 11th December, 1856.

Rev. Henry Holden, D.D., Head Master of Durham Grammar School. 16th June, 1858.

John Dickonson Holmes, Barnardcastle. 4th June, 1867.

The Very Rev. W. F. Hook, D.D., F.R.S., &c., Dean of Chichester. 14th March 1862.

A. J. Beresford Hope, M.P., F.S.A., &c., Connaught Place, Hyde Park, London. 15th December, 1859.

The Lord Houghton, Fryston Hall, Ferrybridge. 30th December, 1858.

Fretwell W. Hoyle, F.G.H.S., Eastwood Lodge, Rotherham. 14th December, 1860.

The Huddersfield Archæological Association. 3rd March, 1868.*

Henry Arthur Hudson, Bootham, York. 7th March, 1865.

William Hughes, 24, Wardour Street, London. 7th March, 1865.

Rev. Thomas Hugo, M.A., F.S.A., The Chestnuts, Clapton, London. 14th March, 1862.

The Hull Subscription Library. 14th March, 1862.

Rev. Henry Humble, M.A., Canon of St. Ninian's, Perth. 31st May, 1849.

Richard Charles Hussey, F.S.A., 16, King William Street, Strand, London. 12th July, 1836.

Joseph Hutchinson, Durham. 6th December, 1864.

Rev. Dr. Hymers, Brandesburton, Beverley. 30th December, 1858.

Rev. H. D. Ingilby, M.A., Ripley Castle, Ripley. 15th December, 1859.

Robert Henry Ingham, M.P., Westoe, South Shields.†

C. J. D. Ingledew, M.A., Ph.D., F.G.H.S., Tyddyn-y-Sais, Caernarvon. 13th December, 1855.

Henry Ingledew, Newcastle-on-Tyne. 1st March, 1864.

Charles Jackson, Doncaster. 14th December, 1860. (*Local Secretary*, 1863-1868).

Henry Jackson, St. James' Row, Sheffield. 15th December, 1859.

William Jackson, Fleatham House, St. Bees, Whitehaven. 7th March, 1865.

Sir Walter James, Bart., Betteshanger, Sandwich. 5th December, 1865.

Rev. Joseph Jameson, B.D., Precentor of Ripon Minster, Ripon. 8th December, 1863.

Rev. Henry Jenkyns, D.D., Canon of Durham. September, 1838.

Rev. J. F. Johnson, Gateshead Fell, Durham. 11th December, 1856.

Rev. J. W. Kemp, M.A., New Elvet, Durham. 8th December, 1853.

Rev. John Kenrick, F.S.A., York. 15th December, 1859.

John Henry Le Keux, Durham. 13th December, 1861.

W. W. King, 28, Queen's Square, Cannon Street, London. 8th December, 1863.

Rev. Francis Kirsopp, Hexham. 7th March, 1865.

Rev. William Knight, Hartlepool, Durham. 13th December, 1862.

John Bailey Langhorne, Wakefield. 31st May, 1849. (*Local Secretary*, 1858-1868).

The Hon. and Rev. Stephen Willoughby Lawley, M.A., Trevayler, Penzance. 8th December, 1863.

George Lawton, Nunthorpe, York. 12th July, 1836.

The Leeds Library. 11th December, 1856.

Octavius Leefe, 61, Lincoln's Inn, Fields, London. 13th December, 1861.

Joseph Lees, Clarksfield Lees, Manchester. 17th June, 1861.

Rev. H. G. Liddell, M.A., Charlton King's, Cheltenham. 26th September, 1837.

The Library of Lincoln's Inn, London. 13th March, 1851.

William Linskill, Ellenbank, Blairgowrie, N.B. 13th December, 1855.

The Liverpool Athenæum. 6th June, 1855.

William Hugh Logan, Berwick-on-Tweed. 18th June, 1862.

The London Library, 12, St. James' Square, London. 13th March, 1851.

William Hylton Dyer Longstaffe, F.S.A., Gateshead. 17th March, 1855. (*Vice-President*, 1859-68. *Local Secretary*, 1858-1868).

Rev. J. L. Low, M.A., The Forest, Middleton-in Teesdale, Durham. 16th June, 1858.

Rev. Henry Richards Luard, M.A., Registrary of the University of Cambridge. 24th June, 1859.

John James Lundy, F.G.S., Assembly Street, Leith. 16th March, 1861.

David Macbeath, 48, Mark Lane, London. 15th March, 1860.

Rev. E. M. Macfarlane, M.A., Dorchester, Wallingford. 7th June, 1864.

John Whitefoord Mackenzie, W.S., Vice-President S.A. Scotland, and M.R.S.N.A. Cop., 16, Royal Circus, Edinburgh. 14th July, 1835.

Messrs. Macmillan and Co., 16, Bedford Street, Covent Garden, London. 7th March, 1865.

The Library of Magdalen College, Oxford. 18th June, 1862.

The Manchester Free Library. 3rd December, 1867.*

The Lord Bishop of Manchester, F.R.S., &c., Mauldeth Hall, Manchester. 11th December, 1856.

James Meek, Middlethorpe Lodge, York. 6th December, 1864.

Walter Charles Metcalfe, Epping, Essex. 13th December, 1862.

Robert Mills, F.S.A., Shawclough, Rochdale. 16th March, 1861.

John Mitchell, 24, Wardour Street, London. 24th June, 1859.

E. J. Monk, Mus. Doc., York. 6th December, 1864.

C. T. J. Moore, Frampton Hall, Boston. 25th February, 1859.

H. J. Morehouse, Stony Bank, Holmfirth. 3rd December, 1867.*

M. T. Morrall, Balmoral House, Matlock Bank, Derbyshire. 16th March, 1861.

W. W. Morrell, Selby. 3rd March, 1868.*

Walter Morrison, M.P., Malham Tarn, Skipton-in-Craven. 1st March, 1864.

George Gill Mounsey, Castletown, Carlisle. 17th March, 1855. (*Local Secretary*, 1858-1868).

The Royal Library at Munich. 14th March, 1863.
Charles Scott Murray, F.S.A., Danesfield Park, Great Marlow. 15th December, 1859.
W. Magson Nelson, High Royd, Leeds. 4th June, 1867.
The Literary and Philosophical Society, Newcastle-on-Tyne. 17th March, 1855.
Edward Hotham Newton, Westwood, Scarbro'. 13th December, 1862.
John Gough Nichols, F.S.A., 25, Parliament Street, Westminster.† (*Treasurer from the Foundation of the Society*).
Thomas S. Noble, York. 5th December, 1863.
Rev. Charles Best Norcliffe, M.A., York. 12th March, 1852.
The Duke of Northumberland, Alnwick Castle. 6th June, 1865.
John Openshaw, Bur House, Bakewell. 15th June, 1863.
John R. Ord, Darlington. 30th December, 1858.
Rev. George Ornsby, Fishlake, Doncaster. 24th June, 1859.
Rev. Sir F. G. Ouseley, Bart., M.A., Precentor of Hereford, and Professor of Music in the University of Oxford, St. Michael's, Tenbury, Worcestershire. 11th December, 1856. :
The Right Hon. Sir Roundell Palmer, M.P., 6, Portland Place, London. 8th December, 1863.
Thomas William Parker, Northfield House, Rotherham. 6th June, 1865.
Edward Peacock, F.S.A., Bottesford Manor, Brigg. 10th June, 1857.
Albert Pearson, Knebworth Rectory, Stevenage. 4th June, 1867.
Joseph Pease, Darlington. 19th December, 1854.
George Peile, jun., Greenwood, Shotley Bridge. 7th March, 1865.
Richard Lawrence Pemberton, The Barnes, Sunderland. 13th December, 1855. (*Vice-President*, 1857-1868).
Hugh Penfold, Library Chambers, Middle Temple, London. 14th March, 1862.
James Stovin Penryman, Ormesby Hall, Middlesbro'. 8th December. 1853.
The Imperial Library at St. Petersburgh. 14th March, 1863.
Rev. Gilbert H. Phillips, M.A., Brodsworth, Doncaster. 30th December, 1858.
Rev. Ralph Platt, Durham. 30th December, 1858.
Francis S. Powell, M.P., Old Horton Hall, Bradford. 7th June, 1864.
The Ven. Archdeacon Prest, Rector of Gateshead, The College, Durham. 7th June, 1864.
James Pulleine, Clifton Castle, Bedale. 14th December, 1860.
Bernard Quaritch, 15, Piccadilly, London. 24th September, 1853.
Rev. James Raine, M.A., Canon of York, York. 12th March, 1852. (*Secretary*, 1854-1868).
Rev. John Raine, M.A.. Blyth Vicarage, Worksop. 18th June. 1862.
Rev. Canon Raines, M.A., F.S.A., the Vice-President of the Chetham Society, Milnrow, Rochdale. 14th December, 1860.
J. R. Raines, Burton Pidsea, Hull. 14th December, 1860.
Stephen Ram, Ramsfort, Gorec, Ireland. 6th June, 1856.
Sir John William Ramsden, Bart., Byram Hall, South Milford, Yorkshire. 14th March, 1862.
The Lord Ravensworth, President of the Society of Antiquaries, Newcastle-on-Tyne. 6th June, 1856.
W. F. Rawdon, Bootham, York. 14th December, 1860.
Arnold W. Reinold, 4, Kingston Square, Hull. 8th December, 1863.
Godfrey Rhodes, Rawdon Hill, Otley. 1st March, 1864.
Charles H. Rickards, Manchester. 13th March, 1851.
The Proprietors of the Ripon Public Rooms. 14th December, 1860.
William Rivington, Hampstead Heath, London. 15th December, 1859.
Clarence Robinson, Osmundthorpe Hall, Leeds. 3rd December, 1867,*
T. W. U. Robinson, Houghton-le-Spring, Durham. 14th December, 1860.
The Very Rev. Daniel Rock, D.D., 17, Essex Villas, Kensington. 14th March, 1850. (*Vice-President*, 1851-1868. *Local Secretary*, 1858-1868).
Rev. H. R. Rokeby, Arthingworth Manor, Northants. 14th March, 1862.

16

John Roper, Clifton Croft, York. 13th December, 1862.
Rev. George Rowe, M.A., Principal of the Training College, York. 7th June, 1864.
Samuel Rowlandson, Durham. September, 1841. (*Treasurer*, 1858-1868).
J. B. Rudd, Tollesby Hall, Guisbrough. 13th March, 1857.
John Sampson, York. December, 1857.
George Gilbert Scott, Spring Gardens, London. 4th June, 1867.
Simon Thomas Scrope, jun., Danby Hall, Bedale. 16th June, 1858.
The Trustees of Dr. Shepherd's Library, Preston. 6th December, 1864.
Thomas Shields, Scarborough. 8th December, 1863.
Rev. E. H. Shipperdson, M.A., The Hermitage, Chester-le-Street. 6th June, 1856.
The Signet Library, Edinburgh. 6th December, 1864.
Henry Silvertop, Minsteracres, Gateshead. 21st May, 1849.
The Library of Sion College, London. December, 1857.
R. H. Skaife, The Mount, York. 6th December, 1864.
Rev. Alfred Fowler Smith, M.A., Rector of St. Mary's, Thetford. 6th December, 1864.
John Smith, Her Majesty's Keeper of Records, Doctor's Commons, London. 13th December, 1861.
John George Smythe, Heath Hall, Wakefield. 13th December, 1862.
George Smurthwaite, Richmond, Yorkshire. 8th December, 1863.
The Hon. Henry Stanhope. 2nd June, 1868.*
The Statistical Society, 12, St. James' Square, London. 30th December, 1858.
George Stephens, Professor of English Literature in the University of Copenhagen. 24th September, 1853.
The Royal Library at Stockholm. 14th March, 1863.
John Storey, 71, Albion Street, Leeds. 6th June, 1865.
John Stuart, New Mills, Currie, Edinburgh. Secretary of the Spalding Club, and of the Society of Antiquaries, Scotland. 24th February, 1853. (*Local Secretary*, 1862-1868).
Rev. William Stubbs, M.A., Professor of Modern History in the University of Oxford. 13th March, 1851. (*Local Secretary*, 1862-1868).
Charles Freville Surtees, M.P., Army and Navy Club, St. James' Square, London. 15th December, 1859.
Henry Edward Surtees, M.P., Dane End, Ware, Herts, 10th June, 1857.
Lady Surtees, Silkmore House, Stafford. 2nd June, 1868.*
Rev. Scott F. Surtees, M.A., Sprotborough Rectory, Doncaster. 14th December, 1860.
William Edward Surtees, M.A., Seaton Carew, Durham. 15th March, 1860.
Sir John Swinburne, Bart., Capheaton, Morpeth. 5th June, 1866.
G. E. Swithinbank, Newcastle-on-Tyne. 14th December, 1860.
Christopher Sykes, M.P., Brantingham-Thorpe, Hull. 15th December, 1859.
John Sykes, M.D., Doncaster. 24th June, 1859.
Henry Taylor, the Colonial Office, London. 6th June, 1852.
Thomas Greenwood Teale, Leeds. 8th December, 1853. (*Local Secretary*, 1862-1868).
Wilfred Tempest, Ackworth Grange, Pontefract. 4th December, 1866.
Christopher Temple, Q.C., Temporal Chancellor of Durham, 15, Upper Bedford Place, London. 6th June, 1856.
The Library of the Inner Temple, London. 3rd December, 1867.*
Rev. Francis Thompson, Durham. 7th March, 1865.
Leonard Thompson, Sheriffhutton Park, York. 13th December, 1862.
Sir Nicholas William Throckmorton, Bart., Coughton Court, Bromsgrove. 13th December, 1862.
William Thwaites, Ripon. 7th June, 1864.
John Tiplady, Durham. 6th June, 1865.
Sir Walter Calverley Trevelyan, Bart., F.S.A., &c., Wallington, Newcastle-on Tyne.† (*Vice-President from the Foundation of the Society*).

The Library of Trinity College, Cambridge. June 5th, 1866.

H. J. Trotter, Bishop Auckland. 4th June, 1867.

Charles Tucker, F.S.A., Secretary of the Archæological Institute, Marlands, Heavitree, Exeter. 15th December, 1852.

E. P. Turnbull, Fellow of Trinity College, Cambridge. 7th June, 1864.

Henry Turner, Low Heaton Haugh, Newcastle-on-Tyne. 12th July, 1836.

Rev. James Francis Turner, North Tidworth, Marlborough, 14th March, 1850.

Edmund H. Turton, Larpool Hall, Whitby. 13th December, 1861.

George Markham Tweddell, West Villas, Stokesley. 6th December, 1864.

The President of St. Cuthbert's College, Ushaw, Durham. September, 1838.

The Earl Vane, Winyard, Durham. 17th March, 1855.

The Library at the Vatican. 14th March, 1863.

Rev. C. J. Vaughan, D.D., Vicar of Doncaster. Chancellor of York, and Chaplain in Ordinary to the Queen. 13th December, 1862.

Rev. Philip Vavasour, Hazlewood, Tadcaster. 8th December, 1862.

The Imperial Library at Vienna. 14th March, 1863.

The Very Rev. George Waddington, D.D., &c., Dean of Durham. September, 1841. (*Vice-President*, 1843-1868).

Rev. George Wade, Fulford Grange, York. 18th June, 1862.

John Richard Walbran, F.S.A., Fallcroft, Ripon. 15th December, 1859. (*Vice-President*, 1860-1868).

Rev. William Walbran, B.A., Radcliffe, Manchester. 6th December, 1864.

John Hope Wallace, Featherston Castle, Haltwhistle. 14th March, 1863.

The Library of St. Edmund's College, Old Hall Green, Ware. 8th December, 1863.

J. Whiteley Ward, Halifax. 3rd March, 1868.*

George Waring, M.A., 2, Park Terrace, The Parks, Oxford. 14th Dec., 1860.

Albert Way, F.S.A., &c., Secretary of the Archæological Institute, Wonham Manor, Reigate. 15th December, 1852. (*Vice-President*, 1859-1868).

Christopher M. Webster, Pallion, Bishopwearmouth. 15th December, 1859.

His Excellency M. Van de Weyer, the Belgian Ambassador, 50, Portland Place, London. September, 1841.

W. W. Whitaker, 32, St. Ann's Street, Manchester. 16th March, 1861.

Robert White, Claremont Place, Newcastle-on-Tyne. 12th December, 1851.

Rev. C. T. Whitley, M.A., Vicar of Bedlington, Newcastle-on-Tyne.† (*Vice-President*, 1836-1868).

John Whitwell, Kendall. 1st March, 1864.

Joseph Wilkinson, Town Clerk, York. 14th March, 1862.

E. J. Wilson, Melton, Brough, East Yorkshire. 2nd June, 1868.*

Basil Thomas Woodd, M.P., Conyngham Hall, Knaresbro'. 8th December, 1863.

William Woodman, Town Clerk, Morpeth. 31st May, 1849.

The Lord Archbishop of York. 15th June, 1863.

The Library of the Dean and Chapter of York. 13th March, 1857.

The York Subscription Library. 16th March, 1861.

Sir Charles George Young, F.S.A., &c., Garter King at Arms, Heralds' College, London.† (*Vice-President*, 1836-1868).

The Earl of Zetland, K.T., Aske Hall, Richmond. 13th March, 1851.

AN ACCOUNT OF SAMUEL ROWLANDSON, ESQ., AS TREASURER OF THE SURTEES SOCIETY.

From 1st January, 1865, to 31st December, 1866.

	£ s. d.
1865.	
Jan. 1. To Balance in hands of Treasurer on last account	116 9 4
Dec. 5. To received of Edward Akroyd, Esq., towards the Printing and Illustrating 2nd vol. of Fountains Abbey	180 0 0
1866.	
Mar. 6. To amount received of Messrs. Andrews and Co., for balance of sale of books (after deducting expenses) for 1865	78 4 4
Dec. 31. To amount of Subscriptions received by Samuel Rowlandson, Esq., and J. G. Nichols, Esq., from 1st January, 1865, to 31st December, 1866	771 15 0
1867.	
May 24. To amount received of Messrs. Andrews and Co., for balance of sale of books (after deducting expenses) for 1866	25 5 5
	£1171 14 1

	£ s. d.	£ s. d.	£ s. d.
1865.			
May 26. By paid J. R. Walbran, Esq., on account			49 10 0
1866.			
YORK WILLS:—			
December.			
By paid Leighton, Son, and Hodge, for binding	16 12 8		
By paid Rev. James Raine, for editing	55 13 0		
By paid J. B. Nichols and Son, for printing	119 18 0	192 3 8	
DEAN GRANVILLE:—			
By paid Rev. Geo. Ornsby, for editing, etc.	54 15 0		
By paid Leighton, Son, and Hodge, for binding	14 8 0		
By paid Gilbert and Rivington, for printing	81 6 0	150 9 0	
THE LINDISFARNE GOSPELS, PART IV:—			
By paid Combe, Hall, Latham, and Co., for printing	89 10 6		
By paid Leighton, Son, and Hodge, for binding	16 19 1		
By paid George Waring, Esq., for editing	49 16 6		
By paid Day and Son, for Chromo-Lithographing	13 7 7	169 13 10	
HEXHAM, VOL. II:—			
By paid Monkhouse and Co., for lithographed plan	3 9 6		
By paid Mitchell and Hughes, for printing	81 1 0		
By paid Leighton, Son, and Hodge, for binding	16 19 10		
By paid W. H. D. Longstaffe, Esq., for expenses	2 8 6		
By paid Rev. James Raine, for editing	43 0 0	146 18 10	
MISCELLANEOUS EXPENSES:—			
By paid Rev. James Raine, Secretary's allowance for 1865 and 1866		60 0 0	
By paid Messrs. A. Johnson and Co., for printing Reports for ditto		15 15 0	
By paid Durham Advertiser, for printing Circulars		0 14 0	
By paid for Postage Stamps, &c., for Treasurer, 1865 and 1866		5 0 0	
By paid Assistant Treasurer, two years' salary		4 4 0	791 8 4
Balance in hand of Treasurer on this account			377 5 9
			£1171 14 1

We, the Auditors, appointed to credit the Accounts of the Surtees Society, report to the Society that the Treasurers have exhibited to us their Accounts from the 1st January, 1865, to the 31st December, 1866, and that we have examined the said Accounts and find the same to be correct, and we further report, that the above is an accurate abstract of the receipts and expenditure of the Society during the period to which we have referred. As witness our hands this 2nd day of September, 1867.

RALPH PLATT, D.D.
JOS. HUTCHINSON.

www.ingramcontent.com/pod-product-compliance
Lightning Source LLC
Chambersburg PA
CBHW021340110726
47900CB00005B/1543